T0301229

Cynthia Harrod-Eagles is the author of the hugely popular Morland Dynasty novels, which have captivated and enthralled readers for decades. She is also the author of the contemporary Bill Slider mystery series, as well as her recent series, War at Home, which is an epic family drama set against the backdrop of World War I. Cynthia's passions are music, wine, horses, architecture and the English countryside.

CYNTHIA
HARROD-EAGLES

The
GATHERING
STORM

SPHERE

SPHERE

First published in Great Britain in 2024 by Sphere
1 3 5 7 9 10 8 6 4 2

Copyright © Cynthia Harrod-Eagles 2024

The moral right of the author has been asserted.

A CIP catalogue record for this book is available from the British Library.

ISBN 978-1-4087-2950-2

Typeset in Plantin by Palimpsest Book Production Limited, Falkirk, Stirlingshire
Printed and bound in Great Britain by Clays Ltd, Elcograf S.p.A.

Papers used by Sphere are from well-managed forests
and other responsible sources.

Sphere
An imprint of
Little, Brown Book Group
Carmelite House
50 Victoria Embankment
London EC4Y 0DZ

An Hachette UK Company
www.hachette.co.uk

www.littlebrown.co.uk

DYNASTY 36 – THE GATHERING STORM

THE MORLANDS OF MORLAND PLACE

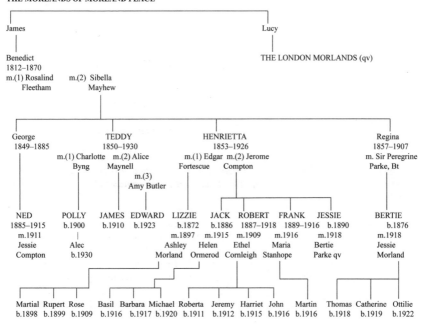

THE LONDON MORLANDS

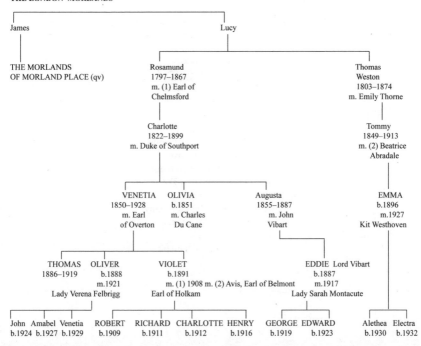

THE AMERICAN MORLANDS

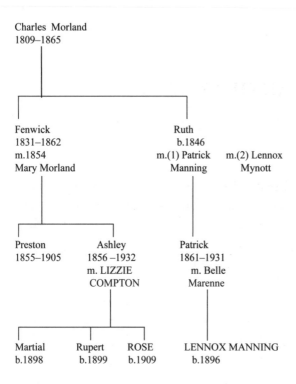

Charles Morland
1809–1865

Fenwick
1831–1862
m.1854
Mary Morland

Ruth
b.1846
m.(1) Patrick   m.(2) Lennox
Manning   Mynott

Preston
1855–1905

Ashley
1856 –1932
m. LIZZIE
COMPTON

Patrick
1861–1931
m. Belle
Marenne

Martial
b.1898

Rupert
b.1899

ROSE
b.1909

LENNOX MANNING
b.1896

AUTHOR'S NOTE

When, in 2022, I realised my next book would be my 100th, I asked the publisher what it should be. We agreed that the most appropriate choice would be the missing last episode of the Morland Dynasty series.

So eleven years after finishing *Dynasty 35: The Phoenix*, I started work on *Dynasty 36: The Gathering Storm*. Before I even began the historical research, I had to go back and re-read quite a lot of the Dynasty series to remind myself of who everyone was and what they were doing. The book has taken me a whole year to produce. As you can imagine, it has been hard work – but very rewarding.

I would like to thank all the readers who kept up pressure on the publishers for there to be another Morland episode. I can honestly say that this book wouldn't have happened without you. Writing the series has been a great privilege, and has brought me in contact with people all over the world who, like me, regard Morland Place as a sort of second home.

For those of you who have been with me all the way, I hope you will find it worth the wait. I have tried to answer some of the questions you regularly ask me.

If you are new to the series, I hope you will enjoy this episode enough to want to read the rest.

Cynthia Harrod-Eagles.
January 2024

For Tony, as always

BOOK ONE

TRAVELLING

But when I draw the scanty cloak of silence over my eyes
Piteous love comes peering under the hood;
Touches the clasp with trembling fingers, and tries
To put her ear to the painful sob of my blood;
While her tears soak through to my breast,
Where they burn and cauterise.

D. H. Lawrence: 'End of Another Home Holiday'

CHAPTER ONE

February 1936

The steward's room was the warmest in Morland Place, with its cosy linenfold panelling and the big fire that had been banked the evening before and stirred back to life in the early morning. The dogs knew it. They had slipped in with John Burton when he arrived and now made a hairy carpet before the hearth.

When Polly came in after breakfast she said, 'I wondered where they'd all gone. You wanted to see me?'

Burton was silent a moment, thinking how fine she looked. For some women, their mid thirties are a time when the dewy but unfinished beauty of extreme youth blends with the serenity and confidence of maturity. Polly had always been a belle in the classical, blue-eyed-golden-haired mould: now she was a lovely woman, with a fine, upright figure in well-cut riding clothes, her golden hair drawn into a tight, practical bun.

She gave him a quizzical look. 'What is it? Have I got a smut on my nose?'

He shook himself. 'No, indeed.' He hurried on: 'I have something to tell you – well, two things. One personal, one business.'

'Personal first, then.' She perched on the edge of the desk.

'I don't know, really, whether it's something you need to

know, or even want to know, but I would feel odd not telling you. Joan – my wife – we are expecting a child.'

'That's wonderful. Congratulations.' Polly's reply was automatic, the product of her careful upbringing, as was her smile. And of *course* it was good news!

But when John Burton had first come into her life as her estate manager, she had been feeling very lonely – a young widow, recently returned from America, her adored father having also died. Of course, she had been surrounded by relatives – she still was – but where was the special person to whom she mattered most in the world, who was interested in every facet of her life? She had longed for that perfect intimacy; had wanted, in a word, a lover.

She had immediately liked and trusted John Burton, and as they had worked closely together, learning the complexities of running the estate, it was natural that a warmth had grown up between them. It had been foolish of her to allow it to develop into a *tendresse*. She had never so much as heard him mention Joan Formby's name until the day he had introduced her as his fiancée. Polly and Burton had spent so much time together, she had forgotten he might have a life outside Morland Place.

She was now ashamed of what her feelings had been. He was her agent, a nice, warm-hearted, straightforward man and an excellent employee: he would be mortified if he ever found out she had harboured a silly fancy for him. 'I'm delighted for you,' she went on. 'When is the great day?'

'Oh, not until September,' he said, pushing back the lock of barley-fair hair that liked to escape and fall over his forehead. 'It's early days – we haven't even told Joan's parents yet.'

'You'll need a larger house,' Polly said briskly. 'Your cottage is really only suitable for a bachelor. Mrs Burton has been very patient to live there for eighteen months without complaint.'

4

'Sixteen months,' he corrected. 'As a matter of fact—'

'You already have somewhere in mind,' she capped him.

'As your agent, I naturally know all the properties on your estate.'

'And which has taken your fancy?'

'Kebble's Cottage, on Moor Lane.'

'Oh, yes. Isn't it the one with the roses all over the front?'

'That's it. There's a good bit of garden at the back, too. The previous tenant worked it well, so we'd be able to grow vegetables. Even perhaps keep a couple of hens.'

Polly had had enough of imagining their domestic bliss. 'Well, you have my blessing to take it, and I wish you very happy there. Now, what was the business matter you wanted to raise?'

He reached for a piece of paper in front of him. 'I've a letter here from York council. To summarise, they are continuing with the slum clearances in the Hungate area, and they want to build council houses outside the walls for the people they displace. You know they did the same sort of thing when they cleared Walmgate and bought the land at Tang Hall?'

'What has that to do with me?' she asked. She had a feeling she would not like where this was going.

'They want to buy twenty acres of Morland land up at North Field, along the Knaresborough road.'

'For housing? But that's good farmland,' she objected.

'Indeed, but when you move people, you can't take them too far from their jobs. And they need access to public transport, so you have to site the estate along a road – which makes it easier to lay in services, too: water and sewerage and so on.'

'My father took years to build up the estate. I'm not going to reduce it,' she said.

Burton gave her a troubled look. 'You may not have a choice, ma'am. Under the Housing Act of 1885, local authorities have the power to purchase land compulsorily.'

Polly's brows drew down. 'You mean, they could *make* me sell?'

'I'm afraid so. It's the law.'

'But the land belongs to me! If they can just take it, we might as well be living in Russia!'

'The thing is—'

Polly turned away abruptly. 'I can't talk about it now. I'm on my way out.'

'We'll need to reply to them fairly soon, or—'

'I'll think about it,' she snapped, and left him.

It was a dry day, but perishingly cold, and not a single dog volunteered to accompany her as she went out into the yard. On the shaded side the frost lay like snow along the foot of the wall; it glistened on the cobbles. One of the grooms, Hodgson, led Zephyr out and helped her mount. She didn't blame him for scurrying back to the tack-room as soon as she had the reins.

Zephyr clattered over the drawbridge and out onto the track, and Polly had a sense of being completely alone in the world. There was no-one about; nothing stirred, not even a bird. The gauntness of February was unsoftened yet by any new growth; even the blackthorn slept. The trees stood stark and bare against a uniform grey sky, and the air was grippingly cold, the sort of creeping chill that worked its way inside your clothes, and numbed your hands.

Zephyr was inclined to be nappy at first, wanting to get back to his stall, but she drove him into a fast canter to warm them both up. They went out as far as Rufforth Grange before she turned back and made a circle towards Twelvetrees, her cousin Jessie's place. She felt the need of advice.

Jessie was in one of the paddocks, lungeing a young horse, with her daughter Ottilie in the saddle. Ottilie, slight with curly fair hair, the image of her mother, was small for thirteen, and Jessie often used her when backing a horse for the first time. The appearance of Zephyr on the other side of the fence distracted the horse and it whinnied and tried to nap towards the gate. Jessie looked round, then waved to Polly and called the horse in to the centre.

'I need to talk to you,' Polly said. 'It's important.'

'Go on, I'll join you in a minute,' Jessie called back. 'I've just about finished.' She turned to her daughter. 'Sit quite still and don't use your legs. I want him to listen to me, not you.' She sent the horse back out to circle on the other rein.

Polly rode on. By the time she had settled Zephyr in a spare stall, Jessie and Ottilie had arrived, walking the young horse between them. Polly heard Ottilie say, 'I'll take him, Mum. You go and talk to Polly.'

Jessie's head appeared over the half-door. 'Come up to the house and have a cup of tea,' she said. Her eyes were watering with the cold and the tip of her nose was red. 'I'm frozen to the marrow. I think we might be in for some snow.'

Polly gave Zephyr a last pat and joined her. 'Oh, I pray not. That's all I need to make a perfect day.'

'Why? What's happened?' Jessie asked. They walked up the path to the house, their footsteps crackling on the skim of ice between the stones. Twelvetrees was a solid, square, stone house, designed to keep out the weather. Jessie and Bertie had had it built to their own plan, with modern amenities, and it was deliciously warm inside.

'This must be the only truly warm house in England!' Polly exclaimed.

'I suppose you were used to central heating in New York,' Jessie said, easing off her gloves. 'I must say, it's a treat on a day like this. It's making me soft, though. I was much hardier when I lived at Morland Place.' She had grown up there. She had inherited Twelvetrees from her father, and she and her husband bred and schooled horses for sale.

'Icy draughts and cavernous spaces,' Polly agreed. 'A little pool of heat around each fire, and Arctic wastes in between.

One of these days I'm going to have central heating put in – when I can work out where to put the boiler. That's the trouble with an ancient pile – especially a moated one!'

Jessie smiled indulgently. 'But you wouldn't exchange Morland Place for any other house on earth.'

'Well, no, but that's nothing to do with it. You should see my chilblains.'

'So, tell me what's ruffled your feathers,' Jessie invited, as they stripped off coats and gloves.

'John Burton's been lobbing bombshells at me. First he tells me his wife's expecting a baby—'

'Why is that a bombshell?'

Polly caught herself up. 'Oh, you know how demanding a first baby can be. He'll have his mind on anything but his work for the next year at least.'

'I'm sure he won't let it affect him. He's tremendously diligent.'

Polly hurried on. 'And then he tells me that the York city authorities want to buy some of my land for council houses. *And* tells me that they can force me to sell. It's outrageous!'

Jessie said, 'This calls for Bertie's wisdom. I think he's in his study. Shall we go and see?'

Sir Percival Parke, who was a cousin to both Jessie and Polly, had always hated his given name and had never been known as anything but Bertie. He had served with distinction in the war, one of the few to fight all the way from 1914 to 1918, winning the DSO and the VC, ending as a brigadier and working afterwards in the War Office. Now he was happy to spend his days quietly at home, farming his estate and enjoying the company of his adored wife and three children.

He was very fond of Polly, and admired the way she had thrown herself into running the Morland Estate. She had bought it from her brother James when death duties had threatened its dissolution. Her late husband, Ren, had left her a large fortune, and James, though a countryman to his fingertips, had no head for business. Polly's head, Bertie reckoned, was as hard as any man's: she had run her own fashion house in New York before her marriage, and *that* was no mean task.

He was studying milk records when his wife ushered Polly in, saying, 'Can we disturb you, dearest?'

'I can't think of anything nicer. What's happening?'

'Polly needs advice,' said Jessie.

As well as the radiator there was a fire in his room, for cheerfulness. Bertie moved chairs and got them all settled around it before inviting Polly to 'tell'.

Polly told. 'I thought an Englishman's home was his castle,' she concluded. 'Magna Carta and all that sort of thing. Is John right? And who dreamed up such a terrible law?'

'Well, I suppose you could say it was an extension, in a way, of the old Enclosure Acts,' Bertie began.

'She doesn't want a history lesson, darling,' Jessie intervened.

'Oh, it was a rhetorical question, was it?' Bertie said, with an indulgent smile.

'They can't really force me, can they?' Polly asked hopefully.

'I'm afraid they can. And before you howl again, think about things like the railways, and new roads. And airfields during the war. On a tiny island like this they could never get them built if landowners could refuse to sell.' Polly was still looking mulish. 'You wouldn't want to be without the railway, now, would you? Quite a bit of Morland land had to be given up for that, if I remember rightly.'

'But this isn't for a railway,' Polly said.

'Compulsory purchase is allowed for projects that are considered to be in the public interest.'

'Why do you object so much?' Jessie asked.

'Because Papa spent his life building up the estate. He

worked and slaved to buy back all the land Uncle George sold, so that he could pass the estate on intact. He'd have a fit at the thought of selling it again. I would never part with any of my land – it would be a betrayal of everything Papa stood for.'

'I wonder,' Bertie said. 'After Morland Place and his family, the one thing Uncle Teddy really loved was York.'

'And the railways,' Jessie added.

'He loved the railways because they brought prosperity to York,' Bertie said. 'He supported anything that benefited the city. Don't you remember how he started the York Commercials during the war?'

Jessie smiled. 'Oh, yes – because Leeds had its Pals unit, so York had to have one too.'

Polly looked from one to the other. 'So you're saying he'd approve of the slum clearances?'

'He helped with some of the early ones,' Bertie said.

'And you think he'd like there to be a council estate on Morland land?'

'I don't think he would fight against it,' Bertie said. 'If you clear a slum, the people have to go somewhere. Another thing to consider,' he went on, seeing that she still wanted to argue, 'is that if you sell at the first approach, rather than waiting to be forced, you may have some say over exactly where the building will be sited. That's worth having.'

Polly sighed. 'I suppose one has accept change,' she said reluctantly.

'I'm afraid there may be more on the way,' Bertie said. 'I had a chat with Jack on the phone last night.' Jack was Jessie's brother, who had been a flier in the war and was now working in aircraft design. 'He said that Hugh Dowding told him there's going to be a big reorganisation in the RAF. It will mean a lot of new airfields being built.'

'Now, darling, don't start Polly worrying about that,' Jessie said. 'To change the subject, tell me, what are James's plans?

Does he have any? I thought he was only coming home for Christmas, but here we are in February and he's still at Morland Place.'

'He's waiting to hear from Mr Bedaux. He and his wife went to America for Christmas and didn't need James with them.'

Charles Bedaux was an American production engineer whom James had met when invited to join his expedition across British Columbia in 1934, and had since worked for in various capacities.

'But I think James is worried he's plunged into some new scheme and forgotten all about him. I don't mind for my own part – I like having him around. I was quite dreading him going. But, of course, now Lennie's coming for a visit, so I've got that to look forward to.'

'Oh, yes,' Jessie said. 'It'll be lovely to see the dear boy again. We must have a dinner for him.'

'When is he expected?' Bertie asked.

'Towards the end of March,' Polly said. 'I hope he stays a long time. It was lovely when I lived in New York and we saw each other all the time.'

'Perhaps he'll stay for good,' Jessie suggested. 'After all, he's got nothing to go back for, really, has he?'

'Except his business empire,' Bertie said drily.

Polly thought about her cousin Lennie – after her father, the person who had always been the most devoted to her. She imagined him at Morland Place, imagined them riding together, walking together, talking. They had so many memories in common. 'We'll have to find something for him to ride while he's here,' she said happily, and the conversation turned, as it so often did quite naturally, to horses.

In Whitley Heights, above Los Angeles, the morning air was cool and scented with pine, and the sun threw long shadows across the terrace from the orange trees that shaded one end.

Lennie, dressed as far as trousers and shirt, looked out over the hills, where the early light lay like silver gilt across the dark trees. The only sound was of birdsong.

On the first terrace below, the gardener was raking a few leaves together on the rectangle of lawn; on the second terrace, the turquoise pool rippled gently, reflecting the sky. Everyone on Whitley Heights had a pool, but lawns were not natural to California. It was that emerald oblong, maintained at such expense, that marked Lennie out as a rich man. He shook his head at the idea. He had made his first million dollars so long ago he never thought of himself as rich. Yes, it was agreeable to have the money to invest in his interests and to see them flourish. It hardly mattered that, flourishing, they then made him even more money.

For the last nine months nothing much had mattered to him. His pregnant wife had been killed in a car smash back in June, and his life had been dark. Only recently had he felt his internal landscape shifting, and this morning he was aware that something heavy inside him had settled into a new position. The day was something to be looked forward to, rather than merely endured. And in this sweet early morning, the planning of the trip he was intending to take was no chore but part of the pleasure. He had a few more things to settle, to ensure that his business would carry on without him, and some last-minute presents to buy. Then there would be just his packing to do.

Wilma, his housekeeper, would want to do the packing herself, and would argue strenuously about it, but holding his own against her would be another sign that he was getting back to normal. She had taken a loving stranglehold on his life these last eight months. She had been with him for ten years, ever since he first came to California, and together with Beanie, his driver, formed the nucleus of a tight, loyal household. The way they schemed to protect him, he sometimes thought they believed him to be a lovable imbecile.

12

He heard Wilma come out of the house behind him: the slip-slap of the dreadful broken-down slippers she insisted on wearing was unmistakable.

'Breffus about ready, Mr Lennie. You want it out here?'

He turned to smile at her. 'Might as well,' he said. She would have squeezed him juice from his own oranges; and her coffee was the best on the west coast. Perhaps she would have made him pancakes.

She didn't smile back. Her lower lip, reliable gauge of her mood, was sticking out. 'Might as well get all o' God's good sunshine you can, 'fore you go to England. How folks can live in all that fog beats me.'

'The sun shines in England too, you know,' he said.

'Nu-huh,' she countered. 'I seen it on the movies. Everybody creeping about in the fog. Enough to make you crazy. They say English folk are all mad. You should stay here, Mr Lennie, an' let me take proper care of you.'

'It's not for ever. It'll only be for a few weeks,' Lennie said – though he wondered. He had a feeling of standing at a crossroads. His life here in California seemed to have paused, as though a phase was completed. And in England there was Polly, whom he had loved all his life, though without return: she had only cared for him as a cousin. But Ren, her husband, was dead, killed in an aeroplane crash shortly before she had given birth to their son, Alec. Now Lennie's Beth was gone too, and enough time had passed for both of them to start thinking about a new future. Perhaps together? She had always depended and leaned on him. She had given her son the second name of Lennox, in his honour. Surely there was something there to work with. Who knew? Perhaps the time was right for them.

'What am I s'pose to do while you're away gallivanting?' Wilma was grumbling. 'Sit on the porch and rock?'

'Oh, you'll find something. Clean the whole house from top to bottom, if I know you. What's for breakfast?' he prompted.

'I'm fixing you pancakes,' she said

13

It was odd how often she read his mind. Or was it vice-versa? 'With bacon?'

'Don't I always fix bacon with pancakes? What kind o' question is that?' She was reluctant to let go of her sense of grievance, and he heard her muttering her way to the kitchen: *No good reason I know of for folks to go skedaddling off to England every five minutes . . .*

She was back too soon, and empty-handed. 'You got a visitor. Mr Rosecrantz. I told him it's too early, but he says it's important.'

'Bring him out here,' Lennie said. If he had to forgo his breakfast, at least he could still have the fresh air. 'And bring coffee, will you?'

He guessed it must be something serious if he had come in person instead of telephoning. Michael Rosecrantz was the agent of Lennie's cousin and sometime protégée, Rose Morland, the young movie actress. As a large shareholder in ABO Studios, Lennie had been in a position to promote and oversee her early career, but as her success grew, he'd advised her to get a proper agent. At that point he had taken a step back; but Rosecrantz notwithstanding, he had been unable to stop feeling responsible for her.

Then a year ago, in March 1935, she had got married, with a great deal of celebrity ballyhoo, to her co-star in *The Falcon and the Rose*, Dean Cornwell. Since then, Lennie had rather taken his eye off her. Between a husband and an agent, to say nothing of a dresser, a secretary, a publicist and a tame lawyer, Rose had plenty of people to take care of her, and he'd felt it was time to let go. Then Beth had died, and he had turned in on himself, with no interest in the outside world. He had not so much as glanced at a *Motion Picture* or *Modern Screen* magazine in months, so he had no idea what Rose had been up to lately.

Rosecrantz, tall and angular, lean-faced with thick dark hair and a fashionable sun-bronze, came striding out onto

14

the terrace, passing Wilma in the doorway, to take Lennie's hand in a firm, professional grip. He scanned Lennie's face with quick, keen eyes. 'You know why I'm here?'

'Haven't a clue,' Lennie said. 'I'm guessing it's something to do with Rose.'

'You haven't heard, then? I thought at least Estelle might have called you.'

'I haven't spoken to Estelle in a year,' Lennie said. Estelle Cable was Rose's publicist. 'What's all this about?'

'Rose was arrested yesterday for public intoxication, coming out of the Parrot Club on Wilshire Boulevard.'

'*Arrested?*' In California, being drunk in public was at worst a misdemeanour, and the police only intervened in extreme cases, when a nuisance was being caused.

'It wasn't just cocktails,' Rosecrantz said impatiently, 'There was cocaine, and who knows what else? She and her companions had been kicking up a row and making themselves unpopular, and when they finally got thrown out, she collapsed unconscious on the sidewalk. Her "good friends" abandoned her as soon as they sniffed trouble, and since the doorman couldn't rouse her, the manager, who'd already called the cops, rang for an ambulance. She was taken to Wilshire Park Hospital and had her stomach pumped.'

'Oh, my God!'

'Some journalist outside the club called Estelle, and she rushed over and got Rose transferred to the Ardmore.'

The Ardmore was an expensive private clinic. 'Is she all right?'

'She will be – sick and sore, and probably depressed, but that's no more than she deserves. It's the hell of a mess, Len. After *Falcon*, and then the wedding, she's big news. This kind of bad behaviour . . . And the stomach pumping in particular . . . Someone at the hospital will talk. We'll never keep it quiet this time.'

15

'This time? Has she pulled stuff like this before?'

Rosecrantz took a breath. 'I forget how out of touch you've been. Estelle's managed to keep her out of the papers, but there's been plenty of gossip. I guess it hasn't got as far as you.'

Lennie was perplexed. 'I thought she'd be happy after she married Dean.'

'That marriage has been a disaster,' Rosecrantz said impatiently. 'I was against it from the beginning, but no-one listened to me. Cornwell's bad news. That clean-cut, boy-next-door image is barely skin deep – he's a troubled creature. And Rose has followed his lead. Wild parties, drugs – she's out of control.'

Lennie raked his hair. 'Why did no-one tell me?'

Rosecrantz shrugged. 'I'm only coming to you now because I don't know what else to do. Maybe you've still got some influence with her. Because I tell you now, Len, this could be the end of her. You know how particular the studios are about their stars toeing the line. ABO's going to kick up. Al Feinstein could cut her loose.'

'But you could talk to Al—'

'I'm cutting her loose,' Rosecrantz said harshly. 'I'm sorry, I really am, because I like the kid—'

'She's made you a heap of money,' Lennie said sourly.

Rosecrantz didn't flinch. 'I made her money, she made me money. That's the deal. But I've got other clients. I've got their reputations to think of. And my own. I can't afford to be associated with this. I'll tell Rose in person when she's fit to be spoken to. But I'm also telling you, because I know you're the nearest thing she has to a father. If you care about her, you need to reel her in. Talk to her like a Dutch uncle before it's too late.'

He rose up to go. Wilma stood in the doorway with a tray of coffee. He said, 'Thanks, but I can't stay. There's a lot of fire-fighting to do. I'll see myself out,' he added, as he passed Wilma.

In the ensuing silence, Wilma fixed Lennie with a reproachful gaze, her lip now resembling a sugar-scoop. Lennie examined her face. 'Did you know about this?'

She didn't pretend not to have been eavesdropping. 'About Miss Rose cutting up frisky? Sure I did. That Beanie, he hears everything. He told me what she's been at, weeks and weeks past.'

'Why didn't you tell me?'

'Not my place,' she said stubbornly. Then, 'You been grieving, Mr Lennie. And far as I knew, you'd dropped her even before that.'

'I didn't drop her, I just – took a step back. My God, if she had her stomach pumped, she must have been bad! She could have died! You can't believe I wouldn't want to know.' Her eyes slid away from his. 'What did Beanie tell you?'

Beanie, his driver, always knew all the Hollywood gossip. There was a network of drivers who exchanged information while they waited outside studios and restaurants and clubs. And everyone who was anyone in Hollywood had a driver.

'Best you talk to Miss Rose about it,' Wilma said. 'Maybe some of it's not true. Alcohol and drugs and all sorts o' wildness. Other men—'

'*What?* She's only been married a few months!'

'That Mr Cornwell, he's no angel. He's led her wrong, you can bet on that. I'll get your breffus now.'

'No, skip it, there's no time. I must get over to the clinic right away. Tell Beanie to have the car ready in ten minutes.' *Other men?* Lennie thought, with a sense of doom. It was supposed to have been a love-match. And while the studios liked their stars to have romances, and *loved* them to get married, they didn't sanction promiscuity. He hastened indoors to finish dressing.

Between 1929, when Talkies became widespread, and 1934, there was a period of freedom in the making of movies.

On-screen violence, profanity, crime, drug use, prostitution, promiscuity . . . nothing was off limits. It was as if, ordinary decent folk complained, bad behaviour was being actively promoted, and they feared it would corrupt society.

In the first half of 1934 a campaign gathered way to persuade the government to take over the censorship of films. The possibility of government interference was enough to frighten the studios into adopting self-censorship as the lesser evil. Under the leadership of Will H. Hays, president of the Motion Picture Producers and Distributors of America, a Production Code was drawn up. Every motion picture released on or after the 1st of July 1934 had to acquire a certificate of approval from the MPPDA.

The Hays Code, as it was generally known, covered everything. Profanity – the use of words like God, Jesus, hell, damn, bastard and so on – was forbidden. There was to be no nudity, even in silhouette; men and women were not to be shown in bed together; no excessive or lustful kissing, especially if one of the characters was a bad person. Crime was not to be treated sympathetically in case it encouraged the impressionable. There was to be no mockery of the clergy or law-enforcement officers or the institution of marriage. Scenes depicting childbirth, surgical operations, or the judicial death sentence were outlawed. And the Flag was to be treated at all times with respect and dignity.

It was natural that, with the content of films so strictly overseen, the studios should clamp down on their stars. In the early days actors, even the females, had enjoyed a free-wheeling, buccaneering kind of life. But now even a big star like MGM's Mr Clark Gable had to conduct himself carefully in public: he was separated from his wife, Ria Langham, but she was unwilling to grant him a divorce, so if he romanced any lady it had to be strictly outside the bedroom. Divorce was acceptable in Hollywood, but adultery was anathema.

Lennie pondered these things as he was driven over to the

nursing home in Wilshire. Beanie glanced at him in the mirror, and finally spoke up when they were halted by traffic.

'Doan worry, Mist' Manning. Dat Ardmore place is the best. Dat whaur William Powell went, time he got his kinney stones fixed. Miss Rose'll be okay.'

Lennie gave him a stern look. 'Oh, you're talking to me now, are you? You didn't say a word before, when I might have helped her.'

Beanie looked wounded. 'I'd have tole you all right, but Wilma, she said notta. She said you wasn't to be upset.'

'And do you always do what Wilma tells you?' Lennie said scornfully.

Beanie thought about it. 'Pretty much,' he concluded. 'She like to whale on me if I cross her any. Wilma, she got a temper on her. She flang a pan o' potatoes at a journalist feller one time, boiling water an' all, jus' cos he trad mud on her clean floor.' He chuckled appreciatively. 'She's some woman, that Wilma.'

At the Ardmore, Lennie found Estelle in the sister's room, sitting at a desk, telephone glued to her ear. Estelle Cable was tiny, but made up for it with enormous masses of hair, dyed a deep, henna red, and flamboyant clothes. She never went unnoticed. The air was blue with smoke. She smoked incessantly from a long-stemmed holder, crushing each cigarette out halfway down, claiming in her harsh bray that she was trying to give up, but lighting another immediately. No-one knew how old she was: her face, under thick make-up, was hatched with fine lines, so that her detractors sometimes referred to her as the Shrunken Head. She was fierce, fearless, inexhaustible, and hugely successful at her job.

She raised her baleful eagle's glare to Lennie as he came in, waved the cigarette at him to wait, barked a few more furious things into the telephone, then slammed it down.

'This is a bad business,' she said. Her voice was as smoky

as a railway tunnel and her accent was pure Noo Yoik. She crushed out the current cigarette and, as though without volition, began fumbling in her handbag for another. 'There's only so much money can do. I can't bribe a whole hospital.' She waved a free hand at the door. 'Oh, this place is sound. Discretion is their sell. But someone at the Park will blab. Worse luck, Phil Stuckey from the *Herald* was outside the Parrot and saw it all. They love all that schmeer down at the *Herald*, Hollywood gossip, especially the bad kind. Most of all when some little Miss Susie Perfect falls flat on her face.' She gave him a skin-stripping look. 'What've you heard?'

'Rosecrantz came to see me this morning. That's the first I knew she was in any trouble.'

'Came to see *you*?'

'He's dropping her as a client,' Lennie admitted reluctantly. 'He thought I'd want to know.'

'Crap,' Estelle said explosively. She had finally fidgeted a new cigarette out of a pack and fitted it into the holder. Lennie fished his lighter from his pocket and leaned across. 'Thanks.' She blew the first cloud politely away from his face, evidently deep in thought. 'That may not be all bad. I like Rosecrantz, he's a great guy, but he's one of the old school. Maybe she needs a different kind of agent now, someone with more pizzazz. I gotta work fast, though, make it that *she* dumped *him*.'

'But there's the drink and the drugs at the club,' Lennie began.

'Yeah, we gotta work out a story. How's this? She was taking tablets for hay fever, had one cocktail, had a bad reaction.'

'But Rose doesn't—'

'I gotta tame doctor'll say he was treating her, warned her not to drink, but she's young, impetuous, she's out for an innocent lark with her young pals, who can blame her for forgetting in the heat of the moment?'

'*One* cocktail?'

She shrugged. 'Bobino, manager of the Parrot, he's one of mine. And he'll keep a hold on his staff. It's the rest of her posse that's the problem. She's pals with some kids that suffer from loose mouths. She's been running with a wild bunch lately. And some of 'em will do anything to get their names in the papers.' She took another mouthful of smoke and absently blew straight at Lennie. 'If we can keep her out of sight for a month or so, it'll give time for things to calm down. We'll say she's suffering with nervous exhaustion from working too hard. What *you* gotta do is talk to Al Feinstein. And talk to *her*. She's gotta shape up.'

'It's a bad business,' Lennie said gloomily.

'It's a shit show, is what it is,' said Estelle, 'and nobody's going to come out smelling like roses. But we'll fix it between us. Now get out of here and let me get on with my job. I got a thousand favours to call in.'

Beanie had been a mine of information. Rose's companions in the Parrot had been Don Acres, Kent Millburn, Tab Minkle, Mimi Cates and Jeannie Hooper – members of a large circle of young film actors, including Dean Cornwell, who in various combinations had been getting a reputation – at least on the drivers' circuit – for wild behaviour. Tab Minkle, brooding star of *Race to the Devil*, he of dark forelock, curling upper lip, and smouldering eyes, was the principal hell-raiser. With a reluctance to meet Lennie's eyes in the mirror, Beanie mentioned that Tab Minkle's driver had told him the two of them were 'having a walk-out' – his euphemism for an affair. Six weeks before, she'd been seeing Kent Millburn.

'It don't mean nothing,' he went on. 'She don't care a rap about either of 'em. I reckon she's just sore about Mist' Howard.'

'Who's Mr Howard?'

21

Beanie's eyes opened wide. 'Why, Mr Leslie Howard, sir, who else?' he said deliberately. 'Played Sir Percy Blakeney in *The Scarlet Pimple-nell*?'

'I've seen the movie.'

'Starring opp'site Miss Merle Oberon? She's English too, like Mist' Howard. After that *Pimple* movie MGM signed her up, and now she—'

'What has Leslie Howard to do with Rose?' Lennie interrupted him before he got too far down the rapids.

'Well, sir, I'm gettin' to it. Last year they was having a walk-out. That was after he stopped seein' Miss Oberon – you know how she played Anne Boleyn in *The Private Life of Henry VIII*? And our Miss Rose, she was Anne Boleyn in *The Falcon and the Rose*? So Mist' Howard's driver, he reckoned Mist' Howard kinda stuck on the character.' He chuckled. 'Ain't that a kick? He's a very romantic gentleman, Mist' Howard – and a real ladies' man. I reckon it's that accent they fall for. Makes everything you say sound classy.'

'But he must be twenty years older than Rose.'

'Yessir, but Miss Oberon only twenty-five. It don't matter in Hollywood.'

'You say it's all over between them now?'

'Well, sir, Miss Rose was partying too hard and I reckon Mist' Howard scared there gonna be scandal, so he skedaddled. But he's over to New York right now, predoocin' a play on Broadway, so it'd be over anyhow. But Miss Rose, I reckon she was fonder of him than he was of her. Maybe that's why she been cuttin' rigs jus' lately. To show like she ain't heartbroke.'

Lennie shook his head, aghast at how much he had missed. 'So tell me,' he said at last, 'what's wrong with Miss Rose's marriage? Why is she having affairs when she's not been married a year?'

'I don't like to say,' Beanie murmured, 'but Mist' Cornwell, he ain't no ladies' man, no, sir, not *at* all.'

'Mr Rosecrantz said Mr Cornwell's a troubled soul.'

'Dat one way of puttin' it.' He hesitated a moment. 'Word is, he pitches for the B team, if you get my drift.'

'Are you serious?'

'Yes, sir.' Beanie gained confidence now. 'And he likes low comp'ny. Mr Cornwell's driver, he takes him to all kind o' dives. Pool halls. Bars down at the docks.'

'And Rose knows about it?'

'That's why she gone a bit crazy, that and Mist' Howard.' He looked anxious. 'She gonna be okay, though?'

'No thanks to you,' Lennie said roughly. But he didn't blame Beanie. He blamed himself.

Rose looked tiny and fragile in the high hospital bed. She raised exhausted, blue-smudged eyes to Lennie, and slow tears leaked out. 'I thought he loved me. He said he loved me.' Lennie took hold of her small, damp hand. 'But it was all just publicity. He only married me for publicity.'

He realised then that it was Dean she was crying for, not Leslie Howard – which was a relief of sorts. 'I expect he did love you, honey. After all, he could have married anyone, but he chose you.'

'Because we'd worked together on *Falcon*.' She accepted his handkerchief and blew her nose. 'I guess when you act being in love day after day, you can start thinking you really are.'

'If you've learned that, you've learned something important,' Lennie said.

'But we really liked each other,' she mourned. 'I just didn't know about – you know what. I'd never even *heard* about that sort of thing. How does it work, anyway? I don't understand.'

'You don't need to know. What we have to do now is sort out the mess.'

'I suppose Dean and I will have to split up,' she said, in a small voice.

'Don't you want to? Are you still in love with him?'

'No, but—' She thought a bit. 'It's sort of like a failure. Like I'm not good enough.'

'You are never to think that,' Lennie said sternly. 'This was all Dean's fault.'

'I don't want to get him into trouble. Estelle says the studios hate that kind of thing. And if it gets in the papers, they might drop him and ruin his career.'

'In the end, it might come down to his career or yours,' Lennie said. He saw steel come into her drawn face.

'Okay. If it's him or me, then the hell with him, pardon my French.'

'Good girl. That's the spirit. Estelle will sort it all out. And it may not come to sacrificing Dean, if some arrangement can be arrived at – I don't suppose he wants publicity of that sort.'

'How—?'

'Leave that to us. I'm going to talk to Al Feinstein. If we can work out something he can sell to the press, I think I can talk him round. After all, I've put a lot of money into his productions, and if he wants to keep dipping into my pocket . . .'

Rose sighed again, and said, in a low voice, 'I miss my mother. If only she'd stayed here she'd never have got pneumonia and died. I feel so bad that she went back east because of me.'

Lennie said, 'Your mother was the strongest-minded woman I ever knew. She went back east because she wanted to. But you've raised a subject that has to be addressed: you can't live on your own, not after this. Everything has got to look ultra-respectable.'

'I don't know what to do.' Tears began to leak again. 'My mother's dead. Dean's a wash-out. Everyone just uses me to make money. Nobody cares what happens to *me*.'

'I care,' said Lennie.

'I wish you were my father. If I didn't have you, I don't know what I'd do. What's going to happen to me? I can't live at Roselands any more. It will always remind me of Dean.'

Inwardly Lennie sighed, but he wasn't surprised to hear himself say, 'Would you like to come and live with me, until all this blows over?'

'Really? Oh, yes!' she cried at once.

'You can bring your people with you – we've plenty of room. Wilma will make you comfortable.'

'Oh, I *love* Wilma,' she said. 'Can I really come?'

'Yes, but there's to be no shenanigans. No drinking, definitely no drugs, no running around with men, no wild parties.'

'I'll behave like a nun, I promise, if only you take care of me. You won't leave me, will you?' For all her fame and fortune, she looked just then very young and very lost.

'No, I won't leave you,' he said. 'As long as you behave yourself.'

Her eyes widened. 'I've just remembered, you're going to England, aren't you?'

'I'll put it off. Don't worry. I said I'd take care of you.'

'You're always so good to me,' she said, smiling at last.

Lennie smiled too, but underneath he could have wept. He thought of Polly, and Morland Place, and felt as lonely as he had ever felt in his life.

'I'd better send a cable,' he said, more to himself than to Rose.

When Polly got back to Morland Place she met James just coming out into the yard, wrapped up to the chin in a thick wool coat, wearing the special hat – deerskin lined with fleece, and earflaps that tied under the chin – that dated from his trip to Bear Island. His Elghund, Helmy, came bouncing past him eagerly. With his thick grey coat, he didn't mind the cold.

'Ha!' said Polly. 'The only dog willing to leave the fireside.'

James looked up at her, resting a hand on Zephyr's neck. 'Are you referring to me or Helmy?'

'Both,' she said. He was tall and handsome, her brother, easy-going and good-natured, affectionate to her, good with animals, idolised by her son, five-year-old Alec. He would have made a fine Master of Morland Place in good times: he was indolent, and not bookish, but he understood the land. And the tenants would have adored him: Polly they viewed with suspicion, though they were getting used to her now, seeing that she had gone four and a half years without ruining the place. But James had been born to the position, and would have reigned over his kingdom with easy grace.

Death duties had put paid to that, and after a period of severe anguish – he simply was not used to having to worry about anything, and the experience frightened him – he had yielded up the estate to Polly with nothing but relief. There was still a part of Polly that felt like an impostor, that James was the true king. But she believed Papa would have approved of her, if he could see her now.

'What are you going after?' she asked, eyeing the gun under his arm. 'Deer?'

'Not with Helmy,' he said. 'I thought I might try for some pigeons. Could you fancy pigeon pie?'

'You get 'em, I'll eat 'em. You seem very jolly. Has something happened?'

'It has. I had a telephone call from Charlie. Typical of him: "Where are you, James? Why aren't you here, James?" As if I should have known by instinct that he wanted me back.'

'Where's "here"?'

'London, but he's going back to Paris soon. He says he's got a big adventure planned for the spring, but he won't tell me what it is yet.'

'How exciting.'

'Well, I expect it will be, knowing Charlie. Oh, and he's having a series of dinners in London at the moment and wants me to help him with them. So I shall be heading off tomorrow.'

'So soon? Oh dear, I shall miss you.'

'I'll miss you too.'

'Well, we've got tonight. I'll have them bring up a good bottle of wine.'

He grinned. 'Already thought of that.' Zephyr, fidgeting, butted him in the chest. 'Better get this nag in out of the cold. I'll see you later.' He passed on, but immediately stopped and turned back to say, 'Oh, and you had a cable while you were out.'

'From Lennie?' she said eagerly.

'I don't know, I didn't read it,' he said, and was gone.

In the great hall, Barlow, the butler, Fand, her dog, and Alec all found her at the same moment. Fand tried to knock her over, Barlow gave her the cable, and Alec wound himself round her waist and begged her to come and see what he'd been doing. She patted the dog, promised Alec she would come, and tore open the cable. It would be details of Lennie's sailing, she supposed. She began to hatch a plan to drive down and meet him at Southampton. It would be fun to surprise—

VERY MUCH REGRET WILL HAVE TO POSTPONE VISIT + FAMILY PROBLEMS WILL KEEP ME HERE SOME MONTHS + HEARTFELT APOLOGIES + LETTER FOLLOWS + LOVE LENNIE ++

It was, Polly thought, enough to make you cry.

CHAPTER TWO

The weather was freezing, but clear: Paris was a place of long blue shadows, skeletal branches, and sooty spires scratching a sky the colour of a Norse goddess's eyes. James liked being back in Paris, and Paris, it seemed, liked to have him back, restoring him to its grubby bosom with a very Parisian nonchalance. He even got his old lodgings back in the tall squeeze of a house in Montmartre: his old room at the very top was let, alas, but the room below that was vacant. It was a little larger and more comfortable, though he missed the view over the rooftops. But leaning out he could see down into the narrow cobbled street and watch its varied life go by. There was a window-box outside his casement, empty now, but he thought he would plant it with geraniums – scarlet ones, which would blaze against the grey stone of the house opposite.

The neighbourhood hadn't changed, nor its cast of characters. They acknowledged him in their varied ways. The pretty brown-haired girl in the blue apron in the *boulangerie* blushed and lowered her gaze. The concierge of the big building on the corner – who on a fine day sat outside on a wooden chair – nodded to him, slightly closing her eyes like a big, dusty black cat. The old man with the empty sleeve pinned across his breast, who always wore his medals as if to advance an explanation, raised his walking-stick in greeting as he stumped by, *Le Figaro* under his arm. Monsieur

Pompier, smoking a foul cigarette at the door of his hardware shop, beneath the entablature of hanging pots and pans, thrilled him with the first '*Bonjour, voisin!*' of his return.

He went to his favourite barber's shop to have his hair trimmed, and the barber smiled and said, '*Ah, m'sieu'. Vous êtes de retour?*' then talked him into a shave with hot towels. He stopped at the café with the blue check tablecloths on the rue des Saules and had his first *café complet.* The proprietress, a wide but curiously flat woman – as if she had been rolled out, like pastry – left her high throne behind the *caisse* and brought it to his table herself, and called him *mignon.* And on his first evening back, he went to Le Grenouille on the rue Gabrielle and had a *tartiflette* that sang with onions, washed down with a beaker full of the warm south, followed by a *financier* that melted on the tongue. The proprietor was a circular man with a round, bald, shiny head, like old ivory, which he nodded as he sent him over a *marc* in a thick, squat tumbler. '*Gratuit,*' the waiter muttered, as he slapped it down, bending to James's ear. He reeked of Gauloises and garlic. *I'm home*, James thought.

The only negative was the absence of Meredith. She had gone home for Christmas, to the family ranch in Wyoming. She had travelled as far as New York with Charlie and Fern, so he had assumed, for no thought-out reason, that she would come back at the same time as them. But on his first day back at the office, when he had asked Charlie where she was, he learned that she was still in Wyoming. Her father, who had been ailing for some time, had died on Christmas Eve. Her three brothers were carrying on the business, but while they were hard workers and skilled with the stock, none of them was the least bit good with the books, so she was staying to run that side of it.

'And she said she didn't like to leave her mother just yet,' Charlie concluded. James always thought Charlie a very Parisian-looking man, short and stocky, with a bullet head, a rubbery, mobile face, and ears that stood out from his head as though he could prick them like a dog at what interested him – which was everything. James had never met a more mentally energetic man. Now Charlie's face creased in sympathy for their absent colleague.

'She told you all this,' James mused, 'so she must have – written?'

'A cable at Christmas, and a long letter in January.'

'Did she – was there any message for me?'

'No,' said Charlie, and then, as if in mitigation, 'It was a business letter, really.'

James was hurt. He had not heard a word from her since she left before Christmas. Now it seemed that she didn't care enough for him even to send a second-hand 'so goodbye, dear, and amen'. It became obvious that she had not shared his feelings. He had been in love with her; for her it had been just one of those things.

'She's never coming back?' James said, subdued.

'Obviously she has some family duties, but stay on the farm for good? That doesn't sound like our Meredith. I told her there's a job for her with me any time she wants it. We'll just have to wait and see. I miss her as much as you, but we'll have to manage.'

James was sure he'd miss her much more than Charlie, and not only on a personal level: he was expected to cover her job.

'I've never done office work,' he protested. 'I don't know how.'

'You'll soon pick it up. Correspondence, answering the phone, making arrangements,' said Charlie. 'Any intelligent person could do it.'

Charlie was kind, and tried to ease him into the job. James did not know shorthand, so he dictated his letters slowly at first, though when his thoughts flowed he tended to forget and gallop ahead. James developed his own scheme of abbreviations, which sometimes he could understand afterwards and sometimes not. Typing was painful at first, with many mistakes, frantic hunting over the keyboard in search of the apostrophe and anguished cries of 'Where's the "q"? I can't find the "q"!' But though he never learned to type with more than two fingers, he got quick enough to give satisfaction.

Making arrangements meant setting up a network of useful contacts, and using common sense, patience and good French. It was more difficult when he had to deal with officials, for Gallic bureaucracy seemed to be designed to make clear a distinction between the mighty bureaucrat and the supplicant citizen. Meredith had obviously had her own methods and short-cuts, and Charlie had never understood the word *can't*, so James laboured to keep up, and went to bed most evenings mentally exhausted.

Much of his work was concerned with Charlie's next 'adventure': a trip to Russia. If French bureaucrats were devoted to arcana, Russian officials were twice as bad, adding a layer of deep suspicion to the passion for secrecy. Getting permits and visas, arranging travel and accommodation, and setting up meetings were all twice as difficult.

The greatest surprise came when Charlie said, 'I think you'd better learn some Russian. You've got a natural gift for languages, so it shouldn't be too hard for you to pick it up. It will make all the difference – even though I believe a lot of them speak French. People are always flattered if you try to speak their language, however badly.'

James looked up from his desk in surprise. 'I'm not going with you, am I?'

'Of course. We were going to take Meredith, and now you're doing her job. Can you shoot?'

'Rifle. I was considered a fair shot back home,' James said, perplexed. 'But—'

'Oh, I'm sure they won't let us carry a gun. I was just thinking out loud.' He slapped James encouragingly on the

31

shoulder. 'There won't be any trouble. Just make sure you have all the paperwork in perfect order. A piece of paper with the right signature on it gets you a long way in countries like that. And learn some Russian!'

'And what is my lovely wife doing today?' Kit Westoven asked. He was magnificent in a dressing-gown decorated all over with exotic birds, his thick glossy hair carefully waved, his chin shaved as smooth as silk. There was nothing impromptu about it when Kit appeared *en déshabillé*: his man, Ponsford, would have died rather than let anyone see his master less than perfectly turned out.

Emma, already dressed, was breakfasting in her sitting-room. His dogs pattered in after him – elegant Sulfi and Eos – and joined Emma's mongrels Alfie and Buster under the table. They hadn't seen each other all night. Wildly waving tails tickled her legs.

'Lunch at the Savoy with Mipsy Oglander and Kitsy Brownlow,' she answered his question. 'I'm hoping to get them to invest in my Macklin Street scheme.' This was the latest of her Weston Trust projects – buying up slum properties, demolishing them, and building blocks of flats for the respectable working classes.

Kit considered. 'Mipsy Oglander, possibly – she has more money than she knows what to do with. But Kitsy Brownlow? Perry isn't exactly swimming in oof, you know.'

'I do know. I don't really expect her to come in, but she's good company and Mipsy can be rather hard work.'

'You know Perry Brownlow's been made lord-in-waiting to the King?'

'I heard. But it was expected, wasn't it, after he was equerry to him as Prince of Wales?'

'Hm, yes, but David isn't exactly known for his deep, abiding loyalty to his chums.' His eye suddenly fixed on the slice of toast that Emma was holding. 'Is that my kumquat marmalade you're spreading about so liberally?' he demanded indignantly.

Emma's hand stopped, knife suspended. 'It's what they brought in. I didn't notice.'

'I do think it's too bad of you! You know how hard it is to get hold of,' he complained.

'I don't actually. From where?"

'Corfu. Marina Kent knows someone who has a villa there with kumquat trees. An elderly grand duchess, I believe – some half-Russian second-cousin in exile. She makes it to earn pocket-money. Or possibly gin-money. You know what these exiled royalties are. Anyway, strings have to be pulled to get it to me via Athens. They smuggle it in the diplomatic bag.'

'I had no idea it was a politically sensitive preserve. Naturally I shall stop eating it forthwith.'

'Oh, you know I can't deny you anything,' he said, but all the same, he took the toast from her and began to crunch it himself.

Philosophically Emma selected another slice from the toast rack, buttered it, and reached for the honey. 'You were late last night,' she observed. 'Good dinner?'

'Rather,' Kit said automatically, but then his eyes flew open. 'Yes, actually, I have things to tell you. Tremendous goings-on – prepare to be amazed! Dinner at Quaglino's, and Belmont and I had just tottered round to the club for a settler when in came Eddie Vibart. He'd been equerrying at York House and he was simply bursting with news. It seems Ernest Simpson went there for dinner with the King. He took his pal Rickatson-Hatt with him—'

'The Reuters man?'

'The very same – and when they'd finished, Simpson says he wants a serious word with HM. So Rickatson-Hatt says, "Point taken, old horse, I'll stagger off and leave you to it."'

'I'm sure he didn't say it like that. He picked up frightful

American slang when he worked in New York, so he'd have been more likely to say—'

'Hush, don't interrupt. This is my story! Where was I? Oh, yes – Hattie proposes to imitate a hoop and bowl away, but Simpson says, "Hold on, old thing, I'd rather you stayed," and gives him a look that says as clear as day, *I need a witness*. Naturally, Eddie is all agog, thinking the Simp is going to slap the King's face with a glove and challenge him to defend his honour.'

Emma, who always enjoyed his style, said, 'He didn't, of course?'

'Well, naturally not, but it wasn't far short. You see – I have to backtrack a bit – Simpson recently applied to join the same Masonic lodge as the King, and Sir Maurice Jenks, who's the lodge president, turned him down. When the King – who had rather encouraged Simpson to apply in the first place, d'you see? – demanded to know why, Jenks said it was against Masonic law to have a cuckolded husband as a member.'

'Oh dear.'

'Yes, rather an "off with his head" moment! But the King then told him – Jenks – that his relationship with Mrs S is purely platonic, so Jenks had to let Simpson in. A mason can't call a fellow mason a liar. Of course, the story's got about and no-one believes a word of it, and now it's got back to Simpson that everyone in London is sniggering about the whole thing.'

'One can't but feel sorry for him,' Emma said. 'Go on.'

'Hence the little tête-à-tête,' Kit continued. 'Simpson feels things have come to a head. It's bad enough that the King is openly running around London with a fellow's wife and lavishing her with jewels, but when people start mocking a fellow on that account, he can't ignore it any longer. He tells HM, man to man, that dear Wally will have to choose between them, and asks what his intentions are: does he mean to marry her?'

'*He didn't!*' Emma was appalled.

'But he did! And here's the thing, Oh best beloved – you'd think the King would *um* and *er* about it and generally look a bit shifty, but in fact he stares Simpson straight in the eye and says he wouldn't dream of being crowned without Mrs S being crowned beside him as his wife and queen! Says it right out, with Rickatson-Hatt as an independent witness – and him a pressman into the bargain! Poor Eddie almost choked on his own tongue, trying not to intervene.'

'My God! But David can't be serious,' Emma said.

'I'm rather afraid he might be. He's absolutely obsessed with her.'

'But surely he can't imagine it could ever happen? What did Simpson say?'

'He said in that case, he would do the decent thing and let Mrs S divorce him, provided the King swore to take care of her. What d'you think of that?'

'I'm aghast. It's going cause terrible complications if the King really starts talking about marriage.'

'Delicious, isn't it? Just like a penny novelette.'

'Except that it's really rather serious,' Emma said reprovingly.

Kit took her hand and kissed it. 'I know, darling. But one can't help seeing the funny side as well. The Hardinges and Wigrams and Halseys at the Palace – all the old guard – are going to be so very, very upset! They're unhappy with the King already.'

'Because he's difficult and stubborn and rude?'

'His father was all those things. They rather expect it of a monarch. No, what they can't stand is the absence of any sense of duty. Obstinacy without a purpose. I must say,' he added, 'that with all her faults, Wally gets more out of him than anyone else. If she were allowed to stay in the background and pull his strings, we might get a better king for it.'

'But this talk of marriage has got to stop,' Emma said firmly.

'Obviously. Eddie will say something to HM when the opportunity arises, for what good that will do. Everything goes in one ear and out the other – there being so little in between to stop it. But it's going to complicate things considerably if Simpson goes ahead with the divorce and Wally becomes available. Our best defence will be gone.' He glanced at the clock on the overmantel. 'Talking of being gone, I must get dressed. Are you in for dinner tonight?'

'I am – are you?'

'I shall make a point of it. Isn't it wonderful that court mourning means there are no heavy engagements? We can have a comfortable coze together – and I'd like to go over your plans for Macklin Street with you. I've had a very clever idea for how to arrange the kitchen, bathroom and coal bunker. Come, dogs!'

And he was gone in a swirl of colour.

As it happened, Kitsy Brownlow chucked at the last moment, so Emma lunched with Mipsy Oglander alone. Mipsy was another Baltimore Belle and had known Wally Simpson all her life, but she seemed not to have heard the latest story – at least, she never mentioned it, and Mipsy was in the habit of mentioning everything – so Emma avoided the subject altogether and talked, when she could get a word in, only about Macklin Street. Mipsy seemed quite receptive, and Emma was quite hopeful of getting a commitment from her, when Mipsy suddenly noticed the time and exclaimed that she had a 'facial' appointment and would have to dash.

Emma said lunch was on her (it never hurt to impose a small obligation) and was waiting for the bill to arrive when her name was called in a loud, harsh voice, and Mrs Simpson came striding towards her, trailing restaurant staff like a magnet trailing pins. 'Emma, just the person I wanted to see!' she exclaimed. She snapped her fingers without looking and one of the waiters darted in to pull out a chair for her. 'Bring me a ham omelette and a salad. And a glass of seltzer. No, make it a glass of champagne,' she said. 'Put it on Lady Westerham's check.' She met Emma's eye, raised an eyebrow, and said, 'I left my pocket-book at the flat. I figured a friend could sock a girl a lunch once in a while.'

Emma nodded assent to the waiter and he went away. Mrs Simpson loosened her fur, emitting a waft of expensive perfume, and said, 'I'm beat. David's been taking me over Buckingham Palace all morning.' Her hard eyes raked Emma as she spoke, cataloguing her looks and her clothes. Emma knew herself pretty in a fresh-faced, curly-haired way, and young for her years – she had just turned forty. Wally had never had beauty, making up for it with style and vivacity, but she looked her age. There were diamonds at her ears and wrists, and her small, close hat was secured by an amusing diamond arrow, but despite their sparkle, Emma thought she looked tired, and not at all well, her skin pouchy and a bad colour. Her red lipstick only emphasised her pallor.

'You're not lunching alone?' Wally demanded.

'I've just finished,' said Emma. 'Mipsy was here – she had to dash away.'

'Oh, Mipsy. Haven't seen her in a while,' Wally said dismissively, and reverted to her own affairs. 'Buckingham Palace is simply ghastly. It's a mausoleum. Dusty crimson velvet, gloomy old paintings and heavy furniture. David and I agreed there's nothing worth saving. We're going to strip everything out and do it up from top to bottom. Light colours, modern furniture, bright drapes, new carpets, everything. Open the place up and blow some fresh air through it. And here's the thing,' She leaned forward slightly. 'I'd like to offer *you* the job.'

Emma was shocked, not so much that Wally had no taste for Victorian interiors, but at her use of the word 'I' in that sentence. She thought for an instant of what Kit would say. 'It's kind of you to ask me,' she said, 'but—'

'Now, Emma, at least think about it before you say no. I liked what you did with Veronica's house. Very fresh. And didn't you do the Talbot-Manners place as well? You have just the sort of light, modern touch we want. And this will be a major, *major* project.'

Now Emma laughed. 'I don't want a major, *major* project, thank you. I haven't time.'

'Your name would be associated with the interior, right down through history, like all those Nashes and Adamses and Scotts. It would absolutely *make* you!'

'I don't want to be made. I'm quite happy – and *very* busy – with my Weston Trust buildings.'

Wally sat back, her interest lost where she could not prevail. 'Oh, yes, your flats for the lower classes. You should talk to David about that. He's very keen on welfare for the poor.'

'Weston Trust flats are not for the poor, they're for decent working people: clerks, teachers, nurses, people like that.'

Wally wasn't listening. 'And, frankly, he needs something to keep him busy. He's all too inclined to lounge about, smoking too much and complaining he's bored. I'll get Elsie Mendl to do Buckingham Palace, if you're really not interested. She'll jump at it.'

'You'll ruffle a lot of feathers if you change things too much.'

'I intend to ruffle feathers! They need ruffling. All those old palace servants and officials, they're like stuffed dummies. Everything has to be done the same way it's been done since 1066 or the sky will fall. David's not going to be that sort of king. We're going to drag this whole show into the twentieth century. Can you imagine,' she said, leaning forward, 'they insist that lunch be served at one p.m., whether anyone wants it or not? And why? Because it's always been served at one p.m..' She sat back, and the waiters seized the opportunity to put her lunch before her. She picked up the champagne glass, but put it down again untasted as she went on speaking. 'I told them, you need to figure out who's in charge around here. If the King wants luncheon at two p.m., that's when it's served. And if he wants a sandwich at eleven p.m. or scrambled eggs at four in the morning, the kitchen's got to be damn well ready to rustle it up. They should remember who pays their wages.' She changed tack. 'He hardly eats anything as it is. He'll eat a lettuce leaf and five grapes and say he's done. I do my best to tempt his appetite when we're at home, but of course I can't always be there.'

She picked up her fork and broke a small piece off the edge of the omelette, speared it, then put the fork down again.

'You don't seem to be eating much yourself,' Emma remarked.

'It's my insides playing up again,' Wally sighed. 'All this conflict is hell on my ulcers. I'm sick of palace officials saying such and such can't be done because it's never been done that way. And looking at me like I'm something the cat dragged in.'

'People don't like change,' Emma said mildly. 'They like to know where they stand.'

'They'll be standing in the dole queue if they don't shape up,' she said. 'I told Alec Hardinge, "The King wants people around him with fresh ideas. If you're going to be his private secretary you're going to have to change the way you think." He's only forty-two, you know, Hardinge. You'd think he was *eighty*-two! They should ask themselves,' she went on pointedly, 'why the King gets on better with Americans than with his own people. It's because *we*'re not hide-bound. We're not afraid of change. We *embrace* the future.' She paused for breath, and actually ate the corner of her omelette.

'I understand Ernest had dinner with David last night,' Emma said tentatively.

Wally looked up. 'How do *you* know about it?'

'Kit told me.'

Wally grimaced. 'Kit always knows everything.'

'Apparently David talked about marriage?'

'It's sheer fantasy,' Wally said sharply. 'He knows it can't happen.'

'Of course it can't. But – wouldn't you like to be Queen?' Emma asked mischievously.

'I've never asked for that,' she said. 'I'm quite happy as I am, in the background, pulling the strings. I just want to get things running smoothly, and put away a little nest egg, so Ernest and I can retire together, financially secure. All I need is another year, maybe two, to consolidate, then I can step back. What I *don't* need,' she went on, with fierce emphasis, 'is Ernest getting himself involved and complicating things.'

'Perhaps he feels a bit left out,' Emma suggested.

'I'm doing it for *us*,' she said indignantly. 'I can manage David if everyone just leaves us alone. And the country will get a better king out of it.'

'That's what Kit said.'

'Kit knows what he's talking about,' Wally said approvingly. 'But we've got to scotch this talk of divorce. Ernest could put me in a very difficult position. He just has to trust me and not interfere.' She put her fork down again, as though it was too heavy to hold.

'You do look tired,' Emma said. 'Maybe you should do the stepping back now.'

'David would go mad if I tried. All this kinging is new to him. He needs me too much.' She didn't say it as though it gave her pleasure. She leaned closer. 'Tell you the truth, Emma, I sometimes think he's gone a little crazy since his father died. He wants to be with me *all the time*. And when he's not, it's telephone calls every couple of hours, and letters, and little notes brought round with flowers. I'm suffocating! He rings me up in the *middle of the night*. I don't sleep well anyway, and it's dollars to doughnuts that as soon as I do manage to drop off, he'll telephone and wake me up again.'

'They ought to find him a suitable princess,' Emma said, interested to see what Wally would say. Kit had explained to her his own idea about how things really stood between David and Mrs S: the King hadn't been lying when he told Ernest his relationship was platonic. 'He needs to get married and produce an heir.'

Wally gave a mirthless snort. 'That won't happen. David's not what you'd call heir conditioned.'

Emma smiled at the joke, but said, 'That's hard luck on the country.'

'Not at all. There's Bertie York and his two little girls. And the Kents have a boy already. There's plenty of cover.' She sighed. 'God, I have *got* to get away for a bit, have a break from all the strain. I'm thinking of going to Paris. First week of March – David's got engagements so he wouldn't be able to follow me. Why don't you come? See the new collections. Do a little shopping. What do you say?'

Emma felt bad about refusing. For all Wally's annoying ways, she couldn't help feeling sorry for her. 'I can't. I'm up to my ears in work. I'm sorry.'

Wally shrugged. 'No matter. I'll ask Mipsy. She's always got time for me.'

James had no idea how he might learn Russian. It was true he had picked up French quickly enough, but one was exposed to a certain level of French all one's life: Russian one never came across. The only idea he came up with was the barman at a little place on the corner of the rue Girardon whose name was Igor, which he thought was a Russian name. Igor was burly and swarthy and had a foreign accent – though in fairness you could say that about a lot of French barmen.

So he called in at the Chat Inquiet on his way home for

a *pastis* and coffee and, having chatted to Igor for a few minutes, he asked, 'Are you Russian, by any chance?'

Igor scowled. 'Are you English, by any chance?'

James gave a placating smile. 'I'm not being rude. You see, my boss wants me to learn a bit of Russian, and I don't know where to go or who to ask.'

'I was born in Russia,' Igor said, without moving his lips, 'but I don't go around talking about it. You never know who's listening.' He swiped a cloth over the bar top while glancing cautiously to left and right.

'Would you teach me?' James asked. 'I would pay you, of course.'

Igor shrugged. 'I've forgotten most of it. Been speaking French for too long.'

'Well, could you suggest anyone else? A friend, maybe?'

'I've only got French friends,' Igor snapped. 'Russians are all bastards, or drunks, or crooks. Or all three.' Then he seemed to relent. 'You serious about this?'

'Yes, I am. I really have to learn some Russian – or I might lose my job,' he added with a hint of pathos.

'Best place for you to go, then, is the Maison de l'Évangile.'

'What's that? A convent?'

'No, it's a charity. An English lady set it up. They help Russian refugees find a place to live and give them money till they find a job, things like that. They're bound to know someone who would give Russian lessons for money.'

'Have you got the address?'

'All I know is it's over in the sixteenth, down by the river, past the Bois. Look it up.' Igor swiped the rag over the bar top again. 'You eating?' he demanded.

Information had to be paid for, James thought. 'I'll have a *croque monsieur*,' he said. 'And a *pression*.'

Igor shouted the order through to the back, and poured the beer. He slapped it down in front of James, then added another *pastis* he hadn't ordered. For a warm instant James thought it was a gesture of friendship, then realised that the profit on *pastis* was greater than on beer.

A smart young woman in a tailor-made was manning the office. She listened to James's enquiry, then asked him a number of questions about himself, making a note of his name, address, and place of work. She knew the name of Charles Bedaux, and that seemed to give James some status. But it was his admission that he was English which finally thawed her. She switched from French into English to ask him where he was from, and elicited a description of Yorkshire. James could always wax lyrical over Morland Place, but he was rather wondering where all this was going, when she said at last, 'We have to be very careful, you see, but I am satisfied now that you are not a Soviet agent.'

'No, of course I'm not,' he said, surprised. 'I don't look Russian, do I?'

'I didn't think you were. But we don't get many people coming in off the street – mostly people come by recommendation. I can arrange with someone to teach you Russian. I'll have to check with her first, so you must come back tomorrow.'

Thus James was introduced to Tatiana Bebidov. She worked during the day as a teacher at an infant school, so their meeting took place, conveniently for James, in the time between his office day and his evening engagements. As well as doing Meredith's job, he was still expected to be available as before to welcome Charlie's guests, make them comfortable, show them around Paris, entertain them. Most evenings were taken up with attending parties or escorting people to the theatre or nightclubs.

Tatiana Bebidov was a tiny person, with an unruly mass of dark brown wavy hair, barely subdued in a chignon. She had large, dark eyes, and a wide, full mouth that seemed always to want to be laughing. The effort of restraining it had given her deep dimples on either side. She had long, expressive fingers and when she moved it was with a grace that he learned later to associate with those who had trained in the ballet. She was vivacious and disarmingly friendly and he guessed her age to be about twenty-three.

She lived in a small, dark apartment in an old house with a particularly ferocious concierge, a large woman with enormous arms like bolsters, who would not allow James in without reading his letter of introduction several times, and inspecting him with an intimidating scowl.

'What do you want with Mademoiselle?' she demanded, at length.

'She is to teach me Russian,' James said. It said so in the letter, but this was obviously not a woman to argue with.

'Why do you want to learn Russian?'

'My boss has Russian clients. He wants me to make them feel welcome.'

'What sort of Russians?'

James had no idea what would be the right answer. 'Nice ones, who like flowers and birds and go to church,' he said, and got ready to duck.

The woman's eyes seemed to bulge, and then she broke into phlegmy laughter and reached out to pinch James's cheek. The pinch hurt quite a lot. 'You are a wicked boy, but I like you. Go on up. I shall knock every half-hour, so no funny business.'

Telling Miss Bebidov about this encounter broke the ice. She laughed. 'That is "Maman" Poussin. She eats strangers for breakfast. Never show fear. She likes bold people who make her laugh.'

'Is there a Papa Poussin?' James asked. 'Somehow I can't imagine it.'

'Oh yes, she is married, but he is no "Papa". He has nothing to do with the tenants. He works for a newspaper.'

'He's a journalist?'

'No, a printer. A compositor, I think it's called. He's a very small man and never speaks. One sees him scurry in and out, but that's all. Your French is very good. You speak like a French person.'

'Thank you. Yours is very good too, Mademoiselle.'

'But you silly, I've spoken it since birth. We spoke it at home, English too. I can talk in English if you prefer. But do not call me Mademoiselle. My friends call me Tata, and we must be friends if I am to teach you properly. Your name is difficult for me. Shems, is that right?'

'Shems will do very well,' he said, amused.

'And you must come every day. You cannot learn with a lesson once a week because you forget everything in between and are always catching up.'

'I can come at this time every day,' James said.

'Good. Then we begin.'

By the time Maman Poussin knocked at the half-hour point, James felt thoroughly at home, though the room had an exotic feeling. The dark red flock wallpaper was almost hidden with framed photographs, icons of saints, posies of dried flowers, silk rosettes, and hanging strips of coloured silks, like scarves. The furniture was old and heavy, with crimson velvet upholstery, rubbed threadbare in places; the carpet was an ancient Turkish, mainly dark red and brown; and every surface was covered with ornaments and more photographs in silver frames. The alcoves either side of the fireplace were shelved and filled with old leather-bound books. In one corner a candle burned inside a red glass before an icon, and in another a samovar, with the silver worn brassily off, bubbled softly.

Concentration broken by the knock, Tata said, 'We will have tea.' She served it to James in a glass in a silver holder, with a saucer of raspberry jam to spoon into it. He found he quite liked it. Gazing about the room, he asked about the candle in the red glass, and she said, 'That is St Basil, my birth saint. In Russia we call it the "beautiful corner". Every house has them.'

'Is the glass always red?'

'Oh, yes. That is tradition. In Russian, "red" and "beautiful" are the same word.'

'Red is a lucky colour for the Chinese people, too,' he said.

'Where did you learn that?' she asked, seeming surprised.

'Charlie – my boss – told me. He has travelled a great deal.'

'You are not very like an English person, Shems,' she said thoughtfully. 'English men are gruff and stiff, though kind underneath. But you are . . .' she waved a hand around, searching for the expression '. . . *souple*. I think you might be quite poetic.'

James laughed. 'You can't call an English man poetic.'

'But there, I have said, you are not like an English man.'

Richard Howard paused and checked the address. Each road in that part of Ealing was lined on either side with identical semi-detached 'villas', as they were known, in red brick with a slate roof and a bay window. Each had a little porch over the front door, edged with fancy woodwork, like the canopy in a railway station. There was a black-and-white diamond path leading from the front gate to the front door, which had two stained-glass panels in the cheerful primary colours of boiled sweets. There was a small garage attached to the side with wooden doors and a tar-paper roof, and the front garden was an oblong of grass with a round bed in the middle in which stood several March-bare roses.

In fact, the villa was distinguishable from its neighbours only by the house number back-painted on the fanlight above the door.

Richard stared up and had a moment of extraordinary double vision, as though standing outside himself and seeing a different view altogether. He had been born Richard Arthur Hampden Fitzjames Howard, the second son of an earl. His maternal great-grandfather had been a duke. His maternal grandmother's godfather had been the Duke of Wellington, in whose honour he had been given the name Arthur, and her sister had been lady-in-waiting to Queen Victoria. His widowed mother had remarried, to another earl, and was now the Countess of Belmont with a large estate in Derbyshire. For a moment, overlying the suburban villa, he saw the ancestral mansion in St James's Square where he had been born and raised. There had also been the great estate at Brancaster in Lincolnshire, and another in Yorkshire, and yet another in north Norfolk that no-one much ever visited.

Until his father's death, he had never lived in a house with a number.

'This is it,' he said. He felt Cynthia's hand tighten on his, and looked down at her. 'What do you think?'

'It's lovely,' she said, in a faint, strained voice.

She was tall for a woman, and rather on the thin side, and you would not have called her pretty, except when she smiled, which she didn't often – not because she was sullen but because she was shy. She mostly resembled her father, with his large-featured face, round blue eyes and curly hair; from her mother, who was small, plump and handsome, she had got only the fairness of the curls. She was wearing a close-fitting wool coat with a black velvet collar and cuffs, and a small round hat trimmed with gold-brown feathers. Her sensible brown shoes were well-polished and her gloves well-kept. She looked in every particular neat, respectable and unremarkable. You would not remember passing her in the street.

She had cried when he had proposed to her. He found that uncomfortable to remember.

'*Really* lovely?' he asked.

'It looks new,' she said approvingly.

In the world he had come from, newness was not looked for in a house. Fitzjames House, where he had been born, had belonged to his ancestors for four hundred and fifty years. But everything was different now. He shook away the double vision.

'It's new all right,' he said. 'It's hardly been lived in. Shall we go in?'

Inside, the house smelt cleanly of wood. He closed the door behind them, and saw how the sunlight coming in through the stained-glass panels made fruit-drop patches on the wall. *This will be my home*, he thought. *My children will be born here*. The house number, seen backwards from inside, was 27. That would be his address – 27 Wellington Road. The streets in this estate were named after Victorian prime ministers, and it was simply chance that they were looking in Wellington Road rather than Melbourne, Palmerston or Canning. His grandmother's godfather. Coincidence.

The house was empty of furniture. Downstairs there was a drawing room at the front, a tiny room behind it, which he supposed might be useful as a study, and then a dining room, with French windows letting out to the garden. Beyond again, in the back-addition part of the house, were the kitchen, scullery, servant's lavatory and coalshed.

Upstairs there were three bedrooms, a bathroom and a separate lavatory. Over the kitchen there was the servant's bedroom. Each of the rooms had a fireplace; electricity and gas were laid on, as well as mains water and sewerage, and there was a boiler in the scullery to provide hot water to the whole house. Behind was a garden with a lawn and flower-beds, and vegetable plots beyond. It backed onto the garden of the matching house in the next road.

Inspection over, Cynthia looked up at him shyly, and it was not possible to tell anything from her face – except that her cheeks seemed a little pink. With pleasure? Or vexation?

'Well?' he said. 'Do you like it?'

'Will it be all right for you to get to work?' she asked.

'Oh, yes. I can drive in, or take the Underground. The Piccadilly Line goes straight through. But what about you? Could you be happy here?'

'It's lovely,' she said again. 'I've never lived in a house before.'

She had lived all her life with her parents in a mansion flat in Earls Court. Her father, his employer – soon to be partner – was buying them the house as a wedding-present. He would pay for the furniture, which Cynthia and her mother would choose. Richard imagined them browsing for linens and china in Peter Jones, and refreshing themselves afterwards with tea and buns in the top-floor café, two quiet, well-dressed ladies, who had never caused a moment's disquiet to anyone in their well-ordered lives.

'Shall we take it, then?' he said. She nodded, looking up at him, and he knew she wanted to be kissed, to seal the bargain, here, in their very first house. So he kissed her, and her soft lips clung for an instant before she made herself release him. She had been brought up to believe a woman must not make too many demands on her man.

He drove them back to Town. All the way he had that same strange feeling of double vision, a sense of unreality, as though at some point he had gone through the wrong door and was not living in his own life any more. He feared that if he looked into a mirror just then, it would not be his face looking back.

Everything had changed, of course, when his father died, leaving them literally penniless. But he was the second son: had his father survived, he would still have had to earn a living. Probably he would have gone into the diplomatic, or the army, his way eased by connections; and in time, given that he had always been popular with the other sex, he would have married a nice girl with a reasonable dowry, and set up

49

house with her. Not so very different, then, from what he was doing with Cynthia Nevinson? But her world was different from the world he had been brought up in.

As he drove along the Uxbridge Road he saw to either side the shops and occasional pubs, the side streets of neat little houses, the omnibuses. This was Suburbia: his sort lived in Town, or the country, or both, but never this in-between shadow land. He saw the people in their plain, modest clothes, going about their plain, modest lives. He thought, I shall be doing that: going to work, coming home on the Underground, letting myself in with a key, having dinner, then a quiet evening reading the paper or listening-in to the wireless. It was how people lived.

And it wasn't that he missed the old way of life. Yet he felt as though he was standing still, while the world tumbled past him, like a stream, waiting for his proper life to start. He did not know how he had got here. And beside him was the girl he would marry in a few weeks' time. A register-office wedding. Then a honeymoon on the Riviera: that part, at least, came from his old life. Ealing people probably went to Bournemouth or Torquay.

Suddenly an image came into his mind, of a poster he had seen for the Cornish Riviera Express, showing a very glamorous man and woman holding champagne glasses and gazing from the carriage window at the sparkling, sunlit sea. Then he remembered one wet day in Dover when his sailing had been delayed and he had gone for a walk along the seafront while he waited. A very drab couple, their coats and hats dark with rain, had been sitting huddled on a bench under a seafront shelter, sharing a saveloy and chips out of a newspaper. They didn't look like that pair in the poster. He thought how different the holiday experience was for the working classes: they would have their precious week at the seaside, where a sour-faced landlady would lock them out of their lodgings from just after breakfast until just before 'tea'. If the weather was unkind they would have nothing to do but sit and shiver under one of the shelters and watch the teeming rain hitting the grey sea. There ought, he thought, to be a better way.

CHAPTER THREE

The Nevinsons' flat was large, dark, filled with old, well-polished furniture and the faint smell of soup. Samuel Nevinson opened the door to them himself. They had a servant, Leah – a cook-general Richard supposed you would call her – but in the way of Jewish people she was more like a member of the family. She and Mrs Nevinson – Hannah – shared the work without much distinction between them, and chatted and complained and sometimes quarrelled mildly, like two sisters. They conspired to protect the man of the house from even the slightest disappointment, and to burnish up the daughter for her hoped-for fine marriage.

Samuel opened his arms as if he meant to embrace them both and said, 'Now tell me, what did you think? Did you like it?'

'I love it, Papa,' Cynthia cried. 'It's perfect. Can we really have it?'

He fondly kissed her brow. 'Of course you can, chick. Richard? What's your opinion? Good enough for Mr and Mrs Howard to start off their lives together?'

'It seems excellently suited in every way,' Richard heard himself say. And now he was embraced, and he felt in the older man's arms a tremor of relief.

Samuel bore Richard off to the fireside while Cynthia went to the kitchen for house and wedding talk with her mother and Leah. Richard heard their light, musical voices rising and falling in the background, like the sound of birds out in the garden.

Samuel made him sit down, served him sherry, then took the chair opposite, and pursued his own thoughts for a few moments. Then he said, 'Have you heard of the Nuremberg Laws?'

'No,' said Richard. 'Nuremberg? That's in Germany, isn't it?'

Samuel sat forward. 'Listen, and I will tell you. They were passed last September, for the protection of German Blood.'

'What on earth is German Blood?'

'There's a belief over there that the different races of human beings on earth can be ranked in worthiness. The Aryan race is the finest, the top of the tree. The Jews are right down at the bottom, inferior to everyone else. Guess which race the Germans belong to?'

'I'd have thought they were mixed, like every other nation,' Richard said.

Samuel almost smiled. 'They have a way to get round that. They say that only pure Aryans are really Germans. Only *they* have true German blood running in their veins. And to stop any more diluting of their wonderful, perfect blood, the first Nuremberg law forbids them to marry or have intercourse with Jews. Oh, and a Jewish household may not employ an Aryan female under forty-five – because you know what ravening beasts men are when it comes to servant girls. And how servant girls have no morals.'

'The first law?' Richard asked, without at all wanting to know.

'The second law says that only pure Aryan Germans are Reich citizens. The rest are state subjects without any rights. And the Jews, along with Blacks and Gypsies, are classed as enemies of the state, so you can imagine how they will be treated.' Richard could think of nothing to say. 'It's true, what I'm telling you,' Samuel concluded.

'It could never happen here,' Richard said at last.

'I hope not,' Samuel said. 'But people anywhere can be worked up to hatred by certain words, or a certain combination of events. I hear a lot of people now who are afraid of the Soviets, who say that we should be friends with the Germans, because they are decent, hard-working, peace-loving people just like the English. But they don't know what is going on over there. We have relatives there, and in Poland, who write to us. It's bad now, but it's going to get worse. As individuals, people are nice and kind, but mobs are cruel and bloody. They do things and think things that not one of them would do on his own. So I want you to be really sure what you are marrying into.'

'I don't understand you,' Richard said stiffly.

'I think you do.'

'But you're not really—'

'We're not observant, but we're Jewish all the same. Have you thought about that? People hate us. They shun us, and they'll shun you too, if you marry one of us. Have you thought how you'll feel when people turn down your invitations, or don't invite you, or don't want to sit next to you? When Cynthia is excluded from the circle of your friends' wives.'

'My circle aren't like that.'

'They won't throw stones or break your windows. It'll be more subtle, but it'll hurt just as much.'

Richard felt his face burn. In the normal course of events, if he had got engaged to a girl from his own set, his parents would have invited hers to dinner or a weekend stay. There had been no invitation yet for the Nevinsons from his mother – not from any dislike, but a nervousness about whether they would require different foods or special arrangements. She only wanted to get it right, but he knew how it must look.

Samuel looked as though he had read everything that had just passed through Richard's mind. 'You see, we're thought of as *different*,' he said sadly. 'So I want to say to you, my dear boy, that you should think very carefully and clearly about it, and if you decide you don't want to go ahead with the marriage—'

'Sir!'

Samuel raised a hand. 'I'm not impugning your honour, I'm saying that if you decide it's wiser to pull out, there will be no hard feelings, not on my part, not on Cynthia's. She'll release you. We'll say she's changed her mind. No shame will stick to you.'

Richard felt slightly sick. 'Doesn't she want to marry me?'

Samuel didn't answer at once, looking at him steadily. Then he said, 'She doesn't want a reluctant husband. Or one who's taken by surprise when things go bad.'

'They won't go bad,' Richard said stubbornly. Underneath, his thoughts were seething. A reluctant husband? No, he wasn't that – not exactly. But he was not in love with her. Had Samuel guessed that? Oh, God, did *she* guess it? He knew how much she loved him; yet she would release him without reproach? No shame would stick to him? Perhaps not in public, but in his head, in his heart . . . He could never forgive himself if he hurt her, or them, so much.

He felt the velvet jaws of the trap close on him. But he must not remain silent, or Samuel would believe the worst. 'Of course I don't want to be released from the engagement. I want to marry Cynthia, and I say that with my whole heart.'

Samuel grunted, as if different words entirely had been spoken. But all he said was, 'You had better tell her that, then, when you see her next. She can't help wondering, poor child.'

'She shouldn't. What have I ever done to make her doubt me?'

'She hasn't seen much of you in the past few weeks.'

'I've been very busy,' Richard said, burning again, though outwardly composed. 'But perhaps I *have* neglected her. I'll put that right.'

Cynthia appeared at the door just then. 'Papa, Richard, dinner's ready.' She looked quizzically at them. 'You look so serious. Did something happen?'

Richard knew then that Samuel hadn't told his daughter he was going to have this conversation.

'I was telling Richard how your mother wants me to retire once you're safely off my hands,' Samuel said.

'But, Papa, you can't retire! Whatever would you do with yourself all day?' Cynthia responded.

'That's just what I said,' Samuel said, and laughed.

Richard chuckled too, to keep up the benign pretence.

Samuel put his arm round Cynthia's shoulders and walked out towards the dining-room. Richard followed their entwined figures down the dark passage towards the smell of soup, now joined by that of fried fish and something richly beefy, and felt so unreal he almost had to look down to see if his feet were still there, and still working.

Basil Compton emerged, blinking, from the Underground at Green Park station and felt the sun warm on his face, unseasonably for March. Across the road, the eponymous park beckoned: its towering plane trees were just coming into leaf; the grass was edged with a cheery paint-spatter of daffodils. Flat-dwellers were walking grateful dogs, nursemaids were pushing perambulators, children were slipping restraining hands and running wildly about after pigeons.

The weather had tempted him from his desk at the *Bugle*. He ought to have been working, but a sunny day in March, he reasoned, must be celebrated lest the Weather Gods be offended and inflict cataracts and hurricanoes instead. He darted across Piccadilly, dodging between taxi-cabs and delivery vans. He'd hardly gained the opposite pavement when he was hailed by someone coming out from Queen's Walk. It was a woman in a loden-green two-piece. Skirts were calf-length this year and slightly flared at the hem, jackets were fitted, with built-up shoulders (he knew this from perusing all sections of his own newspaper most days instead of working) and the two-piece was bang up to the mark. The lady had completed it with a saucy Robin Hood hat decorated with an upright diamond turkey-quill and rather exciting high-heeled ankle boots, and was wearing a black fox fur round her shoulders, proving she was wealthy as well as fashionable.

'It is Mr Compton, isn't it?' she said, extending a leather-gloved hand. 'Gloria Rampling's Mr Compton?'

He remembered her now. 'Mrs Glenforth-Williams,' he said, raising his hat and shaking her hand in the same movement.

'You remember my name,' she said, with a dazzling smile. 'I couldn't be more flattered.'

'I am hardly likely to forget *you*, of all people,' he said, returning the smile.

'And what are you doing here, Mr Compton? Are you meeting Gloria?'

'Sadly, no. She's out of Town at the moment.'

'Paris?'

'Yorkshire.'

'Oh, the poor darling. How *too* sick-making!'

'Not really. She's attending a country-house sale, something she adores. So I believe she's quite happy. And how about you, Mrs Glenforth-Williams?'

'Veronica, please! When people use all my names I can't get it out of my head that they're scolding me. Makes me feel quite put-upon.'

He grinned. 'I can't believe you ever feel anything but superb.'

'Oh, now, after that you simply *have* to let me take you to lunch,' she said, laying a hand on his wrist. 'I was just heading for the Ritz and hoping I'd find someone there to lunch with.'

Basil was flattered, and liked the idea of being seen going into the Ritz with the famous Mrs Glenforth-Williams on his arm, but there was a problem. He made a rueful face and a vague gesture towards his pocket. 'There's nothing I'd like more,' he said, 'but I'm ashamed to say – have to admit . . .' he felt himself reddening, '. . . somewhat financially embarrassed just at present, you see. In fact – absolutely stony. Frightfully sorry.'

The pressure on his wrist increased, and she laughed trillingly. 'Oh, my dear, it's I who should apologise! Of *course* I meant *you* to be *my* guest. I thought that was understood.'

'It's very kind of you . . .' he began to demur.

But she tucked her hand through his arm and turned him towards the hotel's entrance. 'I simply *can't* take "no" for an answer. I loathe eating alone, don't you? Such a bore!'

Basil was only just twenty. She was a glamorous woman, and London society was still thrilling to him. Also he was hungry and his pockets were to let. 'In that case,' he said, 'I shall let my inclination follow my duty.'

'How prettily you put it,' said Veronica. 'Now do say more things like that. I could listen to you all day.'

'I'm at your service,' said Basil.

He had been planning to be seen at his desk again later in the afternoon, but he had never yet got into trouble for not being there, so he was willing to take the chance. To let his inclination override his duty, in this case.

When Basil got home to his rooms in Ryder Street the next day, the porter was not in the hall, for which he was grateful, since he had long suspected him of spying on Gloria's behalf – she owned the lease of his rooms, so the porter ultimately worked for her, and she was generous with tips. Basil would have liked to be generous with tips, but his wages at the *Bugle* fell short of his ambitions; and while Gloria spent lavishly on him, she did not often give him actual cash.

He ran up the stairs two at a time, whistling. Life was good. Gloria would be back that evening and he expected a passionate reunion. He would have to think of some excuse for his absence from work that day, but Gloria had got him the job through a friend of hers who was managing director (he suspected that 'friend' in this case meant 'former lover'), and with so much influence in high places he doubted he would be in trouble.

He opened the door to his set, and was surprised to see Gloria standing in the middle of the room. Before he could say anything she flew at him and slapped his face.

He reeled back, his hand to his stinging cheek – it had been a *hard* slap – and cried, 'What—?'

'Don't you dare say, "What have I done?" Don't you *dare*!'

Basil backed up against the door, staring. He had never seen anyone so angry – she looked almost mad. If she had been holding anything in her hand to attack him with he would actually have run. 'But – darling – Gloria—'

'Don't call me "darling", you – you *swine*!'

He shut his mouth on any further protest. He was beginning to fear he knew what was wrong.

'How dare you betray me with Veronica? Oh, yes, I know about it. When I got home Morton said she'd rung several times but wouldn't leave a message. Then the phone rang again. She called me to *gloat*.'

'I thought you weren't coming back until tonight,' he said, and immediately could have groaned. As soon as he heard himself he realised it was not a good thing to say.

'Oh, I've no doubt about that,' Gloria said bitterly. 'I wonder how else you've been amusing yourself while I was away. No!' She held up a hand, like a policeman stopping traffic. 'Don't tell me. I may be a fool about you, but I'm not an idiot. I dare say you've been tom-catting your way around all my acquaintances, and they're all laughing at me for thinking you actually care about me.'

59

'I *do* care about you,' he said, with all the emphasis he could muster. 'Gloria, darling, please—'

She was cold now, and that was worse than the heat of her fury. 'Veronica called me to congratulate me. She said she understood now why I prized you so highly. Your skills in the bedroom were quite remarkable, she said. You'd given her the best thrill she'd had in ages.'

Oh, my God, Basil thought. What a cat. That horrible spiteful woman! (Though a tiny bit of his brain preened itself over the compliment. He was only twenty, after all.) He knew he was in real trouble now, and thrashed around mentally for a way out.

'But it's you I love! You have to understand—'

'Understand why you did it? No, I don't.'

'It – it just sort of happened. I bumped into her by chance. We had lunch. And a lot to drink. Things got out of hand. It all happened in a flash—'

'No, Basil, these things never happen in a flash. You have to take your clothes off, for one thing. That takes long enough for you to have second thoughts, if you were going to have them.'

'But I didn't mean— I would never—'

'But you did. And you stayed all night.' He was silent, unable to think of anything to mitigate that. 'I'm done with you,' she said, without emotion. 'Pack your things and go. You don't live here any more. And you don't work at the *Bugle*, either.'

'You've spoken to—?'

'That was the first thing I did after I'd taken Veronica's obliging call. You'd better see if she's willing to finance your carefree life, because I won't.'

'Gloria, you don't understand,' he said desperately. 'Veronica doesn't mean anything to me.'

'And while you were in her bed, neither did I,' Gloria said. 'Go and pack. And please don't speak any more. There's nothing you can say that will make this any better.'

He realised that this was literally true. He went into the bedroom and began slowly packing his things – most of which Gloria had bought for him. He was cursing himself for being such a fool. And that cat Veronica Glenforth-Williams! If only she hadn't told, Gloria would never have known, and everything would have been all right. She'd be happy, he'd be happy – and presumably Veronica would have been happy. But – oh, God, why had he done it? It had seemed so exciting in the heat of the moment, but now . . . He'd give anything to wind back the clock and make it not to be. For the first time in his life he had come up against a consequence of his actions that actually mattered. This was not like being expelled from school. He cared for Gloria, he really did, and his life with her was – had been – *just fine*! And now . . .

He was half hoping Gloria would come in and forgive him; that having given him his telling-off, she would soften. He would be contrite, then strong and manly. He would pet her and show her how much he loved her, and she would melt into his arms . . . He would do those things she so liked him for . . .

But she didn't come, and by the time he'd got everything into the suitcase, his mood was of sick apprehension. Was there really no way back?

He stepped out into the sitting-room with the case, chastened and subdued, hoping against hope that she would smile at him. But she was stony-faced. She held out her hand, and said, 'Your keys, please.'

He pulled them from his pocket and handed them over. *This can't be the end. It can't!* 'Gloria, please,' he began desperately

'Don't.' She turned her face away. 'No more words. There's nothing to say. Leave now, please.' And when he didn't immediately move, '*Go!*'

He went.

He walked until he found a bench, and sat down to think. His parents lived in Surrey, and he most definitely didn't want to go to them. His mother had been so proud that he had got a job on the *Bugle*, believing that in journalism he had found his niche. In a disgraceful journey through school the only praiseworthy thing he had done was to edit the school newspaper. She didn't know, of course, that Gloria had got him the job. She – they – didn't know about Gloria at all.

His father has been a distinguished flier during the war, with a DSO and a DFC, the sort of hero that boys worshipped and men looked up to. He could have been a fictional character in a boys' comic paper: Jack Compton, Air Ace, strong-jawed and handsome in that ridiculously attractive flying helmet and fleece-lined leather jacket, fearlessly pursuing the Red Baron through the skies. He had also been a pioneer test pilot and was an aircraft designer. He was impossible to live up to, and Basil had long ago concluded there was no point in even trying. If he was going to invite detrimental comparison, better he should go the whole hog and be a Bad Boy, so that it looked deliberate. Better to be good at being bad than to be a failure at everything.

No, he was not going home to see his father's look of weary disappointment that, once again, Basil had failed to shape up.

Barbara, his sister? He adored Barbara – or, more importantly, *she* adored *him* and could never see any fault in him. But Babsy lived in Petersfield, and he had no wish to be so far from London. And her very dull husband, Freddie, was, Basil suspected, a lot shrewder than he appeared and readily saw through Basil. There was a look he gave him sometimes . . .

Besides, after several false alarms, Babsy was very definitely pregnant, and the atmosphere at Crossways would be too domestic to conduce to his comfort. He was used to coming first with Barbara, but he suspected the baby might oust him from his throne.

Uncle Oliver was tempting. He was immensely rich, so he could easily afford to rescue Basil. He was also very modern-minded, practising as a plastic surgeon despite being an earl and not needing to earn a living. But he was not a real uncle, being in fact a sort of cousin of Basil's father, so Basil had no real call on him. And in actual truth, he was just a wee bit afraid of him.

Then there was Aunt Molly, his mother's sister. He certainly had closer ties with her than anyone else. She was a writer of detective yarns and married to a publisher; and though she would probably berate him for losing his job and make him squirm, she would not let him down. She was obviously the best bet, though he didn't relish having strips torn off him; and she might feel obliged to tell his mother.

He sat for a long time debating internally, until he discovered he was ravenously hungry. Hauling his suitcase, which was growing heavier by the minute, he walked to Albemarle Street, fingers crossed.

Jack Compton came home from work and found his wife Helen standing in the hall reading the evening newspaper, which had presumably just come through the letter-box.

She looked up. 'Did you know about this?'

He looked over her shoulder at the headline: 'GERMANY SENDS TROOPS INTO RHINELAND'. 'Yes, everybody's talking about it at work. Hugh Dowding came to the factory today, and he said the Foreign Office had heard a rumour about it: something that came over the wire from an American correspondent in Berlin.'

They read the article together, standing there in the hall, Jack still in his coat and hat. Twenty-five thousand German troops had marched into the demilitarised Rhineland zone, to an ecstatic welcome by the German population. They had met with no resistance.

'But what does it mean?' Helen asked.

'It means the Germans have violated the Treaty of Versailles. And the Locarno Treaty.'

'But did no-one try to stop them? The French? The League of Nations?'

'Well, the French are in the middle of an election, so they don't actually have a functioning government. Germany chose the right moment. *And* on a Saturday, when diplomats and politicians are all away from their desks.'

The maid was hovering, waiting to take Jack's outerwear, and obviously listening with all her might in order to report back to the cook in the kitchen. Jack shed his coat and hat to her, and sought to deflect her attention towards domestic matters. 'What are you giving me for dinner this evening?'

'Mrs Dyer's done her kidneys in wine sauce, sir.' Ellen said.

Jack managed not to flinch at the thought of eating his cook's kidneys, and said, 'Jolly good. Mrs Compton and I will have a glass of sherry now, and dinner in half an hour.'

'Yes, sir.'

Jack took Helen's elbow and moved her towards the drawing-room.

She had been pondering. 'I don't understand, it says Germany claims it was being threatened by France and Russia,' she said. 'Surely they can't mean the Franco-Soviet Pact?'

'I imagine so,' said Jack. 'I don't see what else it could be.' He walked over to the drinks tray and poured sherry.

'But that's just a defensive treaty – that each will defend the other in case of an unprovoked attack. And even then, only after approval from the League of Nations. Or am I misunderstanding?'

'Your understanding, as always, my love, is immaculate.'

'So how does saying, "If you hit my friend I'll help him defend himself," constitute a threat?'

'It's obviously just an excuse,' Jack said, handing her a glass and sitting down by the fire. 'And after they took back the Saar last year without a word of protest from anyone, they must have thought it was perfectly safe to walk into the Rhineland.'

'Well, they had a plebiscite on the Saar,' Helen said, 'with a ninety per cent vote for reunification. So there wasn't much anyone could do about that – was there?'

'There was a lot of disquiet at the time about irregularities – you remember, reports of intimidation by the Nazis? The League was supposed to conduct an investigation, but I don't think anything came of it.'

'And what is the League going to do about the Rhineland?'

'Probably nothing,' Jack said. He held up his glass to look at the firelight through the golden liquid. 'Hitler took a calculated risk: people don't want another war. And there's an idea circulating that the Germans were unfairly treated by Versailles. I heard someone at work today saying that, after all, Germany was only walking into its own backyard. Is it worth starting a war over that?' He drained his glass. 'More sherry?'

'No, thanks.' Helen watched him go over to the drinks tray. 'Don't spoil your dinner,' she warned.

'The thought of eating Mrs Dyer's kidneys will carry me through,' Jack said.

'I believe it was supposed to be a hash of yesterday's beef, but the joint wasn't large enough, after they'd had their supper. There'll be apple dumplings afterwards.'

'In that case, I'm reconciled.' Jack poured himself another glass. He held up the decanter. 'You're sure?' She shook her head and he returned to the fire. 'The government seems to be working on the principle that going into the Continent in 1914 was a terrible mistake that cost thousands of lives, and that we shouldn't ever do it again. We should let the European countries work out their own problems.'

'That's all very well, until the bombers start flying over London, and it becomes our problem again.'

'Well, at least we're doing something about that,' Jack said. 'Dowding wants a network of spotters, with radio and telephone links, and the lines all buried deep underground so they can't be damaged by bombs. Thousands more fighter planes: the Hurricane will be going into production this year, as you know. And then there's the good old secret weapon – radio detection.'

'If it's secret, should you be telling me?'

'I can't go into details, but the theory's pretty well known. You remember that the biggest problem for home defence during the war was having early enough warning of enemy planes approaching?'

'Yes. By the time our fighters made the height the bombers had been and gone.'

'Quite. So this new idea is to send out radio signals, which bounce off anything they hit. You can tell where the thing is and how big and how fast it's travelling and so on. We're pretty sure the Germans are working on the same idea – you've heard of this Death Ray they're supposed to be developing?'

'There isn't a Death Ray?'

'Not outside an H. G. Wells novel.'

'Thank goodness. The servants will be pleased,' said Helen.

'We think the Death Ray story is just a cover for their version of the radio detection system.'

'And this system – will it work?'

'There was a demonstration down in Daventry last year that impressed Dowding so much he was able to get government funding for more research. Once we get it up and running it will make all the difference. We will be able to detect German bombers while they're still out over the sea.'

Helen's expression changed. She stared at him bleakly. 'You said "we will" not "we would". You talk as if they're really coming.' She got up abruptly, went to the window and stood with her back to him. He was afraid she might be crying.

'Darling—' he said.

'It's all starting up again, isn't it?' she said. 'The war was supposed to be the end of it. There wasn't ever going to be another one, they said.'

He went over and laid a tentative hand on her shoulder. She wasn't crying – she had reached an age where tears were hard to come by – but she turned an impassioned face up to him. 'Oh, Jack, why do we keep ending up in the same place? I can't bear it.'

'If it comes you'll have to bear it,' he said gently. 'But perhaps it won't.'

'I've heard it in your voice – you don't think Hitler will stop at the Saar and the Rhineland. All that build-up of arms – you think we're for it.'

'Darling,' he said, taking her into his arms, 'we don't know what's coming. All we know is that we can see the storm clouds gathering. We hope and pray the storm will pass us by. But just in case, we'd better have a damn' good umbrella. That's what I and Dowding and Tom Sopwith and all the rest are working on.'

She rested her head on his shoulder. 'Thank God I have you,' she said. She thought about the war, the agonising waiting to hear from Jack, not knowing from hour to hour if he was still alive. His two brothers and his cousin Ned – who had been like a brother to him – had fallen in the war. He had been shot down, wounded, captured twice. He and she had survived, but their whole generation had been changed by the ordeal. That had been their war, Jack's and hers. 'If it comes, it will be the children's war – Basil's and Michael's. And Barbara's,' she said.

Jack closed his eyes. He heard the words she didn't say: *You'll be too old to go.* It was one of those things a woman would never understand – that while he didn't want war any more than she did, if it came he would want to go and fight, to protect her, his family and his world. It would be hard, intolerable, to be told he was useless and must keep out of the way.

Ellen's polite cough from the doorway interrupted his thoughts. 'Dinner's ready, madam,' she said.

She would tell Mrs Dyer when she got back to the kitchen that 'they were spooning again'. She and the cook had both had to get used to it. It was nice in its way, to see how fond they were of each other, but that sort of thing was not done in the best houses.

Molly's sharp eyes travelled from Basil's face to the suitcase in his hand. 'You're in trouble again,' she said. 'What is it this time?'

'Not my fault,' he said automatically, then summoned his charm. He leaned forward to kiss her cheek and said, 'Hello, Aunty Molly. You're looking very well. That colour really suits you.'

'Don't flannel me,' Molly said, trying not to smile – Basil out to charm was hard to resist, and she was fond of him anyway. 'What have you done?'

'I lost my job, and I've had to move out of my lodgings,' he said. 'So I was hoping you'd take me in for a little while. Otherwise,' he added pathetically, 'I'll have to sleep under a railway bridge, in the cold and the rain. And that will be so bad for my consumption.' He coughed hollowly into a fist.

'Oh, stop it,' she laughed. 'Of course you can stay here. But tell me you haven't done anything *really* bad, or I shall feel obliged to tell your mother and father.'

'No, I'm not wicked, just rather put-upon and stray-dog-ish,' he said meekly. 'And *awfully* hungry.'

'Dinner will be an hour,' Molly said. 'Vivian's not home yet. I'll tell them in the kitchen to lay an extra place. Can you last until then, or should I ask them to bring you something to tide you over?'

'Just a mouldy crust, or the scraps set aside for the dog will do – anything you can spare,' he said, with deep pathos.

'I'll see what there is,' she said. 'Go on into the drawing-room, by the fire. You can leave your suitcase here. We'll take it to the spare room later.'

In the drawing-room he found Charlotte sitting in an armchair by the fire. On the hearthrug, gazing up soulfully, was a loose-limbed young man in shirtsleeves and a Fair Isle sleeveless pullover, with dark hair flopping over his forehead. From these clues Basil divined that he was one of Aunt Molly's pet poets. Her husband's publishing house, Dolphin Books, published poetry, and Molly took it on herself occasionally to offer sympathy and basic nourishment to the tortured souls who produced it. 'Otherwise they forget to eat, bless them,' she had sometimes said.

Charlotte, who worked as an editorial assistant with Dolphin, was another 'sort-of' cousin – in fact, she was 'Uncle' Oliver's niece, and sister to Richard, who had got Basil his first job after leaving school, driving motor-cars for Nevinson's.

She looked up as Basil came in, and said, 'This is a nice surprise. Molly didn't say you were coming.'

'I wasn't expected,' Basil said, approaching the fire. It was getting quite cold outside now the sun had gone down. He looked enquiringly at the flop-haired boy.

'Oh, this is Leo Cust. Leo, Basil Compton. He's a sort of cousin, works for the *Bugle*.'

The young man looked interested at this connection – the *Bugle* was known for its literary reviews – and began to scramble to his feet, but Basil waved him back down and said 'Don't get up. Not worth your while. I was sacked today.'

'Oh, *Basil*!' Charlotte exclaimed. 'What did you do?'

'Nothing for your ears,' Basil said. He looked at Cust. 'Poet?'

Cust blushed. 'I try. It's what I want to do most in the world. And Mrs Blake says – she's so kind – and Miss Howard—'

'Mr Cust is working towards his first collection,' Charlotte said briskly. 'His poems are rather good. But, Basil, what are you going to do?'

'Aunt Molly said I could stay here for a bit. I suppose I shall have to get another job of some sort. It's either that, or go home to the Aged Ps.'

'What's wrong with that?' Charlotte asked.

'Pained silences and reproachful looks,' said Basil. 'Mother mentally comparing me with Dad and seeing how far short I fall. You don't know what it's like, having an *Übermensch* for a father.'

'I don't have a father of any sort,' Charlotte said.

'Oh – sorry, Charley. I forgot,' Basil said, trying to look contrite.

'Anyway, I think Uncle Jack is a perfect pet,' Charlotte said warmly.

'That's the trouble, everyone does,' said Basil.

Leo Cust spoke up. 'I know what you mean, though. My pater is good at everything. He always knows exactly what to say to everyone, and everyone admires him. And I'm such a clumsy fool, I'm always tongue-tied in company, and the only thing I'm any good at is poetry and the pater thinks it's an awful bust and that I should go into politics or something.'

'Leo's father is Lord Haverfordwest,' Charlotte explained.

'He got a double first at Cambridge,' Cust said gloomily. 'And he was a first-class cricketer. He made sixty-two at The Oval opening with Jack Hobbs in a Players-and-Gentlemen match for charity.'

Basil patted the poet on the shoulder. 'I always feel it's best to find what you're good at and stick to it.'

70

Cust got to his feet. 'I really do have to go. The parents are having a Thing tonight that I have to dress for.' He made his farewells and drifted out.

Charlotte said to Basil, 'Alternatively, you could just get the sort of job anyone can do and jolly well stick at it. Parents tend to forgive you for being a blithering ass if you show that you try.'

'I don't know what you think *you* know about it, Miss Howard,' Basil said, 'given that nobody expects anything of girls – honestly, your sex has the easiest run of it! – but if you think it's that easy to get a job, why don't you get me one?'

'I will,' she said promptly.

Molly came in with a tray. 'I looked in the dog's bowl, but all the scraps had gone,' she told Basil, 'so I'm afraid you'll have to make do with some cheese and biscuits. The biscuits aren't stale and the cheese isn't even mouldy.'

'I'll try not to get above my station,' Basil said, giving her his most fascinating smile.

'Molly,' Charlotte said, with a clear, innocent look, 'Basil needs a job. Couldn't you take him on to help in the ware-house? We're short-handed anyway, and there's going to be a lot more work once we start making the move to Acton.'

Horrified, Basil hastened to deflect his aunt. 'Oh, is the move coming up? I didn't realise your new premises were ready.'

'They're not,' Molly said, 'but it won't be long. The builder expects it to be finished by the middle of May. It's all very exciting.'

Dolphin Books had been working out of a tiny office above a grocer's shop in Theobalds Road, with the warehousing operating from the crypt of a church round the corner in Gray's Inn. Now that the company was making profits, they had decided to incorporate all the activities in a single new

71

building a little further out of Town, where there was more room and the traffic was easier.

'Shall I show you the plans?' Molly went on. There was nothing she liked better than talking about the new head-quarters.

Charlotte intervened: 'Let's fix about this job for Basil first. It's perfect for him. He's young and strong, so the physical work won't bother him, and he's family, so it won't matter that it's so dirty and cold down in the crypt.' Basil made an exquisite face at her, out of Molly's line of sight.

'Oh dear,' said Molly, 'you're not making it sound very attractive. But it's true we are short-handed.'

'Yes, and once we start packing, there'll be masses to do. And I was thinking, if he proves himself by sticking it out, there might possibly be something better for him after we've moved.'

'Well, there's always a place for an intelligent, ambitious sort of chap in our business,' said Molly.

'Yes, and Basil *really* doesn't want to bother his mother and father over having lost his job, so he needs to get some-thing to do straight away,' said Charlotte sweetly.

'May I make it clear, Aunty, that I didn't actually *ask* for a job?'

'Still, we could certainly do with another hand,' said Molly. 'I shan't be able to pay you much, but you can live here, and that will keep your expenses down, so I'm sure you'll be able to manage. And if you're working hard and giving satisfaction, I won't feel I have to tell your mother anything. I can leave it to you to decide when you want to tell her you've changed jobs.'

It was blackmail, plain and simple, Basil thought, observing Charlotte's grin. But it did solve his immediate problem, and he had never lacked ability when it came to being idle while appearing to be busy. And it wouldn't be for long, anyway, because Gloria would forgive him and take him back. He pinned his faith on her missing him too much to stay angry.

'Thank you, Aunty,' he said, eyes cast down modestly. 'I'll take the job. It's very kind of you to look after me.'

'That's what aunts are for,' Molly said, wondering what Basil was up to. She didn't trust that meek, compliant look. But he really couldn't do much harm down in the crypt, moving boxes of books around.

Just at that moment, Vivian arrived home, and Nana appeared at the same moment bringing the bathed and pyjama'd children in to see their papa and say goodnight to everyone. Their faces lit when they saw Basil, who was a huge favourite with Esmond and Angelica, and watching him talking to them, Molly thought that there was a lot of good in that boy, if only he let it be seen.

CHAPTER FOUR

James had settled into a comfortable relationship with Tata, and Maman no longer came and knocked every half-hour. Tata took her tutoring very seriously, but James insisted on breaks every now and then, 'To rest my poor brain. I'm not five years old, you know.'

'*Ça se voit!*' she said sternly. 'Come, Shems, you must concentrate.'

'But also I must get to know my teacher, to generate trust.'

Though she was immediately friendly, she was cautious at first about telling him anything about herself, but that caution was soon eroded. She said to him, in French, on their third day, 'You are a man one perceives immediately to be honest.'

James smiled. 'That's because I am too stupid to be devious.'

'Oh, I don't think you are stupid at all,' she said, looking at him thoughtfully. 'Not at all.'

He soon found that she spoke English almost as well as French. 'We spoke it at home,' she said. 'And German, a little. I had an English nanny, and a German governess. And French, of course, everyone speaks. It is the language of the ballet, and the ballet is in our blood.' After that, their conversations drifted impartially between French and English, and their relationship became friendship.

At tea-time one Friday James got up and walked about, looking at the photographs on the walls. He stopped in front of one showing a scene in a hospital. A bare-chested man was sitting up in a bed, with a bandage round his head and one arm splinted and held up by a string-and-pulley device. A handsome middle-aged woman was holding the arm as if about to adjust the sling, and three other younger women stood around the bed. All four were in white nun-like nursing uniform and stared at the camera. 'Where's this?' he asked.

Tata came and joined him. 'That is the war hospital at Tsarskoye Selo. That's Sister Chebodarev, the head of the hospital. Those two are Natalie Karaulov and Nina Berberov – they're cousins – and that one is Grand Duchess Olga, the Tsar's eldest daughter.'

'What connection do you have with the hospital?' he asked. 'You must be too young to remember the war.'

'How old do you think I am?'

'I thought about twenty-three?'

She laughed. 'Come, I'll show you.' She led him to another photograph on the wall, a larger one of a hospital ward, showing several occupied beds, and a number of other people standing and sitting, crowding together to be in the picture. The men were all in dressing-gowns, some with bandages, all with the large moustaches of the time. The women were all in the same nursing uniform. Standing to one side was a solemn little girl of, he guessed, about ten, in a white dress, white ankle socks and white shoes, with dark ringlets and large dark eyes. 'That's me,' she said. 'I lived in Tsarskoye Selo Before.' It was clear that 'Before' had a capital letter. It did not need to be specified, before what. He had come across it already, with some of Charlie's Russian guests. 'Before' was back then, in the golden time, the lost pre-revolution time that could never be revisited. It might not have been a perfect world, but it was the world you knew, and nothing would ever be like it again.

It meant, James thought, that she must be twenty-eight or twenty-nine. 'I thought Tsarskoye Selo was a palace,' he said, from some vague idea he had gleaned God-knew-where. 'Where the Tsar lived.'

'There *were* palaces, but lots of other houses too. Tsarskoye Selo means the Tsar's Village. I lived there with Papa and Mama. But then Papa went away to the war, and didn't come back. And when Mama got sick and died I went to live with Aunt Masha who was Sister Chebodarev's deputy. So I was often around the hospital. I knew them all,' she said, with a wave of the hand at the nurses in the picture.

He had picked up another photograph, in a silver frame, sitting on one of the many small tables. In what seemed to be a Victorian-style drawing room, very dark and cluttered, three women were in nursing uniform, one seated, the other two standing behind the chair. One of those standing was holding the hand of the same dark-haired little girl.

'That's me and Aunt Masha, in Sister Chebodarev's sitting-room at the hospital.'

James recognised the second standing woman as the sister from the previous photograph. 'And who's this?' he asked, pointing to the seated lady. She had a beautiful, sculpted face and sad eyes.

'That's the Tsarina. She and the two elder grand duchesses were all trained nurses and worked very hard there, but her other three children came too, and visited the soldiers and read to them. Olga was my favourite. She was so quiet and kind, and I think she was fond of me.' She sighed. 'I felt so sorry for her, poor Olichka.'

'Why?'

She led him to another photograph, a family group. James recognised them from newspapers and magazines: the Tsar and Tsarina, four Grand Duchesses and the Tsarevitch. But this was no studio portrait – the Tsar was digging in a vegetable patch, the children were helping, while the Tsarina leaned on a stick and watched. There were other people in the picture: a man in the background, who looked like a servant, holding the handles of a wheelbarrow, and another to one side, a tall, dark-haired man, who was watching and smiling.

Tata pointed to the latter. 'There,' she said. 'That is Thomas Ivanovitch. He was an aide to the Tsar, and he and Olga were in love. But she would never have been allowed to marry him. She was the daughter of the Tsar, and he was only an earl.'

'An earl? Do you have those in Russia?'

'Oh, no, he was an English earl. A rich one, too. But it would never have been allowed. Poor Olichka.' She sighed again, then became brisk. 'Now we must get back to work. Come, we shall talk of travelling – ships and trains and motor-cars. And you must concentrate, Shems,' she added, as he was still staring at the photograph.

'I'm sorry. Seeing them all so happy and laughing here, I was just thinking how terrible and tragic it is, how they all died.'

'Oh, but they didn't die,' she said matter-of-factly. 'Everyone knows that. That was just a story to cover their escape. They were all got away. But where they are has to be kept secret, because the Reds would come after them and kill them if they could find them.' She stopped, looked gravely at him. 'Everyone knows, but we don't speak of it, so don't say anything to anyone. You won't, will you?'

'Of course not,' he said, a little mystified. The story of how all the Imperial Family was killed in that cellar somewhere beginning with a K, or an E, or something, was so well known that it made him blink and inwardly shake his head to clear it. Well, she ought to know better, having been there . . . And, of course, everything coming out of Russia had always been shrouded in mystery. Who knew what had really happened? And – an English earl? Why did that strike a chord with him? He was not, to be truthful, much interested in the Imperial Family. But it did make him much more interested in *her*. He gazed at her with new enthusiasm, and she reddened a little.

'Come, we must work,' she said firmly, and led him away towards the books.

It was cold down in the crypt, the work was hard, and the boxes were dirty. While Basil cultivated a raffish air, he was fastidious, and hated to have dirty hands. Working in the crypt was one of the Circles of Hell, all right. Since he felt like a fraud beside the others working there, he supposed it was the Eighth.

There were no facilities of any sort: to use the lavatory, or even get a drink of water, they had to walk round the corner to the office in Theobalds Road. As his colleagues so rarely absented themselves, Basil felt constrained from going too often. He guessed they looked on him as a trial inflicted on them by his relationship with the management. He wouldn't have expected to care about their opinion, but he came to respect their knowledge of the publishing business, envy their camaraderie, and admire the effortless ease with which they hurled great boxes about.

They also, unexpectedly, took advantage of copies damaged in transit that couldn't be sold, and were widely read. He was shaken one day by a discussion of *Brave New World* – which Dolphin were putting into paperback – over whether the advantages of social stability were worth the loss of individuality. Alf, the foreman, made a comparison with H. G. Wells's *When the Sleeper Wakes*. Petey said he couldn't see anything wrong with a world where everything was clean and everyone was healthy. Harry said the constant sex was all very well, but centrifugal bumble-puppy sounded stupid and he'd miss his football. Bill said breeding people to think they were happy doing rotten jobs was just as wrong as economic coercion. Eventually, Alf asked Basil what he thought of the book, and he had to admit he hadn't read it. It was an exquisite kind of torture.

So there were many reasons for him to be happy one day when Alf had a message for the management and asked Basil to take it round. The first thing he did on reaching the building was to hurry to the lavatory on the landing to wash his hands and his face, comb his hair, and brush the dust off his trousers. Finally he strolled out, feeling more like himself, and bumped into a large, pink-faced young man who had just come up the stairs.

The man, being English, apologised for having been barged into, then said, 'Elphinstone,' and held out his hand.

'I'm Basil Compton,' said Basil. He knew who Lord Elphinstone – 'Stuffy' to his close friends – was: a newly wealthy man who was being persuaded to invest in Dolphin Books.

Elphinstone looked hopeful. 'Oh, you're Charlotte's – Miss Howard's – um, brother?' The mention of Charlotte's name made him turn a shade pinker.

'Cousin,' said Basil, using the shorthand for their more distant and complicated relationship. 'She's a grand girl,' he added provocatively.

Elphinstone now seemed both embarrassed and ecstatic. 'Oh, she is! That is – I wouldn't presume – she's quite – very – not that I—' He pulled out a handkerchief to mop his brow – more, Basil thought, to hide behind it than because his brow needed it – and the muffled words *wonderful* and *tremendous* could just about be heard.

Basil grinned to himself. He now had a fair idea of why Lord Elphinstone had sunk his money into Dolphin Books, and it hadn't much to do with the hope of a financial return – or a romantic one, since Charlotte was engaged to another. Namely, Milo Tavey, who happened also to be the Earl of Launde.

'We're all dashed grateful to you,' Basil said, allowing Elphinstone to re-emerge from his eclipse.

'Oh, glad to be of service. Fact is, one has to put it

somewhere, one's fortune, I mean – and one might as well do some good with it. Books, you know, they're a jolly good thing, aren't they? Everyone ought to read books. Education, and so forth. Expanding the mind.' Basil smiled and looked receptive, and Elphinstone was obliged to continue. 'Read one myself recently. *The ABC Murders*. Rather a jolly 'tec novel.'

'Oh yes, I enjoyed that one myself. Agatha Christie. Did you guess the ending?'

Elphinstone blushed and his eyes slid away. 'Oh. No. Well, when I say *read*, I've started it. Haven't got all the way to the end yet. But it's jolly – awfully—'

'Good,' Basil helped, and decided to stop teasing him. 'It was Milo Tavey brought you and Vivian Blake together, wasn't it?'

'Tavey? Oh, yes, Launde. Frightfully good fellow, known him since school. Fearfully bright upstairs. Always up to some scheme or other.'

'Rather an elusive character, would you say?' Basil was fond of Charlotte, and wondered how much she knew about her fiancé, who had appeared out of nowhere, if her tale of how they had met was true. *Slippery*, was what Basil had thought when he heard it. As one who aspired to be slippery himself, he thought he could spot an eel when he saw one.

'Oh, I wouldn't say that,' said Elphinstone, vaguely. 'Good fellow. Same house as me.'

'And you've been in touch with him ever since?' Basil probed.

'Well. Not entirely.' Elphinstone frowned. 'Fact is, I didn't expect to. Come from different parts of the country. Soon as school finished he disappeared off home to Ireland and it was Hampshire for me. Didn't see him again until last year, when the pater went to grass. Wrote to me. Condolences. Very decent of him.'

'Reminded you of what great chums you'd been at Eton, eh?'

'Well . . .' said Elphinstone, again. He looked as though he suspected he was being made fun of in some obscure way, and Basil changed tack.

'Where is he now, by the way? I must say, if I was engaged to Charlotte, I wouldn't want to leave her side for a moment.'

The troubled brow cleared. This was a concept Stuffy could agree with. 'Absolutely,' he said. 'She's a grand girl. If it was me, couldn't tear myself away.' Loyalty kicked in. 'But – business, you know. Chap has to attend to it. Needs must, and all that. Launde wouldn't go away unless he had to, I'm sure.'

'Go away where, actually?' Basil asked. 'I'm not sure I heard where he went, except that it was abroad somewhere.'

'Oh, yes, it's abroad all right,' Elphinstone said, pleased to be able to help. 'India. Or China. One or the other. Or was it Africa? No, India, I think. Yes, because when I heard, I remember thinking—' He stalled, unable to articulate what he had thought.

'What business does he have in India, I wonder?' Basil said.

'Well, his usual, I suppose,' Elphinstone said vaguely.

'As I understand it, he brings people together: those who want to buy with those who want to sell.'

Elphinstone looked relieved. 'Nutshell. Useful sort of chappie. Well, somebody's got to do it, or how would we all get on?'

At that moment, the office door opened and Charlotte looked out. 'What's all the talkage and chattery—? Oh, Lord Elphinstone. How nice. And Basil. What are you doing here?'

The question was meant for Basil, but Elphinstone's inbuilt shyness made him answer guiltily. 'Oh, just popping in – see how everything's going. No reason really. Anything I can do to help, that sort of thing.'

'You,' Charlotte said warmly, 'are always welcome. Please come in, and I'll make some coffee. Basil – why are you here?'

'Message for Mr Blake from Alf,' Basil said, trying to sound brisk and businesslike. Perhaps he'd be invited for coffee, too. He hadn't had a thing since breakfast.

'You can give it me, and then you'd better get back to work, hadn't you?' Charlotte said, dashing his hopes.

The work in the crypt was mostly physical, and his always overactive mind had little to do. It wanted exercise, something to chew over, and its tendency at first was to chew over the whole Gloria business. He missed Gloria, he longed for her, and he still felt hard-done-by. Why had she not given him another chance? How could the Veronica woman be so spiteful? How could he have been so stupid as to get mixed up with her? He replayed in his mind again and again the meeting by Green Park, and had himself leaving her politely but firmly at the door of the Ritz after lunch. He imagined again and again a successful rapprochement with Gloria, his heartfelt but manly apology and her melting forgiveness, followed by a blissful reunion at all levels.

But reality remained stubbornly uncooperative. He wrote to her, but his letters went unanswered. He telephoned, but her servants had orders not put him through. He hung about outside Sotheby's when he saw a sale advertised that she might be interested in, but she did not appear. He even borrowed half a crown from a gullible fellow employee and sent her flowers, but they elicited no response. Gradually he came to the conclusion that it really was over, and he was surprised (and secretly a little impressed) by how upset he was.

He needed something new to think about, and he found himself replaying the conversation he'd had with Lord Elphinstone about Launde. He badly wanted there to be a mystery about him, and Launde did seem a somewhat shadowy and unsatisfactory character. For instance, why had he not given Charlotte the full account of who he was when they first met? He had 'bumped into her' in a Lyons restaurant – fortuitous, surely, when her mother had recently presented her with a rich stepfather – but only told her that he was Milo Tavey, not mentioning his title. Having inherited a bankrupt estate, he had made his own way in the world, which might be admirable, but how exactly did he make his money? No-one seemed to know. Elphinstone didn't even know which country he had gone to. To be fair, Elphinstone was not the sharpest blade in the knife-box, but still . . .

He felt there was something shady about this Tavey fellow. Someone ought to be looking after Charlotte's interests and asking questions, and since her mother and stepfather were too unworldly, and Molly and Vivian Blake too grateful for the Elphinstone introduction, he decided it would have to be him. He introduced the subject casually with his colleagues in the Underworld. None of them seemed to know anything about him; they had no idea where he was at present or what business had taken him away, and didn't seem to be interested, either, which he chose to see as significant.

These preoccupations lasted until Thursday, when Charlotte came to Molly and Vivian's flat for dinner, and mentioned that she had been invited down at the weekend to Tunstead Hall in Derbyshire, the home of her mother Violet and her stepfather Avis, Lord Belmont.

'Oh, is it a house party?' Molly asked. 'How exciting. Who else is going?'

'It's just a family party,' said Charlotte, 'to meet Richard's fiancée and her parents.'

'That will be nice,' Molly said dutifully.

'Or embarrassing,' Basil suggested.

Charlotte scowled. 'Why should it be?'

'Because they're not exactly out of the top drawer, are they?'

'You're a beastly snob, Basil!' Charlotte exclaimed.

'Not at all,' he said in his most reasonable voice, which only annoyed her more. 'They may be the most worthy people in the land, but it's no kindness to put them in a position where they won't know how to behave.'

'You're forgetting we were all poor after Papa died,' Charlotte retorted. 'We lived in a little house with no servants and did our own shopping and cleaning and everything.'

'Doesn't matter. Being poor didn't change who you were. Just as being rich wouldn't change who they are. *Are* they rich?'

'I wouldn't be so impertinent as to ask,' Charlotte said loftily.

'Basil, don't be provoking,' Molly said. 'You don't know anything about these people, so don't judge.'

'We know he sells motor-cars,' Basil said.

'There's nothing wrong with that,' Charlotte said.

'No, there's nothing intrinsically wrong with buying or selling – or being a go-between for the two,' he added, to see if she would bite. She flung him a scorching glance, and looked away. 'But I gather they've lived in Earls Court for a very long time.'

Vivian intervened: 'Sir Henry Royce, of Rolls-Royce motor-cars, once said, "Whatever is rightly done, however humble, is noble."'

Molly wrinkled her nose. 'Darling, whatever does that mean? In this context?'

He smiled sheepishly. 'Just trying to keep the peace. A quotation usually does the trick. It can stop the most furious argument dead.'

Basil laughed. 'I must brush up my store of quotations. Didn't Socrates say you should improve yourself by other men's writings, so that you gain easily what they laboured for?'

'Socrates also said the only wisdom lies in knowing that you know nothing,' Vivian said pointedly.

'I am justly rebuked,' Basil said meekly. Then, to Charlotte, 'Let me come with you to Tunstead!'

She recoiled. 'No!'

'I mean it, seriously.'

'You'd poke fun and be a nuisance and make everyone uncomfortable.'

'I swear I wouldn't. You know I owe Richard a lot, and I'd never do anything to upset him. Or you. And,' he added, with an innocent look, 'it will make the numbers at table even.'

'You are an atrocious wretch!' Molly laughed. 'Robert will make the numbers even.'

'Not if he takes his fiancée.'

'Robert's not going,' Charlotte said. She avoided Basil's eye. 'He's engaged somewhere else for the weekend.'

There was a brief silence. They all knew her brother Robert disapproved of Richard's choice of bride.

Basil said, in a different voice, one without edges, 'Then you *must* take me. I feel for Richard. I want to do my bit to make his in-laws feel welcome. I'm serious now. Let me show you I can do it.'

Charlotte seemed to be warming to the idea, but she said, 'It's up to Mother. I can't just "take" you.'

'You could send a telegram and ask,' Basil suggested.

Molly said, 'I'm sure your mother will like to see Basil again. And he can behave prettily when he wants to.'

Basil looked at her with narrowed eyes. 'You just want to be rid of me.'

'What – want to spend a rare weekend alone with my beloved husband whom I see all too little of? How could you think it?'

Molly was right: Violet said yes. She and Jessie had been each other's best friend all their lives, Jack was Jessie's favourite brother, and Basil was his son. And she was aware that when Basil had first flown the nest, Richard had taken him under his wing, found him lodgings and a job, so there was a connection there.

Also, though Charlotte had dismissed the idea, she really did like the numbers to be even round her dining table. It was a small matter, and these days lots of hostesses didn't bother any more, but she felt it made things comfortable. And she *was* a little worried that the Nevinsons might feel out of place. She had grown up in a very formal age: Basil, like Charlotte, was of a more relaxed generation. Between the two of them, they ought to be able to keep things going.

The Nevinsons were a little intimidated by their surroundings. Tunstead Hall, in the glorious Peak District, was Elizabethan, built of grey stone with a multitude of small-paned windows so that it glittered in the sun. Inside, a darkness of oak floorboards, family oil-paintings and old furniture contrasted with the daylight from the many windows. There was a smell of lavender wax and an underlying mustiness, like prayer-books. Room led to room in bewildering sequence, with massive fireplaces and ceilings of decorative plaster-work. There was a plethora of servants. Lady Belmont greeted them with a pretty smile and evident kindness, but she was undeniably grand. Like scared children, the Nevinsons put themselves on their best behaviour, sat with their hands folded and their backs straight, and said as little as possible.

Violet was made uneasy in her turn. Richard had assured her that they had no special dietary requirements or religious tabus, but did he really know? She did not want to tread on any cultural sensitivities. In the drawing-room on their arrival she tried to engage her future daughter-in-law in conversation, but Cynthia was even more scared than her parents and she could hardly get her further than yes and no.

Eventually Avis and Samuel struck up on the neutral subject of business, Charlotte and Basil drew Cynthia out on the latest shows and films, and Richard encouraged Violet and Hannah to talk about the proper care of furniture and fabrics, about which Hannah knew everything and Violet nothing. Hannah gave Violet some excellent housewifely hints, and Violet admired her expertise, but it was still very sticky. Both sides were glad of a respite when the visitors were shown to their rooms before dinner.

At dinner there was an incident which made Violet glad that Basil had invited himself. They had just finished the first course, and without thinking Hannah stood up to clear the dishes. At table, when a lady stands, the gentlemen have to stand also, and Basil who was opposite her and Avis who was beside her were both automatically getting to their feet before they had registered what was happening. Startled by the movement Hannah froze, one hand outstretched, her cheeks crimsoning as she realised what she was doing. Out of the corner of her eye she could see the servants waiting to clear, and was mortified.

Basil took it all in with one leap of piercing sympathy. As the other two men began awkwardly to rise and Cynthia, not understanding what was happening, half rose too, he said cheerfully, 'A little cramp, ma'am? Horrid thing, isn't it? I get it too, when I sit for too long. I got a cramp once when I was dining with some very fashionable people, and I stood up so fast I knocked my wine glass over, and the contents landed in the lap of my dinner companion. I've never felt so foolish.'

By now, one of the footmen was standing behind Hannah holding her chair, ready to seat her again, and she subsided into it, her eyes down. Basil prattled on as the men sat again.

'Luckily it was white wine, not red, so it didn't show too much. But the poor lady was terribly put out. She was so obliging as to tell me that it was the first time she'd worn that particular dress: it had come home from the dressmaker only that morning. So I comforted her as best I could by assuring her that I felt much worse about the whole thing than she did.'

Everybody laughed at that, and Charlotte said, 'Oh, Basil, you didn't!'

'I had to. I was afraid she was going to tell me how much it cost, which would have been a shocking solecism. I had to save her from that.'

'Now, young man, I'm sure you're exaggerating,' Samuel Nevinson said, but not unkindly; and across the table, Hannah threw him a silent look of gratitude.

After that, Basil entertained the table, playing the impudent but lovable young rapscallion, and the atmosphere eased until everyone was joining in with the conversation to some extent, even Cynthia.

Later, when the men rejoined the ladies in the drawing-room, Violet came up to him and murmured as she handed his cup, 'That was kind of you. I felt dreadfully for that poor lady.'

'The one whose dress I ruined?' he said innocently. 'I am a clumsy oaf, it's true.'

'Anything but clumsy, Basil dear,' Violet said.

On Sunday morning, Basil was halfway down the stairs when he overheard Violet in conversation with Richard, and paused on the landing out of sight to listen.

'I'd completely forgotten about church,' Violet was saying. 'I really ought to go, and Avis is supposed to read the lesson. But I don't think there's a temple, or whatever it is, anywhere near.'

'I told you, Ma, they're not observant.'

'Are you sure they didn't just say that to be polite? And it would be rude to go, and leave them here.'

'You and Avis should go. They'll understand completely. The rest of us will take care of them. I'll show them over the house or something.'

'That's another thing. Now we've had them here, they ought to invite us down to their place for a weekend. But they haven't got a place, have they?'

'We've discussed that,' Richard said firmly. 'When you come up, they're going to invite you to dinner. That will cover it quite nicely.'

'Oh!' Violet said. She sounded anxious. Basil could imagine her concern. What would their home be like? Would she feel as out of place in it as they had evidently felt in hers?

Now Richard sounded a trifle impatient. 'The food is always delicious. Hannah's a wonderful cook. You'll enjoy it, Ma.'

Basil decided it was time to interrupt, given that Violet had never cooked a meal in her life and might well question the last statement. He clattered noisily down the last flight with a cheerful 'Good morning!' Both of them looked slightly relieved.

Before lunch the sun came out, and they all took a turn around the gardens, naturally separating into pairs according to their speed of walking. Charlotte and Basil soon pulled ahead of everyone else.

'It's a good thing Robert didn't come,' Charlotte said, after a pause in the conversation. 'He's such a snob – worse than you. He'd have done his best to make the Nevinsons feel small.'

'You are horridly unjust to me. I'm not a snob and I get on with everyone.'

She snorted, then said, 'What do you think about it?'

'It?'

'Richard marrying her. It's odd, isn't it?'

'All marriage seems odd to me.' He thought for a moment of Gloria. Would he marry her, if she was free? Yes, probably – but he was quite glad the question didn't arise. 'She seems a nice enough girl, if a little milk-and-water for my taste. But I believe she'll inherit her father's business.'

'Basil! You don't say he's marrying her for her money?'

'Oh dear, you're so romantic! A man has to have *something* to live on. But I'm sure he's fond of her.'

'Fond!' Charlotte brooded a moment. 'They're going to live in *Ealing*,' she said at last, as though it was the world's end.

'Now who's the snob? Anyway, your company's moving to Acton. Right next door.'

She brightened. 'That's true. I could pop over after work. I was afraid we'd never see him again.'

'My dear child, you live in Bloomsbury. The Piccadilly Line runs from Russell Square all the way to Ealing.'

'Basil, you can't call me 'your dear child'. I'm four years older than you. You sound like the vicar.'

'I'll call you Grandmama if you prefer. I'm sure they'll be all right,' he went on seriously. 'Richard knows what he's doing. He's the most level-headed chap I know.'

'You're right. Thank you. I feel better now.'

'I'm more worried about you,' Basil went on. 'Engaged to an invisible man, don't know where he is or when he's coming back. Or, indeed, *what he's doing.*'

She didn't rise to the bait. 'He's earning money so that we can get married. Don't try to annoy me about Milo, Basil, because it won't work. Oh, did you hear that Henry saw Uncle Jack at Hucclestone?' Her younger brother was an engineer apprentice with Hawkers at their Gloster factory. 'He wrote to say that Uncle Jack urged him to take flying lessons, told him that when the next war starts, they'll need all the pilots they can get. *When* the war starts, he said, not *if*. What d'you think of that?'

'There won't be another war,' Basil said. 'Those old fellows who fought in it can't let it go, that's all. It was the best fun they'd ever had in their terribly boring lives, so of course they want to do it all again. But our generation has more sense.'

'I don't think anyone would ever mistake you for someone with sense,' Charlotte said. 'Ow! That hurt!'

Al Feinstein relit the stub of his cigar and clenched it between his teeth, screwing up his eyes against the rising smoke. The narrowed eyes gave him a dangerous, calculating look. He was such a mixture of the crass and the canny, it was hard to say which he really was. Perhaps, Lennie thought, he meant people not to know, so as to keep them off balance. In a world that made money from acting, it became hard to tell when anyone was simply being themselves.

'And she's staying at your place?'

'In one of the guest bungalows, quite separate from the house,' Lennie said. 'She has her dresser with her, sleeping in an adjoining room. Then there's her housekeeper Dola and my housekeeper living in—'

Al's teeth grinned round the stub. 'I wasn't questioning your respectability, Len – though it's as well to be careful. There's some that'll always look on the dark side of everything. But your reputation is sound. I was asking how she's getting on.'

'She's doing well. Off the dope, getting her strength back. Lots of walking and swimming and tennis. Wilma's feeding her up with every vitamin in the book. Steaks, oranges and cod liver oil every day.'

'Okay. So far so good.'

'She's learned her lesson, Al. She just wants to get back to work.'

'Hmph,' Al said noncommittally. The stub had gone out again. He took it out, looked at it in disgust, and put it in the ashtray. 'Cohiba my ass,' he muttered. 'Never buy a stogie from a guy you meet at a poker game. Five bucks a box of ten, the robber.'

'"What this country needs is a really good five-cent cigar,"' Lennie said, quoting Thomas R. Marshall.

Al looked impatient. 'Whaddaya wasting my time talking about smokes for? This situation with Rosie is not so good. And this affects you, too,' he added sharply, throwing a furious look at the other person in the room.

Dean Cornwell's agent, Doris Forman, allowed the look to bounce off her harmlessly. She was used to Al Feinstein trying to bully her because she was a woman, but she was a formidable person, not least because of her connections. She was the sister of David B. Reznik, ABO's leading film director, a second cousin to Louis B. Mayer, and the wife of producer Bernard Forman, who was responsible for a string of hits to rival Feinstein's.

'I'm just waiting for you to get to me, Al,' she said comfortably. 'Take all the time you need.'

Al stabbed a forefinger as thick as a Cohiba and much the same colour at the newspaper lying on his desk. 'What I *need* is some constructive suggestions!' he bellowed. 'God damn it, they've only been married a year. It was billed as the greatest love story since – since—'

'Antony and Cleopatra?' Lennie suggested helpfully.

Feinstein was sidetracked. The finger now poked at Lennie. 'You've said a bundle, Lennie my friend. That'd make a great movie! It's got everything – doomed lovers, Roman soldiers, chariots, pyramids, a snake! And it's never been done! You can't count that Blackton one-reeler in, what was it, 1908? With Florence Lawrence!' He sidetracked himself again, staring into space. 'My God, she was a gorgeous gal! Could act, as well. Signed with Universal eventually, and they nearly killed her – a stage fire got outta hand, burned off all her hair, and she got a fractured spine when the set collapsed.'

'Yes, I read about it,' Lennie said.

'Then those shysters wouldn't pay her medical bills, the bastards – pardon my French, Doris. Not one dime. Wonder where she is now? It's a great idea, Tony and Cleo,' he said, his focus returning to Lennie, 'but we got to get outta this hole we're in first. Rosie and Deanie. Doris, your boy done her wrong. Whaddaya gonna do about it?'

'He doesn't want a divorce,' Doris Forman said, with an air of getting her bid in first.

Al was half out of his chair, shouting, 'I don't give a rat's ass what he wants! Who does he think he is? I eat punk actors like him for breakfast!'

'He could be the next Clark Gable,' Doris said calmly.

'In his dreams he could! He's milquetoast. Rosie carried him in *Falcon*, and you know it.'

Lennie winced, not wanting to get into this kind of exchange. There were enough hard feelings flying around Hollywood without adding to them. 'I think there has to be a divorce,' he said, in a level voice, 'for both their sakes. There's been too much publicity for them to get back together with any credibility, even if Rosie was willing. Let them move on. Get them both talked about with new part-ners – at a very respectable boy-and-girl-next-door level, I mean. A clean divorce without rancour is the best solution all round.'

'I agree,' said Al. 'I don't like divorce, it stinks, but in this case it's the best option. They're both young, youngsters make mistakes, it'll be easier forgotten if it doesn't drag on.'

'It's not going to look good for Dean if she makes out it's his fault,' said Doris.

'It *is* his fault,' Lennie pointed out.

'There are faults on both sides,' Doris said, giving him a look that said, *Don't mess with me, buster.* 'Things could come out she mightn't like. For instance, why has Michael Rosecrantz dropped her if she's the innocent party?'

Lennie gave her a steady look in return. 'A clean, speedy divorce. Otherwise Rose might be forced to look for an annulment, on the grounds of non-consummation.'

Feinstein thumped his desk. 'Ha! He's got you there, Dorrie! You don't wanna open *that* can-a worms! No reason a virile young man wouldn't want to do the business with a gorgeous gal like Rosie, is there? Or *is* there?'

Doris was thinking furiously. As Al drew breath to speak again she held up her hand, stopping him, while she calculated. 'Okay,' she said at last. 'A clean divorce – without recriminations on either side. No leaking little innuendoes to the mags! They made a genuine mistake, found out they didn't suit, no alternative but to split, going their own two ways but still the best of friends. And no financial settlements, either way. No strings. They've both got their careers to support them.'

'What about Roselands?' They had bought the house between them.

'Sell it, split the cash fifty-fifty.'

'Suits me,' said Lennie.

'Al?'

'Deal,' said Feinstein. 'Let's get our lawyers on to it, make it watertight. We don't want anything coming back to bite us in the ass five years down the line.'

Doris stood up. 'I'll talk to Dean. You'll talk to Rose?' she asked Lennie. 'Is she getting another agent? No offence, Len, but she needs someone who knows what they're doing.'

Now, how could I possibly take offence at that? Lennie asked himself. 'As soon as she's ready to start work again, I'll see she signs on with somebody.'

'I'd like to take her on myself, but I don't think it'd be wise for me to rep both of them. Michael's crazy,' she added shortly. 'That gal's going to be big.' And with a nod to each of them, she went out.

Feinstein fumbled in his drawer and pulled out a box of cigars, offered one to Lennie, who shook his head, and went through the business of clipping and lighting it. Lennie didn't know if it was one of the so-called Cohibas, but it smelt like a lit garbage heap.

'Now,' Al said, when he'd got it going, 'talk to me about

Rosie. We got to get her back in harness soon as possible.'

'I agree. She needs to work to keep her out of trouble. A big, meaty part – something like *Falcon*.'

'Yeah, another historical,' Al mused. 'She looks good in all that gold stuff, big skirts and headdresses and all.' He drummed his fat fingers on the desk. 'You got my juices going with that Tony and Cleo talk.'

'Rose is too young. Cleopatra was a mature woman – in her forties, I believe.'

'Hell, that don't matter. In Hollywood she can be any age you like. We could call it *Queen of the Nile.*'

'Good title,' said Lennie, cautiously.

'How about,' he wrote it across the air in block capitals, '*Queen of the Nile*, with Rose Morland as Cleopatra and Leslie Howard as Mark Antony?'

Lennie winced. 'Mark Antony was a highly successful, battle-hardened Roman general. Do you think perhaps—?'

'You could be right. Needs someone a bit more – *rugged*. Less polite. Less British.'

'I still think Rose is too young for Cleopatra. When she has a few more movies under her belt, she could come back to it. The story will still be there.'

'Hmmph. But we gotta get something big, sweeping, *epic* for her. What else you got in British history?'

'What about the civil war?' Lennie hazarded.

Al gave him a boiled look. 'I said *British* history.'

'They had a civil war as well. Cavaliers and Roundheads?'

'Oh, yeah, I heard o' them.' He chomped on the cigar. 'I like it. The guys with the long hair and the lace, and the other guys with the buzzcut and the bad attitude. Who won in the end?'

'The ugly ones.'

'But all the time you want the pretty boys to win, I love it.'

'Two families on opposing sides, the son of one falls in love with the daughter of the other.'

'Your basic Romeo and Juliet.' Al nodded, almost gleeful. 'Is there a book?'

'There is one I know of, called *The Leopards and the Lilies*. By Celia Hardwick. It's a famous novel back in England.'

Al thought. 'Is that too much like *The Falcon and the Rose*?'

'It's a reference to the English royal flag. The lilies are the fleur-de-lys, and in heraldry, lions can only be called lions when they are rampant, otherwise they're called leopards, so since the English lions are passant regardant they're—'

Al waved all that away. 'We can talk about a title later. Get me the book – better still, give me a précis and get the book to the writers.' He gave Lennie one of his narrowest looks, though the cigar wasn't in his mouth at that moment. 'You're gonna want to put some money into this, aren't you, my boy? This one's a banker. Rose on horseback – they rode horses in those days, right?'

'Horses everywhere,' Lennie agreed, amused.

'Any battles?'

'As many as you like. Lances, bows and arrows, swords. Cavalry charges.'

'Yeah.' Al sighed with satisfaction, seeing it in the air in front of him. Then his gaze sharpened again. 'You're gonna want to make a big, fat investment in this, I know it.'

Lennie didn't say yes or no, but he knew he could not leave Rose in her present fragile state, or indeed before the divorce had gone through. Work was undoubtedly the best thing to put her on a steady course, and he would have to stay at least until she was properly engaged with a new project. A sweeping, epic civil-war movie with her as star would be a terrific boost to her career – as long as she didn't fall for whoever they cast opposite her and start another foolish affair. He would need to stay involved with the film until he was sure she was all right. And that was going to mean putting some money into it. But Al Feinstein was a sharp operator, and he was not wrong. As an investment, it seemed like a sound one.

England – the real one, where Yorkshire and Morland Place and Polly were – would have to wait.

CHAPTER FIVE

Over tea one evening, James asked Tata something he had been wondering about, though not with any urgency, for some time.

'How did you get out?'

'Out?' she said, though he saw understanding reach her eyes a moment later. Still, she was cautious. 'Out of where?'

'Out of Russia. If you were there during the war, I suppose you were there during the revolution—'

'We don't talk of that,' she said quickly. 'That terrible time.'

'No, I understand. I just wondered . . .' He was thinking, staring at those photographs on the wall. 'You were just a child. Your aunt Masha – is she in Paris too?'

'No, Shems, she is dead.'

'I'm sorry,' he said, and prepared to change the subject.

But she went on: 'There were secret organisations, lots of them, helping people to get away. There was an American colonel, called Boyle, Joe Boyle – he was a great big man. Aunt Masha called him a magician. She said he could do *anything*. And an English flying officer called Hill, who was his partner, I think. They worked for the Queen of Romania. She was an English princess by birth, cousin to the Tsarina, so of course she cared about them. They helped a lot of people. Aunt Masha and I were got out through Romania. I don't remember much about it. I was a child, and it was a bad time. I remember the travelling, always in the dark, always in a hurry. The pinching hands urging one along, pinch and shake, and the whispering. One must never make a sound. And the fear. The fear most of all. Everyone scared me. The men with guns, who smelt of sweat, demanding papers, always papers. One time, in a railway carriage, I remember a soldier reading our papers, and I don't think he could read. I said, "You're holding them upside down," and I felt the shock all around the compartment. I thought we would be killed. I was just a child, Shems. The memories are all jumbled up. We got out on a ship from Odessa to Romania. But Aunt Masha was never well afterwards. She caught some kind of fever in Odessa – that was a dirty place. She died of kidney disease after we came to Paris. I was always glad that at least she died here, in freedom.'

'I'm so sorry,' James said. 'That must have been terrible for you.'

She gave a French little shrug and was silent for a moment, thinking. 'It is not surprising perhaps that there is so much taking of drugs.'

'Is there?' James queried.

'Natalie's circle – they all take cocaine. There's a lot of it at her parties. But even Before, in the top circle, they all used it. The Tsar took it for colds, and the Tsarina for rheumatism, but also I think for pleasure. I remember Aunt Masha talking about it once with Sister Chebodarev. She said the Tsar had told her it made him feel "absolutely marvellous".'

'But you don't—?'

'No, Shems. I've seen what it does to them. Don't you try it, even if someone offers.'

'I won't. I believe it's illegal in England.'

She shrugged. 'Well, it wasn't in Russia. And no-one thought anything of it, any more than drinking brandy. Now we must get back to work. You have made me think of uncomfortable things.'

'"For old, unhappy, far-off things, and battles long ago,"' he quoted, from some buried childhood rote-learning.

'Wordsworth,' she said unexpectedly. 'Yes, we read English poetry. Why are you surprised? "His little, nameless, unremembered acts of kindness" – that was Wordsworth as well. And my kindness to you will be to make you work harder. Idleness is a sin, Shems, you should remember that.'

'You are a harsh teacher,' he said, grinning. 'I bet your little children at school are terrified of you.'

'Do I terrify you?'

'I'm shaking to the core,' he assured her.

'You are a liar,' she laughed, 'but I like you. Come, we must look at verbs. You are lucky, there are only four irregular verbs in Russian, unlike in English where it seems all verbs are irregular.'

'Ah, but with English, one may speak it very badly and still be understood. That is its great advantage. Unlike French, where the slightest mistake means they'll look at you with stony incomprehension. I never knew people so very good at not understanding.'

'Are we going to be embarrassed tonight?' Emma asked, as she and Kit walked down the marble staircase, dressed for dinner. The dogs rushed past them in a flood, skidding on the corners with wildly flailing paws.

'No more than one usually is by the Simpsons playing host to the King at Bryanston Court. Personally, I find it amusing when Simpson suggests a cocktail and HM heads straight for the drinks trolley and does the mixing, as if he's the host.'

'You have an odd sense of humour,' Emma said. 'I can't help feeling sorry for Ernest. It's his house, after all. But why a *black*-tie dinner? It makes it so awkward to know what to wear.'

'You always look exactly right, darling, whatever you wear,' said Kit.

Emma was amused. 'That is the worst thing you can say to a female. It suggests you either don't care what she wears, or simply don't notice.'

'What I *meant* to say was that your choice this evening is perfect.'

Emma was wearing a bias-cut silk Vionnet gown in broad black-and-white diagonal stripes, calf-length with a little flare at the hem. She wore modest diamond earrings and two small diamond clips in her dark hair. 'But the King being there makes it a sort of royal occasion, and one doesn't want to look underdressed,' she fretted.

'You know my view. Better under than over.'

'I suppose Wally will be hung about with jewels like a Christmas tree.'

'Now, darling, don't be unkind. You are so very beautiful, you don't understand that lesser women have to decorate themselves more to compete with you.'

'She does dress very well, and I must say her style is good. She got shoals of new dresses in Paris. And David gives her a jewel every time she tells him off for something. She got sapphire clips after scolding him for leaving a wine-glass ring on some official paper.'

They reached the hall, where the servants were waiting with their outdoor clothes, and at the sight the dogs came to a halt and sat down on their tails and looked mournful. Kit took Emma's fur from Spencer and hung it round her shoulders. 'Alec Hardinge is in despair about the red boxes,' he said. 'HM reads them in the drawing-room or wherever he happens to be, and leaves confidential papers lying about where anyone could read them.'

'"Anyone", in this case, being Wally, I suppose,' Emma said. 'Alec hates her so much, he's hardly rational about it. He must know HM shows her everything anyway – otherwise how could she advise him?'

Kit took his scarf and gloves from Ponsford and they

walked towards the door. 'I rather think that begs the question,' he said. 'She shouldn't *be* advising him. He has an entire government for that.'

'Ah, but they don't tell him what he wants to hear,' said Emma, passing before him down the steps into Manchester Square. It was a clear, starry night, and sharply cold. Each streetlamp wore a halo of mist. They hurried into the waiting car, and were glad to have the rug tucked around their legs. As Osmond closed the door, Kit sought her hand under the rug and held it. It was one of his fond gestures that made her feel very fortunate in her marriage.

'What is the situation between the Simpsons, anyway?' Emma asked him, when they were moving. 'I thought Ernest was going to arrange for a divorce, but I haven't heard anything more. Has he changed his mind?'

'Oh, I have news on that front. I met Wally in Selfridge's this afternoon and took her for a cocktail—'

'What were you doing in Selfridges?'

'Looking at some Van Cleef cufflinks. Please concentrate on the important point.'

'Did you buy them?'

'The cufflinks? No. So I took Wally for a cocktail—'

'Why didn't you tell me you'd seen her?'

'You only got home just in time to dress. I'm telling you *now*. May I continue?'

'About the divorce?'

'Yes. It's in abeyance at the moment. HM is consulting a new lawyer, one Walter Monckton, who's supposed to be as clever as a barrel of monkeys, and he's suggested a way out – because, you know, as it stands, the King can't marry a divorcée.'

'Wally told you all this? She certainly confides in you more than in me.'

'Of course she does. Everyone does. I'm the sort of person people love telling things.'

'That's true. So what's the new idea?'

'Monckton's suggested instead of a divorce Wally seeks an annulment.'

Emma considered. 'But even if there were some legal problem with her marriage to Ernest, she would still be a divorcée from her first marriage.'

'An annulment of *both* marriages.'

'That sounds a little improbable. Legal hitches in *both* cases?'

'No. Non-consummation,' said Kit, watching her face for her reaction. He was enjoying himself.

'Really? She told you all this?'

'After the second martini she let down her hair. She told me she had never had sexual relations with either of her husbands. She said she would never allow a man to touch her below the Mason-Dixon line.'

Emma frowned. 'The—'

'It's the line that divides the American North from the American South.'

'I know what it is. I just can't believe she used an expression like that to you.'

He shrugged. 'I'm exactly the chum she wants: a man – because she prefers men to women – but one who's never going to want to sleep with her. In fact, she likes me so much, I'm almost an honorary American.'

'She can't be serious about this,' said Emma, getting back to the point. 'The King won't go along with it, surely. Think of the speculation it would unleash. About him as well as her.'

'Oh, he's all for it. Anything that gets him his way. You're forgetting, he's already sworn to Ernest that his relationship with Wally is platonic. And to Sir Maurice Jenks. And he swore the same thing to his father. Now, our King may be careless in a lot of matters, but I don't think he would have lied to his father – not solemnly and to his face, at any rate.'

'Well, it would be better than a divorce, I suppose. But no-one would ever believe it, would they?'

'That's very cynical of you, darling.'

'It's a cynical world,' Emma said.

Wallis greeted Emma with a brisk, hard gaze. 'Emma, darling, you look perfect as always.'

Wallis was also in black and white, which might have been awkward, but hers was a black gown figured all over with white humming-bird shapes, and she had coupled it with a magnificent ruby and diamond bracelet that Emma hadn't seen before. Wallis saw her looking, and touched it in acknowledgement. Her nails were painted a dark red that matched the rubies. 'A little present from David when I came back from Paris,' she murmured.

'You're looking much better,' Emma said. 'You seemed quite pulled after that trip.'

'My nerves were shot, and David was in a state. But things are going better now,' she said. 'I'll talk to you about it all later. David will be here any moment.'

Emma was glad to see that Oliver and Verena were among the guests, and she and Kit went to join them. After some family talk, Kit asked if Oliver had any interesting new cases. 'And by "interesting" I mean something with a stardust element, of course,' he urged. 'You know Raymond is in America, so I'm parched for news.' He adored films, read the magazines for Hollywood gossip, and had a long-standing friendship with silver screen darling Raymond Romano.

Oliver smiled indulgently. 'You know I can't discuss my clients.'

Kit rolled his eyes. 'Don't be coy. I just want names, not details. You do have something,' he concluded. 'I can see it in your face.'

'I can't tell you anything,' Oliver insisted. 'I do happen to know, however, that Vera Bergdorf is coming to Town.' Film stars were a lucrative part of his business. It was how Kit had met Raymond in the first place, when he had come over to consult Oliver.

'Vera Bergdorf? I loved her in *Brunhilda*,' Kit cried.

'She *was* supposed to be coming with Eric Chapel, the artist—'

'Oh, I heard about him,' Emma said. 'He's having an exhibition at the Cavendish Gallery, isn't he? Daisy Fellowes is organising it.'

'That's right,' Verena said. 'He's quite her new pet. I'm afraid he's *very* modern, though. Just squares of colour – nothing really to look at.'

'Don't be old-fashioned, dear,' Kit said. 'Modern art is supposed to make you think.'

'I don't *want* to think,' Verena said. 'I just want to look at a picture and feel pleasure.'

'Bowls of fruit and thatched cottages?' Kit suggested. 'Baskets of kittens?'

'I'm not a Philistine,' Verena said, with dignity. 'There are lots of modern paintings I like. But there ought to be some sort of skill in them, surely. Isn't that what "art" means?'

'I'm with you,' Emma said. 'I can go along with Fauvism and Cubism, but if I want a plain square of colour I can look at a wall.'

'We're getting away from the point,' Kit said impatiently. 'The only reason to be talking about this wretched Chapel daubist is that he's accompanying Vera Bergdorf – the actress with the exquisite cheekbones, the actress who uttered the immortal words, "I am both queen and king to my people!"' He imitated her accent. '*That* Vera Bergdorf. Is she having an affair with this Chapel person?'

'I can't tell you,' Oliver said, 'because if you'd let me finish, I'd have told you he's not coming after all, and the exhibition is off. He's gone back to America.'

'Oh, a scandal!' Kit said. 'Have they quarrelled? Did she thrrrow him out?' He rolled his r like the actress.

'I don't even know if they were a couple. I only know he was supposed to be accompanying her and now he's not.'

'You're no fun at all,' Kit complained. 'At least tell me she's coming to see you.'

'I couldn't possibly say.'

'Smug beast! Probably some tiny, almost invisible mole – you know what these stars are like. It must be something below the neck, anyway, because her face is utter bliss,' Kit said. 'Especially the left profile – *perfect*!'

Wally, who had been circulating, joined them just at that moment, and said, 'Oh, you've heard? About the postage-stamp debacle?'

Kit turned eagerly. 'No, not at all. Is it something delicious? Tell me at once.'

'But I heard you say "left profile". You must know about our row with the Post Office. They want the new stamps to show David in right profile, and he really dislikes the way he looks from that side. He looks much better from the left. But, of course, Alec Hardinge has to interfere and say the old king was shown in left profile and it's the tradition to alternate.' She made an exasperated sound. 'As if *that* was the important thing! David's the King. *He*'ll decide how things are to be done.'

'But tradition is important,' Oliver said tentatively.

'David is not going to be dictated to by tradition,' Wally said impatiently. 'If something wants changing, he'll change it, not be hidebound by a lot of silly, outdated rules. He's going to throw open the windows, I can tell you, and blow away the cobwebs. Oh, here he is!'

She hurried away, as Ernest came into the drawing-room escorting the King. Behind him, they spotted Eddie Vibart, Oliver's cousin, who was evidently equerrying that evening.

'Oh, good, there's Eddie,' said Kit. 'Now we can get some juicy inside information.'

'The first thing to ask him is why Ernest is showing HM in like an usher at the theatre,' said Oliver.

'Perhaps it's an American custom,' Verena said drily.

'How does he manage to go on looking honoured to have the King here,' Oliver said, 'given that his wife is HM's popsy?'

'Because he's a passionate royalist,' Kit said. 'He loves being "inty" with the Crown. "The King of England calls round to my place for cockers." Makes his chest swell with pride.'

'The King's sacking old retainers right, left and centre,' Oliver said, 'but perhaps he'll make a special post for Ernest. He could be Master of the Mistress.'

The next morning Wally called on Emma in Manchester Square quite early, when Emma was still in the nursery with the children, as she explained when she came downstairs. Wally evinced no interest in Alethea and Electra, but enthused over the dogs. 'They're so well behaved. How do you do it? We still have the odd little difficulty with Slipper. Well, more than odd, really. David's valet calls him Mr Loo! Did you enjoy dinner last night? The fried chicken was a recipe from back home – you soak it in milk first. I could see everyone was impressed. It's what this country needs – simple tasty American cooking. I'm so tired of that eternal poached salmon the Tadcasters serve up. Their dinners! Six courses, every single dish cold! I can't stay long, I have a nail appointment, but I haven't had a chance to talk to you for ages. And I may be a little *engagée* for a few days because my oldest friend from back home, Mary Kirk – Raffray, as she is now – is coming to London. She was bridesmaid at my first wedding. And she was the one who introduced me to Ernest.'

'It'll be nice for you to have time together to catch up.'

'That's just the trouble,' Wally said, frowning. 'I simply don't *have* time at the moment. I love Mary, but I wish she'd asked, rather than just land herself on me. David takes up my every minute. If I didn't have hair and nail appointments, where he *can't* come with me, I'd never have an instant to myself. It isn't all a bed of roses, you know, Emma, being the King's friend.'

'I never thought it was,' Emma said. She hesitated. 'This new idea of yours – Kit was saying. About an annulment?'

'He told you, did he?'

'He tells me everything, but I would never repeat it.'

'Oh, I knew he'd tell you. You two are as close as thieves. The famous Westhoven perfect marriage.' It sounded disparaging.

Emma let it go. 'But, Wally, an annulment? Have you really thought it through? Wouldn't there have to be a medical examination?'

Wally winced. 'David would never allow it. I'm sure there'd be a way round it. Sworn affidavits or something. Anyway, it's just an idea. There's no need to act on it. Monckton talks a lot but, after all, his fee depends on sounding positive. I don't believe any of this will ever happen. But as long as David thinks we're on track, he's happy. And if he's happy, I'm happy.'

'I'm glad you're being . . . *realistic* about it,' Emma said.

'I'm a practical person,' Wally said sharply. 'I've always had to look out for myself. God knows no-one else ever did. I'm happy with Ernest, and if David had never come along . . . But the opportunity was there, and I had to take it. I've always had in the back of my mind, though, that one day the dream would have to end. Somewhere, sometime, somehow. It was something I built into my plans.' She looked away pensively. 'Now I almost long for it – for a little peace. What with David, and the Establishment, and all those old courtiers briefing against me . . . Do you know, I think I'm being followed? By the Secret Service, or Scotland Yard – some government agency or other. Is that possible? Do they do that sort of thing in Merrie Old England?'

'Surely not,' Emma said. 'We fought the war for freedom.'

Wally nodded, almost indifferently. 'It's quite something to be hated like the old guard hates me. Sometimes I wish I could . . . But I'm so tangled up in things. I feel as if I'm strangling to death.' She stopped, staring moodily at her hands.

'You could leave him,' Emma suggested gently.

She looked up. When she didn't smile, she looked older than her years. 'He'd never let me,' she said. She stood up. 'I must go,' she said briskly. 'You're coming to the Fort this weekend.'

'Oh, I'm not sure that we—' Emma began.

'It wasn't a question,' Wally said. 'At least there we can be ourselves. Such a relief to get away from protocol. Ernest is coming, and Mary, and some other friends. We'll be going over to the Castle, so that I can show Mary around. And we'll have a movie show up there. David's getting hold of a newsreel of the Grand National – you love horses. And we'll have *King Kong*. I could watch that one again and again.'

April in Paris was a particularly romantic time. The chestnuts were in flower, and the tulips in the place Dauphine were a sight to behold. James was busy, but thoughts of Meredith were never far away. He imagined them having a cup of coffee and a *croque* in the Café Richelieu in the rue de Rivoli, then going for a stroll along the river. They would admire the tulips, perhaps pop into the Sainte-Chapelle – because she would have forgotten over in America how beautiful it was – then they'd browse at the book stalls on the quai Voltaire. They'd have a cocktail at the Hôtel d'Orsay, then dinner at a delightful restaurant he'd discovered just off the Boul' Mich' that he'd been longing to show her. And to finish the evening, dancing at the Florida. Or, perhaps not the Florida, because it was always full of Americans, and he didn't want her to be reminded of home. No, he'd make it

Le Boeuf. It's was little *passé*, perhaps, but the jazz was always good.

But she was not here. And she hadn't written to him – not so much as a postcard – to explain why she wasn't coming back, or when – if ever – he might see her again. And soon he would be off to Russia with the Bedauxs, another world away from where she was. Just a line: she could have sent him just a line! It must mean – he forced the realisation like a stiletto into his unwilling heart – that she didn't care for him. He must get used to this being-without-Meredith because it was to be the norm for the rest of his life.

His lessons with Tata Bebidov helped, because learning Russian was an effort that used up mental energy, and because Tata herself was such fun, good company, and growing, he thought, rather fond of him. He was fond of her, too. Since she had confided in him about her escape from Russia, their friendship had deepened. There was an ease between them that he had not known with anyone else, except perhaps his sister Polly. He felt he could talk to her about anything. And there was an equality between them: with Meredith he had always been courtier to her queen, supplicant to her goddess.

One Saturday evening when he was not wanted by Charlie, he invited Tata to go to the cinema with him. They went to see the just-premièred *Le Deuxième*, with Marcel André as the brave secret agent and Vera Bergdorf as the glamorous enemy spy who was supposed to thwart his plans but fell in love with him instead. In the flickering dark, in the drama of the screen moment, Tata touched his arm, and he took her hand and held it for the rest of the film. It was very pleasant to have the touch of a woman again.

When they came out, Tata seemed excited, and said, 'Did you know that Vera Bergdorf is Russian?'

'No, I didn't. I only know she's a Hollywood star. If I'd thought about it, I might have supposed she was German or Scandinavian.'

'She was born in Russia and her name was Vera Bogolyubov, but she changed it when she got to America because no-one could spell it.'

James laughed. 'Bergdorf sounds much more like a film star, in any case. Do you know her?'

'I've met her,' Tata said, with modest pride. 'She's a friend of Natalie Cooke – who used to be Natalie Karaulov. You know, you saw her picture at my house, working in the hospital.'

'Oh, yes, one of the nurses in the photograph.'

'You should meet Natalie. She knows everyone. And she loves English people. She has very exciting parties—'

'You mentioned those, too. About the cocaine.'

'But there is no necessity to take it oneself. She's having one this week. Would you like to go?'

He hesitated. 'Wouldn't it be rather awkward, as I don't know her?'

'Foolish, *I* know her. I'll take you. And think,' she added beguilingly, 'what good practice it would be for your Russian. Everyone speaks French, but when they get to talking about the old country they generally lapse into Russian.'

'Oh, now you've persuaded me. I really don't enjoy parties, but if it counts as a lesson, I'll go along with it.'

She giggled, sliding a hand affectionately under his elbow. 'Oh, you are *very* foolish! I will try to make sure you don't enjoy yourself. But Vera Bergdorf is in Paris at the moment, because of the film, so she may be there. She and Natalie have known each other all their lives.'

Natalie's rooms were crowded, stifling with the heat of many bodies, blue with cigarette smoke, exotic with wonderfully colourful clothes and jewels. Tata was engulfed with cries of delight, open arms and many kisses, and James was welcomed similarly for her sake. Everyone was smiling, laughing, chattering, affectionate. 'It is not possible,' Tata told him, 'to be sad at a Russian party.' James was given a tumbler of vodka, and every time he lowered the level slightly, someone topped it up. The talk, in rapid and heavily accented French, was hard for him to follow. Sometimes people changed to English to be polite to him, but as soon as they became enthused they slipped back into French.

Tata introduced him to Natalie in rapid Russian that he could not follow, but she shook his hand warmly and looked into his face with keen interest. Tata then switched into French, and Natalie seemed amused to be told that he was trying to learn Russian. 'I will help you,' she said. 'I will speak Russian to you.' As he had to lean close to hear her over the din of voices, he didn't think he'd learn anything useful in the current environment. 'Perhaps not here,' he suggested.

She smiled. 'Whenever you want to practise, you are welcome to come and see me.'

Her English was excellent, and she told him that her husband – now estranged – was an Ulster cloth merchant, and that she had spoken English for more of her life than French. She lived in Paris during the winter, but spent her summers in the north of Ireland, where a wealthy friend regularly hosted lavish house parties for émigré Russians. 'We have such fun – riding, fishing, croquet, parties every night. Talking about the old days. The samovar is never cold, darling. You should come and stay – that's the way to learn Russian. Come and stay for a whole summer.'

He thought she was rather drunk, and in any case was being wholesale with someone else's hospitality, so he made a vague answer, but she clasped her hand around his wrist and said, 'No, no, you must promise to come. You'll meet everyone there – *everyone!*'

There seemed some extra significance in the last word, but before he could answer, a tall, slender man with a pencil moustache, who had been standing behind her for some time, leaned in and said something in her ear in a low voice in Russian. Then he straightened and looked directly, consideringly, at James. He had sculpted features, melancholy eyes and very pale, almost translucent skin, not as if he were ill but as if he belonged to a different species. Natalie did not introduce him to James, but immediately turned away and went with him into another room.

'Who was that?' James asked Tata.

She moved her eyes away, as if checking whether anyone was listening. 'His name is Nicholas Chebodarev.'

'Oh, like the sister at the hospital?' he said intelligently.

'Yes, except that Sister Chebodarev had only one son, and his name was not Nicholas.'

'A cousin, then, perhaps.'

Tata moved closer and lowered her voice. 'Natalie never calls him Nicholas. She refers to him just as "the prince". She likes to keep him to herself and not share him with anyone. And he's rather proud, and doesn't speak to people he doesn't know well.' She looked pensive. 'In Russia, of course, there were many princes, but—'

'Yes?'

She looked up at him seriously. 'I saw him one time with a woman he called his sister. They certainly seemed like brother and sister together. She was introduced to me just as "Lydia". But I noticed that she had a *thing*, a sort of lump, on the third finger of her right hand, here.' She demonstrated on herself. 'She seemed self-conscious about it. When she saw me looking, she covered it with her left hand.' She paused.

'Very well,' James said. 'Not the most exciting thing I've heard tonight, but—'

She gave him a troubled look. 'I told you, Shems, that when I was a child, at Tsarskoye Selo, all the Tsar's children used to come to the hospital. I saw them all, I spoke to them. Grand Duchess Marie had a lump on the third finger of her right hand, where she'd caught it in a car door once. She was self-conscious about it. If she saw you looking, she would cover it with her other hand.'

James stared at her. 'You think this "Lydia" was Grand Duchess Marie? But – then, if this Monsieur Chebodarev is her brother, doesn't that mean—?'

Tata reached up quickly and laid her fingers on his lips. 'Don't say it!' She looked around, to see if anyone was near enough to hear. 'I should not have told you. Forget it, please. I am foolish and talk nonsense. It was just nonsense. Oh, look!' Her change of tone was blatant, and she seized his arm in what looked like excitement, but which hurt in an admonitory way. 'Look, there's Vera, just arriving! Come and meet her.'

He recognised the film star from her motion pictures – the pale, classical face, clouds of black hair and soulful dark eyes. She was wearing a flowing gown of black with a large, swirling, many-coloured pattern. Her hair was decorated with jewelled turkey-quills, and large earrings dangling from her lobes. Her slightly slanting eyes were outlined with kohl, and her full lips matched the blood red of her nails. Despite the heat in the room, a long black crêpe scarf was wound around her neck up to her chin. She looked as though she expected to be looked at – James would have known, even if he didn't know, that she was a film star.

'This is Shems, Vera,' Tata said.

She held out her hand automatically, and he thought she might like a little homage, so he bowed over it and lifted it to his lips in the continental style. '*Enchanté, Madame*,' he said. '*Vraiment enchanté*.'

She examined his face quickly and sharply, like, he thought, a policeman or a border official used to making rapid assessments. Close to, he realised she was considerably older than she appeared at a distance, or on the screen. He guessed – though he was no expert – that she must be about forty. In the Hollywood world where, for a woman, youth was everything, he thought it must be rather frightening to hear Time's chariot wheels behind you. Still, he couldn't help being excited. This was Vera Bergdorf, whom he had seen only days ago on a giant screen at the Grand Rex, closing her enormous eyes and pouting her luscious lips for Marcel André's kiss. This was the same *her*, here, in the flesh. For the first time he felt the awe celebrity engenders.

'I saw you in *Le Deuxième*, Madame,' he said. 'I thought you were wonderful.'

Now she smiled, and her whole face changed. 'Thank you,' she said. 'Tata says you are English. I am going to London on Friday. Do you live in London?'

'I live in Paris now, but I come from Yorkshire. My father had an estate there.'

'Ah, Yorkshire. I was told it is a very beautiful place. I must visit it some time. How do you know Natalie?'

'Tata introduced me. She is teaching me Russian.'

'And how do you know Tata?'

'I was recommended to her by the Maison de l'Évangile.'

'Ah, yes. Mrs Richardson's mission.' This seemed to satisfy all the great lady's curiosity, and she bowed her head slightly to James and moved away.

Tata took hold of his arm and said breathlessly, 'She liked you, Shems! Isn't she wonderful?'

'It's the first time I've met a real movie star,' he said, and she seemed pleased.

'We are all so proud of her. And Natalie likes you, too. I knew she would. Lots of people have been talking to me about you.'

'There's nothing to say about me,' he said. 'I'm nobody important.'

'Nina Berberov thought you might be in the movies too, because you're so handsome,' Tata said.

He laughed. 'Now that's enough of that, or I shall be embarrassed.' He glanced around. 'Would anyone be offended if we left now? The noise is rather overwhelming when you're not used to it. Would you like to go somewhere for a quiet supper?'

'I'd love to,' Tata said.

When they were out in the street, she slipped her hand through his arm, and he pressed it affectionately against his ribs. 'Shems,' she said in English, 'I must say something serious to you.'

He stopped and looked down at her. She gazed up into his face earnestly. 'Are you really going to Russia?'

'You know I am.'

'Then, listen, Shems. You must be careful. The Soviets are bad, crazy people. They watch you *all the time*. You will be followed and spied on. They listen to everything you say. And if they don't like you, they come in the middle of the night and take you away, and you're never seen again.'

'But that won't happen to us,' he said indulgently. 'Charlie was *invited* to go. We'll be there on a government accreditation.'

She shook her head, and gave his arm a little shake, too, for attention. 'You can't trust them. Trust nobody, Shems. Say nothing but yes, no and thank you. I am so worried that you won't come back.'

'I'll come back,' he promised. She still looked troubled. 'I promise,' he said.

Her little face was turned up to his, and it came to him that those full, beautiful lips were wanting to be kissed. So he kissed them. Lightly, briefly, but still it was a kiss, and he knew even as he straightened that by kissing her he had changed something.

She looked up at him urgently. 'Come home with me,' she said.

He hesitated. There was no mistaking the message in her eyes. A sweet enchantment was here, a dream into which he could sink. Was he ready to be entangled? He felt instinctively she was someone who would take a soft but implacable hold on his soul. 'We were going to supper.'

'I don't want supper,' she said. And she seemed to have seen an answer in his face, because she slipped her hand through his arm and turned away, drawing him with her. A taxi cruised by, and he hailed it, the quicker to get home. Like a willing bee to the nectar, he hastened to his fate.

In bed, as out of it, she moved like a dancer. Her body was supple, her skin smooth and honey-coloured; her hair smelt of almonds. Her long fingers caressed him, her full soft lips were more than ready for his. He sank into her with a sensory delight he had never known before, a pleasure that was so piercing it was almost pain. And when she whispered his name in a little, broken breath – the ridiculous 'Shems!' – his heart convulsed with tenderness for her. 'My love,' he whispered back; and his climax almost turned him inside out.

Afterwards she lay on his shoulder and made patterns on his chest with her fingers. 'Your skin is so smooth,' she said. 'I like that. Russian men are very hairy, like bears.'

'Have you known a lot of men?' he asked idly. He saw he had hurt her, and was sorry. He hadn't meant anything by it.

'Not like this,' she said. 'One sees them in the fields at harvest time.' He kissed her contritely.

After a moment she said seriously, 'I am not *vierge*, Shems. I expect you know that by now.'

'You don't need to tell me. I had no right to ask.'

'But now we are lovers you should know. There *was* a man. I was in love – I was seventeen. He was a Romanian officer. His name was Karol. He had to go away to fight the Bolsheviks, and I could not bear to let him go without – without loving him completely. We were going to get married when he came back, so what did it matter if it was frowned upon? It was only a question of timing. But he never came

117

back. He was shot in the neck by a revolutionary and died. And now – now after all that has happened, it seems foolish not to take happiness while one can. Don't you think?'

'I think,' he said. He kissed her again to signify his agreement and, if she wanted it, absolution, and she turned so readily towards him that there was no more talking for a while.

At last she sighed – a contented sigh – and said, 'Have you had many lovers?'

'No,' he said. 'One or two encounters when I was very young. And I was in love once. But that was purely platonic. I have never had *this* with anyone. I have never known anyone like you.' He asked something that he had meant to ask many times: 'Were you a ballet dancer?'

'Not on the stage,' she said, 'but in Russia all girls learn the ballet a little. I should have liked to dance professionally, but with the war coming there was no opportunity.'

'In England, it is not considered respectable for a girl to be a ballet dancer. Girls from nice families wouldn't do it.'

She laughed. 'But the English are barbarians, everyone knows that.' She kissed him, to show how much she liked barbarians. 'In Russia, the dance is the highest calling. All the rich men have ballerinas for their mistresses. The Tsar himself had the great Kschessinska. They say he would have married her.'

'Is that something else "everybody knows"?' he teased.

'In Russia,' she said leaning over him and punctuating her words with kisses, 'one does not care if a story is true, only that it is a good story. Kschessinska was a great dancer and *very* beautiful.'

'*You* are very beautiful,' he said, rolling her over and leaning above her. 'A dark princess. My Scheherazade.'

'And you are my beloved barbarian,' she said, as he lowered his face to kiss her.

March and April were the busiest time, with lambing at its peak, not to mention cows calving, but Polly still kept an eye on the newspapers for the announcement of the exhibition. So far there had been nothing, and she was beginning to worry irrationally that she had missed it, that Erich had been and gone and she had lost the opportunity that had become more important to her as time passed. With James gone and Lennie not coming, she'd had no-one to think about but Erich.

She was looking through the paper in the Steward's Room one morning when her cousin Jeremy, one of the dependants she had inherited from her father, appeared in the doorway.

'What are you doing up so early?' she said.

He was already dressed in his suit and tie and well-polished shoes for his job at the bank – the same bank where his father Robert had worked before he was called up. Robbie had died in a Malta war hospital in 1918 of typhoid contracted in Palestine, where he had been posted after basic training. Jeremy had been only six years old and didn't remember his father, but the bank remembered his long service and had been glad to give Jeremy a job when the time came, and to nurture his career.

'I wanted to talk to you, and you go out so early, it's hard to catch you.' He had caught from his mother Ethel a little of her manner, which was always to sound complaining.

'You don't have to be at work until ten, which is very nice for you, but I have work to do. Sheep don't keep to office hours,' she said.

'The bank doesn't open until ten, but I have to be there at nine.'

'I beg your pardon,' Polly said impatiently. 'What do you want to talk to me about?'

He bit his lip. 'I'm – I'm hoping to get married.'

Polly stared. He seemed so raw and unfinished, but he would be twenty-four in June. It was hard to think of any of her encumbrances as having lives of their own. It was a fact that she never bothered to think about them or ask them

119

how they were getting on. Her father, who had taken them all in because he loved family and could never get enough of it, would have known everything about them.

So she tried for a pleasant tone as she said, 'I didn't even know you were walking out with anyone. Do I know her?'

'Yes, you do. It's Amelia Robb,' he said, fixing her with the hopeful expression of a dog by the table. Polly frowned. 'She works for you,' Jeremy urged. 'At Makepeace's.'

'Oh, not Miss Robb of the lingerie department?' Polly placed her now – a small young woman, with a chalky-pink complexion and curly fair hair. She had round blue eyes, which gave her, Polly always thought, rather the look of a budgerigar. But she was a good saleswoman, with more determination of character than her size suggested.

'That's right,' Jeremy said, with a blissful look. 'We've been walking out for a year now – a year next month.'

'But can you afford to get married?' Polly asked, with the feeling that her burdens were about to increase. Her father would have invited Jeremy to bring his wife to live at Morland Place – it was how he had ended up with Robbie, Ethel and their brood – but she wasn't sure she wanted to commit herself to another generation. Marriage was generally followed by the arrival of children. Where would it end?

'Not immediately, but we're saving up. And we'd like to become engaged.' He blushed slightly. 'She's a very popular girl.'

'Oh, and you're afraid if you don't make it official she may go off with someone else.'

It was obviously what he thought, but he didn't want to say so. 'We love each other,' he said. 'She's a grand girl.'

'I'm sure she is.' She decided to put down a marker, so he understood she would not be keeping him when he was married. 'Where would you live?' she asked.

'We've thought about that,' Jeremy said. 'There are some nice little terraced houses in Bootham you can rent for about twenty-five shillings a week. I'm earning four pounds sixteen now, and I ought to get a rise in June. We should be able to manage nicely. And, of course, I hope to get promoted,' he added modestly, 'and eventually work my way up to manager, and then we could have somewhere bigger. But it will be enough for us to start off.'

'I had no idea you were earning that much,' Polly said, remembering wryly that Jessie had said a year ago she ought to charge Jeremy rent. 'Well, that sounds all right.' Something occurred to her. 'Oh – I suppose you'll be taking Miss Robb away from me, if you get married.'

'Certainly,' he said, rather pompously. 'I wouldn't have any wife of mine working.'

Any wife of mine sounded as if he intended to have them in multiples, but she didn't tease him. 'So what did you want from me? Not my permission, surely.'

He blushed again. 'Oh – well – no. I just thought you ought to know. And – well – I hoped you'd be there when I tell Mother, and sort of support me.'

'She doesn't know?'

'No, and I'm afraid she may object – say I'm too young and so on.'

Ethel was devoted to her sons, and Polly thought she might well object to losing one. 'Well, I'll support your right to make your own decisions, of course,' she said. 'You're over twenty-one. I just wish you weren't depriving me of a good employee.'

'I only met her because she worked for you,' Jeremy said. 'I bought a tie at Makepeace's when she was in gentleman's accessories, and it went on from there.'

'So it's my fault? When do you plan on marrying?'

'Oh, it won't be until next year. We have to save up a good bit first. There'll be lots of things to buy. Though, of course, people may give us wedding presents.'

'I'm sure they will,' Polly said absently. It was customary

for Makepeace's to give a present to employees leaving to get married. There was a sliding scale: a tea service for girls who had been there for more than five years. A dinner service after ten years. Miss Robb had been there a long time, since she left school, so if she was around the same age as Jeremy she could have done ten years. If not, it would not be difficult to arrange for it to be the dinner service.

'Well, congratulations,' she said, and he looked at her so hopefully, she felt obliged to add, 'There'll be something for you from me, of course. I expect you'd prefer cash.' Being relieved of the expense of Jeremy's keep, she could afford to be generous.

When he had stammered his thanks and gone away, she stared at nothing for a while, thinking how easy life was for the Jeremys of this world. He'd met a decent girl, courted her, would marry and probably have two or three children, work his way up through the bank to a respectable height, and retire with a gold watch and grandchildren, all according to a traditional pattern he'd never had to think about. Why couldn't her life be like that?

Later that morning, when she returned from the lambing pens, she went to the telephone and, when Exchange answered, asked for the Cavendish Gallery in London. Eventually a female voice with a very refined accent answered, and Polly asked when the Eric Chapel exhibition would be opening. After a brief pause, the voice informed her that the exhibition had been cancelled, and would not now be taking place.

'Cancelled? Why?' Polly demanded.

'I really couldn't say, madam. There will an exhibition of modern ceramics instead. Would you care to be sent a leaflet about it?'

'No, thanks,' Polly said, and put the phone down, rather harder than was strictly necessary.

★ ★ ★

Ethel was cautiously pleased at Jeremy's announcement that evening, until she understood that it meant he would be leaving Morland Place after the wedding. Instead of having a daughter-in-law added to her entourage, someone she hoped to mould into a useful handmaid, she'd be having a son subtracted.

'Why? she cried. 'This is your home – why would you want to leave it?'

'Amelia and I want a place of our own, Mother,' Jeremy said. 'Anyway, it's not going to happen for a while yet. At least a year.'

'There's still no need for you to go. There's lots of room here.'

That was the beginning. Over the following days, Ethel pointed out to Jeremy in her soft, complaining voice how unkind and selfish he was being in wanting to abandon his mother in her declining years and deprive her of his support and the potential future joys of grandmotherhood. Jeremy reassured her over and again that it would not be happening yet, that he would not be going far away, and that she would see him as often as before. She sighed that this could not be, since she saw him every day now, and nothing could replace the comfort of knowing she was sleeping under the same roof as her darling boy. He wobbled alarmingly under the tender onslaught, and occasionally came close to tears, but with a few bracing looks from Polly he managed to hold firm.

It was all Polly could do to keep her temper with Ethel, especially when she began to comfort herself with the idea that Miss Robb looked a flighty sort of girl and would probably break off the engagement before it got to marriage, which reduced Jeremy to incoherence. It was with relief that Polly received a message from the mills in Manchester to say that the linens for the *Queen Mary* were ready, if she cared to come and inspect them.

'I have to go to Manchester for a few days,' she announced to the family. She instructed John Burton to send a telegram, told Rogers to pack for her, kissed Alec goodbye and told him to be a good boy, then fled.

CHAPTER SIX

It was raining in Manchester. She didn't remember ever going there when it wasn't raining and, after all, this was April. *March winds and April showers bring forth May flowers*. Not that there would be many flowers, except the odd bit of ragwort sprouting at the base of a wall or a dandelion or two clinging to life in a crack in the pavement. The air smelt sooty, and the rain running down windows left streaks behind, but there was a committee waiting for her in the factory yard with umbrellas and smiles.

She was shown up the stairs to the manager's office, an impressive room of mahogany furniture, panelling, rich carpet, bookshelves of impressive tomes with gilded spines, and a large, ornate chimneypiece under which a fire burned vigorously. It was deliciously warm, the lights were on against the dreary day outside, and there was a smell of coffee in the air. The manager, Lesser, came forward with hand extended, and said, 'It's very good to see you here, Mrs Morland. And I hope you don't think me impertinent, but I've someone here for you to meet.'

And he conducted her towards the figure standing by the fireplace, a tall man in some kind of naval uniform. He looked about sixty, with thinning hair carefully cut, a square, clean-shaven face, tired eyes and a fatherly smile. 'How d'you do, Mrs Morland?' he said. 'I'm very glad indeed to make your acquaintance. I knew your father, you know.'

He had a slight Yorkshire accent, eroded by long absences, and he offered her a hand like a plank with thick old man's fingers. Polly had guessed who he was even before Lesser gave his name: Sir Edgar Britten, commodore of the Cunard Line and commissioned to captain *Queen Mary* on her maiden voyage.

She had naturally read up about him when the appointment had been announced: born in Bradford, went to sea at fifteen as a cabin boy on a sailing ship, joined Cunard in 1901 and had been with them ever since.

'I'm delighted to meet you, Sir Edgar,' she said. 'How did you know Papa?'

'With me being Cunard and him being White Star, you mean?' Britten said. 'Oh, we all knew each other in the ocean-racer business. I met him quite a few times at this or that jamboree – more so during the war, of course, with working on the hospital ships. And now Cunard and White Star are under one roof, so we're all one family, and when Clive here mentioned you were coming for a visit, I couldn't resist popping over to make my number with you.'

He beamed, as if meeting her was the greatest treat imaginable. She couldn't help smiling back at him – he was so natural a person, without 'side', that he reminded her a little of her father.

'I'm honoured you could find time,' she said. 'You must be terribly busy. How is the fitting-out going?'

'Oh, very well, very well. She's a fine ship. There are always little snags, but that's what we're there for, to iron them out. We'll be ready for the twenty-seventh of May. My first command, you know, was one ton, and *Queen Mary*'s going to be near eighty, quite a difference! She'll have every luxury you could think of – and the finest crew that ever sailed. I've deckhands and stokers and stewards and stewardesses who had fathers and even grandfathers in the Line. We value tradition, as you know. Your linens, by the way, are beautiful.'

'You have the start of me, Sir Edgar – I haven't seen them yet.'

'I have samples laid out in another room,' Lesser said quickly. 'I'll show them to you later. I thought you might like a tour of the factory before luncheon.'

'Ah, I wish I could join you for that,' Britten said, 'but I must be getting back. However, there's something I want to ask you first, Mrs Morland, and I hope you won't deny me. Your father was always invited on the maiden voyage of any of the ships he supplied for, and Cunard-White Star is anxious to keep up the tradition. I spoke to Sir Percy only yesterday about it, and he agreed with me.'

'Sir Percy Bates, the Chairman of the Line,' Lesser murmured, for Polly's benefit.

'Do you know him?' Britten asked.

'I know of him. I've never met him,' Polly said.

'You will. Delightful feller. At all events, he agreed with me that you should be extended the same invitation we would have given to your father, to sail as our guest on the maiden voyage to New York. Now, do say you will! There's a good chance she may take the Blue Riband, if the weather's kind so she can stretch her legs.'

'You don't need to add any extra inducement,' Polly said, laughing. 'I can't think of anything more delightful. I'd love to, and thank you.'

If what she had read was true, the interiors of *Queen Mary* would be even more wonderful than *Titanic*'s, which her father had described to her, wistfully, in later life. She really wanted a holiday, and the crossing would provide it, with more luxury than any hotel on solid land. And she would see New York again. It was five years exactly since she had left, and though Morland Place was *home*, with all that small word implied, there was a piece of her heart that would always belong to New York, where life had been so full and so exciting; where she had been young with everything ahead of her.

★　★　★

127

Rose was lying on the terrace beside the pool on a steamer chair. She was wearing a bright red bathing costume, a straw hat and enormous sunglasses. She had a tumbler of something in her hand that Lennie hoped was iced tea. Condensation beaded on the glass; the sun bounced dazzlingly off the turquoise water; hummingbirds were feeding on the blooms of the golden currant. Rose, however, did not look happy.

'I hope you're not going to stay out in the sun too long,' he said, coming down the last step. She didn't look at him. 'You don't know what part is going to come up. You know how difficult sun-bronze is to cover with make-up.'

She pouted. 'It doesn't look as if I'm ever going to be offered another part. You told me if I was good and got clean, everything would be all right. I go to voice-coaching classes and fencing classes and singing classes – all I do is go to classes. When is something going to happen?'

'I'm sure—' he began encouragingly.

'And when's this divorce going to be done?' She pulled off the sunglasses.

'It's going through. You know how lawyers like to hang things out.'

'But who's looking after my career? Maybe I should be getting myself an agent. I know you know everybody, but you aren't getting me parts, are you?'

He'd been afraid of this – the restlessness and boredom that would kick in when she began to feel well again. He had shielded her from the bad publicity and the gossip, so it was his fault that she did not know how out of favour she had been. In an odd reversal of the usual order, it was better that she should get the offer of a part first, and engage the agent afterwards, to wrangle the terms. And his influence with ABO was the most likely route to an offer.

'I'm going to talk to Al Feinstein today,' he said. 'Just be patient, honey. Things will take off very soon. And, please, get out of the sun. You're going to get a mark all the way round the edge of that costume.'

'Oh, all *right*,' she said, heaving herself up reluctantly. He dragged the steamer chair into the shade of the trumpet vine, and wriggled an umbrella round. Without the intimidating dark glasses she looked forlorn and vulnerable. 'Are you hungry? Shall I get Wilma to fix you a sandwich?'

Lennie was one of the few people who were shown straight into Al Feinstein's office with no waiting. Joeseph Kennedy was another, and for the same reason – they had both been big financers of motion pictures, often the same ones. But Kennedy lately had been concentrating on politics, supporting Roosevelt's campaign and promoting the New Deal – with eight million still unemployed it was needed more than ever. Lennie had lived his life the other way round, having been involved in politics in the twenties and now finding more to interest him in the movies.

Al greeted him with enthusiasm. 'The Civil War! I was right about it, wasn't I? This book is dynamite, and it's going to make a great movie. It'll be the biggest hit of the decade.'

Lennie was pleased but surprised at the degree of enthusiasm. 'You liked *The Leopards and the Lilies*?'

'The who and the what now?' Feinstein looked genuinely puzzled round the pacifier of his cigar stub.

'The Cavaliers and Roundheads,' Lennie prompted. 'Romeo and Juliet in seventeenth-century England?'

Al made an impatient gesture. 'Christ, no, not that shit! I'm talking about the *real* civil war. North versus South. Southern belles and northern carpetbaggers! This new book! Don't tell me you haven't read it?' He slapped what was evidently a bound proof that was lying on his desk. '*Gone With the Wind*. Not crazy about the title – sounds like a bout of indigestion. But we can change that. Written by some dame or other. Title's supposed to be a "literary allusion", for Chrissake. But the book's the goods all right. It hasn't even been published yet, but we're all fighting like cats in a sack over the movie rights.'

'If it hasn't been published, it's no surprise that I haven't read it,' Lennie said mildly.

'It's hot, I tell you. MGM's reading it. David Selznick is.' The director David O. Selznick had recently set up his own company with the ample backing of the fabulously wealthy Jock Whitney. 'Pandro Berman at RKO. Darryl Zanuck at Fox. Jack Warner at Warner Brothers. And the damn thing isn't published until June!'

'With so much competition, it'll push the price up,' Lennie said doubtfully.

'Yeah, but it's all good publicity. The leading man is perfect for Clark Gable – a big, swashbuckling, womanising bad-boy. The sort to get women swooning. And there's a feisty female lead who stands up to him – the kinda spunky girl Norma Shearer plays.'

'You're thinking, if you get the rights, to borrow them?'

Al cocked his head. 'I can read you like a book, Lennie my friend. You're thinking of Rose for this O'Hara female.'

'That's the character's name?'

'Yeah, there's an Irish father, rough as a dog's arse, self-made man, and a la-di-da Southern aristo mother. Lead girl gets the looks from her ma and the spunk from her pa. Nice twist.'

'It sounds like a good part for Rose,' Lennie said.

Al narrowed his eyes. 'If I'm right about this crap – and I'm never wrong – it'd be the making of her. This is box-office gold.' He did one of his rapid mood changes. 'Or it's a bankruptcy claim in waiting. Who knows?' He shrugged, pushing the proof across the desk. 'Read it. Go on, take it – I got other copies. Let me know what you think. How's Rose getting on?'

'She's ready to work. Eager for it,' said Lennie.

'Divorce not done and dusted yet, is it?' Al always knew these things.

'We're working on it. There's no hurry, is there? They won't close a rights deal before the book's published, will they?'

'Make sure she stays ready. Read the book. It's gonna take a lot of dough. I'm gonna need committed investors. Think about it. This is gonna be big.'

Mrs Simpson barely waited for the butler to withdraw before bursting out, 'I'm absolutely furious! That snake-in-the-grass Mary Kirk! She was always jealous of me because the boys liked me better than her – for all the money she spent on clothes.'

'What's she done?' Emma asked. There were spots of colour in Wally's usually pale cheeks, and her eyes were sparking.

'I *knew* there was something fishy about this holiday. Why did she suddenly decide to come stay with me? And it's been "Oh, it's so lovely to be with you, Wally. We don't see each other often enough, Wally." The time and money I've lavished on that woman – theatre tickets, opera boxes, dinners at York House, weekends at the Fort! She couldn't hope to have that sort of access to royalty any other way. And I've been trailing her round ancient monuments because she *adores* British history. Of course, it wouldn't be because *Ernest* likes all that sort of thing – of course not!'

Emma began to have an inkling of where this was going. 'What has she done?' she asked again.

'She's having an affair with *my husband*, that's what!'

'Oh dear. Are you sure?'

'She admits it. They both admit it. All those times he's been over in New York on business, they were seeing each other – behind my back! She seduced him when he was far from home and lonely. He'd never have fallen for her meagre charms if I'd been around. Now he says he wants to marry her. *Now* we can see what all that sudden divorce talk was about. Not because he wanted me to choose between him and David – because he was choosing between me and Mary!'

'Oh, Wally, I'm so sorry,' Emma said, seeing that she was close to tears. But she thought of Ernest and what had become a comfortless home, a wife who was no wife. She felt sorry for them both.

Wally looked up with stark eyes. 'I'm nearly forty, Emma. I didn't start with money or position like *some* people.' Another dig, Emma supposed, at Mary Kirk – she hoped not at *her*. 'I've had to make my own way in the world, and I've been through some pretty hard times, I can tell you. I never knew any security until I married Ernest, and everything I've done, I've done for *us*, to give us a position in society and solid finances. And now *this*! Stabbed in the back by the two people closest to me.'

She walked away to the window, and stood with her back to Emma for a moment. When she turned back, she was dry-eyed and composed. 'Oh, well, I've always liked a challenge,' she said, with a tight smile.

Emma didn't like to mention the King just then. 'What will you do?' she asked.

'Throw Mary out, first of all,' Wally said briskly. 'I told her to pack her bags and get out. She's going to an hotel. But she let slip that Ernest is looking into the lease of a flat for her in Albion Gate.'

'For both of them?'

'No, I told him he has to keep up the appearance of respectability for the time being. Officially he still lives at Bryanston Court. Of course I can't control who he sleeps with, but he has to be discreet, and at least *play* the devoted husband.' Her eyes moistened again, treacherously. 'He said—' She stopped to master her voice. 'He said he wanted a child.'

'Oh, Wally!'

She shook away the sympathy with a jerk of her head. 'I told him he's already got one, his kid by his first wife, Audrey. Lives with her mother in New York, and precious little he seems to care about *her*. He never sees her. But he said that was the point. He wanted to have another child and do it right from the beginning. And, of course, Mary's at her last knockings as far as *that* goes, so they have to get on with it quickly if she's to have any chance. So it's back to the divorce.'

'You'll go along with it?'

'How can I stop it? That would cause even more scandal. Ernest advised me to consult a lawyer. I suppose I'd better go see Monckton – he's smart.'

'But I thought David was using Monckton? You can't use the same lawyer, Wally. That would look like collusion. When it goes to court, if the judge has any doubts, he won't award the divorce, and that's that.'

'I'm just going to take advice from Monckton,' she said impatiently. 'Ask him to recommend someone. I may as well have the best attorney. David will pay.'

'That's another thing that had better not come out,' Emma said.

'He's just a friend, trying to help a friend,' Wally said, a trifle wearily. Then she became brisk. 'Now, I want you to put a date in your diary: the twenty-eighth of May. We're having the Stanley Baldwins to dinner, and I want you there for moral support, because from what I hear they are horribly dull people. Married forty years, six children, terribly religious. She does all sorts of charity work with the Young Women's Christian Association. They have a theatre in their country home and put on family amateur dramatics – can you believe it?'

Emma was concerned. 'But is it wise? Introducing you to

the Prime Minister is – well, it's a political act, isn't it? It could make things awkward.'

Wally shrugged. 'David insists. He says it has to be done, that sooner or later his Prime Minister has to meet his future wife.' She gave a taut smile. 'You could say that was his proposal of marriage. He's talked to everybody else about marrying me, but he's never actually asked me.'

'Did you say yes?'

'Well, it wasn't a question, it was a statement, so I didn't say anything. We'll see when the time comes. One step at a time. I'll take legal advice, and we'll go on from there.'

Polly had expected to feel excited when she left the shed at Southampton and saw the ship for the first time. What she hadn't expected was to feel lonely. *Queen Mary* towered above her, with her black hull and white superstructure, the three huge chimneys, black with red caps, blocking out the sky. Polly had already crossed the Atlantic twice on liners, but she had been younger then, with other things on her mind. Now she looked at the massive indifference of the ship – an artefact, and yet, like all ships, seeming like a living thing – and felt too small, too lost, too alone. For a foolish moment she wanted to go home.

But, urged on by the pressure of the porter behind her with her luggage, she mounted the gangplank to be welcomed by an officer on the look-out for her, and began to feel better. And as a steward conducted her to her cabin, she was passed by a fashionably dressed woman who stared and cried out, 'Polly Alexander? Is that really you?'

Polly stopped. 'Agatha van Damme,' she responded. It was a former client of hers, a member of the top circle of New York society. 'It's Polly Morland now. I reverted to my maiden name after Ren died.'

'And you're coming back to New York?'

'Just for a visit,' Polly said. She was about to explain her connection to *Queen Mary*, but Agatha rushed on.

'My, that's a cute outfit! Fashion hasn't been the same since you left. Remember that Egyptian-style evening gown you made for me? Heaps of the old gang are aboard. You must promise me to come to my cocktail party tomorrow – I'm getting in early before everybody else thinks of the same thing. What fun that we'll all be meeting every day for five days! It's going to be a marvellous crossing.'

They parted to head to their cabins, and Polly felt comforted. Agatha was a fool, but completely without malice, and it was good to know other old friends were aboard. There was a wonderful smell of newness everywhere, and she looked forward to exploring all of the luxurious facilities.

One of the glories of crossing the Atlantic – perhaps the crowning moment – was going up on deck early in the morning of arrival and watching the Statue of Liberty slowly rise from the misty horizon of the sea, until her gilded torch caught the sun, and flashed its welcome to the world's most exciting city.

One of the facilities in the ship was the wireless-telephone connection to every part of the world, and the telegraph office was one of the busiest places on board. The passengers had been chattering away to friends ashore all the way across, with the result that by the time Polly checked into her room in the Plaza, flowers, messages and invitations had already begun to arrive. One bouquet was from Freda Holland, containing an invitation to her latest exhibition. Across the bottom she had scrawled, 'Welcome back! Call me!'

Queen Mary turned round in two days, and since it seemed absurd to go so far for so little time, she had elected to take the following crossing and stay a week. Her first day was occupied with shopping, and she rediscovered how busy and noisy New York was. She was exhausted by the end of the afternoon, but a long bath in the fabulously appointed bathroom revived her, and she went out to dine with the Whitneys, who were keen racehorse owners. The male Whitneys were polo players and had known Ren Alexander – many of them had profited by his financial advice – while the women had bought Polly Modes, so there was plenty to talk about.

So many invitations were arriving that a week seemed not nearly long enough: she should have arranged to stay a month or two. She would have to prune drastically, but Freda Holland had been so kind in the past she felt obliged to accept her invitation for the opening on the following day. It was an exhibition of modern realist painters, like Edward Hopper, Grant Wood and Thomas Hart Benton, so she hoped it would not be too challenging to the eye. Besides, Freda knew everyone and her launches were always well-attended, so Polly hoped to meet some of the people she would not have time otherwise to visit.

She arrived at half past eleven, when the severely fashionable were only just getting up. None but genuine art lovers and critics were present, though that still constituted quite a crowd. But Freda spotted her at once and came straight over.

'You haven't changed a bit! Still as lovely as ever. Now, someone's going to drag me away any moment, so tell me quickly, what are you doing in New York?'

'I was invited by Cunard-White Star as a guest on *Queen Mary*'s maiden voyage. My textile company supplied the linens.'

'But why alone? Where is Mr Polly? It must be five or six years since you lost the fabulous Ren Alexander. Why haven't you been snapped up?'

Polly said, 'I've been too busy. I have a big estate to run in England.'

'Wasn't there a brother?' Freda said, with a frown of concentration. 'I'm sure I remember someone telling me. They met him in Paris – big, handsome fellow with too much charm for one person.'

'That sounds like James. Yes, he's in Paris, working for Charles Bedaux.'

'Ah, the ineffable Charlie!' Freda said. 'I know him well. I remember now, it was Sophie Talbot-Manners who told me she knew your brother. She and Daisy Fellowes met him at Hélène Gilbert's. Oh, *they*'ve just had a big disappointment, poor things – an exhibition they were planning in London fell through. The work was just too modern for the backers and they pulled out. And the worst thing is—' She broke off. 'Damn, Rathbone Oldfield's just arrived. *The Times*'s critic. Terribly influential and terribly self-important. I'll have to go. He'll expect me to show him everything in person, or he'll take offence and give me a bad review. I'll catch up with you later, darling.' She slid away through the crowd.

Polly thought she should look at the paintings, and found them easy to enjoy – scenes of American life painted in clear and realistic detail. She was absorbed in examining a canvas showing a field being harvested when a very quiet voice behind her said, 'Polly?'

She felt the hair lift on her scalp; even her arms goose-bumped. She knew that voice. Quiet as it was, and with the din of chatter all around, she knew it. Slowly she turned, and he was there, looking at her with a troubled half-smile, as though not sure of his welcome.

He was standing so close he was almost touching her. She could see the fine lines around his eyes, the sheen of his skin over his cheekbones, the tiny scar that ran into his left eyebrow, the slight redness above his collar where it had chafed him. She saw every detail of him all at once, and felt hollow with shock.

Erich. She said his name, but didn't voice it – it was a movement of her lips, without breath. His presence was so overwhelming that for the moment she could not speak or think, only *be*. The whole world had become one small square of space in an art gallery in New York, and the man before her.

'How are you here?' When words came to her, it was as a banal question in an everyday voice.

His answer was commonplace too. Perhaps it was all that was safe in a moment so charged. 'Freda sent me an invitation. I thought I should come, as she's been so good to me over the years.' He paused, licked his lips. His eyes were so blue, it was as though the colour had just been invented. 'I didn't know you'd be here.'

'Nobody knew I was coming. And you – you left Paris?' She didn't quite like to ask him why, so she made the statement a question.

'My exhibition was cancelled.'

'So I heard.' It didn't really matter what they said – it was just a way to stay there looking at each other. She ached to touch him.

'I thought I'd never see you again,' he said. He lowered his voice even further. '*Herzliebste.*'

It was the ultimate act of love for him to speak to her in German, and instantly she felt weak with longing. 'Can we—?' she began.

'Polly? Polly Alexander? Oh, my *Gahd*, I haven't seen you in an *age*!' A whirlwind of colour, expensive perfume, furs and diamonds burst between them. Polly was embraced, Erich displaced by the sheer impetus. Polly recognised a society female who had been one of her couture customers, but couldn't for the instant remember her name. 'How *are* you? What are you *doing* these days?' the intruder gushed.

Polly said something, she had no idea what. It didn't matter. Maggie Belascu – yes, that was her name, wife of a shipping millionaire – did the talking. Polly was terrified that Erich would go away, or be drawn off by some art-lover or critic, and she would lose him; she was desperate to be rid of this interruption. To make polite conversation was more than she could bear just now. As Maggie drew a breath, breaking the flow of words, she plunged in: 'Maggie, darling,

I'm wild to have a real long talk with you but I absolutely *have* to go and speak to Freda right this minute. Forgive me?' And, without waiting for her to respond, she turned away.

Erich was still there – thank God, thank God! Their eyes met, exchanging the same message. 'Now?' he said.

'Oh, yes,' she said.

He took her hand and burrowed his way through the crowds. At the door there was a knot of newly arrived people, fashionable and wealthy and loud people, some of whom Polly knew, and she was afraid they'd be stopped. But the gallery attendant was still holding the door open, and Erich dodged through, drawing her with him, just as he let it go, and it swung slowly shut after them. It was as neat a manoeuvre as a chessmaster's checkmate.

They were out and safe, and she laughed at the thought of the society people gaping after her fleeing back. They were out into the busy street, the clear May sunshine and sharp shadows, the traffic filling the tarmac river of Fifth Avenue like a single articulated beast, gaudy with yellow cabs. He hailed one and they scrambled in. He looked at her. 'Where shall we go?'

New York was full of bars and restaurants and cafés. There was Central Park. There were many places they would not be known to anyone. There was her room at the Plaza, but it would not be respectable to take him there. She knew in that instant that she did not want to be respectable. The social rules, the iron bars enclosing behaviour that every decent woman lived by, were dissolving fast under an over-whelming need that left her feeling weak and almost sick.

'I want to be alone with you,' she said, and the huge confession seemed to release something in her, so that the sickness abated, and what she contemplated seemed the most natural thing in the world, like drinking water when you were thirsty.

He smiled, and the smile flooded her like hot sunshine. 'I've rented a walk-up,' he said. 'Shall we go there?'

The driver had pulled out into the traffic to free space at the kerb for the next taxi-cab. Now he glanced in the mirror and said, 'I ain't no mind-reader, bud.'

'West Third Street, corner of Broadway,' Erich said.

Now I'm ruined, Polly thought. *I'm a fallen woman.* But it only made her smile more. Nothing like that mattered now. His name called itself inside her head over and over like the blink of a flashing buoy – *Erich, Erich, Erich.* She was going home.

She lay in his arms, her head on his shoulder, breathing the scent of his skin. She had forgotten in the years apart how absolutely *right* it felt to be with him. He was the place she ought to be. It was relief, it was *Ah, yes, there you are. Now I can stop looking.*

His walk-up was small, a little shabby, but clean, and monastically tidy. She remembered how when he had worked at White House Farm, Mrs Bellerby had said he kept his room spotless. Above all it was private. There was no doorman or concierge in a place like this. People came and went with their own latch-key and no-one was interested in anyone else's business. They were as alone here as on a desert island.

In one corner of the living room she had seen stacked what she knew was his artist's gear. 'What happened to the paintings?' she asked idly. He grunted a query. 'From the exhibition that was cancelled.'

'A few of the biggest canvases were already in London. Sophie will sell them for me. There are lots of rich Americans in London with walls to cover. The rest I had packed up and sent on board the ship. Freda's taking care of them. She might give me an exhibition, or sell them privately.'

'It seems . . .' She looked for the word. '. . . extreme to leave Paris just because your show was cancelled.'

'It wasn't only that,' he said. 'I had a cable to say my son was ill.'

She had known he had a son, whom he had left at school back in America, and as far as she knew rarely visited. It had shocked her a little at first, but she had told herself that men did not feel the same way about their children as women – and a small, shameful part of her had been glad he did not treasure the offspring of his marriage to another woman. So now it surprised her that he should rush across the Atlantic for a mere illness. She couldn't think what to say. 'I hope he's better now.'

'He died,' Erich said.

Polly sat up so that she could look down at him, to see what he was feeling. It was hard to read his face. 'What happened?' she asked.

He took one of her loose, hanging locks and wound it round his finger as he spoke. 'He was at a special school. He was not normal, you see. After my wife died his grandparents looked after him, but as he got older, they couldn't cope, so the special school was the only solution.'

'I didn't know. I'm sorry,' she said.

'Don't be. It is run by nuns, and they are very kind. I think he was happy there.' He stopped, and started again. 'It was always known that he would not live to a great age.'

'What did he die of?'

'Influenza. One could think of it as a blessed release.'

'Do you think of it like that?'

'Yes and no,' he said, and she understood it was not an evasion. After a pause he went on, 'I wasn't in time to see him. The crossing takes so long . . . But he didn't really know who I was, even when he was well. They had to tell him each time, and even then . . . And he didn't know anyone at the end.'

She lay down again so she could put her arms round him. He gathered her close, and kissed her hair.

'So, are you staying on here now, in America?' she asked at last.

'I haven't decided.'

'This place . . . Not an hotel?'

'Freda found it for me. It's cheaper than an hotel.'

'Aren't you rich?'

He laughed. 'You sound like a little girl! I have money, but I have to be sensible with it. I don't have a steady job and a salary to depend on, like a bank clerk. I have to *make* money, so I can never be sure of it. But my needs are simple and this place serves. And it's private. I'd have thought you'd appreciate that, at least.'

'I do,' she said, turning her face up, hungry for kisses. She adored his presence, his body, his touch, the breath of his words on her ear, the taste of his lips, the smell of his skin, the feeling of him moving inside her. She wanted all of him, every atom, she wanted to consume him and be consumed by him, melt together into one entity. She felt his instant response, and gloried in it. They made love again, and thought was chased out by feeling.

Much later, they were hungry and went out for food. There was an Automat on the corner of Broadway. They sat across the small metal table from each other holding hands, her right in his left, because they couldn't bear not to be touching each other.

'I feel bad about running out on Freda,' Polly said.

'I hope she doesn't think you've been kidnapped. We don't want the cops looking for you.'

'Should I ring her and let her know?'

'Let her know what?'

'That I'm in good hands.'

'She served her purpose, bringing us together. She should be happy.'

They walked a little, wrapped in each other's arms. They walked to Washington Square, where other lovers were, and drunks. The grass smelt of the warmth of the day. The fountain had been turned off, and two ducks were resting on the water, the female asleep with her beak tucked into her back, the male keeping one eye open, guarding her. 'I know how he feels,' Erich said. 'I have longed for five years to watch you sleep again.'

The next day she went back to the Plaza to pack her things and pay her bill. Erich waited across 59th Street on the edge of the Park. While she was in her room Freda rang.

'Well, well, you and Eric Chapel!' she said archly. 'I'd forgotten you knew him from before. I suppose we won't be seeing much of you for the rest of the week.'

'How—?'

'Dolly Armitage passed you in the doorway, darling. She said you and Eric were running away and laughing like a couple of naughty kids on a prank. Are you staying on at the Plaza?'

'No, at his apartment,' Polly said, feeling awkward at having her private idyll pawed over.

'That poky place? It's a bachelor hole, not suitable for a lady. Let me ring round and find somewhere else.'

'No, please, I'm happy there.'

'Well,' Freda said doubtfully, 'you've got my number, if you change your mind. What are you doing with your baggage? It'll never all fit into that hole.'

'I've packed a valise, and the Plaza is going to store the trunk for me in their baggage room. Freda, I must go. Thank you for all your kindness.'

Freda sighed. 'I'll tell everyone you have the *grippe*. But you must at least go to the Cornfelds' party – you can't miss that. I'll find a girl for Eric, if you don't want to be seen arriving together. Not that everyone won't know by then, because Dolly Armitage is like the town crier.'

'I'll think about it,' Polly said, knowing she would not be

going. 'Goodbye, Freda, and thanks for everything.' She put the phone down before there could be any more argument.

Erich didn't seem at all disturbed that they had been found out. 'It was bound to happen. Don't look so troubled. Last time was different – we were married to other people. Now we are both single. We are not harming anyone.' He ran a finger across her brow. 'No frowns – it will spoil your beauty.'

At his touch, desire for him sprang up, and she saw his eyes change as he felt it too. 'Let's get home quickly. I want you,' he said.

After the first frenzied slaking of their long thirst for each other, they didn't need to spend every moment in bed. Everything they did together was satisfying. He had a fancy to draw her, and she posed for him, happy to watch him work. Sometimes he drew her face. 'But I can't do you justice,' he said. 'Your beauty is elusive, like all true beauty. I can only catch its shadow. It's frustrating.'

They had to leave the apartment from time to time to eat. And sometimes they went for walks, arms twined round each other. They wandered along the streets, or strolled in Central Park. Once they went down to Battery Park, more of a park now they'd removed the Els – the elevated train lines that had blighted it – but it still needed improvement. 'It should be the green toe of New York, welcoming the world,' Erich said. 'You do green spaces much better in London.'

'We've had longer to learn how,' Polly said. The river was busy with boats and ferries, barges and tugs, and across the water she could see Liberty on her little island, looking out to sea. A sadness came over her, remembering that her time was almost up. As so often, Erich felt her mood, and came closer, putting an arm round her waist and kissing her ear.

'Home?' he murmured.

She knew he meant the apartment.

'Home,' she said.

But it was not her home, was it?

He leaned up on one elbow, looking down at her, with his free hand brushed away the hair that had stuck to her cheek, damp with sweat. 'I thought I would never see you again,' he said. 'That day when you left me at the cottage – it was like having a piece torn out of me. I didn't know how I could face a life without you in it.'

'But you didn't come and find me when – when your wife died.' She didn't like mentioning his wife. She never spoke of Ren to him.

'You had gone to England,' he said. 'And not just to England – to Morland Place, where people would recognise me and know who I was. You were in the one place on earth where I could not follow you.'

She felt the cold weight of those words in her stomach. *Would people really mind?* But it was not a question. She knew they would. Mrs Bellerby at White House Farm, where he had lodged and worked as a prisoner of war, had approved of his clean habits, good manners and helpfulness, but how could that weigh against her three fine sons who had perished in the mud of the Western Front? At Huntsham Farm, Joe Walton had a patch over one eye and half his left leg missing; his brother Matt had fallen at Passchendaele to German artillery fire. Younger people, who didn't remember the war, and sophisticated people, who travelled and read and thought objectively, might be minded now to forget, or to say that the Germans had suffered enough and should be taken back into the fold. But the older people who had lived through it, and the simpler people, would never be able to get past the horror of it, would never forgive. To them, the Germans were a pariah race, and they would hate them with a visceral hatred until life ended.

In Paris, in London, even, Eric Chapel was a man without a past. But the people of the Morland Place Estate would recognise him, and they would never accept him. Yes, it was true: she lived in the one place he could not follow her.

The place to which she would be returning tomorrow when *Queen Mary* set sail from Pier 90. This was their last day together. Her throat closed up with tears.

'Stay with me,' he said abruptly. 'Don't go back.'

'Stay in New York?' she said. Her voice sounded strange to her.

'It need not be New York. We can go anywhere in the world.'

'How would we live?'

'I can paint anywhere. Paris. Rome. Florence.' He smiled. 'Los Angeles. I could work in Hollywood again. Or we could buy a farm. An orange orchard in Spain. An olive grove in Campania. The light in Italy is wonderful. I see a small whitewashed cottage among the olive trees. A steep track down to the sea. The air is scented with pine and myrtle and salt. We have a lemon tree, and the smell of the blossom is piercing. We grow grapes, too and keep a few chickens. You wear a faded blue linen dress, and your skin is golden from the sun, and your hair silvered with it. Life is simple, our needs are few. We have each other. We grow together like those olive trees whose trunks wind round each other. And at night we sleep by the open window, with the smell of the warm earth and the sound of the sea.'

She saw it, too, just as he described it. Why should she go back? Her heart was here, with him. It would tear her apart to leave him. Life is short, too short not to seize your happiness when you found it. Their future together as he had drawn it for her was as tangible as a taste in her mouth.

But . . .

'I have a son,' she said, in a flat voice.

He was not willing yet to let it go. 'You will bring him

too. He will love the life. And we'll have other children – brothers and sisters for him.'

'I can't, Erich. I can't. It's not only my boy. It's – Morland Place.'

'Sell it,' he said. 'Sell it, and we'll buy another place, where we can be together.'

But I am the Mistress of Morland Place. It was not something she could say to him, because it was something out of the deep past, something almost sacred, passed down from generation to generation, that an outsider would not understand. Her father before her, and his father, and his, going back into history, the land and the people and the house all bound together, to be held together through conflict and disaster, peace and prosperity, the erosion of time and the accretion of memory.

She owned it, but it owned her far more, because her blood and her bones were made by it. When the men of her family had gone to war, it was to preserve Morland Place and to preserve England, and they were one and the same. They had given their lives, and though she was a woman and could not fight, it still demanded her life. The Master or Mistress was the keeper of faith. She could not betray that.

'I can't,' she said. 'They all depend on me. The estate, the tenants – the family. I have to go back.' She saw he did not understand, and there was nothing she could do about that. The piece of land his forefathers had owned, which should have been his, had been seized and sold after the war; his very country – the Germany he had known – was no more. He was without a place in the world, so the whole world was his place; anywhere was the same to him now. She understood, as he looked at her, that he wanted *her* to be his place, as he would be hers. Agony though losing him would be, the loss of her to him would be infinitely worse.

'I can't,' she said again, and it was like dealing a death blow.

*   *   *

Her trunk was at the Customs shed, sent by the Plaza. Erich looked very pale in the bright June light, as though the colour had been washed out of him. He pressed his lips to hers, then held her very close, and she leaned against his hard body and thought *How can I do this?* Finally, they released each other. There was so much to say, and nothing that could be said.

'It should be raining,' he said. The sunshine was heartless.

'What will you do?' she asked, her voice light and hollow.

'Just go on. What else is there?' They looked at each other. He said, 'I think I'll go back to California. It will be easier there. Nothing seems very real in Hollywood.'

He lifted her hand, turned it over and kissed the palm. And folded her fingers down over the place. And then, without another word, he turned and walked away. She watched until he had disappeared into the crowd. Her throat hurt so much she put up a hand to rub it. Just in that moment she wished to die, so that she would not have to face the life she was going to.

If her father had been alive, he would have met her at Southampton with his motor-car. Probably there would have been a picnic basket and he would have regaled her with delicacies on the journey – *foie gras* and quails' eggs and strawberries. She missed him sharply as she came out of the Customs shed to no greeting. In truth, there was no great hardship in travelling first class by train, but she felt lonely and lost. She wanted Papa to make everything right for her, as he had always done.

There was time to wait at King's Cross to send a telegram to say what train she would be on. So, when she stepped down from the carriage at York, the first thing she saw was Jessie's smiling face. And before she'd had time to speak she was hit full broadside by Alec, who flung his arms round her waist, crying, 'Mummeee!'

She bent and scooped him up, and kissed him. He buried his face in her neck and said tremulously, 'Don't go away again.'

She felt a pang of guilt. How nearly she had not come back! No, it would never have come to that. 'I won't,' she said.

He emerged, like the sun after rain. 'I can jump twelve inches now on Mr Pickles. But she doesn't always want to. Josh says she's an idle beggar.' Mr Pickles, despite the name, was a mare.

The porter was dealing with the luggage, and Polly let Alec slide down as Jessie came up to greet her. 'I thought you'd like to be met,' she said. 'Uncle Teddy always met me from the train.'

'I was thinking about that at Southampton,' Polly admitted. 'How is everything?'

'All serene,' said Jessie. 'Bertie and I kept an eye on everything, but there was no need. Your John Burton is terribly efficient. And Laura's been playing big sister to Alec. I've got the car outside.'

'Can I drive it?' Alec asked, taking Polly's hand to tug her along faster.

'Not today,' Jessie said.

'I bet I could,' he said boastfully.

'You need to get taller so you can reach the pedals,' Polly said.

'Josh says he'll teach me to drive Mr Pickles.'

'She doesn't have pedals.'

'Stirrups are pedals,' Alec said, and dropped Polly's hand to run ahead shouting, 'Pedal-pedal-pedal!' at the top of his healthy young voice.

'I don't think he's missed me a bit,' Polly said, smiling.

Jessie linked arms with her comfortably. 'He did.'

They followed the porter towards the exit. Polly looked around at all the familiar things that seemed oddly smaller than she remembered. She supposed it was having been surrounded by thousands of miles of ocean for five days. Thousands of miles of ocean that separated her from Erich. She ached.

Jessie glanced at her face. 'Is it nice to be home?' she asked. 'Or rather not?'

'I haven't taken it in yet,' Polly said. 'Nothing seems real.'

'A bit of a contrast to *Queen Mary*,' Jessie suggested.

'But that was the unrealest thing of all.'

Jessie drove, and Alec sat on Polly's lap, reassuringly heavy, growing bony as he entered boyhood from infancy. His seat bones grinding her thighs were actually painful when he fidgeted, which was all the time. He was beginning to smell like a boy, too, a slight metallic scent, and his voice was always too loud – he hadn't learned to modify it yet. Her son. Her blue-eyed, fair-haired son. She squeezed him in a hug, and he grunted in surprise.

They turned onto the track, and there was Morland Place ahead of them, the stone honey-coloured in the June sunshine. It was waiting for her. Like Alec, it seemed to be saying to her, *Don't go away again*. But when Alec said it, it was love. Just then, Morland Place felt like duty.

CHAPTER SEVEN

With hard work, Dolphin Books managed to relocate into its new premises by the middle of June. The area, in North Acton, had been farmland at the beginning of the century, providing milk, vegetables and hay to the vast market of London, and also, by one of those quirks of history, hosting an unexpected number of mushroom farms. During the war, several munitions factories and army vehicle parks had been sited there, along with a military hospital and a prisoner-of-war camp. After the war, because of the proximity to London and a number of new roads and railways, it had started to develop into what was being called an industrial estate, with nearby housing developments along the Western Avenue and the North Circular Road providing plentiful labour. The last of the farmers sold up, and now factories produced goods as varied as canned food, aircraft parts, ice cream, fountain pens, radio sets, biscuits and agricultural machinery.

Dolphin's new premises were a plain, two-storey, yellow-brick office building facing the road, with the warehousing and packing facilities at the back around a large yard.

'Not pretty,' Charlotte said. 'But much more comfortable.'

The modern steel-framed windows let in lots of light while keeping out draughts. 'The saving on electricity will be enormous,' Molly said. 'And it's so clean. No more splintery, dusty old wooden floors.'

'The outside is bound to look a bit raw when it's so new,' said Vivian.

'The Hoover Building is beautiful. It has actual lawns,' Charlotte mentioned wistfully. It was a gleaming white modern edifice not far away, which had already become a landmark on the Western Avenue.

'My dear child, Dolphin Books is not in the same league as the Hoover Company – but we can have a patch of grass at the front and a flowerbed or two once we've settled in, if it will make you happier.'

'There's quite a lot of research now into working conditions,' Molly said, 'that shows workers are more productive if their surroundings are pleasant.'

'Well, I don't see what could be nicer than working surrounded by books,' Charlotte said loyally, and Vivian laughed.

'And the journey isn't too bad for us, from Arlington Street, when you take the car,' Molly said to him. 'We just have to walk to Bond Street, and it's straight through on the Central Line.'

'There was a plan back in 1902 or 1903 to run the Central Line through our own dear Green Park station, which would have been even more convenient,' Vivian said. 'What a pity it fell through.'

'You know such interesting things,' Charlotte exclaimed.

'I was talking to an enterprising young man the other day who wants to write a history of the London Underground. I think it would make a perfect book for us, for when we start our non-fiction list.'

'Reading about the Tube while on the Tube, with a book bought from a slot machine on the Tube platform,' said Molly. 'Ouroboros in action.'

'Heard anything from Milo lately?' Vivian asked Charlotte.

'Just a postcard last week,' Charlotte said. 'A picture of the Taj Mahal.' She tried not to let her discontent show, but it had not been an informative postcard. And, in fact, he had sent her the same one a month earlier.

Basil had said helpfully, 'He probably didn't even send it himself. I expect he signed a whole batch at once, and left them with some obliging clerk to post at intervals.'

'Why do you say such horrid things, Basil?' Charlotte had said crossly.

'Just trying to keep your feet on the ground, dear. I don't altogether trust your Lord of the Elves and Assorted Little People.'

'In the first place, you have no business trusting or not trusting him. He's not your fiancé—'

'He's barely *yours*,' Basil interrupted.

Charlotte forgot her second point, and said instead, 'I wasn't going to invite you to our wedding, but on second thoughts I shall make you come, just to apologise.'

'Speaking of weddings, your family is rather cornering the market, wouldn't you say?'

June, of course, was the month for weddings, and two of Charlotte's brothers were to tie the knot within a week of each other.

'I do wonder,' Charlotte said, 'whether Robert is doing it to show Richard up. Richard's will be such a little thing, and Robert's so grand.'

'It would make for a much better plot if he was inspired by malice. But remember it's the bride's family who do all the wedding stuff – the groom just has to turn up.'

'Mummy says Robert still hasn't replied to the invitation, so I suppose that means he's not coming.'

'It seems not. Richard has asked me to be his supporter.'

'Do they have supporters at a register-office wedding?'

'I suppose they must, even if they don't call them that. Cynthia is having a bridesmaid, at any rate, Richard told me.'

'Yes, I know – a schoolfriend of hers.'

'It's such a pity I didn't get invited to Robert's wedding,' Basil said, with an air of pathos. 'As a journalist, I would have liked to be able to compare the two – family only at Caxton Hall, and the entire fashionable world at St Margaret's.'

'I'll tell you all about it afterwards,' Charlotte said.

'Perhaps I'll stand outside in the street with the rest of the spectators and take notes as people go in. Will you wave to me?'

'Certainly not,' said Charlotte.

In the train down to Hampshire, Basil pondered on what sort of frosty reception he might meet, not because he had done anything bad lately, but because he was so accustomed to being dressed-down he never expected anything else. But his parents were so happy about the safe arrival of their first grandchild, they hadn't room for any negative emotions.

His mother embraced him with a radiant smile and said, 'Isn't it wonderful? And they really hoped for a boy!'

His father gave a lopsided grin as he said, 'I didn't expect to be this moved. I suppose you can't know until you experience it.'

It made Basil feel such a degree of gratitude towards Barbara that he refrained from saying, when the baby was presented to him, that it looked a poor specimen – which was odd, because Babsy was pretty decent-looking for a sister, and old Freddie must have been handsome when he was young. He peered at the creased brick-red face, which was not improved by the contrast with the lacy white bonnet. 'What are you calling it?' he asked.

'Douglas Frederick,' Barbara said. 'We're going to have a big christening party when I'm out of bed. I want you to be one of his godparents.'

Basil couldn't help it. He roared with laughter. 'I'm sure Freddie didn't agree to that! He's met me more than once. He must be aware of how unsuitable I'd be.'

Barbara shook her head at him with a fond smile. Nothing could disperse her euphoria. 'Don't be silly, Bozzy darling – you'll be splendid.'

He bent to kiss her cheek. 'Your blind faith in me is what keeps me going. But I'm not godfather material. Choose someone else, and save yourself disappointment.'

The nurse came in to say Mother had had enough excitement and it was time for visitors to go, and Basil exited promptly with relief, going downstairs to join his parents.

'Douglas?' he said, as he entered the sitting-room. 'Where on earth did they get that from?'

'It's the name of Freddie's brother, who died in the war,' Helen said. 'And his grandfather, I think. A family tradition, anyway. And Frederick after his father, of course. What did you think of him?'

'The baby? It looks like a slightly shrivelled tomato. Why did they put that terrible hat on it?'

'You're trying to be provoking,' Helen said, 'and of course it – *he* – will look better in a few days. Babies are always crumpled to begin with.'

Jack said, 'In that case, darling, there's no point in asking people what they think about a brand-new baby, is there?'

'Well, I suppose I wanted to hear how he feels about being an uncle.'

'Oh, my God, I am, aren't I? It sounds ancient. Crusty old Uncle Basil. I think I shall start wearing a smoking-cap and harrumphing. How does one harrumph, by the way?'

Jack laughed. 'You'll never get a straight answer out of him. How are you, my boy? How's the job going? Do you like the new premises?'

'I'm so pleased you are settled at last,' Helen added.

Basil was thrown into a quandary. He didn't like the new premises. Even if he played hooky, there was nowhere to go, surrounded as they were by acres of industrial estate. It was an eight-minute walk to the Tube station, and then at least thirty minutes into Town. He hated not being in London, and any day now, Aunt Molly and Uncle Vivian were going to turn their attention to training him properly for a serious, permanent job at Dolphin Books, and his goose would be cooked. Next thing they'd be saying he ought to live nearer the job, and wanting him to move to a room in North Acton.

He had come to the conclusion that he would have to find another job. He was pretty sure that if he chucked Dolphin, Aunt Molly would not want to keep harbouring him in Arlington Street, which would mean getting lodgings, which in turn would mean earning a living. It was a horrible prospect, but far worse to be marooned for ever in the arid waste, caught 'twixt the wind of the railway lines and the water of the Grand Union Canal.

What job he could do – or, rather, what was the least objectionable job that would take him – was one problem; how to sell the idea to the Aged Ps the more immediate one.

He assumed an earnest expression. 'That's something I wanted to talk to you about,' he said.

His mother's face registered dismay. 'Oh, Basil! What have you done now?'

'Nothing,' he said, in a wounded tone. 'I don't know why you always assume I'm in trouble.'

'You usually are,' his father said.

'I'm doing rather well, as a matter of fact. Aunt Molly is very pleased with me,' he said. 'But that's the problem.'

'How is it a problem?' Helen asked.

'You see,' Basil began slowly, having had time now to think of an approach but not all the details, 'living with Aunt Molly, in her house, in her spare room – it's a lot of obligation.'

'I'm sure she doesn't mind—'

'Let the boy finish.'

'Thanks, Dad. I live in her house and eat her food and work in her business. It's like— Well, it's as though I'd never left home. I'm very grateful for all she's done for me, but I

156

think in a way I'm *too* comfortable. I need to get out and fend for myself – prove I'm really an adult.'

'You're not, until next year,' Jack said mildly.

Basil turned to him. 'Yes, Dad, I know, but I want a job that *I've* found, and lodgings that I pay for from my wages. I want to – what do the Americans say? – hustle for myself.'

'But, Basil, what job would you do?' Helen said. 'Have you found something?'

'Not yet. I'm looking at advertisements in all the papers,' Basil said, determining to do just that when he got back to London. 'What I wanted to consult you about,' he hurried on before Helen could develop the question, 'is how best to put it to Aunt Molly. She's taken such trouble with me, I don't want to have her think I'm ungrateful.'

Jack answered, 'You must put it to her just as you've put it to us. Be honest and straightforward. I expect,' he added, with a faint smile, 'she'll be glad to get her spare room back.'

Basil grinned with relief, thinking he'd won over his father. That was more than half the battle – Mum followed Dad's lead more than she probably realised.

Now Helen spoke, musingly: 'There are lots of other publishers in London – hundreds, I dare say. You have some experience now, and I'm sure Molly would put in a good word for you.'

Basil didn't want to stay in publishing. He'd met one or two other publishers at Aunt Molly's parties, and they were not only ancient stiffs, but formidable chaps, with sharp eyes that would not take readily to wool. They would keep a tighter lead on him than Molly did.

'But that would be more obligation to Aunty,' he said earnestly. 'I want to be really independent, or I'll never be able to prove to myself that I can do it.'

His father spoke. 'Well, let's all have a think about it, and talk some more tomorrow.'

'Yes, let's not forget why we're here,' Helen said. 'Oh, did

I mention, Michael's coming tonight? He's got a weekend pass from Dartmouth.'

'Oh, good. How's he doing?' Basil seized the new topic, and felt the spotlight swing away from him.

The whole Russia experience was like a dream – always a strange dream, and often close to a nightmare. Not only was the spoken language incomprehensibly different, but the written language looked like hieroglyphics. Every road sign and shop front and poster – there were *lots* of posters – confirmed that James was very, *very* far out of his way. There was no getting used to it: Russia not only went on being alien, it seemed to get more so with the passing weeks. It was rather frightening, like being marooned on another planet.

Then there was the vastness of everything: the incomprehensible miles of forest and wide unending skies, the length of time it took to cross it in the antique-looking and somehow brutal trains. In the towns, the enormous imperial-era edifices and the vast post-war blocks rose to hide the sun and went on and on, lining the roads to the perspective point. The streets were so wide, and the public squares so *absurdly* wide, they required a new word for wideness that just didn't exist.

And always there was a sense of menace, usually low and in the background, like a distant rumble of a storm that might or might not come your way. Tata had warned him that they would be watched all the time, and they were. They were accompanied everywhere by a government guide, but even so there were often long delays while papers were checked and queries passed up the line for confirmation. He could not count how many hours they had spent sitting on hard chairs in bleak offices while a man with cold eyes barked into the telephone, staring at them as he spoke. The Russian he had learned so painfully from Tata did him little good. He might manage to convey a simple idea to a Russian, but he never had any idea what they said in reply. They spoke so quickly, with such a variety of thick accents; and their vocabulary went so far beyond his, which was largely confined to food, hotels and trains.

Then, along with their official guide and driver, there were the local security details that attached themselves at every stop, and gave them an impressive retinue that would have turned heads if the heads hadn't all been down, concentrating on their work. And beyond all that he sensed the shadowy presence of a further level of government surveillance. Sometimes there would be a man lounging in the hotel foyer with a newspaper open before his face in a manner not quite natural. Sometimes he'd look back and see a solid man in a heavy overcoat and anonymous hat trudging along thirty feet behind them, who met his eyes with a stony look that might or might not mean anything. But mostly he just had the itch-at-the-back-of-the-scalp feeling that their footsteps were being dogged. He began to feel very tired.

In the long, long waits between activities, and during the long, long train journeys, he thought about Tata. Their relationship, begun so suddenly and unexpectedly, had ripened daily. He hurried to her flat as soon as work finished to snatch an hour or so with her before his evening engagements; when he had none, he spent the whole time with her, usually in bed. Her bed, like an Oriental divan freighted with velvet cushions and silk scarves, exotically scented, became a galleon on which he sailed an ocean of sensory delight: not just the love-making, though they made love a lot, but the talking and the touching and just the *being* together. They rarely went out. She shopped hastily on the way home from school or he bought things on the way from work, and they ate in bed, feeding each other delicacies, slivers of cheese, pâté spread on biscuits, sweet white grapes, macaroons . . . After love they slept at last like exhausted puppies, waking to make love again almost with a groan. He had to make himself get

159

up early in the morning so that he could go home to wash and change his clothes.

One weekend when Charlie wanted him for a house party and he could not bear to be parted from Tata, he asked if he could bring her with him. Charlie agreed, and was instantly enchanted with her. He had seen her at one of Natalie's parties, but never spoken to her. Now he and Fern took her into their circle of acquaintance; and Charlie no longer wondered when James arrived heavy-eyed at work in the morning. Instead, he laughed and said it was a miracle he had managed to get up at all.

'She's a lovely girl,' he said. 'You hold on tight to her.'

And James had answered, 'I will,' and was disturbed by the thought that he might not have, out of carelessness. He had parted with her to come to Russia without any contract of permanence, and it seemed an extraordinary omission. His mind was full of her, of the musical sound of her voice and her delicious chuckle, like a delighted child's; the scent of her hair when he thrust his hands into its living mass; her look when, heavy with love, she lifted her full lips to him.

He remembered the way she moved across the room, as though barely touching the floor; the graceful turn of her head, her long neck, her expressive hands. Sometimes in her flat she would dance for him, out of her sheer joy at being in love, and she would tell him where each movement and gesture came from. *This* port de bras *is Cechetti – don't I do it well? Look, this is how Karsavina placed her feet before the* Swan Lake *fouettés. Pavlova did this with her hands in the Dying Swan.* And sometimes her dancing would be simply Tata, a whirling Czárdás of passion, because she was too happy to keep still.

In his mind she danced, and smiled at him, and reached out hands to him, as the sullen train beat its way across the wide empty landscapes; she came to him soft and scented in the moments before sleep in yet another alien, comfortless hotel room. Even when he was busy with his job, even when he was anxious and tense with the subdued menace of the place, he was aware of her under the edge of his thoughts, waiting for him.

Meanwhile, he and Charlie and Fern had meetings and receptions and even banquets. There were smiles, but there never seemed to be any warmth in the eyes to match: at best there was caution, at worst a contained hostility. It was strange to see the magnificent imperial palaces being used by the very people who had slaughtered the occupants as a punishment for having built them in the first place. It was sad to see the old revolutionary damage and the modern, careless damage, but also unsettling to see beautiful interiors that had been expensively restored as a theatrical backdrop for the new regime. The food was dull and unappetising – dark bread, beetroot soup, pickled cucumbers and boiled potatoes could be expected, joined by an anonymous slice of grey meat, or a bony fish. At the banquets there was a little more variety, and often very good wines, though it was hard to relax and enjoy anything when the hairy wrist of the man serving you was lavishly pocked with flea bites.

Even Charlie, whose energy and curiosity had always seemed boundless, began to look worn. The purpose of their visit had been to study labour-management methods – particularly the Stakhanovite scheme – but the reality did not match the glossy Soviet propaganda. The posters showed muscular men and rosy, pretty women performing their tasks with happy smiles, and the text said their output was increasing day by day, thanks to superior Soviet management techniques and the dedication of the loyal workers to the enlightened State that nurtured them.

James began to wonder why the Soviets had let them come, to see for themselves the dirty, dilapidated buildings, the old machinery, the cowed and silent workers; to learn that the Stakhanovite system, far from being an inspiration to free souls to work more efficiently for the sheer love of country, was just another repressive method of getting more work out of weary bodies for the same pay. And when a manager, ordered to do so by their guide, picked out an employee and commanded her – it was usually a her – to answer the visitors' questions, his eyes would flit sideways to the government official inevitably standing at the guide's shoulder, in terror that she might say the wrong thing.

'I'm ready to go home,' Charlie said. 'There *is* no wonderful new efficient way to work here. It's just propaganda.'

The following day, their guide did not turn up. Down in the foyer they spent a useless hour trying to get the hotel clerks to understand the problem, to telephone somebody and find out what had happened, and to get them another guide.

'This is not good,' Charlie said at last, in an undertone. 'I'm worried.'

'He has our passports,' Fern said. She looked at Charlie with fear in her eyes.

James had turned back to the desk to try a fresh appeal, when the street door opened and a man in a quintessentially government suit came in, followed by four uniformed men – soldiers or armed policemen, he couldn't be sure which.

'You will come with us,' the man in the suit said without preamble.

Fern moved instinctively closer to Charlie, and James edged to her other side. His scalp felt cold where his hair had risen. 'What's this about?' he demanded, trying to sound tough.

'You have to answer questions,' the man said. He seemed to be struggling with the English, which was not reassuring. 'Come, please.'

'I am an American citizen,' Charlie said. 'So is my wife. My secretary is a British citizen. We are here at the invitation of the Soviet Government.'

The man's face was as blank as a slab of concrete, which it slightly resembled. 'You will come, please.'

Charlie turned back to the desk, and said urgently, 'Telephone the American Embassy – do you understand me? Telephone the American Embassy and tell them what has happened here. Do it at once.' The clerk looked frozen with fright.

Outside there were two black official cars waiting at the kerb with their engines running. Charlie and Fern were bundled into the back of one, James into the other. Bracketed by the armed men, he heard the doors slammed, and wondered if he would ever see home again.

Later in the weekend Basil managed to have a talk with Barbara, up in her bedroom, with Michael.

'Well,' she said at length, 'I think it's brave of you. I'd much rather live with Aunt Molly and Uncle Vivian than pig it in some horrid rooms, but I suppose it's different for girls. The important thing is deciding on a suitable job. What sort of job do you want, Bozzy darling?'

'I don't want any job, but I have to have one.'

'I'm sure Freddie could—'

'In London,' Basil interrupted hastily.

'But you'd have to stick at it,' Barbara said, as if concluding her sentence.

'You've had three different jobs,' Michael said sensibly. 'Which one did you like best?'

'You liked it when you were working for the *Bugle*, didn't you?' Barbara suggested.

'It wasn't bad,' Basil said cautiously, 'but I can't go back there.'

'There are other newspapers,' said Michael. 'What about the *Clarion*?'

'That's of the opposite political persuasion to the *Bugle*,' Basil pointed out.

'Why should you care? I can't believe you have any political convictions.'

163

'So that's settled, then,' Barbara said with satisfaction. 'You'll get yourself a job on the *Clarion* and work hard, and become a great reporter like – like—' She couldn't think of the name of any reporter. But then, she didn't read the newspapers.

'Don't look at me,' Michael said. 'I like to read the paper when I have time, but I never look to see who's written it.'

Basil could only laugh. 'So you're setting me up for a lifetime of satisfying obscurity, are you?'

'There!' Barbara said. 'You've got such a good way with words, it will be just the right thing for you. Unless,' she added doubtfully, 'you'd rather write novels? It *does* run in the family, after all.'

'No, thank you. Too much hard work.'

Michael looked at him pityingly. 'Hard work is satisfying. What's leisure unless it's leisure *from* something? I should hate to spend all day, every day, doing nothing.'

'Don't condemn it till you've tried it,' said Basil.

Afterwards, James could never remember the terrible fear. He remembered the fact of it – he thought he'd never forget it – but not how it *felt*. At the time it had seemed to go on for days. In truth it was about twenty-four hours.

The Soviets had somehow got it into their heads that they were spies.

'I'm a production engineer and management consultant,' Charlie said, to one stony-faced official after another. 'I developed the Bedaux System of Human Power Measurement. I was *invited* here by your government to look at labour systems. I have permits from the Departments of Labour, Culture and Tourism.'

'You are spies,' was the reply. 'You came to steal Soviet industrial secrets.'

One thing that seemed to interest them particularly was the fact that he had worked for Kodak. 'You have secret camera. You send photographs of Soviet factories to America.'

'I didn't bring any sort of camera with me on this trip. I was only at Kodak to develop a motion study system. And that was years ago,' he protested. They thought he had developed a miniature spy camera that could be hidden in the clothing. 'I was at Kodak solely to streamline their working practices. I had nothing to do with the products. There is no such thing as a spy camera.'

It was infinitely more frightening when they were split up and questioned separately. James had felt protected to an extent by Charlie's presence. In a room containing only a table with a chair on either side, they left him to wait. The single bare light-bulb overhead flickered periodically. The room smelt of sweat and cigarettes. The sensation of being watched intensified minute by minute until his skin crawled with invisible ants. Hidden cameras? Hidden microphones? He was so terrified of being tortured his brain kept stalling, and his heart fluttered like a hurt bird.

He had a succession of interrogators. They snapped questions at him that he could not answer.

'I'm Mr Bedaux's secretary,' was all he could say. 'I'm not a spy. I don't know anything about industry. I'm just a secretary.'

Now and then they switched to Russian, but he could only catch a word or two.

'Why do you pretend you don't understand Russian?'

'I learned some phrases for the trip, that's all.'

'Who did you learn from?'

He was just enough in control not to mention Tata's name. 'People in Paris, where I live.'

'Which people?'

He invented desperately. 'A man called Ivan, who works in a bar.'

'Which bar?'

'The Blue Cat. In the boulevard de Clichy.'

'He sent you here to spy, to steal Soviet secrets.'

It went on. He sweated. He felt light-headed. He lost all sense of time. Was it daylight outside, or dark? But outside was harder all the time to believe in. There was only this – there had only ever been this: this dry-mouthed, gut-shrivelling, unmanning fear. They kept coming back to Ivan, kept asking about cameras, and why he had learned Russian, and what Charlie's business really did. When they left him alone for a time – he supposed it was to make him more anxious, and it worked – he found himself examining the scratches on the table. Some of them looked like letters. What message were they trying to convey? How long had the author been confined in this room to manage to scratch so deeply? What had they used? What had happened to them?

He'd eaten and drunk nothing for – for however many hours it had been. He felt faint, and confused. Had he said anything to the interrogators that might incriminate him? Anything they might use against Charlie? What were they doing to Fern? *Why was this happening?*

The door opened, and he stiffened, not as a hero stiffens in resistance but like a beaten dog seeing the stick. A different man came in with the same stony face but an air even more disapproving, more grim. James's mouth went dry. *Was this it?*

Behind him came a man in civilian clothes who – oh, Lord, oh, thank God! – was so obviously not Russian, was so obviously from the free and civilised West that he wanted to run to him, clutch him by the lapels, and sob.

'I'm so sorry, Mr Morland,' he said, in a mellow American voice. His tone was neutral and he didn't smile, but his eyes were flashing messages at him. James could only suppose they were warnings not to say anything. He would be happy never to say anything to anyone ever again. 'I'm sorry you've been kept so long. My name is McArthur, I'm from the American Embassy. We have a car waiting outside and your

166

friends are on their way down. We had a little trouble straightening all this out, but we can be on our way now.'

McArthur walked briskly, though not briskly enough for James, who wanted to run. They passed to the echo of their own footsteps through the labyrinthine corridors, under the bare lights, past the anonymous doors behind which who knew what horrors were being perpetrated? His senses were stretched to painfulness for a shout from behind to signify a change of mind – a challenge, a clumping of boots, and a detaining hand on the shoulder.

Down flights of steps, and into a large entrance hall, where the armed guards stared at them. But no-one stopped them, and they stepped out into the street. It was daylight. The sky was overcast, the light grey and muted. James could not determine if it was morning or afternoon – and, of course, in June it stayed light until ten or later, so it might even have been evening. Just ahead, at the kerb, was a large black car into which, he saw with vast relief, Charlie and Fern were just climbing. James was squashed into the back with them. Charlie, the always immaculate, smelt of sweat; Fern was white and exhausted-looking and her hair was disordered under her hat. They looked at each other but didn't speak.

McArthur climbed into the front and the driver set off at speed without waiting for a command. McArthur twisted himself round to address them. 'We're getting you straight out of the country. Once the Russkis get suspicious, they don't give up easily. They've let you go for now, but they could easily decide to re-arrest you tomorrow, so we have to get you over the border tonight. I have your passports here.'

'We had all the permits,' Charlie said. He sounded dazed. 'Why did they suddenly turn on us?'

'They're paranoid. Think the whole world's against them.' He grimaced. 'As well it might be. You took a hell of a risk coming here, Mr Bedaux. I recommend you consult the Department of State or your local embassy before you visit any more unstable countries. We've been lucky to get you out at all, and we're not out of the woods yet.'

The last words dropped James back into the nightmare. He hunched in the seat for the rest of the journey, waiting for the official cars to come roaring up behind them and force them over, the glaring headlights, the loudspeaker. Feverishly, he imagined guns and truncheons. No-one in the car spoke; the tension was palpable.

They arrived in the grey light of a Russian White Night at a remote airstrip: a rough field surrounded by pine woods, a tarmac runway, a wooden hut and a windsock, the smell of dry grass and resin on the light wind. A small aeroplane was waiting, its propellers already turning. McArthur shook their hands and got straight back into the car. They hurried up the steps to where a tall, thin young man waited to receive them. He saw them to their seats and strapped in, even as the plane began taxiing, and lurched into his own seat facing them as it hurled itself into the air.

'Just under two hours to Stockholm,' the young man said. 'I've got a flask of coffee and some ham sandwiches – I don't suppose the Soviets fed you. Just sit back and I'll get them to you once we've made our height.'

James was already 'sitting back', pressed into his seat by the climb. He clutched the arm rests. *Stockholm?* his mind queried, somewhat wildly. But then, *Ham sandwiches!* it said, and for the moment that seemed more important.

At work on Monday morning, Charlotte was radiant. 'Milo's back,' she said exultantly. 'He came round to Ridgemount Gardens last night with flowers and a bottle of champagne, and took us all out to dinner. We ate at Driscoll's, and went on to the Kit-Cat for dancing.'

Basil was piqued. 'But why was he away so long? And why didn't he write to you? A few paltry postcards for the woman he loves – supposedly.'

'No "supposedly" about it. Why are you being so beastly?' Charlotte said, but her smile was undented. She was too happy to take offence. 'He was too busy to write, and in any case, the sort of places he had to be, there was no handy stationery shop or a nice red pillar box on the corner. Do stop being objectionable, because we're going to dinner at Mummy's tonight to celebrate and you're invited. Molly and Vivian too, of course. The glorious thing is that he says he's made enough in commission for us to get married. He's going to talk to Avis.'

'I'm glad to hear it.' Basil smiled, to let her think his objections were over. The prospect of eating at the Belmonts' was alluring, but he still didn't trust Launde.

Charlotte went out, and he returned to studying the positions vacant in the morning newspaper he had brought from home.

Robert did not attend Violet's dinner for Charlotte and Launde, but she had expected that – it was very short notice and they were much engaged in the evenings. But her old friend Freddie Copthall, who had known her children all their lives, was in Town and came with his wife Cordelia. And to make the numbers even, she had invited the twin daughters of Lady Partridge for Henry and Basil. They were well-behaved girls, a little sandy like their father, but not unattractive – actually, she wouldn't mind at all if Henry took a fancy to one of them.

'I'm so glad,' she confided to Freddie later in the evening, 'that Launde can now marry Charlotte, and she can give up her job. Living with two other girls in a flat – it's so unsuitable.' Freddie nodded sympathetically. Violet remembered in a warm rush how comfortable it had always been to confide in him, and went on, 'If only Holkam hadn't died bankrupt. Charlotte ought to have had a proper Season and married someone we knew. And Richard and Henry would have gone into the army or the diplomatic corps, instead of getting mixed up with commercial activities.'

Freddie thought about it. 'But if he hadn't popped off, you wouldn't be married to Belmont now. And, do you know, I suspect the boys don't mind at all being mixed up with cars and aeroplanes.'

She looked at him admiringly. 'You always think of the right thing to say. You're such a comfort, Freddie.'

He blushed at the compliment. 'Machines, you know. Chaps love 'em. Always wanted to drive a steam engine m'self. When I was young.'

'Did you really?'

He nodded solemnly. 'Would have given anything. Too late now – never happen. Pity.' He sighed and stared for a moment into the distance, and in a flash of sympathy she saw him on the footplate of a great steam-gushing, gleaming beast, his hand on the shining brass lever, ready to unleash all that power and hurtle off to the horizon. The vision faltered when she tried to imagine the railway overalls and greasy black cap. Freddie's dress was always point-device.

His reverie lasted only a moment. He shrugged it off and said, 'But then I'd never have had Cordelia and the girls. So it all works out in the end.'

'How are the girls?' Violet asked, and his eyes lit as he embarked on what, not even second to the prize pigs he bred, was his favourite topic.

Milo came up to Basil after dinner when coffee was being served. He had been in lively spirits all evening and had been making his way round the room, his laughter lifting over the other voices as he told amusing anecdotes of far-away places and outlandish customs. Now he had reached Basil, who had been talking to the younger and less sandy Miss Partridge. She plainly had as little interest in him as he had in her, and at Milo's approach she took the chance to slip away.

Milo looked straight into Basil's eyes. 'Have you got something against me, Compton?'

Basil hid his surprise. 'Why should you think that?'

'You've been giving me black looks all evening. Is it something I've done?'

'Only *you* know what you've done. I'm afraid the rest of us are in the dark. Including Charlotte.'

Milo gave him a hard grin. 'I think I begin to see where the hitch lies. You wanted Charlotte for yourself. Sorry, old man, but these days females choose for themselves, and she chose me.'

'You're wildly amiss there, Launde. I see Charlotte as a sister, that's all. No, it's you who intrigue me.'

'I'm delighted to hear it. I like to be intriguing. For the rest, I'm happy to supply any information Charlotte's steppapa requires, but I'm damned if I see why I have to answer to you for anything.'

Basil saw by the glitter in Milo's eye and the tightness of his jaw that he had annoyed him. He really had nothing against him except an instinctive dislike, so he had to leave it at that. 'Idlest of idle curiosity,' he said. 'Nothing better to do than wonder about other people's goings-on.'

'Perhaps you need another job,' Milo retorted. 'One that keeps your mind busy.'

'Oddly enough, I've thought that myself,' Basil said, as Milo stalked away.

Charlotte, flushed and pretty, came up to Basil later, and said, 'I saw you chatting to Milo. I'm so happy you've made friends with him.'

'If you're happy, I'm happy. Has your step-papa had the customary "Come into my study, young man" talk with him?'

Charlotte laughed. 'I expect he'll have a discreet word, for form's sake, but he'd never be stuffy about it. And Milo's been making love to Mummy all evening and softened her

171

like putty. He's so good at getting people on his side. I suppose that's why he's so successful at what he does.'

Basil let an opportunity to say, 'And what exactly *is* that?' pass, and instead asked, 'When's the wedding to be?'

'In the autumn, to let the memories of Robert's and Richard's fade. We don't want to be in competition.'

'Good thinking. And shall I be invited?'

'Of course,' she said. 'As long as you behave yourself.'

CHAPTER EIGHT

Chelsea was a little out of the way, but Sybil Colefax, wife of the MP Sir Arthur, gave good parties and knew everybody through her interior decorating company. Argyll House was an exquisite early Georgian building by Leoni, on the King's Road, with a symmetrical brick façade of two storeys, five twelve-paned tall sash windows, and a parapet hiding the roof.

'It's such a pretty house,' Emma said, as she and Kit stepped through the front door into the hall, which was wood-panelled and always smelt delightfully of rosemary. 'Too small, really, for grand parties, but she always carries it off.'

'And what a treat it will be to hear Rubinstein,' Kit said. 'I believe he hardly ever plays for private parties.'

The first people they saw were the Duff Coopers. 'I'm glad you're here,' Diana said. 'You know the King and Wally are coming? And the Vansittarts, and the Hardinges, so just a small table. With the King mooning over Wally, and the Hardinges fuming in silence, we'll need you to keep the conversation going.'

'Lots of others are coming after dinner for the music,' Duff said. 'The Mountbattens, the Winston Churchills, Kenneth Clark and his wife, the Princesse de Polignac—'

'Alone?'

'I believe she's still between lovers,' said Duff. 'Emerald Cunard, Noël Coward—'

'Rubinstein *and* Noël Coward?' said Kit. 'Is Duke Ellington invited, to complete the set?'

'HM requested him.' Duff rolled his eyes. 'I think he's gone completely potty,' he said, barely bothering to lower his voice. 'Not only going to the Ascot races in the middle of court mourning, but parading Wally in a royal coach! Does he think people don't care?'

Alec Hardinge and Nelly joined them and caught the last sentence. '*He* doesn't care,' Hardinge said.

'Even I was shocked,' Nelly said, 'and I've almost got used to his antics.'

'If only he'd marry, he could have any mistress he liked,' Alec mourned. 'Nobody's asking him to be celibate.'

'I heard a rumour they're trying to arrange a marriage for him with Alexandrine of Denmark,' said Emma.

'Desperation,' Diana snorted. 'They tried to get him to marry her mother twenty-five years ago. It will never happen.'

'Perhaps he'll settle down, once he's got used to being King,' Kit said.

'He can hardly carry on like this without being committed to a lunatic asylum,' Hardinge said bitterly.

Dinner was excellent, and afterwards the great Polish pianist was escorted to the piano in the great hall. The guests mingled, chatting, mostly about politics, until Sybil got everyone to sit down and hush. The King made a great fuss about seeing that Wally had a good seat, close to the piano, then seated himself on a stool next to her. Quiet fell, and the maestro began to play an étude by Chopin. It was not long before the King began to fidget, and addressed a remark to Wally in his strangely high-pitched voice and his peculiar accent, part-Cockney, part-American. His talking become more frequent during the second piece, almost non-stop during the third, and when Rubinstein doggedly prepared to play a fourth, the King got up (which meant, of course, that everyone else had to rise) and walked over to the performer to say loudly and terminally, 'We enjoyed that very much, Mr Rubinstein. Thank you.'

It was the royal dismissal. In the shocked silence that fell, everyone could see Rubinstein was furious. 'I am afraid you do not like my playing, Your Majesty,' he said, in a low voice, but the King had already turned away, looking for Wally.

The Princesse de Polignac – formerly Winnaretta Singer, the sewing-machine heiress – was next to Emma and said in a low, angry voice, 'Such appalling rudeness! It would never happen in France.' She was a musician herself and hosted musical salons in Paris. 'Or in America. Mr Roosevelt might have picked "Home On The Range" as his favourite tune, but he knows how to behave to a guest.'

Sybil hastened to thank Rubinstein and, buttering hard, escorted him from the room. The Clarks, perhaps pointedly – he was the Director of the National Gallery and the Surveyor of the King's Pictures, a very cultured man – attached themselves to the group and left also.

The King was not in the least abashed. Happy with Wally once again firmly attached to his side, he asked Noël Coward to play and sing for them. Coward looked embarrassed, but could not refuse a royal command. He assumed the seat just vacated by the world's greatest proponent of Chopin, and hesitated with his hands above the keys as if wondering what on earth it would be appropriate to play.

'My God, the poor sap,' Kit whispered to Emma. 'I hope he doesn't give us Liszt, or HM's head will explode.'

Wally broke the deadlock, 'Let's have "Mad Dogs And Englishmen",' she commanded.

Meekly, Coward complied, and followed it with 'Don't Put Your Daughter On The Stage, Mrs Worthington', and the King applauded each loudly, though as he had talked all through both numbers he could hardly have heard them.

* * *

The Bedaux party stayed in Stockholm for almost a week, partly to get over the shock, and partly for various diplomatic currents to settle. The Swedes were neutral, but had always been more Russophile than the other Baltic countries, so there was a delicate balance to be struck. Charlie, who bounced back in his usual fashion, took the opportunity to visit several model factories – Sweden was known particularly for its arms, automobile and machine manufacturing, and it was a chance to compare with similar American businesses. Fern, whose nerves were very shaken, booked sessions with hairdressers, manicurists and masseurs, until she felt well enough to look at some shops.

James would rather have gone straight to Paris. He was longing to see Tata. And he longed to be somewhere where he spoke the language. Although most Swedes spoke very good English, Swedish was impenetrable to him and the written script had some peculiar symbols, which left him with that same nightmarish feeling of not knowing what was going on.

He was suffering from an underlying feeling of shame. He had been so afraid, and the memory unmanned him. Three of his cousins had fallen in the war, Jack and Bertie had been in it from the beginning, even Jessie had nursed at the Front amid falling shells and strafing Fokkers. James was too young to have fought, but he had always assumed that if the occasion had arisen, he would have faced danger as bravely as they did. Instead, he had quivered like a jelly merely at being questioned. He tried to tell himself that facing shot and shell in hot blood would be different from the horrible creeping terror of interrogation and torture, but it didn't help much. He stayed in his room and brooded, until youth and strength restored his shaken nerves, and boredom drove him out to discover that Stockholm had several very fine art museums.

But at last they were free to leave, and Charlie, as eager as James now to get home, arranged for them to fly. This time, not being afraid for his life, James was able to enjoy the experience, and the many stops they made. Paris grew larger and more beautiful in his mind with every mile travelled, and the image of Tata's laughing face was inextricably linked with it. The strength of his feelings for her had surprised him: he had assumed no-one would ever take Meredith's place, but his love for Meredith now seemed a mere boyish fancy. It was not real. With Tata, he had filled every sense, and satisfied his mind as well. He closed his eyes and daydreamed about how the reunion might go. He was always happy in her company. She was beautiful, intelligent, warm, funny. What more could a man want? Suddenly he knew he must ask her to marry him. The thought sent a flood of happiness through him, and he began to plan how he might do it. A little supper, champagne, perhaps a walk along the *quai* in the moth-haunted June twilight. He would turn to her, take her hand; he would say . . .

It was late when they finally landed at Le Bourget. There was a car waiting for Charlie, and he dropped James at his lodgings and told him to take a few days off. 'We'll talk about all this next week. Fern and I are going to the château for the rest of the week so I won't need you.' He owned the Château de Candé, on the banks of the Indre in the Touraine. 'But drop in at the office now and then to see if there are any messages. You can ring me if there's anything you think I need to know.' He'd had the telephone installed in the château when he'd bought it in 1927, when such a thing was almost unheard of. Telephone and inside lavatories and bathrooms with running hot water . . . The locals had been dumbfounded.

That night James slept like the dead, and woke the next day filled with such relief to be home that he felt light and refreshed. He jumped from his bed to bathe and dress and hurry out, took a *café complet* in the rue des Saules, then walked for the sheer pleasure of it through the familiar streets.

Tata would be at school at this time of day, but it was a poor Parisian who could not amuse himself with strolling and sitting for a few hours, especially when he had a woman with midnight eyes and a dancer's grace to fill his reveries.

As early as it was feasible that she'd be home, he presented himself at Tata's house. The door was closed and the concierge was not in sight, which was odd as it was the sort of sunny day when she would usually bring out a chair and sit. He rang the bell, and had to ring again before there was a grinding of locks and the small door within the double doors opened.

'*Bonjour, Maman – me voici, enfin!*' he said cheerfully.

She looked at him for a long time, her lips pressed tight shut. Her eyes were inflamed, and there seemed to be more lines in her face than before. She seemed bewildered by his presence.

'I've come to see Tata,' he prompted. 'I've been away a long time, and I've quite an adventure to tell. Is she home yet?'

Tears began to gather in Maman's eyes. It was disconcerting, because he had never thought she was capable of crying. A cold finger of dread traced its way down his spine.

'What's the matter?' he said nervously. 'Has something happened? Where is she?'

The rigid lips unlocked at last. 'She's dead,' said Maman.

Maman sat at the table in the dark kitchen of her dark little flat. Heavy lace curtains at the window created twilight; there was a metallic smell of dank water from the drain under the sink. Behind her a dresser was crammed with kitchen china and pots of trailing ivy, and on the middle shelf there was an icon of Our Lady parting her robe to point at her glowing, throbbing heart. She had long, slender fingers, delicately arranged like a dancer's. Ever afterwards, when James thought about that moment, it was the image of the Immaculate Heart

178

that he saw, those white hands, and the green ivy leaves.

It was three days ago, said Maman. Mademoiselle had come home from school just as usual, tired from the day's work, but cheerful – always cheerful. Unlike many of her exiled compatriots, she never let herself sink into melancholy: Maman had heard them often enough, mooing like cows about Mother Russia, drowning themselves in vodka until they fell into a stupor. Mademoiselle was not like that. She kept herself busy and never complained. She had asked Maman if there was any hot water, as she'd like to have a bath. She said she was going to the cinema with Valya Danilov. She had come down from her room at six o'clock, in a pretty red dress and a hat with daisies in it. She said she and Valya would eat at the Oeil du Perdrix before the show, and that she would be back at ten. They were going to see *On Ne Roule Pas Antoinette!* because it was important to laugh, *n'est-ce pas?* Maman had patted her cheek and called her a little pixie, and she had done one of her ballet steps, a little twirl on the spot (Maman spun her finger to demonstrate) and off she went.

That was the last time she had seen her.

Maman had sat up, waiting. She'd had a bad feeling. It was well past midnight when the *flics* had come. They had got Tata's name and address from the *carte d'identité* in her *sac à main*. They had asked Maman many questions, then asked her to go along with them to identify the body.

Maman had met James's eyes at that point, and he flinched.

'Let Our Blessed Lady and the saints witness, that was the worst moment of my life,' she said. 'And I have lived through the war. I had two sons who never came back, and I buried a husband to a broken heart and a daughter-in-law and a grandson to the Spanish flu. But this was worse. To see my poor girl like that, like a bundle of clothes thrown away, all her lovely vitality gone, stolen from her by some dirty murderer! Her poor throat cut right through. Her skin

179

was so pale it looked like alabaster. There couldn't have been a drop of blood left in her body.'

James's mouth was dry. 'Wh—?' was all he managed.

'They found her in an alley not a hundred yards from here. Behind the dustbins. It's a dark alley leading nowhere – no-one would go there. The *flics* said the assassin probably hid there and grabbed her as she came past. A drunk found her – a vagrant. He stumbled in there with his bottle to pass out for the night. He saw a bundle of clothes. Merciful St Martin, he thought he would lie on them to sleep! Then he saw the blood. He was so frightened that he was shocked sober. He ran out and bumped into Monsieur Faucher, who was just coming home from his work at the railway yard, and Monsieur Faucher called the police. And so . . .' She stopped, her mouth wry. 'And so,' she ended flatly.

'What—?' James could not seem to get any further.

'She must have been on her way home. I told the *flics*, she meant to be home at ten. They said that seemed right from the condition of the blood.' She took out her handkerchief and wiped it slowly over her face, not, James thought, because she was sweating, but as a respite for just a moment, as a child hides its head under the bedsheet when the horrors come. 'She was coming home and they grabbed her and cut her poor throat. Why? Why? She was a sweet, good girl, she meant no-one harm. Why would they do that to her?'

They sat in silence as the kitchen clock, on the wall opposite the dresser, picked the seconds out of its teeth and spat them into eternity. Tick-tick-tick, time moving on, moving on relentlessly, leaving Tata behind, further and further in the past, the past which was all she would ever have now.

James roused himself. 'They have no idea, the police, who did it? No suspects?'

She shrugged. 'No-one saw anything or heard anything. Only the drunk who found her – and they believe his story.

They said . . .' she sighed, weary of words. '. . . they said there are murders like this all the time. Three or four every day. Often they end up in the Seine. Often they are girls.'

So they won't investigate, James thought. Perhaps if Tata had been a rich girl or a politician's daughter or someone important . . . But a Russian emigrée infant-school teacher, who cared for her?

Another long time later, he said, 'Can I see her room?'

She looked at him searchingly, but in the end did not ask him why. She heaved herself up from the chair, took a huge bundle of keys from the dresser and wordlessly led the way.

The room was just as he had last seen it, except that the light before the icon in the Beautiful Corner had burned out. 'Night's candles are burnt out.' But there would be no jocund day. The things she had arranged and chosen and loved, the rich colour and interest of the room, seemed faded and life-less, rather pathetic – coloured scarves and cushions, paper flowers and pictures could not make the room live. It was Tata who had done that.

'What will happen to her things?' he heard himself ask.

'Someone from the Maison de l'Évangile will come and take them. She had no relatives. They'll give them to her friends, I suppose.'

His eye took in the elaborate samovar, the glorious bedspread, the many, many photographs, the gilded icons of the sultry saints. Shawls and scarves. In his mind she danced across the room in a twirl of coloured silks. The books. He saw her, patiently trying to teach him from them. Vividly, in his memory, she laughed, her dark eyes flashing.

Beside him was the low table on which stood the framed photograph of her as a child with Aunt Masha and Sister Chebodarev and the sad-eyed Tsarina. She had explained it to him, touching the figures with a slender, tender finger. As

Maman turned away to wipe her eyes and blow her nose, he snatched it up on an impulse and hid it in his jacket pocket.

Out again in the unfeeling day, he hurried, almost ran through the streets to the Maison de l'Évangile. There were three people there, the girl he had met the first day, whose name he now knew was Madeleine, and two older women. One of them was Nina Berberov. They turned and looked at him in silence as he came in. Nina's eyes were red, her lower lip drooping. 'You!' she said.

'I've just heard,' James said. 'I can't believe it.'

'Now you know why we're always so careful,' Nina said. 'What did you do? *What did you do?*' She ran at him and beat his chest ineffectually with her small fists, crying. He caught her wrists and held them, trying to be gentle.

Madeleine said, 'I checked him, Ninochka. I checked everything I could.'

Nina pulled herself free from James and took a step back. 'I don't blame *you*,' she said to Madeleine, dragging a hand-kerchief from her sleeve. She pressed it to her eyes as if she could push the tears back to their source. 'It's *him*.'

James was aghast. 'You think *I* had something to do with it?'

'You went to Russia with Bedaux. I know Tata warned you they would be watching you all the time. What did you tell them? You brought this on us!'

'I didn't!' James protested. 'I didn't say anything to anyone. I was just the secretary. I never mentioned Tata, or any of you.'

'It doesn't matter, Nina,' the other woman said. 'You know they've been watching Natalie for years, and Bedaux has been to her parties. It could have been any of us. There's no reason to think—'

'You think the Soviets did this?' James said, in astonishment. 'How? Why? Why would they want to kill Tata?'

'As a warning to us,' Nina said. 'To teach us a lesson.'

'They want to find – certain people,' Madeleine said. 'They think we harbour their enemies.'

'They have agents everywhere,' the third woman said, in defeated tones. 'The Soviet state has a long arm. They like to remind us that we can never be free of them. They want us to know they can reach out any time, anywhere, and snuff us out.' She made a gesture on the air of pinching out a candle flame.

Madeleine spoke again. She looked dog-tired. 'Someone followed you, James. They established that you were a regular visitor to Tata. Then you went to Russia. There they think everyone is a spy.'

'We—' he began, then stopped. Better not mention that they had been arrested and questioned.

Madeleine went on. 'So they made an example. That's what we think. Poor Tata was chosen. Or perhaps chosen is too strong a word. They told their operative, "Kill someone," and he killed her.'

'It's happened before,' Nina said.

'But – but there's no reason to think . . .' James stammered. 'It could have been just another vagrant, like the one who found her.'

Madeleine gave him a pitying look. 'If it were that, her purse would have been taken, her trinkets. She might have been raped. There would have been a struggle, there would be torn clothes or bruises. This was not that. One cut, no other injuries, the body not interfered with, the possessions untouched. So quick no-one would have seen or heard a thing. A professional assassin. The *flics* know that,' she concluded, with a contemptuous look. 'That's why they won't investigate.'

'Oh, God,' said James.

'So you go, now,' Nina said, moving a step closer to James, threateningly. 'And don't come here again. Don't come near any of us. You smell of death.'

James turned and left, walked out into the street with no idea of where to go or what to do. He walked, without seeing where he was going. In his mind, Tata danced across the darkness, the *placement* of her hands and white arms pure Cecchetti, her hair flying about her face.

The competition for the film rights of *Gone With the Wind* had thinned out. The front-runner, Jack Warner of Warner Brothers, had just dropped out.

'He wanted it for Bette Davis,' Al Feinstein said, 'but she didn't fancy the part.' He was standing at the window of his office, his back to Lennie, looking down onto the lot, his fists jammed into his trouser pockets, jingling his change. It was a hot day, and he had abandoned his jacket. In a blue-and-white-striped shirt and scarlet braces, he looked a yard wide, immovable as an elephant, and oddly festive, like a circus tent. He swung round. 'That's what happens when a star gets too big. They start thinking they run the show. They forget who made them a star in the first place,' he said accusingly.

Lennie, accustomed to Al after all these years, didn't flinch. He had read the book now. 'Bette Davis wasn't right for it anyway.'

'She's young. She's spunky.'

'Not the right sort of spunky.'

'Yeah,' Al conceded. '*She* wouldn't have mooned over that Ashley feller. She'd have kicked his pansy ass. Well, Jack's out. Louis Mayer's out. That leaves us and Fox. Fox has made an offer, but I don't know how much for. I've not made up my mind.'

'The book's doing well,' Lennie mentioned.

'Mixed reviews. The *New York Times* says it's too long.'

'Reviewers don't like long books because it takes too long for the reviewer to read them,' Lennie said. 'The public don't mind. More to enjoy.'

'Hmph,' said Al. 'They're paying three dollars a shot for it – who ever heard of a book costing three dollars?'

'I think you should make an offer,' Lennie said.

'You in?'

'You know my condition.'

'Yeah, Rose gets to be Scarlett. Hey,' Al brightened, 'Rose – Scarlett. She was pink, now she's red.' Al never made jokes, and was pleased with himself. He swirled the cigar from the side to the middle of his mouth and grinned round it. 'Okay, I'll make an offer. You visiting Rose now? She's filming in Stage Three.'

'I know,' said Lennie.

Rose had returned to work, was doing back-to-back movies with the western star, Hoot Gibson – Al had got the idea of Rose on a horse into his head, and matters had gone from there. They were shooting *The Arizona Ranger* at present, a story about a retired ranger and his new young wife: the past returns to haunt him when a cattle-rustler he brought to justice is released from prison, vowing to avenge his brother, who was shot and killed by the ranger in a thwarted raid. Rose, playing the young wife, had some moving scenes. It wasn't a bad part – a little meatier than the usual western offering.

Lennie had resigned himself to looking after her for a while yet – she seemed too fragile to cast off into the wider ocean, but she was definitely better for being at work. He hoped it would not be long.

They were doing the interior filming at the moment, and Lennie slipped into Stage Three and watched for a bit, but it was obvious they weren't close to breaking, so he slipped out again, lit a cigarette, and strolled along the lot's main street. There was always something interesting to see. He stopped by Stage Two, the largest, and looked in. There seemed to be some kind of Roman epic building, and he watched for a moment, wondering what it was. He hadn't heard anything about it.

Then a man who had been bent over some plans at a table just inside the door straightened up, caught sight of Lennie, and came across, his hand out. It was Eric Chapel.

Lennie shook. 'I didn't know you were back in Hollywood. I thought you'd abandoned us for Paris and the world of fine art.'

'I had an exhibition in London cancelled – my work was too modern for them. So I decided to come back to America, where I'm appreciated.'

'And what are you doing here?'

'Working. A man has to eat.' Lennie waved his hand at the set, and Eric went on: 'The interior of the great Library of Alexandria. Make it look Roman, Mr Feinstein said. People like Roman. But it's supposed to be Greek, Mr Reznik said. So, make it Roman with a touch of Greek, said Mr Feinstein. I love the way that man cuts through all problems.'

'By ignoring history.'

Chapel shrugged. 'People don't go to the movies for history. As long as it's magnificent, they don't mind if it's Greek, Roman or Babylonian.'

'What's the film called?'

'*Alexander the Great.*'

'Hmm. I wonder why I haven't heard about it.'

'I think Mr Feinstein didn't want you to know, in case you asked for Rose to have the part of Roxane. You are becoming known, my friend, for your advocacy. Producers and directors run away when they see you coming.'

Lennie laughed. 'I know that's not true. Producers and directors brush off agents like flies.'

'It's just my fun. I see she's working again.' He nodded towards Stage Three. 'A cowboy film?' he queried. 'After *The Falcon and the Rose*?'

'A woman has to eat.' Lennie gave him his own words back. 'And there are bigger things on the horizon.'

'You mean *Gone With the Wind*? I heard the agents are getting quite ambitious. They have turned down the only offer they had, from Fox, because it's not high enough. It would be a good role for Rose, if Mr Feinstein was willing to offer enough.'

'You've read it?'

'Everybody's read it. A strong leading role, but not *sympathique*. I suspect the second-lead Melanie character will steal the show. By the way,' he said, 'I saw your cousin recently. Mrs Alexander that was – Mrs Morland, as she now is.'

Lennie's heart contracted merely at the name. 'In London?'

'I didn't go to London in the end. No, I saw her in New York.'

'What was she doing there?' Lennie was puzzled.

'She came over on the *Queen Mary*. The maiden trip. She was invited as a guest by the shipping company because her factory supplied the linens. Apparently, it was a tradition begun with her father.'

Lennie pushed his hands into his pockets so that Chapel should not see his fists clenched with emotion. 'I wonder why she didn't tell me she was coming. I could have come across and met her.'

'But it was a short visit. Only a week.' He stopped, turned his head away, cleared his throat. 'She went back on the next crossing.'

'I'd still have come. I'd have liked to see her,' Lennie said. 'How did you happen to meet her?' That Polly should have come to New York without telling him was hurtful enough, but if it transpired that she had told *Chapel* she was coming, had arranged to meet *him* . . .

'It was just chance,' Eric said, giving Lennie momentary relief. 'I met her at an art exhibition. I had no idea she was in America.'

187

'Did you see much of her?'

'Quite a bit. She seemed well. It was a pity,' he said, in a changed tone, 'that she had to go back. But that estate of hers is a hard master.'

'Morland Place? Yes, I suppose it is.'

'She will not leave it again, I think?' Chapel said.

There was the suggestion of a question mark, but Lennie was too preoccupied to notice. Why had Polly not told him she was coming over? Was she angry with him for cancelling his visit? Had he offended her in some other way? Or – something he could hardly bear to contemplate – had she entered a relationship with a man back home, and didn't want to tell him? She knew, of course – he had never hidden it – that he was in love with her. Did she perhaps think that the less she saw of him, the better it was for him?

Chapel had said something else, that he had missed. 'I beg your pardon?'

'I said that it is good to be kept busy. And there is always plenty of work in Hollywood.'

'Yes, I suppose there is,' Lennie said absently.

Robert's nuptials would take place while Richard was on honeymoon, so given that neither would be at the other's wedding, Richard asked Robert to a bachelor luncheon beforehand. Robert suggested the Peers' Dining Room at the House. But Richard wanted to be on his own ground. 'No, no, this is my show entirely,' he said, and took him to the Savoy. Over the menus, he suggested the most expensive dishes, and ordered a fine claret to accompany the beef Wellington Robert chose. It was rather pathetic, he admitted to himself, to try to impress, but he didn't want his brother to pity him.

Through the first course, they talked about neutral matters. It was only when the beef, with cauliflower, peas and Jersey potatoes, had been served and the waiters had departed that there was space for personal enquiry.

Robert raised an eyebrow, and said, 'So, you're really going to go through with this marriage?'

Richard quelled his immediate annoyance, and said, 'Why not?'

'Nevinson is rich? I can't find out much about him.'

'Fairly,' Richard replied. 'He's taking me into partnership in the business.'

'Ah!' Robert said, his brow clearing. 'In return for marrying the daughter. I see. What's wrong with her?'

'Nothing,' Richard said sharply. 'There is no condition attached. I am marrying because I want to.'

Robert shook his head slowly. 'I think it's a mistake. Money's useful, but it doesn't make up for everything. You won't be received, you know. Not in the best houses.'

'I have no desire to mingle with high society.'

'But then who *will* you mingle with?'

'We'll make our own friends. We'll meet people through Molly and Vivian, to begin with.'

'Oh, the bohemian set.' Robert said dismissively. 'And you're willing to settle for that? I don't understand you.'

'Don't you? After our father's disgrace?'

Robert coloured slightly. 'Yes, very well, I agree we had to haul ourselves up from the bottom. But you see that I've done it – and done it the right way. Marrying the right sort of girl, whose father has influence. Getting myself known in the House. I shall have a ministry. Suitable directorships. There are lots of things you could have done – still could do, with my help. The diplomatic corps, for instance. But not if you marry into that family.' Richard did not respond, and he went on, encouraged: 'Charlotte, now – I deplore this office-girl, latch-key business she's got herself into, but now she's marrying Launde, she'll leave all that behind. A decent title, as the Irish ones go, and I shall take him under my wing when he comes into the House, make sure he shapes up, put him in the way of something suitable. Charlotte is doing the right thing, and I do think it's too bad of you to jeopardise all that with this *very* unsuitable liaison. It will reflect on her, you know. And on us – Joan doesn't say anything, but I know she's upset. No man is an island.'

Richard noted that he didn't mention Henry. Their father had acknowledged him, but it was common knowledge in the *ton* that Henry was the result of their mother's affair with the acclaimed war artist Octavian Laidislaw. Such things were far from uncommon, and were shrugged off as long as the wife had already presented her husband with sufficient offspring. But Robert had a very rigid sense of propriety, and Henry was rarely mentioned in his conversation.

'Why *are* you marrying her,' Robert concluded, a touch peevishly, 'if you don't have to?'

The easiest thing would have been to say, 'Because I love her.' That's what he *should* have said. But he hesitated just too long for it to sound natural. There was no reason he could give that would make any sense to Robert. They hardly made sense to him. Because the Nevinsons had been good to him. Because he could not bear to hurt their feelings by letting them think he was snubbing them. Because Cynthia loved him. Because he had to do something with his life, and here was a whole path mapped out for him: a business, a marriage, a family.

And now, finally, because he understood the hatefulness of the prejudice that followed the likes of the Nevinsons around, the shadow-presence always in the corner of the room that you tried never to look at, that you hoped never to provoke into showing its face.

In the end, all he could say was 'You wouldn't understand.'

'I don't,' Robert agreed robustly. 'Now, I know it's not the done thing, but isn't there still time to get out of it? If the old fellow turned sticky – well, Avis would probably stand the nonsense. He can afford it, and he'd do anything to please Mama.'

Richard couldn't help smiling at this second-hand largesse. Jilt Cynthia, and if Samuel brings an action for breach of promise, have his stepfather cough up to pay him off. And Robert believed he was occupying the high ground!

'It's no good,' Richard said, quite gently, because he found he rather pitied his brother – there seemed to be a whole dimension missing from him. 'You can't change my mind. I want to marry Cynthia, I like her father and mother, and I shall enjoy expanding the business.'

'Expand into what? Hiring out even more cars? Even more guided holidays?' Robert invested it with scorn.

'Oh, there are big things afoot. I shouldn't be surprised if I ended up a millionaire,' Richard said cheerfully.

Caxton Hall was a handsome, ornate French Renaissance-style building in deep red brick and pink sandstone, dating from the 1880s. It contained two large public halls, used for meetings and musical events, and it also served as the register office for Central London, conducting weddings for those wanting only a civil ceremony.

Despite the modesty of the proceedings, Samuel had not skimped on the arrangements, and one of the finest of his motor-cars arrived at Richard's lodgings to take him and Basil to Caxton Street.

'Nervous?' Basil asked, as they glided through the sunny London streets.

'Not at all,' Richard said. All he felt was a strange, unearthly detachment, as though he was dreaming this whole thing. 'Do you have the ring?'

Basil tapped his breast pocket. 'Safe in here.' He was about to add, 'Queer business, this – a wedding that's not in a church,' but thought better of it.

There was no altar to stand at, and no aisle for the bride to walk down to indrawn breaths of wonder from the congregation. There was almost no congregation. They all assembled in an anteroom, which Basil thought should have been called an anticlimax-room. Violet looked ravishing in a dusky-pink outfit, with pearls, but was clearly nervous and ill-at-ease, though it was only from fear of doing or saying the wrong thing and hurting someone's feelings. Avis was his usual urbane self; Henry stared around in open curiosity and asked his stepfather questions about building techniques that he couldn't answer; Charlotte, looking pretty in pale lavender, seemed to have nothing to say for herself.

The Nevinsons all arrived at once. The bride was in a cream-coloured silk crêpe dress, close-fitting, with a ruched bodice, calf-length and slightly flared at the hem, with a matching coatee, and a small hat with a half-veil. She carried a bouquet of very pale pink roses. Basil thought she looked pale, and wondered if she was having second thoughts. He felt like telling her that Richard was a thoroughly good egg.

Richard noticed her extreme nervousness. Her eyes flew at once to him, as though pleading for help. *Don't leave me! Hold me up!* After that, he couldn't notice anyone else. To the company it looked as though he had eyes for no-one but her, which touched Charlotte and soothed Violet's nerves considerably. In fact, it was a kind of terror that he might let her down, mixed with furious determination that he should not.

The ceremony didn't take long. Basil produced the ring at the right moment, and when Richard tried to put it on to Cynthia's finger, her hand shook so much he had to hold it still with his other one. But it was done, they were lawfully man and wife, and he felt relief at having crossed the Rubicon, as though some horrible madness might have sent him running away to the sound of shattering hearts. It was done, he couldn't run now, and he was glad.

She met his eyes, and he had an awkward feeling that she knew all he had been thinking, had always known it. She smiled – a hesitant smile, and her eyelashes were wet. He

192

took both her hands and smiled down at her reassuringly. Then he bent to kiss her cheek. It was not part of the ceremony, but he felt the moment required it.

The wedding breakfast at the Savoy was lavish, and conversation flowed comfortably. Samuel was a good host, Basil, Charlotte and Henry kept things going, Avis drew out the bridesmaid, who was shy, and Hannah talked to Violet about the hope of grandchildren. Eating brought a little colour to Cynthia's cheeks – Richard suspected she hadn't been able to eat any breakfast – and Basil even made her laugh once or twice. Then it was time to go up and change.

The bride came down in a dark blue silk suit, a sable piece, which was one of her father's presents to her, and diamond ear clips, which were Richard's. (He'd had to borrow the money from Avis, but had been determined to do the thing properly.) Goodbyes went on for a long time. Violet kissed Cynthia and said, 'You must come to dinner as soon as you're back.' Charlotte kissed Richard and said, 'We're only just down the road in Acton. I shall come and see you often.' Henry shook his hand and said, 'You're a lucky dog. I don't suppose I shall ever be able to afford to get married.'

They all trooped outside, and Basil, laughing, threw a handful of rice, which he had concealed in his pocket, as they crossed the pavement to the car.

And so they were on their way. They were silent for a while, and then Cynthia sighed.

'Tired?' he asked kindly.

'A little,' she said. A pause. 'It wasn't the sort of wedding your mother expected, was it?'

'She's still got Robert's show next week.' That wasn't tactful. He asked diffidently, 'Are you disappointed? Not to have . . . ?'

'A church wedding? I couldn't very well, could I? It would always have been a civil wedding for me.' She looked at him. 'Are *you* disappointed?'

'*Me?* Lord, no. I don't think men mind about that sort of thing.' Even as he said it, he thought Robert did mind, very much. 'I just want you to be happy,' he concluded.

'I am,' she said, and slipped her hand into his. 'I will try to make you a very good wife.'

Guilt, shame, remorse, pity – a host of emotions like thin needles pierced his heart. He squeezed the hand she had bestowed so trustingly on him. She was ready to give everything, and asked nothing in return. 'You couldn't possibly make anything but a very good wife,' he said.

She smiled. It was, he thought, not a bridal, but a motherly smile. Just at that moment, she looked like Hannah.

James wandered, walking until he was footsore and weary. But though he would tumble into sleep as down a well, it never lasted long, and he would wake after a couple of hours to tortured thoughts. Staring at the ceiling, he would go over and over their time in Russia, trying to remember every sidelong look, every cryptic remark, every word that had been said on either side. Had he let something slip? Had her name ever crossed his lips? Had he mentioned to Charlie something that Charlie could inadvertently have passed on? He was certain he had never repeated to anyone what she had told him about her life in Russia or her escape from it. And yet, in the stark evil spotlight of her death, how could he be?

Was it that they had followed him here, in Paris? Had he betrayed her simply by going to her house? But why had they picked on her – a person with no political ambitions or connections? Yet she knew Natalie, and they had said that Natalie was watched. Natalie, who had been close to the Romanovs, Natalie with the strange man at her shoulder whom she called the Prince. Was it not more likely it was Tata's friendship with Natalie that had put her in danger? He longed to be absolved. But then there was the timing. He had gone to Russia, and only then had they struck. He had been arrested and interrogated. He had been so terrified while under arrest, he could not be sure now what he had said or not said. It *must* be his fault.

And yet, the very idea that they would maintain, across the world, a spy network, and professional assassins to strike at the émigrés – wasn't that absurd? Wasn't that overwrought, unbelievable, crazy? Yes, he would have said yes, had he not been in Russia himself, and felt for himself that numb, dry-mouthed, unrelenting fear. The émigrés themselves believed it utterly. And Tata had been killed.

He tried going into the office to work, but it was no use. He could not concentrate. He was exhausted to the point where his hands shook as he tried to open mail. His head whirled when he tried to read letters, and he saw only Tata, teaching him Russian, giving him tea, laughing, dancing across her warm cave of a room, with white, expressive arms. Tata, drowsy with sated passion in his arms. Tata, her throat cut, left as a bundle of rags in an alley as a lesson to them all.

When Charlie finally came back to Paris, he had his words ready. 'I have to leave. I can't work for you any longer.'

Charlie's mobile face was set in lines of tragedy. 'I've just heard about it. That poor, sweet girl.' He clasped James's arm, emotion in his biting fingers. James turned his face away. 'I went to see Natalie,' Charlie went on. 'They're all in a state of panic, and no wonder. But it wasn't your fault, James.' James only sighed denial. 'I spoke to someone at Police Headquarters. They say it was some vagrant, who killed her to rob her.'

'She wasn't robbed.'

'They were disturbed in the act. James, James, you can't blame yourself! The émigrés all live in terror of the Soviets, it colours their every thought, so of course they think that's what this was. But even if the Reds *could* strike at this distance, why the heck would they pick on that poor little girl? It doesn't make sense.'

'They were watching, saw me visit her, and then we went to Russia,' James said dully. 'I led them right to her. I'm sorry, but I can't stay here.'

Charlie lifted his hands. 'Don't decide in a hurry. Have a vacation – you can use the château. It's fully staffed. Rest, fresh air, good food. Get some distance from things. I don't want to lose you – Fern doesn't either. Take a break, then come back and we'll talk some more.'

'Thank you. You're very kind. But I have to go home.'

Charlie looked eager. 'Home! Yes, that's right, go back to England for a couple of weeks, see your folks, get things into perspective. And when you're feeling better, come back.'

James shook his head. 'I don't think I'll be coming back.'

Charlie clapped a hand on his shoulder. 'Never say never. Your job's open for you, whenever you're ready. I'm a loyal old cuss, and you're one of mine now, so you just get your mind in order, then come on back to Charlie.'

The wedding of Robert Adelbert Winchmore Fitzjames Howard, Earl of Holkam, to Joan Evadne Forthill Cupar Whittington at St Margaret's, Westminster, was everything a top society wedding should be. As the magazines recounted afterwards in breathless detail, the bride arrived in a landau drawn by two white horses. Six bridesmaids carried her twelve-foot train. Her silk tulle veil was held in place with a tiara of four hundred and ninety-eight diamonds, borrowed from her aunt, the Countess of Duncrammond. The over-tunic to her ivory satin gown was made from antique lace first worn by her great-grandmother. Her bouquet was of white roses, lilies and jasmine.

The wedding breakfast was held at Duncrammond House in Grosvenor Square, the home of the bride's uncle. There were three hundred and twenty guests, and the banquet was designed by Marcel Percevault, the master chef from Claridge's. Seven hundred bottles of champagne were emptied. Eight police officers were on duty in Grosvenor Square to direct the traffic and another four to keep the entrance to the house clear, and Sir Philip Game himself, the Commissioner of the Metropolitan Police, looked in to see that all was well. The wedding presents were laid out on trestles round three sides of the ballroom, and guarded day and night by two Scotland Yard detectives.

The young earl and his new countess finally drove away in a hired Hispano-Suiza for their honeymoon journey to Venice, Florence and Rome; and the thirty-seven reporters from various newspaper and magazines retired to write up their pieces. The *Tatler* magazine had four pages of photographs; *Vogue* had six.

The bridegroom's mother, Lady Belmont, on the short drive home afterwards to Berkeley Square, sighed and said to her husband, 'It's absurd to say it, I know, but I think I liked Richard's wedding better. It was more . . .' She paused for the right word.

'Intimate?' Avis offered.

She moved a little closer and he responded by putting his arm round her. 'I think that must be it.' She stifled a yawn. 'I'm very sleepy.'

He kissed the top of her head. 'Imagine how tired you'll be when it's Charlotte's turn, and you actually have to do all the work.'

Polly was waiting on the platform when the train pulled in. As James stepped down from the compartment she flew at him. 'I got your telegram. Oh, Jamie, Jamie, I'm so pleased to see you!'

She exchanged a heartfelt hug with him, then stepped back to look up into his face. 'What is it? Has something terrible happened?'

'I'll tell you about it on the way home. My God,' he said, 'England is beautiful in June. All the way down on the train,

I kept thinking that. I must try and paint it. That green evening light . . .'

'Are you staying, then?'

'If you'll have me.'

'I want you to stay,' she said, with emphasis. 'I've missed you so much.'

'Well, I'm here now, old thing. We'll be two old folk, crossed in love, leaning on each other, like blasted trees.'

'How did you know I was crossed in love?'

'You have the look,' James said. 'I recognise it now.' He slipped his arm round her waist and they walked out together into the gentle June twilight.

BOOK TWO

MOVING ON

These were the woods the river and sea
    Where a boy
    In the listening
Summertime of the dead whispered the truth of his joy
To the trees and the stones and the fish in the tide.
    And the mystery
      Sang alive
    Still in the water and singingbirds.

Dylan Thomas: 'Poem in October'

CHAPTER NINE

The car that had collected him at Southampton station deposited Jack before the plain brick façade of an office building. It was a hot day, but a little breeze ruffled his hair, bringing the flat, oily smell up from Southampton Water and the distant sound of gulls. He knew that smell and that sound of old. They brought back sharply poignant memories: he had started out here, in Southampton, as a young engineer, designing motor-boats for Rankin Marine – back in the days when powered flight was still a hope for the future. And now just look! Around him were the workshops, hangars, and the big tin shed of the drawing office of Supermarine, since 1928 a subsidiary of Vickers-Armstrong, and aeroplanes were everywhere. He remembered his first ever flight, the first time he had left the surface of the earth, in a Farman biplane – something that today would look hopelessly frail and rickety – and had known he had found his vocation . . .

He was about to go looking for someone when a familiar figure came hurrying out, his broad, pleasant face wreathed with smiles, his thick fair hair escaping from the morning discipline of oil and responding like Jack's to the teasing fingers of the breeze.

'Mutt! By all that's wonderful, Mutt Summers!' Jack said, allowing his hand to be engulfed by a big paw. Joseph 'Mutt' Summers had got his nickname during the war. When they scrambled he would always urinate on the rear wheel of his 'bus before climbing into the cockpit. It was a sensible precaution, given that a full bladder could prove fatal in a crash, but his fellow fliers had joked that he was marking his territory, like a dog. He was a Yorkshireman, like Jack, coming originally from Hull, but younger than him.

'It's good to see you, old man,' Summers said, grinning like a dog.

'Not so much of the "old", if you please,' Jack said. 'Chief test pilot, eh? Now, remember, you're not supposed to leave the cockpit until you've landed.'

Summers laughed. He had been testing an aeroplane one time when it went into a spin, and, unable to stop it, he had tried to bail out. He had actually climbed out onto the mid section when it stopped spinning and went into a dive. With only two thousand feet to go, he had stretched out his leg and pushed the stick with his foot, and was able to level the flight and climb back into the cockpit. 'Never forget that, will you?' he said. 'I was damned lucky that day.'

'Pilots have to be lucky,' Jack said. 'If you're not lucky you're—' The last word was 'dead', but he stopped short of saying it. 'I was damned sorry to hear about Reggie Mitchell,' he said soberly. Mitchell, the chief designer, had died only the week before. Jack had met him many times during his days working on seaplanes for the Schneider Trophy. He'd had a reputation as a difficult man, but all his team had loved him.

'It was a rotten thing,' Summers said. 'The old trouble, you know – it came back. He went on working until a few months ago. Went to Vienna for some new treatment, but no go. Payn's taken over as chief designer.'

'"Agony" Payn?'

'The very same. Large as life and twice as ugly. He's waiting for us in the shed. Wants to pick your brains.'

'Well, I was hoping someone would let me know why I was summoned here,' Jack said, falling in alongside Summers. 'What is it – the Type 300?'

Summers grinned. 'Trust you to sniff it out.'

'I like to keep on top of things,' Jack said. The air ministry had issued specifications for a new fighter plane to several manufacturers in 1931, and with Supermarine keen to widen its range from flying boats, Mitchell had taken up the challenge with the Type 224, an open-cockpit, gull-winged monoplane with a fixed undercarriage and a Rolls-Royce Goshawk engine. It had been unsatisfactory in many ways, and he had started modifying it, until the Type 300 hardly resembled it, with a closed cockpit, oxygen apparatus, a retractable undercarriage, shorter and thinner wings, and a much more powerful Merlin engine. 'Haven't they called it the Spitfire?'

Summers smiled. 'Mitchell thought it was a damned silly name but, then, aren't they all?'

'Have you flown it?'

'Took it up for the first time back in March, at Eastleigh – showing it off for the air min. They were so impressed they ordered three hundred and ten of 'em. Of course, we're still modifying it. Lots to do.'

'You sound worried,' Jack said.

'Oh, not really. I mean, you know yourself, you keep on ironing out the wrinkles, even after they've gone into production.'

'So what is it, then?'

'Well, Sir Robert McLean – you know, the big boss at Vickers? – he got rather carried away by enthusiasm and guaranteed the air min delivery of five 'buses a week, starting fifteen months from the date of the first order. And since the order was put in on the third of June, that means we're supposed to roll the first ones out by next September.'

'That's a tough one,' Jack said.

Mutt leaned closer, and became confidential. 'Just don't see how it can be done. We've only just started fitting out the works for the production. And apart from anything else, we simply don't have the physical space here. This one order is more than double the total number of aircraft we've built in twenty years together.'

'New premises?' Jack hazarded.

'There'll have to be,' Summers said. 'I think they're looking at some empty space further up the river. But for now,' he went on, pausing with his hand on the door of the design shed, 'we have to concentrate on the modifications. Reggie was never shy of picking other people's brains, and Agony doesn't suffer from any false pride, so he suggested we got you here to have a look at the retractable undercarriage, seeing as it was you who designed the bally thing in the first place. Are you game?'

'All in a good cause,' Jack said. 'When the balloon goes up, I want us to have the best there is. What's she like to fly?'

'Oh, she's a honey!' Summers said enthusiastically. 'Fast, light, manoeuvrable – the Germans won't have anything like it. You know how you test for handling by throwing the 'bus into a flick-roll? Well, you can get two and a half flick-rolls out of her!'

'Impressive.'

'She's a bit too sensitive in the rudder, but we'll sort that out.'

'God, I'd love to take her up!'

'We might be able to arrange that.'

'Really?' Jack exclaimed.

'If you can fly a Camel with Archie rattling your ears, you can fly anything. Come on in and talk to Agony and Joe Smith. Jeff Quill and George Pickering are here too – I leave a lot of the test flights to them these days. We're planning to show her off at Hendon on the twenty-seventh – Sir Robert wants to convince the air min we know what we're doing . . .'

Later, Jack telephoned Helen to say that he'd be staying on for a couple of days. 'There's a lot to work out, and they assure me I can be a real help,' he apologised.

'Don't pretend,' Helen said, laughing. 'You *want* to stay. Wild horses wouldn't drag you away.'

'Well . . .' he admitted.

'Have you got oil under your fingernails yet?'

'No. I've been all day in the design shed. We're just heading off for a beer and to find me some lodgings – probably at the Cricketer's. I wonder how much it's changed.'

'Are you wallowing in nostalgia, my love? Revisiting your salad days, before you knew me?'

'I can't imagine not knowing you. Simply doesn't make any sense. Look here, why don't you come down at the weekend? You've nothing on, have you?'

'The diary is clear. I'll come on one condition—'

'That you get to see the Spitfire? She *is* beautiful – and very different.'

'Can you get me in?'

'With your record? I'm sure I can. Did I mention "Agony" Payn is in charge of the design shed now?'

'There's a certain note in your voice, Jack Compton,' Helen said suspiciously. 'What are you not telling me?'

'They said I might be able to take her up. There's an adjustment needed to the rudder, and I said—'

'Jack!'

'It's quite safe. I wouldn't do any fancy tricks – for one thing, I couldn't afford to pay for her if I ditched her.'

'I'm definitely coming,' Helen said. 'If only to pick up the pieces.'

Emma and Kit were summoned to the Fort for the 19th of July, and were pleased to discover that, as well as Fruity and Baba Metcalfe and Eddie and Sarah, Oliver and Verena were guests.

'It certainly helps to have one's own friends here,' Emma said.

'We were caught off guard,' Oliver said, 'without a viable excuse.'

205

'Don't be naughty,' Verena rebuked him. 'Of course we had to come, to show our support, after that shocking incident on Thursday.'

The King and the Duke of York had been returning from a review of the Brigade of Guards in Hyde Park.

'I was part of the escort,' Eddie recounted, 'but in the second row, and I didn't see much. Jack Aird was right behind the King, and he told me all. The band was leading the way, then the King and Bertie York, then us, and the Brigade marching behind. Just as we came out from under Admiralty Arch, one of the spectators brought out a revolver and pointed it straight at the King.'

'Oh, my goodness! Did he fire it?' Emma asked.

'No, because a woman screamed, and one of the police horses was startled and swung its rump round, and apparently knocked the gun out of his hand. It got kicked away under the horse's hoofs, and three bobbies grabbed the man and hauled him away. Whether he would have fired, we shall never know.'

'Who was this man, have they said?'

'I spoke to Sir Philip Game on the telephone yesterday,' Oliver began.

'You really do know everyone, don't you?' Kit grinned.

'Ah, well, he's something of a movie fan. He has a particular crush on Mary Maguire, and thought I might be able to arrange for him to meet her when she comes over.'

'Who is Mary Maguire?' Sarah asked.

'She's an Australian film actress. You know Sir Philip was governor general of Australia until last year? He saw her over there in something called *Heritage* and was struck all-of-a-heap by her nubile dewiness. She's just starred in a film called *The Flying Doctor*, which is a joint British-Australian production so it will be coming here next year, and the rumour is that she'll be coming too.'

'But how do you know her?' Kit asked.

'I don't, but *The Flying Doctor* is being released by Gaumont, and I know Mark Ostrer of Gaumont – removed a little mole for him last year – so I dare say I can arrange something through him for Sir Philip when the time comes.'

'And how does *he* know? No, never mind.' Kit interrupted himself this time. 'We shall never get to the point this way. What did Sir Philip say about the thwarted assassin?'

'That's he's an alcoholic Irishman with a police record and a history of mad antics. He claims he's working for the Nazi government and was ordered to kill the King, but Sir Philip says that's nonsense.'

They had the story over again from the King himself when everyone gathered for drinks before luncheon.

'You were terribly brave, sir, carrying on as if nothing had happened,' Wally prompted him, when he had got to the policeman's horse's rump.

'Oddly enough,' he said, 'I don't remember feeling afraid. I remember seeing something black go flying through the air, and wondering quite calmly to myself whether it was a bomb. I'd have dismounted and got hold of the gun to keep it from anyone else, but my overalls are so tight I was afraid I wouldn't be able to mount again.'

'They caught the madman, at any rate,' Wally said. 'A Communist, or a Fascist – one of the two. London seems to be full of radicals these days.'

'It's lucky that I *wasn't* hurt,' the King went on, 'because I have a busy week ahead. Buckingham Palace garden parties, then off to France to dedicate the Canadian war memorial at Vimy Ridge. We'd hoped to have a few days on the Riviera after that, but apparently the South of France is a hotbed of Communism, and they're afraid there might be an attempt on my life.' He gave a brave little laugh. 'Another attempt, I should say.'

*   *   *

After luncheon, the Kents and the Mountbattens called in. It was a hot day, and the King and Wally had decided on a party by the swimming-pool, but the newcomers had not brought bathing-things, and seemed happier to distance themselves from the noisy group at the water and sit sedately in the shade to talk. The discussion at first was about the situation in Spain, where an insurgent army under a General Franco had marched on Madrid to overturn the Communist government that had been elected in February. News was that the Spanish government had armed the factory workers, and so far the insurgents were being held at bay. But it was plain that it was not all going to be over quickly.

'I've heard that the Germans are supplying arms to Franco,' Louis Mountbatten said. 'If the Russians do the same for the Republican side, we may have a dress rehearsal of the coming European war.'

'We're surely not going to get involved,' Oliver said.

'We and the French have agreed to keep out of it,' said Mountbatten. 'But these things have a habit of spreading. Any group with a grudge takes it as encouragement to do likewise.'

By the pool, the King was much more interested in discussing his upcoming holiday. 'I've chartered the *Nahlin* from Lady Yule for the whole of August, and we're going to cruise the Mediterranean. But I really am annoyed with the Foreign Office. We were going to join the ship at Venice, but Eden insists we mustn't have any contact with Italy because it would embarrass the government. So we shall have to start from Yugoslavia. Such nonsense! These ridiculous sanctions against Italy will do nothing but drive Mussolini into the arms of Hitler. I've told Eden as much more than once. The FO simply doesn't understand foreign affairs. I have relatives all over Europe. I can accomplish more through family connections than ministers ever can. I shall call on Crown Prince Paul, of course. And see what I can do in Greece and Turkey.'

Eddie rolled his eyes at Kit. One intervention by the King could lead to weeks of untangling for the Foreign Secretary.

At a little distance, under an umbrella, Wally was talking to Emma in a low voice about the divorce. 'It's definitely going ahead,' she said. 'Ernest is booked into the Hôtel de Paris in Bray on Tuesday, with someone called Buttercup Kennedy.'

'That surely can't be her real name?' Emma protested.

'It could be if she's an actress – and by actress, I mean dance-hall floozy. But I suspect it's an alias,' she lowered her voice even further, 'for that snake-in-the-grass Mary Raffray.'

'Surely she wouldn't put herself through that?' Emma said.

'She'd do anything to get Ernest. At any rate, once it's done I'm to send him a letter saying that I cannot overlook his behaviour, and he'll move out of Bryanston Court to the Guards' Club.'

She looked gloomy and discontented, and Emma said, 'I suppose none of this is pleasant for you.'

Wally shook herself. 'At least I know I'm making a difference to David. He said to me the other day that he's quite enjoying the kinging, and he never thought he would. I'm just trying not to think too far ahead.'

'You've got the cruise to come.'

'Yes, it will be good to get away from the Bertie York faction for a bit, though I don't relish being shut up on a tiny yacht day after day with David not having anything to do. There's only so much *einem-meinem* talk I can stand, and David playing itsy-bitsy-spider up my arm. I sometimes wish—'

She stopped. 'Yes?' Emma prompted.

'Oh, nothing,' she said.

Emma thought she had been going to say something about wishing she and Ernest had never met David. Exciting though the association with the Prince of Wales had been, now he was King it was all too complicated.

Emma remembered that Kit had seen Ernest in the Aldwych the week before. Kit had been to see Fred Astaire in *Rise and Shine* at the Theatre Royal – Emma had been otherwise engaged – and had bumped into him, walking along twirling his rolled umbrella, a slightly wilted flower in his buttonhole, his hat tipped back on his head.

'He looked as though he hadn't a care in the world,' Kit had told Emma later that evening. 'Between you and me, darling, I don't believe he's really all that heartbroken over Wally. I suspect he's decided that it's all working out for the best.'

Emma didn't tell Wally any of that.

James woke thinking he had cried out, though as the sleep fog cleared he realised it could only have been a grunt at most. He had been dreaming about Tata again – the dream in which he saw her walking into danger and tried to run to her, but was unable to move.

It was still early, but he was too wide awake now to go back to sleep. He got up, washed his face and hands in the cold water in his basin, dressed and went downstairs.

The dogs were not in the Great Hall, so he knew someone was before him – most likely Polly. He headed for the small dining room, where indeed he found her addressing a bowl of porridge, with the entire pack gazing at her adoringly. There was a restorative smell of coffee on the air. She looked up and said, 'You're early. Help yourself to coffee.' Then she noticed his face. 'You look tired. What's up?'

'I was dreaming again,' he said, slumping into the chair nearest her and receiving Helmy's chin on his knee. He caressed his ears automatically.

'The same one – about Tata?'

'I can't get away from the idea that it was my fault.'

Polly poured him some coffee. 'I remember Papa once said that people always feel guilty when someone close to

210

them dies. Doesn't mean they were.' He gave her a look that said she wasn't helping. 'Ring the bell if you want some breakfast. I'm going out for a ride while it's cool – it's going to be hot later. D'you want to come with me?'

At that moment Barlow came in, followed by William, both carrying trays. Somehow the butler had known James was down. Barlow always knew everything. William put the hot dishes under the covers and lit the heaters, while Barlow placed the toast rack and the fresh coffee-pot on the table, and laid a small stack of post beside Polly's place and one envelope beside James's.

When they had gone, Polly got up to get herself eggs and bacon. 'Oh, mushrooms!' she exclaimed. 'Someone must have been out early. I expect one of the milkers dropped them off on their way in.' Turning with her plate, she saw her brother still sitting in the same attitude of dejection, his mouth a grim line of endurance. She wished she could help him. She knew that iron feeling. The helplessness was the worst thing: you could not make it not to have happened; you could not escape it.

'Have some breakfast,' she said gently. 'Food really does make things seem better.'

He gave her a grim sort of smile. 'Nice try, Pol.'

She sat down and reached for the toast. 'Read your letter, anyway,' she said.

He picked up the envelope, and recognised Charlie's handwriting on the typically heavy, expensive paper. Urging him to come back, he supposed. The man had no tact, no understanding of what he was feeling. In his mind, in one of those vivid flashes, he saw Tata laughing, her eyes bright, her loosened hair a living thing around her face.

'Do I see a foreign stamp?' Polly went on. 'Don't forget to save it for Alec. Oh, do open it, James! You can't read it through the envelope.'

So he opened it. Inside was a single sheet with Charlie's

forceful-spiky writing, and a slender, printed booklet. The letter said: *Sometimes poetry helps. Come back to us soon. We both miss you.* The kindness of the simple words moved James, and he felt a prickling behind his eyes, almost as if he might cry – but he never had yet. Men didn't.

On the cover of the booklet it said: '*Black Marigolds*, translated from the Sanskrit by E. Powys Mathers'.

He opened it, and saw two or three pages of close-printed text. A glance told him it was some explanation about the origins of the text. Too boring to read. What was Charlie thinking? Unpronounceable names exasperated him. He leafed past it all, and found beyond, in larger, better-spaced print, the verses of a long poem. He was about to close the thing and throw it down, when some words caught his eye.

Even now
When all my heavy heart is broken up
I seem to see my prison walls breaking
And then a light, and in that light a girl
Her fingers busied about her hair, her cool white arms
Faint rosy at the elbows, raised in the sunlight . . .

He heard himself make a sound that was between a gulp and a sob. The words might have been written specifically for him. He began to read, almost greedily, turning back and forward, snatching at random as though he could find her again.

Even now
I love long black eyes that caress like silk,
Ever and ever sad and laughing eyes,
Whose lids make such sweet shadow when they close
It seems another beautiful look of hers.
I love a fresh mouth, ah, a scented mouth,
And curving hair, subtle as a smoke,
And light fingers, and laughter of green gems.

Words caught his mind like shards of glittering glass, beautiful and painful.

> . . . the essence of her beauty spilled
> Down on my days so that it fades not,
> Fails not, subtle and fresh, in perfuming
> That day, and the days, and this the latest day.

And:

> I call to mind her weariness in the morning,
> Close lying in my arms and tiredly smiling
> At my disjointed prayer for her small sake.

And at last:

> Even now
> I know that I have savoured the hot taste of life
> Lifting green cups and gold at the great feast.
> Just for a small and a forgotten time
> I have had full in my eyes from off my girl
> The whitest pouring of eternal light . . .

He couldn't read any more. He couldn't see the words. Faintly, in the distance, he heard Polly speaking. He thought of what Charlie had written: *Sometimes poetry helps.* Was it help, this awful pain in his throat and chest? He put his hands up to his face, and felt wetness. Helmy was trying to climb onto his lap, distressed. He pushed him down, dragged in a convulsive breath, and then he really was crying. He put his head down on his arms on the table. It hurt to cry, it was ugly and difficult, but he felt something in him loosen. He heard Polly get up, felt her hand on his shoulder, and he turned roughly to put his arms round her waist and cry into the comfort of her stomach.

★   ★   ★

213

The *Messenger* was not a monolith like the *Bugle* or the *Clarion*, but though smaller, it had a good reputation as a go-ahead paper with its finger on the pulse. It aimed to be on top of every breaking story, but devoted fewer pages to the daily doings of the Houses of Parliament and the *ton*.

'If you start with us,' said the news editor, Bill Dickins, who interviewed Basil, 'you can look forward to progressing through the company. We like to give a good grounding and encourage talent and ambition. You'll be expected to muck in wherever you're needed at first, while you learn the trade. We're not like the *Clarion*, where you get shunted into a department and stay there until you're sixty-five. News in the modern world is fast-moving, and we need flexible thinkers who can react quickly and get the job done.'

It was, Basil could tell, a set speech, but he liked it. It suggested to him that it was the kind of place where no-one would necessarily know where anyone else was – perfect for him to disappear when the fancy took him.

'You edited the school newspaper, I understand?' Dickins went on. 'Good experience. And you had a short time at the *Bugle*. Why did you leave?'

Basil had anticipated that question. 'Well, sir,' he said, 'it was like what you said about the *Clarion*. I found it rather – um—'

'Stiff? Hidebound?' Dickins offered helpfully.

'Yes, sir. Exactly.'

'Well, I think we can take you, Compton,' Dickins said. 'A month's trial, with no notice on either side, then if we're happy, we'll offer you a permanent job. We'll start you off as a runner in the news room, so you can get the flavour of what we do.'

Basil smiled. A runner's life suited him perfectly. They send you to fetch something, or look something up, and you can take as long as you like. And no-one passing you anywhere in the building ever questions what you're doing if you're carrying a file or a piece of paper.

'Thank you, sir,' said Basil, and shook the hand that was offered.

'I'm happy for you, Basil,' Aunt Molly said. 'We'll miss you, but I dare say the faster pace will suit you better. When do you start?'

'On Monday.'

'That gives you a few days to find yourself lodgings. You shouldn't have any difficulty. There are plenty of rooms to let in Bloomsbury and Holborn.'

Having told her I wanted to stand on my own two feet, Basil thought, I can hardly complain if she takes me at my word. But such lodgings as he could afford on *Messenger* pay would be modest indeed. He had a spasm of missing Gloria, and the golden days when he'd lived in Ryder Street and dined at the Ritz. He wondered why he had been such a fool as to lose her. He could have kicked himself.

All the same, he couldn't deny that he felt a queasy sort of excitement at the thought of being really on his own at last.

'I hope you're going to settle down this time, and stick to it,' Helen said. 'You can't keep changing jobs. People will think you're unreliable.'

'The *Messenger* is a much better fit for me than the *Bugle*,' Basil said. 'It's a young newspaper, with fresh ideas.'

Helen didn't look quite convinced, but she said, 'Tell me about these lodgings of yours. Are they respectable?'

'It's in Mecklenburgh Square. A shabby old house, but clean. My room's on the third floor. It has a bed, a chair, a wardrobe, and a chest of drawers. And there's a gas ring in the hearth where I can heat soup.'

'Aren't your meals included?' Helen said.

'Yes, but Mrs Morgan's very strict about punctuality. If you don't sit down on the dot, you get nothing, and as a reporter, you can't always be sure when you'll be home. The other lodgers all seem respectable. One's a law student.'

'Oh, yes, it's not far from the Law Courts, is it?' Jack said. He turned to Helen. 'I wouldn't worry too much about his domestic arrangements, darling. I can't imagine Basil ever going hungry. And it will do him good to have to fend for himself. We can't afford to have a nation of soft young people, with another war coming.'

'Oh, Dad! There's not going to be a war,' Basil said.

'Why do you think we're putting all this effort into developing new aeroplanes?' Jack said. 'But it won't be like last time. This will be a specialist war.'

'You mean people like me won't have to fight?' Basil said.

'Of course you'll fight, but you'll be properly trained. And if you want to serve in a good unit, you'll need to get in early. Michael's all set in the navy, but you, Basil, why don't you join the RAF? You ought to get yourself in at the ground floor, so that by the time the war starts you'll have some seniority.'

'I can't believe it'll ever come to war,' Basil said. This thing was getting to be a bit of an obsession with the old man. 'Nobody wants one. Anyway, I could be a war journalist, couldn't I? Someone has to bring the news back from the Front.'

Helen intervened: 'We haven't seen you since Richard's wedding. How was it?'

'Short,' said Basil.

The hot weather had ripened the wheat, and the first fields were ready for cutting. The day was perfect, sunny and settled, the sky cornflower blue with a few high, large clouds like piles of whipped cream. The lime trees were in blossom, and the hedges were full of wild roses and honeysuckle, so they rode through a tunnel of scent.

A robin in the top of one of the hedges sang a sharp-edged challenge as the horses passed by, to Zephyr's leisurely thub-dub and the rapid counterpoint of fat little Mr Pickles as she hurried to keep up. (Alec had been very young when he named her, the complexities of equine gender beyond him.) Her coat, in bold markings of cocoa and cream, was glossy over her summer roundness, and her bright eyes peered out from under her thick, coarse forelock, looking for mischief. Polly noted that Alec was growing again. His legs used to stick out at comical right-angles, but now they hung down a decent amount, despite the pony's barrel sides. It wouldn't be long before he'd need something bigger. It would cause a pang to get rid of Mr Pickles, though. She ought to be a family pony, introducing a stream of children to the art of equitation. But Alec was six now. Polly wondered if he would ever have a brother or sister.

They found James up at Har Piece, an odd-shaped field at the far side of White House Farm. '"Har" means parish boundary,' she explained to Alec.

He wasn't listening. He had seen James at the far side of the field, jacket off, shirt-sleeves rolled, helping the stookers. 'There's Uncle!' he cried, and dashed off.

Polly handed Zephyr to one of the men and went to join John Burton, who was talking to Seb Bellerby, the White House tenant. 'How is Joan?' she asked at once. She asked nearly every day, now Mrs Burton was nearing delivery.

'She can't get comfortable in this hot weather, not even to sleep,' Burton said. 'I never realised what hell we men put you women through.'

'Ah, well, it will all be worth it when she holds her son in her arms,' Polly said. She looked at Alec, who had caught up with James and was bouncing on the spot as he chattered, while James looked down at him indulgently. 'I hope he doesn't get in anyone's way.'

'Those scythes are very sharp,' Burton agreed.

'I mean I don't want him hampering the workers,' Polly said. 'The scythe-men are too skilled to cut anyone by accident.'

'It's fascinating to watch the wheat being cut that way,' Burton said, 'but I was just saying to Seb here, it would be more efficient to use a machine. Lord Lambert has a reaper-binder that cuts the wheat and binds it into sheaves.'

'I wouldn't mind one of them,' Seb said. 'Course, we do have a plain reaper that we use on the other fields, but this 'un is too small.'

'Lord Lambert's reaper-binder is drawn by a tractor,' Burton said.

'Horrible noisy thing!' said Polly.

'Well, you could have a horse-drawn reaper-binder,' Burton said. 'But it's not as efficient. A tractor does a field four times faster.'

'Horses compact the soil less,' Polly countered. 'And they make lovely manure for fertiliser. All a tractor makes is stinking fumes. Besides, you can't put all these people out of work.' She waved a hand at the men and women following the scythe-men, binding and stooking – and the little girls following them, gleaning into their aprons. The boys were too busy chasing mice and rabbits, wielding catapults and boasting about their prowess.

'But what happens when the scythe-men get too old to work?' Burton said.

'There'll be new young ones,' Polly said.

'Young men don't want to learn reaping. They don't want to work on the land. They want to work in a nice clean office or factory, and come home at five thirty to a nice clean modern house and a nice little wife. And at the weekend they

218

want to go to the cinema, or a football match, or go for a spin in their nice little car and look at the countryside that someone else is tending.' Burton shook his head. 'We're becoming a nation of watchers instead of doers.'

'That's right,' Seb said, as if struck by the thought. 'My ma used to play the piano of an evening, and my dad played the fiddle, and us kids'd all stand round and sing. Now folk listen to the wireless or play the gramophone.'

'The war broke the mould,' Burton said. 'A generation left the land to fight. And the next generation has different interests. The old ways have to go.' He cocked an eyebrow at Polly. 'You know that. And you've always been keen to modernise the estate.'

'This field is too small to be cut by machine,' Polly said, rather than say she liked to watch the scythe-men and would be sorry to see the tradition die.

'We ought to grub up the hedges and make the fields bigger,' Burton said.

Polly thought of the roses and the honeysuckle and the robin's song. 'We won't be doing that,' she said firmly.

Seb laughed. 'You looked just like your father then, Miss Polly. He was a fine master and a genial man, but his word was law, and that was all about it.'

'I'm just doing my duty and warning you,' Burton said, without rancour. 'The time may come when you'll have to embrace machinery because you can't get any workers.'

'They've started digging the footings in North Field,' said Polly. 'Once they've built the council estate, there'll be a whole new pool of labour to draw from. They live on my land, what more natural than to work on it?'

Burton was about to say they already had jobs and would be no more likely to want farm work than anyone else, but conversation had to stop as an aeroplane grumbled overhead. A two-seater bi-plane, it was, flying low. Goggles flashed as the two inside looked down, then away.

'That's the other thing,' Burton said, as the noise faded. 'What if it comes to another war?'

The thought of Erich scorched across her mind. She remembered one day, during the war, when she had come upon him mending a dry-stone wall, remembered his care and skill and his sure hands – the hands that had so lately caressed her. She felt the sick, falling-away sensation of missing him, longing for him; and the hateful hopelessness of not being able to change the way things were.

'If the men go off to fight,' Burton was saying, 'what will you do for labour then?'

Polly pulled herself back from the brink. 'Land girls,' she said briskly. 'Like last time. But maybe there won't be another war,' she added, as James and Alec joined them.

'I bet there will be,' Alec piped up. 'I'd like to go and fight. Bam-bam-bam.' He hoisted an imaginary rifle to his shoulder and shot several enemy soldiers who had been creeping up on them.

'If we have to fight Germany again—' Seb began.

But James interrupted him. 'You've got the wrong enemy. Russia is by far the greater threat. I've been to Russia. I've seen for myself what the Reds are like. We *have* to throw in with the Germans to stop them.'

Burton said, 'It's not even twenty years since the Armistice. Memories of what the Germans did are fresh and raw.'

James overrode him. 'We can't ignore the situation. Communism spreads like a poison. Look at Spain, look at France. The Reds won't be satisfied until the whole world is enslaved by them. And the Germans are the only nation with the military strength to beat them. We have to have them on our side.'

Now Seb spoke. 'Begging your pardon, Mr Morland, but the Huns killed all three of my brothers, and Matt Walton over at Huntsham, and I don't know how many more. You only got to look at all the names on the War Memorial. And what I hear is they're making guns and bombs as fast as they can. Well, if the Germans start up again, we have to finish with them, once and for all, wipe them off the face of the earth. And I'll be ready. Any German that sets foot on my land, I'll shoot him like a dog. Begging your pardon, Miss Polly,' he added with an apologetic glance at Alec, who was listening with his mouth open. And he touched his forelock to her and walked off.

Polly watched Seb's retreating figure, and thought *How right Erich was. They would never have accepted him.* A weight settled in her as, finally, she accepted the truth. Some mad, stubborn and unrepentant part of her that had kept hoping turned its face to the wall and died. It was the end. She would never see him again.

James was saying, in an exasperated voice, 'You see? This is just the sort of blinkered attitude we have to deal with. When the red flag goes up over Buckingham Palace, they'll realise too late I was right.'

Alec stared at him intently, catching up. 'I'll fight the Reds, Uncle. And the Germans, too. I'll fight them both.'

James pulled himself together, ruffled Alec's hair and said, 'I don't suppose there'll be any fighting of anybody. The diplomats'll talk everybody out of it.'

Alec didn't know what diplomats were, but he looked disappointed.

CHAPTER TEN

The cruise was not an unalloyed pleasure, and Emma and Kit were glad they had only promised two weeks to Wally and the King, using the excuse of their children. 'We have to take them away for a holiday before school starts again.' They left the *Nahlin* on Monday the 24th of August at Piraeus, having witnessed yet another piece of unpleasantness. As they came into port, the King, wearing nothing but khaki shorts and two little crosses on chains round his neck, was standing on the foredeck, and Jack Aird, who was equerrying, suggested he might like to put on a shirt before they came within range of the press cameras. The King gave him a filthy look and stalked off in a temper, while Wally rounded on Aird and snapped, 'If His Majesty wants your advice, he'll ask for it. Otherwise, you should hold your tongue.'

The stresses between the King and Aird had been much on display during the past fortnight. The King was travelling under the incognito of the Duke of Lancaster, but it had been used so often, no-one was under any illusion as to who was on board, and every landfall had been met by shoals of press and throngs of locals. But the King refused to make any concessions.

Kit and Emma settled into their compartment on the train from Athens with a sigh of relief. The staterooms on the *Nahlin* had been small and airless, and there'd been little to do on board. The King had insisted on sailing past the major sights at night-time, to save Wally from getting too much sun, so they had missed them all. Neither HM nor Wally cared for sight-seeing – it was golf for him and shopping for her, and their guests were expected to fall in with the programme.

'Jack Aird was quite right,' Kit said, as the train rattled across the arid spaces of Greece. 'HM just doesn't see that it won't do for the King of England to be seen paddling in rockpools in nothing but bathing drawers. Or to go on shore bare-chested in espadrilles and a pair of shorts. It's undignified. It hurts our reputation.'

'And Wally doesn't help,' Emma agreed. 'She just keeps saying that a king can do anything he likes. But if one photograph of her holidaying with another man gets back to England, that will be the end of the divorce.'

'It won't, though,' Kit said. 'HM's got an agreement with Harmsworth and Beaverbrook never to mention Wally's name. That's why the ordinary man in the street has no idea who she is. I don't think she realises the lengths that are being gone to to protect her.'

'Oh, well, let's just forget all about it for now,' Emma said. 'I can't wait to see the girls! And the doggies.'

'I can't wait to see their faces when they see the presents we've bought them.'

'You bought presents for the doggies?'

'Very amusing. I say, why don't we stop off in Paris and buy the girls a dress each? I bet it would tickle them to have a Paris mode.'

'They're six and four, they're too young to care about that sort of thing. Buy them a doll, if you want to buy them anything. Oh, I'm so looking forward to Walcote and a bit of peace and quiet!'

'Not *too* much quiet,' Kit said. 'I was planning quite a few parties. And I've invited Raymond to stay.'

Emma sighed. But she had been engaged three times before Kit, during the war, and all three of her fiancés had died.

Kit was a good husband and a dear creature and they loved each other, so she'd had to accept that he was attracted to other men. Otherwise she would lose him, too. He had promised her he would never be unfaithful to her. And they had a good life together. It seemed a small price to pay.

'You don't mind, do you?' Kit asked. 'You like Raymond?'

'No, I don't mind,' Emma said. 'Perhaps we ought to invite some more people, make a house party of it.'

'Excellent idea,' Kit said, and began to speculate aloud on who would be good company. Emma silently bade goodbye to the peace and quiet. But Kit was happy, and if he was happy, she was happy.

Despite being Earl of Overton and Chelmsford, Oliver had no country estate, and if they wanted to get out of London in August, they had to rent somewhere, or rely on friends. This year they had planned to rent a cottage on the Isle of Wight; but Oliver urged his wife to accept Kit and Emma's last-minute invitation.

'They're always good fun,' he said. 'And the children will like playing with their girls. And I want to hear how things went on the *Nahlin*.'

'You have an unhealthy interest in that ménage,' Verena said.

Oliver gave a rueful grin. 'You know how I love the movies. And the King and Wally are pure Hollywood.'

'I object to the word "pure",' Verena said. 'But I suppose I can't change you.'

'You are saintly in your patience, my love. But, honestly, don't you yearn to know how it's all going to come out? Do admit.'

'I *know* how it's going to come out,' said Verena. 'Badly.'

'It's ironic,' Oliver said at dinner the first night, when it was just the four of them, 'that the Matrimonial Causes Bill should be going through Parliament at this particular juncture.'

The cloth had been drawn and the dessert put on, and Emma had dismissed the servants, or he would not have raised the subject. It wouldn't be proper to talk about it in front of them.

'The Divorce Bill, you mean?' said Kit, cracking a walnut, 'Well, the law *is* a bit of a mess. That old girl-in-a-hotel-bedroom ploy – the judges must know it's fake. And the idea that the wife has to be entirely innocent. If the husband and wife have *both* committed adultery, neither can have a divorce. Where's the sense in that?'

'Is there any great appetite for easier divorce?' Verena asked. 'There aren't many of them, are there?'

'About five thousand a year,' said Oliver, drawing the cheese board towards him. 'But there must be many more thousands of people struggling along in unhappy marriages, who would like to be free.'

Emma objected. 'It's a dreadful idea that if you see someone you like better you can simply ditch your current spouse and help yourself to a new one. And it will be the women who suffer. They have no money or any way to earn a living if they're abandoned.'

Oliver cut a sliver of Wensleydale. 'I can only say that there is a feeling abroad, these days, that the pursuit of individual satisfaction is the primary purpose of life.'

'I blame the cinema,' Verena said.

'My dear,' Oliver protested, amused, 'are you starting a moral crusade against Hollywood?'

'I would if I could. It does nobody any good – you wouldn't claim otherwise, I hope?'

'It seems to me films have become intensely moral. The baddies always suffer and the goodies prevail. But let's not argue about that. We were talking about the Matrimonial Causes Bill.'

'What will the new grounds for divorce be?' Kit asked.

'Adultery, desertion for three years or more, cruelty, incurable insanity, incest and sodomy. From what my fellow peers are saying, it will have no difficulty in getting through the Upper House. I only mention it in the context of the King disporting himself publicly with a mistress who will soon have been divorced twice. It might be acceptable to the spirit of the age to pursue happiness at all costs, but the King is supposed to represent an ideal, especially to the lower classes. They won't like it.'

Kit, tired at last of talking about the fabled couple, cracked another nut. 'Since we've dragged your children away from the sea, and we're about as far away from the coast as you can be in England, I thought I'd arrange for us all to go over to the Endberbys at Kilworth tomorrow. They have a splendid lake, for boating and swimming. What do you think?'

David O. Selznick had offered $50,000 for the film rights of *Gone With the Wind*, and Al Feinstein was disinclined to outbid him. In typical fashion he immediately lost interest in the whole thing. 'He wants Clark Gable for Rhett Butler,' he said to Lennie, with a shrug. 'Good luck to him. MGM will never release him.'

'I heard that Warner's offered him Errol Flynn in return for the distribution rights,' Lennie said.

'That movie will never be made,' said Al. 'Anyway, I've got an idea for your girl. Listen, you'll love this. William – Shakespeare!' he pronounced, with a dramatic pause between the two halves.

Lennie was surprised, but pleased.

'Shakespeare's hot,' Al went on. 'Warner did *The Midsummer Dream* last year. MGM's just released *Romeo and Juliet*.'

'I've seen it,' Lennie said. 'Norma Shearer and Leslie Howard. A bit middle-aged for the star-crossed lovers, I thought. But it's a pretty good production. They certainly made an effort to be faithful to the play. They sent the set designer to Verona to make sketches.' He knew that because the designer had been Eric Chapel, any news of whom always caught his eye. He had a morbid fascination with the man, wondering whether there had been anything between him and Polly in New York back in May.

'The buzz is that it's gonna get Oscars. And we'd better get in on the act before all the good Shakespeares are snapped up. Reznik's suggested *The Merchant of Venice*. Gondolas I like, but it reads like a slow day on Wall Street. Loans and interest and bonds? Where's the action? George Cukor got a great fight scene into *Romeo*. Now, Reznik's other suggestion is *Twelfth Night*. Whaddaya think about that? I've not read the outline yet.'

'That could work,' Lennie said. 'It's all about mistaken identity. The heroine dresses up as a boy—'

'Rosie's got a great pair of pins!'

'She goes to work as a page to a duke, and falls in love with him. But he's in love with a rich countess and sends this page to woo her on his behalf. The countess falls in love with the page—'

'Who's a girl, right?'

'Right. Then our heroine's twin brother, whom she thinks is dead, arrives. Everyone thinks he's her, the countess marries him, and the page reveals she's a girl and marries the duke.'

'It's farce, right?' Al said, frowning.

'Romantic comedy. But the heroine falling for a man who doesn't know she's a girl so he can't fall in love with her – that's poignant. A tear-jerker.'

Feinstein's face cleared. 'And no need to splash fifty grand on the film rights, because Shakespeare's dead!' He swivelled his cigar from one side of his mouth to the other. 'Forget the Wall Street doohickey! We'll go with *Twelfth Night*. Have to change that title, though. It's not sexy.'

'If you change it, no-one will know it's Shakespeare,' Lennie pointed out.

Lennie was waiting for Rose when she came off the set at the end of the day's filming and gave her the news.

'Shakespeare!' she said, as they crossed the lot. 'But that's great! I've about had my fill of cowboy movies. How did you talk him into it?'

'It was his idea.'

'It's a romance, right?' Rose said. 'I haven't read it.' He gave her a quick outline of the plot. 'It sounds complicated.'

'But if it's done right, it'll be a big hit for you – as long as you behave yourself.'

'I will. I'm over all that stuff. I just wish—' She stopped, with a sigh.

'Wish what, honey?' Lennie said.

'I wish I could fall in love, and have the guy love me back, like an ordinary person.'

'But you're not an ordinary person,' Lennie said, feeling a little sick at heart.

She looked up at him. 'Is that the price I have to pay for my career? I don't know if it's worth it.'

'Only you can decide that. I would never push you, you know that. If you want to quit, you can.'

She thought a moment. 'But I love it,' she said. 'I love acting, I love being in front of the cameras. When I walk onto a set I get a thrill. And seeing myself on screen. I don't know if anything else would make me feel like that.' She followed her thoughts then said, 'You won't leave me, will you, Uncle Lennie? You won't go away? I don't think I could cope without you there at the end of the day.'

'I'm not really your uncle, you know.'

'But I like calling you that. Makes me feel safe.'

'Go on and get changed. I'll take you out to Perino's for dinner tonight.'

She brightened. 'That's Bette Davis's favourite restaurant.'

'You're going to be twice as famous as Bette Davis. And you're ten times as pretty.'

She laughed happily. 'Perino's! I love you, Uncle Lennie.'

The *Messenger* took Basil to its heart in a way that confounded him. Everyone was openly friendly and helpful. Even the proprietor – normally, at a newspaper, a distant and terrifying figure – was genial. Sir Bradley Perkins, who had made his fortune through a national chain of haberdashery shops, liked to pop his head round the door of every department on his weekly visits and say, 'Well done, chaps! Keep it up!' and had his chauffeur deliver a box of cakes for the employees' afternoon tea.

And everyone was so trusting that it was no fun to bamboozle them. Shirking would have been so easy that he could not work up any enthusiasm for it. Also, to his surprise, he was finding the work so interesting he did not want to avoid it. Even his probationary days went quickly. His immediate boss, news editor Dickins – a spare, rumpled, harassed individual – was generously encouraging. 'Go where you like, see what's going on, ask questions, find out what you're good for. Follow your instincts,' he had said, an open invitation to Bad Basil to disappear for most of the day. But Bad Basil was losing ground to Curious Basil, and he feared that Diligent, Eager and Focused Basil might be close behind.

He had been put under the wing of a junior reporter, Bob Zennor – an enormous young man like a friendly puppy, who had played rugby at Oxford and was only a few years older than him – and went out on 'stories' with him. Dickins gave him back his early attempts at writing them up almost completely obliterated by blue pencil, but still said, 'Good effort! You'll soon pick it up!' Zennor told him not to be discouraged by the blue pencil – even veteran reporters were not immune. A sheet that came back unaltered, he said, would have worried him.

At the end of his month's trial, Basil was given a rosy assessment and was offered a permanent job. He even got a handshake from the newspaper's actual editor, Mr Comstock – a person so exalted a junior reporter hardly ever came across him. 'Hearing good things about you, Compton. Keep it up!'

Basil accepted the manly grip with a sickly grin and muttered thanks, feeling at the same time gratified and oddly nervous. Adulthood was claiming him. He was going to be a grown-up, whether he liked it or not.

While most of the staff were male, there were some females around the building, and on one of his early expeditions, when Zennor was showing him around and introducing him to the lino men and the comps and explaining what they did, they encountered a tall young woman, who greeted Zennor with a brisk 'Morning, Bob!' and gave Basil a look that was swiftly comprehensive. She did not slow to be introduced, and walked rapidly to the stairs at the end of the corridor and disappeared down them.

Basil, who had turned to watch her go, discovered that her back view was almost as enticing as the front. 'Who was that?' he asked.

'Miss Byrne,' Zennor said. The tone of his voice made Basil turn back to look at him, to discover Zennor's big, healthy face had taken on a distinctly 'soppy' look.

'Tell me more,' Basil encouraged.

'Miranda Byrne. She works in the advertising department. She did HMDs before—'

'She did what?'

'Hatches, Matches and Despatches. Births, deaths and marriage notices,' he elucidated, seeing Basil still looked blank. 'But she was in the newsroom for a bit before that. She's *wonderful*!'

'Are you and she . . . ?'

'Lord, no!' Zennor blushed. 'Doesn't know I exist.'

'She called you "Bob".'

'Well, we were pally when she was in the newsroom. But she's much too good for me. I wouldn't have a hope.'

Basil was glad to hear it, though he found himself, inexplicably, saying, 'A girl is just a girl, you know.'

'Not that one,' Zennor insisted. 'Quite apart from—' He made a vague gesture, encompassing Miss Byrne's charms. 'She's Mr Comstock's niece. And frightfully well off.'

'Oh, is she?' Basil said, and changed the subject. Encouraging Bob Zennor to think he had a chance was no longer in the plan.

Kit had been out with Raymond and a group of friends. Arriving home late, he saw a light under Emma's door, and went in, finding her sitting up in bed reading.

'I was hoping you'd drop in,' she said.

He crossed the room to kiss her and sat on the edge of the bed. 'What are you reading?'

'*Regency Buck* – Georgette Heyer.'

'Nice?'

'Pure frivol. I was struggling through *Brave New World* and thought I deserved a treat. Did you have a nice evening?'

'Ish. Dinner was good, but then we went on to Brokespeare's flat for coffee and brandy and the talk turned terribly earnest. Brokespeare's a devoted leftist, and they've all vowed never to enjoy themselves until the New Order is established – perhaps not even then. But he had some divine pieces of early Sèvres, and some rather good ivories, so I occupied myself pottering among them while they saved the world. How was your day?'

'I went to have a look at Macklin Street with John Douglas this morning. He has some good ideas. I'll show you tomorrow – they're on the desk downstairs.'

Kit nodded. 'Lunched where?'

'Here. Came back to change, thought I'd slip over to

Verena's, but I found Wally on the doorstep in a terrible state. So of course I had to ask her in. Mrs Ambrose had to find something for us. Cold watercress soup and omelettes *fines herbes*,' she added, knowing he'd want to know. He thrived on detail.

'And what was the Wally upset about?'

'You were right, she's never realised how much she was being protected from the press. When she left the *Nahlin* she stopped off in Paris, at the Meurice, and her post caught up with her, including a big package of press cuttings from her aunt Bessie in America. Pictures of her with the King on holiday – him in shorts and no shirt as often as not – and lurid accounts of their affair. Plenty of detail, not much of it accurate, but a terrible shock, when she was used to the silence of Fleet Street. It's thrown her into a panic.'

'Yes, I can see that it would. A taste of horrors to come. Sooner or later the dam will burst – I'm amazed the press restraint has lasted this long.'

'Now she's saying she must break off her relationship with the King. I think she really means it. She says she wants to go back to Ernest. She really misses him – talked about how he used to come home from work with the *Evening Standard* under his arm, mix her a cocktail and chat about ordinary things. "We were always good friends," she said. And, of course, you and I know that there's no friendship for her with David – he's like a demanding child.' Emma paused, then concluded, 'I think she's lonely.'

'But she loves the high life,' Kit said. 'She wouldn't really give that up.'

'I think she would now. The price is too high.'

'She's left it too late. Ernest wants the divorce. Even if she withdrew the petition, he wouldn't want to live with her again, and you can't blame him. He must have seen what the American press is saying about him. No man likes to be cast in that light.'

'At any rate, she's writing to the King to tell him she wants to break with him.'

'Ha! Well, we'll see how that goes.'

'She looked awfully ill, poor thing. She said she'd caught a cold in Paris, but I think it's all emotional. I can't say I really like her, but I do feel sorry for her.'

Kit stared at his hands. 'Yes. It's hard to see how this can turn out well. There's absolutely no chance the establishment will let him marry a twice-divorced woman. The country would never stand for it, let alone the colonies.'

'Perhaps he could just marry her in secret,' Emma said doubtfully.

'But that's not what he wants. He wants to marry her in Westminster Abbey in the full glare of publicity, and have her crowned as queen beside him.'

'But that makes no sense,' Emma said in frustration. 'It's madness.'

'It's an obsession, and they never make sense. It's a great pity Simpson decided on the divorce. As long as she was someone else's wife, David's hands were tied.'

Emma got a phone call early enough the next morning for her still to be in bed with her morning tray of tea and bread-and-butter and her post, her secretary Miss Ames sitting across the room and taking notes. When Emma heard Wally's voice, she waved Miss Ames out of the room.

'He rang me last night from the Fort,' Wally said, without preamble. 'He must have just got my letter. He said he will never let me go. He cried. He said if I tried to leave him he would cut his throat.'

'How horrible! I'm sure he wouldn't really—'

'He would. Maybe not cut his throat, but Alec Hardinge told me he sleeps with a gun under his pillow. And there are always pills. He was quite hysterical – it took me ages to calm him down. Then this morning there was a letter from him, saying it all again, swearing if I left him his life would have no meaning and he'd kill himself. He says if I'm not crowned beside him next May, he won't be crowned at all. I'm in agony, Emma. I feel like an animal in a trap. I wish I was dead!'

'You don't,' Emma said encouragingly. 'You're going through a hard time, but you'll come about. Aren't Baltimore girls famous for their grit?'

There was a pause. Then, in a watery voice, 'I don't mind telling you I'm at a low ebb. One thing,' she added, 'Goddard tells me there are so many divorce petitions piled up in London for the fall session, my case will never get called. He said I might have to wait a year for a hearing date. That might solve the problem.'

'Because David wants to marry you before the Coronation?'

'When he knows he can't, he may let the whole marriage thing drop.'

The words were hopeful, but Emma heard the doubt underneath, and shared it. The King's principal characteristic was the sort of dogged stubbornness that got hold of a bone and would never let it go. He would wear Wally down, as he had before, with a mixture of threats, endearments and jewels. And with Ernest determined on a new life, she had nowhere else to turn.

So it proved. She heard nothing more from Wally for ten days, then bumped into her at Ciro's, looking better, though still tense, and wearing a pair of sapphire and diamond ear clips in the shape of arrows. She told Emma that Goddard had got her petition into the Ipswich Assizes, where there was much less competition. It was to be heard on the 27th of October. 'Which would mean a decree absolute at the end of April, just in time for the Coronation on the twelfth of May. Where *is* Ipswich, anyway?'

'Suffolk. In the bit of England on the right-hand side that bulges out,' Emma said.

'Oh. It sounds rustic. I have to go and stay there, apparently. I have to be in residence for three weeks before the hearing. David's got them looking for a house for me in the area. I hope it's not too far from London – you'll come and visit me there, won't you?'

'There are trains to Ipswich from Liverpool Street,' Emma told her, skating over the invitation. 'I believe it takes about an hour and a half.'

'And I'm looking for a house in London,' she went on. 'Bryanston Court was all right for the Prince of Wales, but you can't expect the King to visit me there. Oh, and I'm going to Balmoral on the twenty-third.'

'I know,' Kit said, when Emma told him that later. 'Winnie Churchill told me – he was horrified. It's an official palace, with long traditions of who ought to be asked and how they should conduct themselves. Imagine our Wally barging into the kitchen and pushing the dour Scottish cooks aside to make club sandwiches! And moving the furniture about, and giving orders. Oh dear.' He shook his head, laughing. 'They are a dreadful pair, but they do make life entertaining!'

There was a bigger scandal in store, which they found out about later. Wally and the Rogerses went down by train, but to save Wallis from having to change trains, the King drove himself the sixty miles to Aberdeen to meet them and drive them back to Balmoral. That was bad enough, but he had been supposed to visit Aberdeen Royal Infirmary on that day, and had called off, pleading illness, and made the Duke of York go in his place. He thought that wearing motoring goggles would disguise him, but everyone recognised him, and his actions made it into the Aberdeen *Evening Argus*, which speculated sourly on what guest could possibly have been so important as to require the cancellation of an official engagement.

'The Bertie Yorks are furious,' Kit heard from Oliver, who had it from Eddie, who was staying with them at Birkhall. 'Doing the hospital instead of the King made it look as though

Bertie was complicit in the shockingly bad behaviour. HM asked Wally to act as hostess at a dinner at Balmoral the Yorks were invited to, and when Wally stepped forward to greet them, the Duchess ignored her and walked straight past. So now the Yorks will never forgive David and Wally, and they will never forgive the Yorks.'

Kit told Emma all this that evening, and she said, 'You're not laughing. You said they made life entertaining.'

'I know, but suddenly I don't find them so funny. It's all getting rather . . . shoddy.' He paused, then said, 'I heard a joke at the club at lunchtime: Mrs Simpson got into a cab and said, "King's Cross," and the cabby said, "Oh, I'm sorry to hear that."'

'You're not laughing at that, either.'

'I didn't say it was a good joke,' said Kit.

The King rented a house in Cumberland Terrace for Wally – one of the fine Nash houses on the outer ring of Regent's Park.

'I'm having it redecorated,' Wally told Emma at lunch at the Café Royal one day, 'so it won't be ready before I leave for Ipswich. David will have my things moved in while I'm away. I'm staying at Claridge's for a few days.'

'Where are you staying in Ipswich?' Emma asked.

'Some place nearby – Felixstowe, it's called. Goddard's found a house there for me. By the sea.' She looked out at the dark day, where rain was sheeting down on Regent Street, and the few people hurrying by were sprouting umbrellas like mushrooms. 'I'm stocking up on things to take with me. One never knows if they'll have one's favourite brand of gin. You will come and stay, won't you? David is absolutely forbidden to visit me down there, and it will be a long three weeks.'

'You could do with the rest,' Emma said.

'But will I get it?' she said, raising bleak eyes to Emma's.

Those with friends in America were having American newspapers sent to them. They were full of Wally and the divorce.

King's Moll to Reno in Wolsey's Home Town
Baltimore Cutie Cuts Out British Belles
King to Wed Wally Before Christmas

Still the British press kept its silence, and the ordinary man in the street was in the dark, but everyone in London Society knew, and was rapidly dividing into two camps: those who believed the King should be allowed to marry his One True Love, and those who deplored the whole thing and believed nothing should be allowed to upset Queen Mary.

'You wouldn't think of stopping the divorce?' Emma asked.

'Everything's gone too far now,' Wally said. 'Better to have it over and done with.' She mused for a moment. 'We weren't unhappy, you know – Ernest and I. We jogged along perfectly well together. If David hadn't come along . . .'

Emma was thinking of something Kit had told her that his solicitor Peter Bracey had said to him: that since Wally's first divorce had taken place in America, on the grounds of desertion, it could be challenged as invalid in England, where adultery was the only accepted ground. 'That would mean,' Kit had said, quoting Bracey, 'that her marriage to Simpson was bigamous. And bigamy is a crime. If anyone thinks to raise *that*, she could go to prison.'

Kit had also mentioned something Lord Halifax had said when he bumped into him in the lobby of the House: that the Archbishop of Canterbury was deeply distressed that the King did not go to church, and felt that he would have difficulty anointing him at the Coronation. As for his marrying Mrs Simpson, he said no Anglican cleric would carry out the ceremony. *He* certainly would not.

But Emma kept the thoughts to herself. As Wally said, things had gone too far now.

Basil was reading a report that had come in on the wire from New York, headlined 'MILLIONAIRES' FLIGHT OVER NEW ENGLAND'. The operating company of the German airship

Hindenburg, the Deutsche Zeppelin-Reederei, had arranged a special trip on the 9th of October as an advertisement for their transatlantic service. It was a ten-hour cruise for invited influential persons from New Jersey to Boston and back, with champagne and fine food and the inevitable speeches. The airship was luxuriously appointed, and even featured a light-weight aluminium piano. The public rooms included, Basil was amused to read, a smoking lounge, which he thought was rather risky for a vessel filled with combustible hydrogen. Though, he supposed, given that people *would* smoke, it was probably better to confine it somehow. The smoking lounge, he read, was pressurised to keep out any leaking gas, and was accessed by a single air-lock door behind the bar, so that the steward could check that the passengers coming out weren't carrying a lit cigarette or pipe.

The *Hindenburg*, the largest thing ever to fly over the earth, was, of course, a valuable propaganda tool for the German government. The Nazi swastika was prominently displayed on her keel, and she had been flown over the Olympic stadium in Berlin that summer, dropping leaflets praising Nazi achievements.

What interested Basil most was that among the list of passengers, which included millionaires Nelson Rockefeller, M. G. B. Whelpley and Winthrop W. Aldrich – along with top naval officers, generals, government officials, senators, bankers, industrialists and the bosses of three American airlines – he found the name of Lennox Manning, head of Manning's Radios and former presidential adviser on broadcasting.

'What's up?' said Bob Zennor, who had ambled up behind him eating a Bath bun and looked over to see what Basil was reading. 'Oh, the "Millionaires' Flight". Are you writing it up?'

'Dickins said just a par, but he hinted there might be an article on the Nazi government background and the propaganda value to the Fascists.'

'Yes, he's red hot on Fascists, is our Mr Dickins,' Zennor said.

Basil tapped the sheet. 'Interestingly, I know one of the millionaires.'

'You *know* a millionaire?' Zennor said, in mingled awe and doubt.

'Well, not *know* him personally, but I'm distantly related to him. Lennox Manning. He's a sort of cousin of my father's. Dad's talked about him, and how he lived at Morland Place during the war – that's where Dad grew up. I lived there too when I was a nipper. Don't remember Lennox Manning – I was just a baby – but I've heard him talked about.'

'Morland Place? Where's that? Is that where your people live?'

Basil grinned. 'I don't have "people". There's no money in my bit of the family, I promise you. But it *is* quite a grand place. In Yorkshire. My great-uncle owned it, and my grandmother lived there and sort of ran it for him, so my aunt and uncles all lived there too when they were kids.' He returned to the report, which contained a lot of effusive detail. 'Do you think the old man will want the luncheon menu included? Swallow Nest Soup, whatever that is, cold Rhine salmon, tenderloin steak, Chateau Potatoes, beans à la Princesse, Carmen salad, and iced melon.'

'Not unless you can prove that's what Fascists eat when they grind the faces of the poor,' said Zennor. He looked at the back of Basil's head. 'You seem a bit struck. You like airships? Particular interest of yours?'

Basil looked up. 'My father worked on them, on the R100 and the R101. Mostly the 101.'

'Oh!' Zennor's face creased in concern.

The R101 disaster had so shocked the nation that the airship-building programme had ended there and then, never to be revived. His father had often said it was a pity, since airships were more practical for long distances and for heavy freight. Basil knew, because he'd heard his father talking about it, that the Germans had experimented with using helium instead of hydrogen, because it was an inert gas and did not explode or burn. But helium was also heavier than hydrogen and did not provide nearly as much lift. The Germans must have decided they could not achieve sufficient payload with helium to make it commercially viable, because the *Hindenburg*, and her sister ship the *Graf Zeppelin*, were both hydrogen-filled.

'Oh, Dad was all right. Actually, it's a strange story. He was meant to go on the flight, but he was up a ladder doing a last-minute adjustment before it took off, fell off the ladder and concussed himself. So he was rushed to hospital, and was lying safely in a clean white bed when it came down in flames.'

'That was a piece of luck,' Zennor said.

'Yes,' said Basil. 'When I think about it, he's had a lot of lucky escapes.'

Kit had always been more sympathetic towards Wally than Emma was, but it was Emma who agreed, in response to a frantic telephone call, to go down to Felixstowe for a few days, while Kit said he would rather be boiled in oil.

'Look at the weather!' he said, gesturing towards the window. 'Have you ever *been* to Felixstowe?'

'No – have you?'

'I've been to Aldeburgh, so I know what that coast is like. Bleak, bleak, bleak. The North Sea, darling! Unless Goddard's found a centrally heated palace formerly owned by a rich American, I know just what the house will be like. Cold as a tomb, wind whistling in under the doors and round the window frames, fires that smoke, and damp sheets. No, you can't ask it of me.'

'I don't ask it – Wally does.'

'Well, someone has to stay at home with the girlies. If you're really going, take your own bedding with you. And your furs.'

Emma agreed to go down for the weekend on Friday, the 16th of October. Kit bought her a hot-water-bottle as a going-away present, and packed the car with 'the essentials' – champagne, smoked salmon and books: *The ABC Murders*, *Jamaica Inn*, *Eyeless in Gaza*, *Keep the Aspidistra Flying* and *Ballet Shoes*.

'I'm only going for a weekend,' Emma protested. 'I'll only need one book.'

He looked horrified. 'But think how ghastly if you only took one and found you couldn't get on with it! Wally won't have any in the house, and as for a handy bookshop – you *are* going to the ends of the earth, my cherub!'

'*Ballet Shoes* is a children's book,' Emma said, turning it over.

'Oh, but I adore children's books,' Kit said. 'So restful. And ten times as much imagination as in adult books.'

Emma kissed him goodbye. 'When all this is over, and we have our lives back—'

'What makes you think it will ever be over? But if it is, what then?'

'We talked about a third child.'

'So we did.' He kissed her a bonus time. 'I may hold you to that.'

The house was pretty much as Kit had predicted, cramped and shabby. The prospect was uninviting: the sea was grey, the sky was grey, and a bitter east wind lashed the waves against the shingle and the rain against the windows. Of course there was no central heating. The coal-and-wood fires only made small arcs of warmth, leaving everywhere else clammily cold. Another couple, George and Kitty Hunter, were also staying, and Emma thought Wally could have managed without her and spared her the discomfort, but she seemed almost feverishly pleased to see her.

'I don't believe Goddard could have seen this house before

241

he rented it!' she said. 'And I daren't go out, even for a walk. The detective says the place is crawling with American press, and if they spotted me they'd follow me back here. Then they'd be jamming their cameras against the windows and we'd have to have the curtains shut all day.'

They played cards all evening, with rugs over their knees. Wally seemed to have lost more weight, and even with a rug and the seat closest to the fire, she was shivering. Emma took pity and offered her hot-water-bottle, and with that filled and on her lap under the rug, Wally relaxed a little. But she didn't give it back when it was time for bed, and it took Emma a long time to get to sleep.

She woke early and, longing for a cup of tea, got up and dressed and went downstairs. There was no-one about, and she was waiting for the kettle to boil when the King arrived. The detective at the door let him in, and he stood in the dingy hallway, staring about as if he wondered that such places could exist. Or perhaps he was only astonished to find himself in one.

Then he saw Emma, and gave her a beaming smile. 'Is she up? I want to surprise her,' were his first words.

'No-one's up but me.'

'I drove through the dark so as to get here early,' he said, seeming terribly pleased with himself. 'I want to be the one to take her tray up. Won't she be surprised when she sees me? I wonder what she'll say.' He rubbed his dry hands together, and laughed in childlike delight.

But he was no child. 'Sir,' Emma said, 'you really shouldn't be here. You and Wally aren't supposed to meet until the divorce is over.'

'Oh, don't fuss,' he said gaily. 'No-one will know. And, anyway, what could be more natural than for a friend to visit another friend and give them support when they're going through a difficult time? That's all I am, Emma, a concerned friend.'

'But you know that's not the way it will appear,' Emma urged. 'It could jeopardise the divorce if you were known to have visited.'

His smile went, and the deep frown etched itself between his brows. He hated to be argued with. 'I'm surprised at you,' he said. 'I know the papers say foul things about our relationship, but I thought you knew better.' Emma didn't answer, and his face cleared again. 'All this has been very hard for her, and I look to her friends – I look to *you* – to keep her spirits up. Anything she wants, she must have – you will see to it? And I've brought her a little present. What do you think?'

He took a jeweller's box from his pocket, and opened it for her to see. It was a ruby bracelet. 'It's lovely,' Emma said.

He beamed. 'You think she'll like it? I've had something engraved on the clasp. Look. It says, "Hold Tight." Because we're on the last lap now. She only has to keep up her courage, hold fast a little longer, and everything will be all right.'

His eyes were moist as he gazed into the middle distance, evidently viewing a golden future when he and Wally would be together as man and wife, King and Queen, soul-mates never to be parted for a single minute of any day, ever again.

She would have felt pity for him, had the prospect not made her feel a bit sick.

He stayed the night, and since some other American friends drove down on the Sunday for the day, the atmosphere was more cheerful. The King seemed in high good humour, and Wally relaxed a little. He mixed the pre-luncheon cocktails, and she went into the kitchen to explain to the bewildered locals who had been hired to cook and clean how to prepare cutlets her special way.

The telephone rang after luncheon. It was Alec Hardinge,

243

the King's private secretary, calling to ask Wally – much against his will – if she knew where the King was. The Prime Minister had telephoned Sandringham, where he had believed the King was hosting a shooting party, to arrange an urgent meeting. Sandringham had told him the King had already left for the Fort. Baldwin had rung the Fort, but they'd said they didn't have him. Then he rang Hardinge personally, and Hardinge had had to admit he didn't know where the King was. It made him look a fool. Once he learned the King was there, with his mistress, his voice became very tight-lipped, according to Wally.

When the call was over, the King said that Hardinge had suggested he come straight back. The Prime Minister's business was very urgent: he ought to be granted an audience that same day.

'I know what he wants to say to me, and I don't want to hear it,' the King said. 'Especially not today. It's Sunday – the day of rest. I'm not at anyone's beck and call. Not Hardinge's and not Baldwin's.'

Wally's hands clenched at her side in anxiety. 'Oh, please, sir, please don't antagonise Baldwin. Things are difficult enough. And please don't risk them knowing you're here.'

'I thought you were pleased to see me,' he said.

'Of course I am, but I haven't suffered two weeks in this hellish place just to have my divorce thrown out of court.'

'You fret too much, darling,' the King said, beaming, taking hold of her arm and stroking her hand. The ruby bracelet glinted in the dull light. 'Everything's going to be all right. I'm not worried, so you shouldn't be – isn't that right, Emma?' Luckily, he didn't expect a reply from her. 'I'll go back later today. Can't set off until after dark, anyway, in case I'm seen. Baldwin can wait. Kings don't jump to attention for prime ministers. It's the other way round.'

CHAPTER ELEVEN

The schools inspector, Frank Clarke, was slightly apologetic. His grandmother had been a maid at Morland Place, where she had received such a good grounding that she had made a good marriage, and his grandfather had been educated at St Edmund's School, a free school founded by the Morlands, enabling him to better himself. So where he might have been stern, he treated Polly with something close to deference. It didn't stop him pointing out, however, that universal education was not just free in England, it was compulsory.

'Your son *must* go to school, ma'am,' he said. 'That is the law. And I'm afraid if you don't comply there will be a court order and a serious fine.'

Polly frowned. 'I'm not *keeping* him out of school – it's just that I hadn't thought about it. Our boys have usually been educated at home. I know my father was, and my brother.'

Clarke nodded encouragingly. 'There is no reason that Alexander should not be, as long as proper provision is made. There must be regular hours, and a lesson plan must be approved. And there will, of course, be inspection from time to time to see that he is progressing. You will be engaging a tutor, I suppose?'

'Um,' said Polly. 'Is that necessary?' It wasn't that she didn't want to, it was that she hadn't time. And where did you even start looking for a live-in tutor, these days?

'The education department must be satisfied that your son is receiving as good an education as he would receive at school.' He studied her expression, clearly trying to fathom her thoughts. 'If you haven't an arrangement in place, Mrs Morland, might I suggest it would be easier all round if you sent him to school? I dare say he would enjoy it, you know. Boys like to be with other boys. He would probably be happier at school than all alone in the schoolroom here and no-one to play with.'

'Oh, very well. I expect you're right,' Polly said. 'I'll see to it.'

'Straight away, ma'am,' Clarke said, managing a little strictness. 'He must be in school on Monday morning.'

Polly didn't want to part with her boy. She would miss having him around, and she wondered how he would react to the confinement, when he was used to scrambling about the country on his pony, or going off on expeditions on foot with the dogs. But Clarke was right: he ought to have other boys his own age to play with.

At least there would be no difficulty in finding him a school – St Edmund's was practically Morland property.

She was about to go and find Alec to break the news to him, when John Burton came in, having been out at Eastfield Farm that morning to look at a roof repair. He saw her thoughtful frown and said, 'Is something the matter?'

'The school inspector was here. I have to send Alec to school.'

'Ah. Yes, of course, it is past time. You don't want him getting behind the other boys, do you?'

'I hope they don't fill his mind with rubbish.'

'It's a very good school,' Burton said.

'But he needs to learn about the estate.'

'He needs schooling too. It will make him a better Master.'

'I don't know about that. I went to school, and I don't

think it did me any good at all. I don't remember a single thing I learned.'

'It was all over in twenty minutes,' Kit said to Emma, as they drove down the A1 for a shooting weekend in Bedfordshire. 'She was very nervous going in, but Birkett, her lawyer, simply asked her questions to which she had to reply, "Yes," so she couldn't go wrong. She said the beastly judge had a head cold, and spent the whole time blowing his nose and coughing. There was one moment when he just sat and glared at Birkett without saying anything, and she was sure he was going to deny her the decree. But he was just waiting for a sneeze to arrive. Anyway, he awarded the nisi. The police and detectives bundled her out of the back door away from the press, and she drove straight back to London. She's at Cumberland Terrace now, sorting out her goods and chattels.' He gave a snort of laughter. 'As well as all the stuff from Bryanston Court, HM apparently had a whole vanload of choice pieces from Buckingham Palace delivered – furniture, mirrors, a lot of very valuable silver, even some pictures. And she'd hardly got her furs off when he turned up with cold pheasant sandwiches and even colder champagne. Along with a gigantic emerald and platinum congratulations-darling-you're-nearly-divorced ring.'

'If she goes about sporting what looks like an engagement ring and the King's Proctor gets to hear about it, there goes her divorce,' said Emma.

'Probably better all round if he did block it. I met Bob Boothby in Regent Street, and he said he'd heard that when Baldwin had his meeting with HM, he urged him to call off the divorce, and the King said he couldn't possibly interfere in a private decision of Mrs Simpson's, which he had nothing whatever to do with. Which apparently made Baldwin blink and ask for a whisky-and-soda.'

'Well, nearly everyone thinks they are lovers,' Emma said, with a shrug.

'And then our gallant PM asked if it was absolutely necessary to marry Mrs S, and hinted delicately that certain things are customarily allowed to a monarch that are not allowed to the ordinary man.'

'Brave indeed.'

'And HM pretended to look shocked and said there was no question of that, that Mrs S was a lady, and he was going to marry her.'

'Isn't there *any* way to stop him? What about the Royal Marriages Act?'

'No good. It only says that royal marriages must be approved by the monarch. But for a king to marry against the advice of his government would be unconstitutional. I was talking about that with Boothby. He said if the Cabinet told him he couldn't marry Wally and he persisted, the entire government would resign.'

Emma shook her head. 'But you know what he's like – opposition just makes him more stubborn. And if the government resigned, what then?'

'There'd be a general election, with the King's Matter as the chief issue. That would convulse the country and damage our reputation abroad. Boothby said he'd heard that Baldwin is thinking of appealing to Wally, begging her to go abroad.'

'But David'd cut his throat. Or follow her,' said Emma.

'It's the next left,' Kit said, and waited until she'd made the turn before he went on, 'I don't believe he'd really kill himself. He's too self-absorbed. No, I'm afraid Wally's got him for life, poor thing.'

'Can't *you* persuade her to go away? She listens to you. If she went back to America and didn't tell him where she was going, he couldn't follow her, could he?'

'I could try. But she's almost as stubborn in her way as he is. And, of course, she still doesn't really understand the British Constitution and the limits on monarchy. As long as he keeps telling her it will be all right in the end, she's inclined to believe him because, after all, a king can do anything he likes, can't he? And then she'd be queen, and even with David attached that must be a dazzling prospect.'

'I'm afraid you're right,' Emma said. 'Oh dear, let's forget about it for now, and concentrate on enjoying the weekend. Look, is that the other car up ahead? They've made good time.'

The servants, children and dogs had gone on ahead in a separate motor. One of the nice things about their hosts this weekend was that they had young children and had extended the invitation to the two girls as well. It made it comfortably like home.

Polly was out for a ride with Jessie. 'That's a nice-looking youngster,' she said.

Jessie leaned forward and ran a hand up an ear. 'Yes, I like a horse with long ears. They're always good-tempered. He's for Lady Grey. He's ready now, but she wants me to show him to hounds a few times before she takes him.' She glanced across at Zephyr. 'You ought to start bringing on a new hunter. How old is Zephyr now?'

'Twelve,' said Polly. 'We've a few more good years together.'

'Yes, but a second horse would allow you to stay out longer.'

Polly smiled. 'You wouldn't happen to have a youngster on your hands, by any chance?'

'As a matter of fact, I've a couple of very nice three-year-olds. Come over and have a look some time,' Jessie said, and changed the subject. 'How is the young master taking to school?'

'There was no more resistance once I said he could ride to school. I believe he's the envy of his class. But I think he's enjoying being with other boys. I do miss him, though.'

'At least he comes home every afternoon. My darling Thomas is all the way over in Preston, and only visits one weekend in four.'

'What's the name of the college, again?'

'Myerscough. It's something of a disgrace that Yorkshire doesn't have its own agricultural college, and he has to go all the way to Lancashire. But Bertie's pretty upset that he wants to go to agricultural college at all, instead of learning at his father's feet.'

'I can see that would dent his pride,' said Polly.

'Thomas pointed out that there's lots of new scientific advances, these days, that he ought to know about. He can be terribly tactful for an eighteen-year-old.'

'At least he *wants* to follow in his father's footsteps,' said Polly. 'It must be hard to build up a business and find your son wants to do something else entirely.'

'I told him that, but he misses having Tom around. Then there's Catherine, worrying about her coming-out ball. Afraid no-one will ask her to dance.'

'I'll have a word with James, tell him if there's any lull to throw himself into the breach.'

'That should do it. He's handsome and unmarried, and all the local females look at him with cinema eyes.'

'Cinema eyes?'

'You know – the way the female star looks at the male star.' She did an imitation.

Polly laughed. 'You look exactly like Mary Pickford! James is a worry to me,' she went on, with a sigh. 'He had such bad luck – gave his heart to the American woman, Meredith, and she went back to America without a word to him. And as soon as he transferred his affections to someone new, she got murdered.'

Jessie glanced sideways at her companion. 'You didn't have much luck either, did you? But it's been a long time – have you never fancied anyone else?'

'I think I'm just too particular,' Polly said lightly. They came to the place where the track branched off towards Knapton, and she checked Zephyr and said, 'Let's not go that way. I hate seeing North Field all cut up, and concrete and bricks everywhere. It looks so dreadful.'

'People have to have somewhere to live,' Jessie said. 'It will look all right when it's finished.'

'I know. But let's go on towards Rufforth. We can have a gallop across the grounds of Rufforth Hall, and come back by the Whin.'

They took the left fork, and Polly said, 'Tell me more about the ball. I suppose you'll have it all to do again in a few years' time for Ottilie?'

'I don't think so. Ottilie has two passions – horses and aeroplanes. Her greatest hero is Aunt Helen: she's living proof that a woman can fly. When she found out that women couldn't join the RAF, she cried for an hour.'

The King opened Parliament on the 3rd of November, and appeared, many said, calm and happy and, at least from a distance, young and handsome, like a smiling Prince Charming.

A week later, Kit met Chips Channon, the Member for Southend, at his club, and learned that Mrs Simpson's name had been mentioned in the House. A question had been raised about the arrangements for the Coronation, and a Labour MP, John McGovern, shouted out, 'Why bother, in view of the gambling at Lloyd's that there will not be one?'

There had been cries of 'Shame! Shame!' and McGovern shouted, 'Yes, Mrs Simpson—' and the rest of his sentence became inaudible through the bellows of outrage.

'I think that's a Rubicon,' Kit said.

'You're right,' said Channon. 'I passed Sir John Simon afterwards in confabulation with Eden, and heard him saying that Baldwin is thinking of putting it to the colonies. Not sure if he's hoping they'll say, "Sure, old man, he can marry anyone he likes," or whether he's hoping a robust four-letter response will make HM think again.' He shrugged. 'At least he'll be kept out of harm's way for a while: inspecting the fleet on the twelfth, and a tour of the South Wales coal fields on the sixteenth.'

'I hear South Wales is pretty grim,'said Kit.

'Yes, that ought to take some of the bounce out of him,` said Channon.

It didn't take long for Basil to grasp the limitations of his salary. His Spartan lodgings and landlady's cooking did not shock someone who'd been to an English public school, but having no jingle in his pocket limited his social life, and he was a sociable creature. Bob Zennor often, tactfully, paid for the drinks when they went to the pub after work, but Basil didn't like to leech on him too much. And he had other wants, too. What he really needed was a rich girlfriend.

His interest in Miranda Byrne began when Zennor told him she was privately wealthy, and she had the advantage of being accessible – his job took up a lot of his time. She was undeniably attractive; he had been told she was very intelligent, which he had no reason to doubt; and her clothes showed she had taste as well as money. She seemed in every way qualified to become his companion. But so far he hadn't got anywhere with her. She acknowledged him when he passed her in the building with the same brisk greeting she gave everyone else. He had managed to bump into her 'accidentally' in various places around the building, but despite considerable outlay of charm, she wasn't responding to him.

He had learned that she was rather left-inclined, as indeed was the whole newspaper, so he got hold of a couple of suitable books, and allowed himself to be seen with his nose in them when he encountered her. The first time Miss Byrne only glanced at him and frowned. The second time, she definitely looked at the book, and seemed as though she was about to speak. On the third occasion he contrived to drop the book at her feet and be slower than her in picking it up.

She looked at the sticker on the cover as she handed it back to him. 'The Left Book Shop?' she said. 'I'm surprised you know it.'

Basil had never been there – he had borrowed the book from another fellow in the newsroom – but he'd seen the address on the sticker. So he said, 'Charing Cross Road isn't exactly out of the way. I wonder they can afford the rent, though. I'd have thought somewhere like Peckham would be cheaper.'

'They wouldn't get so many people coming in, in Peckham,' she said.

'I suppose that's true,' Basil said. 'But how *do* they afford it?'

'Wealthy supporters pay for the premises.' She looked at him as though reassessing him. She indicated the book, which was called *Post-Structuralism and the Fallacy of the Chartist Legacy*. 'Are you interested in those sorts of ideas?'

'Isn't everybody?' he said, rather than tell a lie. He'd had difficulty reading the title, let alone anything inside.

'I hadn't realised,' she said. 'I thought you were rather a—'

'Yes?' he prompted hopefully.

She didn't answer directly. 'Would you like to come to a party tomorrow night?' she asked. 'Some friends of mine – they don't live in Peckham, though.'

'I'm quite prepared to forgo Peckham,' he said, and to his relief, she smiled. He'd been afraid she had no sense of humour, which would have made things difficult. 'What sort of a party?'

'Are there different sorts?' she said. So he assumed there'd be food, drink, dancing and – if he was really lucky – the opportunity to steal a kiss at some point. 'Just some like-minded friends talking about important issues,' she went on. His heart sank. But still he said yes. It was progress, wasn't it?

★ ★ ★

253

The earnest young man in the sleeveless Fair Isle pullover was holding forth. Every now and then, at moments of vehemence, a lank forelock of dark hair fell over his pale brow and he had to brush it back. His round glasses shone. Everything about him shone with innocent conviction.

'We must embrace the proletarian life. We must live alongside them and work alongside them. Because the proletariat are the only authentic people. Only they live a truly natural human life.'

Outside, the November evening was cold and sleety, and Basil had put on his warmest sweater over a shirt and undervest. But the party was in a basement, with a fire burning in both the small rooms, and a gas stove in the kitchen alcove where someone was cooking sausages, and the heat, together with that generated by the guests, was making Basil uncomfortable. It was hard to concentrate on what the young man was saying.

'Why should the owner of a factory take all the profits, when his factory is useless to him without the efforts of his labourers? They are the ones who create the wealth, so they ought to share in it. That's only fair, isn't it? You can *see* that.'

The company nodded and murmured. They could see that. It was only fair.

'And since only the state can be disinterested, it follows that the factory ought to belong to the state, so that it can oversee the distribution. So that everyone gets an equal share. We are all equal, aren't we?'

They murmured agreement. They were all equal.

'Communism is the only rational organisation of society. Everything must be owned by the state so that it's owned by everyone. Private property must be outlawed. As Marx said, "Property is theft."'

Basil stirred. 'That wasn't Marx,' he said.

He wasn't even sure he'd said it to be heard, but the

earnest young man was thrown off his stride. He turned the headlamps of his spectacles towards him. 'I beg your pardon?'

'Marx didn't say property was theft. That was Pierre-Joseph Proudhon. Nineteenth-century French anarchist.' He only knew that because, purely by chance, he'd had to look it up for an article.

The young man gave him a stern but kindly look. 'I think you'll find it was Marx,' he said. And then, 'Are you an anarchist?'

All eyes swivelled on Basil. Plainly being an anarchist wouldn't go down well – though he had no idea how they differed from Communists. He waved a dismissing hand. 'Do carry on,' he said.

After a doubtful pause, the young man resumed. 'All work should command the same wages. Why do managers get more than workers? We all have to buy food and clothes and pay rent. The bosses' wages should be taken away from them and divided up among the workers. That's how they do it in Russia.'

Basil saw the beauty of that idea. He would like to receive a slice of the salary of the top earners at the *Messenger*. He had a sneaking suspicion, however, that it could not be quite as easy as that.

'But how do you motivate people to work hard and get on if their efforts won't earn them any more wages?' he asked, when the earnest young man drew breath.

'That's a capitalist question,' the young man said disapprovingly. 'You're coming at it from the wrong direction. You see, in the Communist state we all belong to one another, and the good of one is the good of all. You work hard for love of your brother man.'

Basil could see a problem right there, but the young man went straight on.

'You have to purge the population of individualism. Where you have individualism, you have ownership. Ownership fosters greed, and greed leads to war. You only have to look at Germany. Capitalism *means* war. It's inevitable. Eventually, when Communism spreads over the whole world, conflict will be a thing of the past.'

Someone raised the question of free love, and Basil stopped listening. He wondered where Miranda was. He had got separated from her, and then had become marooned in this corner. Presumably she was in the other room, where more voices were having more discussions, with the addition of music from a gramophone – though turned down disappointingly low. You couldn't dance to that. He was afraid they weren't intending to dance. But he wanted another drink – and he hoped the sausages might be ready by now. It was enough to be worth the effort of getting to his feet.

He just wished the comrades weren't so earnest *all* the time. Surely laughing wasn't a capitalist evil.

The weather, though it was November, did its best for Charlotte: it was cold and a little blowy, but it stopped raining at about half past ten, and by eleven there was even a glimmer of sunshine. It came and went, but it allowed the newly united couple to pause on the steps of the church long enough for the society and magazine photographers to get their shots.

The wedding breakfast was at the Belgrave Square house, which was another reason for Violet to be happy. There was something just a little vulgar, she thought, about having it in a hotel, though of course many people had no choice. And because this time they were marrying a daughter, they were not at the mercy of other people's taste. 'I wish we had another daughter to marry one day,' she whispered to Avis in the reception line.

He pressed her hand, rather than reply. The doctor had said she mustn't have any more babies. Besides, even if she did have a daughter now, they would be in their sixties by the time she was old enough to marry, and surely, he thought, the strange female urge to arrange weddings would have worn off by then.

Almost the best thing about the wedding, in Violet's view, was that Jessie and Bertie had come, and were staying on afterwards in Belgrave Square for several days. It was years since they'd had time together. Jack and Helen had also come, though Jack could not get leave from work to stay on. But they would have Sunday to be all together again, they who had played together as children.

After the receiving line and before sitting down, when everyone was circulating, Richard found his sister. 'Happy?'

'Oh, yes,' she said.

'I'm glad Robert came.'

'He hardly waited to say hello before telling me his wife is expecting,' Charlotte said. 'She looked embarrassed, but he was as smug as could be.' She looked cautiously at her brother. 'Are you and Cynthia—?'

'No,' he said, with a forgiving smile. 'You sound just like my pa-in-law. Every time we see them. Handshake for me, kiss for Cynthia, then, "Anything to tell me?" "Daddy, stop!" says Cyn, blushing like a rose. And he looks unrepentant and says, "Time waits for no man. I want to hold my grandson in my arms before I die." I have the greatest difficulty in not saying, "You could hardly hold him afterwards, could you?"'

Charlotte laughed. 'I suppose that's something I have to look forward to.'

'Except that I can't imagine Avis ever being so vulgar as to enquire. Have you and Launde decided where you're going to live?'

'We've taken a flat at Hertford Street, in one of those new buildings. Straight lines, lots of light, parquet floors. Nothing old or dusty or splintery,' Charlotte said happily. 'Mummy was a bit put out at first, but she's so glad we're on the right side of the Park, and not somewhere like Kensington, she's willing to overlook it. She and Avis want me to choose things out of Tunstead Hall – you know, antiques – and I don't know how to tell them I want everything modern.'

'We didn't have that problem,' Richard said. 'Pa-in-law just provided a cheque, and Cynthia and her mother chose everything from Heal's.'

Charlotte looked hesitant. 'You didn't mind—?'

'Lord, no. Men don't care about interiors – haven't you learned that yet?'

'Not true. Milo cares. Luckily we have the same taste. We're going to have fun doing the flat together.' She hesitated.

'What?'

'Oh, nothing. Well, he did say doing up the flat would keep me busy while he's at work. As if he doesn't expect me to be going back to work at Dolphin.'

'Married ladies don't go to work.'

'Cynthia does,' Charlotte pointed out.

'Only for a few hours a week. And only until they have her replacement trained. Honestly, I wouldn't mind if she wanted to, but her father wouldn't like it. And she seems quite happy pottering at home.' He examined his sister's thoughtful face. 'You may have to get used to it, Charley. Most men don't like their wives to work.'

'I thought Milo was different.'

'Well, perhaps he is,' Richard said hastily, and changed the subject. 'Vienna for your honeymoon, I gather? Will that be nice in November?

'Gosh, yes! Vienna's better seen in cold weather, Milo says. In fact, it's best in the snow, he says. And there'll be plenty to do. Opera, ballet, concerts. The galleries and museums are wonderful, apparently. Lots of intellectual life – he says there's a café on every corner, stuffed with philosophers and thinkers. The wonderful dancing horses. Riding in the park. The gilded palaces.'

'The cake,' Richard said solemnly. 'I believe there is a great deal of cake in Vienna.'

She laughed and smacked his hand lightly. 'Make fun of me if you want.'

'Oh, I will. You're my little sister. It's expected.'

'But we'll have a heavenly time. And we can always do the traditional places another year – you know, Florence and Paris and so on.'

'Be sure when you do that you book a Nevinson's Holiday. Then I can come along as your courier.'

'Ass!

'I'm serious. You have to support my business. Remember I'm a poor second son – we have to make our own way in the world.'

'Eldest sons sometimes have to, as well,' she said. 'Milo didn't inherit anything. He's having to do it all himself.'

'Good for him! And when you've an hour or two to spare, you can explain to me exactly how he's doing it, because nobody seems to know.'

'Ass again!' she said affectionately.

The King came back from South Wales in buoyant mood, having received a warm welcome wherever he went, which convinced him that the People were on his side. He summoned the Prime Minister to Buckingham Palace and informed him brightly that he was going to marry Wallis Simpson as soon as she was free, whether the government approved or not.

Eddie, who had been there, told Oliver about it afterwards. 'Baldwin tried to persuade him that a shock like this could cause the Empire to break up, split the country and cause untold damage to the Crown. But I could see – I could actually *see* – that HM wasn't listening. He was just waiting for Baldwin to stop talking. He had that fatuous half-smile on his face that tells me he's thinking about *her*. And he said if they tried to stop him marrying her, he would abdicate.'

Oliver was shocked. 'He actually *said* that?'

'Yes, but I don't think he meant it,' Eddie said, running

a hand through his hair in remembered frustration. 'It was most peculiar. It was as if there were two conversations going on, Baldwin saying one thing and the King hearing something entirely different. Poor old Baldwin retired baffled in the end, practically in tears, and afterwards the King walked about the room in a state of high excitement asking what Baldwin was up to, and saying it was a plot by the PM and "the nebulous figures around him" – his words – to test the strength of his love for Mrs S.'

'That's madness,' Oliver said flatly.

'I think he *is* actually insane. He said to me that if their real intention was to make him give Wally up by pointing a big gun at his head then they had badly misjudged their man. He said they had struck at the very roots of his pride. He said only the most faint-hearted lover would fail to be roused by the challenge. Nothing Baldwin had said about the Empire, the Crown, the country stuck at all. "They" had impugned his love for Wally, and he was going to show them. D'you know what his last words to Baldwin were? As he shook his hand and sent him away, he said, "She is the most wonderful woman I've ever met."'

Word soon got about that Baldwin had told Sir Donald Somervell, the Attorney General, to start work on drafting an Abdication Bill. Whether he had taken the King seriously, or was merely covering all angles, was unknown.

But Oliver witnessed for himself a few days later the proof that Eddie was right, and that to the King, abdication was simply a counter-threat to prove how serious he was about Mrs Simpson, and that he didn't actually mean to carry it out. Oliver and Verena were guests at a dinner-party given by Chips Channon, at which the King and the Duke of Kent were present. The King was in high good humour. He had been telling Oliver and Kent about his trip to South Wales, and how the people loved him – 'The miners lined up and lit their Davy lamps and sang "Men of Harlech" to me,' and he suddenly broke off to say, beaming at his brother as if it were good news simply bursting out of him, 'I must tell you, George, that I'm going to marry Wally Simpson.'

Kent looked stunned. Whatever rumours he must have heard, he had not before had a direct declaration from his brother. Seemingly at a loss, he asked, 'What will she call herself?'

The King's eyes twinkled with good humour. 'What will she call herself? Why, what do you think? Queen of England, of course.'

'She is going to be Queen?' Kent gasped.

'Yes, and Empress of India – the whole bag of tricks.'

He believed, Oliver realised then, that he could 'get away with it' – could marry Wally on his own terms and make her Queen, no matter what the government, the Royal Family, or anyone else thought about it. He was infatuated, in every sense of the word.

His good humour continued throughout the evening, amounting almost to a state of euphoria. Oliver noted that, whoever he was talking to, he would turn every few moments to gaze at Wally, seated next to Victor Cazalet, the MP for Chippenham, and his face would fill with a radiance of adoration. If it hadn't been so mad, it would have been touching. Oliver looked at Wally in sheer wonder. How could this thin, plain, harsh-voiced woman be elevated in HM's mind to archangel status?

Kit and Emma were summoned to the Fort again for the weekend.

'It's such a relief to get away from London,' Wally said, when they arrived. 'I don't feel safe in Cumberland Terrace. I'm supposed to have armed protection, but all they give me is two detectives who sit in a car outside all night. Probably asleep most of the time.'

'You don't really think you're in danger, do you?' Emma asked.

'There are elements,' she said darkly. 'I've heard there are those who wouldn't mind if I was assassinated.'

'I'm sure that's not true.'

'You're such an innocent, Emma! You don't realise there are all sorts of secret agencies operating in the shadows. MI this and Special that. Secret dossiers and hidden cameras. You Brits are not the folksy innocents you pretend to be. But come on in and have a drink. There's a new idea I want to tell you about.'

The Metcalfes were already there, and after greetings had been exchanged, they sat down and Wally told her news. It seemed that Esmond Harmsworth, the chairman of Associated Newspapers, had suggested, over lunch at Claridge's, a morganatic marriage.

'Apparently it's popular on the Continent,' Wally said. 'It would mean I wasn't called Queen – well, I don't mind being Duchess of Lancaster – and any children of the marriage wouldn't be able to succeed.' She glanced round to see that the King was out of earshot, across the room mixing cocktails, and lowered her voice. 'Well, there aren't going to be any children, so that doesn't matter. So it looks like a good solution to the whole muddle.'

Kit said, 'Morganatic marriage is not in our constitution, Wally.'

She rolled her eyes. 'Again with the constitution! Just because a thing hasn't been done that way before, is it any reason not to do it that way now?'

'Um – well – yes,' Kit said helplessly.

Fruity Metcalfe helped him out. 'There would have to be a special Act of Parliament, you see. Otherwise the marriage wouldn't be legal.'

The King arrived at that moment with a tray of glasses. 'Are you talking about Harmsworth's idea? I must say, I don't like it. Left-handed marriage!' He handed out the cocktails. 'I'm not going to stand for you being short-changed, darling,' he said, putting her glass tenderly into her hand. 'You are to be Queen, not the Duchess of Lancaster.'

'But if it means we can marry without all this trouble,' Wally urged.

'Baldwin and the whole bally lot of them would still have to approve it. Why should they have the final say? I don't see why we should make all these concessions. It smacks of grovelling, to me.'

'Well, let's just think about it,' Wally urged. 'There's no harm in Esmond putting it to Baldwin, and seeing how we get on. Put some music on – something lively to cheer us up.'

Later, on the way up to change, Fruity stopped Kit on the landing and said, 'She doesn't realise it would have to go before Parliament, and Parliament would almost certainly reject it.'

Kit agreed. 'Not only that, the Dominions would never wear it. Australia and New Zealand have Catholic prime ministers. And the Irish Free State would have a fit.'

Fruity sighed. 'I have a feeling that Harmsworth only put up the idea to put Baldwin in a spot. He must know it's a non-starter. He wants Baldwin to bungle the whole Wally business and have to resign.'

'That's very profound of you, Fruity,' Kit said. 'I haven't heard you make so much sense since 1919.'

'I do have the occasional idea,' Fruity said modestly.

Emma was dressing when Wally sent her maid to summon her. Emma put on a dressing-gown, her hair still loose, and found Wally dressed, but without make-up or jewellery, her Indian-black hair hanging on her shoulders. Her eyes were red. She waved Emma to a chair, from which she had to eject the dog, Mr Loo, first. He lifted a resentful lip at her, then disappeared under the dressing-table's skirt.

'Has something happened?' Emma asked.

'We've had such a row,' Wally said. 'Beaverbrook rang him, and David told him about the morganatic idea. Beaverbrook said he should withdraw it at once. It gives Baldwin too strong a hand. He said the best thing would be for me to go away until after the Coronation. Let that take place, he said, then let the country and the Commonwealth get to know me gradually through charitable works and public appearances, until they realise what a good thing I am for David and for the throne. I told David I was quite happy with that, and he absolutely exploded.'

'Oh dear!'

'He said it was all part of a plot started by the Hardinges, that they'd been angling to get rid of me from the beginning. He said he absolutely would not allow me to leave the country. He said nothing would stop him marrying me. I begged him to think about it – I said we had time, the divorce won't be final until April – but there was no reasoning with him. He started raving about everyone being against him. He said, let them find out how they'd get on without him. I said, "What are you talking about?" and he said if the government would not approve the marriage, he would be ready to leave the throne.'

It was not the first time, of course, that Emma had heard of the threat, but it seemed to be the first time Wally had.

'I started crying – I begged him not to talk like that. I said it was the last thing I wanted, to come between him and the Crown. But he wouldn't listen. He said if I didn't agree to stay, he would summon the Prime Minister right away, that very minute, and tell him he was abdicating.'

'I'm so sorry,' Emma said. 'How did you leave it with him?'

'I said I'd stay, of course.' She sighed heavily. 'I feel so ill. My nerves are in shreds. My ulcers are killing me. And now my heart is playing up – palpitations.' She looked up. 'I'd give anything for this to be over. You know I've had poison-pen letters? Threats to my life. I've had stones thrown at my windows. I hardly dare leave the house. Every time a flashbulb goes off I think it's someone trying to shoot me.'

'What will you do?'

She was silent a long moment. 'I'm going to go away. Promise me you won't say anything to David? I can't tell him because I know what would happen. I'll make up some excuse about being fitted for gowns in Paris, and go abroad until after the Coronation. Or perhaps for ever,' she added, in a low voice. Another pause. Then she said, 'I think everyone would like that – apart from *him*, of course. After a while my name will be forgotten.' She brooded, staring at her hands in her lap. 'It's all Ernest's fault. I never wanted the divorce. And Mary – she was always jealous of me. This last month . . . You don't know what it's like, Emma. Used by politicians, hated by jealous women, accused of everything. I'll never forgive the American press for what they've done, stirring up people against me. I'm flattened out.'

'You'll come about,' Emma said.

Wally looked up sharply. 'Of course I will. I'll get out from under this load some time. But just now . . . My God, Emma, I'm so darn tired.'

The British press had kept quiet, and only a thin little trickle had leaked out to those with access to the American press. But on the 1st of December, the Bishop of Bradford, addressing the annual diocesan conference, criticised the King for his non-attendance at church. The criticism had necessarily to be indirect, so he couched it in oblique terms – so oblique that the press barons believed he was referring to the situation with Mrs Simpson. When the speech was reported in a northern newspaper, they thought the paper had broken ranks, and they were afraid of being left behind. The floodgates burst: on the 2nd, there were photographs of the King and Mrs Simpson everywhere, articles and critical editorials in the leading papers.

The King and Wally were at the Fort, and it came as a terrible shock. Accompanied by Eddie, who was equerrying, the King drove up to London and summoned Baldwin to a meeting at Buckingham Palace. As the car passed an underground station, the King said, 'Look at that!' The paper-seller at the station entrance had his placard on display, and the words stood out, heavy black on white, like a bellow: 'THE KING AND MRS SIMPSON'.

'How dare they?' he cried, his face darkening.

It was in an ill mood that he received Baldwin, furious about the bishop's impertinence and the treachery of the press. Baldwin tried to calm him, but he had no good news to impart: he'd had the replies from the Dominions. The prime ministers were strongly opposed to a morganatic marriage; so were the Cabinet, the leader of the Opposition and the leader of the Liberals. Indeed, in Canada, Australia and New Zealand they would not countenance any kind of marriage between the monarch and a twice-divorced woman.

'Well, there are very few people in Canada and Australia,' the King snapped, 'so their opinion doesn't count for a great deal.'

Patiently, kindly, as though talking to a child, the Prime Minister tried to make him understand the responsibilities of the Crown, to see that there were things more important than his personal life, but he said stubbornly, furiously, that the only important thing was their happiness, his and Mrs Simpson's, and that the people understood that, if the government didn't. He should make a broadcast, he said, place himself at the mercy of his people.

Baldwin paled, and said it would be unconstitutional to appeal to the people over the heads of their elected representatives. It would be a threat to democracy itself. The King's reply was that Mrs Simpson was the most wonderful woman in the world and he was determined to marry her. Two minds with such divergent templates could never come together. The audience limped to an end.

'One more thing, sir,' Baldwin said, as the King prepared to depart. 'I think it only fair to warn you that Geoffrey Dawson, the editor of *The Times*, has told me he is to publish a very hostile leader tomorrow, a strong attack on Mrs Simpson.'

'But you mustn't let him!' the King exclaimed. 'You must have it stopped!'

'Sir, I cannot do that. It is not within my power. We have a free press in this country. The government *cannot* interfere with it.'

Baldwin did not say 'even if it wanted to', but Eddie supplied it in his mind. Dawson was a staunch supporter of the government, unlike Harmsworth or Beaverbrook.

The King was silent on the way back to the Fort. At one point, Eddie dared to ask him, 'Do you mean to abdicate, sir?'

'Oh, no,' the King said. 'I think I might go to Switzerland, and let them have to call me back. Then I'll say I'm only coming back if Mrs Simpson is by my side.'

At the Fort, he told her about the hostile leader expected in *The Times* the next morning, and said it was no longer safe for her to stay, even at the Fort. He had evidently been thinking it out during the journey. 'Kath and Herman Rogers keep offering us their villa at Cannes. You must go there, and stay until it's safe to come back. Perry Brownlow can travel with you, and the detective. Ladbroke can drive you to Newhaven and you can catch the ten o'clock ferry to Dieppe. You can be at the villa by Sunday afternoon.'

Wally, white and exhausted, only nodded. She had nothing more to argue; she was only relieved to be getting away.

Tears flooded his eyes. 'You must wait for me, darling,' he said. 'No matter how long it takes. I will never give you up.'

'My patience with him is frayed to the limit,' Eddie said, when he dined with Kit and Emma on Sunday night, his current period as equerry over, 'but even I couldn't help being moved when they said goodbye.'

'Tears?' Kit asked.

'Floods. He clung to her hand until the last minute – she had to wind the window up to make him let go. And he said, "Wherever you reach tonight, no matter what time it is, you must telephone me. God bless you, my darling." Then she drove off, and he watched until the car was out of sight.'

'It sounds like something in a movie,' Kit said.

'All day yesterday he kept talking about her, wondering where she was, how far they'd got, when she would telephone. I've been hoping that once she was out of the way he'd gradually return to normal and we might work on him. But I'm not sure that's going to happen. Without her, he's like a lost dog. He doesn't seem to function at all. He must have told me a dozen times that she was the most wonderful woman in the world, and the best friend he ever had.'

'Let's hope the press don't get on her trail.'

'She's terrified of assassination,' Eddie said. 'She wrote out her will before she left, you know, just in case.' He brooded a moment. 'I had a few words with her, while they were carrying her bags down. She said to me, "You and the others must find a way to make the King forget this marriage completely. He must end the crisis and keep the throne." I said something noncommittal, and she looked at me pretty sharply, and said, "Do you think I wanted any of this? I have to get away to keep my sanity." So I said I didn't think any of us could change the King's mind about anything, and she said, "You must try. The Coronation *has* to go ahead. And one day, perhaps, I can come back as royal mistress. That's all I wanted."'

Kit shook his head. 'I expect she really means it now. But it was open to her at any point to withdraw the divorce application. She still could.'

'I don't think she thinks of that,' Eddie said. 'I think she feels completely helpless.'

'You men don't understand what it is to be a woman,' Emma said. 'We have no power to direct our lives. Men command us, until we lose all will of our own.'

Kit startled them by bursting out laughing. 'There speaks the woman who drove an ambulance at the Front amid shock and shell, ran her own decorating business, and uses her fortune to build blocks of flats to house the working classes. I am completely in awe of her, and hardly dare speak in her presence, unless she speaks first.'

'You are a dreadful man,' Emma said, shaking her head. 'What am I to do with you?'

'Anything you like,' he said, grinning.

Events staggered on, with Cabinet meetings, speeches in Parliament, anguished telephone calls. Influential figures scuttled in and out of Downing Street at all hours, collars turned up against the freezing fog. There were articles in every newspaper, even some demonstrations in the streets: crowds gathered outside Buckingham Palace shouting, 'We want the King.' Others marched along Piccadilly with placards saying, 'No to Mrs Simpson' and 'Remember the War Dead.' As Kit remarked to Emma, 'HM and Wally still believe the working classes are for them. But they, above all, want their monarch to be virtuous.'

'A lot of the younger set are for the marriage. They think it's romantic.'

'But it's the Dominions that matter,' Kit said. 'There's no way past that.'

Preparations for the Coronation had been halted, dealers were trying to buy up Edward VIII postage stamps, and the King still would not make clear his intentions. Even Baldwin had no idea – as he constantly had to tell ministers, ambassadors and high commissioners – when or even if the King would go.

The person suffering the most was the Duke of York, who

pressed for an interview with his brother and was constantly put off. Frail, desperately shy, and with a crippling speech impediment, he was terrified of having the throne thrust upon him. To add to his troubles, his duchess, on whom he relied heavily, was ill with influenza and unable to support him. Sick with dread, he called at Number Ten every day, going through the garden entrance to avoid being seen, to beg Baldwin for clarification. The rest of the Royal Family might be starting to think that perhaps David had better go, since he couldn't be trusted any more, but Bertie would have done anything to keep him on the throne, had there been anything he *could* do.

It wasn't until the 9th of December that the King finally told the prime minister that he had decided to abdicate.

'Apparently what made up his mind,' Eddie told Kit, 'was a visit from Goddard. He said someone might be about to make a formal application to the King's Proctor to investigate the Simpson divorce. HM was convinced it was part of a plot by the Beaverbrook press to scare Wally into giving him up, so he decided to pre-empt it by announcing his abdication.'

So now frantic negotiations and preparations began.

'You know,' Kit said to Emma, 'I don't think he realises even now how serious this is. Eddie told me he heard from Sir John Simon that he was cheerful and smiling when he told Baldwin his decision. *I* think he believes that he can give up the throne without giving up the privileges, just go back to the life he enjoyed as Prince of Wales, while poor Bertie York does all the disagreeable duties. He thinks he'll have a honeymoon trip abroad with Wally, then come back refreshed to his old position. I don't think he understands that he'll have to live in exile, that he will never be allowed to come back.'

Emma thought about that. 'Poor Wally,' she said.

'Yes, she's for it, now. Imagine spending a lifetime with

him, in exile, on a budget, with nothing whatever to do. Golf and shopping for all eternity.'

'And not so very much shopping, either, on a budget.'

The Instrument of Abdication read:

I, Edward the Eighth of Great Britain, Ireland and the British Dominions beyond the Seas, King-Emperor of India, do hereby declare my irrevocable determination to renounce the Throne for Myself and My descendants, and My desire that effect should be given to this instrument of Abdication immediately.

'To give up the throne and the Empire because he wants to marry Mrs Simpson,' Emma said, wonderingly. 'All that for so little.'

At 1.52 p.m. on Friday, the 11th of December, the Instrument took effect, and from that moment the Duke of York became King and Emperor. His names were Albert Frederick Arthur George, and he'd always been known in the family as Bertie, but he'd been advised that Albert was too Germanic a name to sit happily with the British people. So he was to be King George VI. The ex-King was to have the title Duke of Windsor.

At the Royal Lodge, Windsor, there was a farewell dinner that evening for the royal family only: the Queen, his brothers and sister, and the Queen's brother and his wife, who had been staying with her since the beginning of the crisis. An effort had been made with flowers and pretty china to lighten the gloom of the occasion, and the Duke of Windsor at least seemed cheerful, though the Queen was nervous about what he might say in the broadcast he had persuaded the government to allow him to make. Sir John Reith and Walter Monckton were waiting for him in a specially prepared room in Windsor Castle, and he began speaking at ten o'clock to the nation.

271

At long last I am able to say a few words of my own. I have never wanted to withhold anything, but until now it has not been constitutionally possible for me to speak.

A few hours ago I discharged my last duty as King and Emperor, and now that I have been succeeded by my brother, the Duke of York, my first words must be to declare my allegiance to him. This I do with all my heart.

You all know the reasons which have impelled me to renounce the throne. But I want you to understand that in making up my mind I did not forget the country or the Empire, which, as Prince of Wales and lately as King, I have for twenty-five years tried to serve.

But you must believe me when I tell you that I have found it impossible to carry the heavy burden of responsibility and to discharge my duties as King as I would wish to do without the help and support of the woman I love.

And I want you to know that the decision I have made has been mine and mine alone. This was a thing I had to judge entirely for myself. The other person most nearly concerned has tried up to the last to persuade me to take a different course.

I have made this, the most serious decision of my life, only upon the single thought of what would, in the end, be best for all.

This decision has been made less difficult to me by the sure knowledge that my brother, with his long training in the public affairs of this country and with his fine qualities, will be able to take my place forthwith without interruption or injury to the life and progress of the Empire. And he has one matchless blessing, enjoyed by so many of you, and not bestowed on me – a happy home with his wife and children.

During these hard days I have been comforted by Her Majesty my mother and by my family. The ministers of the crown, and in particular, Mr Baldwin, the Prime Minister, have always treated me with full consideration. There has never been any constitutional difference between me and them, and between me and Parliament. Bred in the constitutional tradition by my father, I should never have allowed any such issue to arise.

Ever since I was Prince of Wales, and later on when I occupied the throne, I have been treated with the greatest kindness by all classes of the people wherever I have lived or journeyed throughout the Empire. For that I am very grateful.

I now quit altogether public affairs and I lay down my burden. It may be some time before I return to my native land, but I shall always follow the fortunes of the British race and Empire with profound interest, and if at any time in the future I can be found of service to His Majesty in a private station, I shall not fail.

And now, we all have a new King. I wish him and you, his people, happiness and prosperity with all my heart. God bless you all! God save the King!

'It was a pretty good speech,' Emma said, turning off the wireless. She had found herself unexpectedly moved, close to tears. It was so momentous, so colossally sad and unnecessary, that things had come to this.

'It was a very dishonest speech,' Kit said. He had also been moved, not for the King personally but on behalf of the country, the people, and history itself. '"I was only thinking of what was best for everyone,"' he quoted. '"There has never been any constitutional difference between me and the government." I especially liked "I did not forget the country or the Empire." How many times were they invoked to his deaf ears?'

'But I suppose there were things he had to say,' said Emma, 'or they wouldn't have let him speak at all.'

'Well, it's over now. For him, at any rate. For poor Bertie York, it's just beginning.'

After the broadcast, the ex-King went back to the Royal Lodge to say his final farewells to his family, before his departure for Austria, where on Monckton's strict instructions he was to wait out the period before the decree absolute. He did not linger long. He embraced his mother, kissed the Princess Royal and Princess Alice, shook hands with the men, bowed to his brother the King. All were making a tremendous effort to keep their upper lips stiff, and pretend that it was just the end of another day.

His black Buick was brought round, and he climbed in without looking back. Footmen closed the heavy door with a quiet click, and the Buick rolled away into the swirling fog, a very big motor-car carrying a very small man into the darkness.

As they went up to bed, Kit said, 'I wonder if Eddie will be made equerry to the new king, or if there'll be a purge.'

'But Eddie and Sarah have always been friendly with the Yorks. They live next door to them, for goodness' sake,' Emma said.

Kit yawned. 'True. But you and I might have seen our last royal invitation. We shouldn't have spent all those week-ends at the Fort.'

'As if we had a choice!' Emma exclaimed. She paused at the bedroom door. 'I keep thinking of those little York girls. They're princesses now. And quiet, good little Elizabeth will almost certainly be Queen one day.'

He recognised the tone of her voice. 'I'm sad too, darling,' he said tenderly. He examined her expression. 'Would you like me to sleep with you tonight?'

'Would you?' she said gratefully.

He put a companionable arm round her, and they went in together.

CHAPTER TWELVE

Lennie had found Rose an agent. His name was Forrest Van Kerk; nearly everyone called him Van, but those closest to him called him Woody. Lennie liked him from the first because he had been a movie actor, having played dozens of supporting roles, so he knew what was involved in standing in front of a camera. He had inherited from his father a pickle-canning company – Van Kerk pickles were a favourite in northern California – and had successfully run it before, during and after his acting career. He'd gone into agenting accidentally one day on set by representing a shy and tongue-tied fellow actor's perfectly reasonable demands to the management, and now had a small but impressive stable of clients.

He was in his forties, with a pleasant face that could look handsome in certain lights; he was patient, calm, intelligent, sensible, tenacious and very likeable, upending the accepted belief that, to be successful, an agent had to be a ferocious brute. The first meeting with Rose went well – she said to Lennie afterwards that she particularly liked his 'furry' voice – and Lennie felt comfortable about entrusting her to Van, who was surely too old and too pleasantly ordinary to be the object of one of her crushes.

Van liked Al Feinstein. 'He's a great guy. He knows the business inside out.'

'But it's important that he's not allowed to walk all over

Rose,' Lennie said, thinking there was such a thing as being *too* nice.

'I've always found his underlying instincts are sound,' Van said. 'The old boy is cinema to the bone. He likes to pretend he's a fire-breathing dragon, but he doesn't scare me. We understand each other pretty well.'

So Lennie felt able to step back once again from Rose's concerns, and look to his own business. Rose was still living in the guest villa at his mansion, Bel Air, with her own household, as well as Lennie's housekeeper, to watch over her, so he took a trip to New York, where he owned a radio station, W2XKX, and had the headquarters of his radio-manufacturing business. 'I want to see how they're getting on with television,' he told Rose.

She wrinkled her nose. 'Television? Nobody's interested in that.'

'That's what they said about the movies, honey. Then they said Talkies would never take off.'

'I saw one once, in a shop window. It was all grey, and only about a foot square. Why would anyone want to look at such an itty-bitty screen when they could go to the movies?'

'I'll tell you why – because people are fundamentally lazy. Okay, television's not good enough as it stands. But let's say one day they can get the picture as good as it is on the big screen.'

'Could never happen.'

'Just suppose. If you could give people a movie theatre in their own home, you'd kill cinema stone dead. People wouldn't have to put their shoes on and get the car out and drive into town, and wait in a queue with a lot of strangers to buy a ticket, and maybe have to sit next to a fat sweaty guy, or behind a woman in a crazy hat. Why, they could sit on their own sofa, in their own lounge, in their slippers. They'd have beer and pretzels right there in the kitchen. They could go to the john whenever they wanted.'

'Uncle Lennie!'

'It's a factor,' Lennie insisted. 'And at the end of the movie, they can just switch off and shuffle up to bed. No drive home, no putting the car away, no coming back to a dark house. Maybe it's cold and wet outside. I'm telling you, honey, television could be the next big thing.' Rose only sniffed. He went on reflectively, 'You probably don't know, but President Hoover put me on a special White House committee for television back in 1929. I've taken my eye off the ball since Hoover lost office. Had other things on my mind. But television must have moved on a lot since then. And if it's a question of investing – well, the man who gets in on the ground floor is the one who makes the gravy.'

Rose gave him an indulgent smile. 'I think this is all just excuses because you're restless and want to take a trip.'

He grinned. 'You got me.'

'Well, go with my blessing. I've been taking up a lot of your time lately, and I'm sorry. But I'm okay now, and you don't have to worry about me any more.'

'I'll always worry about you,' he said, standing up and leaning down to kiss her forehead, 'but I'm not worried now. And if you need me, I'll come back in a hurry. I could even fly back if I had to.'

'Fly?' Rose exclaimed.

'TWA does a flight from New York to Los Angeles, with just three stops, and it only takes about twenty-five hours.'

'You'll meet yourself coming back one of these days,' Rose said wisely.

'You sounded just like your mother then.'

When Lennie had been involved in it, television meant shining a neon lamp through a spinning Nipkow disc, which was punched with equidistant holes in a spiral pattern. As it revolved, the disc split the image into slices, which were projected onto a sensor as a pattern of light and dark lines.

It was a simple and cheap system, and John Logie Baird had demonstrated it in Selfridges in London as early as 1925. From 1929 the British Broadcasting Company transmitted experimental programmes using Baird's 30-line system, while W2XAB transmitted in New York on 48 lines from 1929 to 1931. The BBC had improved the image by an intermediate film process, where footage was shot onto cinefilm, which was then scanned. Now it was broadcasting a limited range of programmes from Alexandra Palace in 240 lines. But the mechanical system was limited. The more lines, and the quicker the spin, the clearer the image, but there was a limit to how big and how fast you could make the disc. The fact was that mechanical-scanning television had never yet been good enough to tempt the general public.

Now Lennie caught up with Allen B. DuMont, whom he had met at Westinghouse in New Jersey when he was working for the Television Commission. DuMont was working on electron currents in vacuum tubes, creating an electrical field that accelerated the passage of electrons from the cathode to the anode. The electron scanning process was infinitely better than the mechanical, and DuMont had started his own company in New Jersey to work on manufacturing long-lasting and reliable cathode ray tubes.

Lennie spent a very interesting day with DuMont, who was just a few years younger than him – and, amusingly to Lennie, viewed him as something of a pioneer of the air waves – and was pondering to himself whether DuMont's company might be something to invest in. But DuMont let fall the information that EMI, which had just merged with Marconi, had developed an all-electronic scanning system, which they had improved to 405 lines, and that the BBC was already trying it out. EMI-Marconi, Lennie reckoned, was already too big for him to get in on the ground floor.

That evening, he met Joseph Kennedy at his club, the Metropolitan on East 60th, for dinner and a long chat. He and Kennedy had been co-investors in the early days of movies. Kennedy had moved on now, investing mostly in real estate and importing liquors – such lucrative fields that his fortune was said to be $180 million. But he still loved the movies, and was interested in everything Lennie had to tell him about the Hollywood scene. When Lennie mentioned television, however, he lost interest. 'Just a toy.' He dismissed it. 'It'll never amount to anything. But you've made your fortune, haven't you? Manning's Radios are everywhere.'

'You know as well as I do that you can't stand still,' Lennie said.

'Okay – but politics, Len. That's where you should be pitting your energies. Controlling events, not following in their wake. I got Roosevelt back in – shut down that renegade Coughlin. Roosevelt's eighty-one per cent of the Catholic vote? He owes that to me! And he won't forget it. I'm in for a big position, once he gets his feet under the table. An ambassadorship – a good one. And come 1940, I'm gonna succeed him to the White House.'

'You're going to be president?' Lennie said, more amused than amazed.

'What d'you think I've been working towards all these years?' Kennedy said, flashing him a grin with his great white tombstone teeth. 'First I'm gonna be president, then my son, Joe Junior. I'm gonna make it hereditary!' He laughed infectiously.

'I wouldn't be a bit surprised,' Lennie said, laughing too. 'If kings can do it—'

'Kings nothing! They get it handed on a plate. I worked for mine from the bottom up. I deserve it – and I'm gonna have it. And my nine kids are all gonna benefit. The Kennedy Dynasty. It's got a ring to it, don't you think? But what about you, Len? You married yet? No? You ought to think about it. People trust you more when you're a family man. And you can't get far in politics if you're single. You should get married and get a family going. You're not getting any younger, you know.'

'I haven't met the right girl yet,' Lennie said. 'Or, rather, I met her, but she met someone else.'

'There's thousands of girls out there,' Kennedy said cheerfully. 'And I'll tell you a secret,' he added, with a wink. 'One's pretty much the same as another, when you get right down to it.'

Kennedy was a famous ladies' man, despite having a high-energy, politically engaged wife. Or perhaps, Lennie thought, because of it. He had met Rose Kennedy a few times and had found her exhausting. And a little bit frightening.

The next morning Lennie, feeling idle, decided to stroll along Fifth Avenue, look in the shop windows and take note of the fashions so that he could report them back to Rose. It was a still day, very cold, but dry and bracing, and in his coat with the big fur collar he felt impervious. He was staring at a display of hats in Saks's window and composing an amusing letter in his mind when he was accosted by a lady just coming out of the store – a tiny round thing bundled up in furs, tottering on high-heeled boots. 'Lennox Manning, I declare! I didn't know you were in town!'

He submitted dutifully to an embrace from Mimi Niebling, one of New York's noted hostesses. 'I'm just here for a few weeks on business,' he said. 'You're looking wonderful, Mimi. I swear you get younger every time I see you.' There wasn't much of her to be seen between fur hat and fur coat, but it was the right thing to say.

She giggled like someone a quarter of her age and girth. 'You and your silver tongue! You get that from mixing with all those Hollywood types, I suppose. Oh!' Her eyes widened as she thought of something. 'Now, that's a wonderful co-incidence. You'll never guess who's coming to my cocktail party this evening.'

'No, I never will,' Lennie said solemnly.

'Anthea Taylor! There! What a lucky thing I bumped into you! You must come and meet her!' Most of Mimi's utterances came with exclamation marks. 'You know her, of course?'

Anthea Taylor was one of MGM's stars, and on the rise. Sifting through his mind, he remembered that he had read she was starring in a play on Broadway between pictures. 'Not really,' he said. 'I know who she is.'

'She's my guest of honour. We're celebrating her Academy Award nomination,' Mimi beamed. 'You must come and help me look after her. She'll be feeling a little lost, so far from home, and you'll be a friendly face. Now, say yes! I must have you! And we'll make up a party for dinner afterwards. That's settled, then.' She beamed again, certain she had got her way. It was her practice to ride over obstacles like a tank across no man's land. 'Come early! Bless you! Now I must dash!'

'Let me call you a cab.'

'No need!' she said, and produced from nowhere a small silver whistle, which she blew piercingly. As if by magic, a large yellow cab scorched to the kerb, and she waved a fur-gloved hand to him as she climbed in.

Lennie smiled to himself and strolled on. He'd had no plans for the evening, and he felt he might as well submit to Mimi as anyone. Her hors d'oeuvres were always excellent; and through the wealth and connections of her husband, who it was said 'owned half of everything', she was able to command the most interesting guests. It would be worth putting on a tuxedo for.

On the corner of Tottenham Court Road, Oliver bumped into a small, wiry man with horn-rimmed glasses, a scarf wound up to his chin and a soft hat pulled down to his eyes. He was carrying a canvas bag, which he now clutched to his chest as though fearing it might be snatched away.

'Good gracious!' Oliver exclaimed. 'Beefy Oxenford, as I live and breathe!'

The little man looked up and blinked, 'Oh, hello, Winchmore,' he said mildly.

'Old Beefy!' Oliver said, grinning. 'I haven't seen you since the Armistice! What are you doing these days?'

'Oh, this and that,' Beefy said vaguely.

The nickname Beefy was one of those ironic labels, Beefy being notably slight of build. But he had a wiry strength. He had been an anaesthetist during the war, and had served with Oliver in many a sticky part of the Front, where delirious soldiers often had to be restrained as they were being put under.

'Still passing gas?' Oliver asked. He knew most of the gasmen in London, and he hadn't heard Beefy's name mentioned. But there were other cities.

But Beefy said, 'No, I gave that up after the war. Never wanted to go into another operating theatre.'

'I don't blame you,' Oliver said. 'That was quite a picnic, wasn't it? Come and have a wet, and tell me what you're up to.'

The Rising Sun on the corner of Windmill Street was just a step away, one of those old pubs full of oak panelling and acid-embossed glass screens. Established at a table with two pints of beer, the men looked at each other. 'I say, do take off all that muffling,' Oliver said. 'You look like Sergei Sokolov, the Sinister Spy. What's in the bag?'

'Nothing in particular,' Beefy said, unwinding the scarf. 'Just some bits and pieces. For my hobby.' He thrust the bag under the table.

They talked a bit about the war, and the fate of various people they both remembered, and Oliver spoke briefly about his plastic-surgery work. Beefy then admitted that after demobilisation he had had what was nowadays called a 'nervous breakdown', and had gone home to live with his parents in

Stevenage. He had been shaken out of the state by the sudden death of his father. Having to comfort his mother and sisters and deal with all the practicalities had put his feet back on firmer ground. He had inherited a large slice of his father's fortune, and, on the death of his mother in 1928, he had sold the family house – his sisters being settled in marriage by then – and had come to London, where he lived modestly on his private income, and devoted his time to his hobby.

'Television.'

'Good Lord!' Oliver said. 'I thought you were going to say you've been working on some wonderful new surgical invention. You always *were* interested in machinery and gadgets and so on. But television?'

'I've been working with Baird,' he said, unmoved by Oliver's sceptical tone. 'But the fire was a terrible blow.'

'The fire?' Oliver said vaguely.

'Crystal Palace. You must know it burned down. It was in all the papers.'

'Of course, I heard about it.' The fire had broken out in the night of the 30th of November, and the blaze had been seen as far away as Willesden and Haywards Heath.

'Well, that's where Baird had his workshops and studio and so on. All destroyed. And now Reith has dropped the Baird system in favour of EMI.'

'Who's Reith?'

'John Reith, fellow in charge of the BBC. You've heard of the BBC?'

'Of course.'

'They were doing experimental television radiations, using the Baird system and the EMI system on alternate weeks. But Reith hates Baird, something to do with their schooldays – they're both Scots, you know – and the fire was the final excuse to drop him. But to be fair, the EMI system *is* better. Vacuum cells. Electron scanning.' He frowned, staring into the distance. 'All the same,' he said, coming back suddenly, and fixing Oliver with a stern look, 'Baird is a true visionary. He's already working on colour transmission and larger screens, which is more than the other lot are. But mechanical scanning will only take him so far. Look here!' he said. 'Have you got an hour or two?' Oliver made a cautious noise. 'Come back to my place, and see the receiver set I'm building. That's what's in the bag – parts I've been scavenging. There are all sorts of useful shops in Tottenham Court Road. Have you ever seen television?'

Oliver admitted he hadn't.

'Well, then, come back to my place and I'll give you a demonstration.' He looked at the clock on the wall. 'We can catch one of the regular BBC programmes. And I can show you the new improved receiver I'm building.'

'What was it like?' Verena asked later, over dinner.

Oliver considered. 'Human fish swimming in dishwater.'

'Oliver!'

'It's true. Like figures viewed through the fog. And the sound was a bit foggy, too. Poor old Beefy! He says it's because they don't have enough lines in the picture for his larger screen, whatever that means. He says Baird reckons he can get a thousand lines before long.'

'It sounds like a school punishment.'

'The conventional set he had was better – still grey and strangely two-dimensional, like a post-Stilton dream, but not so foggy. But the screen was so small – about six inches square. After squinting at it for half an hour, I had quite a headache. Beefy says that's why the BBC only broadcasts for an hour at a time, twice a day – concern for the welfare of the "lookers-in", as they seem to call them.'

Verena seemed bemused. 'It all sounds most unsatisfactory.' She helped herself to the fish from the dish the footman was holding for her.

'Well, it's early days. One must suppose it will get better.

I dare say radio was pretty sad when they first started it. And you remember how jerky the old cinema films used to be. But I can't see the point of television, I must say. If I want to see a play, I'll go to the theatre. If I want to hear a political talk, I'll go to the town hall. If I want a variety show—'

'I take the point,' Verena interrupted. 'What *did* you see, by the way?'

Oliver gave a rueful smile. 'A variety show – dancers, singers, jugglers, and a man telling jokes. Oh dear!' He took potatoes from the offered dish, and waited for the sauce to be handed. 'However, Beefy said that this Reith fellow is negotiating with the Postmaster General for the right to show the Coronation on the television. I don't suppose there are more than two hundred people in the country who have a receiver, but as a general principle, looking to the future, that might be something worthwhile – to show great national events. After all, not everyone can attend them in person.'

Verena looked up from her plate. 'Surely they won't film inside the Abbey.'

'Good heavens, no. Just the procession.'

'Oh.' She looked down again, and separated a forkful of fillet. 'But it's bound to be on the cinema newsreels, anyway. So nobody needs a television receiver.'

'Quite,' said Oliver.

Basil turned twenty-one in January 1937, and went home for the weekend for this remarkable fact to be celebrated. Barbara came with her husband and child, and everyone made a very pleasant fuss of him. His father shook his hand, and said, 'Now we're not responsible for you any more,' and though he smiled, Basil suspected he wasn't entirely joking. He gave him a handsome watch; Barbara and Freddie gave him a silver hunting flask engraved with his name; and Michael sent a telegram from Yorktown.

'You're looking better than when I last saw you,' Helen

said, automatically brushing back a stray lock of his hair. 'I think you're turning into quite a handsome man.'

Barbara protested: 'He was always handsome, Mummy.'

'Is he turning into a responsible man, that's the question,' Jack said. 'How are you getting on at work?'

'I'm working hard,' Basil said. 'It's interesting.'

The incorrigibly honest part of himself, which he was not able completely to suppress, acknowledged that it was partly Miranda Byrne who was interesting. Since that first party they had gone out together every week, always – was it tact on her part? He was never sure – to things that didn't cost money: galleries, exhibitions, lectures, political meetings. There were parties now and then, very much like the first one, where people talked earnestly about the injustice of the way the world was run, and what ought to be done about it.

He longed sometimes for a night-club and some dancing – anything frivolous. But when it came down to it, it was better to go out even to a Communist rally with Miranda than to rot alone in his room at Mrs Morgan's. He was being exposed to new viewpoints, and as he naturally went to Miranda for analysis, he was inevitably beginning to take on some of her seriousness. In bed at night he sometimes mourned the passing of the old Basil – or at least his retreat into hiding – but at any rate, it was a novel pleasure to have his parents approve of him.

'But do you have a sweetie?' Barbara asked impatiently. 'If so, we have to meet her, to see if she's good enough for you.'

'Oh, she's far *too* good for me,' he said unwarily.

'So there *is* someone! Is she pretty? Does she love you?'

'Steady on, Babsy. It's not like that. She's a work colleague. We go to meetings and things together, but we're just friends.'

'Oh, *poor* Bozzy! What a horrid girl! How can she be so hard-hearted?'

He laughed. 'She's the boss's niece, that's how!' And he changed the subject.

In truth, he didn't know how Miranda felt about him. She treated him with the brisk matter-of-factness she seemed to show everyone at work. And yet he felt there was undeniably a tension between them, the sort that was always there between a man and a woman, rather than, say, a brother and sister. It gave him hope that something would develop. He had had a lover once. He missed it.

All the comrades, as Basil called them in his own mind, were very exercised by the Spanish Civil War, to which he had paid little attention before. It was interesting to learn from Miranda that while general opinion and most news articles talked about there being two sides – the Fascists under Franco, and the Republicans,who had formed the legitimate government they had ousted – there were in fact three.

'It's not just a civil war any more,' she told him. 'There's a revolution going on. The Communists don't want to restore the old government, they want a complete change, government by the people, Soviet-style. Complete equality. If you saw how the peasants live, how badly the working classes are treated, Basil, you'd want revolution for them too.'

Miranda's Uncle Gilbert was also deeply interested in the war, and ran a series of articles on the subject in the *Messenger*, to which Basil contributed. His name did not appear on any of them, but Mr Dickins was impressed by his work and told him so, and Miranda somehow came to hear about it, congratulated him, and looked at him, he thought, in a more respectful light.

One dull February day, when they met after work, Miranda said, 'There's a café just along the road. Let's go and have a cup of tea. I've got something I want to talk to you about.'

The café was warm and steamy, full of people in damp coats and the smell of bottled coffee. Luckily two people were leaving as they entered, so they got the reversion to a tiny table in the window. Outside it was already dark, and the damp pavement glistened, smeared with colour from the traffic lights and illuminated street signs. People hurried past, huddled under umbrellas, figures that were strangely elongated by the rivulets running down the window. There was something rather French Impressionist about the scene and, not for the first time, Basil wished he could paint.

His reverie was interrupted by Miranda smacking down two cups of mahogany tea, scraping out her chair, and sitting, elbows on the table, leaning forward for emphasis. 'Have you ever thought about going to Spain?'

'No,' he said. 'Why?'

'Several newspapers have sent reporters over there, for eye-witness accounts. The people deserve to know what's really going on. We ought to have our own special correspondent in Spain.'

'But what has it got to do with us?' Basil asked tentatively.

'The future of Europe could be at stake! Aren't you frustrated by the lack of information?' She leaned forward another inch. 'You know how keen Uncle Gilbert is on the war. I bet he'd be all for it, if it was put to him – especially if he knew there was someone ready and eager to go.'

'You mean *me*?' He couldn't quite mask his horror.

'Imagine actually being there, while history was being made, and seeing it all for oneself, with one's own eyes! And, better still, being able to influence the outcome! If I were a man, I wouldn't hesitate to volunteer. I can't go – but you could!'

Her eyes shone, and having initially rejected the idea as potty, he began to think about it. There was a part of his mind that reeled at the idea of settling down and becoming a respectable tax-payer. A part that wanted excitement and adventure. And, besides, if he did this, clearly she would admire him for it. Nothing else so far had worked.

'It's a funny thing,' he said. 'My father was talking about another war coming and how I ought to get myself into one of the services so as to be ready. And I told him I would rather be a war correspondent, because someone has to report from the Front.'

'I knew you were the right person! Oh, Basil, it will be the best thing you ever did!'

That was a fairly narrow field, Basil thought, but Miranda had reached a hand across the table and clasped his, the first time she had voluntarily touched him. He was so entranced, all reason fled. 'I'll do it!' he said.

Dickins had not shown any surprise when Basil accosted him the next morning and asked to be allowed to volunteer to go to Spain. He simply nodded and said he would take him to see Mr Comstock right away. That ought to have seemed odd to Basil, had he been thinking straight.

And, strangely, Mr Comstock did not question the idea at all – as if it had already been decided. He simply stood up and reached across the desk to shake Basil's hand, and said, 'Excellent, my boy! You're exactly the sort of chap we want for the job. We'll make all the travel arrangements, and you'll be on full pay, plus reasonable expenses. Sit down, sit down!'

Basil learned that he was to proceed to Barcelona to join a militia, and send back regular reports on the progress of the war. He would have full press accreditation, which should secure him access and privileges everywhere, and enable him to ferret out the political and strategic thinking behind the actions he witnessed. But, most of all, he was to be one of the ordinary soldiers, and report on their day-to-day life. Basil was too excited, and too impressed with his own daring, to wonder how they had thought it out so quickly.

'You won't be going alone,' Comstock said. 'Mr Zennor has volunteered to go as well. You'll be able to support each other and compare notes.'

'Mr Zennor?' Basil said, bewildered.

'Mr Dickins says you get on well.'

'Yes, sir. I like him,' Basil said, beginning to think of questions.

'And you've worked together before on stories. Very good. Run along now, and Mr Dickins will talk to you later with more details.'

Dismissed, Basil went straight to find Bob Zennor, who looked rather the way Basil felt, as though he had been smacked on the head and wasn't sure what had happened to him.

'What's this about your going to Spain?' Basil demanded.

'Have you volunteered? I hoped you would,' said Zennor. 'I must say, I'm relieved there'll be two of us.'

'But – but Miranda Byrne only suggested it last night, and I went straight in this morning to volunteer. How did you hear about it?' Basil said, bewildered.

Zennor shook his head, as if shaking water out of his ears. 'They've been planning it for days – the editor and Mr Dickins. They asked me yesterday morning if I'd go. Apparently, they think I'm the right man for the job because I was in OTC, and I'm not married or anything. And Miss Byrne—'

'Miss Byrne?'

'Well, she knew about it, because of the editor being her uncle. She hinted you might be the other bod. I can see why – you're the adventurous type. It's much more in your line than mine. I don't know, really, how I came to say yes, but she talked and talked and made it all sound so marvellous. Well, you know how she is.'

'I thought I did,' Basil said.

'Am I right in thinking the whole thing was your idea?' Basil demanded. 'That you put your uncle up to it?'

'Of course not. He was already thinking about it. I just helped him make up his mind.'

'They'd already recruited Bob Zennor. You pretended to me that it was a new idea, that nothing had been settled.'

Miranda was unrepentant. 'I didn't pretend anything. You drew your own conclusions. But what does it matter who thought of what, when? You've volunteered for an exciting expedition, something that will change your whole life. Most men your age would give their eye teeth to go.' She gave him a sharp look. 'You're not going to back out?'

'No,' he said, 'but—'

'I knew I wasn't mistaken in you. My hero!' She laughed as she said the word, as though it was ironic, but he thought there was a new warmth in her look.

She had manipulated him, Basil thought. But as she smiled at him, he decided it didn't really matter after all. He was going to Spain. It was the most exciting thing that had ever happened to him. And when he got back, she would see him in a different light. He *would* be a hero then.

Nothing in Barcelona surprised Basil as much as finding himself there. It was the first time he had been abroad, and he was glad of Bob Zennor's large, solid presence. Zennor didn't have any warlike qualities, as far as Basil could tell, but he seemed unflappable, and he had the inestimable value of speaking some Spanish. 'Learned it as a nipper,' he said, when Basil asked why. 'Had a Spanish nanny.' He anticipated another question and added, 'M' father was in mining, spent a lot of time in Bolivia. I was actually born out there. Don't remember it, though. We came home when I was still a baby. But we brought the nanny with us.'

On the long journey to Barcelona, Basil learned as many words and phrases from him as he could. He found it not dissimilar to Italian, of which he had a smattering from schooldays; he thought he'd pick it up quickly.

As the train pulled into Barcelona station, he had one of those moments of suddenly seeing himself clearly, and a wash of shock went over him. *What on earth am I doing here? I'm not a soldier. I don't know anything about soldiering. I don't really care about this war – why should I? I don't even know what they're fighting for. I don't want to get shot at. I don't want to get killed.*

Zennor was up and collecting their bags; Basil was rigid, gripping the edge of the seat. 'This is us,' Zennor said, seeing he hadn't moved.

'Aren't you scared?' Basil heard himself ask.

Zennor only looked mildly puzzled. 'What of?'

Basil was comforted. He wasn't going to be outdone by a feather mattress like Bob Zennor. He was Basil Compton, the scamp, the outlaw, the dare-devil, the scorner of rules. If anyone was going to be a hero, it had to be him.

Barcelona looked rather shabby. Boarded-up shops; some windows broken, others mended with brown paper; peeling paint, damaged stonework, missing cobbles; rubbish lying in the street. And – the most noticeable thing to Basil, having come from London – a complete absence of well-dressed people. Everyone looked poor, and was dressed either in coarse peasant clothes or workers' blue overalls.

'Bit of a dreary place,' he commented.

Zennor said, 'I was here five years ago with my parents, and this street was full of expensive shops and rich people. It's called Las Ramblas, and it was the main street for strolling about and being seen. But now everything belongs to the people.'

'Well, the flags are jolly,' Basil said doubtfully. All the big buildings were draped in red or red-and-black flags; red and blue posters were plastered on every surface. There were no private motor-cars, but the trams had been painted red-and-black. And loudspeakers along the street bellowed out songs with simple, catchy tunes. Revolutionary songs, Zennor told him, about the brotherhood of man and the newly won

293

freedom of the proletariat from oppression. A man in a uniform of some kind thrust a leaflet at him, and he folded it into his pocket for future reference, remembering that he was supposed to be taking notes for his first report to the *Messenger*.

'Where are we going, anyway?' he asked Zennor.

'The Lenin Barracks, to enlist. Don't you remember?'

'Why name it after him?'

'Why not? He was the father of Communism. It all started with him.'

'But wasn't he a dictator? Didn't he have thousands of people killed?' Basil asked, from some vague memory of history lessons.

'You can't have a revolution without the spilling of blood,' Zennor said simply. 'The birth-pangs of a new civilisation.'

Basil mentally banked the phrase.

The Lenin Barracks were a block of buildings from another age, handsome and stone-built, though beginning to have the knocked-about look that Basil was already coming to recognise. They had been a cavalry headquarters, so the buildings included stables and a riding-school, and several enormous courtyards where mounted drills had been conducted. There was an office just inside the entrance, where an officer sat at a battered wooden table, surrounded by piles of papers, which seemed to be mostly lists, and some very frayed maps. He looked up with a fierce frown. His face was rather impressive and hawk-like, with sharp cheekbones and a jutting nose. He looked like Basil's idea of a guerrilla commander.

Zennor addressed him in Spanish, and he seemed to listen impatiently until he called him '*señor*'. Then he burst into indignant speech. Basil managed to catch enough of it to understand that he was saying there was no more '*señor*' in Spain: everyone was equal, everyone was a comrade. Then he looked sharply from Zennor to Basil, and said, '*Inglés?*' They assented, at which the officer stood up and shook hands with them, and said, 'We like very much English. Many English come. Maybe soon we get all English *centuria*. English good soldiers.'

He reverted to Spanish with apparent relief, sought out a particular list and added their names to it, spelling them laboriously letter by letter. Then he said something else in rapid Spanish, waved a hand expansively, and called forward a shabbily dressed man who had been toiling at another desk and consigned them to his charge.

'What did he say?' Basil asked, as they followed the shabby little man into the yard.

'He said we'd be going to the Front very soon, when we finish training.'

'Surely,' Basil said, suddenly nervous, 'training takes weeks and weeks?'

Zennor shrugged. 'We'll find out. I expect they do everything differently here. Can't expect it to be like the British Army.'

Basil knew very little about the British Army, but he was sure the Lenin Barracks would have sent any British NCO into fits. The place was filthy, every window opaque, the stonework chipped and streaked, rubbish lying about. Every corner seemed to be filled with broken saddles, dented brass helmets, smashed furniture, scraps of paper, rags, rotting food and human waste. The smell of horses was strong, even though there had been none for months – they had all been commandeered for the Front.

The clerk explained that they were to be part of a new *centuria* – roughly equivalent, Zennor decided, to a British Army company – being formed. It was being housed in one of the stables. In a stall with high wooden sides, bars going up to the ceiling, and a manger across the back, Basil and Zennor were to bed down on the stone floor. High on the wall was a wooden plaque bearing the name of the previous occupant: Tormenta. Zennor said it meant Storm, a good name for a military horse. Basil, however, took it gloomily as an omen.

As the days passed, the stable block filled, with more recruits arriving every day. They were all young men, mostly around seventeen or eighteen, some as young as fifteen being brought in by their parents for the sake of the ten pesetas a day wages. They were shy, friendly, eager, and filled with revolutionary fervour. They spoke a dialect of Spanish that even Zennor found challenging, but goodwill and a uniformity of ignorance about what they should be doing drew them together. Space soon ran out, and they were crammed in three and four to a stall, with others sleeping in the passageway, but Basil and Zennor were not disturbed from their regal occupancy of Tormenta's stall. Their Englishness was evidently a revered characteristic.

Uniforms began to be handed out from the first day, but piecemeal, as items arrived from the factories frantically rushing them out, so there was no uniformity of appearance. Corduroy knee-breeches formed the basis, along with a grey cotton shirt, but some men were issued with puttees and some with corduroy or leather gaiters. The quartermaster, impressed with Zennor and perhaps seeing in him officer material, issued him with long leather boots, and found another pair, with a sort of shrug, for Basil. Jackets were of wool in various colours, or canvas, or leather, and there were no uniform caps. Some felted forage caps were handed out, and even some wartime kepis, but most men wore a round knitted hat, pulled down low for warmth. The one uniform element was the red-and-black scarf tied around the throat – they all had one of those, for pride. Red and black were the colours of the Party.

Training began the following day, under the instruction of a rosy-cheeked young man in a smart uniform who explained to Zennor that he had been a regular army lieutenant. He told them foreigners did not have to attend instruction: there seemed to be a belief among Spaniards that all Englishmen had military instruction from the cradle. Basil would have accepted the exeat and gone and found a heap of straw somewhere to sit and read quietly, but Zennor said on behalf of both of them that they needed to learn the drill like anyone else. What followed was not drill in any sense: the recruits were ardent revolutionaries and longing to get to the Front and trounce the enemy, but they had no idea of military procedures, and were actively averse to discipline. They would not even stand in line, constantly wandering off to chat to someone else they had spotted, swapping cigarettes and sweets, and talking non-stop like a treeful of starlings. And they had absorbed the revolutionary code of equality to the point that if they were given an order they didn't like, they would leave the rank and go up to the officer to argue about it vigorously.

Gradually, day by day, in a shambling manner, they learned to stand in ranks, and to march in formation of a sort round the big cobbled yards. Coming to attention was not the clump-thump that Basil had witnessed at home: it was a prolonged rattle-and-shuffle as everyone achieved the position in his own time, and adjusted it as he thought necessary. Many of the recruits did not know their right from their left. Javier, the young man who drilled beside Basil – it was all Christian names in the militia, surnames being deemed part of the old order and unacceptably deferential – was particularly baffled. On the order to march he would stare with desperate, frowning concentration at Basil's feet, and try to copy him, frequently clutching Basil's arm in the effort to stay upright as he tripped over his own boots or collided with the man in front. Eventually, Basil pulled a red thread from his already frayed scarf and tied it through an eyelet hole of his left boot. '*Rojo*,' he told him, again and again. 'Red first.'

Eventually Javier got the hang of it, and forced grateful cigarettes on him every time he saw him.

After a week, it was decided that the *centuria* marched well enough to be seen in public, and they were taken out of barracks to march through the town and up and down the pleasure-gardens, which were the common parade ground for the militias. The men were desperately proud to be seen, though their uniform was still hopelessly patchy, and their drill would have made a British sergeant weep, but for three hours each time they marched stiffly up and down, throwing out their chests and trying to look like soldiers, but fatally grinning and waving every time they saw a girlfriend, mother, grandfather or neighbour they recognised.

Drill took up the mornings. Afternoons had no military shape, and often the recruits played unregulated games of football, up and down the riding-school, or found a quiet spot to sleep – they were great sleepers in the afternoon – or wandered off into the town. Basil often persuaded Zennor to go with him to a café in the Plaza de España to attempt to supply the deficiencies of the barracks mess. The evening meal was always the same, a kind of stew served in greasy tin pannikins, with great lumps of bread, and a thin local wine, which they drank out of a common *porrón*, a bottle with a long spout from which you could direct liquid into your mouth without the lips touching it. At the café they could get coffee, and sausage, and boiled potatoes, and a kind of dry, grainy yellow cake – nothing very tempting, except that it was different.

Basil had always thought of himself as a rebel, but he had always lived in a tightly structured world where *he* was the disruptive element. Finding himself in a place where nothing was as it should have been threw him off balance. His mind automatically searched for order and discipline against which to brace himself. And he had always been personally fastidious.

He didn't like to be uncomfortable. It offended him to be dirty. Many times in those early days, he thought about leaving and going home.

But gradually he became fond of the other recruits, who were so very friendly, as well as touchingly dedicated to their cause. Physical discomforts didn't concern them at all. And there was the effortless way in which Zennor seemed to fit in and cope with everything, and the quiet enthusiasm with which he looked forward to the next stage of the adventure. So Basil squared mental shoulders and dug in, telling himself there was nothing he could not stand for a few weeks in the cause of making a name for himself back home.

The most troubling thing was that there was no rifle drill. Zennor, talking to the officer after drill one day, learned there were no rifles in the barracks, other than those issued to the sentries. Rifles were in desperately short supply, he said: militiamen going up to the Front would take over the rifles of the men coming out of the line to rest.

'But you know how to shoot,' the officer said, more a statement than a question, but with a hopeful look.

'Yes,' Zennor said, frowning, 'but—'

'Then you will be all right,' the lieutenant said. 'Rifles will be issued. Everything will be done, in due course.'

Basil, whose Spanish had improved no end in the past couple of weeks, took his friend's arm as they walked away. '"Rifles will be issued"? We haven't even got full uniforms. What have we got ourselves into?'

'Oh, I expect it will be all right. I've noticed that these chaps lack any kind of order or routine, the way we know it, but things get done, more or less. Eventually.' He looked at Basil frowningly. 'You aren't thinking of chucking, are you?'

'Well—' Basil began.

'Please don't go,' Zennor said urgently. 'The chaps need us. They're splendid fellows. And the cause is a good one.'

Actually, Basil had only the vaguest idea what the cause was. But the fellows certainly were splendid.

Zennor, looking down in embarrassment, said awkwardly, '*I* need you. Don't want to do this alone.'

That clinched it. When an Englishman went so far as to express his inner feelings, you had to take it seriously.

Basil had just settled in to the lack-of-routine, and had come to believe that they would never go to the Front, when one evening the order came to be ready to go in two hours. There was a stampede for the quartermaster's stores to try to get hold of equipment, most of which was still not available. And suddenly the barracks filled with women, wives and sisters and mothers of the recruits, who had heard the news of departure on the town's grapevine and had come hurrying in to help them pack their kitbags, press parting gifts on them, and smile and weep simultaneously with pride and apprehension. Blankets were rolled, pannikins slung from knapsacks, bottles of wine and lengths of sausage forced in among the socks and shirts.

The train would be leaving the station at eight o'clock, they were told, but it was already ten past when they were finally paraded in the barracks square, still fumbling with fastenings and searching pockets for stray items, chattering, questioning, laughing. Then there was a further delay as a commissar in a smart uniform and bright boots climbed up onto a box and addressed them in what was evidently a rousing speech, though his accent was so strong Basil under-stood only one word in five. Two attendants had unrolled a great red banner to hold above him as he exhorted them in the name of the revolution; some of the men had tears in their eyes; at the end, there was a great roar of approval. How strange it all seemed: Basil had another moment of standing outside himself. Torchlight flickered, gleaming off a buckle here, a curved, wet female cheek there; voices echoed off the stone walls; above the barracks square, the sky was black and indifferent.

On the march to the station, nothing at all seemed real. They were taken on a circuitous route all round the town so that everyone could see them, and everywhere they were acclaimed by crowds shouting and waving flags, while revolutionary songs pumped out from the loudspeakers, and the men grinned as they marched, basking in the love and pride, close to believing themselves heroes.

The train was so crowded there was not room for everyone to sit. Basil and Zennor were ushered by their own particular comrades into a favoured corner of a compartment: they were, Basil realised, the equivalent of a good-luck mascot. The last-comers had to stand, so crushed together they could probably have gone to sleep on their feet without the slightest chance of falling down. The train gave a melancholy *wheep!* and began to crawl out of the station, where still crowds, mostly women now, called in high, echoing voices like a colony of seabirds, and were left behind.

Now Felipe passed round cigarettes; Ramón hauled out a bottle of wine; chattering resumed as the train gathered speed to a heady twenty kilometres an hour, clattering and lurching on the ill-maintained track. And Basil, out of his pervading sense of unreality, stared across at Zennor, struggling to extract a lump of dried red sausage from his pack, and thought, *What on earth have I got myself into?*

CHAPTER THIRTEEN

Polly and James had taken to going to the cinema once a week. It was Ethel who had got them into the habit. She had become very keen on the pictures, which had taken the place of table-turning in her life. The medium to whom she had been going for years had suddenly disappeared, and had subsequently been exposed in the local newspaper as a fraud. Ethel stubbornly maintained faith in her, and insisted that professional jealousy had driven her out. But she had cooled rather towards the whole idea of spiritualism. The messages from her dead husbands had become rather monotonous. There were only so many times you could hear that everything on the other side was lovely, without craving stronger meat.

She had invested so wholeheartedly in the movie world that she bought magazines and followed the lives of the stars and the directors, knew who was signed with which studio, whose wonderful new film was 'coming soon', whose marriage was imminent and whose was on the verge of ruin. It was all she cared to talk about; but to Polly it was a great deal better to have Hollywood chatter at every meal than have Ethel lying on a sofa all day complaining about her health.

Ethel did not like to go to the cinema alone, and the previous autumn her usual companion, Mrs Chorley, had moved away from York. Her daughter Harriet was back living at Morland Place – having done a teacher-training course at Maria Grey College in London, Harriet had been fortunate

in securing a post at the Mount School – and could sometimes be persuaded to go with her, but Harriet was studious,
keen on self-improvement, and would only go to serious
films. So Ethel looked to the nearest alternative companion,
and badgered Polly to go with her. It was only when James
said he would go as well that Polly gave in, and found she
rather enjoyed it. To be taken out of oneself for a few hours,
transported to another world where different rules applied,
was rather shamefully delightful. James, of course, being a
natural hedonist, saw no shame in it.

One night they went to see Dorothy Lamour and Ray
Milland in *The Jungle Princess*, and between the second feature
and the main film there was a newsreel. It contained a report
on the 9th Academy Awards ceremony which had just taken
place at the Biltmore Hotel in Los Angeles. The camera was
focused on the red carpet, along which the stars walked
between the ranks of journalists and fans. Another limousine
door opened, another glamorous woman in evening dress
emerged. 'And here's Anthea Taylor,' the disembodied voice
explained, 'hotly tipped for the Best Supporting Actress award
for her part in *Three Wishes* . . .'

Emerging from the car behind her, a man in the stark
black-and-white of evening dress. The woman, in what looked
like silver lamé, long white gloves and a white fox cape, waited
for him, slipped her hand through his elbow, and then hugged
his arm to her as she smiled ravishingly at the camera. The
man smiled too, looking pleased with himself, his hand laid
over her gloved one.

'. . . and supporting *her*,' the voice went on, 'is her latest
companion, a new flame who seems to find the task very
congenial.'

Presumably the commentator did not know who the 'new
flame' was, or did not think him famous enough to name.
But Polly knew. She didn't see anything more of the newsreel.
She was thinking, *Now I know why he hasn't been writing to*

me. Lennie had a new love, a famous – and beautiful – film star. Of course she couldn't compete with that.

She dreaded having to talk to Ethel and James afterwards about it, but it seemed neither of them had recognised Lennie on the screen. Perhaps they had been concentrating, along with the commentator, on Anthea Taylor. And, of course, neither had seen Lennie for a very long time. On the way home, Ethel quarrelled with James, who had laughed all the way through *The Jungle Princess*, while Ethel had thought it romantic and touching. Polly concentrated on driving, and was glad for once of the conflict.

It is usually only in retrospect that a person knows he has changed. Basil was privileged – if that was the right word – to witness the process in action, as day by day layers of the old Basil were stripped away. It was very hard for him to bear being dirty. He had flattered himself that he really didn't need much, but he had never regarded hot water and soap as a luxury. And, for a young man who had promoted anarchy, he discovered that he didn't like disorder. Ugliness, broken and damaged things, strewn rubbish, inefficiency, wilful stupidity – they offended him. And they were all around him.

Lorries had taken his *centuria* up into the mountains, but there had been heavy rains and the roads further on, they were told, were impassable: they would have to march the last few miles. It was not, of course, a march – it was barely a walk. After fifteen minutes the column straggled so badly the rear of it was out of sight. The road was narrow and unpaved, and the unplanned-for passage of men and vehicles had sunk it below the level of the fields to either side, which had not been cultivated since last year's harvest. The occasional mud-and-stone farmhouse they passed was always deserted, and they saw no animals, no cows, horses, sheep, even chickens – the militia had taken them all.

The village they arrived in at last was a collection of mean cottages, with barns and mule stables behind, huddled round a primitive church. It had the desperate, battered look that the passage of soldiers always left behind: things carelessly broken, vandalised, dirtied. In addition, some houses had obviously been bombed from the air or shelled, and had gaping roofs or part-collapsed walls, while others were pocked by rifle fire from when the village had been fought over earlier in the war. And he encountered for the first time the smell of the front line: a mixture of excrement and rotting food.

They saw animals now, but only pi-dogs and strings of mules pulling rough farm carts. The houses had no gardens, only a backyard featuring a dung heap; and there was nothing green to be seen anywhere. If there had ever been trees, they had been cut down for firewood long since, and the passage of feet and wheels had turned everything else into mud, through which they had to pick their way.

It was not only mud, however: there was no such thing as a latrine in the whole village and, as far as Basil learned, never had been. The local people, before the war, had used their dung heaps. Now the passing soldiers went wherever they happened to be. The *comandante* of the *centuria*, a Belgian mercenary, who had taken a liking to Basil and Zennor, kindly warned them to watch where they stepped: there was hardly a square foot that was unsullied. They spent days in the village before they went up to the line. The church, which had been shelled and was missing its roof, had been used so extensively as a latrine that it was useless for any other purpose; the fields on either side of the road and every abandoned building likewise. The first time Basil had to relieve himself in the stinking stubble, another layer was stripped away from his old self. He tried once to imagine himself in Gloria's bed in her pink and scented boudoir, and it seemed like a fantasy scene from a Hollywood movie, nothing to do with him at all.

It was Bob Zennor who got him through it: he never

305

complained, took the filth and the privations so much in his stride that Basil felt compelled to match him in stoicism. He took out his frustration on his notebooks, writing up graphic details every night, in tiny writing to save space, because obviously there would be no replacing his notebooks until they got back to a city like Barcelona, and he had no idea when that would be.

The front line, they learned, was about three miles away, obviously quiet at present as there was no sound of shelling and no wounded being brought back. There was nothing to do in the village but sit and smoke. So it was a moment of diversion, even excitement, when on the second day half a dozen Fascist deserters were brought in. They were not ideological Fascists, but conscripts who had been doing their national service when the war broke out, and had no desire to fight. They had taken the chance of a quiet period to slip across to the Communist line and surrender.

The *comandante* allowed everyone to go in batches and look at them, and in a state of festering boredom Basil and Zennor did not refuse their turn. The enemy turned out to be very like themselves, skinny young men, unshaven and rough-haired, indistinguishable from their own side except that they had khaki uniforms, and were more ragged, with boots falling to pieces. They were being held in an abandoned cottage by the armed Communists, who had brought them down from the front line. One of them was clearly terrified, and shook like a horse, his eyes white and rolling, probably believing that the Reds were feral beasts who intended to torture and kill him. Food was brought to them, and being faced with a pannikin of stew, the lad – who appeared to be no more than fifteen – did not seem to know what to do with it. His guard stroked his shoulder and made crooning noises as he would to a horse, and finally took the spoon, wrapped the boy's fingers around it, and dug it into the steaming mess. Once he started eating, the boy shovelled with desperate haste. The guard grinned at Basil, patted the boy again with a proprietorial air, and said in Spanish, 'You see, the Fascist troops are always starving. That's why they're no match for us.'

On the third day, a covered mule cart arrived with the rifles for the *centuria*. They were unloaded at one of the larger barns, and the men gathered there to have them handed out. Basil and Zennor examined what they had been allocated, and Basil exclaimed, 'What in God's name is this?' It was a German Mauser, and the date stamped under the manufacturer's name was 1896. It was rusty – the bolt so rusted it wouldn't move – and the stock had a split you could put a pencil into. Zennor's was no better. He looked down inside the barrel and said, 'It's completely corroded inside. It will never fire.' The other rifles were as bad. The boy next to him was turning his round and round and staring at it in bafflement, and Basil could see at a glance that if he ever managed to load and fire it, it would explode and take his hand off.

'What are we supposed to do with these?' Basil said, his voice high with frustration.

'Look,' Zennor said. Two young lads had just come back with something obviously newer and less rusty, and were nudging each other and grinning in self-congratulation. They were two of the youngest in the company, only fourteen, and from the way they were holding their prize rifles obviously had no idea how to use them. Zennor asked them for a look, and they showed him reluctantly, without actually letting go. They were dated 1926, and though dirty, were intact and not rusty. 'I'm going to talk to the sergeant,' Zennor said, in a determined voice Basil had never heard before. 'Obviously the best rifles ought to be given to people who can shoot. That's only common sense.'

Before Basil could say anything, he was pushing his way through the throng and was addressing the sergeant. Basil could not hear what was said, but saw the sergeant's face redden, saw the fury on it as he bawled at Zennor, and made a furious gesture of dismissal.

He came back, not chastened, but quietly angry. 'He said you and I are foreigners, and the best rifles go to the good Communists, those most loyal to the cause.'

'But that's . . .' Basil was lost for words.

'I know. And how could those little beasts ever have done anything for the Party?'

Later they learned that one of the lads, Manuel, was the sergeant's nephew, and the other, Mateo, always known as Rubio for his fair hair, was his best friend at school. But there was no time now to worry about it. After five minutes' instruction on how to load the rifle, they were told to get their packs and form up. Then, without further warning, they set off for the front line. Basil felt only relief at leaving the stinking village behind. Fear of death had not managed to find room in his head yet, though he was anxious about his useless, rusty rifle.

'Don't worry,' Zennor said calmly. 'We'll have the good ones off them when we get to the front. Rubio will do anything for chocolate, and Manuel is a blockhead and does whatever Rubio says.'

'But what about the sergeant? He'll make us give them back, and punish us.'

'He won't. The sergeant will do anything for cigarettes,' Zennor said. Basil could only admire his confidence and resourcefulness. Back in London he had thought him rather pathetic, like the swotty boy in specs at school who was always bullied, but before Basil's very eyes he was turning into a hero and a solid, grown-up man. Basil could only hope he would do as well.

It was wild country, a chain of bare rocky hills that supported no growth but low scrub, with outcrops of limestone sticking through the thin earth like bones. The sides were steep and ribbed with rock, slashed with deep ravines. There was no possibility here of a continuous front – rather, there was a series of fortified posts perched on the hilltops wherever the ground was flat enough, facing across the ravines the similar posts of the enemy.

'They must be five or six hundred yards away,' Basil said to Zennor, observing the faint line of a parapet, like a scrawl along the hillside, over which a red-and-yellow flag flew, and behind which tiny figures moved in ant-like occupations.

'Beyond rifle range,' Zennor said. 'Even if we had working rifles.'

The last part of the journey to the front had been in single file, scrambling up a steep mule-track that looped back and forth across the hillside. As soon as they reached the top, they could smell the rotten stink: everything got thrown over the escarpment, where it accumulated on ledges and in clefts, the ordure of all the months past. Unsurprisingly, there was no animal life to be seen, not even a bird, though it was the kind of country where you might normally expect to see an eagle or a buzzard cruising the rising air currents. Beyond the human sounds of the position – conversational voices, the clink of stone or metal, the occasional cough or laugh – it was eerily quiet.

The company they were relieving were desperately anxious to get away. They looked like scarecrows, filthy, unshaven and ragged. A corporal, a very dark Frenchman from some-where in the south, picked out Basil and Zennor as obviously different from the crowd, and on learning they were English, showed them round, seeming grateful to be able to commu-nicate in something other than Spanish. The stronghold, or position, as he called it, was semi-circular and about fifty yards across, enclosed with a parapet of limestone boulders reinforced with sandbags. In front of the parapet was a series of narrow trenches with firing loopholes made of piles of limestone; then came the thick loops of barbed wire. Beyond that the scarp plunged down vertiginously into the ravine, whose bottom was out of sight. Even Basil, with no experience of such things, could see that it was unassailable by infantry.

Zennor asked the corporal if the enemy had artillery. 'They have a couple of guns,' he said, 'but no ammunition. Now and then they manage to get a few shells brought up from Zaragoza, but so few they never find the range. We've never been hit.'

Inside the parapet were forty or so dug-outs, and the corporal showed them his, where his packed kitbag was still stowed. 'You should take this one,' he said. 'It's one of the better ones.' When they thanked him, he said, 'No need. We have to stick together, we foreigners.' He kicked moodily at a stone. 'This is not a war, you know, it's a comic opera, without the fancy uniforms. And with the occasional death.' He shrugged. 'Not death in combat. We've lost five men since we got here, and had a dozen more injured, but all by accident, at their own hands. Be especially careful after dark. These boys poop off at the least sound.'

'So there's not much chance of action here?'

'It's a stalemate. Has been since last autumn.' He stared across the parapet at the ribbed hills opposite. 'The maddest thing,' he said, 'is that those boys over there are exactly the same as our boys here. There's no reason for them to be trying to kill each other. Ours've been told the Fascists are murdering swine who want to rape their sisters, but when we get deserters, you can see they're just Spanish boys like ours, scared and hungry and fed up and wanting to go home. They could be cousins – they just happened to have lived on the other side of the valley, and got recruited by the other lot. Politics! Bloody politics!' He turned to them abruptly. 'For instance, why are *you* here?'

Basil let Zennor answer. He wasn't sure he could make a coherent account of himself. 'To help drive the Fascists out and restore the legitimate government,' Zennor answered. He sounded comfortingly sure about it. 'Fascism has to be stopped. If it gets a foothold here, it could spread throughout Europe.'

The corporal looked at him for a long time, as if he debated correcting everything that was wrong about that statement. Then he shrugged. 'Well, good luck to you. I hope it's worth it.' And he heaved up his kitbag and walked away to find his men.

Spring had come, even up there in the sierra, but it was still wretchedly cold at night and when the mysterious fogs rolled in. One moment you might be sitting on a rock, enjoying a cigarette in the sunshine under a sparkling-clear blue sky; the next you could be enveloped in thick, white, damp and distinctly chilly mist. Sometimes in the morning the valley would be hidden under a sea of milk, while the hilltops rose up from it like blue-grey islands. And always in the distance the huge, snowcapped peaks of the Pyrenees stood clear, guarding eternity.

The days passed in a monotonous cycle of sentry-go, camp duties, and foraging expeditions. The enemy fired occasionally. Sometimes there were positive volleys, as though frustrated children were lashing out; and then the excited Communists fired back, wild fusillades accompanied by cheering, abusive shouts, and the singing of partisan songs. Now and then a rifle bullet would come far enough to hit the parapet, almost spent, but mostly they fell harmlessly into the valley.

The foraging expeditions were for firewood. The hills could never have yielded much in the way of vegetation, but months of occupation had stripped them bare. Foragers had to go further afield all the time to collect enough miserable little twigs to cook the rations. Down on the valley floor in front of their position there were some bushes, stunted oaks, and reeds that, when dry, burned effectively. But foraging there was hazardous, for the bored enemy sentries loved to shoot at anything that moved. Basil learned that they generally fired too high, and the bullets would whine overhead like hornets. But occasionally one would strike the rock close enough to fling shards of limestone into the group, upon which they would throw themselves flat on their faces, no doubt affording satisfaction to the Fascists – until they got up again and went on.

When they had been at the position two weeks, Basil and Zennor were made corporals, each in charge of twelve men. 'I suppose it's because we're educated,' Basil said, 'and we know how to shoot.'

'Well, if they're going to give us responsibilities,' Zennor said determinedly, 'at least we should have rifles that work.'

They succeeded in swapping with Rubio and Manuel, each using his own tactics. Basil got Rubio's good rifle away from him with a mixture of threats and cigarettes; Zennor subjected Manuel to a long and earnest lecture about one's duty to the cause and the importance of loyalty to one comrades that had him close to tears.

'In the end, he begged me to take it.'

'You're a lot less of a typical Englishman than you appear at first sight,' Basil said admiringly.

Being a corporal conferred little other than responsibility. The militias were political entities, and run on lines of complete equality. There were no badges, no titles, no deference, no saluting, no increased pay or extra rations: the unit was a democracy, not a hierarchy. Officers and men called each other 'comrade'; orders were requests, and always required discussion. Before a comrade would do as you asked, he had to understand why the thing needed doing, and why it was his duty to the Party and the cause to carry it out. He would often want to propose counter-arguments, to the end itself, or to the method of achieving it, that could take ten minutes. It troubled Zennor, who had British Army ideas, much more than Basil, who was more inclined to find things funny than annoying. His Spanish improved rapidly. 'Not so much conversational Spanish as argumentative Spanish,' he said to Zennor one evening.

'I read somewhere, before we left Barcelona, that they're raising a non-political army now, along conventional lines,' Zennor said. 'Thank God for that, I say. They'll never get anywhere with this crazy system.'

'But they're good fellows underneath,' Basil said, enjoying the first evening cigarette, in anticipation of dinner. Wild rosemary grew below the parapet, and some genius on kitchen duties had added a handful to the stew – he could smell it. 'And I rather like the fact that they understand why they're obeying an order, rather than being drilled into unquestioning obedience.'

'That's because we're not under fire. You'd soon see how unquestioning obedience matters if we were fighting a conventional battle. And I don't see the moral difference between parade-ground drilling, and the political indoctrination these boys have undergone.'

'Mind drilling versus body drilling,' Basil said. 'Which is worse? I suppose we'll never know.'

'We might learn by the end of this war,' Zennor said.

'I don't think war ever teaches anything,' Basil said idly. 'You never find out who was right. You only see who is left.' He saw Zennor raise his eyebrows at that, and thought it quite a nifty phrase. He would record it in his notebook – he was still writing it up every night, though he was unsure what use his experience would turn out to be to the newspaper.

Meanwhile, was it being useful to him? It was certainly moulding him. After three weeks, he had stopped fretting about being dirty. He had almost stopped noticing it. It was impossible to take off one's clothes or boots: you simply added or subtracted layers according to the temperature.

Nobody shaved – water was in short supply. There was none on the mountain, so it had to be brought up on mule-back from the valley, and was issued for drinking only, a quart a day per man, horrible cloudy water, which gave him diarrhoea for two horrific days before his body adjusted. There were no latrines and everyone defecated outside the barricade anywhere they could squat, so the smell of excrement was the first thing you noticed when coming out of the dugout in the morning. It became second nature to watch your step anywhere beyond the walls. Occasionally he thought that if London Basil could have seen him now, he would never have come, but most of the time he didn't think about it.

Apart from the water shortage, they had adequate rations: food was also brought up by mule, but there was enough of it, and it wasn't bad – usually some kind of stew and bread for dinner, sometimes rice or beans; bread and bacon for breakfast; the occasional ration of dried sausage and cheese. They were also issued with a pack of cigarettes each per day. What they lacked was military supplies. They had little ammunition, and much of that useless. They had no tin hats, no bayonets, no grenades, no range-finders, no field glasses, wire-cutters, flares, electric torches; unsurprisingly no maps – that area of Spain had never properly been surveyed. They didn't even have any cleaning materials: the pull-through had never been heard of, and there was no gun oil. They had to grease their guns with olive oil when they could get it; sometimes bacon fat.

To alleviate the boredom, Basil often volunteered for patrols, which took place at night or in foggy weather, and were not popular with the others, who saw no reason to exert themselves or face danger for no material benefit. Basil surprised himself the first time he heard himself volunteer – another way in which he had changed, he supposed, because he realised only then that the danger did not bother him. There was a chance of being shot by the Fascists, certainly,

314

but he backed himself to be wily. There was more likelihood of being shot on your return by your own sentry, who had probably fallen asleep and, waking with a start, assumed the Fascists were coming and started firing wildly. The challenge and password were forgotten in such moments. They were usually elevated revolutionary sentiments like *progreso*, *solidaridad*, *unidad*, or *adelante*.

To go on patrol was a change from the deadly routine, a chance to exert the body and exercise the mind. There were no paths down the ragged ravine sides: Basil enjoyed having to pick a way like a mountain goat from foothold to foothold – and to remember the way back – then across the valley floor and up the other side, trying to make no sound, to approach the Fascist stronghold. Dislodge a pebble or break a twig, and the darkness would fill with bullets whistling overhead.

One misty night he and his section of four got as far as the barbed wire, and crouched there, listening to the Fascists talking inside their compound. He couldn't make out what they were saying, and didn't suppose it was anything worth hearing. He doubted these patrols answered any military purpose. But he felt oddly alive creeping about on the dark, stark hillsides.

He was preparing to leave when he heard the clump of boots as someone came up to the parapet, and he made an urgent sign to his men to keep down. He smelt a cigarette, heard someone muttering to himself. A sentry, he supposed. Cautiously he shifted his position so as to crane upwards, and saw a shadowy figure standing there, looking out, the position of the face marked by the glowing end of a cigarette, like the red bull painted on a target. Basil froze, making a mental note to remind his men later not to smoke on guard duty. Had they been heard? Was the man scanning for them, with a view to opening fire? He could see indistinct movements, but did not know what the man was doing, until suddenly a thin stream of liquid arced over the barbed wire, luckily a few feet away. He heard the man next to him draw a breath to curse, and jabbed him warningly with his elbow. The sentry aloft cleared his throat and there was a gigantic hawk-and-spit, but he did not see where that landed.

Someone called from further away, the man answered and left. Now Basil had only to alert his men and creep, carefully and noiselessly, back the way he had come. Javier, the soldier he had helped with his marching down in Barcelona, was in his section and had developed a dog-like devotion to him, which meant he always volunteered alongside him and while out on patrol kept so close he was in danger of tripping over him. Now, Basil rose to a crouch and turned, he knocked into Javier, who was squatting just behind him, and the man overbalanced, went down on his behind, and let out a muted cry. There were sharp stones all around – Basil assumed he had landed on one. He grabbed Javier and slammed a hand over his mouth, but it was too late. Someone up above called an alarm, there was the sound of multiple boots, and then an excited jabbering as four or five Fascists came up to the parapet, telling each other it was a possible raid and asking each other if they could see the raiders.

Basil felt the hair rise on the back of his neck. He pushed Javier down, and lay flat himself, glad to see his other men instinctively followed suit. He gestured to them to begin the crawl away; he felt Javier beside him trembling all over and, afraid he might cry out in his fear, he caressed his shoulder and squeezed it comfortingly. He saw the white roll of eyes as the boy looked to him for instructions, and gave him a little shove and nodded, and began to inch forward himself. The others were already ahead, almost at the bushes, which would cover their retreat. But the loose stones were treacherous, and someone dislodged something. The sound, which would have been trivial in daylight, seemed monstrous in the dark. At once a cry rose from the Fascists, and they began firing. Basil felt an instant of rippling fear. He could hear the

316

whine of the bullets, but couldn't tell how close they were. But the Fascists knew their general direction. There was no point now in stealth, and grabbing Javier's upper arm he got up to a crouch and scuttled forward, dragging the boy with him. There was a pinging sound and a sharp pain in his thigh, and he thought he'd been hit, but his leg didn't fail. Seconds later they were in the scrub, fell flat again, and continued their progress wriggling like snakes. The rifle fire continued, but it was wild, spraying back and forth above their heads until, as they got far enough away to begin to feel safe, it petered out and stopped.

Basil called a halt, ascertained that no-one was hurt, and examined his leg with some trepidation. But it must only have been a sharp stone that had hit him – there was no blood. Javier was weeping quietly, and with an odd insight Basil knew it was with shame, not fright. He said something to reassure him, and started leading them back towards their position. He was interested to find, now it was over, that his fear had not been for being hit, but rather not knowing *where* he might be hit: leg, shoulder, back, head? It had made his whole body feel exposed and vulnerable. Once he'd felt the pain in his thigh, the general terror had gone away: he knew the worst.

Minor though the incident was, it was the nearest thing to war he had yet experienced. And, absurdly, it confirmed in Javier's mind that he was a genuine leader.

Helen and Jack were at breakfast in the dining room. The day was warm and dry, though overcast, and the French windows onto the garden were open, letting in the May smell of growing grass and the sound of birds. All was peaceful, with nothing but the clink of knife on plate or cup on saucer. Jack had finished reading his letters and picked up the paper. A few moments later, without a word, he dropped the newspaper, got up, and walked out into the garden.

317

Helen half rose, thinking he might be choking, but she saw the headline, and understood. She reached over, and read the news article. The giant airship, the *Hindenburg*, while docking at the Naval Air Station at Lakehurst in New Jersey, had suddenly caught fire, dropped to the ground, and burned so fiercely that within seconds nothing was left of the vast superstructure but the bare bones of the metal frame. Thirty-five people had perished.

Jack was standing with his back to her, staring down the garden. She hesitated but, seeing him fumble out his cigarette case, she went to him, and was in time to take the lighter from his hand, which was shaking, and light the cigarette for him.

'Thanks,' he said. And then, 'Those poor souls.'

She slipped a hand through his arm and stood silent for a while. Then she said, 'They don't seem to know what caused it. Could it have been a lightning strike? Conditions were stormy.'

'It doesn't matter,' Jack said. 'It was bound to happen, sooner or later.'

'But the other one – the *Graf Zeppelin* – has made hundreds of trips without trouble.'

'Don't you understand?' Jack said harshly. 'Hydrogen is highly flammable when even small amounts are mixed with air. And it's not possible to prevent all leakage when you're dealing with cotton gas bags, no matter what you dope them with. They'll never be completely airtight. Those ships build up huge amounts of static electricity in flight. The slightest spark—' He stopped and took a draw on his cigarette. 'The whole concept is faulty. Sooner or later, it had to happen. There's no safe way to use hydrogen for lift. We learned that six years ago, but the Germans . . .' He shuddered. 'They used them for propaganda, Helen! "Look how wonderful our engineering is, look how go-ahead we are."'

'I suppose this will be the end of it,' she said after a

moment. 'I mean, no-one's going to want to travel by airship after this. Not even the Germans.'

'They weren't planning to use hydrogen, you know, at first. *Hindenburg* was designed for helium. But the only commercial supply of helium comes from America, and the Americans banned any export of it.'

'Why?'

'Didn't trust the Germans. Didn't want them developing rigid airships for military use. I believe the Germans thought they'd change their mind – that's why they went ahead with *Hindenburg*. But they didn't, so it had to be hydrogen.'

They were silent for a while longer. Helen felt him gradually relax beside her, and finally asked, 'Are you all right?'

'I will be,' he said. 'It was a shock.'

'I know. For me, too. I'll never forget that night when I thought you were on the R101 and I heard—'

'Yes. Don't.'

'I'm so grateful I have you. We're so lucky. When I think of everything we've been through . . .'

He looked down at her, and gave a twitch of the lips that was almost a smile. 'There *has* been a lot,' he acknowledged. 'Uniquely blessed, aren't we?'

'*I* think so,' she said stoutly.

He stubbed out his cigarette and turned with her towards the house. 'I wish men would learn from the past. After the R101, they still built the *Hindenburg*. After the Great War, they're still heading hell-for-leather for another. Every new generation thinks they're the first people to tread the earth. I'd make studying history compulsory for politicians. At least five years of it.'

'That'd larn 'em,' Helen said. 'I'm going to ring for fresh toast – that lot'll be leathery.'

He followed her in. 'Did you know that *Hindenburg* was built using eleven hundred pounds of duralumin salvaged from the R101?'

Helen stopped and looked back. 'But it wasn't the frame that failed,' she said at last. 'What are you saying – that *Hindenburg* was cursed?'

'Don't be silly,' Jack said. 'That's superstitious nonsense.'

But Helen remembered the war. Fliers were all superstitious. Perhaps all people risking their lives daily in times of war were.

Oliver tapped the newspaper. 'A milestone,' he said. 'In a very small paragraph.'

'What's that?' said Verena.

'The Simpson divorce,' he said. 'A notice here that the decree absolute has gone through. I imagine the ex-King is galloping to her side even as we speak.' He put the paper down. 'It's interesting how completely they've been forgotten, isn't it?'

Verena was decapitating her egg and didn't look up. 'I suppose so. You never read anything about them in the papers now.'

'I think the whole country is just relieved it's all over. And the new King and Queen are doing very well. They're tremendously popular everywhere they go.'

'He did awfully well at the Coronation,' Verena said. 'Considering the strain there must have been on him, and all the awkward things he had to say. I was afraid there would be embarrassing silences. You know how he gulps, and his jaw works when he can't get a particular word out.'

'Oh, he had a speech tutor, who went through the whole thing with him. Rehearsals every day until he was comfortable with it.'

'I didn't know that,' Verena said. 'Who is he?'

'The tutor? An Australian fellow – used to help shell-shock victims after the war, who had trouble with speaking.'

'I haven't heard anything about that.'

'I don't think the King would want it generally known,'

said Oliver. 'He's pretty sensitive about the stammer. But I've spoken to the fellow professionally once or twice. He has rooms in Harley Street, not far from mine. We've consulted about hare-lip patients – I did the surgery, and he did the speech therapy. He has no professional training – I'm afraid some of my colleagues dismiss him a quack – but he's had some good results. He's a very nice fellow, infinitely patient and kind, which helps when dealing with children.'

Verena buttered a piece of toast. 'He must have been working very hard with the King, to get him through the wireless broadcast after the Coronation. I didn't hear any stammering at all. There was just that pause at the beginning when nothing happened – I was afraid he'd got stuck and would never speak at all.'

Oliver smiled. 'I heard about that from Tommy Lascelles. It was just a mistake of timing. The King was supposed to walk from the anteroom into the studio while the National Anthem was playing, and take his seat in front of the microphone just as it finished. But they'd timed it wrongly, and the anthem finished before he got there.'

'I see. Well, it was a very nice speech. I think he'll do very well, don't you?'

'We're lucky to have him. And the Queen.'

'It makes you realise how unsuitable the Simpson woman would have been. Imagine her being crowned in Westminster Abbey, kneeling under the canopy, being handed the sceptre and rod and so on.' She shuddered. 'She would probably have wanted to "modernise" the whole thing.'

'She'd have ordered jazz singers instead of the Abbey choir. "I Got Rhythm" instead of "Zadok the Priest". But it would never have happened: Cosmo Lang would never have crowned her, let alone anointed her.'

Verena put down her knife. 'Yet here we are, talking about her again. Let's not. We've got the Buckingham Palace dinner party on the seventeenth, and Lady Sutherland's ball on the eighteenth to look forward to.'

'Have you decided what to wear?' Oliver asked. 'Apparently the King's asked the Queen's dressmaker to design her something based on those Winterhalter portraits of Queen Victoria – you know, crinolines and lace berthas.'

'Hmm. Well, I suppose it would suit her. She is quite . . . round.'

'I like roundness. It's cheerful. Better than being stick-thin and miserable like—'

'Don't say it! We are not going to talk about Wallis Simpson any more.'

'Who? I don't know who you're referring to,' Oliver said solemnly.

'According to Fruity,' Kit said, as their car conveyed them to the ball, 'David caused deep offence to Kitty Rothschild, after she'd lent him her château for all those months. When she left for Paris, he didn't bother to get out of bed to say goodbye to her, let alone thank her. Now he's bundled off to join Wally without tipping the servants, and he's left behind a socking great telephone bill – all those long-distance chats with his beloved. Fruity said he asked Wally to ask David to do something about it – even a nice thank-you letter would help – and got a very sharp retort.'

'She was never very keen on paying bills,' Emma said. 'I can't see her pressing David to do it. And doesn't he claim to be hard up, these days?'

'He pretty much has to, given that he's trying to prise a pension out of the government. But I imagine her real disgruntlement is about not being an HRH.'

'I didn't understand that,' Emma said. 'I thought once an HRH, always an HRH. David's been one since birth, so wouldn't that make his wife an HRH too?'

'In normal circumstance, yes,' Kit agreed, 'but the argument by the Lord Chancellor was that in renouncing the succession, he also renounced his royal rank. And according to Clive Wigram, by abdicating in order to marry Wally, David accepted that she wasn't fit to be queen. So, logically, she must be unfit to be a member of the Royal Family. Wigram says the brothers agree, and the old Queen does, of course, and the Dominion prime ministers.'

'So what are the Letters Patent about?'

'Well, the King is still fond of him, even after all he's done. So the Letters Patent say that the D of W shall, notwithstanding the Act of Abdication, hold and enjoy the style of Royal Highness, but that his wife and descendants shall not. A wee wedding gift from one brother to another.'

'A gift that will annoy the recipient no end,' Emma remarked. It was raining again, the drops slapping against the window beside her and running diagonally down the glass. It had rained most of Coronation Day, too.

'Apparently Wigram hinted the same thing, and the King said that, far from taking anything away from David, he was *giving* him a title he would otherwise have forfeited when he abdicated.'

'David will never see it that way.'

'No. Even after all this, he's incapable of understanding the pain he caused everyone. Fruity says he's simply bewildered by his family's inability to see how wonderful Wally is.'

'Oh, well, it's all over now,' Emma said, as the car glided to the kerb in front of the lighted building. 'Let's forget about it and enjoy the evening. I don't suppose we'll ever see them again, anyway.'

'Almost certainly not. They are now in the category of old, unhappy far-off things and battles long ago, and we shall think of them no more. Here we are, beloved, and may I say you look ravishing tonight?'

'You may, provided you promise to dance with me and

not spend all evening frowsting in the smoking-room with your chums.'

'The only thing that would stop me dancing with you is not being able to get near you for your hundreds of admirers.'

There was a saying: God laughs when men make plans. It was the next day that Kit was called from the breakfast table by a telephone call.

'That was Fruity,' he said, returning to Emma.

She studied his face. 'Something wrong? They've heard about the Letters Patent? What did they say?'

'David said that Bertie would never do such a thing, and that it's a plot by the Hardinges to insult Wally.'

'What does she think?'

'Fruity says she wasn't surprised – she's been telling David ever since she left England that his family would never allow her to be an HRH. She said that the British monarchy is a matriarchy in pants: the King's wife runs the King and the King's mother runs the King's wife. But that's not the worst thing.'

'Oh dear. You'd better tell me. I can see it's shaken you.'

'Fruity says David wants us at the wedding on the third of June. We are commanded to propose ourselves, on pain of – well, whatever level of displeasure we care to imagine.'

'Oh, heavens! I don't want to go.'

'You still haven't heard the worst. Despite the Letters Patent, he says everyone has to call Wally HRH. And to get into the swing of it, he's making everyone curtsy to her.'

'Kit, I can't, I really can't, curtsy to the double-divorcée from Baltimore who left me to pay restaurant bills even when *she*'d invited *me*. And who borrowed a pair of pearl and diamond earrings from me and never gave them back.'

'Did she, by gum! Then I shall wrestle them out of her if I have to pin her to the floor.'

'You don't mean you're thinking of going?'

'Sweetheart, I think we have to. Apart from Fruity and Baba, and Kath and Herman Rogers, there'll be no-one there.'

'Whose fault is that?'

'Don't be so unforgiving. The poor old chap can't help being a little bit mental. He was hoping that one of his brothers would come and be his supporter, but the King's forbidden it. Monckton's on his way, but David's down to one equerry – Dudley Forwood – and a detective.'

'You used to be sorry for Wally, now you seem to be sorry for him,' she accused.

'I'm sorry for both of them. When I think of the future that awaits them, I shudder. They ought to have *one* happy day to look back on.'

Emma stared at him. 'You *want* to go,' she accused him.

He gave her a shamefaced grin. 'Come on, don't you want to be able to say you were there? It's a little piece of history.'

'I'd be happy to *say* I was there,' Emma grumbled. 'It's the having to *be* there I mind. And I haven't anything to wear. '

'Bless you, you've days to choose something. We won't stay afterwards, I promise. They'll go straight off after the wedding breakfast, and we can leave the next morning.'

'Wally will expect a wedding present.'

'There's that silver chafing dish she gave you for your birthday last year. Give her that.'

'She didn't buy that for me, you know. I saw it at the Fort. David took it from Buckingham Palace.'

'So that makes it a fittingly royal gift,' said Kit.

'You are very wicked,' Emma said admiringly. It seemed she had agreed to go, without ever agreeing. 'But I won't curtsy,' she added, in final defiance.

CHAPTER FOURTEEN

Polly was in the Steward's Room one morning, looking at accounts, when James came in with a telegram in his hand. 'For me?' she said, looking up.

'No, for me,' James said. 'It's from Charlie.' He handed it to her.

WE ARE AT THE CHATEAU + GREAT THINGS AFOOT + I NEED A GOOD MAN + PLEASE COME AT ONCE + FERN MISSES YOU ++

'What great things?' Polly said.

'Now, how would I know?' James said impatiently. 'But if he needs me, I think I should go.'

'You've forgiven him for the Russian business?' Polly asked.

'That wasn't his fault. I never blamed him for it. I just couldn't stay in Paris, or be around them, with all the memories. But I'm over that part now. And he's not in Paris, anyway. He's at the château.'

Polly smiled. 'The fact is you're restless, you want a new adventure. You don't need to justify yourself to me, Jamie. You can come and go as you please.'

'Yes, but I know you depend on me. I couldn't just go if you're not happy about it.'

'I'll be fine. Go with my blessing.'

His face cleared. 'I'll go and cable Charlie.'

He got a reply within hours, telling him to catch the five-thirty ferry from Dover, and detailing the trains to take from

Calais to Paris and Paris to Tours, where he would be met by Charlie's car. This was the sort of thing he would be doing, he thought, looking up trains and arranging travel. It was what he had done in Paris. And what 'great thing' was Charlie planning now? A ripple of excitement went through him.

'The five-thirty ferry!' he exclaimed. He counted up journey times in his head. 'I'll have to get a train about noon. I must go and pack.'

'I'll come and help you,' Polly said. 'And I'll drive you to the station.'

'Thanks, that will be a help.' He headed for the door. 'Do you think I need to pack my evening clothes?'

'For Charlie Bedaux and his "great things"? Certainly,' Polly said, hurrying after him. Of course she would not try to stop him going. But she felt hollow already, knowing how she would miss him.

Clouds had obscured the twilight, and it was dark when James arrived at Tours station, with its magnificent façade of pale stone and vast semi-circular glass canopies, the elaborate columns topped with allegorical figures. He had expected to be met by Charlie's Hispano-Suiza, but there was only a battered taxi sitting out front, gently chugging as though waiting for him. The driver – a villainous-looking individual with a beret pulled down almost to his eyes – nodded to him.

James slung his luggage into the back and got in beside him. The taxi stank of French cigarettes; a rosary and a baby's shoe dangled from the mirror. He looked at his watch. It was well past nine o'clock. They would have finished dinner, and he was starving. But what he wanted most was a hot bath. Fern and Charlie's improvements to the château had included a bathroom for every bedroom, with a hot-water system so effective it could fill and empty a bathtub in less than one minute.

Soon after leaving the town, they turned off the main road onto a country lane.

'This isn't the way we came last time,' James said, wondering if he was being kidnapped. The driver looked capable of it.

'We go in the back way,' the driver said tersely. A few minutes later they slowed, and James saw a man sitting on a white staddle-stone at the side of the road. He stood as they approached, holding his shotgun in front of him in a casual-but-ready manner. The driver flashed his lights, the man stepped back, touching his hat-brim, and they turned into a gap in the hedge James had not noticed until then.

It was a track barely wide enough for a car – branches scraped against the taxi on both sides – and to judge from the jouncing it was a rough one. Branches met overhead so they crawled along a green tunnel, lit before them by the headlamps and closing in black behind them. Eventually the taxi turned sharp right through a gateway and stopped. The driver turned off the engine in a terminal manner, and James climbed out into what was evidently the service yard of the château. On one side the massive stone walls rose to the sky; on the other sides there were lower, less grand annexes. He'd not seen this part before.

A door in a cottagey building on the right opened, letting out a slice of yellow light, and James went towards it. A comfortable black-clad servant greeted him in French, told him that Monsieur and Madame were occupied with their guests and begged his indulgence. Was there anything Monsieur desired? Something to eat and drink, James said. She would have a *plateau* sent up to his room *tout de suite*, she said.

She took him to his room, pointing out the bathroom and WC on the way. The passages and stairs were covered with plain drugget, the walls were painted white, and he guessed this was the staff quarters. His room was plain but pleasant, and everything seemed to be new: there was a faint smell of fresh plaster. The bed was covered with a mauve-and-white cotton counterpane, and someone had put a vase of marguerites and mauve stocks on the dressing-table. In a corner there was a wash basin, where the water gushed from the tap piping hot, and a fresh cake of soap sat in a china dish. Such little touches made him feel like a welcome guest, even though he was there to work.

He'd had time only to wash his hands when the tray arrived, brought by a rosy-cheeked maid who blushed when he thanked her in French and scuttled away without speaking or meeting his eyes. After a bowl of soup, bread, a wedge of delectable pâté, some fruit and a carafe of wine, he felt too sleepy to bother with a bath, so he contented himself with a good wash at the basin and climbed into bed.

He woke very early the following morning. No-one would be up yet, he thought, but it was already light outside and the sun was slanting through the curtains, so he decided to get up and have a wander around before the day claimed him. Outside the early air was chilly but with the promise of heat; collared doves were hooting monotonously somewhere, and the air smelt of dewy grass. A striped cat stalking delicately across the yard hoisted its tail in greeting and veered out of its way to brush his legs in passing. In the left-hand corner of the yard he found a narrow, stone-flagged path that went under an arch and round the side of the main building to the front.

Here there were the beautiful lawns he remembered, with an edging of trees, and beds of flowers. The château was enchanting, a fairy-tale confection of bulbous towers and spire-topped turrets, all in a pale creamy stone now gilded in the first light of a summer morning. On one side the lawns fell quite steeply to a river; on another there was a broad gravel sweep that stopped abruptly at a drop-off, with a fine view across a valley to a magnificent many-arched viaduct. The grounds were extensive, mostly wooded, running down to the river below – he could just see the gleam of it between the trees. From the gravelled sweep a tree-lined avenue passed down to the front gates.

When he saw a servant opening the main door, he decided there was a good chance of something to eat if he returned to the staff quarters. He retraced his steps, encountered the rosy maid again and asked if anyone was up. Not yet, but soon, she told him. Madame and Monsieur were always up early, as was also His Royal Highness, who liked to perform *la gymnastique suédoise* first thing in the morning.

'His Royal Highness?' James queried.

She looked at him, wide-eyed, seeming surprised at his ignorance. It was here at the Château de Candé that the wedding was to take place, did he not know?

The wedding? he asked.

The wedding of His Royal Highness and Madame Saint-Saëns. It was very romantic. His Royal Highness was only lately arrived, but Madame Saint-Saëns had been staying here already many weeks.

She had pronounced the name in French, and her accent was strong and rustic, so it took him a moment to realise that Madame Saint-Saëns was in fact Madame Simpson, and the Royal Highness must therefore be the Duke of Windsor. So *that* was what Charlie wanted his help with. James had had no idea they were involved with it. They were lending them their exquisite château for *les noces*.

And James was to witness the wedding that had changed history, the wedding everyone would surely be talking about.

'Good God,' he said.

The *centuria* moved at last, from the high sierra north and eastwards to a plain in Aragon, where the Communists were besieging a small town that had been occupied by the Fascists since the autumn. The high plain was subject to fierce, cold winds, but there were more signs of life: this flat land had evidently been cultivated, and though it had been abandoned when the war began, Nature had reasserted itself, so that the bare sticks of the grape vines budded, the green blades of winter barley thrust through where the fields had not been trampled, and the orchards first blossomed, then came into leaf. There were unlifted potatoes in one field, which made a welcome addition to the diet, though the field was closer to the Fascist line and under observation. They had to lie flat and dig them up with their hands, and if they were spotted the machine-gun fire would throw up earth and stones all around them. But there was always somebody in the company who thought the reward worth the risk.

The new position was a couple of miles from the Fascist line, behind mud and stone parapets. To their rear a former farmhouse was much battered, and most of its roof was missing, but with its outbuildings it provided enough shelter to serve as cook-house, store and headquarters. Behind that was a swift-running stream, foaming over rocks, whirling in deep glass-green pools. Basil made use of it for the first bath since leaving Barcelona. He stripped naked, stepped in, and gasped. The water was grippingly, agonisingly cold.

On the bank, Zennor laughed. 'Where do you think that water comes from? It's snow-melt from the mountains.'

'Don't care,' Basil replied, between clenched teeth. 'Worth it!'

He stayed in as long as he could bear it, and rubbed himself all over with the sliver of gritty soap he had been saving. Zennor contented himself with washing face, hands and feet. 'I'll go in when it's warmer,' he promised.

The main action was on the other side of the besieged town, but there was intermittent shell fire most days. The noise at first was horrifying: not a bang or boom, Basil discovered, but a shrill, tearing, clashing noise, like metal being ripped apart by giant torturing hands. It was hard to bear, but he discovered again that you could get used to anything; and he very quickly learned to tell simply by the pitch of the noise how close the shell was likely to fall. Quite often the shells did not explode – the Fascist ammunition was almost as bad as theirs – so the dud would be picked up and fired back at the enemy.

The only military activity they had was going out on night patrol, into no man's land. Creeping about the fields among the remains of abandoned crops and inching along drainage ditches was at least different from the rocky places they had been used to, and occasionally they would find something fit to eat – a brick-like ear of corn, or a wizened piece of fruit. Once they were required to make a feint to draw the enemy's attention from an attack going in from the other side. They advanced, firing and yelling, until told to retreat, and whether it did any good they never found out. But that night a file of ambulances came down from the main action, jolting on the terrible roads. Basil wondered how the injured inside could bear it. If their wounds didn't kill them, the ambulance journey might well.

'I don't understand what we're doing here,' he complained to Zennor one evening. The nights were still cold, but the daytime temperature was rising, and enough heat lingered in the evening to smoke a cigarette outside after the meal.

Zennor thought about it. 'Well, I suppose if we weren't here, there wouldn't be a siege and the Fascists could just go where they wanted.'

'That's it? We're just a fence across the road?'

'If it wasn't us, it would be some other soldiers. Maybe they're more needed in battle than we are.'

Basil poked moodily at the ground with a stick. 'It's not that I really want a battle – I mean, when you think about being wounded or killed. But—'

'I know. I've heard the men say the same thing: when are we going into action?' He shrugged. 'I suppose it's our nature, as men.'

'You're a philosopher,' Basil said. It wasn't a compliment.

Charlie greeted James with cheerful warmth. Tall, elegant Fern kissed him on both cheeks in the French manner.

332

'I'm so glad you're here,' Charlie said. 'There's still a heap to do, and I need someone I can trust, someone who knows how I work. Just one thing. I'm sure I don't need to tell you, but not one word to any journalist – in fact, not to anyone outside these walls, because they're cunning devils and they'll try anything to get a story. They're camped outside the front gates, have been for days. That's why we go in and out by the back entrance. They haven't found that yet. I send my motor out of the main gates every now and then as a decoy to keep them focused.'

'I saw your armed guard,' James said.

'He's meant to be seen.'

'But he wouldn't really shoot at people, would he?'

Charlie hesitated for a telling second. 'Only into the air. Although,' he added, 'a peppering of shotgun pellets in the backside is a pretty good deterrent.'

'Charlie!' Fern said warningly.

'The *threat* of a peppering, is what I mean, of course,' he added hastily.

It turned out that the Bedauxs were staying in the staff quarters too. 'We've given our bedrooms to the happy couple. And it's more convenient to be over here,' Fern said, as they went into the small parlour where they breakfasted. The smell of coffee and new bread was torturing James.

'We can come and go more easily, and don't get sucked in,' Charlie agreed.

'Sucked in?' James queried.

Charlie looked a little embarrassed. 'The Duke's accustomed to having equerries, you see, and he's no good at being on his own. He tends to buttonhole you, and I haven't time to hang around and chat. Don't take me wrong, he's an excellent fellow, and we're very proud to be hosting his wedding, but with so much to do in such a short time . . .'

James's duties did not take him into the château very often, but he did encounter the Duke now and then, walking the dogs around the gardens, or setting off for a round of golf on the eighteen-hole course in the grounds. His bow was met each time with a blank look and the merest twitch of acknowledgement. James was sure the Duke had no idea who he was.

He was an odd-looking soul, James thought, so thin and small and undeveloped – James towered over him – that he looked from a distance like a fourteen-year-old boy. His hair was flaxen and still thick, but close to, his face was covered with fine lines, like the glaze on an old piece of china, and there were heavy bags under his eyes, and a wattling of the flesh under his chin. And his left eye was noticeably lower than the right. Even when he smiled, his expression was sad: he didn't seem at all like a bridegroom. But one day James saw him approaching the house just as Mrs Simpson stepped out of the front door, and then his face lit up with an expression of almost religious adoration.

Mrs Simpson, when he was presented to her, looked him over intently but unsmilingly. She was terribly thin, with bad skin, a big nose and a big chin with a slash of scarlet mouth in between, shiny black hair tightly drawn back, smart, elegant clothes and some very sparkling jewellery. He could not for the life of him see what there was about her to make her worth a kingdom – and yet, there was that look on the face of the Duke. It was, he thought, like the rapture of a lost toddler who suddenly spies its mother again.

His job involved a lot of driving: meeting people at the station and fetching things from the town. He had to collect Mr Main Bocher and his retinue of assistants, who brought The Dress and conducted a final fitting; the next day it was a Mrs Spry to do the flowers, and Mr Cecil Beaton, to do the official photographs in full costume. The rosy-cheeked maid, whose name, he had discovered, was Cécile, was upset about that, saying it was bad luck to wear the wedding dress before the wedding day. James was called into the château to help with the photography session, since Mr Beaton was making all sorts of demands about moving furniture, lights, mirrors and drapes, which Mrs Simpson was countermanding as fast as he ordered. Neither of them spoke any French. He was approaching the door of the Red Sitting-room when he heard Mrs Simpson's harsh bray: 'Where's that young man, the tall one – Bedaux's assistant? He speaks French. Get him here – he might as well earn his keep.' And when he entered the room, she said, 'Oh, there you are!' as though he had been keeping her waiting. 'Tell these people I want that armoire moved – it's hideous. And I want the two lamps from the Music Room brought in, the ones with the glass shades. And the blue-and-green rug from the Library, the one by the window at the far end.'

The Duke, in his morning-suit, with a gardenia in his button-hole, was standing by, looking on helplessly. He reminded James of a clockwork toy that hadn't been wound up.

Later he had to collect the clergyman from the station. Under French law, there had to be a civil ceremony before the mayor; but the Duke was determined they should be married by the Church of England rite. The Archbishop of Canterbury had forbidden any Anglican priest to have anything to do with it, and things were looking desperate when a letter came from a Reverend Robert Jardine, the vicar of a poor parish in Darlington, offering to perform the ceremony.

Jardine was a short, red-faced man with thinning black hair carefully eked over his scalp; his suit was worn at the seams. He chatted to James all the way back to the château. He thought it a disgrace, the way the ex-King had been treated. If a man had a sincere desire to wed the woman he loved under the auspices of the Church, no man, even the archbishop, ought to deny him. He didn't care a fig for the archbishop, anyway – Lang was an ecclesiastical cad. Suppose the ex-King were to have his throne restored to him, where would Lang be then, having snubbed him? The Church, in any case, was stuffy and outdated, riddled with prejudice and back-scratching. There was no future in it for a modern thinker, or an ambitious man without the right contacts. He was thinking of emigrating to California.

At the château, they set about creating something like a chapel in the Music Room with a massive oak chest for an altar and a fine white tablecloth for an altar cloth. Chairs for the guests were arranged before it. A plain silver cross and silver candlesticks had to be borrowed from a nearby Protestant chapel to stand on it – Jardine wouldn't have a crucifix. Then Mrs Simpson demanded more candles: the whole ceremony was to be candlelit. Electric lamps were tacky. She ordered more mirrors to be brought in to reflect the candles, and directed where they were to be put. Here. There. And there. A little more to the left. A little higher. That's it. James wondered what Fern would think about the nails being hammered into her newly restored woodwork.

On the eve of the wedding James had to go to Tours station and meet the last two guests. Emma, in a close hat and a fox fur over a dark cloth suit, stopped in astonishment, then came towards him with outstretched hands. 'James! What on earth are you doing here? Surely you don't know David and Wally.'

'No, I'm Charlie Bedaux's assistant. I've worked for him on and off for years.'

'Well, it's wonderful to see a friendly face,' she said.

Kit shook his hand. 'How are things at the château? Is it all tantrums and scalded cats? Or is everything proceeding calmly, like a liner gliding across a tranquil sea?'

'A bit of one and a bit of the other. I think we've got it all set out now, barring last-minute changes. I can't help feeling,' he added, carrying Emma's bag to the car, 'that a wedding would go off much more smoothly if there were no bride and groom involved.'

'Especially this bride and groom,' Kit said, heaving the other bag in beside Emma's.

'I'm sorry about the car. The press are everywhere, and they know the good motors by sight, so we have to trundle about in these battered things we've borrowed from the neighbours. Charlie calls them the Old Contemptibles.'

'Who else is here?' Kit asked.

'The Metcalfes, of course. Mrs and Mrs Rogers have arrived, and I picked up Mr Monckton this afternoon. Mrs Simpson's Aunt Bessie has been here for a while.'

'Is that all?'

'I understand so. Well, there's Charlie and Fern, and me, of course – if you count us.'

Kit looked at Emma. 'So it's come to this – only seven English people will witness the wedding of the man who just six months ago was King of England and Emperor of India.'

'Actually, I'm not sure if I'll be at the ceremony,' James said. 'I'm not a guest, you know, just an assistant, and I'm staying in the staff wing. In fact, I may even be told not to talk to you once we get there. Mrs Simpson doesn't like the staff taking liberties – she likes the distinctions to be maintained.'

'If I know Wally,' Kit said, 'and I do, she'll want you at the wedding, for decoration. She likes handsome young men. I hope you have a good suit with you?'

The wedding day was fine: sunshine, clear skies, and a very light cooling breeze. Charlie went over to the château after breakfast, and returned with an order from Mrs Simpson that James was to attend the ceremonies, 'in case any translations need to be done'. So Kit had been right, James thought.

The mayor arrived promptly at noon to perform the civil ceremony in the Library, wearing over his suit an immense red-white-and-blue sash.

'It's lucky they're the colours of America and Great Britain as well as France,' Baba Metcalfe said to Emma, 'or it might be seen as a revolutionary taunt to a king without a throne.'

The civil ceremony was short, registers were signed, and then everyone passed into the Music Room, where the carefully placed mirrors reflected a prodigious twinkling from the multitude of candles, and from the bride's diamonds. Wally was in her Main Bocher gown: floor-length and close-fitting in ice-blue crêpe, under a tight, boxy jacket with long sleeves and a ruched bodice, and a halo-shaped straw hat with a tulle half-veil. Fruity Metcalfe was the Duke's supporter, and Herman Rogers gave away the bride.

'I think the hat is a mistake,' Kit murmured to Emma. 'Straw? Too picnic-like. I'd have thought a tiara . . .'

'Ssh!' Emma said.

'She looks tense,' he went on, unrepentant. 'And I think David's going to cry.'

Emma pinched him and he subsided. The Duke *did* cry when they were pronounced man and wife. Wally remained rigid throughout, evincing no emotion of any kind, as though she had braced herself to go through with it at any cost. When it was over, the Duke turned to her and took her hands, as though he expected some gesture, a smile, perhaps, or a kiss, but she merely rearranged him, folding his arm across his stomach so that she could put her hand through the crook, and turning him to face the company for their congratulations. No-one seemed to know quite what to do next, until Fern, always the thoughtful hostess, said in a quiet but carrying voice, 'Shall we retire to the Drawing-room for champagne? Luncheon will be served shortly.'

The newly-weds walked out, and the guests formed a little procession behind them as they moved to the Drawing-room, where two footmen stood with trays of glasses. The flower arrangements were magnificent in every room, almost more than the rooms could stand. 'There can't be a paeony left standing anywhere in France,' Kit said. 'I wonder if Mrs Spry will get paid. I don't think Main Bocher has ever had a penny for any of his efforts.'

'He gets the publicity,' Emma said automatically.

Kit left her to go and talk to Herman Rogers.

'What a sad little wedding,' Baba said, appearing at Emma's side as she took a glass from a tray. 'The final act in a tragi-comedy that nearly toppled an empire. Why was Wally so granite-faced?'

'The poor thing broke out in spots this morning,' Emma said, 'so I imagine her stomach's been playing up these last few days. It's usually a sign.'

'She's got her man,' Baba pointed out. 'She should be happy.'

'She never wanted this,' Emma said. 'Any of it.'

'Well, she's got it now, so she might as well make the best of it. You can see the love is all one-sided,' she said, gesturing towards the couple, standing at the other end of the room. The ex-King was looking at her adoringly; her face was taut and turned away from him. 'I'd feel warmer towards her if I'd seen one loving gesture from her today – if she'd just touched his arm, or once looked at him kindly.' She emptied her glass and met Emma's eyes. 'She's like a woman unmoved by the infatuation of a much younger man.' She took another glass from a passing attendant. 'Talking of younger men, who is that Adonis, whom you seem to know? Bedaux's assistant?'

'James Morland – a distant cousin of mine. I used to go and stay at his father's house, Morland Place, when I was a girl. I loved it there – the house was always full of people and servants and dogs, and Uncle Teddy made it such fun, with riding and picnics and games and dancing.'

'You sound positively nostalgic!'

'I was always happy at Morland Place. Uncle Teddy taught me to shoot and my cousin Jessie taught me to drive. And Aunt Hen – she was Uncle Teddy's widowed sister, she lived there and ran the place – she was a mother to me, when my own died.'

'And is he married?' Baba asked.

'Uncle Teddy? He's dead now.'

'No, the divine young man – James Morland, you said?'

Emma frowned. Baba was famed for having affairs – Emma knew of at least six lovers, including, a little awkwardly in the circumstances, Walter Monckton. 'No, he's not married – I really don't know why. You're not thinking of—'

'Oh, no, I don't get involved with unmarried men. But he's rather delicious. Why on earth hasn't he been snapped up? Perhaps he's an invert – the pretty ones often are.'

Luncheon was lobster and champagne followed by strawberries. Neither bride nor groom ate much – the Duke never did eat luncheon, and the new Duchess looked unwell. Immediately afterwards they left for their honeymoon at the Schloss Wasserleonburg in Austria, lent to them by a cousin of their friend Lord Dudley.

'Another mistake,' Baba said to Emma. 'The last thing those two need is to be alone together. They should have gone to Vienna.'

At the very last, when Emma said goodbye to her, Wally's iron control wavered. Her lips trembled as Emma leaned in to kiss her cheek, and her hands gripped Emma's tightly for an instant. But she said nothing, turned away and got into the car.

Fruity, who really loved the Duke, wept a little as he said goodbye to him; and the Duke's eyes were wet.

Then they were gone. The guests turned away to walk back into the house. 'Are you crying?' Emma said in amazement, seeing Kit run a knuckle under his eye.

'No!' Kit said immediately. Then, 'A little, perhaps. That really is the end of it.'

'What will they do from now on?' Emma wondered.

'We've seen enough exiled royalty since the war to know how it goes. They'll wander from place to place, fêted by excitable second-raters, staying wherever anyone will give them a lavish enough welcome. Until their hosts discover they're too expensive and hint them away. Everything gradually getting smaller and shabbier as their glamour fades and they're forgotten.'

'No, that's too sad!' Emma protested.

'They should go to Hollywood,' Kit said, 'and attach themselves to the movie-celebrity circuit.'

'You're not serious?'

'Why not? They'd fit in perfectly there. Hollywood loves royalty. He still has a certain cachet, and she's very smart and fashionable, and knows how to work a room. They'd do very well, going to parties, opening nights, galas, being photographed with movie stars. He could play golf with celebrities. She might write fashion notes for a newspaper. And living is quite cheap in California, I understand. You can make a splash without huge expense.'

Emma shook her head, unsure if he was joking. The wedding stood in her mind as a terribly lonely thing, and the thought of that pointless, nomadic future was lonelier still. 'We'll never see them again,' she said, and it was half a question.

'No,' said Kit. He took her hand into the crook of his arm, and looked down at her. 'It's all over now. We can go home.'

James was helping the servants to dismantle the chapel and put the house back as it had been, when Charlie came downstairs from taking back his bedroom and said, 'James, there you are! What are your plans now?'

'I haven't any,' he said.

'I hope you're not thinking of going back to England right away? Please don't. We're having a few days here to get over it all. I'm sure you need a rest too. But then I'm going back to Paris. Lots to do. And I want you with me, if you'd care to have your old job back.'

James smiled slowly. 'I'd like that,' he said. He'd missed Paris. Morland Place would always be home, but it would always be there for him. He was ready for a new challenge.

'Good. Well, I'll have them move your things over to one of the guest rooms – no need to rough it in the staff quarters now there's plenty of space in the house. Enjoy yourself for the rest of the week. Make use of the facilities, golf, tennis, the gym. There's the lake to swim in, lovely walks. You can use one of the cars if you want to go out. And I can borrow a horse for you, if you'd like to ride. Then we'll go up on Monday and make a start.'

'On anything in particular?' James asked.

'Yes – as well as the regular business, I'm going to arrange a trip to Germany for the Duke and Duchess in the autumn. I've already mentioned it to him, and he's dead keen. He wants to cement relations between the two nations, and study housing and working conditions in Germany, now the Nazis have cleared up the mess left by the war. And I've got business interests there. The Duke's name could be useful. You'll help me?'

'I'd be happy to.' Closer ties between England and Germany could only be a good thing – an alliance to face down Communist Russia.

Charlie slapped his shoulder. 'Good man!' he said. 'And after the Germany visit, I've got something else up my sleeve: a royal tour of America. What do you think? Would you like a trip to the States with us?'

'I'd love it,' James said. *America!* Morland Place seemed very far away.

It had grown very hot on the Aragonese plain. Routine work, such as digging trenches and replacing sandbags, was now carried out under a burning sun. The temptation was to strip off, and there were many cases of sunburn, one or two of sunstroke. The heat also triggered tremendous thunderstorms and torrential rain. The rain was at least a relief, but quickly turned the ground into a quagmire, and the ditches into streams. There were more foreigners now in the *centuria* –

two more English men, Williams and Kellerman, and three German students who had run away to join the Communists out of a dislike of Fascism. Most German combatants were on the Fascist side, and Basil wondered how these three would feel about shooting their own people, if it came to it. They were full of idealism and high courage, and seemed very young to him, making him realise again how he had changed in the months he had been there.

The heat brought other problems: mice and rats, which ate everything, including leather belts and cartridge-pouches, and would even nibble at boots; clouds of black flies that flew into your mouth as you panted under the sun shifting sandbags; and lice, which were worst of all because they were actually inside your clothes, living on your body. Basil went through another crisis of revulsion, and knew he would never be reconciled to the sensation of something running across his skin. He bathed in the still-icy stream as often as he could; and one of the older Spaniards showed him how to burn the eggs, which nestled along the seams of clothing, with a metal rod heated in the fire. It kept the numbers down, but nothing could eradicate them completely.

There were shortages now, of candles, matches and oil. Replacements for uniforms, which had been hastily made and were falling apart, came through rarely. Everyone's boots were coming to pieces, and there were no new ones. Worst of all was the shortage of tobacco. The daily pack per man had gone down to an issue of ten cigarettes, then reduced to five; then for a week there was no issue at all, and men were scouring the ground for long-discarded cigarette ends. Basil wondered whether anyone at home had sent him parcels, as promised: he hadn't received so much as a letter. He indulged in fantastic dreams where a parcel arrived, full of cigarettes and soap and chocolate, tea and cake and biscuits and jam, razor blades and socks, but it never happened. Williams said he'd heard that the Post Office would not accept mail of any sort for Spain; Kellerman said he'd heard parcels were stolen as they passed through France.

One day in July, Basil and Zennor were told they were going on leave. They had been at the Front for three and a half months, and Basil had not even considered the possibility of leave. He had sunk to a point where the daily tedium and privations seemed like the eternal order. They cleaned themselves up as best they could, and with a dozen others – eight Spaniards, two Belgians and two Frenchmen – they climbed with their kitbags into a lorry and were jolted away over the appalling roads to the nearest railway station. There was a long wait for the train, and when it came, belching black smoke from the inferior grade of coal it was burning, they found the carriages were all ancient, third class, with bare wooden benches, and no glass in the windows. More and more lorries had disgorged more and more militiamen onto the station during the wait, and now they all crowded in, packed close together. In holiday mood, they laughed, bellowed revolutionary songs, and passed bottles of wine and *anis* from hand to hand.

The train made frequent stops, and at every one, local peasants forced their way in with bundles of vegetables, chickens tied together by the feet, and sacks of live rabbits, which kept writhing across the floor and having to be retrieved. Basil's group had been told they were going to Barcelona, but a little conversation with the peasants revealed they thought they were going to Tarragona. Zennor was quite worried – he whom nothing in the war so far had troubled – that either the soldiers or the peasants would end up lost and stranded. But when the train finally pulled into Tarragona, there were lorries waiting for the militiamen, and the peasants tumbled out onto the platform and dispersed, evidently familiar with the place.

They were driven to what had been a convent, from which the nuns had long been ejected: the Communist side was very anti-religion, as opposed to the Fascists, who were strongly Catholic. The main block was now a hospital, and the militiamen were accommodated in the former guest-house. As soon as they were settled, Basil and Zennor went out to explore. Tarragona was an ancient stone-built city and a modern port. There was a medieval old town and numerous Roman remains, and pleasant walks along the ramparts and the riverbank. Strangest of all was to see the beach, with its promenade and cafés and striped deckchairs, where prosperous-looking Spaniards enjoyed a seaside holiday, sitting on the sand and bathing in the sea, as though they had never heard the words 'civil war'.

The convent had extensive grounds, mostly being cultivated for fruit and vegetables, but there was also a garden, where the wounded were sometimes wheeled out to sit in the fresh air. It had a green lawn and beds packed with red, white and pink flowers, and in the centre a fountain featuring a nude nymph tilting an amphora from which the water tinkled into the bowl. After the first couple of days, Basil gravitated naturally to it. There was a rose climbing across the sunniest wall, covered in enormous pink flowers with a heady, slightly spicy scent. He liked to sit on his own on a bench in the shade and smoke and think his thoughts, while Zennor went out with the others for more conventional fun.

He was sitting there one day when a young Spanish woman appeared, carrying a basket. She was slender and high-coloured with glossy black hair, and she gave him one long, considering look from under thick lashes before beginning to work, dead-heading the rose, clearing up fallen petals and leaves, pretending to ignore him. He finished his cigarette, got up, and strolled slowly around the path until, arriving in her vicinity, he coughed discreetly and, when she looked up, smiled and greeted her.

They chatted. Her name was Consuelo. He explained that his name was that of a herb. Some discussion established

345

that it was probably *albahaca*. She said they had some growing in the vegetable garden – would he like to come and see? They strolled through the arch in the garden wall, while she told him that she had worked in the garden when the sisters had lived here, and after they had gone, the garden fell into disarray, until several of them in the town formed a group to take care of the grounds. Some of the vegetables went to the sick in the hospital; the remainder they sold in the town and the money went to the Cause.

Basil told her he was English, and she said she could tell, although his hair was dark enough for a Spaniard and he spoke Spanish very well. Her brothers, she said, were in the militia. She hadn't seen them since December. Her father had a lame leg and could not serve. He told her that his father had been an *aviador* in the war. She found the patch of herbs and pinched off a leaf for Basil to smell, and he agreed that it was the right one, though he really had no idea. Further on there was a patch of strawberries, bright red and as glossy in the sunshine as if they had been lacquered. She picked a fat one for him, put it into his mouth, and watched his lips as he ate it. So he was pleased but not surprised that she agreed to meet him that evening to go for a walk.

Along the riverbank there was a strip of greenery, trees and bushes and rough grass, providing cover and seclusion, a traditional haunt, he suspected, of young lovers. Consuelo was willing, passionate and evidently not inexperienced. He indulged her afterwards with love-talk about seeing her again and finding her when the war was over, but though she listened and seemed to enjoy it, he had a strong feeling that she knew it was nonsense, and didn't care. She was surprisingly hard-headed, and he guessed she had got what she wanted out of the encounter, even as he had.

346

CHAPTER FIFTEEN

Vivian raised a glass. 'To Porpoise Books! May the first nine vessels we have launched on a choppy sea bring their cargoes of enlightenment safely to harbour and enrich the minds of the readers.'

'Hear, hear,' Molly said. They drank the toast, and she added, 'And they might as well enrich our pockets while they're at it. It was a leap of faith on our part to sink so much money and time into them.'

'But the first month's sales have been good,' Charlotte said. 'And they've been awfully well received by the trade?'

'Yes, I fancy one or two other publishers are kicking themselves that they didn't think of it first,' Vivian said. He seemed in buoyant mood.

Porpoise had been launched at the beginning of June with nine titles from eminent thinkers and established literary figures who were sympathetic to the scheme. The books were *Practical Economics*; *A Short History of the World*; *Collected Essays in Popular Science*; *A Guide to Communism and Fascism*; *An Introduction to Modern Architecture*; *Nineteenth Century Art – an Introduction*; *Childhood and Society*; *Beasts and Maidens – A Modern Guide to Greek Mythology*; and *The Open Door – Social Anthropology Explained*.

Already prominent people had expressed approval of the list and an interest in contributing, including H. G. Wells,

J. B. Priestley, George Bernard Shaw, George Orwell and Winston Churchill.

'It's just the right time for something like this,' Molly went on. 'There's such a desire for self-improvement and self-education among the striving classes these days. The war broke down many barriers to advancement. There's a hunger for knowledge and for culture.'

Vivian picked up the copy of the *Spectator* he had been reading aloud from before. '"If there is any sense in saying that the culture of the world should be accessible to all without distinctions of wealth, such publications are helping to make it true."'

'That's an accolade worth having,' Molly said.

'Further down the line,' Vivian said, 'I think there might be a strong argument for an imprint for the classics. Including poetry.'

'How far back do you have to go before something's a classic?' Charlotte asked. 'The nineteenth century? Obviously Blake, Shelley and Byron are, but Tennyson and Hopkins only died – what? – around forty years ago.'

'I think he means epic poetry,' Molly said. 'Virgil and Horace. Not my pink-cheeked boys.'

'I think modern poetry belongs in the Porpoise catalogue,' Charlotte said. 'It's self-improvement, surely. Something to do you good, rather than enjoy?'

'Oh, you wicked girl!' Molly laughed.

And Vivian said, 'I'm ashamed to say I half agree with you. You can't call yourself an educated person without having read the great poets, but to sit down by the fire after dinner with a volume of it? I'd sooner have one of Molly's novels.'

'Blatant flattery!' Molly said.

Vivian turned to Charlotte. 'I've forgotten – why wasn't Milo able to come this evening?'

Charlotte was caught out by the change of subject. 'Um

– he had a business meeting. He sent his congratulations, of course, with his regrets.'

They didn't divide after dinner, but Vivian went off to his wine cellar to find a particular cordial, which he had been talking about, to go with their coffee, and Molly took the opportunity to say to Charlotte, 'You're looking thinner since I last saw you. And a trifle less blooming, if one might say so. Are you quite well?'

'Oh, quite,' Charlotte said, avoiding her eyes.

'Are you increasing?' Molly asked bluntly. Then, 'No, you'd have told me straight away if you were, I'm sure. Is something bothering you? You know you can confide in me.'

Charlotte shook her head. After a bit, she said, 'I wish Basil was here. He ought to have been raising a glass with us – he seemed to be so much a part of it all, in the early days.'

'I suppose you haven't heard from him? No, I imagine there isn't much of a postal service from Spain, in the circumstances. I couldn't be more surprised that he went, could you?'

'I don't know. He used to talk about having adventures.'

'Hmm. But he always seemed to me to be wedded to his comfort. I can imagine Basil in a silk shirt sipping a cocktail, but in khaki and biting a cartridge?' No response. 'Do they still bite cartridges? I don't really know much about firearms.' No response. 'Charlotte, dear, what's wrong?'

She looked up at last. 'It's seeing you and Vivian together. That's what I thought marriage would be like. And we used to talk so much before we were married. Or, at least . . .'

'Yes?' Molly encouraged, after a pause.

'We did, before he went away for that long trip abroad.' She bit her lip, thinking. 'He changed, you know. When we first met, he was just – a sort of vagabond, devil-may-care, easy-going. He reminded me a bit of Basil, except he's much more intelligent and better educated.'

349

'Oh dear. I shan't tell Helen you said that. When I think what those two spent on his education! No, go on, dear, I'm sorry.'

'He didn't care about money and titles and society and all that sort of thing. That's why Mummy disapproved of him at first. At least, Robert disapproved of him – Mummy just wasn't sure about him. But he was such fun to be with. After he came back from that trip, he was different. He seemed the same on the surface, but underneath he was – harder.'

'But you still married him,' Molly said.

'I loved him,' she said simply. 'I *love* him. But I don't feel I – quite – know him now. Not as I used to.'

'Specifics?' Molly said briskly. Vivian would be back in a moment.

'His business friends, whom we have to entertain. I don't feel that they're like us. And why *do* we have to entertain them? *You* don't do that.'

'We have authors to dinner.'

'That's different. You don't have to impress them.'

'You have to impress these – business friends?'

'Dinner has to be very good, the best wines. I have to have new gowns all the time. And be charming.'

'It's the hostess's job to make her guests feel welcome. Look at your mother.'

Charlotte frowned. 'I know. But it's more than that. I can't explain it. And there's this business of not wanting me to work.'

'Ah,' said Molly. She'd been wondering about that. Since her marriage, Charlotte had been doing some editing and proof-reading at home, part time. 'So you won't be coming back to the office?'

'He says I wouldn't have time, with running the house and entertaining. But I don't think it's that. I think he just doesn't want me to have a job.'

'A lot of men don't like it,' she said. 'Probably the majority,

350

if we're honest. Even Vivian, though he's the most enlightened of men, sometimes feels a little put out that I'm not his helpless little woman. He really likes it when I have a day at home writing, and have it all put away in time to greet him when he gets back from work, with my frock changed, my hair brushed and a cocktail mixed ready for him. Sometimes it's a nuisance for me to stop when I'm in the throes of inspiration, but I make a point of not letting him catch me still pounding away at the typewriter when he puts his key in the door. Marriage takes compromises, you know.'

Charlotte tilted her head. 'Isn't it always the wife that has to compromise? I don't see with Vivian – and I really like him, honestly I do! – what he's had to give up.'

'Ah, well,' Molly said. 'That's the way the two sexes were created. You'd have to ask God to explain that one. The caveman went off to hunt, and when he got back with the mastodon steaks, he expected the cavewoman to have collected the firewood and have the cave warm and tidy.'

'But—' Charlotte began, and broke off as Vivian came back in, holding a bottle.

'It was in completely the wrong bin,' he grumbled. 'I don't know how things move around on their own when one's back is turned.'

Molly look amused. 'My dear chap, if you're thinking that I, or the servants, go into your wine cellar while you're at work and play around with the bottles for fun, I can assure you—'

'Oh, no, of course I don't think that. I expect I moved it and forgot.' He caressed some dust from the bottle and displayed it proudly. 'Now, this is a Frapin vintage cognac from 1906. It's something you ought to try once in your life – if you're lucky enough to be offered it.' Belatedly, he looked at them, scenting an atmosphere. 'Did I interrupt something?'

Charlotte looked away.

Molly said cheerfully, 'Not at all. Ring the bell, and they'll bring the coffee. I didn't want them bringing it in until you were back or it would have got cold.'

When the *capitán*, a Belgian called Dupont, asked for volunteers to make an attack on the Fascist redoubt, Basil was surprised to see his own hand go up even before Zennor's. They had come back from leave to find that the line had been moved about a thousand yards further forward, so it was now only a couple of hundred yards from the Fascists. The point of the proposed exercise was to draw fire away from the main attack, which was to go in on the other side with the aim of cutting the road that supplied the besieged town.

Williams and Kellerman put up their hands, and grinned exuberantly across at Basil as Dupont outlined the plan, like children promised a treat. Basil's shadow, Javier, also volunteered, and prodded his skinny younger brother Jorge, who had come out recently to join him, to do the same.

'Action at last, eh?' Zennor said to Basil. He seemed as calm as always, but Basil sensed excitement in him. 'If it doesn't get cancelled again.'

'It won't be cancelled this time,' said one of the Spanish boys, known as Primo – Primo meant 'cousin', but it also had a slang meaning of 'mug' or 'dupe', and Basil could never determine which applied to him. 'Aguila told me.' Aguila was Primo's cousin, who was second in command of the battalion. Primo often presented himself as possessor of inside information. 'There'll be seventy *tropas de asalto* attacking the next position, on the right, so we can take the redoubt by surprise.'

Dupont was at that moment saying the same thing, so it seemed Primo's information was right this time. The redoubt was positioned at a point where the Fascist parapet bent round almost at a right angle, making it a natural weak spot, and the next position was two hundred yards further along. The storm troopers were the elite of the militia, and a determined assault by them would take attention away from Dupont's action. 'We'll sneak in and take a chicken while the farmer's chasing the fox,' said another of the Spanish boys.

They were issued with cartridges, and three bombs per man. They set off at midnight across no man's land, creeping in the pitch dark, bent double, tripping over the rough tussocks, slipping on the mud, stumbling into drainage ditches that were full to waist height after the recent rain. Before they even reached the wire they were all coated with mud, wet and cold.

A halt was called while the wire-cutting party went forward. They were close enough now that they were in range of the Fascist machine-guns, and it was essential to be absolutely quiet. In the black, still, damp night, the snip of the cutters sounded horribly loud, and Basil crouched, cold dread in his stomach, expecting any moment a shout from up ahead. Then the night would light up with whirring death. At this range, the gunners would not need to aim, only spray bullets from side to side.

But the wire was cut, and they filed through the gap and moved on. There was a second line of wire only twenty yards from the Fascists, and the parapet was just visible now, a looming darker shadow in the blackness. Basil felt they had been creeping forward for hours, so slow was their progress, and he scanned the sky anxiously for signs of dawn. But it was still black, the dead black of the small hours. Still there was no sound from the enemy. They crawled through the gap in the second line of wire. Basil was just behind Dupont; he heard Javier's noisy breathing as he came up on his left; shadows, more felt than seen, crept past him as the men spread out to form a line. Then Dupont lifted his arm, swung it back and hurled a bomb over the parapet. It exploded with a noise that was huge in the silence, but immediately, as if at a signal, the night lit up with a roar, with vivid light and black shadow, as a whole line of enemy rifles opened fire at once – twenty or thirty, Basil guessed. The attack was no surprise after all: the Fascists had been waiting for them.

Basil flung himself flat, pressing his face into the mud as the bullets whined overhead. The darkness spat with flame and heaved with noise as the more ready of the loyalists hurled their bombs. Basil dragged out the first of his, wrested away the pin, rose to his knees and flung it wildly, then dropped again to the mud. He had no idea where it went. The Fascists were throwing bombs now too: one burst a little to Basil's left, in a red glare and a gout of heat, and he heard a high-pitched scream close by him. Javier gave a cry. 'He's hit! Jorge, Jorge!'

Basil felt him try to get up, and reached out a hand to yank him down. 'Stay down, you bloody fool!' In the heat of the moment, his Spanish abandoned him. He fumbled out his second bomb and threw it, and saw it hit the parapet with a burst of light and dust. He dropped again, hearing the bullets sing around him. How could he not be hit? He was aware of Javier wriggling away from him, presumably trying to get to his brother, whom he could hear crying for Javier in a voice of childish fear.

'I'm coming, *pequeño*!' Javier replied.

Basil actually heard the bullet strike – a solid smack, like someone pounding a steak – and a gurgling grunt from Javier. But the firing intensified just then, and Basil burrowed into the mud, unable to look.

After what seemed like an eternity, the firing suddenly died, and Dupont at once got up and shouted, in Spanish and then English, 'Come on! Forward! Charge!' Basil was on his feet without volition, only desperately glad to be doing something rather than waiting passively for death. He staggered forward, weighted with mud, following Dupont. He saw Zennor to his right, and was vaguely glad, saw, to his amazement, skinny Jorge to his left, limping gamely, but no

Javier. Dupont threw another bomb, and Basil did the same with his last, seeing it burst well inside this time, in a satisfying fountain of debris.

There was a short slope leading to the parapet. It proved to be made of sandbags, which gave a foothold, enabling them to scramble over easily. Basil assumed there would be a Fascist waiting for him on the other side, and how could he possibly miss at that range? But there was no-one, only a scene of devastation from the bombs they had thrown: shattered huts, gaping holes, splintered wood and flung corrugated iron, here and there a dead body. They had driven them off; or had they rallied to the other attack point? Off to the right there was still firing, rifle flashes stabbing the darkness, greenish against the red of fires. The sound was oddly inconsequential, like water rattling over stones.

Dupont waved a hand. 'See what you can find, lads. Ammunition, rifles, food. Anything.'

Zennor came up to Basil. There was a shallow cut across his brow, and he had smeared blood into his hair as he'd brushed it out of his eyes. 'We ought to try and find the machine-gun,' he said. 'If we can get that back . . .'

'Right.' Basil turned and banged into Jorge, who was standing so close behind him he was almost touching him. He was trembling all over. Remembering that he had been limping – and remembering the scream – Basil said, 'Are you hit?'

'My foot,' Jorge said. 'But it doesn't hurt.' He plucked at Basil's sleeve. 'Javier's down. He's wounded. Hurt bad. You must come.'

Basil pulled away. 'I can't. I have to—' He waved vaguely at Zennor's retreating back.

'Please!' Jorge cried, the whites of his eyes showing in the darkness. 'Help me, for the love of God. I can't go back without him. Mama will kill me. Help him!'

He clutched again but Basil wrested himself away and

went after Zennor, who was disappearing into a structure that must have been a machine-gun nest. He ran to catch up. As he reached the doorway, he saw that there was a tripod and stacked boxes of ammunition, but no gun – they must have carried it away. And as Zennor turned to say the same thing, someone who had been hiding behind the stack rose and came out. Basil cried a warning, even as he saw the soldier, his face wild and stretched with panic, lunge forward, saw Zennor jerk at the impact, saw his puzzled, almost enquiring look. Then he pressed his hands to his chest, made a gulping sort of noise, and crumpled to the ground, pulling the soldier's bayonet out of his hands so that it clattered to the floor.

Basil found he had lifted his rifle into the firing position without even knowing it. The soldier screamed, a high-pitched sound like a girl, and clapped his hands to his cheeks in terror. Basil saw that he expected to be shot, even as he also saw he was a scrawny youth, probably not seventeen. It seemed only sad and pointless now, but he felt obliged to do it. With a sense of weariness, of a terrible weight rolling over him, he pulled the trigger. The boy was flung backwards, smacked into the wall, and slithered down into a sitting position. He stared a moment at Basil, and then his eyes closed and his chin fell onto his chest.

Zennor was trying to get up. He had got his hands and knees under him but seemed unable to lift himself. Basil put his rifle down carefully, as though it might go off again, and knelt beside Zennor. He was too heavy for Basil to get him to his feet, so he helped turn him into a sitting position, supporting him with an arm. Zennor seemed to be about to speak, but instead he coughed, a horrible choking, gurgling sound, expelling a great gout of blood, that soaked the front of his tunic. He tried again to say something, staring into Basil's eyes as though willing him to understand, but only coughed again, and the blood this time was a wet flood. Basil was going to say, 'Don't try to talk, old man,' when he realised Zennor wasn't looking at him any more. The eyes were fixed, but not on him. He had never seen anyone die before, but he discovered that the difference between a living body and a dead one was too profound to be mistaken. His friend had gone.

The *tropas de asalto* secured their position and joined up with Basil's unit. The Fascists were already regrouping, but they were able to hold out against them for twelve hours, long enough to get the dead and wounded back, before making a controlled retreat, abandoning the redoubt, but taking with them a quantity of ammunition, a few rifles, and some rations. The machine-gun they never found. The main objective, to draw fire, had been carried out, but the attack on the other side had not succeeded: the road had not been cut. So was it a success, or wasn't it? Had it been it worth the cost?

Javier had been hit in the head, neck and chest by a spray of bullets, and never regained consciousness. He was pronounced dead on arrival at camp. Only then did Jorge allow his wound to be looked at. The front half of his foot had been severed by shrapnel, and only the mud and blood had bound foot and boot together. Even so, neither the camp doctor nor Basil could understand how he had continued to get along on it for so long. He was taken off with the rest of the wounded to the hospital in Siétamo for treatment and discharge from the militia. Basil watched him go, so dazed with grief for his brother he had no fears for his own future as a *guerra discapacidados*.

It was two days later that Basil was wounded, and his own state of shock and grief for his friend probably contributed to it, making him incautious. He was out on patrol in no man's land, crawling on his belly through the swampy reed beds. Longing for a clean breath of air, he had raised himself up, forgetting that the movement of the tall reeds would have given away their position. He had just put up his hand to wipe the sweat out of his eyes, and before it reached his face, a sniper bullet went through it. After the initial shock of the blow, he felt no pain at first; when it did arrive, it was terrible. Morphine was in short supply after the recent action, and reserved for the worst injuries. Eventually there was space in an ambulance to take him to the hospital. He was thrown about so violently by the jolting over the ruts that his head bounced from the roof to the side. He couldn't use his hand to save himself.

The doctor who cleaned, dressed and plastered his hand was not sympathetic. 'Serves you right,' he grumbled. He was well educated, had visited England several times in his student days, and his English was excellent. 'What are you doing here anyway?'

Basil roused himself from a haze of pain and hopelessness. 'I volunteered,' he said. 'I wanted to help.'

'Help? How are you helping?'

'Fighting Fascism. Helping Spain.'

'Spain does not need your help. We can manage our own affairs without foreigners barging in. You arrogant English think you can teach us poor Spanish peasants about democracy and the rule of law? Spain was an old civilisation when your barbarian king was cutting off his wives' heads.'

'I'm sorry,' Basil said wearily. 'My friend was killed in the last action.' It sounded weak, like a plea for compassion – which he supposed it was. 'We only wanted to help.'

'And see how it turned out!' He paused while he finished smoothing the plaster, eyed Basil for a moment, then leaned closer and said in a kinder voice, 'You don't want to be here, my friend, do you? You want to go home.'

Home! The word cut through the fog in Basil's mind like a breath of clean air in a stifling room. He met the doctor's eyes, hope in his own.

The doctor nodded, as though a question had been answered. 'This hand will be long healing, and you will never get full use of it again,' he said clearly, as though someone might be listening. 'What a pity it is your right hand, your rifle hand. You cannot pull a trigger now. I must certify you medically unfit, and recommend you for discharge.'

'Discharge?' Basil repeated.

'You are no use to us now. You will leave the militia and go home to England.'

It turned out to be a simple process. The doctor gave him a certificate on which he was 'declared useless', which he took before the hospital medical board. They endorsed it, and sent him to the militia headquarters, where his papers were stamped for discharge and he was given a travel warrant. Then he caught a transport to the station where, after the usual delay and contradictory announcements, he was able to board a train for Paris.

His mood lifted a little as the train travelled slowly north, away from the bleak mountains and into a green and fertile land, away from the sights and smells and concerns of war and into a landscape of agriculture and rural affairs. He thought of England, and considered where he should go when he got back there. Not to the office, not yet, not to Aunt Molly's. He did not want to be with anyone who would want to talk about the war and what he had achieved – which was absolutely nothing. People had died, a land had been convulsed, and for what? He could not believe that it would end well for the Spanish people, whichever side won. But he could not talk about any of it, not yet. His hand was injured; and his heart hurt. There was one person who would welcome him, respect his silence, would always accept him, whatever his worth. He would go home to his mother.

Lineman's was a well-kept secret in Los Angeles – a small, discreet restaurant just off Wilshire Boulevard where important Hollywood people ate on the rare occasions when they *didn't* want the attention of the press. Lennie went there sometimes for a quick solo lunch, because they did the best Reuben sandwich outside New York. He had finished and was on his way out one September day when he heard his name called, and turned to see, to his surprise, Al Feinstein beckoning from a corner table.

The surprising thing was that Feinstein was alone. Lennie couldn't have imagined him ever being allowed to be alone. He was as recognisable as the Eiffel Tower or the Leaning Tower of Pisa, as impossible to hide; and there was hardly anyone in Hollywood who wouldn't have wanted something from him if they'd spotted him. In that moment Lennie realised fully the awfulness of fame and was glad he was largely unknown. He changed direction and went across to him. 'Al! Lunching alone?'

'They just left,' Feinstein said, waving a cigar in the direction of the door. 'Coupla nice gals up from Ohio, wanting an audition.' His merry eyes gleamed from their nests of wrinkles, challenging Lennie to make something of it.

'Oh,' said Lennie. He knew of Al's reputation. Though he was probably too fat and too bronchitic now actually to get into the saddle, he did still like a little canoodling when he had the chance, with chorines and eager ingénues who wanted to get into films. It was reprehensible, of course, and Lennie was glad he had not come upon him sooner, and perhaps have felt obliged to warn the girls, risking a scene.

Al waved him to a seat. 'Siddown, I want to talk to you. What'll you have? They do a great custard tart here. They call it *torta della nonna*.' His Italian accent was surprisingly good for a man who pretended Philistinism.

'Thanks, I've just eaten.'

'Coffee and brandy, then,' Al said, waving to a waiter, then again at Lennie. 'Siddown, you're making the place untidy.'

Lennie gave in. He wanted to hear what Al had to say, in any case. Rose's agent, Forrest Van Kerk, was friendly with David B. Reznik, ABO's lead director, who had an interest in Rose's career and had discovered what he thought was an ideal script for her, a thriller called *Into the Night*. He and Van had together taken it to Feinstein and persuaded him to take it on, with Rose as the ordinary Brooklyn housewife who finds herself under attack, first by anonymous telephone calls, and then increasingly sinister and troubling incidents. Since most of the action happened in one indoor location, with a small cast, production costs would be low, and Lennie would not be required to put a lot of money into it. And it was a good dramatic part for Rose, not in the mainstream mould of *The Falcon and the Rose*, but a good way to bridge the gap between the westerns and the big Shakespeare role Al had been promising. Lennie hadn't heard any more about that for a while.

'How's the Shakespeare project coming along?' he asked, as the waiter put coffee and brandy in front of him. He refused Al's silent offer of a cigar. 'Have you decided yet? Is it *Twelfth Night*?'

Al waved it aside. 'My guys rewrote it a whole bunch, but it still reads like a dog's breakfast.'

'It's a celebrated part of Shakespeare's canon,' Lennie said, with slight reproof.

'Gave me a headache figuring out who knew who was what and when. And if I can't figure it, what chance the audience will? *Romeo and Juliet* it ain't! I wish we'd got to *that* little honey before Cukor grabbed it. Can't do it again for five years, minimum.'

'Well, what about *As You Like It*? *The Merchant of Venice*? *A Midsummer Night's Dream*?' Lennie urged.

'I got my doubts about all of 'em. *As You Like It*'s the same mess all over again. And the *Merchant* thing? If I wanna do a courtroom drama I'll set it in present-day New York. Wait, that could work!' A costive look indicated the arrival of an idea. 'Did you see *The Witness Chair*? Or Jean Arthur in *The Defence Rests*?'

Lennie refused to be distracted. 'Is that what you've got planned for Rose after *Into the Night?*'

'Who said I'm making *Into the Night?*' Al said, narrow-eyed.

Lennie was not impressed. 'You did. In your office two – three? – weeks ago. I can look up the date, if you really want me to. I remember you talking about it using the studio capacity nicely until you were ready with the Shakespeare project. You said—'

'Yeah, yeah, don't have a conniption. You're like a cat with one kitten. I like *Into the Night* okay. Like I said, it'll keep things ticking over until the big production – the spectacular, box-office-busting extravaganza. Listen to this, you're gonna love it. It's the bee's knees, it's got action, romance, every damn thing, including a great part for Rosie. How d'ya like this, Len?' He blocked the title across the air. '"Shakespeare's *Robin Hood*, with Rose Morland as Lady Marian".'

Lennie blinked. 'Shakespeare didn't write *Robin Hood*,' he objected.

Al looked belligerent. 'How do you know?'

'Nobody wrote it. It's a legend.'

'Legend, schmegend! Guys in tights, bows and arrows. If that's not Shakespeare, I don't know what is!'

'And it's Maid Marian, not Lady Marian.'

'I don't like "Maid". Sounds like she's gonna start cleaning the bathroom! "Lady" is classy. And I've got a great actor for Robin Hood. One of Hollywood's best: Dick Randolph!'

'I heard you'd poached him from MGM,' Lennie said.

Al looked pleased. 'You heard that, did you? It wasn't easy, I can tell you. But the old man's still got it where it counts. Anyway, Dick's perfect for this Robin guy. He's tall, hunky, *and* he can do an English accent.'

Lennie groaned inwardly. 'Al, you're not going to do this with English accents? It never works.'

'Why the hell not? It's Dick Randolph's speciality.'

'I've heard him,' Lennie said, 'and the accent he does is not English, it's more like Welsh.'

Al didn't like being opposed. 'What the hell is Welsh?'

'From Wales. A far-flung region of Britain with a very different accent. Just imagine making a movie about a hot-shot New York lawyer, and the actor plays it with a Deep South accent, like a Georgia Cracker.'

Al contemplated that, then said, 'Yeah, but nobody's gonna know the difference from a British accent. Bottom line is Dick Randolph is big box office, and he likes doing the accent. You should be concentrating on Rose – I'm offering her the lead role! She's gonna be the only female on screen, except for a servant girl, a nun and the wicked queen. And it's a great script. It's got action, sword fights, tight bodices, galloping horses, romance, a near rape—'

'A what, now?'

'The second male lead, Sir Bedevere, Mr Sexy but Slimy to Robin's Stand-up Guy. I had to beef up the script a little. He gets Marian backed into a corner, then Robin swings down from a tree, like Tarzan, and snatches her away. That's a great scene! I tell you, this movie is gonna be big. The script's got everything!'

'A bit more than everything,' Lennie said. 'There was no Sir Bedevere in Sherwood Forest.'

'Why the hell not? Sidekick to the evil King of Nottingham. King's gotta have knights, right? Sir this and Sir that. There's even a fat one, great comic relief. Think Oliver Hardy, Guy Kibbee.'

Lennie was floundering in a sea of error. 'It's the Sheriff of Nottingham, not the King.'

'King is better. I'm thinking Charles Laughton. Don't tell me *he* can't do a British accent.'

'Yes, but Sir Bedevere? Shakespeare didn't—'

Al grew impatient. 'Who the hell knows what this Shakespeare guy didn't write? It's English, it's historical, it's right down his street. We'll call it one of his lesser-known novels – who's gonna argue? And I'm telling you, Len, if Rose doesn't want this, there's a hundred other actresses will bite my hand off for it, so don't do me any favours. I'm just telling you first because I know you got her best interests at heart. Have a word with her and Van and let's get this thing moving and make us all some serious moolah.'

Lennie went straight to Van Kerk's office, and found him more than ready to talk about *Robin Hood*.

'There's a bit of background to it that I'm guessing Al won't have mentioned. He's supposed to have poached Dick Randolph from MGM by employing great cunning, but the fact is they were willing to let him go because of his drinking problem. Now Al wants to use him in a smash hit so as to spit in Louis B. Mayer's eye. You know the rivalry between those two – friendly on the surface, deadly underneath.'

'A drinking problem?' Lennie groaned.

'Don't worry, he's in the Ardmore right now, drying out. ABO's paying. He's getting clean, lean, and ready for the screen. I believe he'll knuckle down, all right – he needs this role to restore his reputation.'

'What about Rose's reputation? She wants to do serious parts.'

'Of course the script needs some work, but there's some touching scenes between Marian and Robin, and some real menace from the bad guys.'

'Including Sir Bedevere?'

Van shrugged. 'The handsome bounder, trying to seduce the virtuous girl? And she nearly falls for him? It's classic,' he said. 'They've got some great dialogue together. We can get the names changed.'

'And what's this about a nun?'

'One of Robin's ex-girlfriends – took the veil when he went off to the Crusades. That'd make a great movie on its own – *The Earlier Adventures of Robin Hood*. But the nun's a small part – won't take the shine from Marian. Likewise the Wicked Queen.'

'Who is . . . ?'

'The Sheriff of Nottingham's wife. She won't be called the Wicked Queen in the finished film – that's just shorthand for now.'

'It sounds as if you've made your mind up,' Lennie said, 'but Al seems to think you need persuading. What's the snag?'

'I've told you the project is really about showcasing Dick Randolph to put one over on Louis B. Mayer. The fact is that Al only wants Rose for the part of Marian because he doesn't want one of the big-name actresses taking the attention away from him. But that doesn't make it any less of a good part. We just have to let Al think he's pulling the wool over our eyes. Between us Estelle and I will make sure she's not sidelined.'

Lennie examined his face. 'There's something else, isn't there? You brushed that objection away too easily.'

Van hesitated. 'It's not a problem, it shouldn't be a problem, but it's just something I'll have to sell to Rose. I need to find the right way to put it to her.'

'Put what to her?' Lennie said suspiciously.

'They want Dean Cornwell to play Sir Bedevere.'

'Oh.'

'The official version is that their divorce was mutual and they remain the best of friends, but I don't know how she really feels about him. I'm a little worried about how she'll feel, being at close quarters on set with him.'

Lennie was thinking hard. 'When is all this likely to come off?'

'There's a lot to iron out, but without major snags, first photography ought to start in the spring.'

'That's far enough from the break-up for them both to be grown-up about it. And Rose is a professional.'

'I've just been pondering how best to put it to her.'

'Point out that Dean will be playing the loser, the man she gets to reject. And that he'll be playing second fiddle to Dick Randolph, while she's the leading lady.'

'Good thought. Yes, that's a positive way to go.'

'And point out that she could make a very great deal of money.'

Van Kerk laughed. 'You really think that matters to her?'

'I never knew an actress it didn't matter to.'

'Well, thanks. You've given me something to think about.' He drummed his fingers on the table a moment, thinking, then came back to the present. 'How is Anthea? Are you two still a couple?' he asked politely.

'Hardly that. We like each other's company. It suits us both to have someone's arm at parties and premières and so on. We're friends.'

'Good friends, is what I heard,' Van said, twinkling.

'Who told you that?'

'Rose. But don't worry,' he responded to Lennie's quick frown. 'She wasn't upset. Her attitude was "Good old Uncle Lennie. There's life in the old dog yet."'

James was only Charlie's assistant, but since he opened the post each day, he could not help knowing that there was a great deal of resistance back home to the idea of the Windsors' tour of Germany. The King and the Foreign Office had both declared it a very bad idea, given international tensions. If the Duke insisted on going, it must be made clear that he had no official status. The ambassador must not meet them on arrival in Berlin, the embassy must not entertain them, there must be no official engagements, and invitations connected with the tour must not be accepted by members of the embassy.

The Duke didn't blame his brother: it was the Hardinges, Baldwin and the Establishment who were set on humiliating them. 'They've been so bloody to me, why the hell should I do what they want? They've denied my wife her rights. And look at the shameful way I've been treated ever since I left England in December! When they see how we're received in Germany, they'll realise they can't do without us.'

The Duchess said, 'They're small-minded people, with drab little lives. We'll show them how things ought to be done. Show them a bit of sparkle and glamour.'

'*You*'ll show them, darling,' the Duke said adoringly.

Charlie was unconcerned by the disapproval at home. 'The Duke's going to study labour conditions, that's all. And anything that improves Anglo-German relations can only be a good thing. Nobody wants another war. I'm coaching him on how to further world peace through labour reconciliation.'

'Um – what does that mean?' James asked.

'Labour must be well treated and content if we're not to see the breakdown of the capitalist system, like in Spain. The Duke's always been concerned with the lot of the working man. What better leader could you find to head the movement?'

It sounded praiseworthy, but James suspected the Duke's interest in working conditions was not as fixed as Charlie believed, and that his real purpose in visiting Germany was to give the Duchess a taste of a state visit: he was angry that she'd been cheated of being queen, and wanted her to see some red carpets and guards of honour.

James was also doubtful about the man he was liaising with in Germany, a Dr Robert Ley, head of the Nazi National Labour Front, who impressed him as rather a shady character. Still, Dudley Forwood, who was still the only equerry, told James the Duke believed strongly that the British and German races were of one origin and should always be united, and that mankind was in great danger from the Bolsheviks. 'And,' Forwood went on, 'the Duke says that while he hopes there

367

will never be another war, if there is we must be on the winning side, which means Germany, not France.'

James didn't really know what to think. All he could do was his job – making sure that the tour went smoothly, and was a credit to Charlie's organisation.

It started well. On the 11th of October, the train pulled into Friedrichstraße station, and the Duke and Duchess were received by a contingent of top Germans, headed by Dr Ley and a brass band, with a fleet of impressively large Mercedes cars waiting. The embassy was represented only by the Third Secretary, but the Duke and Duchess seemed delighted with the reception nevertheless, and James noted that Dr Ley bowed deeply to the Duchess and called her 'Your Royal Highness', which won him the Duke's approval. The cars took the party to the Kaiserhof Hotel, with an escort of storm troopers. The procession passed through streets lined with a cheering crowd waving flags. They were, James noted, black-and-red Nazi flags, but there was no doubting the enthusiasm of the onlookers.

That evening there was a magnificent banquet attended by the Otto von Bismarcks, the Himmlers, the Goebbelses, Herr Hess and Herr Ribbentrop. Everything glittered, flowers were massed in every corner, an orchestra played softly and, best of all, everyone bowed and curtsied to the royal guests. A thousand press bulbs lit up the night. James had to admit that Ley had come up to scratch.

The rest of the tour went smoothly, with a punishing schedule of visits, starting at eight in the morning each day and finishing at five in the evening. The Duke visited housing projects, hospitals and youth camps, factories, a coal mine, new highways, a veterans' home, a foundry, a military airport, public gardens, a training school for Hitler Youth, a war museum, sports facilities, a Turkish bath. And in the evenings there were more banquets, exhibitions of folk dancing, dinners with eminent Nazis, a performance of *Lohengrin* – even a visit to a beer hall. Everywhere they were received rapturously, photographed by press from a dozen countries, wafted seamlessly from Dresden to Nuremberg to Stuttgart to Munich in the glossy limousines. James couldn't fault the organisation. It was a great success.

The climax was a meeting with the Führer himself, Adolf Hitler, at his mountain home, the Berghof, near Salzburg. He came down the steps to greet them in person, and bowed and kissed the Duchess's hand, which pleased the Duke. The Duke, Forwood and Hitler then went to the Führer's study for a private meeting, while the Duchess was given afternoon tea by Rudolf Hess.

On the way back to the car afterwards, James heard the Duke say to the Duchess, 'We hit it off immediately. I found him thoroughly agreeable. Of course I didn't allow myself to get into a political discussion, but I could tell we had a lot in common. He only wants a fair deal for his country, and who can argue with that? We mustn't let scaremongers drive a wedge between us.'

Despite this warm endorsement, James heard later from Forwood that the Duke had been greatly annoyed that Hitler had provided a translator, one Paul Schmidt, even though he, the Duke, spoke flawless German. He had told Hitler that he did not require a translator, and Hitler had replied coldly that the Duke was to speak in English. The interview continued awkwardly in that way, with the hapless Schmidt in the middle, and the Duke saying to him irritably every few minutes, 'That's not what I said to the Führer,' or 'That's not what the Führer said to me.'

On the 23rd it was all over, and they took the train back to Paris, where the Duke and Duchess went to their usual suite at the Meurice. James was able to relax at last, and consider the visit. His impression was of everything in Germany being very clean, lots of new roads and buildings, of people seeming to be well-fed and well-dressed, of everything being efficiently organised. There was no glimpse, as you had in London, of slum side-streets and grimy alleys. It was as if the whole country had been washed and dressed in its Sunday best. Of course they had only been shown the bits they were meant to see. Still, it was an achievement, was it not, for the battered and destitute Germany he had read about after the war to have come so far?

But there had been an incident that had bothered him. In Leipzig, they had not been able to stay in the best hotel, but had been taken to one that was definitely inferior. James had questioned Ley, who had said at first only that the original hotel had been closed and was unavailable, but when James pressed him, he told him that the state had closed it, because the owner was Jewish. It was said as though that was sufficient reason.

It troubled him, too, that whereas crowds lining the street in London would be kept in order by ordinary policemen, in Germany it was by armed soldiers. And there had been an awful lot of swastika flags all over the place, hanging from buildings, painted on vehicles, waved by the onlookers. Being English, he was just a little uncomfortable with too much flag-waving. It was not the British way.

CHAPTER SIXTEEN

Basil was on sick leave from the *Messenger*. His bosses were sympathetic for now, but it was obvious that sooner or later he was going to have to show that the paper had got value for money in sending him to Spain. Miranda sent him a letter, sympathising but asking when he thought he might be able to come back to work. Though his right hand was out of action, she said, someone could be made available to take down his account in shorthand and transcribe it.

But the reckoning was delayed. His parents were not happy with the Spanish doctor's diagnosis that he would never get back full function of his hand, and insisted on paying for him to see a specialist, with the result that Basil was whipped off to a nursing home in Devonshire Street for an operation.

While he was there recovering, he received a visit from Oliver, alerted by Emma, who had heard from Molly, who had heard from Helen. 'You should have come to me straight away,' Oliver said, holding the X-ray photograph up to the light.

Basil was embarrassed. 'I didn't realise it was your area,' he said.

'Hands and faces. I've put more back together than you've had hot dinners, my lad.' Basil tried to smile at the joke, and Oliver gave him a sympathetic look. 'In a lot of pain? They hand out morphine with an eye-dropper in these places. They don't seem to realise that pain delays healing. I'll get them to increase your dose – no reason for you to suffer.'

'Thank you, sir,' Basil said.

'And the good news is that Tompkins seems to have done a good job – almost as good as I would have done myself. I see no reason why you shouldn't regain full function. There's no significant nerve damage, and though tendons take a long time to heal, heal they will. Then,' he put on a mock stern face, 'you must come to me for cosmetic reconstruction – we don't want you to go about with a mangled hand, putting off the ladies. No need to thank me,' he added quickly, holding up his hand. 'Family is family, after all. Tell your parents, no charge for a war hero.'

Basil felt close to tears. 'I'm not a war hero. I didn't achieve anything. It was a complete waste of time.'

Oliver patted his unwounded hand. '*War* is a waste of time – believe me, I've been through one. But when somebody starts one, you have to finish it. All any of us can do is our best. You lost a friend, I understand? That's something you never get over. But you learn to live with it. And you're in a better position than many – you can write about your experiences, and you've a platform ready and waiting to publish. All old fogeys like me can do is bore our colleagues at the club with our reminiscences.'

'But I think what my paper wants is a political analysis,' Basil said. 'They'll want me to say why the Fascists are wrong and the Communists right.'

'You were there and they weren't,' Oliver said. 'Write what you saw. If they don't want to publish it, someone else will.' He looked serious. 'Words have power, and that confers a responsibility on you. The worst thing you can do is to write a lie. Lies kill more people than guns.' He stood up. 'I can see I've exhausted you. I'll go and have a word with the house surgeon, get you some more morphine.' He patted Basil's hand, and went away, a glamorous figure in his beautifully tailored suit, with a gardenia in the buttonhole, every inch the great consultant.

Basil soon got his extra dose. 'Uncle' Oliver was famous for many reasons, not least for being London's leading plastic surgeon and head of the Winchmore Hospital, but Basil thought it was probably just his charm that always got him his way.

Charlie and Fern had gone to the château, leaving James to hold the fort in Paris. He stayed in the flat above the office, which was good and central, and convenient for obeying the Windsors' frequent summonses to the Meurice.

All attention was now on the American trip. They were to sail on the *Bremen* on the 6th of November, arriving on Armistice Day in New York, and taking a train immediately to Washington DC to lay a wreath at Arlington Cemetery on the Unknown Soldier's tomb. A visit to the White House was hoped for, followed by a broadcast on NBC about world peace.

Then there would be the tour of factories, for the Duke to study working-class conditions and industrial practices: Charlie was in touch with a number of major companies such as General Electric in Schenectady, Eastman-Kodak in Rochester, Standard Oil in Bayonne, and Du Pont in Wilmington. The tour was to continue to Virginia to visit Wally's wealthy cousins the Montagues, and on to North Carolina and Georgia; then Ohio; Detroit, to visit General Motors, Dearborn, where Ford was based, and across to Washington and Oregon; then into California, to call at San Francisco, Los Angeles, and Wally's old stamping-ground of San Diego. The tour would finish in mid-December, with some suggestion that there might be time for a dash to Hawaii before returning to France.

On the 27th of October, Charlie and Fern sailed to New York to firm up the schedule, to try to persuade the US government to give official recognition to the tour, and especially to secure an invitation by President Roosevelt to the White House. James was left to liaise in Paris. It was he who booked the Bedauxs' passage on the *Europa*, and he was amused to note from the passenger list that, by coincidence, Ernest Simpson was also aboard, on his way at last to marry Mary Kirk Raffray. He kept that detail from the Windsors.

But there were uncomfortable reports coming in every day, about hostility to the Duke's German visit. References to the Jewish lobby in America, especially comments that no-one who was a friend of Germany could also be a friend of Jews, made him do some research. He came across the Nuremberg Laws, and was disturbed by how much they restricted the civil rights of German Jews. The vague unease he had felt after the tour increased. The Duke believed that the Germans were the only people who could effectively counter the Bolsheviks, that England could sit it out while the Nazis and the Reds fought each other. But at what cost?

He was in the office one day when a telephone call came through from Walter Monckton, who said the King and Queen were very unhappy about the proposed USA trip. 'The King is trying to establish himself, and win the affection of his people, but the Duke is constantly courting the limelight. They resent it, especially since the Duke abandoned his responsibilities and dropped them onto his brother's shoulders.'

James murmured something about factory visits.

Monckton went on, 'I can tell you Their Majesties don't believe this interest in working-class conditions is sincere. There's an element in the country that supports the Duke – a pro-Fascist group – and they believe he's intending to stage a comeback.'

'I haven't heard him say anything about that,' James said cautiously.

'It was his duty when he left the country not to embarrass

the King, and now he wants to conduct a quasi-state visit to America? I can tell you, Lindsay is very uneasy.' Sir Robert Lindsay was the British ambassador to the USA. 'A lot of Congress is fiercely anti-Nazi. Lindsay says the State Department's been sending out a snowstorm of memoranda about the visit, none of them positive.'

James remembered that at that very moment the Duchess was having fittings at Main Bocher for a very extensive wardrobe. 'It's not my place to say anything, sir,' he said cautiously.

'No, of course not. Excuse me, I was letting off steam. I'll have to try to get through to the Duke. Do you know where he is?'

'I believe he's playing golf this morning. And this evening there's a reception at the US Embassy.'

'Ironic,' Monckton said. 'I'll try to catch him this afternoon, then, at the hotel.'

James did not hear the result of that phone call, but a day or two later he heard from Charlie, telephoning from the States, to say it had all gone to pieces. The labour leaders in Baltimore, the Duchess's home town, where a triumphant visit was planned, had sworn to boycott them and if necessary demonstrate against them in public. 'I'm hearing it was Mrs Roosevelt who put them up to it. Lindsay can't get the invitation to the White House because they're expecting a tour of the States and Canada next year by the King and Queen and it wouldn't look tactful. And apparently Vansittart has sent an instruction that the Duchess is not to be referred to as HRH, or curtsied to, and the US State Department has agreed to go along with it.'

'The Duke won't like that,' James said.

'He and the Duchess have been labelled as Nazi sympathisers, and with the Jewish lobby being so strong in the States, that's a big problem.'

The final blow came when the New York longshoremen announced that they would refuse to unload the *Bremen* when it came in, if the Duke and Duchess were on board. They referred to them as 'National Socialist bedfellows'.

James was in the suite at the Meurice when the final flurry of telephone calls was taking place, and overheard enough to understand the situation. Lindsay told of the weight of public opinion against the Windsors in America; Bullitt, the US ambassador to France, said the Duke should go ahead with the tour, but without Bedaux, who was unpopular with American unions. And Sir Eric Phipps, the British ambassador to Germany, said he should definitely not go – the very success of their German tour would play against them in the USA.

In the end, James believed it was the potential snub to Wally that changed the Duke's mind. After the royal welcome she had had in Germany, he didn't want to expose her to slights in the New World. He issued a statement to the press the next day, saying they had decided to 'postpone' the trip. The statement also announced that they would soon be making a trip to the Soviet Union.

James for once overstepped his role, and addressed the Duke on the subject. 'Sir, that's most unwise,' he said. The Duke scowled, and James hurried on, 'Sir, I've been there, I know how dangerous it is. You've always said the Soviets are a bigger threat than the Fascists.'

'Ah,' said the Duke, looking cunning, 'but, you see, after all this nonsense about my German tour, a tour of Russia will balance it out.'

In despair, James went back to the office and telephoned Charlie at the New York Plaza, only to be told that he and Fern had checked out that morning, without saying where they were going. He waited all day for a telephone call or a wire. He had no idea what he was supposed to do next, even if he still had a job. He was now thoroughly confused in his mind about whether he should hate the Bolsheviks or the Nazis more. He was disappointed that he was not going to see America, but realised he did not really like the Duke and Duchess, who seemed both silly and selfish, and he did not want to be involved in any more of their antics.

The next day brought only more silence, and annoyed, worried and upset in about equal proportions, he wrote Charlie a note and left it on his desk, packed his bags, locked everything up, and went home to England.

January could be a hard month, an anticlimax after the bright colours and warm cheer of Christmas. January 1938 began with grey skies and bitter cold. There had been heavy snow-fall in London towards the end of December, and the roads and pavements were dangerous as the snow turned to slush and ice. English houses were not designed to cope with extreme cold, and even with the fire built up, the sitting-room at 27 Wellington Road was not cosy. There was a semicircle of warmth around the fire, but insidious draughts wriggled their way in round window frames and under doors. Richard was aware that, while the skin of his face was hot, his ankles and feet were icy.

When Cynthia, seated opposite him darning socks, sighed for the second time, he lowered the evening paper and said, 'What's the matter, dear?' She didn't answer at once, and he said, 'Is it something I've done?' He was guiltily aware that he had been very busy for some time past with his plans, and probably had been neglecting her.

'It's not you. It's me,' she said, without looking at him. Her face reddened, as if she was going to cry. 'I'm a terrible wife,' she concluded, low and miserable.

Dropping the paper over the side of the chair, he thrust himself across to kneel in front of her and place his hands over hers. 'How can you say that?' Her chin trembled, and there were drops under her lowered eyelashes, catching the firelight. 'Tell me what's wrong, darling. What's troubling you?'

Almost too low to be heard, she said, 'It started today. My – you know.' She was blushing again, wouldn't look at him, and spoke the next words without moving her lips. 'The monthlies.'

He knew how shy she was about bodily functions, and had long since stopped trying to jolly or persuade her out of it. He knew what menstruation was, and had grown used to its regular interruption of routine, but he didn't know, of course, how a woman felt about it, and since it was something they could not talk about, he supposed he never would.

He was at a loss. 'Does it hurt, dear?'

She shook her head, pulled her hands back and fumbled out a handkerchief to dab her eyes and blow her nose. He remained where he was, one side of him uncomfortably hot, but wanting to be supportive of her in her trouble.

'It's not that,' she said, putting the handkerchief away, and he saw she had decided to be brisk and practical, and it hurt his heart, just a little, because he knew she was doing it to save him embarrassment. 'It means I'm not pregnant.'

'Oh,' said Richard.

She gave him a faint smile. 'You don't have to stay there,' she said. 'You'll burn.'

He resumed his seat, but he sensed her distress under her façade of common sense. 'Did you think you were?'

'I hoped.' She swallowed hard, so as not to cry. 'I want to give you a son. But it looks as though . . .' She had to stop, and pressed her fingers to her mouth, closing her eyes against the tears.

'Please don't cry! There's no need. We haven't been married very long. I'm sure lots of people don't get a baby straight away. You have to be patient, that's all.'

She plied the handkerchief again. 'I went to see Dr Saloman,' she said. 'He's not the doctor here, he's our family doctor from when I was a child. He knows me, and I felt more – comfortable talking to him. He – he examined me.'

She didn't even like saying the words, and he considered the courage it must have taken her to undergo such intimacy and shame. 'He says I'm not quite right inside, and that I'll probably never have a child.'

Richard rallied. 'Probably. He said probably. Not definitely. Doctors don't know everything.'

'Why do we consult them, then?' She folded her hands tightly in her lap, and he saw she had come to the thing she felt she had to say, but didn't want to. 'If you want to divorce me, I'll understand. A barren wife is no use to a man. Mummy and Daddy will take me back. I'll be all right.'

He was appalled at her gallantry. 'Of course I don't want to divorce you! Please don't ever suggest it again. As to being barren – I don't believe it. We've got all the time in the world. You *will* have a baby. And if you don't, well, we'll deal with that together.'

'Oh, Richard,' she said, in a voiceless sigh.

'I want to make you happy,' he said. 'Isn't there anything I can do?'

She thought for a long moment, her pale face rosy in the firelight. 'There is something I want,' she said at last.

'Anything,' he said. He had a flashing thought, that a puppy or a kitten might amuse her. Or a canary in a cage.

'I want to go back to work in the office,' she said. 'I'd like to know I'm helping the company. You're always telling me there's a lot to do, and not enough people to do it. And I'd like to be busy. The days can be awfully long here when you're at work.'

'I don't know what your father would say,' Richard began.

'Leave Daddy to me,' she said, surprisingly firmly. 'If you say I can . . .'

'Of course you can, if that's what you want,' Richard said. 'We could certainly do with someone experienced and efficient.'

She looked pleased. 'Is that what you think of me?'

379

'Not think – it's a matter of plain fact,' he said, and her smile was his reward.

January was a quiet time in the office, since few people wanted holidays or to hire a car at that time of year. So when Richard arrived at the open door and looked into Samuel's office, he was not surprised to see his father-in-law dozing in his chair behind his desk. In respect for his dignity, Richard withdrew, coughed loudly, and rapped sharply on the door frame before inserting himself into view again, by which time Samuel was sitting upright with his eyes open.

'Can I come and talk to you?' Richard asked.

'Of course. Anything wrong?'

'No, it's a new idea I've had. Something in the business line that I think could make us a fortune.'

Samuel waved him to a seat. 'More holidays, is it?'

'Yes,' said Richard, 'but not for wealthy people. I've been thinking for a long time about what a wretched time the working classes have of it.' He explained what he had seen in Dover that day, the couple huddling out of the rain. 'They only have a week away from their toil, and what with unkind landladies and unreliable weather, it must be a struggle for them to squeeze out a little enjoyment before they have to go back to the daily grind.'

Samuel was not yet impressed. 'And why is that your problem? Or mine, since I'm guessing you want to involve me in your charity scheme.'

'Not charity, sir. A business proposition.'

'You can't charge the working classes the same rates as you charge the rich, so where's the profit to come from?'

'From economies of scale,' said Richard. 'There are a lot more of them than there are of the rich – and I'm including the lower-middle classes too. And don't they deserve a little comfort and fun just as much as anyone?'

'Deserving is not my business. I leave that to God. Tell me your proposal.'

Richard made a signboard in the air with his hand. 'Nevinson's Holiday Camps.'

'Camps?'

'Or Resorts, perhaps. My idea is that we buy a plot of land, ideally somewhere next to the sea with its own access to the beach. We build a village of wooden cabins: they can be very simple, and with prefabrication they can be run up quickly and cheaply. There will be sanitation huts, with bath cubicles, showers, lavatories – one hut to so many cabins. A dining hall, where three meals a day will be served, of good, tasty food, and perhaps a late-night supper in addition.' Samuel's eyebrows rose at this largesse, and Richard said quickly, 'They manage that even in the third class on the White Star liners, so there's no reason we shouldn't too.'

'Hm. Go on.'

'There must be a comfortable sort of lounge where they can go and sit when it rains, and read the paper or play cards or board games. Perhaps with a piano – there's always someone who can play. A billiard room. A cinema. And there will be entertainments laid on – little competitions and quizzes, dances, organised games, races for the children, perhaps music-hall performances or something of the sort. And,' he finished with emphasis before Samuel could say anything, 'my principal idea is that there is one flat charge per person per week. Once they get there on the train or motorbus and enter the camp, everything is covered. Food, entertainments – they don't have to pay for anything more. No need to carry money with them. Think how comfortable that would be after the struggle of their everyday life.'

'What's to stop everyone for miles around coming in without paying?'

'Oh, that's easily arranged. There'll be a fence around the

perimeter and a gate, and our visitors will be issued with an identification of some kind – a token or badge they have to show.' He stopped talking to let it sink in.

Samuel pondered. 'You think there's land to be had at the right price, do you?' was his first question.

'I know there is. Agriculture is so depressed at the moment that farmers will be glad to sell their land. And local authorities will welcome us for bringing business and employment to the area – builders in the initial stages, then cooks, cleaners, laundresses, suppliers of all sorts once we're up and running. Everyone will love this idea, sir. You'll be a popular hero!'

Samuel stared into the fire. 'Nevinson's Holiday Camp?' he mused. 'I don't like the sound of Camp. Makes me think of soldiers. Tents. Latrines with buckets.'

'Resort?'

He shook his head. 'Village,' he decided at length. 'Nevinson's Holiday Village.'

Richard smiled with relief. 'You like the idea, then?'

'It will take some thinking out. And, by God, a lot of money to set up.'

'But if we get it right—'

'It'll be big – the biggest thing ever. We could have them all over the country. Like you say, there's a lot of decent working folk out there, millions of 'em, and if you treat them right, they'll come back year after year. By God, Richard, I think you've come up with something!'

'I've been working on it for some time – I've got a lot of the details settled in my mind. I've even identified the right place to start: the east coast. The land's flat there, which will make building easier, and it's cheaper – most people head west when they go on holiday. Land in Devon and Cornwall would be much more expensive.'

'Hmm,' said Samuel. 'But the North Sea? Doesn't sound all that attractive.'

'Sir, they'll find so much to enjoy about the holiday camp—'

'Village.'

'—village, they won't care where it is.'

Samuel gave a slight smile. 'Holiday villages on the moon, eh?'

'Not yet, but in the future – who knows?'

'I like ambition in a man! But let's get the foundation right first. We'll have to run it past Hannah. I never embark on any new venture without my Hannah's say-so. And Cynthia's head is screwed on the right way. You're lucky to have her.'

'I know that, sir,' Richard said humbly.

Basil's hand healed quickly after the operation, and apart from some stiffness, he had full use of it. The Spanish doctor had either lacked expertise or, more likely, had been trying to scare him away. His mother was eager for him to have the cosmetic treatment Oliver had suggested, and he said he would think about it, but for the moment it didn't bother him. It seemed a small matter in the scale of things. Going back to work only made him think more often of Zennor, and the terrible waste of his death. It irked him to be surrounded by people so enthusiastic for the Communist cause in Spain, who spoke so blithely of sacrifices being worth while.

He didn't want to talk about it but, of course, he had to, since that was his job – and keeping his job depended on it. Dickins liked his first draft, but seemed doubtful that Mr Comstock would. 'I don't think this is what he was thinking of when he sent you out there,' Dickins said.

'It wasn't what I was thinking of either,' Basil muttered. 'If I'd known what it was like—'

'You wouldn't have gone? That's not the line to take with Mr Comstock. Or with me. A reporter has to face up to unpleasant facts when he's on the track of a story. If you don't know that, Compton, you might be in the wrong job.'

383

Mr Comstock, it transpired, liked it 'as far as it went'.

'Lots of colour,' he said. 'You write well, Compton. But where's the political analysis? The horrors of war are all very well, and we can use so much of it, but we need the political context to make sense of it all. Otherwise all we have is a bunch of men kicking their heels in the trenches. Luckily, we've got Bob Zennor's accounts as well.'

'You have?' Basil said stupidly.

'You brought his kitbag back with you. It was full of his notebooks. Didn't you look?'

'I didn't think it was my place to, sir.'

In the end, a series of articles was published, and Basil could tell they were a mixture of his accounts, with commentary from inside the office – written by Dickins or one of the others, probably Digbeth who was a senior reporter – and what he assumed must be Zennor's work. It seemed that Zennor had found time while out there to talk to officers and the better-educated volunteers, and assemble a great deal of their political thinking. He had talked to officials in Barcelona and Tarragona, too, while Basil was otherwise occupied. It was obvious that he had thought about things a lot less viscerally than had Basil, who felt rather a fool now. He had allowed himself to be bowled over emotionally by the whole thing, while Zennor, whom he had always thought of as rather a pudding, had dealt with it all far more professionally.

And yet he couldn't help thinking, a little resentfully, that his account was just as much the truth. He thought of the waste and the muddle, the dead and the wounded: all those cheerful boys, like faithful, dog-like Javier, and little Jorge facing an uncertain future walking for ever with a crutch. What did that have to do with Fascism or Communism or any other ism, with governments and coups and shirtsleeved men making deals in smoky rooms?

It was a little galling, when the articles came out, to see them headed 'View from the Spanish Front by Bob Zennor', and to have his name only at the bottom as 'additional material by', with Basil Compton coming after Bill Dickins and Arthur Digbeth, but he supposed it was fair. And Zennor needed a memorial, because that was all he would ever have.

However, it did get Basil a promotion, from junior reporter to reporter, and a rise in salary that allowed him to move into better accommodation. It was in Chancery Lane, which was closer to work, just one room on the first floor with a bed in one corner and a kitchen – double gas ring, marble-topped cupboard and sink with hot-water geyser – in another. He had to share the bathroom and lavatory with the rest of the house; but there was no landlady on the premises, no-one watching him or checking up on him. He let himself in with his own key at whatever time suited him, and cooked for himself when he ran out of funds to eat out.

Too bruised to seek pleasure, he decided to buckle down at work and concentrate on his job. He took Dickins's corrections seriously, asked his advice, studied the other men's reports to learn how better to use the language and get the story across. He read not just the things that interested him but everything, and followed up stories and lines in other places – rival newspapers and books. When Dickins praised a piece of his work, and gave it back with so few blue-pencil corrections the original black was still visible, he felt his effort was paying off, that he *could* make a career in journalism. He went home one Sunday to his parents and told them he had turned over a new leaf, and was now virtuous, diligent, happy and productive, all the things they had ever wanted for him. He could hardly blame them for looking sceptical, though it hurt a little.

Cynthia took to the holiday-village idea at once. 'We must paint the cabins in cheerful colours – nice pastels – pale blue, pale green, pale yellow. And we shouldn't call them cabins. We should call them chalets. That sounds much better.'

'Go on,' Richard said, amused.

'You're laughing at me,' she said suspiciously.

'No, I think it's a very good idea. What else?'

'You'll need a manager to oversee everything,' she said. 'Someone experienced in running a big hotel. He'll have the same sorts of things to deal with – cleaning, catering, maintenance. He'll have to deal with the staff *and* the guests. People will want a lot of telling to begin with, because this is something new and they won't know what to expect.' She pressed a finger to her lips while she thought, and he actually saw the idea come to her. 'There should be guides, like the couriers on our tours abroad – nice, cheerful young people who patrol the camp—'

'Village,' he corrected.

'—answer their questions and make them feel welcome. And they can keep an eye open for repairs that need doing, or dropped litter – it's best to keep on top of such things or the place will start to look shabby.'

'How will the customers know who the couriers are?'

'We'll put them in uniform. Oh, not military uniform, don't be silly,' she said, when he made a face. 'Just something neat, like flannel trousers and a blazer, with a badge to identify them.'

'These are all good ideas,' Richard said. 'You should write them down.'

'I shall. I am doing,' she said. He was glad to see her look so animated.

Hannah was less enthusiastic. 'Why do we need to expand? We're doing all right. And my Samuel is no spring chicken. I don't want him to work himself to death.'

'I won't let that happen,' Richard said. 'I'll do everything.'

She gave him an old-fashioned look, but said nothing more, only took Cynthia away to work on the financial details. 'We have to know how much we can charge before we can see if a profit is there,' she said. They investigated the cost of a bed, breakfast and evening meal in various seaside resorts, the cost of additional meals, cinema tickets, deckchair hire, entrance to piers and shows and attractions, and so on.

Then they had to estimate what staffing costs would be, food, laundry and maintenance. The capital costs of building the village they left to Richard.

Cynthia voiced a problem. 'It's going to sound expensive, next to what they pay for bed and breakfast. We have to find a way to make them understand that it includes all the other things they pay for when they're on holiday.'

'Advertising,' Richard said.

'That's another expense.'

'We'd have to advertise anyway, to let people know the place exists,' Richard said.

'And keep on advertising, for the first few years, until people start to know what Nevinson's Holiday Villages are.'

'Villages – plural?'

Cynthia gave him a smile. 'No sense in wasting a good idea.'

Polly had been glad to have James back, especially when the mild December they'd been having suddenly turned on them and showed its teeth. The heaviest snowfall in living memory blanketed Yorkshire, and there was so much to do: getting animals in, feeding them, exercising horses, checking on elderly neighbours and pensioners, repairing fences and roofs. And when work was done, there were the long hours of being confined to the house, when James's ingenuity and cheerfulness were worth more than gold.

Once the snow departed and things got back to normal, James threw himself into the project for getting Alec a more suitable pony – he would be eight this summer and was growing tall. James and Polly had agreed that a New Forest pony would be ideal, being a nice, narrow breed, and very hardy, if they could find one big enough: many of them were only twelve hands, or twelve-two. After a great deal of enquiry and many visits of inspection, James found a six-year-old fourteen-hand bay gelding with a white star, elegant dark stockings and a sweet nature. Alec was instantly enchanted by him, didn't mind that he had been ridden hitherto by a girl, didn't even mind that he was called Shady, when he had told everyone that he was going to call his new pony Thunder. 'Horses don't like to have their names changed,' he told Josh loftily.

Shady was well-mannered and reliable, but with enough 'go' to satisfy the young master. And, unlike Mr Pickles, the pony had no objection to jumping. Alec began talking about jumping him in horse shows. Polly didn't want to sell Mr Pickles, but Jessie found a good family to lend the mare to.

Polly saw that, having completed that task, James became restless. She tried to interest him in routine matters, but kept finding him looking at books of travel memoirs. He got out his old journals of the trips to Bear Island and Canada, was often found poring over the big atlas from the library. He mentioned his disappointment at the American trip's being cancelled, and began to talk about going there under his own steam, buying a motorcycle and travelling around the country. And in the end she was not surprised, though she was sorry on her own account, when he announced that he was going back to Paris for a while.

'To work for Charlie?' she asked.

'I think I'll just see what turns up. I can earn enough with my painting to keep myself in a modest way. I wonder if I can get my old lodgings back? And there'll be a few people who'll be surprised to see me,' he said, with a happy smile.

Polly saw she could not keep him, and only said wistfully, 'Remember there's always a home for you here. Alec will miss his favourite uncle.'

He seized her in a bear hug. 'I won't forget my favourite sister,' he said. 'Don't worry, I won't be gone for ever – just a few months. *You*'re my home, Pol, my real home. I'll always come back.'

And the next day he was gone. Alec was disconsolate. 'I wanted to show him how I've taught Shady to shake hands,' he complained. 'He's *nearly* learned it perfectly.'

Gone With the Wind was once more in the news, because Selznick had announced he was to scour the country for the right person to play the heroine, Scarlett O'Hara. 'It says here that he's going to audition two thousand unknowns,' Rose said, nose in a magazine.

'I heard fifteen hundred,' said Lennie, looking up from his morning pile of post. They were breakfasting on the terrace, and the smell of waffles and coffee was in the air.

Rose shrugged. 'A nationwide casting call, it says here. I don't see why he can't find someone in the usual way.'

'Of course he could,' Lennie said, 'but this way he gets a lot of publicity for the film. Think of all those pretty girls in small towns across America who dream of being a movie star, and their excitement about maybe getting an audition. Their mothers and aunts will be in a frenzy, and when the movie eventually comes out, they'll all go to see it so they can say, "You'd have been much better than *her*, honey."'

Rose laughed. 'You're such a cynic, Uncle Lennie. Maybe there is a wonderful unknown actress out there, waiting to be discovered. They have to get started some way.'

'The fact of the matter is,' Lennie said, 'that Selznick is determined to have Clark Gable for Rhett Butler, and MGM never loans him. He can't start production until he's sorted that out, so while he works on Mayer to change his mind, he might as well be doing something useful. He's paid fifty grand for the rights, after all, so he's got to drum up some publicity for the end product.'

'But if MGM *won't* lend Clark Gable—'

'Oh, there's a deal to be made,' Lennie said. 'Louis B.

Mayer is Selznick's father-in-law. He won't hold out for ever or his daughter will cut up rough. It just has to be juicy enough on both sides. Meanwhile, a national frenzy over the female lead keeps the interest up.'

'I bet it will be Norma Shearer,' Rose said. 'I read in a magazine that Selznick wanted her.'

'I read somewhere that the author of the book thought Miriam Hopkins was the closest to her character. But Selznick thinks she's too old.'

'How old is too old?'

'Mid-thirties, I think. But that's the same age as most of the other front-runners – Joan Crawford, Norma Shearer, Tallulah Bankhead. If it were me, I'd be looking for someone your age.'

Rose looked up sharply. 'You think I should do it?'

'Have you read the book?'

'Not all the way through. I flicked. There was a lot of history in it. And honestly? I thought Scarlett was pretty dumb, always thinking about her looks, and chasing that Ashley character when it was plain he didn't want her. But I can see it'd make a good movie. Do you think I could get an audition?'

'You're going to be pretty busy, honey. When *Into the Night*'s wrapped up, there'll be the *Robin Hood* film.'

'Woody says I ought to keep going to auditions, even when I don't need the part. He says you have to keep your audition skills honed, and put your name out there.'

'Did he suggest you try for Scarlett?'

'I haven't discussed it with him. But I bet he would. *Robin Hood*'s still not tied up, is it? It might still not happen.'

'I'll talk to Al Feinstein again,' said Lennie.

There had been a lot of work done on the script by the story editor, Kay Courtney, who had experience of countering Feinstein's wilder aberrations without alienating him. So the

Robin Hood/King Arthur entanglement was largely unpicked, the baddie was back to being sheriff, rather than king, and Sir Bedevere – since a dangerously attractive cad was thought to be a strong element – was now Lord Bedford, one of the sheriff's rich henchmen. The other knights were out, the comic relief was toned down and was now a fairly muted Friar Tuck, who had a rather touching romance with Marian's faithful maidservant Jenny, the nun was out, and the wicked queen was now the sheriff's proud and haughty wife, who had once had a *tendresse* for Robin, which explained his exile in the forest – the sheriff had found out and threatened to kill him – and her hatred of Marian – jealousy because Robin now preferred her. It was not essential, of course, as Lennie knew, that a script make sense – it was more important that the movie was action-packed and engaging – but all other things being equal, it was more satisfying if it did.

The problem with Al Feinstein was that if too many problems were rolled into his path, he tended to lose interest in a project and change direction. Lennie was worried that that might have happened with *Robin Hood*. He contrived to bump into him on the lot one day in March and saw from Al's immediately narrowed eyes, and the aggressive way he manoeuvred his cigar from the corner to the middle of his mouth, that he expected to be harangued about Robin and bullied for a decision.

So Lennie changed his attack. 'How about Selznick and this nationwide casting call?' he said. 'That's a smart move, Al. I wonder you haven't thought of it.'

'It'll cost him a hundred thousand bucks if it costs him a cent,' Al said. 'And for what? Running round the country rounding up girls instead of letting the agents do the screening? Crazy!'

'It's good publicity,' Lennie said. 'But the end of it will be someone from the regular circuit, courtesy of an agent, just like you say. I heard Warner's offering a package of Bette Davis and Errol Flynn in return for distribution rights.'

'Tchah!' Feinstein said in disgust. 'Stale news. Selznick's already turned down Bette Davis.'

'Good publicity, too, for the girls who get as far as a screen test,' Lennie persisted. 'I was thinking, Van ought to put Rose up for it. She'd make a great Scarlett. And even if she didn't get the part, just being considered would get her name known.'

Al scowled dreadfully. The cigar rolled to the corner of his mouth so he could get the words out. 'Known? Her name's already known! D'you think I'd let Selznick and Mayer get their grubby hands on my girl? I coulda bought *Gone With the Wind* if I'd wanted it. I tell you, it's got disaster written all over it. That movie will never be made. You tell Rosie I'm not having her audition for that piece-a garbage. She's under contract to me. And she'll be far too busy with *Robin Hood* even to think about it – tell her that.'

'So *Robin Hood*'s going ahead?' Lennie said innocently.

Feinstein champed the cigar to the other corner. 'Going ahead? Course it's going ahead! What kind of a damn fool question is that?'

'Oh, it's just that I hadn't heard anything in a while, and I need to be sure I've got enough finance liquid when it's needed.'

Al removed the cigar so that he could jab it in Lennie's direction. 'You get yourself liquid, my boy. Contracts are being finalised as we speak. They'll be out to you end of this week. I was gonna tellya, but you jumped me with all this *Gone With the Wind* shit. Stale news, Len, stale news. You oughtta keep more on top of things, a guy like you.'

And, pleased with himself for this parting shot, he turned on his surprisingly small, springy feet and rolled away.

BOOK THREE

GOING HOME

I say more: the just man justices,
Keeps grace; that keeps all his goings graces;
Acts in God's eye what in God's eye he is –
Christ – for Christ plays in ten thousand places,
Lovely in limbs, and lovely in eyes not his,
To the Father through the features of men's faces.

Gerard Manley Hopkins: 'As Kingfishers Catch Fire,
Dragonflies Draw Flame'

CHAPTER SEVENTEEN

Le Chapeau Rose was up in the hills above Los Angeles, and the view was spectacular. The food was exceptionally good, featuring French delicacies such as *tripes à la mode de Caen*, sautéed frogs' legs with *fines herbes*, calf's brains, s*alade Niçoise*, and guinea hen with chestnuts and sage. It was very much a 'celebrity' restaurant, which meant there were always reporters and photographers hanging around to see who was there and with whom, and Lennie had been slightly surprised that Anthea had asked him to take her there. But, after all, he reasoned, she had to keep herself in the public eye.

His first hint that something was afoot was when the maître d' escorted them to 'your special table, *M'sieu*'. A glance at Anthea's complacent expression told him that she must have telephoned ahead and arranged it. The table was in the corner with the best view over the hills, but was visible to the press, who were corralled on the terrace below. A waiter arrived with champagne almost before they had been eased into their seats and had their napkins tenderly laid in their laps. Anthea was wearing a very low-cut and almost backless black evening dress glittering all over with jet spars, her hair piled up and held with jet ornaments and black feathers. She wore diamond earrings – a gift from him, as it happened – and a pendant necklace, which was not from him and which, if it was a real diamond, represented a significant investment by some other benefactor. He suspected it might be imitation, but it sparkled all right in the candlelight.

Lennie waited until they had ordered and the staff had gone, then raised his glass to his companion, sipped the champagne, and said, 'What's all this about? Am I missing something?' A guilty thought struck him. 'It's not your birthday, is it?'

She answered, with a vivacious smile, 'I'd soon let you know if you'd forgotten that! Besides, there's nothing to celebrate about being a year older, is there?'

He thought she wanted reassurance. 'You are ageless, my dear.'

She made an impatient gesture. 'I didn't bring you here to discuss that.'

He smiled. 'I thought I brought you here. If you hope to pay for my dinner, I have to tell you that I cling to some old-fashioned views, and one of those is that a lady doesn't pay.'

She leaned forward a little, allowing him a glimpse of her creamy bosom. 'I like that you know how to treat a lady. You would never raise false hopes in a girl and then let her down.'

'My dear Anthea, what *are* you talking about?'

She waved a hand around, indicating the restaurant, with its starry candles, gliding waiters, hushed-voiced clients, and the view over the hills, across the fairy-lit terrace below. 'Romantic, isn't it? Just the sort of place young lovers would choose to come to celebrate their love.'

'I doubt young lovers could afford it,' Lennie said. 'It's definitely for those who've already arrived.'

Now she was cross. 'I'm trying to set an atmosphere here. Couldn't you at least hold my hand across the table?'

'I think that sort of thing is frowned on at Le Chapeau. And, besides, there are certainly people from the press down there watching your every move.' He studied her face. 'Or

396

is that part of the plan? Am I sensing there's an agenda to this evening?'

She reached across and took his hand, and he was too much of a gentleman to pull away. 'How long have we been seeing each other, Lennie dear?'

'Several months, I suppose,' he said warily.

'Over a year. We met in New York last January. Don't you think it's time to move things on a little?'

'Move on? We are already sleeping together.' He saw her blush of annoyance. 'Though of course no-one but us must ever know about it. Except your maid, of course. And my driver – but he's as discreet as an oyster. You needn't worry. Your reputation remains unsullied.'

She pulled her hand back crossly. 'You are deliberately misunderstanding me. It's not polite to pretend you don't know what I'm talking about. When are you going to ask me to marry you?'

He had, of course, realised by now what she was driving at, but had hoped being obtuse would warn her off without having to come to specifics. With a sigh, he said quietly, 'I have no plans to get married. Not now, and not ever.'

'You can't say that! Everyone knows about us. We've been seen everywhere. And we're good together. Aren't we? Don't we have fun?'

'You are a delightful companion. But, Anthea, tell me truthfully – do you love me?' She didn't answer, avoided his eyes, and wriggled a little in the chair. 'Then why this sudden desire to marry me?'

'It's not sudden. I've been thinking about it for a while. You go out with someone for long enough, you're supposed to marry them. People expect it. And, just think, Lennie,' she leaned forward again and recaptured his hand, 'we could have a fabulous wedding. The Hollywood wedding of the year! A wonderful honeymoon – Palm Beach, Paris, anywhere! Set up house together. The dinner parties we'd give! We'd be the golden couple – people would kill for an invite! Wouldn't it be wonderful? Really, don't you see?'

'I can see that there would be endless articles about us in all the magazines,' Lennie said. Her expression was eager. 'It would be good for your career, wouldn't it?'

She almost said *yes*, then spotted the trap, and pouted. 'You're just being mean. I can't help it if publicity is a consideration. You always knew I was an actress.'

'I don't want to be mean. I respect your career, and I've never minded being seen to escort you. I'm glad if that's helped you along. But I can't marry you purely for publicity.'

'It's not *purely* for publicity. Of course I *love* you, as well.'

'Do you?'

'Of course I do. Let me tell you, there are dozens of men who want to go out with me, and I've turned them all down for you.'

Lennie sought to ease the slight for her. 'I'm not the right man for you. You need someone more flamboyant, someone who's happy in the limelight.'

'But—'

'I have to tell you, I have no heart. I gave it away a long, long time ago.'

She looked suspicious. 'We're not talking about Rose, are we? Really, that would be so—'

'Of course it's not Rose! It's not anyone in Hollywood. Please, can we drop the subject now? I'm as sorry as can be, but I can't marry you.'

The waiters arrived with their first course, and she subsided into silence. Lennie was afraid she might storm out, make a scene, but when they were alone again, she addressed her plate with the appetite that was one of the things he had always liked about her – some stars didn't like to be seen to eat in public, preferring to project an image of a spirituality above food. After a few forkfuls she said, 'Well, that's a bust! Still, can't blame a girl for trying.

At least smile at me, can't you? Try to look as if we're having a romantic evening.'

He realised that, knowing the press was down below watching, she would not want them to report they'd had a disagreement. It was a mad thing, this relationship between Hollywood and the fourth estate. Perhaps all Hollywood stars were a little mad because of it. He wondered if she would want to go on seeing him now – whether that would fit her narrative. He knew, however, that he did not want it. He had enjoyed her company all these months, but now he was not sure who it was he had been enjoying.

At the end of the war, Austria had been a broken country, stripped of its empire, its economy in ruins. The idea of *Anschluß* – joining together – with Germany to form the new country of Greater Germany had first been raised in the 1870s. It was expressly forbidden by the Treaty of Versailles and the Treaty of Saint-Germain, but still it enjoyed some support in Austria; though nationalists, along with Jews and many Catholics, were hostile to the idea.

'This is one of those European problems that's been simmering for generations,' Bertie said to Jessie, as they rode side by side one fine, blowy March day. 'Originally it was Austria that proposed a union of all Germanic states, under Austrian leadership. But of course Prussia wanted to be top dog, and after a couple of quick wars, Bismarck got his way, united Germany under Prussia, and excluded Austria entirely.'

'Didn't that settle it?' Jessie said, turning a lock of mane back the right way. The horse turned an enquiring ear back to her, then pricked it again, knowing they were heading home.

'A lot of Austrians are German by blood, and most of them are National Socialists, so union with Germany is back on the agenda.'

'Who cares?' said Laura, riding up on his other side. One

of Polly's dependants, she lived nominally at Morland Place, but spent more time at Twelvetrees than there. She'd been having difficulties with the youngster she was riding, and had hung back to teach him some manners. 'Austria, Germany – it's nothing to do with us, is it?'

'We can't let German expansion go unchecked,' Bertie said. 'If they're allowed to take the rest of Europe, they'll come for us next.'

Jessie knew that Bertie was abstracted. The subject had been triggered that morning by an item in the newspaper saying that the Austrian chancellor, Kurt Schuschnigg, a nationalist, had announced a referendum on Austrian independence.

'Are you really worried, dear?' she asked him. 'Will the Austrians vote for union with Germany?'

'I'm afraid it hardly matters,' he said. 'The Germans take what they want. They took the Saar, they took the Rhineland. Austria is the obvious next step. Hitler is Austrian by birth, you know.'

'I didn't know,' said Jessie.

'He'll have heard all the unification arguments in his youth. It'll be like the religion you absorb from the cradle. And Austria might be in decline, but it's got raw materials, it's got skilled workers and factories lying idle, it's got large gold and foreign currency reserves. It's a rich prize.'

Laura had lost interest and had taken the young horse off to the side of the path where some fallen saplings – victims of a recent windy period – made natural cavaletti.

'We needn't get involved, though. We don't have a treaty to defend Austria, do we?' Jessie said.

'No,' he said. 'But you can see the pattern. Small states, weak states fall, or get absorbed, Germany gets bigger and stronger, and sooner or later Hitler goes for the big prize, France. Then we have to act.' He stared ahead bleakly. 'Five years,' he said. 'They took five years of my life – of our lives, yours and mine. I'm too tired to face all that again.'

'You won't have to go,' Jessie said quickly. Their eyes met, and she knew that didn't help – or not very much. Thomas was nineteen, her precious son; and then there were Jeremy, John and Martin at Morland Place, Jack's Basil and Michael, Violet's sons. And the girls – though they would not fight at the Front, they would suffer too, as her generation of women had suffered: privation, struggle, loss, heartbreak. 'It can't happen again,' she said fiercely. 'It *mustn't*.'

'We should have finished them the first time round,' Bertie said. Laura came cantering back, and he made a small movement of his hand, cancelling the subject.

'Did you see?' Laura called, elated. 'He did it perfectly.'

'We saw,' Bertie answered, smiling. 'Do it again.'

The referendum was set to take place on the 13th of March. On the 10th of March Adolf Hitler moved two army corps into position on the Austrian border and in the morning of the 11th demanded the cancellation of the plebiscite, the resignation of Schuschnigg, and his replacement as chancellor by the Nazi-supporting Seyss-Inquart. Schuschnigg desperately sought support from other nations, but it was not forthcoming, and under the threat of invasion he resigned at eleven p.m. that day. At two o'clock in the morning of the 12th, the German 8th Army crossed unopposed into Austria. Later that morning, Seyss-Inquart assumed presidential powers as well, and raised a bill in Parliament to revoke Austria's sovereignty and declare it to be a province of the German Reich.

'As easily as that, Austria ceases to exist,' Basil commented. In the *Messenger* newsroom, everyone was poring over bulletins and analyses coming in over the wire from correspondents in Europe and America.

'Hitler wouldn't have objected to the referendum if he'd thought it would go his way,' said Jimmy Cutler. 'He wouldn't have needed to invade with an army.'

401

'There was a telegram from Seyss-Inquart last night, saying people were rioting and he needed German troops to restore order,' said Palmer, another junior reporter.

'Those riots were faked,' said Digbeth. 'Local correspondents say they were organised by Nazi supporters to justify the invasion.'

'Obviously, it was all planned,' said Cutler.

But as the day went on, reports came in that surprised them. As the German Army advanced through Austria, it had been welcomed by cheering crowds waving Nazi flags, throwing flowers, making the Fascist salute. In the afternoon, Hitler crossed the border with a four-thousand-man bodyguard and in the evening arrived in Linz, to an hysterical welcome.

'Look at these photos, these faces. You can see they're smiling,' Dickins said, of the crowds packing both sides of the road. 'These people are really glad about it.' They crowded into windows, lined roofs. Boys climbed up onto lampposts and statues. Girls ran out from the crowds to give flowers to the soldiers, women held up their babies to wave, veterans in Austrian Army uniform saluted with tears of pride. 'We thought the majority of Austrians opposed *Anschluß*. Everybody thought so. Obviously even Hitler thought so, or he wouldn't have gone in with an army.'

'He could have saved himself the trouble,' Basil muttered.

On the 13th of March, Seyss-Inquart announced the abrogation of the Treaty of Saint-Germain, and the bill uniting the two states was signed into law. Hitler continued a triumphal tour, arriving in Vienna on the 14th, where a vast crowd gathered in the Heldenplatz to hear him speak. Newsreel images showed more beaming faces, waving flags, thousands of civilians giving the Nazi salute. 'The oldest eastern province of the German people shall be, from this point on, the newest bastion of the German Reich,' Hitler declared, to roars of approval.

'I can only think,' Dickins said, 'there's an element that's always resented the fact that Bismarck excluded Austria from the original unification, and that they've been longing ever since to take care of unfinished business.'

'But where does that leave us?' Digbeth asked. 'Aren't we obliged to uphold Saint-Germain and Versailles?'

'Yes, what about the League of Nations?' Basil put in.

'The League!' Cutler snorted. 'When have they ever stood up to anyone about anything? They'll just say it's Germany walking into its own backyard, like they said about the Rhineland.'

'Can you see Britain and France mobilising for the sake of Austria?' Dickins said. 'Our governments are desperate to avoid war. Especially after this demonstration of popularity. The Nazis have covered themselves. They'll claim they were invited in.'

'There must be Austrians who don't like it, though,' Basil said.

'Of course there are,' Dickins replied. 'But with the clashing boots of the 8th Army marching down your street, and your pro-Nazi neighbours screaming themselves hoarse all around you, would *you* go out and make a show of your opposition? As John Stuart Mill said, "Bad men need nothing more to compass their ends, than that good men should look on and do nothing."' Dickins reached for his cigarettes. 'I tell you one thing,' he said, 'I wouldn't like to be a Jew in Austria right now.'

'And what happens next?' Basil asked after a respectful moment.

Dickins gave Basil a hard look. 'Don't ask questions like that, Compton. Haven't you got any work to get on with?'

James did not know how Hélène Gilbert had found out he was back in Paris but one day in late April he received a hand-delivered invitation to one of her parties at her apartment in the rue Auber, and went along, anticipating good food and wine and interesting talk. He was amazed to find himself lionised by Hélène, who presented him to her other guests as though he was the reason for the party, telling them he was a fine artist and a *vrai homme du monde*. There was always a mixture of nationalities at Hélène's parties, and this one seemed to feature a large number of very rich Americans. It was not long before one woman's polite interest in his painting wore away to reveal the base metal underneath: was it true, she asked, that he had been at the Windsor wedding?

He was trying to think of a polite way to avoid talking about it, when he saw Hélène looking at him across the room. She gave him an encouraging nod, and he realised that this was to be his payment for the hospitality. Reluctantly, he admitted that he had helped to organise it, and a flood of questions was released. He answered the factual ones – what was she wearing, who else was there – and avoided the speculative ones – was he really mad about her, was she in love with him – and, finding they were quite happy making up their own stories once he'd got them started, he managed to slither away.

He sought out Hélène to expostulate, but she forestalled him. '*Chéri*, you were so wonderful, so discreet! They are all mad for information. I will not let them bother you again tonight, but thank you for doing that for me.'

'I didn't have a choice, did I?' James complained. 'And I thought the Windsors weren't popular in America any more, after the German tour.'

'With the Jewish set, they are not, and the *bien-pensants*. But the Americans who come to Paris are in love with romance, and what could be more romantic than a king giving up his throne for the woman he loves? It is like a movie story. It costs nothing to please them, *n'est-ce pas*? And then they will feel happy and generous.'

'And buy your expensive paintings?' Hélène was an art dealer, among other things.

'*Tiens.* You used not to be so cynical. But by all means, *mon cher*, do not speak of the German tour – that would not set the mood at all.' She drew him a little aside. 'Tell me, *petit*, what are you doing in Paris without the good Charlie? My spies tell me that you are selling paintings to the tourists, little nonsenses of wet cobbles and pink blossom.'

'They pay the rent,' James said.

'But only just? They tell me you are in quite poor lodgings.'

'Have your spies been following me about?'

'Don't be cross. I am interested in you. And I would like to make a proposition to you.' James wondered if she was proposing he should become her lover. She was regarding him with a certain speculative look, and she had hinted at it the last time he had been involved with her.

'What sort of proposition?' he asked warily.

'You are so helpful to me, talking to my guests and helping to keep them happy. And I have recently lost my secretary. I know what you did for Charlie, organising everything – would you like to do the same for me? I am offering you a position with a salary.' She laid a tender hand on his arm. 'I hate to think of you struggling for money. Starving in a garret is very well when one is young and full of dreams, but a mature man should have a decent place to live, good food and proper clothes.'

'You don't like my clothes?' he said, amused.

'You are *un peu mal soigné*, it must be said. But of course,' she waved a hand to indicate his face, 'always beautiful.' Suddenly she became brisk, told him the salary she would pay, and what she would expect him to do: sending out invitations, meeting people at stations, finding them accommodation, ordering food and drink for her parties, booking tickets for shows, doing research, writing letters, accompanying her to galleries and first nights . . . It was, as she had

405

indicated, the sort of thing he had done for Charlie and knew very well how to do, and the salary was generous. As long as she did not want him in her bed, it would afford him a very pleasant life.

'And that's all?' he said, when she stopped talking. 'That's all you want me to do?'

She laughed. 'If it's not enough, I can always find you more.'

'It's enough,' he said. 'I accept.'

So he was able to move out of lodgings and into a small, modern apartment on the second floor of a six-storey building in the rue Lepic, on the corner of the rue Véron. She wanted him to be somewhere nearer, and he could have afforded a more fashionable district, but he was happy in his old stamping-ground of Montmartre. The rent was reasonable, and as he ate so often at Hélène's expense, he found himself comfortably in funds. He was able to buy new clothes that satisfied Hélène, who was particular in the matter of shirts and ties. He could afford also to give up his 'tourist nonsenses' and, in what little leisure time he had, go back to more serious painting.

One day when he was walking from his flat to Hélène's he passed an antiques shop on the boulevard de Clichy and, glancing in, saw someone he recognised inside. The man looked up and met his eyes blankly. Then a smile of recognition spread over his face. He put down the piece of Sèvres he was holding – to the obvious disappointment of the shop's owner – and came dashing out to seize James's hand.

'James Morland, is it really you?'

'Emil Bauer, as I live and breathe! I haven't seen you in—'

'—too many years to remember,' said Bauer. 'We are both older and wiser, I hope.'

'How come I haven't bumped into you before?'

'I've been in America for a couple of years. Washington – politics. Frightfully boring. Don't ask! I only got back last week. What are you doing here?'

'I'm working for Hélène – a sort of factotum-cum-secretary. You remember Hélène Gilbert?'

'Of course. I was intending to renew my acquaintance as soon as I got settled. I remember her parties fondly.'

'My God, it's good to see you,' James said.

They had met back in 1932 on the expedition to Bear Island, which Emil's father's money – he was a Swiss millionaire – had helped to finance.

'Same goes for me,' Emil replied. 'Paris has changed so much while I was away, I don't seem to know anybody. And everything's got so shabby somehow. I am very much in need of a congenial friend to restore the gaiety in my life.'

'I'd be happy to be of service,' James said, with a grin. 'I'm in need of a friend, too.'

'How is the lovely Meredith?' Emil asked.

James's grin faded. 'She went back to America for a visit. Then her father died and she stayed. I haven't seen her since.'

'Oh. I thought you two were . . .'

'So did I. But apparently not,' James said. 'What about you? Is there a Mrs Bauer?'

'Not even in prospect. My *affaires* are strictly frivolous. Can something be strictly frivolous? I mean I am strict about remaining frivolous. At the moment I am in pursuit of a delicious young lady called Florence who dances at the "Windmill". I saw her perform last week, and fell hopelessly in love, but taking things any further is fraught with difficulty. I can't even get past the stage door. They seem to guard the girls like nuns.'

'I think I might be able to help you there,' James said. The Moulin Rouge, a burlesque theatre, was on the corner of James's street, the rue Lepic and the boulevard de Clichy. James explained that he knew the manager and the front-of-house staff well, through having booked so many tickets for Charlie's guests, and now Hélène's. 'I can get you complimentary tickets whenever you like. More importantly, I can get you a backstage pass.'

407

'Really? What an invaluable friend you are!'

'But I would have to guarantee your good behaviour, so I have to ask if you have honourable intentions.'

'Well, I can certainly start with them,' Emil said, 'and see how it goes. I say, are you free tonight? Won't you dine with me? My treat, but you can choose the place – you probably know better than me where's good to eat.'

'I'd love to. As it happens, there's a restaurant I've been wanting to try. La Vache Souterraine. Apparently they have a particular way with duck.'

'Say no more! Eight o'clock? I'll pick you up – where are you burrowing these days?'

James fingered a card out of his pocket, handed it over, and they parted with another hearty handshake.

So for the moment, James was happy, usefully occupied, in funds, painting what he wanted to, and he had a friend to do things with. What more could a reasonable man want? It was only at night, in the moments before sleep claimed him, that he knew he was lonely. He thought about poor Tata, but was at last beginning to be able to live with the guilt over her death. He thought about Meredith, and wondered what she was doing, imagining her astride a horse, helping her brothers to round up cattle, living a bright and breezy outdoor life. His imaginings were informed by the cowboy movies he had seen, though he edited out the guns and outlaws.

And the horses made him think about Polly, back in Morland Place. He would write her a long letter to cheer her up. But when it came to it, his daylight hours were so crowded, he only managed to send her a postcard.

One day in May, Hélène said to him, 'The English painter Eric Chapel is back in Paris. I heard yesterday he is to design sets for Billancourt Studios for their *Jeanne d'Arc* film.' She shrugged. 'It is a fad, this having famous artists to design

408

sets. It is foolish, when there are French set designers like Trauner and Lourié wanting the work – but there! All the studios are doing it. Look at Dalí! There is a very silly man – though he can paint.'

'But Eric Chapel designed sets in Hollywood,' James said, amused by her patriotism. 'It's quite respectable.'

She smiled and patted his cheek. 'Respectable. What a word! So *classe moyenne*. I want you to find Monsieur Chapel for me, speak to him.'

'Where are the Billancourt studios?'

'At Boulogne-Billancourt, of course, but you do not need to go all the way out there. He is staying at the Crillon. You can catch him there. I want to know what happens to his original artworks for the sets, and whether I can buy them. I can sell them for a great deal of money to my Americans. And invite him to one of my parties.'

'Which one?'

'We will make one around him, of course. Do not ask foolish questions.'

The Hôtel de Crillon was an eighteenth-century stone palace on the corner of the place de la Concorde, where once Louis XVI and Marie-Antoinette had lived – and in front of which they had died under the guillotine. It had been turned into an hotel in 1909, and was the smartest and most expensive place to stay in Paris, along with its older and more traditional rival in the rue de Rivoli, the Meurice, which James knew well from his time with the Windsors.

He waited outside the hotel for a while, then went in and lurked in the sumptuous foyer. He was just considering a more direct approach – telephoning to Chapel's room – when the lift doors opened and the man himself appeared. James saw at once that he had not changed much since he had seen him last. His years sat lightly on him: his face was still taut and unlined, his pale hair still thick. Under an admirable suit

409

– he was obviously prosperous – his body was lean and agile. He was quite tanned, as was to be expected if he had recently arrived from California, and his eyes were startlingly blue in his brown face. They were also sharp – they picked out James almost as soon as James spotted him. He came across with a pleasant smile, and a slightly quizzical air.

'It's James Morland, isn't it?' he said, holding out his hand.

'I'm surprised you remember me,' James said.

'I have a good memory for faces,' he said. He saw that James was looking with polite enquiry at the woman on Chapel's arm, and said, 'My wife, Emilie.'

'I didn't know you were married,' James said, shaking the delicate hand held out to him. She was very slender, petite, and strikingly beautiful, with dark hair and eyes.

'It's very recent. Emilie was Emilie Delancourt before she did me the honour of accepting my hand – one of Warner's rising stars. You may have seen her in *The Glass Forest* and *We Three*.'

A movie actress. That made sense. James made a polite murmur, not having seen either of those films. 'And what brings you to Paris?'

'We are on our honeymoon,' Chapel said. 'April in Paris – what could be more romantic?' He lifted a hand. 'I know, it's May. We started off in April, but it takes time to cross the Atlantic. The intention was sound. Later, we hope to see a little of Italy. I had a desire to visit Europe one last time.'

'Last time?' James queried.

Chapel's face grew serious. 'War is coming, and it will be bad. If there is anything left afterwards, it will not be fit to visit for a generation.'

'Do you really think there will be a war?'

'Don't you read the papers? Don't you know what's going on in Germany?'

Emilie gave him a minatory look. 'Darling,' she reproved.

He laid a hand over hers where it rested on his arm. 'You

410

are English, you were spared the full horrors of the last war. The next one will be even worse.' Then he made an obvious effort and smiled. 'Your sister, how is she? Well, I hope.'

'Yes, she's well, thank you.'

'She's not here with you?'

'No, she's back in England. At Morland Place.'

'Ah, Morland Place!' James had heard the edge of eagerness in Chapel's voice, and apparently so had Emilie, because she frowned slightly, and glanced at her husband. 'She spoke about it so often, I feel as if I know it,' Chapel went on, and added to his wife in explanation, 'Morland's sister was a well-known New York hostess many years ago.' Then to James, 'Send her my regards, will you, when you write?'

'Of course,' said James. He drew a breath to begin on his own business, but Chapel seemed to have lost interest in him. 'It was good to see you again, but we should go,' he said, beginning to turn away. 'I am due at the studios later today and I promised Emilie a look at the shops first.'

James was not to be put off that easily. 'I wonder if I might walk along with you for a few moments. This meeting wasn't entirely accidental . . .'

As James explained later to Hélène, he was only partly successful. It would have been too awkward to bring up the subject of the artwork originals straight away, but he had secured Chapel's agreement to come to dinner at Hélène's, and an invitation for himself to visit the studios, so there would be plenty of occasions for introducing it more subtly.

At home after work, as he was changing his trousers to go out with Emil, he thought about Chapel and his new wife, and that little awkwardness when he had asked after Polly. James had got the impression on a previous meeting that Chapel was carrying a torch for his sister, whom he had obviously known quite well when they both lived in New York. He wondered whether he should tell Polly about the

411

meeting. But there was no suggestion the torch was reciprocated – and, besides, it was clear Chapel was not intending to come to Europe again.

It occurred to James then that Chapel had said something odd, and he paused, trousers at half mast, while he tried to prise it out of his memory like a raspberry pip from between the teeth. Ah, yes, that was it: talking about the coming war, he'd said, 'You are English, you were spared the full horrors of the last war.' *You* are English. But wasn't *he* English? And if not, what was he, and why had his war been worse?

He thought about it for a bit, then shrugged, and finished dressing. Probably just a slip of the tongue.

He sent Polly a postcard at the weekend, and he did mention the meeting with Chapel. He was not a natural correspondent, and it was something to say. He always struggled for content, even with only a postcard to fill.

Polly was troubled about the increasing number of aeroplanes passing back and forth overhead. There were now two new RAF airfields, one to the north of York at Linton, and another at Church Fenton, which was not far from Morland Place, just to the south, outside Sherburn–in–Elmet. She knew now that Yorkshire was in a strategic position with regard to northern Europe, and especially Germany, and evidently, whatever ordinary people thought about the possibility of another war, the RAF was in no doubt it was coming. And ever since the council had purchased land from her to build a housing estate (she still avoided riding that way, hating the sight of all those raw new houses where she should have had crops growing), she was aware that compulsory purchase could be exercised in case of works for the public good. As she rode about the estate, she couldn't help noticing flat fields that would convert easily to airstrips; and if the government decreed it, there would be nothing she could do about it.

An airfield had to come with buildings – offices, hangars,

workshops, accommodation for the airmen – and roads, for the supply of food and ammunition and other heavy goods and the to-ing and fro-ing of personnel. Proper roads, not beaten tracks. Was her whole estate to be covered with concrete and tarmac? And what of the animals? Driven into panic by the roaring machines overhead, the cows would go off milk and the hens off lay, and the horses and sheep would bolt and get hung up on fences and break their legs. And that was even without contemplating that, if there was a war, the air bases would become targets for enemy bombers. Morland Place had stood for five hundred years. Would it still be there in another five hundred? Or fifty, or five?

It was at times like these that she needed James most, someone to talk to who would put her fears into proportion – probably, knowing James, laugh her out of them. He had been sending her postcards, which was an improvement on his usual absence of communication, but from the tone of them, it looked as though he was settled in Paris. She could only hope for one of his mercurial changes of mind.

She came in one day from inspecting the pigs at Moon's Rush and saw a postcard lying on the silver tray on the hall table, the picture of the Eiffel Tower telling her it was from James. It was always the Eiffel Tower. Couldn't he at least put some thought into it and send her a different landmark? There must be some, or people wouldn't keep going there. She stripped off her gloves and dropped them onto the table, and stopped to read it where she stood.

There wasn't much room on a postcard once you'd written the address. He'd done his best, starting at the very top, but the franking ink had covered the first two lines, so she was no better off. Then a name made her eye jump to the end of the tight screed. *Met Eric Chapel, on honeymoon, married a film star. Apparently he's doing film sets here. Sends his regards to you.*

She stared at the words, frozen to the spot. *He's married?*

413

Married a film star. He had got over her – enough, at least, to give his heart and his body to another woman. Well, that was easier for men than for women. And when they had last parted, they had both known it was for ever. He could not come to Morland Place; she could not leave it. He was a handsome, virile man in the prime of life. It would be unreasonable to expect him never to touch a woman again. But his heart? She thought she could bear it if she could know he still loved her. She had to bear it either way, but it would hurt less.

She stared at the elaborate marble fireplace of the Great Hall, but what she saw was a dusty track, baked hard by summer, a dry-stone wall, a young girl on a horse, a young man with his shirt sleeves rolled up, his hair bleached white by the sun, his eyes as blue as the unblemished sky. He was the great love of her life, but he was gone. She would never see him again. This message had been a little breeze come out of the past to ruffle her hair briefly and die away, a message from the gods that it was all, *all* over and she must accept it.

There was a place in her heart where he would live for ever, unchanged, untouched by time, as much as if he had really died back then. Perhaps it would have been better for her if he had. She could have moved on, and perhaps have come to love someone else, instead of living in this limbo. Because she realised that even in her marriage to Ren, there had been a dishonesty – a little piece of her she withheld from him. Had he known? But Ren had always been sufficient unto himself. He let her in only to those parts of his life that did not touch the core of him. He had been dishonest too, as she was only now coming to realise.

And that had been her life, a series of near misses. Where did it leave her now? She was approaching forty, a wealthy woman, with a growing child, and a house full of dependants. What did the future hold for her? She wanted love – oh, she wanted it so badly! – but where could it be found for someone in her position?

A polite cough alerted her to the presence of Barlow, who had glided out from the kitchen passage and had been, now she became aware of it, waiting for her attention for some time. She looked up and met his eyes.

'Mr Ordsall called, madam, and requested an interview with you. I believe he wants to discuss the wedding arrangements.'

'The wedding?' she said blankly. *But he was already married. He had married a film star.* Barlow waited, his eyes steady, and she slid back down to earth. Jeremy's wedding. They had been engaged for two years and now had saved enough to take the next step. 'Oh, yes. Of course,' she said. 'I'll give him a ring later.'

'Shall I have a luncheon tray sent in to you, madam?'

'No, I'm not hungry,' she said, and walked away, blindly, just to get away from watching eyes and questioning minds. Barlow would have read the postcard, of course he would. She was under no illusion about the interest servants had in the lives of those they served. They would never open a letter, naturally, but a postcard was fair game. He would be wondering what there was written on it that made her look like a Greek mask of tragedy. She walked towards the steward's room, and changed direction at the last moment to go into the chapel. No-one would follow her there.

It was cold, smelling of furniture wax and damp, and a faint, ghostly odour of snuffed candles. It was dark, too, with only the glow of the sanctuary lamp, and what little light the stained-glass windows admitted. Outside it had clouded over, threatening rain. She sat in her favourite place, at the end of a bench, against the wall where long ago someone had carved the outline of a bear in the stone. When she sat here, she sometimes wondered who had done it and why, wondered how many other Morlands, in ages gone past, had run their fingers, as she did, over the outline.

In the stillness she felt the weight of the house around her, the watchfulness of her ancestors, whose bones lay in the crypt under her feet. She had run away, half across the globe, and found Erich. She could have stayed with him. They could have gone anywhere in the world; but the house had called her back. She had glimpsed a bright garden; but Duty was the stern sentinel that stood at the door and said, 'You may not pass.' Now she would never leave.

In the crepuscular gloom, she heard the message, breathed out of the ancient stones of the old, brooding house that owned her. *You have so much. You must not ask for more. Be grateful. Take care of what you have. Do your duty.* And then a codicil, even more sobering. *Your concerns are very small and selfish, when war may be coming.*

Morlands had fallen in the last war, family and employees and tenants, their bodies left in foreign fields, their names inscribed on the Monument. She had a little surge of gratitude that Alec was too young to fight. But there were so many others in her extended family who would be called to go. She wanted to pray, but she had no words. It would be dishonest, when her mind was so full of her own troubles.

Lennie came back from a trip to New York to find Rose fizzing with excitement. 'I've got something to tell you!' she cried.

The first photography of *Robin Hood* had been going well enough for him to feel comfortable about leaving her for a few weeks. She had had a couple of scenes with Lord Bedford, and he had asked her whether it was awkward, working with Dean Cornwell again. 'No, it's fine,' she said. 'There's nothing between us now – Deanie's just a friend. It's a bit like having a brother opposite me.'

'And how is it, working with Dick Randolph?'

The smile disappeared. 'Oh, he's all right, I suppose. He's no *trouble.*'

'What does that mean?'

'Well, just at first he was kind of flirty. Ugh!' She made a face.

Lennie was amused – and relieved. 'He's quite a heartthrob in the cinema,' he pointed out. 'Women swoon over him, they say.'

'But he's so old! It'd be like kissing your father.'

'He's not that much older than me.'

'Well, he looks it.'

'Or Van.'

She looked surprised. 'Woody's not *old*. He's really cool.'

'If Dick Randolph is bothering you—'

'Oh, no. He stopped being flirty after the first day. But now he tries to be helpful and "teach me the craft" – as if I needed teaching! At least, not by him. I'll take direction from Mr Reznik, but not from *him*.'

'Hmm. Well, if you have any trouble from him, let me know.'

'You don't need to worry about me, Uncle Lennie. I can handle it. And he's all right, really, just a bit . . .' she thought for a moment '. . . pathetic.'

How are the mighty fallen, Lennie thought. It didn't bode well for the love scenes if the heroine thought the hero pathetic, but it was far better than having her develop a crush for Randolph. And Reznik was a good director – he'd find his way round any problems.

So he went to New York.

And now, arriving back with a present for her – a whole Lindy's cheesecake in a box – he found her sparkling. 'Don't tell me you've fallen in love,' he said.

'*No-o!*' she said, as though it were a totally ridiculous suggestion. 'I'm going to England!'

'You are?'

'We all are. Mr Feinstein wants to do location filming in the real Nottingham Forest. Woody says it's because George

417

Cukor sent researchers to the actual Verona for his *Romeo and Juliet* movie, to make sure it was authentic, and Mr Feinstein wants to go one better. Woody says it's an Authenticity Auction. He's so funny.'

'I'm very pleased for you. It will be a great experience for you to see England – and Nottingham isn't all that far from Yorkshire where your mother came from.'

Her eyes opened wide – she could make them so big, she looked like a cartoon puppy, and it always made him laugh – and she said, 'Oh, but you'll come too, won't you? *Please*, Uncle Lennie – oh, you must! It wouldn't be any fun without you.'

'Your fun isn't dependent on me.'

'It is – a bit,' she qualified. 'And, anyway, you'd love to come, you know you would. You had to cancel before because of my trouble, and I feel so bad about that, so now you have to go to show you forgive me. So I don't have to feel guilty any more.'

Lennie shook his head. 'It's always best to put forward one reason and stick to it, rather than throw a dozen out there and not believe in any of them.'

'I believe in all of them,' she protested. 'But if you want just one reason, okay: I *want* you to come. And you'll enjoy it.'

'That's two.'

'No, because you enjoying it is why I want you to come. You've been so good to me, looking after me all these years. It's time you had a bit of pleasure.'

'Looking after you is a pleasure. But now I've had a chance to get over the shock, I think I *would* like to see England again.'

She whooped. 'Oh, I'm so happy! I've got to ring Woody and tell him.'

She clashed in the doorway with Wilma, who had emerged to see what the whooping was about. Rose squeezed past her. 'I'm so excited!' she cried, and disappeared.

Wilma gave Lennie a very old-fashioned look. 'It ain't good for that girl to get her own way all the time.'

Lennie cocked his head. 'You know what she's excited about?'

'It ain't difficult knowing what's on her mind. She don't exactly hide it. And *she*'s got to go where she's told. I don't know any reason *you* got to go. She don't need looking after any more.'

'I'm not going to England to look after her. I'm going because I want to.' He studied Wilma's expression. Her lower lip was sliding out further every instant. 'It's not the season for fog over there. And no ship has gone down since the *Titanic*. So I'm not going to get pneumonia or drown.'

'There's more ways of not coming back than fog and icebergs,' she said mysteriously.

'Would you like to come with me?' he said. 'You've never been out of the country, have you?'

'No, sir, I have not, and I ain't going to start now. You go to England if you have to, Mr Lennie, but I'm stayin' right here. I'll look after things so's it's all here for you to come back to. So's you got the choice.' And she turned and went back to the kitchen. Lennie thought he'd miss the slip-slop sound of her movements if she ever left him.

And then he thought, England! So green and beautiful, it made your heart ache just to look at it.

Sherwood Forest. He didn't know it, but English woods were lovely, intimate and charming, not like the great wild forests of America. It would be nice to see Sherwood Forest.

And he could pretend all he liked, but he was just delaying thinking about Polly. It would be more than nice to see Polly, even if he was only Cousin Lennie to her now. Just to see her again – and dear old Morland Place, which held so much of his heart. He felt as though he had been in exile, and was being allowed a chance to go home.

Home! He realised now that that was what Wilma feared

419

– not that he'd die, but that he'd stay there. She was so smart, it was frightening.

Lennie came across Al Feinstein on the back lot, standing in the sunshine in his shirtsleeves, hands jammed into his pockets as usual, talking to the assistant producer, Dorothy Fitch. He broke off when he saw Lennie coming, removed his hands from his pockets and made an expansive gesture. 'So, Len, you've heard? I see it in your face.'

'You're taking the company to England?'

Dorothy turned to him. 'I've been saying, we could find a suitable forest right here in California. And a castle façade can be built on the lot for next to nothing, out of plywood and papier-mâché.'

'Small thinking!' Feinstein dismissed her argument. 'This movie is gonna be big, the biggest thing since *Cleopatra* and twice as good, and we're not gonna stint on it.'

'We're not?' Lennie said wryly. As a major shareholder, much of it was his money.

'Don't worry,' Feinstein said, patting his shoulder. 'It'll all come out of budget. This is advertising, Len – you got to advertise, these days. And it'll cost a lot less than Selznick's dumb "search for Scarlett" stunt. Which, by the way, is a total crock, because I hear on the grapevine he's already got an unknown English actress tucked in his top pocket, not that he's letting on. Those screen tests are totally phoney. Not like our trip to Merrie Old England! See the difference? It's already catching the headlines. "ABO to Major in Authenticity" – *Motion Picture Journal*. "Feinstein backs the Real Deal" – *Movie Mirror*. We're knocking Selznick and MGM outta the park.' He slapped himself on the chest in congratulation. 'The old man's still got it. *Gone With the Wind*!' he said witheringly. 'Kinda title is that? Sounds like a plug for Andrews Liver Salts!'

'What's the plan, then – going to England?' Lennie asked, knowing a smokescreen when he saw one.

Feinstein raised his hand placatingly. 'Controlled, every inch of the way. Small cast, just the principals, small crew. We'll recruit technicians and extras over there. Much cheaper. Six weeks' location shooting in July and August – the weather's more reliable then. Right, Dotty? Get over there, get it done, get back. Nottingham Forest, the real one. Authenticity.'

'The forest is not a problem,' Dorothy said, looking anxious, 'but we're having trouble finding the right castle.'

'England's lousy with castles,' Al objected.

'Yes, but most of them are ruins. And owned by some obscure branch of the British government, which adds to the difficulties and the paperwork. I've got an agent over there looking, and he says there's one in Scotland that might do, but that's a long way from Nottingham, and he says the roads are bad.'

'Scotland can be hard going,' Lennie agreed. 'I'm sure there must be one nearer than that.'

'The problem is, we need one with a working drawbridge for the siege scene. Honestly,' she turned back to Feinstein, who met her with a stony face, 'we ought to think about a back-lot façade.'

Lennie suppressed a smile. 'You want a privately owned castle with a drawbridge, not too far from Nottingham? I think I know just the place.'

'You do?' Dorothy said, hope struggling with doubt in her expression. 'How do you know about it?'

'I used to live there,' said Lennie.

CHAPTER EIGHTEEN

Woolthorpe was a tiny village, with few inhabitants, mostly fishermen or graziers, a poor place, with the church roof suffering for lack of wealthy congregants. 'No-one to object, you see,' Richard said. 'In fact, they'd welcome the influx of money.'

Failing to find anywhere suitable in Suffolk or Norfolk, Richard had cast his net further north, into Lincolnshire, an even less populous region. He and Samuel had taken the train to the nearby small and well-kept seaside resort town, where the agent had a car waiting for them.

'How far is it?' Samuel asked, as they started off.

'Two miles,' Richard said. 'Special motor-buses could be laid on to bring the guests from the station to the camp—'

'Village,' Samuel corrected automatically.

'—village, which would give us an extra element of control, to prevent outsiders getting in without paying. Not that there are many outsiders around – and most of them will probably end up working for us anyway.'

Samuel noted the change of tense from the conditional. 'You're pretty sure this is the place, then?'

'Look around you,' said Richard. 'Flat land, flat as a pancake. All poor grazings. And wait until you see the beach! Miles of golden sand. That's why people come here, of course.' He gestured behind him. 'The town council made a concentrated effort before the war to bring in holidaymakers by providing them with one or two facilities.'

'Well, then, won't that be too much competition?'

'No, because our people will have all the facilities thrown in. And they won't be locked out of their lodgings all day. Think of the luxury of being able to go back to your room to fetch a cardigan. Or if your new sandals pinch. Or if you take too much sun and need to lie down for a bit.'

Samuel, who had never been on a seaside holiday in his life, let alone stayed in a bed-and-breakfast, grunted. 'It's a deserted sort of country, all right,' he said, staring out of the car window. 'Too far from London?'

'Nowhere is too far, if the railway goes there,' Richard pointed out. 'People go all the way to Cornwall for holidays.'

'I suppose that's true.'

The car stopped at the side of the road, and they got out, standing on the grass verge and looking eastwards towards the sea over rough grazings separated by thin hedges. In the distance a square church tower stood above a huddle of cottages. 'That's Woolthorpe,' the agent said, 'and this,' with a wide wave of his hand, 'is the area in question. As far as that line of hedges, and up to the village boundary. And, of course, all the way to the sea.'

'It's bigger than I was thinking of,' Samuel said.

'The land is cheap now,' Richard said, 'and if – when – the village is a success, you'll want to expand. By then, it'll be more expensive. What if someone else has the same idea and wants to build a rival camp next to ours?'

Samuel nodded. 'You've got me there. Well, can we have a look at the beach? And a poke around the village wouldn't come amiss.'

It was a fine day, with real warmth to the sun after a chilly April. The sky was a tender blue, and the sea shaded from sapphire to ultramarine on the horizon, the foam of the little waves breaking on the sand turning it brilliant turquoise. The sand was golden, and there was no sound except the occasional bird cry, the susurrus of the breeze in the rough grasses, and the soft murmur of the waves breaking on the beach. Richard stood contented as a horse at rest, simply enjoying the sweet, clean air and the lovely prospect in front of him. After a long pause, Samuel said, 'I dare say it can get very windy here.'

'Canvas wind-breaks,' Richard said.

'And it won't always be sunny.'

'It rains far less on the east coast than in the West Country. It's the driest area in England. And when it does rain, there'll be the indoor things for them to enjoy.'

'What if it rains all week?'

'They'd have to contend with that wherever they were. And in the ordinary resort they'd have nowhere to go.' He looked at his companion. 'Are you having second thoughts?'

'It's only good business to think about what can go wrong.' He waved an arm encompassing, it seemed, the immensity of the Lincolnshire flatlands. 'I wasn't expecting there to be so much of it. I thought we were going to start small and work up.'

'We have to build the communal facilities at the same time as the first chalets,' Richard said, 'so it makes more sense to start with as many of them as possible. It's economy of scale that will make the thing viable. The owner of the land is the Earl of Ormsby, and he's willing to give us a long lease on all this land at a very attractive rate. But if economic conditions change, we might not get the same rate another year.'

'He owns most of Lincolnshire,' the agent put in. 'Except the bits the Church owns.'

'Got a monopoly on the land, has he?' Samuel said. 'So he can charge what he likes. Why's he putting a low price on it?'

'Agricultural depression,' Richard said. 'Returns are low, so land is cheap.'

They walked, and Richard talked about his plans. 'You

know I suggested we should look at having the huts prefabricated out of timber and just assembled on site? Well, I've been in contact with a contractor – name of Goodman, of Goodman Timber Merchant and Building Supplies. I've been to the factory, or mill, or whatever it's called. They prefabricate sheds of all sizes, and they've got the spare capacity to take our order. He's very keen. He's going to get a suggested design to me this week. And I've found a builder, local man called Hewson, lives in Seathorne, for the construction work – the foundations, roads, drains, sewerage and so on. Best of all, he's willing to manage the whole thing.'

'I thought you were managing it,' Samuel said. He sounded tired.

'Of course I'll manage the overall scheme, but we'll need someone on site to manage the day-to-day work. There will be sub-contractors to keep an eye on.'

'Sub-contractors?'

'It's a big project, and firms up here are small. He'll need to have others involved to get the capacity needed.'

Samuel stuck his chin down into his collar, a gesture of escape. 'I feel as though I'm biting off more than I can chew. You got me all excited about Nevinson's Holiday Village, but I never realised it would be so complicated.'

'It's not complicated,' Richard said cheerfully. 'It just has to be organised, and I'm more than happy to do that. Honestly, you can leave it all to me, and be no more involved than you want to be. I'm not feeling at all daunted.'

Samuel eyed him. 'You look as though you're thriving on it.'

'I am,' Richard said, and then, tactfully, 'that and marriage. I'm afraid my wife is feeding me too well – I'm putting on weight.'

Samuel laughed, and some of the strain left his face. 'I thought you looked as if you'd been on good grazing. Cynthia learned from the best – Hannah is a wonderful cook.'

'I know, sir. And Cynthia is taking after her.'

'How are things at home, now she's come back to work? Have you got the servant problem sorted out?'

'We've got just the one girl, but she can manage, with all those wonderful gadgets you gave us. Electric carpet-sweeper, electric iron and so on. Oh, and the electric refrigerator is a marvel. I'd never seen one before.'

Samuel looked pleased. 'It's an economy in the long run, because it cuts down spoilage. I wanted to get one for Hannah, but she prefers the old ways. I think she's a little bit afraid of electricity, if truth be known,' he added confidingly.

'Well, Cynthia loves it,' Richard said, glad to have got his father-in-law on to a happier topic. 'She made a jelly for supper the other day and it set in no time in the refrigerator.'

Samuel was not to be distracted by jelly. 'You've gone over all the figures, haven't you?' he said, after a brief pause. 'And you're convinced you can make this work?'

'Yes. I think it could be the start of something big. I envisage an empire of holiday villages – with you as the emperor.'

'Not me, my grandson,' Samuel said. 'Who I hope I'll be holding in my arms before too long.'

Cynthia had obviously not shared her fears with her parents. Richard accepted the amendment without comment, and Samuel seemed happy not to probe further.

In the train on the return journey, however, he was quiet and thoughtful, and when finally he leaned forward and said, 'I've something serious to talk to you about,' Richard feared he might be about to be put on the spot about his failure to provide an heir.

Still, there was no help for it. 'Yes, sir?'

Samuel took a moment in which he seemed to be struggling to find the right words. Finally he said, 'I want to be sure that if anything happens to me, you'll take care of Cynthia.'

'Of course I will,' Richard said, puzzled.

'And Hannah.'

'Of course. I take my family responsibilities very seriously.'

'Don't take offence,' Samuel said. 'You've had other things on your mind lately, and you might not have realised how bad things are abroad.'

'In Germany, you mean?'

'It starts there, but it won't finish there. I'm an old man, and my heart isn't good these days. If I'm not still here when things go bad, I want to be sure you'll take care of my Hannah and my Cynthia.'

'This isn't Germany. Things won't go bad here,' Richard said.

'They went bad in Austria! Do you know the first thing they did in Vienna after Hitler marched in? They rounded up seventy thousand Jews, and marched them off to a concentration camp.'

'I didn't know,' Richard said humbly.

'Half the Jews in Austria are Polish, and I have relatives still in Poland. They keep me informed. And if it starts up here, I need to know you won't sit around thinking it can't really be happening, and leave it too late to get them out.'

'Get them out where?' Richard asked, feeling bewildered.

'If England goes, America will be the only safe place. I don't know which will be the safest route – Southampton or Liverpool. Or you might have to get them across to Ireland and find a sailing from there. Ireland'll claim to be neutral but secretly back Germany, like last time, so it might not be safe. You'll have to decide at the time. But don't get caught out. Things will move fast. Don't trust anyone. Don't tell anyone your plans. I've told them to have a bag packed ready to go at any moment. You won't find they argue. They'll obey orders. They know what's at stake.'

Richard started to say, 'I'm sure you're worrying unnecessarily,' and realised in time that it was a pointless thing to say. Instead he said, 'I understand.'

'You'll get them away safely?' Samuel insisted. 'I know *you* won't want to go – you'll want to stay and fight – but war isn't women's business. I've transferred assets over there to support them until you can join them. Or bring them back – if there's anything to come back to.'

'You really think . . . ?' Richard began, but it was another pointless remark. 'I'll see to it that they're safe,' he said instead. And added, 'I promise.'

Samuel visibly relaxed, and sat back. For a moment they both stared out of the window at the passing world. The countryside of May, the loveliest month, unreeled mile upon mile, the hedges thick with hawthorn, the verges with kex and moon daisies, England all in green and white and gold, decked for a wedding. It was beautiful almost beyond belief, and Richard wished he had someone to share it with. The most human of urges is to say, 'Oh, look!' So much of art, he thought – paintings and poetry and much of prose and music – is someone with unusual talent saying, 'Oh, look!' at the world we all see and have no words for. Richard gazed, and felt a tremor of love that was almost fear for the timeless beauty of a timeless land: the fields and woods and villages of England, unchanged for hundreds of years.

After a while, Samuel spoke again. 'Hard to believe, when you look at all this, that anything could ever touch it,' he said, jumping uncannily into Richard's thoughts. Richard met his eyes, startled, and he went on, 'I know you think I'm a foolish old man, but you'll see. There's a monster over there, in Europe, feeding on men's hearts, and growing bigger every day on their blood. I'm a Jew, we're an old people, and we've seen enough monsters to recognise them, however they disguise themselves.'

'I'll take care of them,' Richard promised again. It was all he could say.

He didn't mention the conversation to Cynthia when he got home. They talked about the site at Woolthorpe, and the construction plans. She told him some ideas she'd had about the entertainments they might arrange for the visitors – games and competitions that would cost little or nothing to put on – and he invented some ridiculous competitions to make her laugh. Then they went to bed, and made love, and he held her while she fell asleep, thinking of the Jews in Vienna being rounded up, and wondering what it was that made men do vile acts. One was tempted to say they behaved 'like animals', but animals never did such things. They were governed by nature. Only humans could be so unnaturally cruel.

It was on the following evening, after dinner, that the thought came to him. The wireless was on, playing dance music, turned down low, while Cynthia knitted. Richard put down the book he was reading and left the room to go upstairs.

He found the bag under the bed, pushed well back – he had to lie down and reach full stretch to touch it. A leather Gladstone, worn but sturdy: inside he found clothes, a wallet containing a copy of her birth and marriage certificates and the passport she'd had to get for their honeymoon, a jewel-case, empty, ready to put her valuables into at a moment's notice, and in an envelope, family photographs, of Hannah and Samuel, of Cynthia as a child, an old sepia print of stern-looking strangers, probably her grandparents, and the studio portrait of her and Richard taken for their engagement, her seated and him standing behind with his hand on her shoulder, he smiling confidently, she with a faint smile that looked almost bewildered. At the bottom there was a large amount of money, still bundled in a bank's paper sleeves. Hundreds of pounds. Samuel must have provided it. Passage to America cost around forty pounds, so he was making sure they had enough to get themselves established. Or did he think they might have to bribe their way onto a boat?

He replaced everything in the same order, pushed the bag back where it had come from, and stood up, dusting his hands. His heart hurt. She had taken her father's warning seriously, but had not mentioned it to him. Did that mean she didn't really believe there was a danger, or believed and was afraid Richard might ridicule it? He had a flash of imagination, a bleak image of her and her mother coming down the gangplank at a dock in New York, two very small figures in a huge city, facing an uncertain future, the archetypes of refugees everywhere. What must it be like to be Jewish and know yourself not welcome anywhere? He felt a fierce determination to protect her. In the short time he had known her, she had climbed inside his heart and curled up there, and he could not remove her without destroying himself. But he didn't want to remove her. It was a warm and belonging feeling, to care for somebody. What was one's life for, but to be part of someone else's?

He wished he could give her the one thing she really wanted – a child.

Morland Place was excited about Jeremy's wedding. Mr and Mrs Robb, the bride's parents, had been unwilling at first to agree to it taking place there: a girl got married from her own home, Mr Robb said stubbornly, and that was that.

But the couple had been walking out for a year before they got engaged, and for another two years before they got married, which was long enough for hardened attitudes to be eroded. An invitation to dinner to celebrate the engagement had begun the softening. They had never set foot in Morland Place before, and Mrs Robb was visibly impressed, though – to her credit – not at all overpowered by the magnificent rooms and the even more magnificent servants. Little Miss Robb, having seen what she might be denied, had begun working on her parents soon afterwards. The chapel was very pretty, she urged: how lovely it would be to walk down the aisle there. The Robbs thought the very idea of *having* a chapel in a house was Popish; but she assured them the ceremony would not be conducted by some unknown Romish priest in league with the Devil but by Mr Ordsall, the vicar, whom everyone knew and liked. And to have the wedding breakfast in that lovely dining-saloon! How convenient, just to walk from the chapel, and not to have all the muddle and inconvenience of cars from church to hotel. By the time the actual date for the wedding was being discussed, the walls had been breached, the fort taken, and the Robbs could not remember when they had actually agreed to it, only that they had.

The engagement had gone on for so long that even Ethel was resigned to the marriage. During that time, Jeremy had been promoted at the bank to under-manager, with an increase in salary that not only enabled him to look at renting a three-bedroomed house in Sycamore Terrace – which would mean a bedroom for her to stay in when she visited them – but to afford to run a little motor-car, meaning he could visit her at Morland Place more often.

When she heard about the larger house, Polly had allowed herself to dream that Ethel would go and live with them permanently, but it was not to be. Ethel herself had vetoed the idea. A young couple should have the chance to be alone at the beginning of their married life, she said, with a senti-mental look, and she could not abandon Polly and leave her to run that big house all on her own. Polly believed Ethel had decided her creature comforts would be better served in a household with many servants than in the new house with only a cook-general and a girl for the heavy work. Besides, she had discovered that, despite her soft pink looks, Miss Robb was anything but soft and pink inside, and indeed these days received Ethel's helpful criticisms with tight lips and a militant light in her eye. At the moment Amelia had to take what Ethel dished out, but once under her own roof, she looked likely to make her own rules and want them followed.

So Ethel had all the fun of a wedding without any attendant

trouble to herself. Polly made sure Miss Robb got a substantial discount at Makepeace's for her wedding dress – made by Makepeace's own seamstresses – and trousseau from Makepeace's ready-made department. Her fellow employees clubbed together to buy her a silver-plated filigree cake basket, and from the management, Polly arranged a forty-eight-piece dinner service, comprising twelve dinner plates, twelve dessert plates, twelve side plates, two serving platters, two vegetable dishes with lids, one vegetable dish without lid, one gravy boat with saucer and one sauce boat with lid and saucer. Jeremy's bank gave him a striking mantel clock.

The Robbs were able to be generous to their daughter, since all the expense of the wedding ceremony and wedding breakfast had been taken off their shoulders, and it was they who bought the little second-hand Morris 8, two years old, one careful owner, and also paid for the honeymoon. Jeremy's brother John was the best man – he worked at Hanbury's garage and it took him a week to get his hands and nails clean enough, a week during which Mr Hanbury kindly put him on driving-only duties, and John looked on like a cat watching birds through the window while other employees plunged their heads under bonnets and crawled under chassis.

Alec had been persuaded, through a shocking level of bribery, necessary because he was almost eight and said he was too old to be subjected to silk stockings, to be a page-boy. He complained bitterly right up to the day itself, but then found he rather liked being the centre of attention. He didn't like having his hair ruffled and being told he looked 'sweet', but he discovered the plaudits often came with tips – Mr Robb excelled himself and pressed a half-crown into Alec's hand – which all went towards the construction kit he was saving for.

The groom's sister Roberta came to the wedding, having asked if she could bring her employer, Mrs Maddox, as a guest. Polly said yes, though it seemed an odd request. She thought she understood better on the day when the pair turned up, with Roberta driving Mrs Maddox's motor. She had grown tall and handsome since leaving home to work in the racing stables at Stillington, but she was very slim and probably, Polly guessed, rode at no more than nine stone. Her hair was cropped as short as a boy's, but was curly enough to pass muster with her mother. She and Mrs Maddox were both wearing light tweed suits, the jackets cut rather like hacking jackets – Polly wondered if they served a dual purpose – and in them they looked like sisters. Polly immediately felt the closeness between them. Roberta had gone as a management trainee six years ago, but from the way they stood together, a little apart from everyone else, and talked together in low voices, and managed to exchange information with looks alone, she thought they were more like a married couple. Ethel bustled up to get Roberta to talk about how well she was doing, wanting something to boast about, but Roberta would only talk about the horses, and how well *they* were doing. She had the habit of referring her comments to Mrs Maddox: 'Didn't he, Hilary?' and 'Don't they, Hilary?' and 'Was that in 'thirty-five or 'thirty-six, Hilary?' Mrs Maddox didn't talk much, but she smiled a lot, and when she did speak, it was to praise, so everyone thought well of her.

When the wedding feast was finally over, the young couple set off for Scarborough, Jeremy looking very proud behind the wheel of the Morris 8. Polly, waving them off, thought Miss Robb, now Mrs Jeremy Compton, looked relieved as much as anything. Ethel retired to a sofa, claiming exhaustion, and indulged herself in comfortable tears. And, seeing it was June and wouldn't be dark until ten o'clock, Polly escaped upstairs, changed into riding clothes, collected the dogs and went round to the stables, saddled Zephyr, and cantered away into the green and glowing evening.

* * *

Lennie stepped down from the carriage and saw Polly waiting exactly opposite him. It was an overcast, humid August day, and she was wearing a fitted silk dress in milk-chocolate brown figured with white, a belted waist, slightly flared skirt to just below the knee and cap sleeves, white gloves and a small hat with a very long pheasant feather. His heart swelled.

'How did you manage to be waiting in just the right place?' he called, instead of saying what was in his heart and embarrassing himself.

'I know where the first class stops, of course.'

She looked at him uncertainly for a moment, then he put down his valise and held out his arms to her, and it seemed perfectly natural to step into them instead of shaking hands. He was a sort of cousin and she had known him nearly all her life, after all. And Americans, she knew, were much more demonstrative than the English. It felt good to be held against his strong male body. His grey overcoat, made from the lightest, softest wool, was delicious against her cheek, and he smelt lovely. She had forgotten how tall he was.

Lennie held her slender body close, closed his eyes, and ached. Then forced himself to release her.

'You're all on your own?' she said, looking up at him and automatically straightening her hair.

'Yes, everyone else comes tomorrow. I wanted to make sure everything was all right before they descend on you.'

'I was half expecting to see elephants and camels in special loose boxes, and clowns leaning out of the windows.'

'It's a film company, not a circus,' he reminded her.

'I know, but I'm so excited, my mind keeps giving me circus images. Will we have to meet them from the train?'

'No, Dorothy Fitch will have arranged transport. You're not to worry about anything – she's tremendously efficient. Just enjoy the ride.'

'I will. Let's go – where's your luggage?'

The car was parked outside. 'That's a big beast,' Lennie

434

remarked. 'Is it new?' It was a Vauxhall GY saloon in maroon-and-black.

'I got it last year,' she said. 'I wanted something with plenty of room. It's got a big engine – pulls like a lorry up hills.' There were three dogs in the back, jostling to hang their heads out of the window. He could see what looked like a forest of waving tails. 'You don't mind them, do you? They insisted on coming. They never go in front so those seats are quite clean.'

He laughed. 'It wouldn't be a real Morland Place welcome without dogs,' he said.

The luggage stowed, they settled in and she drove off. There was a little silence, but she was concentrating on the traffic and getting out of the station yard onto Queen Street. Her gloved hands on the wheel looked strong; her bare arms, between the cuff of the gloves and the sleeves of her dress, were brown. 'Everyone's terribly excited about this whole thing,' she said at last.

'It's very good of you to let the company come,' he said.

'Good of me? They're paying me a fortune!'

'I'm sure it's not a fortune.'

'Maybe not to an American, but it seems one to me, especially as I don't have to do anything for it.'

'Dorothy will make sure there's no damage,' he said, 'and I'll keep an eye on things too.'

'I had the estate carpenter look at the drawbridge, and John – you know, Robbie's son? He works in the motor trade – John found a mechanic to check the machinery. It was funny, really, virtually every male in the house, plus the grooms from the stables, found an excuse to be in the yard that day. Men are so fascinated by anything mechanical! Anyway, it was all in surprisingly good order, just needed oiling and a bit of tightening up here and there. But you know, don't you, that it doesn't just drop down? It descends quite slowly. The script you sent me – thanks for that, by

435

the way – seems to have people dashing across seconds after the order's given.'

'Don't worry about that,' Lennie said. 'You can do anything with cameras. They'll just cut from starting to lower it to the dashing part. You'll never know from the finished film how long it took.' They were out on Blossom Street now, and the traffic moved freely. He took a breath. 'Polly—'

She anticipated him. 'I never heard from you for months, years. I was so hurt. You were supposed to come and visit, and then you weren't coming, and then – silence.'

'You came to New York on the *Queen Mary*, and never told me you were coming. I could have flown across to meet you there if you'd told me. So I supposed you didn't want to see me.'

'I thought you didn't want to see *me*.'

'I've *never* changed the way I feel about you,' he said, and managed to stop there.

'Oh,' she said. 'It seems we've been at cross purposes.'

'It does. I was so glad you said yes to ABO's proposal. I thought you'd forgiven whatever it was I'd done and we could make a fresh start.'

And, to his immense relief, she laughed. 'Oh dear, how silly and awkward it sounds now – positively childish! And what a waste of time it all was!' She glanced at him. 'Now I'm actually with you, I can't imagine how I could ever have supposed—'

'Me too,' he said.

'Can we forget it ever happened, and pretend we're just the same as when we last met?'

'Okay by me.'

'"Okay by me". You're very American. I forget. I always think of you as being English.'

'It will wear off,' he said. 'By the time I've been here a week I'll sound as English as you.'

There was another little pause, as Polly thought, *Only a*

week! His life is in America. He'll go back. I mustn't get too comfortable with him. She cast about for something to say. 'Jessie and Bertie are coming to dinner tonight, and the children. They can't wait to see you. Jessie's particularly glad that you're hiring horses from her, though of course any pleasure is tinged with anxiety, because they're all her babies. She worries that you may make them fall over, the way they do in cowboy films.'

'We won't. Horses have to be specially trained to fall like that – otherwise they could hurt themselves.'

'I'm glad to hear it. I hate to see it on a film myself – all I can think is, Oh, the poor horses.'

He smiled at her. 'Tender-hearted Polly.'

She looked away, biting her lip. After a moment she said lightly, 'It's such a long time since you were at Morland Place, I wonder if you'll notice any changes.'

'You haven't changed a bit,' he said, 'so I don't suppose anything else has. Except that Alec's bound to be a lot bigger. He won't remember me. Does he look like Ren?'

'Not at all,' she said shortly. 'He looks like me.'

'Lucky boy,' he said.

As an avid picture-goer, Ethel was in her seventh heaven. The film company was being accommodated in various lodgings and local hotels, but inevitably spent much of each day at Morland Place. As well as the external scenes, there were several to be shot inside the house, using the Great Hall, which had had to be stripped of all furnishings. Here, the wicked Sheriff of Nottingham fought a duel with Robin Hood; here Lord Bedford pressed his malign attentions on Lady Marian. In addition, the dining-saloon had been set aside for Costume and Make-up, again requiring the removal of its usual furnishings. Everything had been taken to the gentlemen's wing, out of bounds for the week.

Joy and profit had been brought to a large swathe of York

people. The film company was ferried back and forth by a fleet of motor-cars, to the satisfaction of John's boss and other motor-garages. Jessie and Bertie had been commissioned to provide horses. She hired those of her own that were temperamentally suitable, and found more in other local stables, along with grooms to handle them. Provisioners of all sorts made an unexpected and very welcome profit. The tradesmen of York enjoyed a golden period as the film people spent their spare time exploring, eating, drinking and buying souvenirs, while their presence drew in people from all around hoping to catch a glimpse of them, spending money in the process. Even the cinemas cashed in by showing Dick Randolph films and *The Falcon and the Rose* to packed houses. And a fencing school on Monkton Road was delighted to provide two instructors to act as doubles and perform the duel for a handsome fee.

But for Ethel, having real film stars under her roof, especially the three principals – Rose Morland, Dean Cornwell and Dick Randolph – brought her to the edge of ecstasy. The drawing-room was made available to them to relax between shots, prepare and read over their lines. They were in and out of the dining-saloon, being costumed and made up. They took refreshments in the small dining-room, where the house's inhabitants actually got to sit down with them. These people she had read about in film magazines and seen on screen were *actually in her house*! Quite unconsciously, she took on the aspect of grand lady of the manor in front them, as if it was her house and not Polly's. She wore her Sunday best every day, her accent underwent a noticeable gentrification, she offered them the hospitality of Morland Place and assured them that *anything* they desired would be provided for them. She listened with flattering attention to their least sentences and laughed trillingly at their little jokes. She was condescending, charming, arch, gracious, and blushingly admiring by turns.

She was particularly excited about Dick Randolph, whom she had always adored on screen, and perhaps not realising that Ethel was *not* the châtelaine, Randolph played up to her. He bowed over her hand and kissed it, calling her 'dear lady' in what he thought was an English accent. He extravagantly opened doors and pulled out chairs for her, to the confusion of the footman whose job it was. Ethel blossomed under his attentions, and allowed herself a little fantasy, at night in bed, where he fell in love with her English charms and whisked her off to California to marry him and live in his Hollywood mansion. At the back of her mind she knew it was only a fantasy, but it was sweet all the same. She had been a widow a long time.

The maids were divided between gazing adoringly at Dick and at Dean Cornwell. Dean was pleasant to everyone in a schoolboyish way and especially friendly to the younger footmen, but Lennie, keeping an eye on him, did not see anything untoward taking place. He seemed on his best behaviour – and it would be only a week, after all. Martin, another of Polly's dependants, was home from college, and befriended him, and Dean seemed to take to his unstudied naturalness.

Rose was very excited to be at Morland Place, which she had heard so much about but didn't remember, and on a day when her schedule was light she begged Polly to give her a tour of the house. Polly had seen *The Falcon and the Rose*, and was prepared for Rose to be the grand actress, but she was friendly and natural, and seemed almost shy with Polly, as if unsure she would be liked. By the end of the tour, during which Rose showed a great appreciation of everything, Polly felt genuinely attached to her. They were, after all, cousins, and Polly was happy to talk about their shared ancestors.

The servants and estate workers were excited about witnessing the making of a film, and people from the village and the housing estate also flocked over to see what was going on, so that a perimeter had to be set up to keep them from interfering with the action. John Burton saw to it, and arranged for it to be patrolled by some of the largest estate workers. The Morland Place people were besieged by picture-goers with requests for information about the stars' actions, habits and preferences, and Alec did a brisk trade in auto-graphs for his schoolfriends.

The pinnacle of joy came when a number of the servants were recruited to act in some of the scenes.

'It's very nice of your producer-lady to ask them,' Polly said to Lennie. 'They couldn't be more thrilled. They'll talk about this for the rest of their lives.'

Lennie smiled. 'Don't you realise that Dorothy's saving money? Your people are happy to do it for nothing, which saves her having to hire extras.'

'Oh, is that it? Well, they're delighted, anyway.'

'It's particularly useful to have people who can ride. In Hollywood, extras with skills cost more.'

The inconvenience to Polly of the invasion was amply repaid, not only by the money ABO were paying her, but by the fun of watching the business of movie-making. She was surprised that the outside scenes required enormous arc-lamps, running off a large generator – daylight was apparently not enough. And at how often there seemed to be nothing going on, everyone standing around in their costumes waiting for . . . she knew not what. The director, a gaunt, saturnine person who seemed to inspire awe even in the principals, was brought to rage by the passing of aeroplanes overhead, which meant the filming had to stop, and the producer, Dorothy, had to go and placate him. Polly overheard her saying to Lennie that he ought to have told her the place was so close to an airfield. At least they weren't rained off. The weather remained perfect, sunny, not too hot, with picturesque large white clouds in a blue sky. Lennie told her that when they didn't have attractive clouds they sometimes added them to the film later, and she wasn't sure whether to believe him.

There was a day when they spent some hours filming horses, ridden by extras in costume, galloping back and forth across one of the fields – from which the cows, of course, had been removed to a safe distance. Polly couldn't see what this had to do with the story, but Lennie told her that as they had hired the horses, they might as well use them, and that you could always find a place in a film for a few hundred feet of galloping horses.

The drawbridge worked perfectly, and the estate carpenter watched it go down and up with parental pride, and murmured to Polly that he had never been to the pictures but he would make an exception when this film came out. 'It's the star of the whole show, is that,' he said. 'I shall take the missus. Wouldn't miss it for the world.'

Perhaps the biggest sensation was caused by the butler, Frederick Barlow, a tall and handsome man, when he agreed to get into costume and play the part of the sheriff's major-domo. It was Dorothy Fitch who persuaded him. He had only to conduct Robin Hood, in disguise, into the sheriff's presence, bow, and retreat, but Dorothy was so impressed by his height, looks and manner that she persuaded the director to give him a line. 'A messenger from Sherwood, sir,' he had to say. It caused a such a ripple among the maids, they had to be restrained from crowding into doorways to watch the rehearsals and the 'takes'. They begged him nightly in the servants' hall to say his line, then sighed and cooed when he did.

'You'll have to keep an eye on him,' Lennie said to Polly. 'Dorothy's after him.'

They were taking the dogs for a last walk round the moat; the evening was mild and sweet, and a gibbous moon was washing its face in the still black water. It had been less than half full when Lennie arrived. The week was almost up.

'After him?' she queried.

'I heard her talking to him last night, saying that with his

441

looks he could make a fortune in Hollywood. She even offered to arrange auditions for him if he came over.'

'She can't take my butler,' Polly said indignantly. 'It took years to train him.'

'I don't think she cares abut his butlerishness. I rather think she's enchanted by his smouldering masculine magnetism,' Lennie said. 'She sees the screen potential. And she *is* a woman, after all.'

'Barlow doesn't smoulder. Besides, handsome men are ten a penny. Experienced butlers are impossible to replace.'

'I don't think you need to worry,' Lennie said. 'Your Barlow listened to her with exquisite politeness, then said he didn't think Hollywood would suit him, if she would excuse him, madam, and might he bring her a little more sherry.'

Polly laughed. 'I can just hear him saying it. All the same, it's not cricket to accept my hospitality, then try to poach my servants. I shan't feel safe until she and the whole film company have packed up and gone.'

She heard the words just after she said them, and looked up at Lennie, whose smile faltered. 'I can't believe the week's almost over,' she said. 'It's flown past.'

'Yes,' he said, and seemed to be hesitating on the verge of saying something, when Kithra, the youngest of the dogs, dashed up with a stick and obliged Lennie to throw it.

'Not in the moat!' Polly cried. 'He'll come back and shake, and soak us.' Lennie threw the stick as far as he could and Kithra dashed off, and Polly used the hiatus. 'I wish you weren't going away. We haven't had any time to talk – not properly.'

'I don't have to go,' Lennie said, looking down at her.

She caught her breath. There was so much in that look. 'Don't you?'

'I'm a free agent. I can stay as long as you like.'

'Don't you have to take Rose back?'

'She'll travel back with the company. There are plenty of

442

people to look after her, on the journey and in California. And she's a grown woman now – off my hands. Would you like me to stay, Polly?'

She felt ridiculously shy, as if she were eighteen again. 'I wish you would,' she said awkwardly. 'You haven't so much as been on a horse yet. All you've seen is the house. I expect there've been lots of changes on the estate. I could take you round the farms: the tenants would love to see you again. And I know Jessie would like to entertain you at Twelvetrees. And—' She heard herself babbling, and stopped. Kithra came running up again, and as Lennie removed his gaze from her to deal with the stick-throwing, Polly was able to shake herself into composure again, and say politely, 'I would like you to stay.'

He looked down at her for a long time. But he only said, 'Then I shall.'

CHAPTER NINETEEN

Peace descended on Morland Place with the departure of the film company. Furnishings were brought back, pictures rehung, rooms restored to order, routines re-established. The servants gradually descended from their exalted state, like autumn leaves whirled up by a wind falling gently to rest. They would talk about it for the rest of their lives, but almost as something out of a dream. Excitement would re-emerge when the film came out, but for the moment, things were back to normal.

The fine weather held, and Polly kept to her promise of riding with Lennie around the estate, pointing out changes, reintroducing him to the tenants and neighbours, who remembered him kindly from his salad days. She saw how instantly liked he was by the younger ones who had not known him, how instantly trusted. She watched him interact with them, seeing him with fresh eyes.

She had borrowed a horse for him from Jessie, a safe one, unsure how much riding he did in California. Very little, was his cheerful answer when she ventured to ask. But he rode confidently, though in a rather American style at first, sitting well back, with loose reins that encouraged his mount to misbehave. He seemed amused when she corrected his seat and told him to shorten his reins, calling her 'schoolmarmish', but he adjusted easily enough, especially as the English saddle was not designed for the American seat.

Sometimes Alec, still on holiday, rode with them on Shady. He was interested in but a little wary of Lennie – or perhaps, Polly corrected her perception, a little in awe of this tall new 'uncle' with the strange clothes and accent, the air of coming from an infinitely larger world. She noticed that Lennie didn't press his attentions, but responded fully and seriously to Alec's comments and questions without either condescending or trying to ingratiate himself. Like most children, Alec was quick to perceive inauthenticity, and he responded to Lennie's quiet and genuine worth. He was surprised and intrigued when Lennie told him he had been there at his, Alec's, birth, and over several days teased various details out of him. His heart was won when Lennie bought him, as a belated birthday present, a Telsen wireless construction kit, and further, when he didn't immediately offer to help him build it, but waited until Alec asked.

The round table in the drawing-room, of an evening, was a place of pliers and snips of wire, and the air pulsed softly with murmured conversations about tuning capacitors and valves, circuits and coils. Martin and John were soon drawn in. While Harriet read and Polly played the piano, Ethel would look up from her sewing and ask John what a grid bias battery was, or a high impedance load, secure in her confidence that he could explain, seeing he was an engineer or as good as. And when John, tongue-tied and shy, stared at her in dismay, turned red and stammered, Lennie would catch Polly's eye across the room and they would share a complicit grin, before Lennie stepped in and rescued him. 'What John's trying to say is . . .' Soon he was John's hero too. Though he was a trained motor-mechanic, John had a natural feeling for any sort of machinery, and the radio fascinated him. Lennie was happy to answer his questions, and was encouraging when John shyly confided that he wouldn't mind changing careers and 'going in for' radio electronics instead. It would be a good move, Lennie said. It was the

445

science of the future. He opened his mouth to suggest that if there was a war, it would stand him in good stead, but then he saw Ethel's pink and proud face and didn't say it.

Meanwhile, on their rides and whenever they were alone together, Polly and Lennie talked. They shared their memories of Morland Place during the war, of Teddy and Aunt Henrietta, of Jessie when she was young, of Robbie and Frank and Ned. They talked about New York, and common acquaintances, Polly's fashion business, Lennie's first forays into the world of radio. They remembered his early radio broadcast channel, and how he had given Rose her first break, acting in radio plays. They talked about his political career under President Hoover, which led them naturally to talk about Ren, and Polly found she could discuss him with Lennie without hurt or embarrassment. It was all so long ago now.

They talked about Lennie's first ventures into cinema, and his early investments at the urging of Joe Kennedy. In March that year Kennedy had arrived in London with his family, having been appointed American Ambassador to the Court of St James. Lennie told Polly how Joe had boasted to him that he would get an ambassadorship. 'You ought to go and see him,' Polly urged, half joking. 'Perhaps he'd introduce you to the King.'

'I wouldn't put it past him,' Lennie said. 'If ever a man had an excess of brass neck, it's him. And a complete lack of diplomacy – why on earth Roosevelt thought he was ambassador material I can't imagine! He's put me in the way of one or two things in the past, and I'm grateful, but I can do without him now. No, if I were to go and see anyone, it would be Sir John Reith. I'd like to find out how broadcasting is going to be organised in this country – quite differently from back in the States, I guess. And then there's radio detection.'

'What's that?'

'It's a way of bouncing radio waves off moving objects so

that you can tell where they are and which way they're moving. It's being developed in several countries at the moment, the States and here, probably France, probably Sweden – the Swedes are very good at that sort of thing – but everyone's working in secret, for fear that some other country will get there first. Whoever has a working system will have an enormous advantage if there's another war.'

'Why?'

'Because they'd be able to detect enemy aircraft approaching in time to shoot them down.'

'Oh,' said Polly. She didn't want to think about the possibility of war.

'They're pretty sure back home that the Germans are working on it too. So it's vital any advances we make don't get to them.'

They were out riding, and had reached Cromwell's Plump. She led the way up onto it, and slid from the saddle, looping the rein over her elbow. Another thing she'd had to cure Lennie of was the tendency to drop the reins when he dismounted. American horses, it seemed, were trained just to stand still when that happened; English horses might stand still, but they were more likely to head off at a brisk pace for home, leaving the rider with a long walk back.

He reached her and dismounted; they sat on the ground on the edge of the Plump, and the horses grazed on the short grass behind them.

'You've gone quiet,' Lennie remarked, after a moment. 'Was it something I said?'

She debated inwardly the wisdom of speaking, and finally said lightly, 'Oh, you called America "home".'

'It was your home once,' he reminded her.

'That was when James was the heir,' she said. 'He was going to be Master of Morland Place, so I could go anywhere I wanted.' She was silent a moment. 'I can't forget that I let Papa die without seeing me again.' He reached out and took

447

her hand to comfort her. 'He never saw Alec – his only grandchild.'

There was nothing to say about that. Instead, he said, 'Do you think James will have children?'

'I don't know. It's hard to imagine. He's never even been married. He had a – an *affair*, I suppose you'd call it, in Paris, with a Russian émigrée, and she died. Was murdered actually – it was really shocking. Well, he told me he'd intended to marry her, but I don't know. Perhaps that was just his reaction to her death. He's very romantic, though people don't realise it. It would be wonderful if he were to marry and have a family, but somehow one can't imagine him ever settling down. He's always off having adventures.'

'So it all depends on you,' Lennie said, 'to keep the line going?'

'Yes.' She sighed. 'And there's just Alec. I don't think Papa would ever have expected the family to hang by a single thread.'

Her hand was warm in his. Behind them they heard the steady tear and crunch of grazing with the accompanying clink of bit-rings, the occasional thump of a hoof: comforting sounds, the essence of happy horses and normality. Before them, her land spread, green and peaceful; somewhere far away a sheep bleated. Next to her she could feel the safeness of Lennie's size and quiet presence. She would have liked to stay like this for ever.

'Do you think you'd ever like to marry again?' he asked, very delicately, so that the question slipped out onto the air as though without human agency.

She didn't answer for a long time. It came too close to a painful place. Then she said, very quietly, 'I'd like to, if the right person asked me.'

The question, *But who would be the right person?*, hung between them, unvoiced.

It took a great leap of courage – only afterwards did Polly

448

appreciate how great – for Lennie to go on, only helped by the fact that they were not looking at each other, and that she had not withdrawn her hand. 'You know, don't you, that I've always been in love with you? I didn't make any secret of it when we were young. But I've never changed. I've never felt any differently about you.'

'You got married,' she said – not as an accusation, but because she didn't know yet what to say.

'Yes,' he said. 'Beth needed me. It was good to be needed.' He didn't say, *You never did*. He also didn't say that Beth had reminded him a little of Polly, in looks, never in character. He had the sensation of walking on a thin sheet of glass over a chasm. He had no idea if it would take his weight.

'You went out with film stars,' she said. 'Did you never want to marry them? Ethel told me – she saw it in a magazine – last year you were with Anthea Taylor.'

'I was never "with" her. I escorted her. It's a Hollywood thing. Film actresses don't like to arrive at public events unescorted. They like to have a man's arm.'

'All women do,' Polly said, in a low voice. Then, 'Didn't she want to marry you?'

'I didn't want to marry her.'

'Poor lady.'

'No. She fancied herself in love with me for about five minutes, that's all. It wasn't real. It was just because I was there, and apparently unattached.'

'Apparently?'

'There was always you.' Now he looked at her. 'I don't know how to say it to you. Now I'm here, I feel as if I've never been away. Morland Place feels like home. But you are – you're Polly. So far out of my league—'

'Out of your *league*?' she queried, screwing up her nose.

'It's an American expression. It means I am not worthy of you. You are my goddess.'

The glass might have shattered then, but instead Polly

449

started laughing, a healthy, natural laughter. '*Goddess!*' she choked. 'You are ridiculous!'

He smirked, reluctantly. 'That's right, trample on my tenderest feelings.'

'I'm not a goddess,' she said, looking at him at last. The next sentence broke from her as if she hadn't meant to say it. 'I'm lonely.'

He squeezed her hand. 'You needn't be,' he said. 'I'm here.'

'But you won't stay. You'll go back to America. You called it "home".'

'Slip of the tongue. I don't want to go away. I never want to go away. I'll stay as long as you want me. As your friend, your cousin—'

She felt a sharp disappointment. 'I have enough cousins.'

'Friend, then?'

'I don't want a friend.'

'What *do* you want?' he asked, hardly daring to breathe.

She met his eyes seriously, staring at him as if measuring something, questioning something. He felt, as if it were a tangible disturbance of the air, the awakening of her physical desire. 'It's not fair to make me say it,' she said, in the breath of a voice. 'The man ought to.'

'I'll say it then. Do you want a husband? Because I want you that way. As a wife.'

She didn't answer, but he knew this was the moment to kiss her.

Zephyr jerked back in surprise at the movement, as their arms went round each other, but was checked by his reins. He observed, ears pricked, for a moment, then resumed grazing. The kissing went on for a long time.

As part of the re-drawing of borders after the war, under the Versailles settlement, the Czech Republic was merged with Slovakia into a new country. Czechoslovakia was a parliamentary democracy, but it was held together only by a fragile coalition in government. There was high unemployment in the industrial areas, which had never recovered from the Depression, and nationalist Slovaks wanted independence.

Another problem was that certain territories of the old Austrian Empire – sections of northern and western Bohemia and northern Moravia near the Sudeten mountain ranges – had been designated part of the new Czechoslovakia. These areas were inhabited by three million German-speaking, German-leaning people, who from the beginning wanted autonomy within the Czech state.

Their demands escalated after the Austrian *Anschluß*: the Sudeten German Party under Konrad Henlein was Nazi in all but name, and wanted Sudetenland to secede from Czechoslovakia and become part of Greater Germany. The Czech government grew nervous. In May, rumours had abounded that Hitler was intending to invade and seize the whole country. Sudeten Germans threatened uprising and the Czechoslovak government ordered a partial mobilisation. Europe held its breath.

Over the summer, France and Britain, under the auspices of the League of Nations, tried to broker a solution, hoping to gain enough concessions for the Sudeten Germans to calm things down. Above all they wanted to avoid war. But on the 12th of September Hitler made an inflammatory speech at the Nazi Party rally on the Czech 'menace'. The Sudeten area responded with violent uprising, the Czechoslovak government declared martial law, Heinlein and other Sudeten leaders fled to Germany.

'That's why Chamberlain went to Germany, to meet Hitler face to face,' Richard explained to Cynthia. It was a cool, damp September evening, and Cynthia had had the fire lit. It was burning rather sulkily – the weather had been so warm until now that this was the first fire in months so the chimney was cold and wouldn't draw properly. She was a little distracted from the conversation by wondering whether to get down on her knees with a sheet of newspaper, or to pile on more coal and hope for the best.

'It was pretty brave of Chamberlain to fly over there,' Richard went on. 'Apparently, he'd never been in an aeroplane before, so you can see how serious he thought the situation was. He and Hitler agreed between them that, to avoid worse problems, the Sudeten Germans should be granted self-determination. Now Chamberlain has to persuade the Czech government to let them go, and in return Hitler promises not to invade.'

Cynthia frowned. 'That doesn't sound like a very fair bargain. What right has Hitler got to invade anyway?'

'The same right as he had in Austria,' said Richard. 'The right of arms. He'll do it because he can.'

'You don't think it's settled, then. You think he *will* invade?'

Richard stared at the feeble flames. 'France is bound by treaty to support the Czechs, and we're bound to support France. If the Czechs let the Sudetenlands go, it will calm things down for a bit, but for how long? We know what Hitler's ambitions are. And you've only got to look at a map. The Czech state is completely surrounded on three sides by Greater Germany. He'll want to draw that line across the fourth side and have it all.'

'Countries aren't a matter of straight lines,' Cynthia said.

'I know, dear. I wasn't being flippant. But that's how dictators think. They don't consider real people. It's toy soldiers on a paper battlefield to them.'

'Are there Jews in Czechoslovakia?' she asked, after a moment.

'Yes,' he said, having had the same conversation with Samuel earlier that day. 'I don't know how many, but I think about three hundred thousand.'

She was silent.

'Britain and France will warn Hitler of the consequences if he invades Czechoslovakia,' he said, hoping to reassure her, though it didn't reassure him. On that day, the 27th of September, the Royal Navy had mobilised. Expectation of war was heavy in the air, like approaching thunder after hot summer days.

She was looking at her hands, clasped in her lap and twisting uncomfortably. 'I went to see the doctor this morning,' she said.

War was forgotten. 'Are you all right? I thought you were looking a bit pale. What did he say?'

Now she looked up. 'He said I'm going to have a baby.'

He didn't know what to say. He slipped to his knees in front of her and took her in his arms.

'Are you pleased?' she said at last, muffled by his shoulder.

'Oh, my dear,' he said, 'so pleased!' He set her back a little and scrutinised her. 'But how are you feeling? Is he worried about you? What did he tell you?'

'He said I'm all right. He said I must be careful, that's all. Not to exert myself. Not to lift anything heavy. Are you *really* pleased?'

He smiled at her. 'I'm very, very happy. Do your mother and father know?'

'I haven't told them yet. I wanted to tell you first.'

'We'll tell them together, then. Tomorrow. You'll have to give up working at the office.'

'I don't lift heavy weights at the office,' she objected.

'But he said not to exert yourself.'

'I don't want to be left here all alone day after day for months and months.'

'Perhaps you ought to move back in with your parents.'

She gave a painful smile. 'Don't be silly. I'll come to work with you in the car and come back at night. You mustn't fuss, Richard. Women have been having babies for thousands of years.'

'But they weren't you,' he said, standing up. 'Shall I make you a cup of tea? Do you want a hot-water bottle?'

'Just a cup of tea,' she said, her eyes shining with amusement.

'Richard!' She called him as he reached the door, and he turned. 'I love you,' she said.

It was not something they commonly said to each other. 'I love you, too,' he said.

So now there was a child to worry about, he thought, as he lay in bed that night. His promise to Samuel to get Hannah and Cynthia out, if there should be trouble . . . This Czech business – all of Europe was expecting war. He hadn't told her, but the Czech government had already rejected the idea of ceding the Sudetenland. He thought about getting his wife away in her delicate condition: surely such a flight would be the very definition of stress. And if it was later in the pregnancy, even worse. Or if somehow matters were delayed, if it happened after the baby was born . . . Getting the two women and a tiny baby away, probably Samuel as well . . . And how could he let her go without him? It was his duty to protect her, and a tiny baby even more so. If it came to it, he would have to take them, not send them. Leave England in her time of peril and save his family. He remembered how people had spoken of those who had fled to America to avoid the last war . . . He didn't want to be branded a coward. But he had a duty to take care of his dependants . . .

She stirred beside him, sighing in her sleep. He froze until she had settled again and was breathing steadily. And then he thought, *A baby!* He would have a son to follow him, to follow Samuel in the business – Samuel would be pleased. Or a daughter to wind herself around his heart and enslave him to the tenderest of loves, a father's for his daughter. It was how Samuel must feel about Cynthia. That request to him now made absolute sense, and he felt for Samuel that, fearing his own weakness, he had had to ask it. Inwardly he renewed the promise to the old man. I *will* take care of your treasures, whatever it takes.

★ ★ ★

William L. Shirer, son of a Chicago lawyer, had broadcast, from London, the first eyewitness account of the *Anschluß*, after he had fled Vienna where he had been reporting for CBS. Now he was in Berlin, and the newsroom at the *Messenger* was poring excitedly over his report of the 27th of September, which had just come in over the wire.

'"A motorised division rolled through the streets at dusk, heading for the Czech border,"' Dickins read out to the assembled staff. 'Timed to catch the hundreds of thousands of Berliners pouring out of their offices on the way home, Shirer supposes.'

'Sounds likely,' said Palmer. 'Hitler's nothing if not the showman.'

'Ah, but Shirer says it didn't work this time,' said Dickins, reading on. 'He says they ducked into subways, refused to look on, and the few that did stop at the kerb and look did so in utter silence – not a cheer to be heard.'

Digbeth was looking over his shoulder now. 'He says Hitler is reported as being furious. He says a policeman came up and told him and the others standing at the kerb to go to the Wilhelmplatz because Hitler was on the balcony reviewing the troops. But nobody moved.'

Dickins resumed reading. 'He says, "I went down to have a look. Hitler stood there, and there weren't two hundred people in the square." He says Hitler looked grim, then angry, and soon went inside, leaving the troops to parade unreviewed.'

'So what was it about?' Basil asked.

'Shirer says it was a demonstration that the German people are dead set against war,' said Dickins, dropping the report on his desk.

'Well, that's good, isn't it?' Basil said.

Rosco, another senior reporter, spoke round his cigarette, rolling it to the corner of his mouth. 'I wouldn't get too excited, young 'un. It might be a setback, but old Adolf won't let a lack of public enthusiasm stop him.'

'He rode to power on a wave of adoration,' Palmer said, 'but now he's there, he's got sharper weapons to hand.'

Another wire came in shortly afterwards. 'Mussolini's offered to broker an international conference to settle the Sudeten issue. In two days' time. In Munich. Between Germany, Britain, France and Italy.'

'Not Czechoslovakia?' Jimmy Cutler queried.

Rosco grunted. 'Who cares what they think? They're as good as finished. The Germans have had military plans in place since May to roll up Czecho completely.'

'But if Hitler's agreed to talk, it must mean he wants to avoid a crisis,' Basil suggested.

'He'll be furious at being made to back down,' said Dickins. 'I'm not sure an enraged dictator is good for anyone's health.'

But for the moment, the crisis seemed to have been averted. An agreement was signed in the early hours of the 30th of September, allowing Sudeten union with Germany, though there remained many arguments about the exact geographical boundaries of the Sudeten area, and in return Hitler undertook to occupy the areas without invasion from the 1st of October onwards. Czechoslovakia was told by Britain and France it must either agree, or resist German military might alone. It submitted.

Shortly afterwards Neville Chamberlain met Hitler privately in his personal quarters, and both signed a piece of paper renouncing war between Britain and Germany and agreeing to consult on any major differences that arose between them. Chamberlain was greeted on his return home by jubilant crowds, overjoyed that the threat of war had passed. Chamberlain waved the piece of paper as he came down the steps from the aeroplane.

Later, outside 10 Downing Street, he addressed the assembled crowds and pressmen, reading out the agreement, and concluding, 'My good friends, for the second time in our history, a British prime minister has returned from Germany bringing peace with honour. I believe it is peace for our time. We thank you from the bottom of our hearts. Go home and get a nice quiet sleep.'

That same day, fifteen thousand people protested in Trafalgar Square against the Munich Agreement, but only the *Messenger* reported it. Other newspapers, and the BBC, suppressed reporting of the event out of loyalty and a desire not to inflame the public mood.

Richard breathed a sigh of relief for the respite, but he did not believe it was 'peace for our time,' only a pause to draw breath. He packed a bag of his own, along similar lines to Cynthia's, and kept it in the bottom of his wardrobe. Just in case.

Polly and Lennie walked up the stairs together and paused at the top where their paths diverged. The tension had been building all evening, an evening of quiet family occupations, where the drawing-room seemed full of Ethel and John and Harriet and Martin, and Laura – who was more often there now Martin, her half-brother, was at home – yet seemed perversely to make them so aware of each other to the exclusion of the rest that they could almost hear each other breathing. And now, as they stopped on the landing, that awareness was hot and heavy between them, almost tangible, impossible to ignore.

'Well,' Lennie said at last.

They looked at each other, and the question crystallised out of the air. He didn't ask it, but she answered it. 'Yes,' she said. His heart skipped, he swayed minutely towards her. 'Later,' she whispered. 'When the servants are in bed.' And turned away to her own room.

She lay naked in the dark waiting for him, only the sheet covering her, hearing the small sounds of the last servants going up to bed, the house settling into sleep. She felt an excitement that was almost painful: every inch of her body seemed hypersensitive, the touch of the sheet almost unbearable. But underneath that, like a somnolent bass-note, was a sense of absolute rightness. She seemed to have arrived at a point to which her life had been directed for a long time.

The door creaked uncertainly; there was a peep of light and a dark shape, undefined. She knew he could see her in that glimmer. She stretched out her arm, her welcoming hand. The door closed, the light was gone, and he came to her in the dark. She could hear his uneven breathing, the thump of her own heart, the rustle of his shed clothes. And then he was there, with her, and there was that unmatchable moment when skin touched skin for the first time. She trembled. It had been so long since she had been touched by a man. She had forgotten these sensations. She remembered now.

He cupped her cheek tenderly with his hand. 'Polly,' he whispered. 'You're sure?' After all this time he still could not trust his astonishing fortune.

She took the hand, kissed the palm, drew the arm around her. She was aching for him. She stretched her whole length against him. Then they were kissing; she smelt the scent of his skin, tasted his mouth. She wanted him unbearably. She slid her hands up through his hair, the better to pull him against her. And then without pause or difficulty he was there, inside her, and she felt every nerve ending swoon at the sensation.

She lifted to meet him, drawing him further in, and they strove together, matching rhythm, matching need, harder and faster. She wanted everything, everything. There was no sound but their ragged breathing; she clung like one drowning, feeling a great, hot wave of glorious, agonising pleasure build until it overwhelmed her, and she cried out and heard him make the same sound, felt him pulsing inside her; and it was as if they were falling weightlessly into a hot, dark place of silence.

Warm and safe in his arms, she slept, knowing he had drifted off before her, glad he had known he could. The sentinel part of her mind told her he must go back to his own bed before the servants were up; but when it woke her in the first grey light before dawn, and she lifted her head, she saw his eyes were open. He was watching her with such a great gladness of love she wanted to cry a little.

'Is it all right?' were his first words.

She pushed herself up onto one elbow so that she could look down at him. This was Lennie, whom she had known most of her life. Lennie. But this morning he was something else as well: a man, a male animal, just unknown enough to make his familiarity thrilling; just familiar enough to make his unknowable maleness safe. She could venture out onto him, daring as a child on the ice, knowing he would not let her fall through. In wonder she traced his features with her free hand, his brow, eyes, cheek, nose. When her fingers reached his lips he kissed them, then captured the hand, and said it again, needing an answer. 'Is it all right?'

She didn't speak, but eased her body over him, felt with a smile that he was already hard for her, manoeuvred herself to take him inside, and in a strangely unemphatic movement, like seaweed swayed by the current, they mated again.

Afterwards she lay on her back and *he* propped himself up to look down at *her*. 'Polly,' he said.

'It's all right,' she said, smiling up at him.

'Did I—?'

'I wanted it as much as you did,' she reassured him. 'Everything's good. I can't feel anything but safe with you.'

A slight shadow seemed to pass across his face. 'Only safe?' He hesitated. 'I want to take care of you, of course I do. I would never let any harm come to you. But – but I don't want to be a father figure to you. That's not what I want at all.'

'Oh,' she said, with a smile she hadn't known she had in her, almost a wanton smile. 'I don't think of you as a father figure, not in the least. That's not what this was about.'

He kissed her then, for a long time. She felt she could not get enough of kissing him. It had been nothing like this with Ren, nothing like this with Erich. This felt so complete, as if every sense and particle and aspect of her was involved, engaged, and satisfied. This was everything. This was what she had wanted always, and had never had a name for.

When he stopped kissing her at last, he lifted the hand his still held captive to his lips, and said, 'Will you marry me? I want to be married to you.'

'I think after last night we really had better be, don't you?'

It was all right to speak lightly. That was part of the everything.

'You said you'd always felt the same way about me,' she went on. 'And, you know, I was in love with you, too, when I was young. Somehow I took a wrong turn. I was so head-strong and sure of myself then. But all of that feels like a shadow to me now – only this is real. I don't know why it's taken me so long to realise that you are the only person I could ever have married. You're the only one who understands who I am.'

He kissed her hand again, unable to speak.

'But you must go back to your own room now,' she said. 'The servants mustn't see you leave my room.'

'But – I can come to you again? Tonight.'

'Every night,' she said. 'Please.'

Basil halted in front of a woman exiting Fortnum's and said, 'Good day and well met, madam!'

Charlotte looked up from putting on her gloves. 'All hail

460

to you too, sirrah!' They exchanged a handshake. 'Why the Shakespearean language?'

'Covering my shyness,' he said.

'You, shy!'

'You have no idea.' He eyed the prettily wrapped parcel in her hand. 'Buying frillies?'

'Sugared almonds for a dinner party. Frillies indeed! Where did you get such an expression?'

'Isn't that what they're called? I wouldn't know,' he said blandly. 'You're looking very prosperous. I like the hat.'

'And you're looking . . .' She surveyed him. '. . . absurdly handsome. Quite terribly film-star-ish. Please tell me some happy lady is getting the benefit of all this . . .' she waved a hand over his *tout ensemble* '. . . fine edifice.'

'Sadly not,' Basil said. 'I am forced to embrace the tranquillity of celibacy.'

'So what are you doing here? Working?'

'Charity lunch at the Ritz, the Vigo girl and her set, including the American ambassador's daughter. I was sent to have a look at her and write a paragraph or two, now she's been presented.'

'Which one was it, again?'

'The second one, Kathleen. Friendly soul, very natural. Freckles, big smile. The image of her father.'

'Oh, have you met Ambassador Kennedy? What do you think of him?'

'Well, he's clearly a crook, but a very genial one. His wife is terrifying, that's all. And all his children have far too many teeth.'

'Oh, Basil!' She laughed. 'How come I never see you? I never see anyone I like any more.'

'Who *do* you see?' he asked, enjoying her appreciation.

'People Milo invites.' She made a face. 'Significant people.'

'What's he selling these days?'

'Don't be rude. He doesn't sell, he *brokers*. And at the

461

moment it's arms, so it's trips to America and Sweden. They take so long, I hardly see him. I wish they'd hurry up and start a flying service to America. It must be ten years since Lindbergh flew across the Atlantic – you'd think they'd have got it going by now.'

He shook his head. 'Would *you* take the chance of flying over that big, empty ocean in a tin box?'

'I might,' she said defiantly. He saw the idea come to her. 'Oh, Basil, *you* must come to dinner tonight. It will probably be poisonously dull, but you'll cheer me up. I can promise you a good dinner – we have a first-rate cook at the moment.'

'Good wine?' he said suspiciously.

'I can't tell one from another, but Stuffy knows about that sort of thing, and he says Milo has an excellent cellar.'

'Dear old Stuffy Elphinstone! Is he still hanging around you, looking like a lovesick puppy?'

'Don't be mean. You wouldn't recognise him,' she assured him. 'He's quite changed. He's doing terribly well in the War Department, one of Hore-Belisha's boys.'

'I've heard Hore-Belisha isn't much liked by the Army Council. Haven't they nicknamed him Horeb-Elisha?'

Charlotte looked stern. 'That's horrid antiSemitism. Please don't repeat it. Remember my favourite brother married a Jewish girl – oh, have you heard that they're expecting a baby?'

'Yes, Richard wrote to me. I sent a card. Happy news.' He tilted his head at her. 'Nothing in that line for you?'

'Milo says it's not the right time for us,' she said, and he couldn't for the life of him tell whether she minded or not. 'So you'll come tonight? Eight o'clock. You know we're in Charles Street now?'

Milo must be doing well, Basil thought, noting the change from the modern flat in far-flung Baker Street to a handsome four-storey Georgian house right in the heart of Town, handy for Whitehall, the clubs, the Palace and everything important. Here they could really entertain 'significant people' and be taken seriously. Milo, he concluded, was intent on being a player in the high-stakes game.

And Basil saw at once what Charlotte had meant about Stuffy Elphinstone. He had lost a lot of weight, fined down a great deal, and with the fleshiness gone from his face he was revealed as being tolerably good-looking. But more than that, he seemed noticeably older – or, rather, more grown-up. It was as if he had suddenly moved a generation further on from Basil. Perhaps, he thought half ruefully, it was only that he, Basil, had not moved on as he should. He still didn't feel entirely grown-up.

It was very much a grown-ups' dinner. Charlotte was the only woman, and he watched her, half amused, half impressed, as she played the hostess with quiet confidence, as if she had been doing it for years. Perhaps she had absorbed her mother's skills without being aware of it. The other guests were very much Milo's invitees – people of substance, business men, financial men. A Swedish industrialist who spoke English so perfectly that he stood out among the drawling, slurring natives like a lodge in a garden of cucumbers. Basil hadn't realised that Sweden was one of the world's top manufacturers of arms, along with the United States. Political men. An army man, Brigadier Jenner, who was Deputy Military Secretary to the War Office. And along with Lord Elphinstone, another War Office man, the under-secretary, Lord Culbeath.

As they mingled before dinner, Culbeath came over to Basil and said, 'Compton? We went to the same school – Felixkirk?'

'Indeed, sir?'

'Not at the same time, however. I left the year you joined. But you'll have known my younger brother Fraser – he was in the year above you. Fraser Kerr-Anstruther.'

'Oh, yes, I remember him,' Basil said, recollecting a gawky

youth with pale red-gold hair and an unfortunate tendency to blush and stammer. 'We served on the school newspaper together.'

'Yes, the good old *Felix Culpa*,' Culbeath laughed. The paper had actually been called the *Felix Dies*, but the boys had changed that – unofficially. The headmaster Mr Cockburn had thrown Basil head first into editing the thing, his cunning plan to tame Basil and make him toe the line. 'My brother had a bit of a hero-worship for you, you know. He was always telling me about your exploits. Thought you no end of a gay dog. That time you climbed up the flagpole on top of the main wing and replaced the flag with a pair of bloomers, for instance. Tell me – he'd love to know, even now – where *did* you get them from? Rumour had it they were Matron's.'

'I couldn't possibly comment.'

Culbeath laughed. 'That's right. Always protect your source. And didn't you once release a fox in the chapel vestry?'

The – surprisingly youthful – brigadier had drifted closer. 'What, Angus? Is this *that* Compton? I didn't realise it was the same person.' He shot out a hand and Basil shook it, bemused. 'I've heard good things about you from Gilbert Comstock.'

'Thank you, sir,' Basil murmured. He was surprised the editor had ever spoken about him to anyone, though he was not surprised he knew the Deputy Military Secretary. The Editor seemed to know everyone.

'Seems to think you did rather well in Spain,' Jenner went on. 'I read the articles. Jolly good! Damned shame about young Zennor, though. I knew his mother before she married – distant cousin of mine.'

It confirmed in Basil a belief that all the important people in Britain were related to one another: it was, in fact, how the trick was worked.

'I expect you and he were close, thrown together in diffi-cult circumstances,' Jenner went on.

Basil thought again, painfully, of Bob Zennor's wasteful, pointless death. He tried *not* to think about him too often. He shut his lips tight.

Jenner and Culbeath exchanged a glance, and Basil somehow gleaned that his reaction had not been held against him – the contrary, in fact.

'Look here,' Jenner said, lowering his voice a little, 'when the balloon goes up, we're going to need men like you.'

Basil was surprised at such directness. 'You think there *will* be a war?' he said. 'What about "peace for our time"?'

'Don't be taken in by that,' Culbeath said. 'Delaying tactic. We'll have to deal with the Germans sooner or later, but the PM has to hold them off until we're ready, got all our pieces on the chessboard and so on.'

'*Are* we ready?' Basil asked. He was flattered that these senior people were talking so frankly to him – but nervous too. He suspected something was about to be asked of him. You didn't get that sort of voluntary exposition for nothing.

'Working on it,' said Jenner. 'Next year, or 1940 at the latest. And when it comes, it's not going to be like the last war. We'll have to employ different tactics. We're going to need men who can think on their feet.'

'Irregulars,' Culbeath said, nodding.

'Of course,' Jenner said, with an air of placating jealous gods, 'there's nothing wrong with the regimental system. Backbone of the army.'

'But we've already discussed recruiting . . . shall we say *special services*?' said Culbeath, with emphasis. 'Men of ingenuity, who can operate outside the conventional.'

'I see,' Basil said. He didn't, but he had an odd feeling he was going to.

'Just keep it in mind,' Jenner said, patting his arm. 'When the time comes . . . Comstock knows all about it. He'll keep you in the picture. This is all hush-hush, by the by. You won't mention this little conversation to anyone.'

'Of course not, sir.' Basil felt he was being rolled up. He tried a last-minute protest. 'I was never in OTC, you know. Didn't go to university.'

'We know,' said Culbeath.

'What I mean is, I have no military background.'

'All the better,' said Jenner.

'Irregulars,' Culbeath said again. 'Like you were in Spain.' One of the other guests was approaching, and he ended the topic. 'We'll talk some more at a later date. Enough of this now. Tell me, your father was a fighter pilot in the war, wasn't he? Quite a hero. Air ace, taken prisoner twice, decorated at the highest level. VC, wasn't he?'

'A lot to live up to,' Jenner said.

They both gave Basil a pointed look that went on a little too long to be comfortable. The approaching guest was one of the financial people, and the conversation turned to the stock exchange, about which Basil had nothing to say. He eased his way backwards out of the group and drifted away to find another more congenial. He felt as if he'd been scoured.

Polly and Lennie had been walking in the rose garden, where Polly had been trying to find enough late blooms to decorate the table; Lennie helped by singing 'The Last Rose Of Summer' in his surprisingly fine tenor. The dogs had come with them, never ones to miss the opportunity of going out, but no-one else had followed. It was a space of precious privacy.

The flowers cut, they sat down on a bench. The dogs came and sat before them, looking willing, and then, seeing that talking was the order of the day, settled down to wait in the hope of better things to come.

The subject was their future together – one still so new to Polly that she could not tire of it – and the immediate topic what Lennie would do after they were married. He was talking about radio.

'The market in the States is so mature there really aren't the opportunities any more to make big profits. Television could still take off. Once they've sorted out the technical stuff, it could be the next big thing over there. But the radio market here is wide open. Demand for radio sets is growing, and I can replicate my manufacturing operation here, with the added advantage that, as far as I can see, no-one else is doing much about it yet. I can get in first and clean up. A Manning's radio in every home!'

'I like the sound of that.'

'And I've got an idea for a combination radio-gramophone apparatus. English homes are so small, compared with American, that something compact that covers both functions ought to be a winner. With some kind of storage cupboard built in, to hold the gramophone records. All in a nice walnut veneer case – a handsome piece of furniture in its own right.'

'Go on,' she said. 'What else?'

'Once I've got my feet under the table, I shall be in the right place to exploit the television market too, as soon as they get the broadcasting properly up and running. Though I'm not sure letting the government control the whole thing is the right way to go about things. Licensing it all through the General Post Office! I can't tell you how quaint that feels – like hitching radio to the Pony Express!'

'It's a different country over here,' Polly said. 'We do things differently.'

'You can say that again. It really stifles innovation when you remove competition and pass everything through a government department. It doesn't look as if I'll ever have my own television channel, the way I have a radio channel back there – my good old W2XKX.'

'It's so much easier in America to get a new business off the ground. Are you afraid you won't be able to get anywhere over here?' she added anxiously.

'Don't worry,' he said. 'I'm a pretty warm man. I can

promise you I'll always have enough to support you in the style to which you've become accustomed.'

'I've heard you're a millionaire.'

'Who told you that?'

'Ethel. She read it in one of her magazines, when you were going out with that film star.'

'It's a vulgar phrase, but I suppose it's true. Will you feel all right about marrying a millionaire?'

'When?' she asked bluntly.

'Whenever you like. You choose the when and the how. But I will have to go back to the States for a while.' Polly's face fell, and he reached out for her hand and took it back into his own lap. 'Don't look like that! It will only be for a few weeks, while I settle my businesses and see to some financial and personal matters.'

'Personal matters?'

'I haven't got secret mistresses and a dozen love children, if that's what you're thinking.'

'I wasn't, but now I am. Why wouldn't you? You're a millionaire, and a very handsome man, now I look at you properly.'

'I am, and always was, a one-man dog, pretty Polly. But there's Rose – I have to make sure she's happily settled. And my staff. They've been with me for years, especially Wilma and Beanie, and they're very loyal. I'd like to bring them with me—'

'Well, do,' Polly invited.

'—but I don't suppose they'd come. And if they don't want to, I'll have to make sure they're all right. Then there'll be the matter of transferring funds. That's bound to be complicated. Fortunately, in this age of wonders and electronic communication, I'll be able to oversee my businesses from here, but it will have to be set up that way, and the right managers put in place. So you see.'

'I see. How long will all that take?'

He hesitated. He wanted to be reassuring, but there was nothing to be gained by underestimating and later having to let her down. 'Three months ought to do it.'

'Three months!'

He closed the other hand as well over her captive one. 'You trust me, don't you? You don't think I'd go over there and not come back?'

'No, I don't think that. But it's such a long time to be without you. And anything could happen.'

'Darling, anything could happen anywhere. The world is not a safe place – never was.'

She looked at him, and believed he was thinking about his Beth, killed when a car shot out of a side turning as they were passing and smashed into theirs. A horrible random accident. And she thought of the young son of one of her tenants who had been playing on top of a haystack, fell off and landed on a pitchfork, which went through his heart. 'No, the world is not a safe place,' she said. 'That's why you have to be with the people you love.'

'We will be together. I'll see to this business, and come back, and we'll never have to be apart again. I'll be with you so much you'll get sick of me.'

She didn't smile. 'What if this war comes?'

'If it comes, we'll deal with it together.' They were silent a moment. Then he said, 'Do you want to get married right away? Before I go?'

'When are you thinking of going?'

'In a few days. I hate to leave you, but the sooner I go, the sooner I'll be back.'

'How could we get married in a few days?'

'Special licence. Register office.'

'I should make sure of you, you mean, before you escape.'

He saw she was joking – at least partly. 'Will that make you feel safer?'

'No. Anyway, I want to be married in the chapel, properly,

with everyone in floods of tears, and a wedding feast, and a Mrs Starling cake the size of a cartwheel, and oceans of champagne. I'm the Mistress of Morland Place. I want our wedding to be remembered for decades.' She met his eyes. 'So it will have to wait until you come back.'

He lifted her hand and kissed it. 'That gives you three months to arrange it all. Will that be enough?'

Tears came suddenly. He took her into his arms and she cried into his collar. The dogs stood up, waving their tails anxiously, and Fand tried licking Polly's hand, the only bare skin he could reach, in case that helped.

It was over quite quickly, and Polly pushed herself upright again. 'Sorry about that. I'm not usually a spouter. Have you got a handkerchief?' Fand pushed in again and licked her face. '*Voilà, service!*' she laughed, pushing the dog away. 'When you come back, then.'

'When I come back. The whole shebang. No half-measures.'

'And we'll tell everyone before you go that we're engaged.'

'As soon as you like.'

'But you still can't be seen going in and out of my room. We'll have to keep that part secret.'

'From?'

'Well, Ethel would be shocked. And Alec might be upset. And the servants—'

'My dear love, in my admittedly limited experience of servants, they always know everything. I'll bet you dollars to doughnuts they're already discussing in the servants' hall how soon we'll come clean.'

The next day he drove Polly into York and left her at Makepeace's to conduct some business, saying he would stroll around and come back for her. And on the drive back to Morland Place, when they had left the road and turned onto the track, he stopped the car under a tree, switched off the engine, and produced a jeweller's box, which proved to

470

contain a very handsome engagement ring: a large sapphire surrounded by diamonds.

'A sapphire to match your eyes – not that it comes close. Yours are more cornflower, but it was the best I could do. Polly Morland, will you marry me?'

'Lennox Manning, I will,' she said. He slipped the ring onto her finger, where it felt heavy and strange, but nice, and then they kissed. A blackbird was singing in the tree above them the whole time – she always remembered that.

That evening, they announced the engagement to everyone, and Barlow came back with the champagne at the right temperature suspiciously quickly, which tended to confirm Lennie's thesis, that the servants always did know everything.

CHAPTER TWENTY

The Boeuf sur le Toit had moved to new premises in the rue de Penthièvre, but it was still the best place in Paris to listen to jazz. It had always been an *avant-garde* gathering place, frequented by famous names like Picasso, Diaghilev, Milhaud, Cocteau, André Gide, Camus, Ernest Hemingway, Charlie Chaplin. On a jolly evening, Artur Rubinstein might play the piano, with Milhaud on drums, or Maurice Chevalier might sing Gershwin; later on, Josephine Baker, tired from a performance, might come in, and sing something slow and sad. Above all, it was about the music. Virtually founded by the group called Les Six, it attracted leading composers, like Stravinsky, Poulenc and Satie, but James and Emil went there for the jazz. It was such a magnet for talent, jazz musicians from other Paris clubs would turn up after hours and play long into the night for the joy of it. In Paris, to have a jam session was called *faire un boeuf*.

It was also a well-known meeting place for homosexuals, but James and Emil had no beef with that. 'It's just a pity they don't come here for the jazz,' James said one evening, when he and Emil, accompanied by Florence – the affair was still going well – and a fellow Folies dancer called Huguette, were at a favourite table. The girls were tired and hungry after the show, but scrambled eggs and champagne perked them up.

'Look at *them*, for instance,' James went on.

At the next table, a very handsome young man, with large

eyes, a tender mouth and a dimple in his chin, was entertaining an extremely swarthy youth, who seemed to be in a bad temper. Neither of them was paying any attention to the music – in fact, it looked as though a quarrel was brewing.

Emil shrugged. 'As long as they pay for the drinks,' he said. 'You can't legislate for taste.'

'No, but he's in here a lot, using up a seat that a music-lover might like,' said James.

'You know who he is?' said Emil.

'He works at the German embassy in some lowly capacity,' James said. 'German nobility by birth, apparently – it's odd how they can become Nazis.'

'Oh, I know who you mean,' said Emil. 'Vom Rath. He's a rising star in the Sturmabteilung, and a bit of a pet of Ambassador Welczeck. I didn't know he was that way inclined. He'd better not let his superiors find out. I believe the beloved Führer is rather down on that sort of thing.'

'I'm surprised he's got this far without being found out,' James said, looking across at vom Rath's current surly interest. 'He seems to like the rough trade.'

Huguette interrupted, bored with the conversation: 'Can't we dance? I'm tired of talk about Germans. They're so dull.'

'I was only sitting still out of respect for your feet,' James said. 'I'll dance with pleasure, if you're rested enough.'

It was a good session, and the four of them didn't leave until two, and then James had to see Huguette back to her lodgings, and walk back to his own. So he was fast asleep the next morning when Emil woke him up with intemperate banging on the door.

'What's the matter with you?' James asked, strangling his waist with his dressing-gown cord as he opened the door. 'Can't you sleep?

'Sleeping at night is a waste of time. And Florence was very lively,' Emil said, walking past James and into the small kitchen.

'I don't wish to know that,' said James, following.

'Are you alone? *Still* not sleeping with Huguette?'

'I have no wish to follow any more closely in your footsteps. Especially when it means being this energetic first thing in the morning.'

'It's nearly noon, old man. Coffee is the order of the day, I think. And then I'll tell you the news, since you evidently haven't heard it.' He filled the kettle and put it on to boil.

James slumped at the table. 'Tell me, and then leave me to die.'

Emil turned, leaned back against the kitchen cabinet, folded his arms, and said, with barely suppressed excitement, 'Who do you think has been assassinated?'

'Someone we know?'

'We were sitting next to him last night. Pretty little Ernst vom Rath.' James stared. 'Yes, apparently a swarthy youth walked into the German embassy in the rue de Lille this morning, asking to speak to the ambassador, saying he had a most important document to hand over. Welczeck had just left, so the duty clerk asked vom Rath to see him. He was shown into vom Rath's office, and the youth pulled out a pistol and shot him five times.'

'Oh, my God. You don't think it was the same person we saw him with last night?'

'Couldn't say. Might be. But his taste seems to run that way so it might be an entirely different swarthy youth. In any case, it seems he didn't ask to see vom Rath by name, so it might not be personal at all. He didn't make any attempt to escape. From what I've heard he's an illegal, a Polish Jew with no papers – on the run from the police, who want to deport him. He said his motive was to avenge persecuted Jews.'

'If it was a lover's tiff, he might still have said he was avenging the Jews, since he is one.'

'Point.'

'Is he dead – vom Rath?'

474

'In hospital, but not expected to live. Shots to the abdomen – not a nice way to go. One almost feels sorry for him.'

'Well, there'll be more room at the Boeuf now for a real jazz lover,' James said, yawning. 'Is that coffee nearly ready?'

On Tuesday, the 8th of November, Basil was greeted when he arrived in the newsroom by Jimmy Cutler, who said, 'That embassy chap who was shot in Germany yesterday?'

'What about him? He wasn't anyone important, was he? Third secretary, or something.'

'He's important now. The German government's using it as an excuse to pass more anti-Jewish laws. Our man in Berlin says they're banning Jewish children from state schools, banning all Jewish cultural activities, and forbidding them to arm themselves. Twenty years in a concentration camp if they're caught in possession of any weapon.'

'More sinister than that,' said Digbeth, overhearing them, 'they've stopped the publication of all Jewish magazines and newspapers. Cutting off ordinary Jews from their leaders, stopping them finding out what's going on. Fragmentation, you see. Divide and rule.'

'It's going to be the leader article,' said Cutler. 'I've suggested, "The move is intended to disrupt the Jewish community and rob it of the last frail ties which hold it together." What d'you think?'

'Shouldn't it be "that", not "which"?' Basil said.

'You're missing the point, sonny,' said Rosco, from his desk. 'This won't be the end of it. A Jew shooting a handsome, firm-jawed, promising young diplomat going about his lawful business? Have you seen the pictures of him? He's an Aryan sweetheart. And you know what tomorrow is?'

'The ninth of November,' Basil said patiently.

Rosco rolled his eyes. 'God help us! Don't they teach any history in schools these days?'

'I left school a long time ago,' Basil muttered.

'It's the anniversary of the Beer Hall Putsch,' Rosco enlightened him, 'and they hold a big Nazi rally in Munich for it every year, with Hitler making a grand speech to round off the evening. Want to put money on what his subject will be this year?'

Vom Rath, who had lingered in hospital for two days, died the next day, the 9th of November. Reports came in on the wire that the news had been brought to Hitler on the platform, that he had spoken briefly to Goebbels and abruptly left the hall, and that Goebbels had then made the closing address on his behalf, a vitriolic speech urging 'spontaneous demonstrations' by Party members and the German faithful of their anger against the Jews.

The hatred that had been carefully fed and nurtured for five years came to monstrous flowering. All through the night the news came in to the *Messenger*; no-one went home; the wires never stopped humming. Across Germany, across Austria, in the Sudetenland, in cities, towns and villages, the windows of Jewish shops and businesses were shattered and their contents looted; the homes of Jews had their windows broken and were ransacked, some set on fire. It was begun by the SA and the Hitler Youth – the uniforms were noted – but in an escalation of horror, the public soon joined in. Synagogues and prayer rooms were invaded; prayer books, scrolls, ceremonial items, artworks and sacred texts were carried out to be burned on bonfires, and the buildings were set on fire. Jewish cemeteries seemed a particular focus of hatred: tombstones were uprooted and smashed, graves violated, the remains dug up and scattered. Warehouses were burned down. Jews unfortunate enough to be caught out on the street were beaten by the mobs, and many died; some were dragged out of their houses and killed. And by a neat reversal of logic, the German authorities blamed the Jews for the riots, and during the night a huge number of Jewish men

– it was estimated in the tens of thousands – were arrested and taken to concentration camps.

One English correspondent in Berlin wrote, 'Racial hatred and hysteria seemed to have taken complete hold of otherwise decent people. I saw fashionably dressed women clapping their hands and screaming with glee, while respectable middle-class mothers held up their babies to see the "fun".'

In the newsroom at the *Messenger* they received and collated the reports in unprecedented silence. Outrage had gone beyond expression: there was nothing it was possible to say. Newspapermen were accustomed to reporting on the worst aspects of human life, and grew thick-skinned. But this seemed a different order of horror. Phones rang, wires came in, typewriters rattled, sheets were passed up to be subbed, passed back to be rewritten, approved, sent to the comps for setting, and the individuals avoided each other's gaze and did not speak.

Basil felt numb. He didn't understand how people could do such things. Why the Jews? What need did this hatred fill? What was this sump of darkness that existed in men's hearts? He felt he had aged years in one night. And he sensed the beginning of a clear path ahead of him. He wasn't sure where it led, but felt he would know when he saw it. It was Duty.

Rosco said, towards dawn, when Basil, passing his desk, accidentally caught his eye: 'This is not the end.'

Richard and Cynthia had been at the Nevinsons' for supper when Leah, who had been listening to the wireless in the kitchen, came in, pale and shocked, to tell them to listen. As the first reports were given by clipped, neutral BBC voices, supper was forgotten, and they gathered round the set in grim silence. Samuel sat slumped in his big armchair; Hannah leaned on the back as if her legs would not properly support her; Leah stood by the door, constantly wringing her hands in her apron. Richard and Cynthia stood together, and her hand crept into his.

477

When the bulletin ended, Samuel leaned forward between his knees as if he was going to be sick. He put his hands over his face and rubbed; Hannah patted helplessly at his shoulder. When he emerged, he said only, as if to no-one in particular, 'It begins.'

Richard and Cynthia did not go home that night. Leah and Hannah made up a bed for them. They talked quietly in bed for a long time.

'I don't know how Papa will stand this,' Cynthia said. Richard held her close in his arms, so her mouth was by his ear. She felt very cold to him, and he tried to put warmth into her with his body. 'He hasn't recovered from what happened two weeks ago. And now this . . .'

On the 28th of October, some twelve thousand Polish Jews had been expelled from Germany, ordered without notice from their homes in the night, told they could take with them just one suitcase each. What they left behind, reports said, was looted by their neighbours, once any valuables had been seized by the Nazi authorities. They were marched to railway stations and put on trains to the Polish border. But the Polish government had said that Polish Jews who had lived abroad for five years were no longer citizens. The border guards refused to admit them and sent them back to the German side.

So for days in the pouring rain they were stateless, unwanted, trapped at the border, without food or shelter. One British newspaper reported that they were 'lying about, penniless and deserted, in little villages along the frontier near where they had been driven out by the Gestapo and left'. Four thousand were finally admitted, but the rest were sent to refugee camps, where conditions were so grim that, according to a report, some in desperation tried to escape back into Germany and were shot by frontier guards.

'Stateless,' Cynthia said. 'Nowhere to go. No-one wants them. It could be us next.'

'No, never,' he said. 'It wouldn't happen in this country.'

'You don't know, you don't know,' she cried softly. 'Why do they hate us? What's going to happen to my baby? Condemned before he's even born to be hated and cast out.'

'He's my baby too,' Richard said. 'He will never be stateless.'

But she was in the grip of an ancient grief, older than her by centuries, and she rocked against him and moaned softly, as Jewish women had rocked and moaned under the black pall of persecution throughout history. He held her close and murmured to her, and kissed her head helplessly.

When she was quiet, finally, he said, 'Do you want to go away? Would you feel safer in America? I can arrange it, if you want.'

'Papa said—' she began, muffled by his neck.

'I know about your running-away bag,' he said gently. 'He told me, if things go bad, I must get you away. All of you,' he added, in case she objected to leaving them. 'But if you want, we can go now. It will only take a few days to arrange—'

'No,' she said. 'Papa wouldn't go, not yet anyway. And he's not well, and Mama wouldn't go without him.' She lifted her head from his shoulder and looked at him, determination in her face, though her chin quivered. Her courage made him want to cry. 'I'm staying. I want to stay with you. We'll – we'll face what we have to together.'

'I will always take care of you,' he said. 'I promise.'

'I know,' she said.

The pogrom was called afterwards the Night of Broken Glass, or Kristallnacht in German, because of all the broken glass from Jewish windows that paved the streets and glittered in the streetlights. The German government ordered Jews to sweep it all up. They further imposed a fine of one billion Reichsmarks for the murder of vom Rath, which they levied by confiscating 20 per cent of all Jewish property. And they diverted six million Reichsmarks of insurance money, which would have been paid to Jews for the destruction of their

479

property on Kristallnacht, to the government's coffers. This, they said, was 'damages due to the German Nation'.

It emerged in reports that Hitler had approved the pogrom, ordering officials not to intervene, and while that was shocking, it was not any more surprising. It could be seen that since 1933 the Nazi government's intention had been to get all the Jews to quit Germany, leaving their wealth behind. But after Kristallnacht, it came to be feared that something more sinister was behind the relentless persecution. On the day after, Hermann Göring said at a news conference, 'The Jewish problem will reach its solution if, in any time soon, we will be drawn into war beyond our border – then it is obvious that we will have to manage a final account with the Jews.'

'You see,' Cynthia said to Richard, 'we are not people, like you. We are a problem.'

They were in the office, and Samuel had not come in that morning – Hannah rang to say that he was feeling very tired and she had insisted he stayed at home and rested. Later that day there was another phone call, from Leah this time – very nervous about using the telephone and under the impression she had to shout because they were a long way away. She said the master had collapsed, and as he was unconscious, the mistress had called for an ambulance, using the new '999' service, and he had been taken away to hospital. Patient questioning by Richard elicited that he was at St Stephen's in Fulham Road. He and Cynthia got their coats and hats and went outside to hail a taxi.

Samuel did not regain consciousness, and died two days later, after a second stroke. He was, Richard thought, though he never said it aloud, one more victim of the pogrom.

Lennie had gone. Polly missed him, but once she had received his wire from New York saying he had arrived safely, she felt calm and hopeful. She had plenty to do, including the arranging of a wedding, though she decided not to put any specific orders in place yet, from a superstitious fear that it would be tempting Fate. In any case, he had said three months, but that did not give her an actual date to work towards. She decided to wait until Christmas. He might have a better idea then of how much longer he needed. Three months would have him arriving back in England in February, when the weather was likely to be hard. March, or even April, would be better for a wedding. She had waited all this time, she could wait a little longer.

In all their talk together about being married, he had always taken it for granted that they would live at Morland Place. She remembered the very first man to propose to her, back when she was a foolish girl, and his assumption that she would live with him in London – far from her home, and not even in the country. No horses and dogs, no wide spaces to roam over. When she had queried that, he had proposed that at some point they might have a country house in Surrey. *Surrey!* But Lennie had understood. It had never been in question. She was Morland Place and Morland Place was her. How could it have taken her so long to see that he was the only man she could happily marry?

Meanwhile, she kept busy. There were many visits of congratulation after the engagement was announced in the papers, with commiseration that her betrothed had had to go away. She held a dinner for the family and favoured guests, and out of kindness to Ethel, who seemed a bit miffed for reasons Polly couldn't guess – had she wanted Polly to remain a widow like her? Did she fear being thrown out after the wedding and made to go and live with Jeremy and Amelia? – she asked Jeremy to act as host. He seemed as much nervous as pleased, but in the event he did it very well, and she was impressed by his gain in maturity since he had married. During the mingling part of the evening, he came up to Polly quietly and told her that Amelia was expecting, which perhaps explained it: assistant manager of his branch, a married man, and now about to become a father. He said he had wanted her to know, but didn't want to steal her thunder by announcing it generally at her party. Polly thanked him, was touched, and when they got to the toasting part of the evening, and she had to stand up and reply, she announced it herself. Jeremy looked startled and pleased, Amelia blushed fierily, and Ethel burst into tears. It was a happy evening – as Polly told Lennie in a long letter.

Alec seemed pleased about the engagement, and to Polly's careful questions said he liked Uncle Lennie and asked would he have to call him 'Father' after the wedding. Polly said that was up to him, and he should wait and see what came naturally – there was no rule about it. But after a few days he seemed to feel differently, became anxious and silent, and finally, when Polly got him alone and ready to talk – she took him out riding, feeling it was always easier to open your mind when you were side by side and moving, rather than face to face and immobile – he confessed that a boy at school had put the wind up him. 'He said that stepfathers always hate you, and beat you, like in *David Copperfield*, and turn your mother against you, and then your mother dies and you're an orphan and your stepfather steals your inheritance and sends you to the workhouse.' He was staring ahead through Shady's ears, biting his lip so as not to cry, because he was eight years old now and big boys didn't.

Polly bit her lip too, so as not to laugh, though she wanted to cry as well. When she had control of herself, she said seriously, 'I think you're being a little bit silly. Nothing like that can possibly happen.'

'Can't it?' he said, in a small voice.

'For one thing, there aren't any workhouses any more. And I'm not in the slightest bit likely to die. The mother in *David Copperfield* was a weak, silly woman, but I'm not, am I?'

'Well . . .' he allowed doubtfully.

'She'd never done anything but sit around in pretty dresses

482

and drink tea. She hadn't run businesses like me. So she was easy for her new husband to dominate. I don't see anyone being able to turn me against you, do you?' He didn't answer. 'And besides all that,' she went on, 'Uncle Lennie isn't anything like Mr Murdstone. David Copperfield had never met him before the wedding, but you *know* Uncle Lennie. You've talked to him and gone riding with him and sat at breakfast with him, and he helped you build the wireless set. You like him and he likes you.'

Alec thought about that. 'He wouldn't change, through being married? You both wouldn't change?'

'Not a bit. We'll just be happier than ever, and that'll make us be nicer than ever to you.'

'Oh,' said Alec. 'You're sure?'

'Completely, absolutely sure.'

Alec thought for a while as they rode on. It was a chill and foggy November day, the only colour the last few leaves clinging to the sycamores, gleaming like fool's gold through the misty greyness. Shady had already grown his winter coat. Polly thought they would have to have him trace-clipped if Alec was to hunt him this winter.

Finally Alec sighed, not an unhappy sigh but a concluding sigh.

'Thought it all out?' she asked. He nodded. 'You're not scared any more?' He shook his head. She could tell he had something else to say. 'What, then? Spit it out!'

'Mum, do you think Uncle Lennie would buy me a camera?'

She wrote to James to tell him about the engagement, and he wrote back expressing his delight. 'You ought to have been married long ago – it's such a waste your being single.' He sent her as an engagement present a beautiful little Schiaparelli evening jacket in scarlet silk with an enormous gold honey-bee embroidered on each breast, and a promise that he would come to the wedding. 'You've chosen the right man,' he wrote. 'I think he'll make you very happy. And if you have some more children, it would do a lot to assuage my guilt over leaving you in charge.'

And then a new paragraph – the ink slightly different, as if he had added it later: 'The world is a pretty horrible place at the moment. I'm very glad that you will have someone to look after you. And we need all the occasions of joy we can get. Your wedding will be a beacon in the dark. All the love in the world from your devoted brother, James.'

Another early-morning invasion by Emil, though this time James was up and dressed. 'What's happened now?' he asked, letting his friend in.

'I've had a phone call from my father in Switzerland. Your blessed country has agreed to allow unaccompanied Jewish children under seventeen to refugee to Britain without visas. Papa says they're talking about five thousand initially. It's the reaction to Kristallnacht, of course. And, wonderfully, the Germans have agreed to let them go. Papa's helping to finance the operation, because of course *they* won't. And my aunt Lotti – Lotti Kaufmann, she's only a sort of step-aunt-in-law, but she and Papa played together as children – she's helping to organise things in Germany, and he wants me to go and assist her. So we have to go, right away.'

'Now? This minute?'

'You can have enough time to pack a bag, but otherwise, yes, this minute. The Germans are in favour of the scheme at the moment, but there's no knowing when the bastards might change their minds, so every hour counts.'

'I have a job, you know, unlike you. I'll have to get permission from Hélène,' James said.

'Not permission, just tell her you're going. This is more important than any job. Don't stand there arguing, go and pack! We'll get a taxi and call at Hélène's on the way. I'll telephone Aunt Lotti from the station to tell her what train

484

we're taking, and she'll meet us at the station in Berlin.'

He urged James into his bedroom and stood fidgeting in the doorway, watching him pack.

'You know I don't speak German, don't you?' James said.

'You'll pick it up. I'll teach you some phrases on the train. Anyway, I speak it fluently. I'll be your translator.'

'Then what am I for?'

'Another driver, for one thing. Another body to do the paperwork. Another child-handler. Also, and specifically, you are tall, fair, blue-eyed and handsome, and you'll appeal to the Nazi officers who have the power to make things difficult, much more than short, dark me. Put in that blue pullover – it brings out your flaxen milkmaid complexion. And don't forget your passport.'

Unexpectedly, Hélène made no objection. The international reaction to Kristallnacht had been instant and condemnatory, and the world of fine art, which was her milieu, contained many Jews. After the horrors of the pogrom, it was coming to be understood that there was no future in Germany for Jewish people, and the question was only when and how they might get out, not if they would have to. But getting out, and finding a place to go, was hard.

Hélène listened to Emil, and said at once, 'Of course you must go, James. This may be the most important thing you ever do. But be careful, both of you. These are not rational people you will be dealing with. They can turn on you at a word. You have enough money, Emil?'

'My father has arranged an unlimited draft on his bank for expenses for both of us.'

'You had better have some cash to be going on with. Bring me my bag, James.' She took out her purse and extracted a wedge of banknotes. 'An advance on your salary,' she said, pressing it into his hand. 'You can stop at the bank on the way and change it.'

'That's too generous,' James protested.

'No. I would go myself if I were a man. Go save people. And come back. Your job will be waiting for you.'

It was in the taxi on the way to the station that James caught up with all the words that had been said. He turned to Emil. '*Unaccompanied* children?' he queried. Emil only looked at him. 'But will the parents let them go?'

'Wouldn't you?' Emil said.

On the train, Emil said suddenly, 'You know I am, don't you?'

'You are what?'

'Jewish.'

'No, I didn't.' James frowned. 'You don't go to synagogue or anything, do you?'

'No, but it doesn't matter to the Nazis. To them Jewish isn't a religion, it's a race. The Nuremberg Laws say if you have three or four Jewish grandparents, you're a Jew.'

James thought about it. 'Are you scared?'

'Not for me. You and I have two of the three safest passports in the world.' He stared out of the window for a moment. 'If I was German, I would be,' he said, after a while.

Lotti Kaufmann was a woman in her forties, smart, energetic, efficient. She was fair-skinned and blue-eyed, her face made up to enamelled perfection, her clothes fashionable but business-like – expensive suits, silk blouses, hand-made but practical shoes – and she smoked incessantly with a short ivory cigarette-holder, using it to punctuate her speech. Her English was excellent, as was her French. She seemed one of those fortunate beings who could not only learn a language easily but master the idiom and accent as well.

She had been working for a Jewish refugee agency for some time, and had developed a good relationship with German officials in various positions.

486

'They want the Jews out,' she told James briskly. 'All of them. And most of the Jews are now willing to consider going. The difficulty is finding somewhere to send them. Countries that sympathise aren't always eager to admit them. We had been settling a lot in Mandatory Palestine, but that hasn't been so easy lately, with the Arab unrest there. It's different with children. The British are the first to offer, but there are murmurs now from Switzerland, Sweden and Japan. The idea is that they'll eventually go back, so it's only a temporary resettlement. Remarkably, almost every parent we've asked was willing to let their children go. They have a high degree of trust in the United Kingdom. But we have to work quickly. We have a window of opportunity here, boys. We don't know when it will shut.'

Though he never spoke of it afterwards, James never forgot those days. The solemn, bewildered children – so many round dark eyes in pale faces, tracking from adult to adult, trying to understand what was going on. The older ones trying to comfort the younger ones. The youngest frightened, in tears. So many hand-knitted woolly hats pulled down over small ears; so many home-made gloves and mittens; the rubbed collars on the 'best' overcoats; the skinny, stockinged legs ending in stout, scuffed boots. It was late November, bitterly cold, the cleared streets edged with packed grey ice. The fog made everything grey, shrouded the tops of buildings, hung in dripping veils from bare trees, made twilight of midday; in the grey cities under the grey skies, the only colour was the bloody red of the swastika flag.

And the parents, trying to be glad: the fathers stoical, resigned, the mothers bright-eyed, trying to smile, being brave for the children. The hugs and kisses – oh, the lingering embraces, the lingering hands pulling a knitted hood straight, wiping a nose one last time. It's only for a little while, they told small Hansi and Minnie and Leni and Willi. Just for a little while, then you'll come back. A nice lady will look after you. Just be good, do as you're told, say please and thank you. It's only for a little while.

One particular parting remained in James's mind, not because it was different, but because it was typical. Most of the windows of the flat were still boarded up, so they had to have the lights on – they had not been able to afford re-glazing yet. There was not much furniture, and what there was showed signs of damage. The father had the scar of a recent wound across his brow, the woman's drawn cheeks and haunted eyes told of suffering not yet forgotten, and the fear of its return. Her lips trembled under the effort of smiling, and the little girl, five years old, would not let her go. In the end, the father snatched her from her mother's legs and put her into Emil's arms; he pushed the boy, a little older, to follow, out of the door and down the stairs. James hesitated, wanting to say something, anything, that might help, but the father stepped across to his wife's side and said tersely, 'Just go – please.' And James saw in his face the know-ledge that it was not just for a little time; saw the terrible acceptance that they would never see the children again; that they, the parents, were doomed.

James nodded and turned away, feeling sick and empty with vicarious grief. And as he closed the door, a single cry of pain broke from the woman, quickly cut off. It was that cry that haunted him. He and Emil were doing good work, vital work, extracting the children from the increasing dangers of the Nazi programme, seeing them on their way to a place of safety.

The plans were in place: James drove them to the railway station where the helpers saw them onto trains for the docks. The long sea crossing to Harwich would not be pleasant at this time of year, but from Harwich port they would be taken by bus to a nearby camp at Dovercourt, a haven run by a matron and volunteers, where there would be food and beds and games and kindness, until a foster home was ready to receive them. He did his best to encourage and comfort the children and told them they would be well treated and that it was only for a short time. Some were relieved, some even looked forward to the adventure, but mostly they looked at him with troubled, patient, ancient eyes, eyes that had witnessed centuries of cruelty and lies; and when he lay down to sleep, it was the woman's cry he heard.

Polly was just about to enter Makepeace's, where she was to consult the manager, Mrs Harrison, about the window display for the Christmas period, when she was hailed from further up the street. Mrs Hughes was coming towards her, waving to attract her attention. She was in her fifties, the wife of a Quaker and very active in charity works. The year before, she and Dorothy Ditcham had founded the York Refugee Committee, offering financial support to refugees, mostly Jews, from Europe. The committee found them homes and jobs, and two employment bureaux had been set up, along with sports and social clubs. It was exhausting work when there were so many displaced people needing help, but Mrs Hughes worked tirelessly, and had already placed almost a hundred Jewish refugees in the area. Polly had frequently been approached by her for funds, and had put her in touch with charitable acquaintances in New York who might swell the coffers.

Polly raised a politely enquiring eyebrow, thinking Mrs Hughes looked more than usually tired and fraught. Her cheeks were hollow and there were dark shadows under her eyes.

'Mrs Morland! I was going to drive out to Morland Place later to speak to you, but here you are! Have you time for a word?'

'Of course. Would you like to come up to my office? We can be private there.'

'You're most kind.'

'I think you may be overdoing things,' Polly said, as they mounted the stairs together. 'You look worn.'

489

'Oh, I daren't slow down, because if I get behind I can never catch up. Every post brings more demands, and such pitiful cases! But I'd sooner die from doing too much than live and do too little.'

'You make me ashamed that I don't help more.'

'Oh, but you are always generous,' she protested. 'Some friends one can always rely on.'

Mrs Harrison was hovering at the door of Polly's office with a sheaf of drawings in her hand, and Polly said, 'Would you give us fifteen minutes, Mrs Harrison? Mrs Hughes wants to discuss something with me.'

'Of course,' Mrs Harrison said, taking a step back. 'Shall I bring you both some tea?'

'Not for me, thank you,' Mrs Hughes said, with a distracted frown at having to deal with an inessential question.

'I'll have mine later,' Polly said, and ushered her visitor in, shutting the door behind them.

When they had sat, Polly said, 'Well, what can I help you with? Another donation?'

'Yes, I'm afraid so – but there's more this time. Something more personal.'

'Ask away.'

'You've heard about this scheme to bring Jewish children to Britain, from German-occupied Europe? Germany, Austria and the Sudetenland – and of course the wretched displaced Poles, sent back and forth from pillar to post, because no-one wants the poor creatures.'

'Yes, of course. Are you involved in that?'

'We simply have to be. The government has said that they will put no limit on how many children can come, but there are conditions. All the agencies involved must find homes for the children, and there must be funds, a guarantee of fifty pounds for each child to finance their eventual re-emigration – because they are to be here only temporarily and they must not be allowed to be a burden on the public purse.'

'So you want me to sponsor a child?'

'I knew you would offer, and thank you. Any funds you can spare are, of course, most welcome.'

'But?'

The frank, weary eyes met Polly's. 'I'm hoping I can persuade you to offer a home to one of the children. It's getting harder all the time to find people willing to take in refugees. I feel that every Quaker house should be ashamed of itself if it doesn't have at least one refugee in it, but *will* they come forward? And I hate to have to harry people and nag, but what is one to do? And now the children . . . Oh, Mrs Morland, you are not a Quaker, of course, but your family has a tradition of charitable works in York – your good father was always the first to offer help – and given that you have such a large house—'

'—A small child would be hardly noticed?'

'I'm sorry – I hope I haven't offended you?'

'I'm not offended. You are quite right. I do have plenty of room, and I know if my father were alive now he would be the first to offer.' Her father, indeed, had always thought the house could never be too crowded. 'You may put me down to give a home to one of these poor children. When are they likely to come?'

'Very soon,' said Mrs Hughes. 'The first shipload has already arrived on the east coast, and more will be arriving every day. I will give you as much notice as I can, of course. Have you a preference as to age, or will you take anyone in need?'

'Well, it would be nicer for them, I should think, if they were about my Alec's age, so that he could befriend them, and for the same reason a boy would be preferable. But I leave it up to you.'

'You are very good,' said Mrs Hughes. 'And the financial pledge . . . ?'

'I can write you a cheque,' said Polly.

'No need, the guarantee is all that's required. I know *you* won't let us down.' She stood up. 'I'll be in touch as soon as I have a child for you. And *thank* you. If only everyone were like you,' said Mrs Hughes. 'Forgive me, I must dash now. I have to catch Mrs Ditcham before she goes to Leeds.'

And she was gone, like a kindly, brown-haired whirlwind.

Ethel, predictably, raised an objection, but when she discovered everyone else was very much *for* the idea, she switched sides and became unbearably sanctimonious. 'It's our Christian duty,' she said. And 'People in our position must set a good example. We who have so much must never forget the needy.' And, most annoyingly, 'Suffer the little children,' which she repeated frequently with a sweet, saintly smile.

Polly was driven to mutter privately to John Burton, '*She* won't have to suffer the little children. It'll be someone else's job.'

He laughed. 'It's important that you have *one* thorn in your rose bed, or the gods might get jealous.'

'I know. It's not much to put up with, when I'm so happy. And Alec is being really sweet about it, looking through his toys to see what he can spare for the refugee. He's borrowed a German language book from a master at school to learn some phrases.'

'He's an ingenious boy. How will he share his pony, I wonder?'

'Hmm. I wish now we hadn't parted with Mr Pickles. Oh, and Nanny's as pleased as a cat with one kitten. Alec's too old for her petting, but she's licking her lips over a poor homeless child. I think she's imagining a barefoot ragamuffin saved from the gutter. I'm worried the first thing she'll want to do is burn his clothes and put him in a carbolic bath.'

'Even if he comes from a fairly prosperous home, he's going to find Morland Place overwhelming, let alone all the strange people,' said Burton.

'Some stranger than others.'

'Well, if there's anything I can do . . .' he concluded.

Mrs Hughes was able to give twenty-four hours' notice of a little boy called Benjamin – Bibi for short – who was eight years old, and an orphan. 'His mother died when he was very young,' she told Polly, over the telephone. 'His aunt went to live with them, but then his father was taken away during Kristallnacht to a concentration camp, and died a few days later. Terribly tragic.'

'How horrible,' Polly said. 'The poor child. I hope he won't be too—'

'I expect he will be. So many tragedies in one short life. His aunt was naturally eager to get him away. But are you worried about taking care of him? If you think it will be too much—'

'What? You'll send him to someone else? I don't imagine you have a large number of alternative homes lined up.'

'None,' she said bluntly. 'But—'

'I have a houseful of people to help me. And Nanny is so eager for it, she would never forgive me if he didn't come now. Don't worry, it will all work out for the best, I'm sure.'

The following day the snow came, and from midday it started to settle, but it was not yet so heavy as to make travel impossible. Everyone was wound up, waiting for the child to arrive. The servants kept finding things to do that meant passing through the Great Hall. Alec had been jumping around like a clockwork toy, so much so that he had finally exhausted himself, and had fallen asleep in the big armchair by the drawing-room fire. Ethel was knitting a colourful scarf from left-over wools, hoping to have it finished by the time of arrival. They had no idea when that would be. Lunch was delayed, until Polly said they had better have it and get it over with.

The afternoon advanced and the early winter dark came.

493

The snow had stopped, and it was freezing hard. Burton went home to his wife and child, telling Polly he'd be in early the next day in case there was anything he could do. John got back from work, bringing a miniature dynamo he had made that he thought the boy might like. Alec started to say why couldn't *he* have it, then nobly stopped himself.

And finally there was the sound of the door knocker, and everyone jumped, and hurried into the hall.

Barlow let in Mrs Hughes, alone. Her eyes sought Polly even as she brushed away Barlow's efforts to take her coat. 'Mrs Morland, I must speak to you. There's been a development.' She took Polly's arm and stepped aside with her.

'A problem?' Polly said.

'Not necessarily. A development.'

'No Bibi?'

'Bibi is here – he's waiting outside in the car.'

'Well, bring him in,' Polly said impatiently. 'It's cold out there.'

'He's not alone,' said Mrs Hughes. 'There's a little girl, Miriam, Mimi for short, nine years old—'

'And you want me to take her as well?'

'It turns out,' Mrs Hughes said, scanning Polly's face for reaction, 'that there were two of them, but a mistake was made. Bibi was registered with his father's surname, but for some reason the little girl was put down under her aunt's. So, of course, we didn't know they were brother and sister. Arrangements were made to foster them separately. But naturally they are upset by the whole evacuation business, not to mention their father's death, and I really don't want to make it worse by separating them now.'

'No, of course not,' Polly said.

Mrs Hughes hurried on: 'The little girl was to have gone to a family in Leeds, but they haven't room to take two. Oh, Mrs Morland, if you could take them both, just for the present, it would help me so much! It will take time to find another home that has room for two children, but room is not the problem here, and it's late and it's cold and—'

Polly held up her hand to stop her – she could see the loquacity was the result of tension, anxiety and exhaustion. 'Please don't worry. Of course we'll take both children. It would be monstrous to part them. They can have a home here for as long as they need it, until they go home to Germany. As you say, we have plenty of room. Do go and bring the poor things in – they must be perished.'

Mrs Hughes looked so relieved, Polly thought she might cry. But she was made of sterner stuff. She pushed a stray strand of hair back behind her ear, smiled, and said, 'You are very good. I'll fetch them.'

She went out to the car, and Polly used the interval to send people away, thinking how overwhelming a crowd of staring strangers would be. Everyone but Nanny and Alec drifted reluctantly off; Barlow remained at the door, and presently opened it again to admit Mrs Hughes ushering two children in winter overcoats, woollen hats and stout boots. The girl had on black woollen stockings, but the boy's knees were bare and red-blue between his short trousers and long socks. His coat was navy, worn pale at the seams; hers was brown, with a brown velvet collar that must once have been a touch of smartness and was now rubbed shabby. She put down beside her a cheap cardboard suitcase; he had a knapsack on his back. They were both pale and looked exhausted, and their dark eyes were wide with apprehension.

'This is Bibi and Mimi Lohmann,' Mrs Hughes said, a hand on the shoulder of each child. She gave them a little shove, and they took half a step forward.

Polly thought they looked like calves arriving at the slaughter house. She smiled at them, laid a hand instructively on her chest and said, 'I am Mrs Morland. You are very welcome. And this is my son Alec.'

Alec had been practising for this moment. *'Ich heiße Alec,'* he said very clearly. '*Sie sind hier willkommen.*' He beamed at the children, but there was no reaction, and he looked up at his mother, puzzled. 'Didn't I get it right?' he whispered penetratingly.

The boy's lip began to tremble, and the girl was holding back tears, both still looking as if they thought they might at any moment have their throats cut.

Nanny had had enough. She surged forward, gently pushing aside her mistress and the young master. 'Now then, there's no need for long faces, never mind tears,' she said. 'You're tired out from the journey, and hungry too, I expect.' She inserted herself between them and took a hand of each. 'You come along with me, and we'll get you out of those coats and boots. There's a nice fire in the nursery, warm as toast it is, and I've got some hot milk and biscuits ready for you, while you warm yourselves up. Then you can have a nice hot bath, and have your supper by the fire in your pyjamas. And it'll be early to bed for the both of you, because I never saw two children look so worn out, indeed I never.'

They could not, of course, understand what she was saying, but a nanny is a nanny in any language, and they went with her without resistance and without looking back. Alec went to follow, but Polly caught him back. 'Leave them to Nanny for tonight.'

'But I've got presents for them,' he said, disappointed.

'They're too tired to want presents just now. Wait until tomorrow. They're going to be here for a long time – you don't have to do everything at once. Your best present was talking to them in German. You did that very well.'

'I can see they're in good hands,' Mrs Hughes said. 'Your nurse is a treasure.'

'She couldn't be happier than having two new children to spoil – and children who really need it, too, not like Master Alec here. Won't you come in by the fire and have a glass of sherry? And stay to supper?'

'Thank you, but no. You are very good, but I just want to get home. It's been a long day. I'll check on you all tomorrow.'

'I put them in beds next to each other, madam, at the other end of the nursery from Alec,' Nanny reported to Polly the next day, 'but when I went to check on them a bit later they'd got in together and were huddled up like two puppies. I don't hold with girls and boys sharing beds, not when they've got to that age, but with your permission, madam, I think I'll let them, just at first.'

'I expect it will give them comfort. They've come through such a lot, poor things.'

'Poor things is right, madam – puny, I'd call them. The boy is the same age as Alec but not nearly so well grown, and both of them pale as milk. City complexions, I suppose – not rosy and healthy like Alec. They need feeding up, plenty of good country food and running about in the fresh air.' She glanced doubtfully at the window, outside which the snow was falling again, softly and heavily, obliterating the view.

'Playing outside may have to wait a day or two. But feed them up by all means. How are they this morning?

'Very quiet. Creeping about like they think we mean them harm. Start when you speak to them. Sit where you put them, as if they're scared to move. I don't know what was done to them where they came from . . .'

'It's all a big change for them,' Polly said. 'And this house will be a lot to get used to – so many rooms and so many people.'

'That's what I was going to suggest, madam, that for the first few days, I keep 'em up in the nursery, till they get used to things, then they can see the rest of the house gradual. And no-one to come up there but me and Jenny and Doris.' Jenny was the nursery maid and Doris was the housemaid who did the nursery fires and cleaned. 'And Alec, of course. And you, naturally, madam.'

'I think you're quite right,' Polly said. 'Let them get used to things gradually. Do they speak any English? Do they understand anything you say?'

'They understand what I *mean*,' Nanny said, 'and I make sure to tell them the words for things – milk and fire and bath and so on. They'll soon catch on.'

'I'll come up later and see them. For now, I think you're doing just what's right, Nanny. Thank you.'

'Thank *you*, madam.' She hesitated.

'What is it?'

'Well, I understand they're not Christians. And I wouldn't hold it against them, poor things, given it's the way they're brought up. But I like to see prayers said at night before bed in my nursery, and I make sure Alec says them, but what about these two? It'll set him a bad example if they don't say 'em, but—'

'I'm sure Jewish children say prayers before bed too. They worship the same God, you know, Nanny, just in a different way. Let them do it in their own words when Alec says his. I'm sure it will comfort them.'

'Very good, madam.'

When Polly went up, she took the dogs with her. Like nannies, dogs were the same everywhere, and excellent ambassadors where language was a problem. She found Bibi and Mimi sitting on the hearth-rug by the nursery fire looking at a picture book. Mimi was wearing a dark red woollen dress she seemed to remember had been Laura's, and Bibi was in shorts and a jumper she knew Alec had outgrown last year. Evidently Nanny had decided everything they had brought with them needed cleaning. They looked even paler than they had the night before, which might have been the result of professional washing by a determined hand, and their hair was clean and shiny – mid-brown hair, slightly wavy. They scrambled to their feet as Polly came in, and looked at her warily, though with a degree less fear than the night before. She smiled and said good morning, but there was no answering smile or speech.

And then the dogs surged in behind her, and the ice was broken. Fand could never see a face he didn't want to wash, and they were within easy reach of a tall Morland hound. Kithra didn't want to be left out of any fun or affection that was going, and Helmy bustled in to give a laughing greeting and then check the hearthrug for dropped toast or biscuit crumbs. The children started, then smiled at last, and soon were patting and stroking the dogs. Alec, who had been fetching another book, came back in time to tell them the dogs' names.

'I'm teaching them English, Mummy,' he explained earnestly to Polly. 'I've given them a picture book, and I point to the things in the picture and say what it is in English. And now I've got one with words as well.'

'It's lucky the snow's keeping you off school today,' Polly said. 'You're being a good host to them.'

Alec smirked under the praise. 'It's going to be my house one day, so I have to, don't I? Will they be going to school?'

'Eventually, of course. You'll be breaking for Christmas soon, so perhaps after that, when they've had time to settle in. It's a big change for them. Have they spoken to you about their home?'

'They don't really speak much at all,' he said. 'Should I ask them about home?'

'I think that would be a good thing. Encourage them to talk to you. But don't worry if it makes them cry. People need to cry sometimes, and their father died.'

'My father died too,' he said.

'But that was before you were born. Theirs died not long ago, and they must be very sad.'

He gave her a determined, grown-up look. 'Don't worry, Mummy. I'll look after them.'

CHAPTER TWENTY-ONE

The snow was down in New York, giving it a magical look. Everything seemed cleaner sketched in black, white and grey. Central Park was like an illustration from a Hans Andersen story: any horse-drawn carriage might prove to be the Snow Queen's sleigh. In the streets, steam rose from gratings like a giant's tea-time, and hot-chestnut vendors in bright-coloured stocking hats hopped from foot to foot and blew on their fingers. The shops along Fifth Avenue were lit up with Christmas displays, and in front of Saint Pat's a choir collecting for charity sang carols.

Lennie had done a great deal of business, but had also been saying goodbye, not knowing when he would see it again. He visited some old haunts, ate in favourite restaurants, saw a few Broadway plays – *Androcles and the Lion*, *I Married an Angel*, and *Danton's Death* – and went to a number of parties and dinners. He was still a popular guest, and could have gone to two or three every night if he'd wanted to. He didn't tell anyone it was a farewell: he didn't want any fuss.

Then he took the train back to California, where there was no snow and very little mention of Christmas. Wilma was glad to see him back. 'People been asking 'bout you, when you're coming home,' she said.

'What people?'

'Folks in general.' She rolled her eyes. 'And females in particular, 'quiring 'bout the big party, and who you're taking

500

with you. I'm just about sick o' saying I don't know. Miss Adeline Colby, she brung me a basket o' fruit,' her voice rose in indignation, 'spectin' me to put in a good word for her.'

'Is that what she said?' Lennie asked, amused.

'She never said it, but I know that's what she want. Bribin' me! And what would I want with a basket o' fruit? If I want a peach, I'll go out and buy maself one. It was mos'ly jus' one big pineapple, anyways, makin' it look bigger,' she sniffed.

'How's Rose?'

'I couldn't say. She ain't hardly been at home, goin' out gallivantin' every evening.'

Lennie was alarmed. 'She's not getting into trouble, is she?'

'I don't think so, Mr Lennie. Mr Van, he's been squirin' her around. He'll take good care of her.'

'It wasn't Van every time, though, was it?'

'Pretty much,' Wilma said, which meant yes.

Rose returned late that evening, and came rushing straight in to see Lennie and flinging her arms round him in a bear hug. 'You're back! I'm so glad to see you!'

'How come? What have you been up to?' he said suspiciously.

'Working hard,' she said. 'You'll see. All the photography's done on *Robin Hood*, and they're editing now. And there's a lot of press interest. I guess Mr Feinstein was right about going to England to shoot – I get asked about that all the time. It was good publicity.'

'And what's the big news?' Lennie asked. 'What's everyone talking about?'

'Well, Mr Selznick has been seen out to dinner with Alexander Korda, and they say they were discussing some English actress he's got under contract – Mr Korda has – that Mr Selznick wants to screen test for Scarlett O'Hara. But Woody says *Robin Hood* will easily do better than *Gone*

With the Wind, and in any case I don't care about it, because Mr Feinstein's got a new script for me. It's called *Anastasia,* and it's about the last Tsar of Russia's daughter who doesn't get killed with the rest of them but secretly escapes, but the Reds find out and chase her all over Europe, and this gorgeous White Russian prince has to save her, and they fall in love and – well, you'll see! Woody says it's a really good part for me. He says Scarlett O'Hara is two-dimensional.'

'He's probably right. What else?'

'Oh – Anthea Taylor is getting married. It's a big sensation because she's marrying Romano Ortez, and he's only twenty-five, and they've only known each other a few months. They met on the set of *The Lion of Burgos.* He was El Cid and she was Chimena.' She looked at him anxiously. 'You don't mind?'

'Why should I mind? I escorted Anthea a few times, that's all. We parted ways on good terms.'

'Oh, good, because they're bound to be at the ABO party – she's sure to want to show him off. You *are* going, aren't you?'

'Of course. How could I miss it?' The ABO Christmas party, held at Al Feinstein's vast pale pink mansion – which was loosely modelled on a French château and filled with reproduction Louis XV furniture and chandeliers the size of cartwheels – was one of the highlights of the Hollywood year. Everybody who was anybody would be there, while anybody who had ambitions to *become* anybody would get up to any trick they could think of to secure an invitation.

'And who will you be taking?' Rose asked.

'Nobody that I know of.'

'Uncle Lennie! You can't not take someone – what a waste! There are thousands of actresses out there who would give their hair to go. You have to take *someone.*'

'I'll take you, if you like.'

502

'But I've got an invitation on my own account. I'll ask Woody to choose someone for you.'

She seemed bent on it, so he let her, and Van Kerk came up with Leona Gaye, a young actress who had just had her first movie speaking part in *The Unvarnished Truth*. She was not only pretty but good company, and would be grateful for the opportunity.

The party was as such parties are – glittering, loud, lavish, full of people more interested in being seen enjoying themselves than actually enjoying themselves. The press lined the red carpet on both sides of the entrance, and beyond them crowds of movie fans gathered to see the cars arrive and decant the stars who made their lives more interesting.

Lennie did his bit for Leona Gaye by walking slowly and making sure he did not mask her from the photographers. They had just reached the doorway when he glanced back and saw that the next car had disgorged Anthea Taylor and her new husband, who was willowy, tanned, and had black curly hair, lustrous black eyes and a superfluity of very white teeth. Anthea was looking radiant, smiling and waving as though all her dreams had come true. As perhaps they had, Lennie thought, and turned his attention to his date. She was very sweet and, as Van had said she would be, very grateful. He walked about with her, introduced her to as many people as he could, and when he had presented her to William Wyler of Universal, Hollywood's youngest director, and had seen that he was quite taken with her, he felt able to leave her there and slip away to be on his own.

All around him were the biggest names in California, and not only movie people: there were politicians and businessmen, artists and composers, authors, millionaires and moguls, socialites of all sorts. All around him were bare shoulders and bare backs, glossy hair and sparkling teeth, silk and satin and sequins, jewels both real and paste, laughter both real and forced, heaving bosoms and meaningful smiles, opportunities sought and chances offered. There were friends of his here, too, old acquaintances and business partners. But he would leave them all without pain. This had been his world for many years, but just now none of it seemed real. In his mind a cooler, greener place called to him, and a woman without artifice whose least smile, unenhanced by orthodontic procedures, shook him to the bones.

Now coming to find him was Rose, elegant in backless black tulle weighted with bugle beads, her hand through Van Kerk's arm, the smile of a transcendent angel lifting her beauty above the worldly. 'Uncle Lennie,' she said, a little breathlessly, 'I've got something to tell you. Or ask you.' She glanced at Van and laughed. 'I don't know which! I've been making up my mind to ask you – tell you – but I didn't know how. And just this minute I saw you looking all pensive and a little bit sad, and I thought, This is Uncle Lennie. What am I scared of?'

'That's what I said to you,' said Van Kerk.

'I know, and you were right. Uncle Lennie, I want to get married. I'm *going* to get married. I know I don't need your permission, but I'd really like your blessing.'

Lennie's heart sank a little. Now what had she got up to? Had she got herself mixed up with some preening male actor again? Another disastrous marriage could prove fatal to her career. Who was it? Not someone from *Robin Hood*, or he'd have heard. And if Wilma didn't know, she must have been keeping it very quiet indeed – which suggested it was someone she knew he wouldn't approve of. But opposition would only harden her resolve, so he refrained from barking, and said mildly, 'This is very sudden.'

'Um, not really. It's been building up for a long time. I just hadn't realised, which was crazy of me, because I can see now there isn't anyone else in the world I could love the way I love him. Only you, but that's different, you're my darling Uncle Lennie, and he's— Oh dear, I seem to be

504

making a mess of this.' She laughed, and looked up at Van Kerk again.

Lennie looked at him sternly. 'Did you know about this? You've been encouraging her?'

Van smiled indulgently. 'Not at first,' he said, 'but once I saw there was no changing her mind . . . and I have to say that when I really thought about it, the idea absolutely enchanted me.'

'You said you were appalled,' Rose objected. 'You said it was out of the question.'

'It grew on me,' Van said.

Lennie looked from one to the other. 'What is going on?'

'Haven't you guessed? Oh dear, you're very slow,' Rose said. 'I want to marry Woody, of course.'

Lennie stared. 'Is this true?' he asked Van Kerk.

'I'm afraid so. I am shockingly in love with her, and apparently she loves me too, so would you mind terribly much if I took her off your hands? I promise to take the best possible care of her, and look after her person, her mind, her heart and her career with equal diligence.'

A slow smile spread over Lennie's face. Now he thought about it, it was obvious that Rose would have to have an older man she could look up to, not some Dean Cornwell or Romano Ortez pretty-boy in love with himself and with nothing to offer beyond his looks. Rose was a smart young woman, and canny, too, when she wasn't distracted. Van Kerk was clever, charming, sensible, good at his job – and generally no end of a man. He was just right for her.

He turned to Rose. 'You do know how lucky you are, don't you?'

'Oh, I do, believe me, I do. So you don't mind? You think it's all right?'

'I think you've chosen the best man you possibly could. I'm delighted for you both. When are you going to do the deed?'

'As soon as possible,' Van said. 'Just waiting for your good offices.' He looked at Rose. 'January all right with you?'

'You will give me away, won't you?' Rose asked Lennie.

'I'll give you away and dance at your wedding. And then I shall be going.'

'Going?'

'Like you I couldn't think of the right way to tell you. But this seems to be the moment for big news. I'm going to England to marry Polly and live at Morland Place.' Rose looked stricken, and he went on, 'To borrow your words, there isn't anyone in the world I could love as I love her.'

Rose pulled herself together. 'I suppose I should have realised. Oh, Uncle Lennie, I'm going to miss you like anything!'

'You'll be too happy and busy to miss me – married to Van and working on your new movie.'

'I shall anyway. You will come back sometimes, won't you?'

'I'm sure I will. And you can come and visit me. But with your husband and your career and a houseful of lusty young Van Kerks, you'll have trouble finding the time.' He bent to kiss her cheek, and she clung to him for a moment. 'What a happy ending for all of us. Like something out of Hollywood.'

'Oh, Lord,' said Van Kerk, 'don't say that!'

Richard had been out all day, and returned home late to find Cynthia waiting for him in the hall. The sound of Hannah's and Leah's voices came from the kitchen, along with clashing pans. There was a smell of soup in the air, but to him, the flat in Earls Court always smelt of soup. He and Cynthia were still living there, she being reluctant to leave her mother at that time. The house in Ealing languished unused, and he worried occasionally about damp and possible leaks, but Earls Court was more convenient for him for the office and for meetings in Town.

'Something wrong?' he questioned his wife's pensive look.

'Oh – no,' she said. 'Let me take your coat. Is it still snowing?' She brushed at the shoulders.

'No, it's stopped. That fell off a tree as I went past.' He removed off his hat, and she took that too, but stood holding it and his coat. 'What's the matter? There's something on your mind.'

'Oh.' She shook herself and hung the things up. 'Mummy had a telephone call this morning. From an old friend, Mrs Margolies. She's working with the Movement for the Care of Children from Germany. Well, she *was* with the Central British Fund for German Jewry, but they're all grouped together now for—'

'Yes, I know – for bringing Jewish children over here. I heard about it on the wireless. What about it? Was she looking for a donation?'

'She wants Mummy to help. And Mummy really needs something to do, to take her mind off things.'

Richard laid a hand on her arm. 'Her husband died. Your father. It's all right to grieve.'

'We do, and we will. But this is an emergency, Richard. All those children . . . It's something we can do, don't you see? In a world of hate, it's a little bit of love we can show.'

'We?'

'I want to help too.'

'Of course you do. Where do I come in?'

'Oh, to give your permission, of course.'

'You don't need my permission!'

'But it will take us away from the office work.'

'There isn't much of that, and enough people to do it. It's the quiet time of year. To be honest, I don't think there's going to be much call in future for holidays on the Continent. And there's not much happening with the holiday village, with the winter weather and Christmas coming up, so you won't be needed. You couldn't really think I would object?'

She hesitated. 'It's – it's publicly associating ourselves with

507

Jews. There are people who won't like that. It could affect the business in the future.'

'I don't believe it. Look here, darling, do you want to help with this children thing? Well, then, do it. What does it actually entail?'

'Well, you know Sir Samuel Hoare put out an appeal on the Home Service for foster homes for the children? It seems they've had over five hundred offers, and now the Movement needs volunteers to go and inspect the homes to see if they're suitable. Mrs Margolies asked if Mummy and I would be willing to help.'

The sounds in the kitchen had stopped, and at the end of the dark passage he saw that Hannah had come to the door, with Leah behind her, to listen.

'I think it's a splendid idea. In fact, I'll volunteer as well. I dare say it will be useful for them to have someone with a car – all the homes might not be so easy to reach.'

His reward was the way Cynthia's face lit up. '*Would* you? Oh, I think that would be wonderful, all of us helping.'

'I'm not sure I'd know a good Jewish home when I saw one, though – you might have to give me some hints,' Richard said.

Hannah had come hurrying to join them. 'Rachel Margolies says they don't have to be Jewish homes. And she says we can't be too fussy, given how many children there will be, and how urgent the need. All we have to see is that the homes are clean, and that the families seem respectable.'

'I think I can do that,' Richard said. 'When do we start?'

Cynthia and her mother exchanged a glance, then said, at the same moment and in the same tone, 'Tomorrow?'

And Richard laughed.

Jack and Helen went down to spend Christmas with Jessie and Bertie. Basil preferred to stay in London, and Michael was in Malta. And while the pull of Barbara and Freddie and their two little boys, Douglas and Peter, was strong to devoted grandparents, Barbara was pregnant again, having a hard time with morning and evening sickness, and didn't feel up to company.

And Jack said, 'Who knows what's going to happen next year?'

In the hall at Twelvetrees, Jessie hugged her favourite brother for a very long time, her thoughts running on the same lines as his. Then they went into the drawing-room and a good, big fire. 'So much nicer to look at than coal fires,' Helen said.

'We lost a big sycamore in the storm before last Christmas,' Bertie said, 'so we've got plenty of nicely seasoned logs now.'

The girls brought sherry and mince pies. Thomas was home from college, having arrived just the night before, and listened intently as his mother asked, 'Are you keeping busy?' and his uncle Jack said, 'Very, what with the Spitfire and the Hurricane coming off the production lines, and the Typhoon to work on. And so many new bases being set up.'

Jessie laughed. 'You're not a construction worker.'

'No, but I seem to be consulted about everything. Jack of all trades.'

'I'd sooner you were a consultant with your feet on the ground than flying.'

He smiled at her. 'There speaks a woman. What man of spirit wouldn't sooner be flying?'

'Do you miss it?' Jessie asked.

'Yes, I miss the sky,' Jack said. He looked at his wife. 'You understand.'

'Ah, you've remembered at last that I was a flier, too.'

'How could I forget? But I keep my hand in,' Jack went on. 'Enough flying hours to keep my ticket. You just never know, do you, when it might be needed?'

'Not at your age,' Helen said bluntly. 'You're fifty-two. Your reflexes are not quick enough. It's young men who are needed.'

'She's cruel, isn't she?' Jack said, reaching out a hand to press Helen's to show he wasn't really hurt.

'But not wrong,' Helen said. 'You were pretty old for the last lot, darling – they all called you "uncle". All those boys in your squadrons were eighteen, nineteen, twenty.'

There was a brief silence as Jack, Helen, Jessie and Bertie all remembered at the same moment how many of those 'boys' had died. And before anyone could tactfully change the subject, Thomas cleared his throat and said, 'You really think there will be another war?'

He was addressing Jack, who, with regard to a mother's feelings, said, 'The government seems determined to keep us out of one.'

'But the RAF must believe it's going to happen, or why are they making new bases and building all those planes?' Before Jack could answer, he said, 'I know they do, as a matter of fact, because we had a recruiting officer come to address us at college last week.'

Helen said, very quietly, 'Oh, no.'

'He said this war will be a war of the air. Ground forces are all very well, but they get bogged down, and they're vulnerable. It's important to be agile and quick. The nation with the best air force will win.'

'There's a lot more to it than that,' Bertie began.

But Thomas turned a passionate face to his parents. 'I've volunteered. I was going to tell you last night but – well – things got away from me. You know, with all the chatting and kissing and everything.'

'You've volunteered?' Jessie said. 'You have to have permission, you know. You're not twenty-one yet.'

'I know, but you'll say yes, I know you will.' He stared at them earnestly, then appealed to Helen and Jack, 'You know how important this is. Every man has to do his duty. And I want to fly.'

Helen met Jessie's eyes. 'When the war comes, there'll be conscription. He'll be called up, and probably offered his choice. It may be better to learn now, without pressure, if he's going to go anyway.'

'Perhaps there won't be a war.'

'Then he'll have a nice, gentlemanly profession for a few years, and do something else. Jack flew passenger runs to France.'

'That was still flying,' Jessie said accusingly. 'I know how anxious you used to get.'

'I'll be twenty-one next June,' Thomas said, watching the ball pass from one to another. 'But I'd sooner go now, with your blessing.'

Bertie spoke. Perhaps a little more of age had settled into his face. 'If we can't stop you – and it seems we can't – then we have to be proud of you. You have my blessing. I can't speak for your mother.'

Jessie remembered all the years of being parted from Bertie, believing she would never be able to be with him. And the anguish of conscience when she gave herself to him and conceived; and the pain of separation from her family while she carried Thomas and gave birth to him. Parents did not have favourite children, but Thomas had been so hard-won, the child she never thought she'd have, and Bertie, having lost his son by his first wife to a German bomb, adored him. To lose him would be a crippling blow. But she looked at her handsome boy, and read the eagerness in his beautiful eyes, and knew that there was nothing she could do. As Helen said, he would go anyway. At least this way she kept his heart.

'Of course you have my blessing,' she said, and her reward was his joyful smile. She had to say something else, to turn the attention from her, because she didn't want to cry. 'What is the training like? Where do you have to go?'

Thomas was happy to expound. 'The officer told us all about that. First you have to do a two-month course at an Elementary Training School – there's one at Brough, near Hull, so they might send me there, and I'd be able to come home at week-ends. That's a civilian school. They teach you aviation theory, and you log fifty-five hours of flying, about half of it solo. Then you go to Flying Training School and that's a six-month course. That's service-run. You have to log ninety hours, two thirds of it solo, and you learn about night flying, and formation, flying on instruments, and navigation and gunnery. And then you get your wings, and you go for specialist training, either fighters or bombers. It's very thorough, Mum.'

'Much more so than in my day,' Jack said. 'We didn't get anything like that amount of preparation. We had boys coming out to France with only twelve hours solo.'

Helen didn't say, *And most of them died*. 'Aeroplanes are much more complicated now. Anyone could fly those old balsa-wood kites – they practically flew themselves.'

'Well, I'm glad to hear that you'll get so much practice,' Jessie said. 'And you'll look very handsome in your blue uniform. Air force blue.'

'Do you remember, when the RAF was first formed, and we were all in our khakis,' Jack said, 'because nobody knew what colour the new uniforms would be, and there wasn't any material anyway?'

Helen laughed. 'And then the War Office got a whole lot of bolts of spare cloth from Russia—'

'—which had been made for the Semenovski Guard. It was a brilliant sky blue, and we all said we'd desert if they made us wear it!'

So the moment was lightened.

Bibi and Mimi were settling down, no longer started at every sound. They were still solemn, as was to be expected, but they were learning words quickly, and seemed to trust Alec.

He gradually showed them round the house, and introduced them to its inmates. The dogs were a great help – the children were always more relaxed when they were present. The good food was putting roses in their cheeks; and Polly took some of their clothes to Makepeace's for the size and bought them several ready-made new outfits, which clearly pleased them.

When they had begun to trust her, she took them to the stables, and was pleased to see that they were not afraid of horses. With a mixture of fractured English, gestures, and Alec's help, Mimi told her there had been a greengrocer back home who had come round with his pony and cart and always stopped outside their building; and Tante had let them go down and stroke the pony, and the greengrocer had given them broken bits of carrot to give it, and how soft its mouth had been.

'When the snow's gone,' Polly said, 'I'll teach you to ride.'

When she understood what that meant, Mimi's face lit. 'Dank you!' she cried. 'Dank you!'

Polly got a long letter from Lennie just before Christmas, telling her about Rose's intended marriage.

The wedding will be at the end of January, and promises to be a grand affair. Van is very well liked, and Rose is becoming quite the star – and of course the studio won't miss a chance of all that good publicity. So I feel I have to stay for it. I hope you understand. But I know I can entrust Rose to Van, that he will keep her safe, so I shall be able to leave her without worrying. I can use the time before the wedding to get things done, and feel sure of being ready to leave by mid-February. I can sail on the 15th and be with you on the 21st. I leave it entirely up to you to choose the wedding day.

Polly decided on the 11th of March, for no better reason than that the previous Saturday was the 4th of March and she didn't like the sound of it. It gave her two months to plan everything, which she thought would be enough.

Christmas was a good distraction for the two little refugees, who might have been expected to be very unhappy at being so far from home. But the bringing in of the Yule log was exciting, and then the erecting of the enormous tree in the Great Hall had their eyes popping. They were thrilled to help decorate it, and when Bibi was given the star to put on the top, which involved being held out over the gallery railing by a footman, he giggled with delight. Mrs Starling invited the three children into the kitchen to make and decorate spiced gingerbreads in the shapes of trees and snowmen and holly leaves. And to keep them busy, Polly sent them out to help collect holly, ivy and mistletoe to decorate the hall.

The church choir came on Christmas Eve to sing carols under the tree, and Bibi and Mimi seemed to know some of the tunes, and sang along with their own words. And they were familiar with the notion of hanging up stockings by the fireplace in the nursery. John Burton explained to Alec that many of what had become traditions were German in origin, including the tree and the stockings, brought over in Victorian times by Prince Albert. The Yule log, the holly and mistletoe were older, English and pagan.

Polly didn't know, because Nanny didn't tell her, of the tears that followed the hanging of the stockings, prayers, and being tucked up in bed. Bibi crept into Mimi's bed, and they cried themselves to sleep. They didn't remember their mother, but Papa was dead, and Tante was far away, and however kind people were to them here, it was not home.

But Christmas morning brought fresh wonders, the magically filled stockings, a walk with Alec, Martin and John and a snowball fight, then the magnificent Christmas dinner of gilded goose and plum pudding. And then, by the blazing log fire in the Great Hall, it was time for presents.

Everyone had wrapped something for the little refugees,

but without doubt the star present came from Polly, though she let it be Alec's present, to strengthen the bond between them. One of Fand's daughters had had a litter in October and the whelps were old enough to leave their mother now. Polly picked out a large, confident one, and Alec gave it to Mimi and Bibi, 'For your own, to share.'

The memory of that Christmas for her was of the children sitting on the floor by the fire with the puppy tumbling and scrambling over them, and their high, happy laughter at its antics. She told them his name was Kai – a traditional Morland hound name, and easy for them to pronounce.

John Burton had been doubtful about the wisdom of the gift. 'What happens when they go back to Germany? They may not be able to take it, and that will mean more heart-break for them.'

She gave him a level look. 'Who knows when they'll be able to go back? The way things are going, there'll be war next year, and they'll have to stay here. And by the time that's over, they'll be old enough to cope with leaving a dog behind. It may be the least of everyone's worries.'

Richard and Cynthia were invited to Tunstead Hall for Christmas, and he was eager for them to go, wanting a change and a rest for his wife, who he thought was looking peaky. Cynthia didn't want to leave her mother, but Hannah and Leah were invited by the Pullingers, a family who lived in the same building – Mrs Pullinger was Jewish but not obser-vant, like Hannah and Samuel. The two families had often had Christmas together, which they celebrated with a large piece of beef followed by *Apfelstrudel* and songs around the piano.

So Tunstead it was, and they arrived to find Emma and Kit, Oliver and Verena and their children there, so the house was gloriously full and rang with the sound of happy laughter. Robert and Joan had been invited but had preferred to go to Joan's people. Charlotte was there without Launde, who was on his way back from Switzerland.

Everyone was interested in the work Richard and Cynthia had been doing, and Richard tried to let Cynthia answer the questions, but she was still too shy, so he had to do the talking.

Kit was very amusing about a dinner he and Emma had been summoned to in Prince's Gate, the home of the American ambassador. 'I couldn't think why they wanted us, since we're not really in diplomatic circles, but it was soon obvious that we were there to be pumped about Wally Simpson – was she really so elegant and witty? Was she really worth giving up the throne for?'

'You're wrong,' Emma said. 'The real reason we were there was so that Mrs Kennedy could boast about their having spent a weekend at Windsor Castle.'

'Nonsense – she could have boasted about that to anybody.'

'She probably has. It was our turn, that's all,' Emma said imperturbably.

'What did she say about the King and Queen?' Oliver asked, amused.

'She was very gracious about the Queen – said what lovely skin she had,' said Kit. 'In my experience, when a woman praises another woman's skin, she means that woman has nothing else going for her.'

'Oh, no! Too cruel!' Violet said. 'I'm sure she didn't mean that.'

'Well, she's thin as a rail, and Her Majesty is nicely plump,' Kit said, 'and I heard her murmur something about having had nine children while the Queen's only had two, so I drew a conclusion.'

'There was mention of a return match,' Emma said. 'Their Majesties to dine at Prince's Gate. Mrs K said she was sure they had to go to so many banquets they'd be sick of them, and would be longing for a simple meal. So she's planning to give them "good, plain American food", as she put it.'

'Shad roe, baked ham and strawberry shortcake,' Kit said with glee. 'Just like Bryanston Court! You remember, darling, the first time Wally served hot dogs and cold beer to the Pragga Wagga, as he then was?'

'Oh, those Bryanston Court suppers!' Emma sighed. 'She said the same thing, that he'd appreciate good plain food—'

'—while the fact was he'd have eaten a chewing-gum sandwich if she'd been on the other side of it,' Kit concluded for her. 'Dear me, how long ago it all seems now,' he added, with a sigh. 'Long ago and far away, and they are so forgotten, it's hard to believe they were real, not just a fairy story.'

'Hmm,' said Oliver. 'I've heard that Ambassador Kennedy has said he thinks David would have made an excellent king, and it was a pity more wasn't done to keep him, because he knew how to get on with Hitler.'

'Yes, I've heard that, too,' said Kit. 'He thinks Britain ought to be bypassed and an understanding reached between the United States and Germany. He thinks Hitler has the answers to world problems.'

Avis intervened, seeing Richard's wife looking very small and vulnerable. 'Violet had a letter recently from Jessie,' he said, firmly changing the subject, 'with some very good news.'

Violet took the cue. 'Yes, it seems that Polly is getting married. The wedding is set for March, and the person she's marrying is dear Lennie Manning.'

'Tremendous news!' Oliver said. 'I'm so glad Polly's found someone at last. She's been a widow for far too long.'

'Yes, and Lennie Manning!' Kit said. 'Not only a very nice person, which is good for her, but he's a real movie tycoon, which will be good for us.'

'How so?' Oliver asked, amused.

'Why, because Morland Place will be filled with movie stars and directors and we'll naturally be invited for Saturday-to-Mondays to meet them.'

'We will?'

'Of course. We're Polly's oldest friends and practically relatives. I'm still a little hurt that she didn't invite us down when they had that film being shot there, and she'll be anxious to make it up to us.'

'When will that film be coming out?' Violet asked. 'I'd like to see it.'

'You never go to the cinema,' Richard objected.

'I know, dear, but to see a place I know so well actually on the screen.' She sighed. 'We could have gone down there ourselves if only Shawes hadn't had to be sold.'

Avis looked at her tenderly. 'We could buy it back. I've heard they can't find a tenant for it, and it's getting a bit dilapidated.'

Kit clapped his hands. 'Oh, do! Do buy it back, and make it a home from home for all us movie fans! Then we won't need to depend on Cousin Polly's generosity – about which, frankly, I know too little to be confident.'

'*Cousin* Polly?' Emma queried.

'I'm sure there's a connection somewhere in the family tree,' he said serenely.

'You're hopeless!' Emma said, laughing.

On the 27th, Avis, Oliver, Kit and Richard took the guns out, and took Oliver's son John with them – he was fourteen, and it was his first inclusion in the grown-up sport. The loaders who went with them carried sandwiches and Thermos flasks of soup for everyone in haversacks, and they lunched in the woods, and stayed out until the declining sun took the meagre warmth out of the day. They walked back with their breath clouding on the icy air, the sky dusky pink behind the black lacework of the bare trees, the tired dogs trotting beside them through grass already beginning to stiffen with frost.

When they came in sight of the house, there was a small black Ford car on the gravel sweep. 'Hello! More guests?' Kit said.

'No,' said Avis. 'That's Dr Ramsay's car.' He speeded up, and the others hurried after him.

Violet was in the hall, waiting for them as the butler opened the door, looking tense and worried, Verena and Emma behind her. Avis reached her and seized her hands. But she looked past him and met Richard's eyes. 'It's Cynthia,' she said. 'Her pains started. We got her to bed and sent for Dr Ramsay.'

Richard made to go past her, but she caught his arm. 'You can't go up there,' she said. 'You'd only be in the way. The doctor's there, and my nanny, and my maid, who's seen me through all my childbirths. They're doing everything possible, Richard, I promise you.'

'It's too soon,' Richard said. 'I have to see her.'

Avis slung an arm round his shoulder. 'Violet's right. There's nothing you can do. It's women's work. Come by the fire and I'll get you a whisky. You look as though you need it.'

'I'll go up and see if there's any news,' Emma said quietly.

The waiting was a nightmare, and seemed to go on for a very long time, but the clock had only just struck six when the doctor came down, looking weary. He scanned the room, and picked out Richard. 'You're the father?' he guessed.

Richard stood, but couldn't speak. He noticed the doctor's dishevelled hair, and his beard starting to come through from the morning's shave; he noticed a fleck of blood on his cheek.

'This is Mr Howard,' Avis supplied.

'I see. Well, I'm sorry. I wish I had better news for you. The baby never lived – it was born dead. Your wife lost a lot of blood, but we've stopped the bleeding now and she should be all right, with rest and good food.'

Richard stared, reaching for understanding. 'She's been working quite hard, recently, instead of resting—'

The doctor smiled kindly. 'People always ask that in these

situations – was it something I did? It very rarely is. Pregnancies are very resilient: women in undeveloped countries labour in the fields up to the last moment and give birth without trouble. Sometimes babies die, and the truth is we don't know why. These things happen – no comfort to you, I know, but it's part of the natural process, very sad but not something to brood about. The likelihood is that she'll have no difficulties the next time.'

Richard cleared his throat. 'Our doctor told her there was some – abnormality. Inside. He didn't think she could conceive.'

'Oh. I'm sorry. I didn't know about that. Well, I recommend you seek his opinion. I can only say, for the moment, I think she is out of danger, but she should be kept quiet, and should not attempt to get out of bed for several days.' He looked at Violet. 'I'll come and visit her tomorrow, my lady, if that's all right.'

'Of course.'

'The nurse and your maid are very competent. I have no anxiety about leaving her with them, but if you want to call in a professional nurse . . . I don't believe it's necessary, but sometimes, for reassurance—'

'Can I see her?' Richard broke in. 'I must see her.'

'In a few minutes more. I'll just see she's comfortable, and then I'll send the maid to fetch you. But please don't upset her. Be calm and reassuring – that's what she needs now.'

She looked very pale, as pale as the sheets. He took her cold hands and kissed them, and she looked up with tear-filled eyes. 'I'm sorry,' she whispered. 'I'm so sorry.'

He sat on the edge of the bed. 'There's nothing to apologise for.'

'I lost your baby. I'm so sorry.'

'It wasn't anything that you did or I did. The doctor said these things just happen, more often than you'd think, and that it's not anyone's fault. Oh, darling!' He freed a hand and wiped the tears from her cheek with a tender thumb. 'Don't cry. It's sad, but we'll have another. The doctor said there's no reason to think that next time—'

'There won't be a next time,' she said, suppressed sobs breaking her voice. 'There shouldn't have been a this time. Dr Saloman said there was something wrong with me—'

'Well, it shows doctors don't know everything, doesn't it? There *was* a this time, and next time it will all go well and you'll have a lovely baby.'

She shook her head drearily. 'I'm no use to you. You should never have married me. I'm a Jew and everyone hates us, and I can't even give you children. You should—'

'No more of that. I won't hear it. You are my wife and I couldn't want a better one. Whatever happens to us, we'll face it together. When you're well again we'll go and see another doctor, get another opinion. And if it turns out that we can't have children – so be it. I still wouldn't change you for anyone else in the world. Now rest, darling. Close your eyes. I'll stay with you. Everything will be all right.'

Still clinging to his hands, she fell into an exhausted sleep. He watched her, her shallow breathing, the shadow of her lashes on her pale cheek. His guilt was huge and hot, like a stone in his chest. *What have I done to you?* Her present suffering was directly caused by him. He should never have married her – he had brought her only grief. But if she had been unmarried when her father died, who would have cared for her and Hannah? And, as uneasy as the world was now, he feared it was only going to get worse. He must protect her. He had promised Samuel. More than that, he had promised himself.

CHAPTER TWENTY-TWO

Rose's wedding took place in Lennie's home, Bel Air, in Whitley Heights. A flower-entwined arch was built at one end of the lawned terrace, under which the minister would perform the ceremony. Chairs stood in two ranks facing the arch for the most important guests, and the stone terrace above at the back of the house formed a grandstand for everyone else. Afterwards a lavish buffet lunch was served, people could wander between levels as they wished, a small orchestra played, and the pool on the bottom terrace was available for the younger people and children. Five hundred guests were invited, and an auction had been held among the newspapers and magazines for a select band of journalists and photographers to record the event, the money raised given to charity.

With a final flurry of photographs and an incontinent throwing of rice, the couple set off for their honeymoon at Palm Springs, and Lennie was left alone to pack and carry out his final preparations. The problem of Wilma and the other staff was elegantly solved by giving Bel Air to Rose and Van Kerk as a wedding present: the staff would stay on and serve them. Van's modest downtown apartment was to be retained as a *pied à terre*, and Rose had only to move her personal things from the guest bungalow into the main house; and, when she returned from honeymoon, completely redecorate and refurnish the entire place, with an interview and photographs afterwards in a chosen leading magazine.

Wilma had dreaded being asked to go to England, but equally dreaded refusing and being put out of work and home. She scolded Lennie every time they met for abandoning them all, but she was so glad to have the decision taken from her she sang about her work when she thought no-one was listening; and in her room at nights she worked on a silk waistcoat as a present for him, appliquéd with California poppies – the state flower – which she embroidered round the edges in gold thread.

Lennie paid a farewell visit to ABO, where Al Feinstein treated him to a private viewing of the first cut of *Robin Hood*. Lennie thought it impressive. In particular, Morland Place looked much more substantial and convincing than the fake back-lot castles that were usually seen in movies. He said as much to Al, who preened himself. 'Yeah, worth every penny,' he said. 'And we got great publicity. Box office over there is going to be huge.'

'I'll make sure everyone I know goes to see it,' Lennie promised.

Al gave him a thoughtful look. 'You gonna stick over there? I hear it's a primitive place. Terrible plumbing.'

'It varies,' Lennie said. 'But I'm marrying the love of my life, so of course I'm going to stick.' Al harrumphed, and he added, 'I'm not quitting ABO. I'll still be in touch by cable. I'm interested in this new vehicle you've got for Rose – *Anastasia*?'

Al brightened. 'Yeah, we gotta keep the momentum going. If they like her as Lady Marian, they're gonna love her as the Tsar's daughter. Reznik says they're not called princesses, that right?'

'Grand duchesses,' Lennie confirmed.

'Don't like it. Sounds fruity, like some old dame with a blue rinse. Princess is better.'

'They had princesses, but grand duchess was a higher rank,' Lennie said, but he saw resistance in every line of Al's face. Well, that was a battle for another day – and Reznik

523

could fight it. He patted Al's arm affectionately. 'I'm going to miss you, you know.'

Feinstein's eyebrows shot up. 'Get outta here!' he said, in outrage.

Basil had been to interview a Russian émigré who claimed that the last Tsar of Russia was alive and living under an assumed name in Ireland. These stories surfaced from time to time and were popular with the readers. Mr Comstock did not approve of courting popularity, but the proprietor had said sometimes you had to give the readers what they wanted rather than what you thought was good for them.

The man, who called himself Ivan, was working backstage at a theatre in Charing Cross Road. Basil met him on a corner, huddled into his coat with the collar turned up, looking as nervous as a horse in a field full of pigs. He took him to a little café and bought him tea and a bun to lubricate his story.

Ivan said that he had been a footman to the imperial family when they were exiled in Tobolsk, and had had to flee because of his loyalty to them. He claimed that the whole family had been extracted by agents of the British government and replaced with doubles during the move to Ekaterinburg.

Despite the story, Basil was quite impressed with him. He both looked and sounded like a Russian, and when Basil tried to confuse him with questions, his story remained the same. He appeared scared, constantly looking over his shoulder, and insisting on speaking in a low voice with his mouth close to Basil's ear – disagreeably close, since his breath smelt strongly of onions. Basil was interested that, rather than the Bolsheviks, it was the British Secret Service he was most afraid of – he hadn't known there was such a thing. When he asked why Ivan was telling the story now, he said he wanted money so he could leave his current job and go to Ireland to seek out the Little Father and offer his devotion.

Basil thought it would make an entertaining short piece – if Dickins would run it at all. 'Get names and addresses,' the boss had told Basil more than once. It was the foundation stone of journalism. But Ivan was adamant he could not do that – and, when Basil pressed, seemed even to be regretting he had said as much as he had. On the whole, Basil thought it had been a waste of his time. He had been authorised to give up to five pounds for a good story, but without names and addresses he told Ivan it was worth nothing – though he relented at the end and gave him a quid for his entertainment value.

A little bit of sunshine in February was not to be sniffed at, and after leaving Ivan, Basil walked down to Trafalgar Square and sat on a low wall to enjoy it, contemplating where he might go for refreshments. He closed his eyes and basked, imagining the warmth on his face was the summer sun, until an uneasy feeling of being watched disturbed him. He opened them to see someone a few feet away staring at him. His heart skipped. 'Gloria!' he said. He stood up. 'Where did you spring from?'

'National Gallery,' she said tersely. But she was still standing there, not taking the opportunity to hurry away. 'What about you?' she asked at last.

'I've been on a story,' he said. 'I'm a journalist.'

'I know,' she said. 'You threw away the job I got for you, and now you're working for some trashy rag.'

'The *Messenger*. It's well respected in certain circles.'

'I know what circles.'

He didn't want to waste time arguing about the newspaper. 'You are looking wonderful,' he said. 'More beautiful than ever.'

She examined him. 'You've grown up,' she said at last.

He wasn't sure if it was said in compliment or disappointment. 'No bad thing,' he said. 'I was a callow boy when I first met you.'

'You were very pretty.'

'But any good qualities I have – and I know there are people who think I don't have many – I owe to you.' She said nothing, seemed to be waiting for some development. He didn't know what. He dropped the lightness of tone and said seriously, 'I've missed you so much.' Still she didn't speak – but also didn't move away. 'Will you let me buy you lunch?'

She shifted her feet, and turned her head a fraction, as though buffeted by a cold wind. For some reason, it encouraged him. She didn't want to march off, head in air, righteously offended. She wanted some way to continue talking to him, without losing face.

He moved a fraction closer. 'Gloria,' he said seriously, 'I did a bad thing, and hurt you, and believe me, I've regretted it every day since. I was young and stupid and spoiled, but I've learned my lesson. I've grown up. I've been in Spain and seen people die.'

'I know. I read the articles.'

'Did you? Well, that sort of thing makes you realise what really matters. If I had the chance again, I would treat you in the way you should be treated.'

'Why do you care?' she questioned, watching his face.

What would be the right words? 'You're the only woman I've ever cared for,' he said, and held his breath.

She gave a brisk little nod, as if agreeing the price of some not-very-important purchase. 'Then you can take me to lunch,' she said.

He suspected it was still a trial, so he hailed a taxi and told the driver to take them to the Criterion. It wasn't very far, but it was cold and Gloria was not shod for walking.

It seemed to be the right choice because, once settled at a table, she thawed, and they were soon chatting with their previous freedom – except that he was no longer a boy, and had things to contribute. It was with regret that he had to

526

go back to work, but she said she would see him that evening. He suggested the theatre, and she told him to call at her flat in Park Street, and they would decide then where to go.

He arrived, correctly togged in evening dress, with a taxi at the kerb, but she opened the door herself and told him to pay off the taxi. And they didn't go out at all that evening.

Lennie stepped down from the train, and Polly was there, waiting, bundled up against the cold in a fur coat that he remembered from New York, before Alec was born: Ren must have bought it for her. It was a very American affair, a glossy dark mink, large and lavish and long, with a huge collar.

'I bet no-one else in York has a coat like that,' he said, putting his bags down to free his hands.

'I've been mistaken for a film star, all due to the coat,' she said.

'It's not the coat, it's you,' he said, took both of her hands and bent to kiss her cold cheek.

'Everyone wanted to come and meet you, but here I am alone, no children, no dogs. You have no idea what an achievement that is. But I'm afraid when we get home there'll be a welcoming committee, and no chance of being alone for the rest of the day. Alec is beside himself with excitement. Mrs Starling has been planning dishes for days. Jessie and Bertie and the girls are coming over for dinner, and Jeremy and Amelia.'

'Ah, well. There's always after lights-out. Shall I find the door barred, if I come creeping?'

She looked up at him with sparkling eyes. 'What do you think?' They picked up a bag each and walked towards the exit, their free arms linked. 'Oh,' she said, 'Alec and the Lohmanns have something planned – some sort of revue, I believe. I know singing is involved, but I think there's playacting as well. They've been rehearsing up in the nursery all week.'

'How are they settling in, the little refugees?'

'Better than I hoped. I was prepared for months of sullenness and misery, but they've perked up wonderfully. They've even started school, which will make them learn English quickly. Alec's been wonderful. He treats them rather like exotic pets, showing them off to people, but he takes great care of them. He's even given up riding to school for the moment because they can't ride with him. Though I suspect the weather made that an easy choice. It's been so cold! It must be very strange for you – what was the weather like in California when you left?'

'Hot, sunny,' Lennie said. 'Though remember, I came here via New York, and you have no idea how cold it is there in winter.' He waved a hand at the frosty world around them. 'This is like a balmy summer day in comparison.'

Polly said she didn't need his help in any of the wedding plans, so he spent his days setting up the English office of Manning's Radios, and looking for a suitable site for a factory. A very few enquiries led him to the premises in Leeds of Cosway Radios. In 1932, radio enthusiasts Mr Cosgrove and Mr Waynfleet had sold Mr Cosgrove's motor-bicycle for the capital to begin making radio receiver sets. They now had a workshop employing ten people.

They had, of course, heard of Manning's Radios, and were flattered to be approached by Mr Manning himself. He showed them technical drawings of new models he had planned, talked inspiringly of expansion and new markets; and it did not take much persuasion for them to sell their business, on the modest condition that the best of the new models was named 'The Cosway' in their honour. They also knew of a vacant factory – in fact they had been eyeing it for themselves to expand into, but they didn't have the capital. Lennie set his agent to buy the new premises; he retained all of the Cosway staff and, liking the energy and enthusiasm of Mr Cosgrove and Mr Waynfleet, he employed them in higher management roles on generous salaries. Mr Waynfleet was to oversee the transfer of the Cosway kit and staff, the purchase and installation of new machinery, while Mr Cosgrove, who was unmarried, was to go on the road, in a new suit and smart haircut, to secure outlets for Manning's Radios in Leeds, Manchester, Liverpool, Birmingham, and thence to every other large conurbation.

Lennie, who had for some time employed others to do the bread-and-butter work of his business, thoroughly enjoyed getting in at the bottom again, and was happily employed by day. Evenings were spent with Polly at home, often entertaining or being entertained by various friends and neighbours who wanted to inspect him. It was rather, he thought, as though he were a foreign prince brought in to marry a queen regnant. Would he be a passive George of Denmark or an active Albert of Saxe-Coburg and Gotha? He thought he would endeavour to set a new template – supportive, discreet, modest, but nevertheless interesting – and be loved by all.

He heard whispers he was not meant to hear, that he was a millionaire, which was a cause of some excitement, and seemed, oddly, to tell against him slightly. Who knew what a millionaire might get up to? On the other hand, it was also passed around that he was a Morland by descent, through the American branch of the family, which meant he was made of the right stuff. And nobody seeing them together could doubt Polly adored him, so that had to be all right, hadn't it?

And at night, after the house was quiet, he slipped discreetly into the Great Bedchamber to sink into Polly's arms and a vast ocean of bliss. And this, he told himself, was only the beginning.

Polly had not heard from James with any regularity since he began helping to bring the Jewish children out of Germany. She had written telling him the date of her wedding, and begging him to come home for it, but hadn't had a reply, and she wondered if he had even received it. But on the 3rd of March a telegram came, saying merely, 'WOULDN'T MISS IT,' and she had to be satisfied with that. The wedding plans were all in place. Bertie was going to give her away. Alec and Bibi were to be pages, Ottilie, now seventeen, and Mimi bridesmaids. Mr Ordsall was to conduct the ceremony. There was to be a sit-down wedding breakfast for fifty in the large dining-saloon, and everyone else was to come in the evening for dancing and a buffet supper.

After which, Lennie would be licensed to enter the royal bedchamber openly and as of right.

'No honeymoon?' he asked, when Polly told him the details.

'It's a bit awkward at the moment,' she said. 'So much to do. And the weather isn't good. Could we have a week later in the year – in May or June, perhaps? We could go to the seaside. I'd like that.'

'Whatever you want,' he said. 'The rest of our lives will be our honeymoon.'

She kissed him. 'You say the nicest things.'

Speculation was rife about what the groom would buy for the bride for a wedding present, with the smart money on diamonds. Bagrath's the jewellers on Stonegate confidently redesigned their window display to show their choicest pieces – including a delicate tiara, such as would become a beautiful golden head, and must appeal to a millionaire in love.

But on the Thursday before the wedding, Lennie interrupted Polly in the steward's room and asked if she would come with him for a moment. 'It's your wedding present. I can't give it to you on the day, and I expect you'll be busy with last-minute arrangements tomorrow, so I want to give it to you now.'

'How mysterious you're being,' she said, but she got up from the desk obediently.

John Burton hesitated, and Lennie said, 'You can come too.' He led the way into the Great Hall, where already a number of people, including servants, were hovering, and Barlow was stationed at the great door, his face so wooden it was obvious he was trying not to grin.

'What on earth . . . ?' Polly said.

Barlow opened the door, and Lennie took her hand and led her through. In the yard, at the foot of the steps, Butterfield, the head man, stood with the reins in his hand of a dark bay thoroughbred gelding of fifteen-two.

'He's four years old,' Lennie said. 'His name is Orlando. Jessie and Roberta helped me find him. He's by Dante out of Enigma, which I'm told is a very respectable lineage.' He looked at Polly. 'You haven't said anything. Don't you like him? Roberta says he's very fast and he jumps, and Jessie says he's good to handle.'

Polly turned a shining face to him, 'He's *beautiful*,' she said. 'How did you think of such a thing? I thought you'd buy me a necklace or something.'

'Judging by how much time you spend in jodhpurs, that would have been rather a waste. I know Zephyr's getting on a bit, and that you'll need a new hunter soon, so this seemed a more *personal* present.'

She kissed him, more eloquent than words, and went down to steps to meet her horse.

James arrived on the 10th, looking tired, rumpled and smutty from the journey. Polly hugged him hard for a long time, then said, 'You smell of trains. You must want a bath.'

'I can't tell you how nearly I didn't get here. I should get top marks for effort. And I'm hoping someone will have some suitable togs I can borrow, because I wasn't able to pack much.'

'I'll see you kitted out,' Lennie said. 'We're about the same height.'

'Thanks. You're looking well,' James said, shaking his hand. 'Are you going to make this sister of mine happy?'

'If I don't, you'll hunt me down to the ends of the earth,' Lennie said.

'How did you guess what I was going to say? Alec! You rapscallion, what have you been up to? No good, I bet.' He swept the ecstatic Alec off his feet, into the air, hugged him, and deposited him again.

'I've been very good,' Alec protested. 'I'm going to be a page at Mummy's wedding and she says it's all right to wear breeches and stockings because the King does, at court. And Bibi is too, and Mimi's going to be a bridesmaid and throw flour at people.'

'I think that's flowers, isn't it?' James corrected. 'Are these your new friends?' He shook Bibi's hand in manly fashion, and bowed to Mimi, and won their hearts by addressing them in German.

'I didn't know you could speak German,' Polly said.

'I've had to learn. I'm proud of you, Pol, for taking in these two. I wish more people would. How have they been?'

'They seem to have settled very well.'

James nodded. 'I can't tell you the things I've seen. The terrible partings.' He stopped abruptly. 'I'm for a bath. And then I hope there's something substantial for dinner, because I haven't eaten all day.'

At dinner that night, James told them more about the state of affairs in Germany than they could have gleaned from the newspapers. 'Hitler has vowed to exterminate the Jews, in revenge for them "stabbing Germany in the back", as he puts it, in 1918. Everything is their fault, apparently. At his big annual speech to the Reichstag in January, he said that if there was another Great War, it would be their doing, and it would result in the annihilation of the Jewish race in Europe.'

'As I understood it,' Lennie said, 'the only person who wants a war is him.'

'Of course. The Jews are just an excuse. It's all about getting *Lebensraum* for the Fatherland, which is code for Germany spreading out and taking over any country it fancies. He's got Austria – Czechoslovakia will be next.'

'But Chamberlain brought back that piece of paper,' Polly objected.

'Czechoslovakia's not a stable country. The Slovaks want independence, and Hitler will use them to break it up and take it over. And some say he has Poland in his sights, too.'

Perplexed, Polly said, 'But what does that mean for us?'

'Britain, you mean? I don't know, Pol. I think it has to mean war in the end. However little we want to fight, we can't let Germany go on like this. You know what happened last time.'

'Well, I don't believe it,' Ethel said. She looked pale. 'There's not going to be a war. You shouldn't talk like that, James, spreading alarm. We got caught up in it last time, and for what? Let the French and the Belgians and the rest sort it out for themselves.'

Polly only gave her a glance, her eyes still on James. 'What will you do?' she asked.

'We won't be able to keep operating in Germany much longer,' he said, 'and I don't want to get trapped in France. As soon as it starts to look dangerous, I'll come home. If you'll have me.'

'Of course I will. It's what I want, to have my people here,' Polly said.

Lennie looked at her. Didn't she realise that if – when – the war started, James would be called up? Ethel knew that – she had two sons of fighting age. That was why she didn't want to believe war was likely. As an American citizen he, Lennie, would not be conscripted, but he had volunteered in the last war, and would he feel able to keep out of it if

533

things went bad? But Polly turned her eyes to him just for a moment, and he saw that she knew, all right. She wanted to have her people around her while she could; she knew it couldn't last.

Oliver came round his desk to shake Richard's hand.

'It's good of you to see me, Uncle Oliver.'

'What can I do for you?' He scanned Richard's face, smiling. 'I can't make you any more good-looking than you already are. That wouldn't be fair.'

Richard smiled too. 'It's not your surgical skills I'm after. It's your advice.'

'Oh. Well, sit down, and tell me all about it.'

It was hard at first for Richard to put it into words. It was all so very personal. Cynthia had recovered physically from the miscarriage, and the doctor had signed her off. But she was not herself. She was too quiet: she brooded, and her attempts to hide it and be jolly for him were painful. And at night, in bed, she kept turned away from him. When he tried to touch her, she flinched and pulled back. He wanted merely to hold her and comfort her, but she evidently viewed any contact as a prelude to sexual congress, and she very clearly didn't want that.

When at last he had – as gently as he could – tried to talk to her about it, she had burst into tears and begged him to leave her alone. 'I'm afraid,' she sobbed. 'I'm so afraid.'

From her barely coherent broken phrases, he gathered that she did not want to conceive again. The pain and distress of the miscarriage were things she did not want to revisit. She believed she was 'all wrong' inside and that she could never bear him a child. If they made love, and she conceived, it would only lead to another disaster.

And to the fear was added guilt. 'I'm no use to you,' she wept. He hated the idea that she saw him as a threat; he hated himself for doing that to her.

534

'I don't know what to do. I must help her, but I don't know how. And I thought – I hoped . . . You were so good to us when Papa died. And you know everything. I thought you might be able to tell me what to do, who to go and see. Recommend a specialist, perhaps, who could help us. I don't care what it costs.'

Oliver rubbed his chin, thinking. 'Do you believe it's her mind that most needs help, or her body? Do you want me to recommend a psychiatrist or a gynaecologist?'

Richard looked taken aback. 'She's not *mad*,' he protested.

Oliver lifted his hands in a soothing motion. 'Of course not. I didn't mean to suggest it. I should have said, would you like her to see a psychoanalyst? They talk to the patient, tease out the basis of the aberrant behaviour, help them to confront the cause and thereby achieve healing of the mind. Or do you think there is something physically wrong with her reproductive organs? In which case, a specialist in that field might be able to help.'

Richard, trying not to blush at the words 'reproductive organs', managed in the end only to say, 'I don't know.'

Oliver eyed him sympathetically. 'Of course you don't. Women's bodies are a mystery to most men. And what we don't understand scares us. Am I right?'

'I don't want to let her down,' Richard said miserably.

'Which doctor has been attending her?'

'Well, she saw Mother's doctor at first, of course, down at Tunstead. And since then, her old family doctor, Saloman, in Earls Court.'

'Old family doctor. Agreeable old fossil who knew her from a child?' Oliver suggested. 'And whom, therefore, she trusts implicitly, even though he qualified before the war *and* has no specialist knowledge of female reproduction?' Richard nodded uncertainly. 'Well,' Oliver said, 'it seems to me that the first thing is to find out whether there *is* any physical problem, and whether, if there is, it can be dealt with. And after that, if necessary, we can look at healing the mind.'

535

Richard felt a surge of relief. 'That sounds sensible.'

'Good. Then I recommend you make an appointment for her to see Felix Young, who is a gynaecologist I can recommend wholeheartedly – not only very knowledgeable, but also very *sympathique*, quite accustomed to dealing with shy and nervous patients. For some reason it helps that he is very handsome, and also – appropriately to his name – young. In medical terms. Mid-forties. You needn't worry that he doesn't know his stuff.'

'Thank you, Uncle. Thank you so much.'

Oliver got up and went to the door. 'Miss Holcombe. Can you look up Felix Young, and write down his address and telephone number for Mr Howard?' He came back and shook Richard's hand. 'Remember, this is very recent for her, and a shock of the sort we men can't really understand. Get the facts first, then deal with them. Miscarriages are quite common, and most probably there is nothing wrong with her, and the next time it will all go well.'

'Thank you.'

'And come and see me again if there's anything else I can do.' He smiled. 'Try not to worry too much.'

Richard smiled too, but it was a frail thing. 'There seems to be so much to worry about, these days.'

It was hard to persuade Cynthia to agree to consult Mr Young. She didn't want 'any more doctors messing me about' and she queried why he was only a mister and not a doctor. Richard explained that surgeons always called themselves 'mister'. That alarmed her. 'I don't want an operation!'

'I'm not suggesting one. Just a consultation to find out if there is a problem – inside. After all, you've never seen anyone who really knew what he was talking about. Apparently this Young fellow is the best.'

'You want a son to follow you, I know,' she said drearily.

He took her hands and gave them an encouraging shake.

536

'That's not what this is about. This is about putting your mind at rest. There's nothing worse than not knowing the facts. Let's find out, and then we can decide what to do. Or not do.'

'I won't have an operation,' she said, her lip trembling.

'No-one's saying you will. Just go and see this man, and find out if you're all right. You're probably worrying about nothing.'

To Richard's surprise, Hannah was on his side. 'See the specialist,' she urged. 'Dr Saloman is a good man, a wise man, but about women's problems he doesn't know. And he's getting old. There are new things being found out all the time. Go and see this young man who knows what he's talking about.'

So the appointment was made. Richard drove her to Harley Street and sat in the waiting room, holding her hand until she was called. She had dressed in her best for the occasion, in her good wool suit with a silk blouse, smart hat, baum marten piece around her neck, leather gloves. Richard guessed she had her best underwear on underneath, though he was not privy to that information. He knew what an ordeal his wife was about to undergo, simply in being examined by a strange man. She didn't even like him, her husband, to see her naked body.

She was in the consulting room for a long time. Richard sat in the waiting room and leafed through a copy of the *Lady* from the table. He read the small-ads. He got up and walked around, smoked a cigarette, sat down again and started on an article by Nancy Mitford. He looked at the clock, and smoked another cigarette. Examined the fashion drawings. His wife was tall, but even she didn't have legs that long. And at last the inner door opened, and Mr Young looked out, smiled, and said, 'Would you like to come in?'

He entered with trepidation, but Cynthia was fully dressed

and sitting on a chair on the near side of the desk. She wouldn't meet his eyes, and her cheeks were red, but she seemed calm. Young placed a chair for Richard beside her, and went round the other side to sit down.

'I thought you would probably like to hear what I've already told your wife,' Young said, clasping his hands on the desk top. He *was* good-looking, Richard thought, and he'd have bet a lot of his patients fell in love with the fair curly hair, the kind brown eyes and the crinkly smile.

'Please,' said Richard.

'After careful examination, I cannot find anything abnormal in Mrs Howard's physiology.'

'Then why did the other doctor say—?'

'I'm sorry to say it of a fellow practitioner, but perhaps he didn't know what he was looking at. But I assure you, this is my area of expertise. I see no reason why she should not be able to conceive and carry to term in a perfectly normal way.'

'That's good to hear,' Richard said.

He turned to smile at Cynthia, and reached out a hand, but she didn't take it, and gave him only a glance before turning her head away. There was no responding smile.

The 11th of March was a damp, windy day, but mild, and not actively raining. Lennie had slept apart from Polly that night, at her request. Her maid, Rogers, came in early with tea and toast, and went through to run her bath, with an anticipatory smile: she was an experienced lady's maid, and it was not often that she had a chance fully to exercise her skills.

Polly had long ago decided that it would not be appropriate to her age or widowed status to wear white. She had designed the wedding gown herself, and her own Makepeace ladies had made it up. It was of pale yellow figured silk, fitted at the bodice, with long sleeves, the skirt falling straight in front, with wide pleats at the back to create a modest train. She wore a circlet of yellow and white flowers, twined with pearls, on her head.

'You look lovely, madam,' Rogers said, when she had finished.

'For goodness' sake, don't start crying or you'll set me off,' Polly said. 'I don't look too old to be a bride?'

'You look like a fairy princess,' Rogers assured her. 'Mr Manning is the luckiest man in the world.'

When she went downstairs, everyone was gathered in the Great Hall, and when Mimi stepped forward to give her a tiny posy of jonquils and winter jasmine to carry, they burst into spontaneous applause, and several of the women into tears. Bertie came forward to give her his arm. The pages and bridesmaids, all in cream silk, fell in behind, and they processed to the chapel. Daffodils had been massed on every available surface, like pools of sunshine. James was acting as supporter, and Lennie stood at the altar in sober morning suit, made resplendent by Wilma's waistcoat, yellow and gold poppies on a background of forest green.

Polly had no idea what expression was expected of a bride at this moment, but she knew that at the sight of him and the realisation that she was really marrying him, her face had broken into a smile of delight so wide it was practically an urchin grin.

So they were married. And Morland Place rejoiced in a very traditional manner, with so much joy it must have soaked into the walls inside, as the sunshine was warming the stones outside.

The fate of Czechoslovakia was being decided even as Polly was getting married. Slovak agitation had become so violent that the government in Prague had declared martial law on the 10th of March. On the 11th Hitler sent two emissaries to Bratislava, the Slovak capital, to urge the nationalists to declare independence from the Czech republic. But they hesitated, so on the 13th he summoned Tiso, the leader of the Slovak People's Party, to Berlin, berated him for his pusillanimity, and forced on him a document to sign, prepared by the German Foreign Ministry, declaring Slovak independence and dated the 14th. German troops were already in position on the Czech border. Hitler then summoned the Czech president and foreign minister to Berlin, and told them they must accept Slovak independence and a German protectorate, or Germany would bomb Prague. At four o'clock in the morning of the 15th, they gave in, signed away Czech sovereignty and agreed to hand over Czech military equipment.

'And two hours later, the German troops marched in,' said Basil, 'and Hitler was in Prague by the evening, giving orders for rounding up anyone considered dangerous to the new order. Not even a pretence of getting consent from the people this time. This looks like a new phase – blatant occupation by force. And so Czechoslovakia has ceased to exist.'

'You really have changed,' Gloria said, running a finger over his bare chest. 'Two years ago you hadn't the faintest notion of politics or world affairs.'

He turned on his side and stroked her shoulder. 'There are better things to talk of with a beautiful woman.'

'Don't do that,' she said. 'I'm not a silly girl. I'm quite capable of talking about world affairs, even in bed.'

Basil preferred to kiss her, and found her ready for love, despite her words. It felt very natural to be back in her bed. He'd have called the experience comfortable, except that the word suggested the love-making was not exciting, which it was. Sex was always exciting to a healthy young man, of course, but now, two years on, it was more than that. It was satisfying in a way he had not expected: it was not something *he* did, but something *they* did. Was he becoming a less shallow person? If so, he owed it to her, which was funny, because he could never tell his nearest and dearest the cause of his improvement.

After love, they sat up and lit cigarettes, and talked some more. 'Do you think it will all end in war?' she said.

He thought about it seriously. 'I used to pooh-pooh the idea, but now I can't see how it can be avoided. If you let a burglar into your house and watch him take your silver without saying anything, he's not going to thank you politely and go away, is he? He's going to take everything else in the house. The question is, at what point do you say, "Enough!", and grab for the poker?'

'We haven't reached that point yet,' she said.

'No, evidently. But I can't see this particular burglar stopping until either he's defeated, or one of his own side murders him.' She was silent. He went on, 'There is one other possible defence – make your house impossible to break into.'

'What do you mean?'

'Make our armed forces so powerful that Mr Hitler decides to leave us alone. But that will take time, given that we've never maintained a large standing army. And arms are even harder to get hold of than men – in the final event, you can force the population into uniform, but you can't just will guns into existence.'

'So we're playing for time?' Gloria said. 'For how long?'

'I have no idea,' Basil said. 'Mr Chamberlain doesn't confide in me.'

'I was thinking, you see, of Anthony. He finishes at Eton in June.'

Basil preferred to forget she had a son; he didn't like being reminded of how old that son was. 'They won't send an eighteen-year-old to the Front,' he said shortly.

'No, but a nineteen-year-old they will. They did last time.' Basil couldn't deny it. 'Have you thought what you'll do, if there is a war?'

He thought of the dinner party, and Lord Culbeath, and

541

Special Services. But that was secret stuff. 'Oh, I'll do something in Intelligence, if I get the choice.'

'You may not,' Gloria said. 'You'll have to go where they send you.'

'Well, one has to do one's duty.'

'Cedric wants to run away to America, and take Anthony with him.' Cedric was her husband. He was thirty years her senior, and they lived more or less separate lives, he mostly at their house down in Surrey, while Gloria stayed in Town. Anthony spent most of his time when he was not at school with his father in the country. 'I don't want him to make Anthony a coward. He says he can't risk losing him because he's his only son – but he's my only son too!'

He said awkwardly, to comfort her, 'No-one in this country wants war.' That was not true, he knew: there were always hotheaded young men who couldn't wait to get out there and biff the enemy – and belligerent old men who couldn't wait to send them.

'But you wouldn't run away, would you? You want to fight?'

'Well . . .' He hesitated. '. . . it's not exactly that I want to fight. But it would be awfully poor spirited to scuttle off and miss all the fun. Does Anthony want to go?'

'I don't know. Cedric won't let me ask him. But he's not of age, so if his father takes him away, he has to go.'

'What about you? Will you go?'

'Not on your life! I'm staying. If the Germans come, they'll have to come through me.'

Basil laughed and rolled her into his arms. 'Wildcat! That's the spirit!'

'I think war is going to let a lot of things off a lot of leashes,' she said, between kisses.

Oliver walked into the House of Lords bar, and raised a hand to Kit.

542

Kit nodded to him, and said to the barman, 'Two pink gins, George.' He brought the drinks to the table where Oliver had settled, and said, 'Well!'

'Well!' said Oliver.

'A defence pact with Poland. I didn't see that coming,' said Kit.

'Nor did I. It was only two weeks ago the Old Man was saying everything in Europe is serene. I thought he'd do anything rather than precipitate war.'

'Better a deal with the Devil than a plunge into the fiery pit,' Kit said.

'I can't tell if that was approval or irony,' Oliver said.

'Oh, approval. Anything but war. It's all right for old fellows like you. I'm forty-six, still within range for being called up.'

'May I remind you that conscription went up to fifty-five in the last war? And that there was no practical limit for the Medical Corps?'

'May I remind you that I don't practise medicine any more? They'd chuck me in the Poor Bloody Infantry, and that'd be the end of me.'

Avis came in, spotted them, ordered whisky-and-soda, and came over to sit down. 'Well!' he said.

Kit nodded. 'That's exactly what we said.'

'I've been talking in the corridor to young Elphinstone from the War Office. They're still hoping a deal can be done with Hitler over the Polish Corridor and Danzig: let him have his route to the sea and he'll leave Poland alone. But just in case . . .' His whisky came. 'Just a splash,' he told the waiter with the siphon. When he'd gone, Avis gulped some of his drink as though he'd needed it. 'Now we've made this pact, if Hitler *does* move against Poland, that will be that.'

'We need time,' Oliver said.

'Exactly,' said Avis. 'The French are in a mess, nobody knows which way the USSR will jump, the Dominions are wobbling, and you can't rely on the USA giving up its neutrality. And Halifax believes it's by no means certain that Hitler *will* move against Poland. Elphinstone said the Americans think he'll invade Holland.'

'Which makes much more sense,' said Kit. 'Nice and handy for jumping to Blighty. In any case, what's Poland to us? We didn't object to the wee moustached one taking over Czechoslovakia.'

'That's because France wouldn't defend the Czechs but she will defend the Poles,' said Oliver. He intercepted Kit's raised eyebrow. 'I talk to people too. Why do you think I have all those dinner parties?'

'To be sure of getting decent grub,' said Kit, promptly. 'But Belmont here just said the French were in a mess.'

'Yes, but they're arming as hard as they can go,' Avis said.

'They have more to fear than us,' Oliver noted.

'And they still have twice as many men under arms as we do,' Avis concluded. 'In the end, they're the only Allies we can count on.'

'All the more reason not to go to war,' Kit said.

Avis nodded. 'You can be sure Chamberlain will do anything he can to avoid it, whatever Churchill and his friends say.'

They drank in silence for a moment. Then Kit said, 'So, what now?'

'Well, the die is cast,' said Oliver. 'We'll have to go all out for rearmament.'

'That's what Elphinstone told me,' said Avis. 'Apparently the order's already gone out to double the size of the Territorial Army. And they're planning to have in place an expeditionary army of two corps – four divisions – ready to go to France at the outbreak of war.'

'And when,' Kit asked with delicate irony, 'will that be?'

'God knows,' said Avis. He drained his glass. 'Another?'

544

CHAPTER TWENTY-THREE

The April weather was unexpectedly benign, and Richard was busy with the finishing of the holiday village site. The chalets were all built and only wanted painting, the sanitation units were just waiting to be furnished and connected, and the construction of the public buildings was well in hand. They would be ready for a summer opening – ironically, considering the low rumble of expectation about a war coming. If they went to war, there was little chance anyone would be going on holiday. And what would he do then? Unused, the buildings would deteriorate, to say nothing of having no return on his investment. The last war had gone on for four years.

One day he received a letter from the Air Ministry, asking him to attend for a meeting. He didn't tell Cynthia, knowing she would jump to the conclusion that it would be something bad. She'd seemed a little happier after seeing Mr Young, and her appetite had improved, but she still turned away from him in bed, and he knew her recovery was fragile. He'd tell her afterwards, when he knew what it was about. He thought it must be something to do with procuring or hiring motor vehicles.

When he presented himself at Adastral House on Kingsway, and gave his name, the porter at the desk looked him up on a list, and told him he was to see the Administrator of Works and Buildings, and summoned a messenger boy to conduct him there. The administrator, a pleasant-faced but worn-looking man in his fifties, sat Richard down, offered him tea, and told him kindly that the Air Ministry was going to requisition his whole holiday camp site.

'It's ideal for our purposes,' he said. 'As you know, the east coast will be one of the first targets for enemy aircraft.' He didn't name the enemy – Richard gathered that the Air Force, at least, had no doubt they'd be fighting the Germans in the near future. 'The land in Lincolnshire is flat and we're building several new airfields there. Your holiday camp will provide us with accommodation for the officers, and administration and works buildings.'

'Holiday village,' Richard corrected automatically.

'I beg your pardon?'

'Not holiday camp, holiday village.' Samuel had been insistent on that point.

The administrator gave him a strange look. 'If you wish.'

'So,' Richard went on, 'do I have any choice?'

'I'm afraid not. That's what "requisition" means. There will, of course, be compensation. And it will be returned to you at the end of the emergency, either restored to previous condition, or with a grant for you to restore it.'

'The emergency? The war, you mean?'

'We call it the state of emergency,' he insisted politely.

When he got home that evening, he knew at once something was up. Cynthia met him in the hall, and Hannah and Leah were behind her, waiting in the doorway of the sitting-room.

'What is it?' he asked at once, Nevinson's Holiday Villages forgotten. 'What's happened?'

She took a shaky breath. 'A man came to the door just a little while ago. He had an armband. He said he was the warden for this building.'

'What sort of warden?'

She wrinkled her brow. 'He did say. Something about air raids.'

'Air Raid Precaution? ARP?'

'That was it,' Hannah said. 'He had the letters on his armband.'

'I didn't know anything about it,' Cynthia said. 'Air raids, Richard?' She looked tearful.

'If there's a war,' he said.

'He asked how many were in the household,' she went on. 'Adults, children and babies. I told him four adults. And he left *those*.'

She gestured with her head, and he saw, on the hall table, a stack of four square-ish cardboard boxes. He took the top one and opened the lid. A black rubber face, with a hose for a snout and big round glass eyes, like the head of a nightmare pig, glared balefully at him. 'Gas masks.'

'He said everyone in the country would be given one eventually, but they were starting with London and the Home Counties because that was the most likely target. For gas attacks. He said we had to practise wearing them so as to be ready. We tried them on—'

'It's not easy,' Hannah said. 'There's instructions on the box, but it's not easy to get it on.'

'The smell is terrible,' Leah blurted out.

'It's hard to breathe,' Cynthia said. 'You have to drag the air in. It tastes of rubber and it makes you feel sick. Oh, Richard! Gas?'

'It's just a precaution,' he said helplessly. 'It might never happen.'

She walked away from him abruptly, went into the sitting-room. He was still in his coat and hat. Hannah, a little shame-faced, said, 'She's upset, that's all,' and helped him off with them. Then she hustled Leah towards the kitchen. 'I'll get supper on, now you're home.'

Richard went into the sitting-room, where Cynthia was standing, her back to him, apparently studying the fire in the grate. 'Darling,' he said hesitantly.

She turned. There were tears on her cheeks. 'I can't bear it,' she said.

'Nobody wants a war. But if it comes, we have to be ready.' She shook her head – *It's not that*. 'What is it?' he asked gently.

'I don't want a baby if there's going to be a war,' she blurted out. 'What kind of a life would there be for it?'

'There've always been wars, but people go on living, babies go on being born. More than ever, when times are bad, we need hope. A new generation.' She shook her head again – this time *I don't agree*. 'Tell me,' he said. 'What do you want?' She looked at him with hopeless, miserable appeal, and he had to guess. 'Do you want to go to America?'

'Oh, Richard!' she said, and then she was crying properly.

He took her in his arms and let her cry into his collar. 'You want to go to America? Soon?' She made a noise of assent. 'Then you shall go.' She made another sound. He was getting good at interpreting. 'Of course, your mother and Leah too. That was always the plan.' She murmured against his wet neck. 'I will take you myself,' he said. 'It will only need a few days to arrange. Don't worry, darling. The war is still a long way off.' Though he didn't know, of course. Did anyone know?

'You'll take us?' she said, detaching herself and dragging out a handkerchief.

'Of course.'

'And you'll stay too?' His hesitation was her answer. She emerged from blowing her nose to stare.

'I can't abandon the country now,' he said. 'If the war comes, I'll be needed.' He was thirty-eight, in the prime of life. 'I'll have to fight. They'll need everyone they can get. We have to keep the Germans out. We have to defeat them.'

'You'll leave me there?'

'I'll see you settled. You'll be all right. And when the war's over, you can come back. I'll come and fetch you.'

She turned away from him again, stared at the fire, picked up the poker and prodded it a little. With her back still turned, she said, 'I'll stay with you. Mummy and Leah can go.'

She turned at last, and searched his face. It came to him that this was a deciding moment, but he had no idea what to say or do. He had no idea even what he was feeling. He said hesitantly, 'It's up to you.'

He saw something die in her face, and knew he had not said the right thing, whatever that might have been. 'I'll go, then,' she said. 'Mummy will need me. I think Daddy would want me to take care of her.' She turned and knelt down to put more coal on the fire. 'Will you stay here, or go to Ealing?'

'Here, I suppose,' he said vaguely, still trying to think it out. 'I'll have to sell the Ealing house. We can't keep leaving it empty. We can buy somewhere else after the war.' She said something, but he didn't hear through the rattling of the fire-shovel. 'What was that?'

'I said, when can we go?'

'On Monday? Will that give you enough time to pack?'

'Yes, thank you,' she said. She stood up, brushing her hands off, and said, 'I'd better go and see if they need help with supper.' And she went.

He didn't know what had just happened, but he felt he had crossed a line – whether starting or finishing he couldn't say.

She hadn't even poured him his evening glass of sherry. He had to get it himself.

James came in out of the chilly April rain, shook himself off, and went into the canteen. The small former factory near the station, which they had taken over as headquarters, was warm inside, and the canteen was steamy with smells of food and cigarettes. He received a tin plate of sausage and bean stew and a tin mug of coffee, and went and sat down at one of the long trestles. The canteen was full, but he got himself

549

onto the end of one of the benches and saved the space next to him.

He saw Emil come in, and waved to him; but Emil stopped just inside the door, in deep conversation with Tante Lotti. Eventually, they came over together.

'James, we have to talk to you,' Lotti said. She took the space at the end of the bench; Emil stood at her shoulder.

'Has something happened?' he asked. He hoped it was nothing that would require a lot of talk. He was starving, and the food in front of him smelt good. He hadn't eaten since their early breakfast.

Emil said, 'I've had a cable from my father. He wants me to come home.'

'Oh,' said James, blankly.

'Things are becoming dangerous,' Lotti said. 'You know that your government has signed a pact with Poland, guaranteeing their independence? Well, yesterday Britain and France extended the guarantee to Romania and Greece. It has absolutely infuriated the Führer. He was quite deranged with rage, they say. He said if England wanted war, it should have a war, one of destruction beyond imagination. He said no English town would be left standing.'

'But that's just—' James began.

She went on without waiting. 'The point is, James,' she rested a hand on his forearm, 'your British passport will no longer be a protection for you. Rather the opposite. Much as we have valued your work, you are no longer safe here.'

'I don't care about that,' he said automatically.

'But if you were arrested, it would endanger the whole operation. Your part in the Kindertransport is done, my friend.'

'And I'm going back to Switzerland,' Emil said. 'Papa wants me – he's planning some sort of resistance movement and I have to help with that. And Mama's getting nervous about me. So I think I'll go.'

James looked at Lotti. 'But you'll stay.'

'For the moment.' She read his thought. 'No, James, you can't help me. I shall have to leave too, in the end, but now it is time for you to go back to Paris. But, if you take my advice, don't linger there too long. Remember France has signed the pact as well. When the war comes, France won't be safe.'

And so, as abruptly as that, it was over. The next morning James took the train to Paris.

He went straight to see Hélène. '*Chéri!*' she cried. '*Tu voici?*'

'I went to my apartment and was told someone else was living there,' he said.

She shrugged. 'I needed somewhere for someone, and an empty apartment is an abomination. I have your things. You can stay here for the moment, until I find you somewhere else. Depending on what your plans are. Are you going home?'

He felt restless. The ending had been too abrupt; he hadn't adjusted yet. 'Not at once,' he said. 'I need something to do. Have you got anything for me?'

'As it happens,' she said, 'there is something that you would be perfect for.'

'Escorting your American guests?'

'No, *chéri*, they are all going home, or have gone already. But all my artworks and beautiful things are here, and I want to get them to safety before – what do you English say? – the balloon goes up? Our friends Charlie and Fern are back at Candé, and they have offered to store them for me. So I want someone to help pack everything up and drive it down there. I have a small lorry but it will take several trips. You are strong in the arms and the back.' She stroked an upper arm admiringly. 'And you are a good driver. Would you like this job?'

He didn't hesitate. It would tide him over until – until what? Well, whatever came next. 'Yes, I would.'

'And how long are you saying? Must I find you a lodging?'

'I don't know how long. But I will go back to England when the war begins.'

'You had better have my spare room. You can unpack in a little while. First, we must go out to luncheon. I suppose you have not had anything good to eat in a long time. We will go to Prunier – I have a fancy for oysters.'

It was only when they were in the street, and James was demonstrating his undiminished ability to summon a Paris taxi, that she said, 'Oh, there is one American who has come back instead of leaving. *Comme c'est pervers!* She used to work for Charlie Bedaux – I expect you know her? The Mademoiselle McLean.'

'Meredith?' James heard himself say.

'*C'est ça.* Meredith. You will see her tonight – she comes to dinner. And I have other guests – you will be a good boy and help me entertain?'

'Of course,' said James.

Polly was happy. She could not have imagined beforehand how happy she could be, because before her dreams had been of Erich, and everything about loving him had involved some strain, some unnatural effort. Hopeless longing could only result in a bliss intense, yes, but perilous. It was a fairy tale full of tests and trials, dragons and ogres to overcome, and the airy spires of the palace she strove to reach were insubstantial, dislimning into the clouds.

Lennie was real. He was solid and warm and so very *there*. He could be touched and talked to and argued with. He responded, he understood, he engaged with what interested her; he cared for what she cared for. She loved every moment when she was with him, and when she was not with him, she stored up everything she saw and heard and thought to share with him when they were together again. He was the litmus paper to her life that proved it was real. She felt safe with him, knowing she was loved. She never doubted him for a moment. She *knew* him.

But at night, in the darkness of the bedchamber, he was anything but ordinary. She loved the smell of his skin, the touch of his hands, the taste of his mouth. In the dark, she thought you would never suspect daytime Lennie was like this, and it was delightfully secret and slightly wicked . . . Except that sometimes, in the daytime, she would catch him looking at her, and for a moment their eyes would meet and a shiver would run down her spine, because the eyes that looked back were the night-time eyes . . .

Alec had forgotten his Mr Murdstone fears, and evidently trusted Lennie as he trusted his mother – and probably found him more interesting. He always rushed to him the moment he got home from school with some question, or tale of what he'd done, or scheme for an adventure. His only difficulty was what to call him. He couldn't quite call him 'Father', and Lennie didn't require it. Mostly it was Uncle Lennie, but sometimes the 'Uncle' slipped. Lennie didn't seem to mind.

Lennie kept them all informed about world affairs, which otherwise could get pushed aside by local matters. It was he who told Polly that on the 15th of April, President Roosevelt appealed to Germany and Italy to give a ten-year guarantee not to attack any of their neighbours – an idea that Hitler rejected out of hand. It was Lennie who explained the importance of the Polish corridor, a strip of land, formerly part of Germany, that linked the greater part of Poland to the sea at the city-state port of Danzig. Danzig had been made a free city after the war, when the corridor was created. Berlin wanted a road and rail link across the corridor, and the termination of the 'free' status of Danzig and its return to Germany.

'Poland's always been afraid of the Soviet Union,' he said, 'but they've had good relations recently with Germany – they signed a non-aggression pact in 1934. Not to mention that Danzig has a National Socialist government.'

'That means Nazi, doesn't it?'

'Yes. So, of course, Hitler must think that Poland will be glad to throw in its lot with Germany as a defence against Russia. He'll expect it to be a tame satellite country. But the Polish leaders may not trust him not to go further. You see, the Polish corridor divides the main bulk of Germany from the East Prussian part, making East Prussia an enclave. So much easier all round, then, for Germany to seize the corridor and link the two parts again. And then, well, why not take the rest of Poland too, while they're at it, and make a nice, tidy job of it?'

'I see,' Polly said.

'And since we did nothing to defend the Czechs, Hitler must believe we'd make a big noise if he took Poland, but wouldn't actually *do* anything.'

'You make it all so clear. Thank you.' She thought for a moment, then said, 'I have to go to Manchester for a couple of days to visit the mills. Would you like to come with me?'

'Enticing prospect. But I have to go to London for a couple of days on business, so it would make sense to do that at the same time.'

'Business?'

'Setting up financial and supply chains. And I want to go to Harrods, and persuade them to stock Manning's Radios. The King and Queen shop there, apparently. It would be a fine thing if they bought one.'

'Manning's Radios, By Royal Appointment,' Polly said. 'Why not?'

Lennie's trip overran, so Polly was at home without him when, on the 27th of April, she came in to breakfast and found Ethel pale and tearful, John staring at his hands, his ears red with embarrassment, and everyone talking at once.

'What's going on?' she asked.

It was Harriet who answered. 'It's in the newspaper today,'

she explained. 'They've passed something called the Military Training Act. Men between twenty and twenty-two have to register for military training.'

'It's a sort of conscription,' Martin added. 'It's interesting, because it's the first time there's ever been peacetime conscription—'

'*Interesting!*' Ethel cried savagely. 'Don't you dare call it interesting! You're talking about my boy being ripped from my arms and sent to war. I won't have it! They'll have to take him over my dead body!'

John actually spoke for himself. 'It's not that bad, Mum. You do six months' military training, and you come home again. And then you're on the active reserve.'

'Which means they can take you back any time. I won't allow it.'

'When you get the letter, you have to register,' he said. 'It's the law.'

'Well, if they come for you, we'll hide you,' Ethel said. 'You're not going to fight!'

'Daddy did,' he said. 'You always said you were proud of him for going to fight.'

Polly saw Ethel had been put on the spot. Robbie had gone to war and not come back, and once someone was dead, you had to say you were proud of them. But Polly had heard Jessie say that Ethel had been outraged at the time when Robbie was called up, and had demanded he get himself out of it by whatever means possible. She'd even urged him once to claim to be a conscientious objector.

'That was different,' Ethel said weakly.

Polly intervened. 'If we go to war, he'll have to go anyway,' she said. 'Isn't it better for him to get thorough training now, in peacetime, when they can take their time about it and do it properly, rather than do it in a rush in wartime and get sent out without all the skills he'll need?'

Ethel opened her mouth and closed it again. Then she

jumped up and cried, 'Oh, what do you know about it? You don't have to worry about *your* son!' And she rushed out of the room in tears.

There was a short silence, then John rose, muttered something about going to work, and slunk out. Polly felt sorry for him. He demanded so little of life: just to mess about in car engines all day, and not be harassed by his mother at home.

Martin got up as well, and said, 'I must be off too.' Since leaving university, he had got a 'temporary' post at St Peter's School, teaching Latin and Greek, until he decided what he wanted to do with his life. But he had been there almost a year already, and the temporary looked like becoming permanent. Polly suspected that the will-there-be-won't-there-be question of war with Germany had made him think there was no point in long-term plans. He caught her eye, and as if he had read her thought, he said, 'I'll be getting a letter too.' He shrugged. 'No point in bleating about it. Coming, Harriet? We can get the bus together.'

Harriet crunched the last of her piece of toast, stood up, and they went out together.

Lennie had been surprised and slightly perplexed that Morland Place didn't have a radio receiver set. He had helped Alec build his little crystal radio from a kit, and Alec loved it, so he knew he had a natural ally, and asked him one Saturday if he would like to come with him to Leeds to choose Mummy a birthday present.

'Is it a secret?' Alec asked.

'Definitely,' said Lennie. 'We'll hide it somewhere so she won't find it.'

'Is it another horse?'

'That would be hard to hide. Besides, I'm capable of thinking of a different present this time.' He was about to add, 'I'm not a one-trick pony,' but desisted, realising it would lead to confusing dialogue.

Polly obligingly evinced no curiosity about where they were going, and saw them off in the Vauxhall, Alec sitting in the front seat beside Lennie, looking proud enough to burst. He was rarely taken on trips, and everything interested him, from the new lambs in the fields, stotting away madly as they went past, to the different buildings of Leeds as they drove through the suburbs and into the centre. And he loved being shown the Manning's Radio factory, seeing the manufacturing processes, being smiled at and petted by the workers. He examined the finished sets with brow-buckling seriousness and, pondered their performance like a small, scab-kneed professor. He was beguiled by their exotic names: the Manhattan, the Belmont, the Hollywood. Lennie honoured him with the final choice of set for his mother's birthday, and barely needed to guide him towards the Manning Baby Grand, because it was the biggest and most luxurious in the place.

When it had been carefully manoeuvred into the back of the Vauxhall, wrapped in blankets for safety and secrecy, Uncle Lennie rounded off the perfect outing by taking Alec to luncheon in the restaurant at Schofield's, the department store. They had steak with fried potatoes, and after that Alec had a Knickerbocker Glory, which was simply too marvellous for words. Plying the long spoon, through layers of ice cream and fruit, sponge and cream, glutted with sensory pleasure, Alec blurted, 'This is the best day of my life, Dad!'

He plainly didn't realise what he had called Lennie, and Lennie didn't comment. It might never happen again, but it was a token of the feeling between them that Lennie treasured. Young David had never called Mr Murdstone 'Dad'.

May was a beautiful month in France, and nowhere more beautiful than in the Touraine, with its meadows and trees and winding water. The lavish greenness was almost dazzling: it made James envy the cows for being able to eat that lush grass. It looked so delicious.

557

He'd thought his first meeting with Charlie Bedaux might be embarrassing, because he had left him so suddenly and not kept in touch, but Charlie did not hold grudges. He met him with the same warm openness as always.

Bedaux's fortunes had sunk since the aborted visit to the States planned for the Duke and Duchess of Windsor. After the German trip, the Nazis had returned to Bedaux his confiscated company, seized in 1933, and unpleasant rumours had circulated in America that he had been given it in return for unspecified services to them. In fact, it had cost him fifty thousand dollars, and the Nazi government seized it back again only six months later, without his ever having had any income from it. But his unpopularity in America was secured, and he was forced to flee to Europe when presented with a tax bill for a quarter of a million dollars. Since then he had been pursuing interests in Turkey, Greece, India, South Africa and other places, trying to recoup his fortunes.

James learned he was just back from doing unspecified business in Germany, and gave him a doubtful look. But Bedaux said, 'Come on, James, I thought you knew me better than to believe those lies about me. I'm no Nazi sympathiser. I'm on the same side as you. I know about your Kindertransport efforts, by the way – well done!'

'So what *were* you doing in Germany?' James asked.

'It has to be kept secret – you understand why – but there's a lot of high-level opposition to Hitler. If he can be brought down before he invades another country . . . I'll say no more. How's my friend Hélène? She was flourishing, when I last saw her, despite the international situation. She's the sort of person who falls on her feet. I like lucky people – they're always better company.'

And James, remembering how kind he had been, not just after Tata's death, but all through their association, allowed himself to sink back into the warm embrace of Charlie's charm.

'Tell me,' Charlie said, 'what's Meredith been up to since she left us?'

This conversation was taking place on the occasion of the first delivery to the château: Meredith and Fern were having tea in the drawing-room, and Charlie had invited James outside for a smoke.

It had been, of course, the first question he had asked Meredith, when they'd met at last at Hélène's. She had looked exactly the same to him as when he had last seen her –beautiful, intelligent, out of his reach. He had not been able to get much of her story that evening, among the other guests and the usual noise of a dinner party, but she had come again the next morning, before Hélène was up, and James had sat with her in a sunny bay window overlooking the street and they had talked for a long time.

In short, she had been at her father's ranch until November 1938, helping her brothers run the place, feeling unable to leave her mother to their tender mercies: they were outdoorsmen, good people, but short on social graces and even shorter on conversation. But in September two things had happened: her mother, who had been growing frail for some time, died quietly in her sleep; and almost immediately, both her brothers had got married.

'I was taken completely by surprise,' she told James. 'You think you know your own family, don't you? I had no idea they had any interest in women. I'd never seen them do any courting. But the Cunninghams, who own the next spread to ours, are Scottish-American like us, run cattle and horses the same as us, and they had two daughters and no sons. So it was logic rather than romance.' She laughed. 'I'm not sure my brothers even knew until the last minute which one each of them was marrying. Maybe they tossed a coin. I don't know. Maybe it doesn't even matter. There was a double wedding, two Cunningham females moved into our house, and there it was. Suddenly I wasn't needed any more. I could have my life back. And I knew I didn't want to spend it in Wyoming. I knew I was going to go back to Europe, but I didn't know where. Then I read about the refugee camp in Perpignan.'

In December 1938, half a million Spanish refugees, fleeing the civil war, poured over the Pyrenees in the most terrible winter weather, and into southern France, where the authorities did their best to care for them, but were overwhelmed by sheer numbers.

'They needed all the help they could get, every volunteer who could be mustered. So I went,' she said simply. 'Administration. Just recording their names and trying to reconnect divided families was a huge job. Driving, first aid. Trying to find somewhere for them to go. The USA took thousands, chartered a ship to take them, but it all had to be organised. I stuck at it until April, and then I decided I wanted to see Paris again, while I still could. You know, the rumours of war? And the obvious person to go to in Paris was Hélène. And here I am.'

She clasped her hands between her knees (she was wearing trousers – since Marlene Dietrich it was daring but acceptable, at least in France) and looked pensively out of the window. James admired her profile, wondering whether she remembered that day on the Pont Neuf when she had refused his offer of marriage but had given him permission to court her – surely an indication that she might one day say yes.

'Why did you never write to me?' he asked. Until he heard his voice, he hadn't been sure he was going to, because the obvious, most likely answer, was the most hurtful one, wasn't it? And he didn't want to be hurt again. That magical evening, looking down at the river . . . So much water had passed under the bridge since then.

She turned back from the window and looked at him sadly, and he thought she was going to tell him the horrible truth, that she didn't care for him, had never cared for him. She would try to do it kindly, let him down gently.

560

'Oh, James,' she said. 'What would have been the point? I couldn't leave the ranch. There I was in Wyoming, and there you were in Paris with half a world between us. As far as I knew, I was never going to be able to leave. Or, at least, not for years and years. And by then, your life and mine would have moved so far apart.' She stopped, looked down at her hands, freed them from between her knees and folded them together. It looked like a casual movement, but he saw her knuckles whiten. 'For all I knew,' she said, 'you were married.' She looked up at him. 'Why aren't you?'

This was not the moment to mention Tata. 'Why aren't you?' he countered.

She gave a dry bark of a laugh. 'Have I not given you an idea of what life is like on a ranch in Wyoming? Who on earth could *I* have married? But you, with all the women in Paris no doubt chasing after you?'

'But they weren't you,' he said.

She looked at him with disbelief. 'Don't tell me you never looked at another woman after I left.'

He thought the truth – or some of it – was safer: she was an intelligent woman. 'I didn't say that. I did look. I even kissed a few.' She lifted a hand as if to stop him going further. 'But they weren't you. I asked you to marry me, don't you remember?'

'Boy-and-girl romance,' she said dismissively. But her expression was not indifferent.

He said, 'You told me then that I could court you. May I now?'

She laughed shakily. 'What a nice, old-fashioned English word.'

He unfurled one of her hands from the other and held it in both of his. 'May I?' he asked again.

She looked at him and, no, she was not indifferent, but she was afraid. 'I had no idea when I came here that I would meet you again. It's almost as if I was never away, we were

561

never apart. But the world is very different now. It's a bad, dangerous place. Night is coming. It's dusk already. We have so little time.'

'All the more reason to hold on to what's precious,' he said. He lifted her hand to his lips and kissed her fingers, very lightly. 'May I?'

'Court me? Here at the end of the world?'

'Before night comes. Two people who've found each other again, against all the odds. May I?'

'You may,' she said.

Together they packed up paintings, furniture, silver, porcelains. They did the Candé runs together. They were entertained lavishly at both ends, by Hélène and by the Bedauxs. And at Candé, one evening at the end of May, they went for a walk in the green, river-haunted twilight, with the soft flicker of bats above them and the melancholy calling of owls echoing back and forth across the valley; and when they stopped at the edge of the scarp, where the ground dropped away, she turned to him, and he saw that it was all right. He took her in his arms and kissed her, and she kissed him back, for a long time, as twilight turned to darkness.

Two people at the end of the world.

June was the best month for Scarborough, when the weather was fine but the holiday hordes had not yet arrived. Polly and Lennie had only a week, but it was good to be away on their own. They slept late, ate heartily, walked a lot. The sea was still too cold for bathing, but they took off their shoes and paddled at the edge of the water, and enjoyed the brilliant light and the exhilarating freshness of the air. Sea and cliff and beach, waves endlessly trundling in and turning over with a sigh and a suck, gulls riding the moving air and crying plaintively: it all seemed so eternal. It must always have been like this. And surely it would always be.

One day, just for variety, they got the car out and drove up the coast to Robin Hood's Bay, down the steep, cobbled street to the harbour, and had a luncheon of fish and fried potatoes in the Bay Hotel, sitting out on the terrace over the sea. 'It's a good thing Al Feinstein didn't find out about this place,' Lennie said. 'He'd have found some way of setting a scene for Robin and Marian here. Probably would have squeezed Bonnie Prince Charlie and Grace Darling in, too.'

Polly laughed. 'When is that film going to come out? I really want to see it. My actual house is in it!'

'Morland Place looked magnificent,' Lennie assured her. 'I should think it will come out in the autumn in the States, and probably January or February over here. If—' He didn't finish that sentence. 'What I want to know,' he said briskly, to cover himself, 'is how Rose is getting on as Anastasia.'

'You're worried about her?'

'Not at all. Van Kerk will look after her. I'm just interested. I always will be, you know.'

'That's all right. I'm not jealous. I'll always be interested in James.'

On the way back, their route took them along an ordinary street of Scarborough houses, where a crowd of people had gathered on the pavement around a lorry parked at the kerb. Lennie slowed, and Polly said, 'Oh, do let's find out what's going on.' So he stopped and they got out. On the back of the lorry there was a load of corrugated steel, in what looked like curved sections. The lorry driver and several men, presumably residents, were staring at a piece of paper the driver was holding. As he got nearer, Lennie could see it was a technical diagram of some sort.

'Can I help?' he asked.

The crowd – women in aprons, some wearing head-rags, men in shirtsleeves, and children of both sexes in a state of excitement – parted willingly, and the driver looked relieved. He pushed his cap back in order to scratch at his head, and said, 'It's this 'ere plan, maister. Ah'm trying to explain to this gent—'

'He's got it upside down,' the gent – presumably the householder outside whose house they were planted – said indignantly.

'It doesn't matter which way oop Ah hold it, you daft—' the driver began, in exasperation.

Lennie played peacemaker. 'May I see?'

Polly could see they were both glad to defer to him. *Solomon and the baby*, she thought with amusement. 'What's all this about?' she asked the woman beside her, whose carpet slippers suggested she came from the house too.

'Anderson shelter,' the woman said. 'In case of air raids. T'council's givin' 'em out. Poor folk get 'em for nowt, but we have to pay seven pund,' she added proudly.

'Oh,' said Polly. 'How does it work?'

'You've to dig a hole, like, then them round bits go over it, then you put the muck you dig out over the top. It's simple enough,' she added confidentially, 'but you know men! Got to make a song an' dance out of everything. Look at 'em!' she said fondly, nodding to where Lennie, the driver, and three or four responsible householders all had their heads jammed into the small space above the diagram. 'Lord save us if Ah'd to look at a recipe every time Ah cooked dinner!'

Polly smiled dutifully. 'So, is everyone getting one?'

'Aye, miss, everyone in t'town 'at's got a garden. Our warden, Tom Battersby, said 'at folk as haven't'll have to shelter in t'cupboard under t'stairs, or under t'kitchen table. God help 'em,' she added charitably.

'I suppose it's necessary,' Polly said doubtfully.

The woman looked stern. 'Folk forget, but Scarborough was bombed in the war. Hundreds killed. You got to be prepared, miss. Ey oop, your man's got 'em sorted out, seemingly. Now mebbe we'll get some action.'

The confabulation broke up. Polly saw from Lennie's

posture that he was ready to go into the back garden and see the job through, but she caught his eye and gave him a stern look, and he said something to the men, caps were touched and hands shaken, and she got him back.

'Damned interesting,' he said, when they were in the car. 'Those curved sheets are bolted together, with steel plates at either end. The corrugation makes them very strong.'

'That lady said they put them up over a hole in the ground.'

'Yes, they're half buried, which makes them even safer.'

'But you'd be sitting on the cold, damp earth. And if it rained, I bet it would flood – what's to stop it?'

He glanced at her. 'It won't be an ideal situation,' he said. 'But better than being blown up. Scarborough's situation on the east coast makes it a likely target. In the last war—'

'I know. That woman told me. It was bombed.'

'Shelled, actually, from the sea, but bombs are more likely this time. Better to take precautions.'

'She called it an Anderson shelter,' Polly said on an enquiring note.

'After Sir John Anderson, who's been put in charge of Home Security. He commissioned an engineer to design it, and the steel is manufactured at a steel works in North Wales.'

'You've read all about it.' He shrugged. 'It's not just Scarborough, is it?'

'Anywhere they think might be a target. London, of course, and the south-east. The east coast. Anywhere near military installations, or docks. Or railway centres.'

'York?'

'Yes.'

'And you didn't tell me?'

He smiled faintly. 'I had better things to talk to you about. I knew you'd find out sooner or later.'

'But what do we do about Morland Place? All the servants . . .' She frowned. 'I seem to remember that people went down into their cellars in the war.'

'I don't think that would be a good idea. We're surrounded by a moat. I don't know how thick the walls are between the water and the cellar, but if there was even a crack, and the water poured in . . .'

'So – what, then? Do I have to have a lot of these Anderson shelters built out in the fields? Or one big one?'

'I wouldn't worry. I don't think Morland Place is likely to be bombed directly. And I think it's strong enough to stand up to anything randomly falling nearby. Just tell people to keep away from the windows, in case of broken glass.'

'You've thought about this,' she said.

'It's my job to take care of you all.'

'It's my job too. But I just never believed . . .' She stared out of the window. They had come down onto the Esplanade now, and she could see the sea, vast and quietly moving in its massive indifference to the transitory concerns of man. 'It's really going to happen, isn't it?'

'I think so,' he said unwillingly. 'It's like a runaway train – I can't see how we can stop it.'

'And what about you?'

He didn't pretend not to know what she meant. 'I'll serve in any way I can. But I'm not a British citizen, so I won't be called up to fight.'

She nodded, and was quiet all the way back to their hotel room. Then she put herself into his arms, and said, 'It's our last night here. Let's not allow this to spoil it. Let's be as merry as possible.'

They dined in the hotel. They had a lot of champagne, and after dinner they danced together until the orchestra stopped playing and packed up their instruments.

When they got home, they learned that the first call-up under the Military Training Act had taken place on the 3rd of June. John, Martin, the footman Sam, and two of the grooms had all left for training camp.

CHAPTER TWENTY-FOUR

The flat was too big and too empty. Richard couldn't sleep. There was no-one to cook meals for him, so he took to eating at a café on the Earls Court Road on his way home. He had too little to do to tire him out. The holiday-village scheme was dead for the foreseeable future, the European driving holidays had stopped, and ever fewer people were hiring cars, chauffeured or un-chauffeured. He sold the house in Ealing without regret – it had never seemed like home to him – and that eased his finances. With the Air Ministry compensation he now had capital but not much income. He didn't like to turn off staff, and kept everybody on, thinking the situation would resolve itself anyway, when the war started. Two of his drivers had left already to volunteer, and others were talking about seeking other work.

When he lay awake at night, he mostly thought about Cynthia bravely managing not to cry as they said goodbye. They had gone first of all to a distant cousin who lived in the Williamsburg district of Brooklyn. Since the Williamsburg Bridge had been completed in 1903, a large number of Polish Jews had moved across from the Lower East Side, and there was now a substantial community of them in Williamsburg. There were Jewish associations, Jewish baths, synagogues, bakeries and kosher butchers; familiar foods, familiar accents, familiar ideas that made Hannah and Leah feel safe, and Cynthia feel that they were now amid a community that welcomed them and did not think them hateful. Cousin Sala said she would help them find an apartment of their own, and that it would not be difficult. Thanks to Samuel's foresight, they had plenty of accessible money. And if they had to stay a long time, there was plenty of work in the area, if they wanted to boost their income, in a multitude of offices, schools, restaurants, shops, aid bureaux – even the mustard factory.

So he was not worried about their immediate safety and comfort. Williamsburg seemed a nice place, and the Nevinsons had several families nearby who regarded themselves as distant relatives. It was even just a short trip across the bridge, by bus or subway train, to Manhattan and all its multiple pleasures, if they felt settled enough to consider enjoying themselves. As he travelled back to England and London and the dreary preparations for war, he even envied them, and wondered if he ought to have stayed. When he kissed her goodbye at Sala's door – he had forbidden them to come to the station – her tears wetted his lips. He felt her heartbreak, and wondered, as he knew she was wondering, if they would ever see each other again. He felt that in some indirect way he had broken his promise to Samuel. But he had a duty to his country, and to a wider morality. If war came, it would be to defeat Hitler and his mad territorial ambitions; but it would also be to punish him and his followers for their hateful anti-Semitism. He owed Samuel that, too.

It took several sleepless nights of soul-searching, but he decided in the end to leave the Earls Court flat. He couldn't live there alone, without them. But it had been Cynthia's childhood home and he didn't quite like to sell it, so he let it, furnished, putting their personal effects into storage. He was prepared to move into lodgings – all he wanted was a bed and someone to cook for him – but he had mentioned his situation when he rang his mother down in Derbyshire to tell her he was back from the States. And the following day he received a message from Uncle Oliver's secretary asking him to call in at his consulting rooms in Queen Anne Street.

Oliver got straight down to business. 'Your mother rang me last night. She told me about your wife and mother-in-law going to America. My condolences – but I can't say I blame them. Tell me, did that other matter resolve itself?'

'Not entirely,' Richard said. 'Mr Young said there was nothing physically wrong with her, but anxiety about the war, the terrible news coming from abroad . . .'

'I understand,' Oliver said. Richard thought that probably he was the only one in the family who really did. 'Now, your mother tells me you are virtually homeless and about to move into lodgings.'

'The flat's too big for me on my own,' Richard. 'And I've never learned to cook.'

'But it's absurd for you to rough it when your favourite uncle lives in an enormous house in Pall Mall. So I want to offer you a home with me.' Richard opened his mouth to protest and Oliver lifted a hand. 'I promised your mother I'd make you accept, so please don't make a liar of me.'

'It's very kind of you, Uncle, but I don't think I'm cut out for that sort of life any more.'

Oliver gave him a sympathetic look. 'You mean you wouldn't be in the right frame of mind for society banquets and glittering *ton* parties every night? My dear boy, what sort of life do you think I lead?'

'Well, I—'

'I quite understand that you want to be independent. As it happens, there is a very nice little apartment in the garden wing – just a bedroom, sitting-room, bathroom and small kitchenette – and the offer comes with a housemaid who will pop in to clean, deal with the laundry, and cook an evening meal for you as and when required. It's not needed by us at the moment, and it's yours for as long as you need it. I should add that there's no requirement to see anything of Verena and me if you don't want to, but you'll be welcome to join us as often as you like – and I do hope that you will sometimes accept an invitation. After eighteen years of marriage we get very bored with each other's conversation, you know.'

Richard laughed. 'I am absolutely sure that's not true! This really is very kind of you – above and beyond.'

'Nonsense! The least I can do. Now, have I addressed all your nonsensical objections? Do you accept?'

'I accept, with the greatest gratitude.'

'When will you move in?'

'Today, if I may. I have everything packed up.'

'Excellent. Call at the main house for the key. And you will dine with us this evening – that's a command, not a request. It's the least *you* can do. The children want to see you. It's just a family dinner, so we won't dress.'

A few months ago, Richard reflected, he'd had a house, a business, a wife, and a child on the way. Now he had none of those things. His life seemed to be going backwards.

Barbara's third child was born on the 28th of June. Thanks to the convenience of the telephone, Helen was able to hurry down and be there the same day. Jack followed on the Friday night, and Basil arrived on the Saturday morning to stay for the weekend.

It was a girl this time. Freddie was happy. 'I hoped we'd have one. I began to think we could only produce boys.'

'It's nice to have a variety,' Jack said. 'One girl and two boys, the same as Helen and I had.'

'You're assuming they'll stop there, Pa,' Basil said.

'Oh, I don't think I want to put Barbara through it all again,' Freddie said, taking him seriously. 'Three is enough. Though, of course, it's up to Barbara.'

'I'd stop there if I were you, Babsy,' Basil said, when he saw his sister alone for a few minutes. She was looking remarkably unruffled this time, as if having a baby was as easy as shelling peas. Perhaps, he thought, it was a matter of practice. 'It's not as ugly as your first two, but you can't depend on improvement every time. What if it's a parabola and you've reached the apogee?'

'I have no idea what you're talking about,' Barbara said, gazing at the baby's face with satisfaction. 'She's beautiful.'

'Of course, all babies are beautiful to their mothers. I expect even you were.'

'Oh, don't be horrid!' she said, without heat. 'You're just trying to tease me, and I won't be baited. Do you want to hold her?'

'All right, I don't mind having a go.' The baby was tiny and unexpectedly light. He held it and felt an unexpected tremor of emotion. He was an uncle again. And this time to a girl – not a nevvy to be rough-and-tumbled, like Douglas and Peter, but a fragile china doll to be protected and cherished and petted. He thought briefly of the harshness of the world this little thing had been born into. And then he thought of Gloria, and himself, and felt sad that he would probably never have a child of his own. Gloria would not want another. And in any case, when the war began, he would be off to do his bit. He might not survive; and even if he did, when it ended – who knew how many years later? – what would be left? This was probably the nearest he'd get to fatherhood.

'She *is* rather nice,' he heard himself say.

Barbara flushed with pleasure. His compliments were rare. 'I'm glad you can see it at last. You're not a bad old animal really, though you like to pretend.'

'What are you going to call her?'

'Helena. After Mummy.'

'That's nice.'

The nurse came in and said it was time for Mother to rest, took the baby and drove Basil away. 'I'll come up and see you again later,' he promised his sister at the door.

571

Downstairs, they were not talking babies, but aeroplanes.

'The first ever commercial transatlantic passenger flight,' Jack was saying. 'You must see how important that is. And the baby was born on the very same day. The 28th of June will be a significant date for ever. Think of Blériot, Alcock and Brown.'

'I see that,' Freddie said patiently, 'but I still don't think it warrants calling the baby Dixie.'

'I didn't mean as a first name,' Jack urged. 'A middle name. Helena Dixie.'

'I adore the name Dixie,' Basil said, 'but I'm not seeing the connection.'

'Basil, don't stir,' Helen said sternly.

'The Pan American flying boat that flew this momentous first crossing is an NC18605 Dixie Clipper,' Jack explained.

'It's also a Boeing B314,' Helen said, 'but you're not proposing to call the baby Boeing.'

Jack lifted his hands. 'All right, I withdraw the suggestion. But you have to be excited, at least. This is what we've been waiting for for years. It's a new epoch in air travel. Now anyone can fly across the Atlantic in twenty-four hours!'

'As long as they have the money,' Helen added.

'I'll be excited with you, Dad,' Basil said. 'I know how much it means to you. And I must say, I'd like to visit America that way, in one day rather than five. Tell me all about it.'

He had read most of it in the newspapers, of course, but he was fond of the old man, and knew he'd enjoy telling it all again. And it stopped anyone asking questions about *his* life.

'Well, they've been doing proving flights for five weeks, of course, carrying mail only,' Jack said. 'And then there was an inspection flight with just twelve passengers, members of the press, before they could get the CAA certificate – that's the Civil Aviation Authority. But they've been testing mail routes since last year. The problem has always been how to carry enough fuel. The mail clippers used up so much of their internal space with fuel tanks there wasn't room for passengers.'

'They tinkered with the idea of air-to-air refuelling,' Helen said. 'You know, Alan Cobham's probe-and-drogue system. But I doubt they'd ever get permission to do that with paying passengers on board.'

'I don't suppose the passengers would care for it much, either,' said Basil. 'Anyway, I must say, if I were crossing all that water, I think I'd like to know it was on a sea plane, just in case.'

'Darling, you can have no idea how nearly impossible it would be to put down a sea plane safely in mid-Atlantic,' Helen said.

'So what's the point, then?'

'Being able to stop and refuel at places without air strips,' Jack said. 'Like Horta on the southern route to Europe, and Ireland and Newfoundland on the northern route to America.'

'I expect it was very luxurious,' Basil said.

'They did their best,' said Helen. 'The bunks convert into beds. Dinner was silver service, six courses, with chefs trained in four-star hotels. Separate lounge and dining areas. Male and female dressing rooms so they could change for bed. I read an account by a passenger who said it was all so nice she forgot she was flying.' She shrugged. 'I can't quite see how that was possible, given the noise. Aeroplanes are never quiet. I suppose it was poetic licence.'

'Given enough champagne and caviar, people can ignore anything,' Basil said.

'These flying boats are only an interim measure, anyway,' Jack said. 'They're too slow, and the choice of routes is restricted. Lufthansa flew an airliner non-stop from Berlin to New York last year as a proving flight for a landplane service across the Atlantic. I've heard they're working towards a regular passenger service. It would be a pity if we let the

Germans get ahead of us, like they did with the airships. Especially given the situation.' He looked at Basil speculatively, a question forming in his eyes.

'Have you heard from Michael recently?' Basil asked, desperate to keep the conversation going.

'Yes, last week. He's just been commissioned into a frigate, HMS *Fortunate*,' Helen said. 'You know he's a sub-lieutenant now?'

'He'll be made up to full lieutenant automatically as soon as the war starts,' Jack said. 'Promotion's always quicker in wartime. And what about you, Basil? When are you going to start taking this seriously?'

So they had arrived at him at last, despite his efforts. 'I take everything seriously, Dad,' he said. 'I'm a reporter. We see all the worst aspects of humanity. It doesn't exactly make for frivolity.'

'And yet here you are being frivolous,' Jack said.

'Darling,' Helen protested.

Jack was not diverted. 'Where will you be when war is declared? You could have volunteered and been in uniform by now. Are you hoping to stay a journalist all through? You know that's not a reserved occupation, don't you?'

'I have plans in place,' Basil said.

'What plans?' Jack said suspiciously.

There was no help for it. 'I have been approached by – certain people. High-up people. But I can't tell you more than that. I've been told not to talk about it.'

His father was still bristling with doubt, and Basil couldn't blame him, given his history. So he smiled at his mother, who came to his rescue.

'Of course, if you can't talk about it, we must respect that,' she said. She was giving him a searching look, but he thought it was not a suspicious one – more that of a mother hoping that whatever he was going to do would not be too dangerous. Unfortunately, she was deflected onto his personal life. 'How

574

are things with you in general? Have you met any nice girls? When are you going to bring someone home for us to meet?'

'You know me, Mum,' he said. 'You're the only woman in the world for me.'

'Flummery,' Helen said. 'I'm sure you—'

Time to divert attention again. 'I think you really ought to call the baby Dixie,' he said to Freddie, who had been following the conversation like someone at a tennis match. 'It's a delicious name – and unique. What do the boys think about their new sister?'

There was nothing Freddie liked talking about more than his children. The topic lasted until tea arrived, and the nanny brought in Douglas and Peter to entertain the company.

'There's another one!' Basil said.

'Another what?' Richard asked.

'Woman carrying a gas-mask.'

'Oh, yes,' said Richard.

They were walking in Green Park, looking for an empty bench, having bought sandwiches at the coffee stall by the gate. Richard had phoned to suggest they had lunch together, but when they met, Basil said it was too nice to be indoors.

'Apparently, the wardens are telling people they should get into the habit of carrying them about all the time,' Basil said. 'I heard that some women are treating them as a fashion item. The Army and Navy are even selling a special gas-mask bag you can wear over your shoulder.' It was Gloria who had told him that. She'd said it was a ridiculous idea, and the bags were hideous.

'Here's a bench,' Richard said.

They sat and opened their sandwich bags, and at once, as if by magic, the path in front of them burst into a full bloom of pigeons.

It was another lovely day in what had been so far a lovely summer. The weather was clear and hot, with no oppressive mugginess. 'This is nice,' Basil said. 'I'm glad you suggested it.'

Richard gave a rueful smile. 'I don't have much else to do. My business is in the doldrums, and my family is far away.'

'Yes, I'm sorry about Cynthia. But I expect she feels safer over there.'

'She writes cheerful letters,' Richard said, 'but with a hint of second thoughts, if I'm reading between the lines. It was a drastic solution.'

'Are you still working with the Kindertransport scheme?'

'We're busier than ever. We've got to get as many out as possible while we still can. It gives me something useful to do, at any rate.' He examined his sandwich, and took a bite. 'You're the one with the best access to the news. What's going on over there?'

'Oh, the German press is full of anti-Polish propaganda, trying to destabilise the Polish government and whip up German fighting madness. You know that Hitler revoked the non-aggression treaty they had with Poland?'

'Yes, I read that.'

'And the German ambassador in Moscow, von Schulenberg, is busy trying to woo the Soviets – which, after the years they've spent denouncing Jewish Bolshevism as the greatest threat to civilisation, would be quite funny if it weren't so serious.'

'But I thought *we* were trying to woo the Soviets,' Richard said.

'We are – us and France,' said Basil. 'With the greatest reluctance, of course. Our leaders would much rather come to an accommodation with Germany, which is at least a civilised country. And the prospect of a Soviet Union bolstered by victory is horrifying – except to my editor and the Left Book Club. So we woo, but without much enthusiasm. And it's anyone's guess which way Uncle Joe Stalin will eventually jump. At the moment, I understand, the Reds simply don't believe the Germans are serious about a *rapprochement*, so that works in our favour.'

'If they side with us, will that be enough?'

'To prevent war? I don't know. When you've got a madman drunk on fantasies of conquest, rational decisions can't be relied on. There's no doubt that Hitler's *planning* an invasion of Poland – has been for months. Whether it will go ahead depends on whether he can be persuaded out of it.' He looked at Richard. 'Frankly, I'm not holding out much hope.'

Richard nodded, and they were silent for a while, eating, watching the endless stream of passers-by, lulled by the burbling of the pigeons, the soft background sound of conversations and the further-off murmur of traffic. The world seemed like a big, peaceful humming top, spinning on the point of Green Park.

Then Richard said, 'There's another one. God, I hate the sight of those things! I think it was the gas mask that was the last straw, as far as Cynthia was concerned.'

'They're pretty ugly,' Basil agreed. 'And I've never liked anything over my face – makes me feel panicky. I find it a bit sinister that the special mask for small children has a safety catch to stop them being able to get it off. Now *that* would have had me in hysterics when I was a kid.'

'Better than being gassed, though,' Richard said. 'Uncle Oliver saw the effects of gassing during the war. He doesn't like to talk about it, but when he does . . . Well, you wouldn't want to go that way.'

'No, I suppose not. How is it, living there?'

'Altogether too easy,' Richard said. 'They're so tactful. I'm welcome to come through any time, but they never bother me. One of their housemaids comes in when I'm out and cleans, and if I leave a note saying I'll be in for dinner and what time, she cooks and serves it.'

'You're spoiled. If I eat in, I have to manage for myself.

Sausages feature heavily on the menu. If I were you, I'd accept every invitation to dine with my dear old uncle. Have you seen anything of Charlotte, by the way? Does she visit them?'

'I haven't seen her at all,' Richard said. 'And, no, she doesn't. She and Launde seem to live a completely separate life from everyone we know.'

'I hear his name mentioned now and then,' Basil said. 'When there's talk of rearmament. One of our biggest concerns, apparently, is that if we started conscription tomorrow, half of them would only have broomsticks to practise with.'

'I understand it was the same in the last war,' Richard said. 'So the longer we can put off the fateful day, the better.'

'Oh, good Lord, look at that!' said Basil. A smart woman was passing with a small dog on a lead, and strapped on the dog's back was a small square bag. 'Do you think that can possibly be a gas mask for the dog?'

Charlotte came home from a little desultory shopping to find all the evidences of a husband's return: open doors, voices, a man's overcoat and hat left on the hall table. A maid, scurrying from one room to another, curtsied in flight and gasped, 'Oh, my lady, his lordship's back.'

Charlotte shed her hat and gloves and, in the absence of anyone to take them, added them to the delinquent heap, and tracked Milo down to his bedroom. He was talking to his man, Foley, and didn't notice her at first. There were piles of clothes on the bed, drawers and wardrobe doors were open, and Milo was bright-eyed and evidently wound tighter than a clock spring.

'You're home,' she said, to gain his attention. 'I didn't know you were coming.'

He said, 'I'm sorry, I didn't have time to send a telegram. Sudden change of plans. Thank you, Foley. Make a start elsewhere – I'll ring for you.'

Foley collected one of the piles on the bed and backed out with no more than a half-bow to Charlotte as he passed. When they were alone, Milo crossed the room to catch her by the upper arms and kiss her hard but briefly on the lips. It was one of his distracted kisses that she had come to recognise – rather like a man patting a dog when his mind was elsewhere.

'How are you? Well?' he asked, but didn't wait for an answer. He turned away and was rummaging in a drawer before she could draw breath.

'What's going on? Milo – what's happening?'

He turned back, frowning, and made a visible effort to clear his mind for her. 'The British and French talks in Moscow have collapsed. Molotov has presented Schulenberg with a draft non-aggression treaty. And a trade treaty is under discussion – Soviet agricultural produce and oil against German machinery and military equipment. It looks as though the Soviets have decided the Germans aren't bluffing – they're throwing in their lot with them. So it's time for us to go, while we still can.'

'Go? Where? And who's "us".'

'You and me, dear wife,' he said. 'To Switzerland.'

'*Switzerland?*'

'A very civilised country. You'll love it. Everything's new and clean. Electric trains. Every modern convenience. Everyone speaks English. And, of course, they'll be neutral, and given that everyone deposits their surplus cash there, no-one, not even Hitler, will dare attack it. So you see?'

'No, I don't see,' Charlotte said. 'What are you saying? That we're going there, you and me? For a holiday?'

'No, darling, for the duration of the war, which I'm sorry to say looks like being a long one. So we'll take everything with us. I've already taken the precaution of moving most of my assets out there – you may thank me later for my fore-sight!' He grinned. 'I shall leave enough here for a base for

579

when we come back, but I'm selling this house. We'll find something else if and when we need it.' He cocked his head at her. 'It's not as if we've been here long enough for you to get fond of it, so don't look like that.'

'I'm not looking like anything,' Charlotte said. 'I'm just trying to understand.'

'Oh dear, you're being very slow,' he said. He came back across the room, took hold of her upper arms again – she realised suddenly that she'd never liked that gesture – and said, with exaggerated clarity, 'Try to concentrate, dear. We are going to live in Switzerland for the next few years, where it's safe and I can carry on my business without the interruptions that will inevitably occur if we remain in this country while it's at war. I've got aeroplane tickets to Zürich booked for Thursday, so that gives you two days to pack. I know you haven't flown before, but Swiss Air uses nice, reliable American planes, Douglas DC3s. You'll be perfectly safe.'

She extracted herself from his grasp. 'No,' she said.

'No what?' He wrinkled his brow in his endearing puzzled smile. He often used it on her when she didn't want to do something, as if he didn't understand how anyone could diverge from his utterly rational course. He always got his way.

'No, we're not going to Switzerland.'

The smile disappeared, like a rabbit down a hole. 'I beg your pardon?'

'How could you even think it? If there's going to be a war, we're not running away and leaving our country in the lurch. We're staying to fight and defend it with whatever strength we have.'

'Oh dear. In the first place, this is barely *my* country. My forebears were Irish. In the second place, what on earth do you think you could do in a war, Lady Launde?'

'Lots of things,' Charlotte said hotly. 'Women served in the last war, and they'll be needed more than ever this time.

There'll be all sorts of voluntary services. Or I can join the ATS, or be a nurse, or even join the Land Army. Don't tell me there's nothing I can do. I'm not some fragile doll, you know. I'm a capable, educated woman.'

'I know you are. That's why I want you with me,' he said, in a more conciliatory tone. 'I'll be working for victory over there, you know, not just sitting on my rear enjoying myself. I'll still be carrying on my business, and you can help me. Did you think I was just abandoning the old country?'

'That's what it sounded like a moment ago,' she said, a degree less forcefully. Had she misunderstood him? But he'd said— 'You said this wasn't your country.'

'*Barely* my country was what I said. You must make allow-ances for my love of rhetoric – you know what I'm like, Charley! Anything for a *bon mot*. I don't always mean every single syllable.'

He was smiling, charming her, and it had always worked before. Why wasn't it this time? Because, she thought, this was too important. 'I'm still not going. I don't know how you can even ask me.'

'Because you're my wife, and you go where I go. Haven't you read your Bible?'

'Don't bring religion into this.'

'It's already in. We were married in church, as I remember. For better or worse until death. I'm going, and you're coming with me, and there's nothing more to say. Now I suggest you find Tasker and start your packing. I won't be dining in tonight, so there'll be nothing to interrupt you. I have to go and see Leslie Burgin at the Ministry of Supply and try to put some steel into his backbone. Then I'll try to catch Sam Hoare, and one or two others, so I'll dine at the club.' He dropped a kiss on her forehead and turned away to go on with what he had been doing.

She stared at his back, fighting tears. She thought back over the time she had known him, and wondered what he had ever felt about her. He had declared love many times, of course, but words came easily to him. As he had just said, he didn't always mean every single syllable. What she knew about him, really knew, was that he was single-minded in the pursuit of his primary aim: to restore the fortune his father had lost, to restore the earldom of Launde to its former glory.

And where did she come in? She looked back on how they had first met. He had eavesdropped on a conversation between her and some friends in a Lyons Corner House, had followed her and scraped an acquaintance. She was the daughter of an earl, great-granddaughter of a duke, and had the status and connections he needed. Had he known that from the beginning? Had he chosen her for that reason? Had he *used* her all along?

It had been fun at first, when they didn't have much, and had muddled along. But for a long time now she had been discontented, seeing little of him, running his house and acting as hostess to his dinner parties when he was at home, being the wife he needed on his arm to make the right impression on the world. She had been more than discontented, she realised: she had been unhappy. She was, she felt now, a useful piece of kit to him, nothing more. That was why he'd not wanted children. They didn't fit into the plan yet. When they did, he would order them from her as he might order a pair of boots from Lobb's: two sons, she supposed – an heir and a spare. Possibly a daughter, if he saw a use for one – to make a marriage with someone who would benefit his plan.

All this rushed through her mind in a flash, leaving her feeling cold and calm. *I am not loved,* she thought, *but I am his wife. I will give him one more chance.* 'I am not going to Switzerland,' she said quietly and clearly.

He turned with an exasperated look. 'You are, Charlotte. Make your mind up to it.'

'I am staying in England, and you can stay with me. But if you go, that is the end of it.'

'The end of what?' he said impatiently.

'The end of us.' She swallowed, and continued bravely: 'I will divorce you.'

He looked at her in silence for a moment. He seemed surprised, but not shocked. She thought he would say something patently disparaging along the lines of *Hysterical women, don't really mean it, think better of it tomorrow, take an aspirin and lie down.* But at the end of his scrutiny, he said, 'If that's what you want.'

In that silence he had been calculating, she realised: deciding the possible damage and whether he could do without her. Her resolve hardened. 'It seems to be what *you* want.'

'Very well,' he said, and there was no fun in his face, no charm, no softness. He seemed to her stripped back to the essential Milo, and there was nothing there for her. The end of their relationship had been that easy. Like a shallow-rooted tree, the first strong wind had blown it over. 'Stay if you want,' he went on, 'but I'm still selling this house, so you'll have to find somewhere else to live. If you want to divorce me, have your lawyer talk to my lawyer in Switzerland. I'll leave you his address. And now, if you'll excuse me, I have a lot to do.'

She left him, without another word. She went to her bedroom and sat on the bed, staring at nothing. She was shaking, but no tears came. Oddly, the only thought that came to her was *Basil never trusted him.*

Her maid, Tasker, came in at last, hesitantly, and said, 'Did you want me to pack, my lady? And Cook says, will you be dining in?'

Charlotte stood up, resolve hardening. 'No, I won't be dining in,' she said. 'Pack me an overnight case. The yellow linen for tomorrow will do, with the two-tone shoes. I shan't need you with me. I'll be back tomorrow afternoon, and I'll talk about the rest of the packing then.'

Polly and Lennie were coming back from a ride, talking about the harvest. The wonderful dry, clear weather had resulted in an excellent wheat yield, which they had been able to get in early. Now in August the oats were about ready, and there would be a good second cut of hay.

'Second cut always smells so much sweeter,' Polly said.

'It's more nourishing, too,' said Lennie.

She looked at him. 'How would you know that?'

'John Burton told me,' he admitted. 'Don't laugh at me. I have to learn these things. Are you going to put the sheep onto the stubble fields?'

'Yes, Farmer Giles! They help to manure it. At Moon's Rush they put pigs on the stubble – they're as good as ploughing for turning over the soil.'

They had reached the Monument and Morland Place appeared at the bottom of the slope before them. Polly halted automatically. 'I love seeing it from this viewpoint,' she said. 'It looks so welcoming. Does it look like home to you now?'

'I think it always did,' Lennie said. 'Remember I lived here during the war. And back in the States it was always only an apartment. I don't think you can get attached to an apartment in the same way. Look at it! Dreaming in the sun the way it has for five hundred years. It looks so unchangeable.'

Polly laughed. 'Cross your fingers when you say that.'

They started down the slope. They heard the sound of an aeroplane's engine, but paid no attention. There were so many of them now, it had become something you didn't bother to notice.

'It's just a trainer,' Polly said, when it came into sight, heading across her view from right to left.

'An Avro 621,' Lennie said.

She was amused. 'Do you know everything?'

'Very nearly,' he said. 'Probably some lad's first solo flight.'
She frowned. 'But he's much too low. He needs to pull
up!'

It happened so quickly. Even as her voice rose in alarm at
the end of the short sentence, there was a tremendous bang
as the fixed undercarriage hit the chapel roof. The plane
ricocheted up, missed the top of the gatehouse by a whisker,
rocked wildly as the pilot fought to regain control, skimmed
across the track and the rails on the far side, hit the grass,
stuck its nose down and flipped over onto its back.

Polly and Lennie were already cantering down the slope.
People came running out of Morland Place, across the drawbridge, vaulting or climbing over the rails. Thanking heaven
she was on Zephyr, Polly popped him neatly over into the
field, and shouted to Hodgson, one of her grooms, to come
and take him. Lennie could not get his mount to jump into
the field, scared of the alien thing in it, and had to grab
someone to hold it while he climbed over.

The first-comers had reached the plane. It looked so
pathetic and helpless on its back, with one wheel still spinning, the other missing, presumably torn off. The pilot was,
thank God, already crawling out, and willing hands grabbed
him and hauled him to his feet. She shouted to everyone to
get clear, in case it caught fire, but he said, 'It's all right, I've
switched off.'

He pulled off his flying helmet as she reached him. He
was as tall as her, and skinny, He looked, to her eyes, about
fourteen. They were so young! He had straight dark hair,
flattened by the helmet, and blue eyes. There was a big red
mark on his forehead, already swelling into a lump, but he
didn't appear to have any other injuries, except for seeming,
understandably, shaken.

Behind her, she heard Lennie tell someone to go back to
the house and telephone the base. 'They'll have to send a
lorry to fetch the machine.'

The boy turned his attention to Lennie, instinctively recognising authority. 'I'm awfully sorry, sir,' he said. 'Is it your house?'

'It's my wife's,' Lennie said, reaching Polly's side just as she answered, 'Yes,' to the question. 'Are you all right?' Lennie went on.

'Yes, sir, I think so. Oh, Lord! I'm frightfully sorry about . . . I hope I haven't done too much damage. Oh, God, Wing's going to slaughter me.'

'Very likely,' Lennie said. 'What happened?'

'I don't know. I misjudged it. I tried to pull up, but . . .' He looked round at the Avro and registered the missing wheel, the other damage to the undercarriage. 'Wing's going to kill me,' he whimpered.

'You'd better come back to the house, and we'll put something on that bump,' Polly said.

He put a vague hand to his forehead, but said, 'Oh, no, thanks awfully, ma'am, but I must stay with my 'bus, make sure nobody touches her. Oh, Lord, I've busted your house! They're absolutely going to kill me.' He looked as though he was about to cry. 'My first solo, and I've made such a mucker of it.'

Polly and Lennie exchanged a look. 'I'll go back and see what's happened,' Lennie said. 'You stay here until they send someone. They won't be long.' He patted the boy's shoulder. 'Take it easy, son. It doesn't look as though you've done too much damage, and the government will pay.'

The words didn't seem to comfort him much. He looked so miserable that he plucked at Polly's motherly instincts. She suggested he sat down, and said a cigarette might calm him. 'I don't smoke,' he said. But he sat on the grass, rather suddenly.

Inside Morland Place it was rather like a kicked ant's nest, with people dashing about, apparently trying to save precious things and carry them out of the house or down to the cellars, while one or two of the maids were huddling, wide-eyed with fear, unable to do anything useful. Oxton, the under-butler, rushed at Lennie with evident relief, saying that it was Barlow's afternoon off and he had gone into York. Lennie took charge and was able to bring order quite quickly by assuring everyone that it wasn't a bomb, that the war hadn't started, and that the Germans weren't coming. He told everyone to stop moving things until he'd seen the damage, compelled Oxton to accompany him, and walked calmly through the staircase hall and to the chapel.

As soon as he opened the door, a cloud of dust billowed out, and it was a few moments before it had settled enough to see anything. Then he could see a patch of daylight above where there shouldn't have been one – a hole in the roof. At first it seemed shocking: the air was full of dust, there was a litter of wood splinters and split panels, broken slates, twisted bits of lead and lumps of plaster and stone. The impression was of devastation. But as he looked more care- fully, he could see that most of the damage was to the Lady Chapel, where a substantial beam had come down right on the Lady altar, and was lying across it with the far end resting on the marble memorial to Eleanor and Robert Morland. There were no windows on the moat side of the chapel, so fortunately none of the glass had been broken. They had got off pretty lightly, he thought.

He backed out, closing the door. 'All right,' he said. 'No-one is to go in for the time being. Can this door be locked? Very well, do it, and bring me the key. And let's get someone here right away to put a tarpaulin over that hole in the roof, in case it rains.'

'Yes, sir.'

'And fetch the estate carpenter as soon as possible to look at the damage.'

He left Oxton to find the key to the chapel door and went

back to the Great Hall, to reassure everyone that the damage was repairable. 'These old places were built to stand up to cannon-fire,' he reminded them. 'There's no danger it's going to fall down, so you can get back to your work.'

As the door to Molly's flat was opened by the maid, Clara, Charlotte saw trunks and cases in the hall, and had an attack of déjà vu that made her feel slightly sick.

Molly appeared behind Clara, and beamed a welcome. 'Hel-*lo*! What an unexpected surprise!' She spotted the bag. 'Have you come to stay?'

'What's happening?' Charlotte asked. 'Are you going away?'

'The children are. They're going on a lovely, lovely holiday in the country!' Charlotte blinked in surprise, and Molly said, 'I'm practising my jolly-and-bright tones for tomorrow because we don't want any tears. Emma and Kit are taking their two down to Walcote and they're calling here tomorrow to take my two with them. Vivian's pretty sure the war's going to start within weeks, and it's as well to get them settled before the balloon goes up.'

'You're leaving London for the duration?'

'No, no, just the children. You can't think we'd want to miss all this! But come into the drawing-room – no need to stand in the hall like a visitor. Are you staying for dinner? Vivian is dining at his club this evening, so it's just me. Mrs Munday will be glad to do something more than an omelette on a tray, which was what I ordered, and which she thinks an insult to her art. Clara, tell Mrs Munday to rustle up dinner for Lady Launde and me for half past seven. And bring the cocktail tray.'

'I thought Emma and Kit were in Cannes,' Charlotte said, seeing that Molly had realised there were secrets to be told and was filling in time with light conversation until they were properly alone.

'They were. They came back this morning. They said

everybody was in Cannes this year. Marlene Dietrich, Delly Cavendish, the Duke and Duchess of Windsor, poor Ena Spain, Ambassador Kennedy and his vast brood. Did you know Billy Hartington is courting one of his daughters – Kathleen? Apparently, it's quite serious. Of course, lots of upper-class boys are marrying American girls these days, and she seems a nice enough little thing. Wholesome and friendly. The Devonshires are putting a brave face on it, but they can't much relish having Mr and Mrs Kennedy as in-laws.'

'Are they going to stay down at Walcote – Emma and Kit?' Charlotte asked.

'I'm not sure. Emma was a bit mysterious about it on the phone. Cocktail?'

The maid put down the tray and departed, and as the door clicked softly closed behind her, Molly said, 'Now, do you want to tell me what's up?'

She mixed martinis while Charlotte told her the story, then put a glass into her hand and said, 'Oh, Charlotte, I'm so sorry. Is it really not mendable?'

'I don't think so,' Charlotte said. 'I know so, really. It hasn't been working for a long time. I feel as if it's all been an illusion, like a magician's act at the music hall, and everyone knew it but me.'

'And he's really selling the house?'

'Yes. Well, as he pointed out, we haven't been there for long, so it's not as if I've put any real effort into making it a home.'

'Well, you must come and live here,' Molly said firmly. 'The spare room is comfortable, and you can have the children's bathroom to yourself, so it will be like a little suite for you.'

Charlotte's eyes filled with tears. 'Thank you. You're so kind.'

'Nonsense. It's pure selfishness – I shall be miserable

without the children, so you'll cheer me up. What will you do, d'you think? Get a job?'

'I'll certainly want to do something,' Charlotte said. 'I thought of joining one of the services – the ATS, perhaps, or the Wrens.'

'No, dear, don't do that. All the other girls will be so much younger than you, it will make you feel lonelier. There'll be plenty of civilian jobs, just as important to the war effort. Vivian and I will find the right thing for you. And you can help me at Dolphin until you find your niche.'

At breakfast the next morning, the children were very bright-eyed. 'Auntie Charlotte, Esmond and me are going to live in the country, with Alethea and Electra,' eight-year-old Angelica said.

'It's Esmond and I,' her brother corrected sternly.

'That's what I said.' Angelica asserted. 'We have to go to the country because of the dirty Huns.'

'Angelica! Who told you that?' Molly said.

'Nanny did. I heard her say it to Clara. The dirty Huns are going to gas us all.'

'You shouldn't repeat things you hear that people that don't know you're listening say,' said Esmond.

'Ungrammatical, but correct,' said Vivian.

'Are you coming too, Auntie Charlotte?' Angelica asked.

'No, I have to stay in London,' Charlotte said. 'But you'll have Alethea and Electra to play with. That will be nice, won't it?' Kit and Emma's two, at nine and seven, were the right age to be playmates.

'But they're just more girls,' Esmond objected. 'And I'm ten. I'm too old for them.'

'But they'll need you to look after them, old chap,' Vivian said. 'I depend on you.'

Esmond looked wistful. 'I'd sooner stay and fight the Germans.'

Emma and Kit arrived so soon after breakfast they must have risen with the lark. Their two daughters looked pale and strained, and Molly sent all the children away to play for ten minutes while she told Emma and Kit Charlotte's story.

'Oh, good Lord!' Kit said. 'What a beast! I must admit I've been completely taken in by him. I thought he was charming.'

'But that's the thing about charm,' Emma said. 'It charms you.'

'When you think of the etymology of the word,' Vivian said, 'it comes from the Latin for incantation. In Middle English it meant magic spell, or to cast a spell.'

'Milo did that, all right,' Kit said, discontentedly. 'I say, isn't that a splendid title for a book: *The Etymology of Charm*. Or a film, even better. Starring Leslie Howard and Olivia de Havilland?'

'Which reminds me,' Molly said, 'are Oliver and Verena sending their children down to Walcote? They don't have a country place of their own.'

'It would rather be putting all our eggs in one basket, wouldn't it?' Kit said. 'No, I believe they're staying put, but the nippers'll be sent down to Tunstead Hall if things turn bad. Oliver won't leave his practice, and Verena won't leave him. Oh, by the way, did you hear, Charlotte, that young Henry is engaged to the younger Partridge girl? The less sandy one.'

'No, I hadn't heard. That's rather sudden, isn't it?'

'A bit of war fever, apparently. Oliver said they're going for a quick wedding because Henry's volunteered for the RAF.'

'I suppose we'll see a lot of that,' Molly said. 'What about you two?'

'We're already married,' Kit said blandly.

'Don't be foolish. I mean, are you going to stay down with the children? Emma turned cagey on me when I asked her.'

Emma and Kit exchanged a look. 'I suppose there's no harm in telling you all now,' Emma said. 'We hadn't decided last night whether to stay down or not. Because, you see, I'm having another baby.'

'Oh my dear! How wonderful!' Molly exclaimed.

'It is, rather,' Emma said, looking pink and pleased. 'We've talked about having a another for ages, but the time never seemed quite right. But now, with the world going to pieces—'

'Anyway, the deed is done,' Kit said, 'and I couldn't be more happy.'

Emma smiled at him. 'I had to persuade him not to delay any more. I'm forty-three, you know. I can't afford to wait any longer. The only thing I regret is that I won't be able to contribute to the war effort, like last time.'

'The baby will be your contribution,' Kit said.

Everyone thought of the same thing, that babies would be needed to replace all the young men who were going to be killed. And everyone saw that everyone else had thought it too.

Emma cleared her throat, and said, 'So I'm staying up for a while, until I get too large to be comfortable, and then I'll go down to be with the children. Unless it starts getting bad, and then I'll go sooner.' She looked at Charlotte. 'You'll have to do it for me – help the war effort.'

The suggestion was tacit, Charlotte thought: *It will keep you busy.* 'I will,' she said.

CHAPTER TWENTY-FIVE

It was not until the next day that Polly went to look at the damage to the chapel. She was shocked at the sight, but Lennie told her it wasn't as bad as it looked. 'Once the debris is cleared away, you'll see.' Workmen had been up on the roof already, to stretch a tarpaulin over the hole.

'But the Lady altar!' Polly said. 'We must get that beam off it straight away. It's not respectful. Oh, and the memorial!'

The marble memorial to their ancestors was in the form of an elaborately carved sarcophagus, though it was thought the bodies were not actually inside, but down in the crypt. On the top life-size marble effigies of the couple lay side by side, hands folded in prayer, Robert's head resting on a lion and Eleanor's on a unicorn. Around the frieze ran the words, 'The brave heart and the pure spirit, faithful unto death. In God is death at end.' But the impact of the end of the beam had chipped off a corner of the lid's lip and broken away the 'ath' of 'death' and all of 'In'.

'It's nearly as old as the house. Can it even be repaired?' Polly mourned.

'Anything can be repaired,' Lennie said. 'They're only material things. Just be thankful no-one was hurt.'

She had turned her attention to the altar, on which the main body of the beam rested. It had split the wooden panelling right down the front to the ground, but more alarming, the ancient wooden statue of the Lady was missing. 'It must be under all the rubbish,' Polly said, anguished.

Lennie saw she was about to get down on her knees and search, and caught her arm. 'Leave it for now.'

'But she looks after the house. It would be terribly bad luck if anything has happened to her.'

'I never knew you were so superstitious.'

'It's not superstition,' she said indignantly. 'There are lots of stories about how she weeps real tears if anything bad is coming to the house.'

'Stories.'

'Not stories as in fiction. Things that really happened and have been handed down.'

'All right, but she's probably under the beam, and you can't look for her until that's been taken away.' He patted the beam. 'Amazing, this old oak – it's so weathered, it's like iron. You'd never be able to drill into it.'

'Lennie!'

'Don't be upset. I'll get some men together this after-noon, and we'll see how best to lift it. Some kind of crane-and-pulley system.' He looked up. 'We'll have to see if it can be used to repair the hole – put it back where it came from. It's no use for anything else. You couldn't cut it up for firewood, for instance – you'd never get a saw through it.'

'I should think not,' Polly said, obscurely comforted by 'crane-and-pulley'. It was lovely to have a man again, to do the man things in her life.

Charlotte got back late from Charles Street, where she had supervised the packing of her personal belongings. She wasn't taking any of the furniture, but she had still accumulated a worrying amount, given that Molly and Vivian lived in a flat with no cellar or attic. But the guest room was large and well provided with cupboards, and Molly had said her trunks could be stored in the nursery for the time being, since the children were away.

She didn't see Milo while she was there, which was a relief. She said goodbye to the servants. They hadn't been with her for long enough to be tearful, and – having called at the bank on her way there – she gave them all a parting tip. She knew they would easily find new positions: good servants were hard to come by in London. And in any case, as soon as the war started, there would be a multitude of other things they could do, and perhaps would have to do.

When she got back to Arlington Street, it was almost dinner time, and Basil was there. 'How did you know?' she demanded.

He kissed her cheek. 'That's not much of a greeting.'

'Hello, Basil. How did you know?'

'Kit rang Uncle Oliver, and he rang me. Was it meant to be a secret?'

'Not really, but I wasn't expecting my shame to be broadcast all over London.'

'Oh, Charley, there's no shame to you,' Basil said, so tenderly that Charlotte's eyes filled with tears. She was used to being teased by Basil, not petted.

'But you never trusted him,' she said. 'I should have listened to you.'

'No, you shouldn't. My prejudice was just that – a prejudice. It wasn't based on anything. And you were in love with him. And he made you happy.'

'Yes, he did. For a while. I don't regret that part.'

'You should never regret anything. It's a terrible waste of time and energy. Do what you do, then move on to the next thing. Which is?'

'Everyone keeps asking me that. Something useful, if I can. Is there really going to be a war? Vivian is sure of it. I expect you know more than most, being in the news business.'

'I'm afraid it's probably coming quite soon,' Basil said.

'Have you heard of the Molotov-Ribbentrop Pact? It's a treaty between the Soviets and the Germans, not just promising to be allies but we think there's a secret protocol to carve up Eastern Europe between them – Lithuania, Estonia, Latvia, Finland and Poland. So that puts an end to the hope that the Soviets would be on our side.'

'Would they really have been good allies?' Charlotte said doubtfully.

'Better than having them as an enemy. Now Poland's surrounded, Germany one side and the Reds the other. And if Hitler attacks Poland, we have to go to their aid.'

'Do you think he will?'

He hesitated. 'The *New York Times* reported German troop movements on the Polish border yesterday, but today it's gone quiet. It's possible that the Anglo-Polish pact has put the wind up him. But I wouldn't depend on it. It's a respite, that's all – in my opinion.'

Charlotte was silent, staring at nothing, thinking about Milo scuttling off to Switzerland. Was it sensible, or cowardly? He'd said he would be doing war-work over there. Perhaps she should have given him the benefit of the doubt. But if war was coming, she wanted to be here, at home.

Basil, watching her face, said, 'You'll find your useful thing.'

She came out of her reverie. 'A woman's thing? Helping in a canteen? Serving tea and keeping up the morale of the troops?'

'Someone has to do it,' he said.

'I was toying with the idea of the ATS.'

'Toy by all means, but no more than that. You don't want to be a typist or a driver. You've got brains.'

'So have you. What's your great contribution going to be?'

Basil thought back to earlier that day when he had been summoned to the editor's office. It was a rare thing to see the great man face to face, and he racked his brain for any egregious misdemeanour he had committed recently. But though Comstock had been grave, he had not looked disapproving. He had come straight to the point. 'Ah, Compton. I've had a communication about you from Lord Culbeath at the War Office.'

'Yes, sir?' Basil said, a little surprised.

'We are old friends,' Comstock explained, 'and we've been working together for some time on various aspects of war planning. However, all you need to know is that you have a file in a special unit of the War Office. They know all about you there. When the National Service Act comes into force, you will receive a letter requiring you to present yourself to that special unit, but after that you will come back here and continue in your usual job at the *Messenger*. I have agreed with Culbeath that you will work here until they're ready for you.'

'When will that be, sir?' Basil had found his mouth unexpectedly dry.

'I have no idea. You will be told. In the meantime, the *Messenger* will provide cover for you. In the last war, men who were not in uniform were subjected to unpleasantness, and we don't want that. You will mention none of this to anyone, of course.'

'Of course, sir.' The interview seemed to be over. 'Thank you, sir,' Basil had said, and left.

Now he said to Charlotte, 'I'll come when I'm called and go where I'm sent, just like everybody else.'

Polly had put a team of servants with brooms and buckets to clearing up the debris, among which they unearthed the Avro's missing wheel. 'I suppose they'll want this back,' she said.

'Well, we don't need it,' said Lennie.

'I don't know. Alec might. I remember in the last war, boys collected war souvenirs like anything. This could be a real prize – no-one else would have one.'

597

Lennie smiled. 'Give it back. It's government property.'

'They took my land. It's a fair swap,' Polly said.

Once the beam was lifted the statue of the Lady was found at once, and put into her hands. 'It's believed she's much older than the house,' she said to Lennie. 'The wood's as hard as stone. Look, she's not even scratched.' She held it reverently. 'I'm so glad no harm came to her. I'll put her on the main altar for now, until we can put her own altar back together.'

The sweepers had started on the debris that had been under the beam, and footman William found the chunk of marble that had broken off the sarcophagus, obviously along a natural fault in the stone. He handed it to Lennie, who said, 'I'm pretty sure marble can be stuck back together. Ought to be quite easy.'

'But the altar panelling will have to be completely replaced,' Polly said. She knelt down to look more closely, put her fingers into the split and pulled. The whole front came away, spitting splinters and ancient dowels. 'I never knew what it was made of, under the wood,' she said. 'I assumed it was a solid stone, but look – there's a sort of recess at the bottom. Almost like a cupboard.'

'Maybe it was meant as a cupboard originally,' Lennie said. 'Yes, look, aren't those dowels hinges? A cupboard for putting altar things in – the cup and plate and so on.'

'But I don't think they would ever have used this altar for serving communion,' Polly said. 'It's too small.' She bent her head sideways to look into the recess. 'There's something in there, though. I can see it, right at the back.'

She got down even lower, stretched in, felt around with her fingers, and finally drew out a small object, a metal box about six inches square and three deep. 'It's really heavy,' she said, standing up with it.

Lennie took it from her. 'I think it's gold,' he said. 'It hasn't tarnished at all, though it must have been in there a

598

long time.' He shook it gently, and heard a rattle. 'There's something in it.'

'Open it, then,' Polly urged.

The lid didn't lift. 'It's locked,' he said. 'I need a chisel or something.'

'Don't damage it,' Polly protested.

'Do you want it opened or not? Unless you've got the key . . .'

'That could be anywhere. If it still exists. I've never heard of anything being kept under there, so it must be old, or Papa would have told me about it, or Aunt Hen.'

They took it to the steward's room, where shortly Barlow brought a fine-bladed chisel, and everyone who had been helping gathered round while Lennie set the blade into the gap between the lid and the box and levered gently. Then less gently. Then with considerable force. The lid flew back violently, breaking one of the gold hinges that held it on.

Inside, the box was lined with velvet. 'In surprisingly good condition,' Lennie said. 'It must have been absolutely dry in there, or it would have rotted away.'

Polly leaned over to look. 'Black beads,' she said, in disappointment. 'I thought it would be diamonds, or gold sovereigns at least.'

Lennie took one out, and lifted it level with his eye between finger and thumb. 'Not beads,' he said. 'This is a pearl. A whole lot of black pearls.' He peered in again. 'I suppose they were strung when they went in, but the thread has worn away.'

Polly snapped her fingers. 'Black pearls!' she said. 'There's a painting in the gallery of one of our ancestresses, wearing a necklace of black pearls. I remember now, Aunt Hen saying they would have been really valuable, because I'd said I thought they looked dull and wondered why she'd had her portrait painted wearing them. I wonder if these are the same ones.'

599

'Hardly likely there would have been more than one necklace of them,' Lennie said. 'Black pearls are pretty rare now, probably even more so in those days.'

The whisper was being passed back through the onlookers to others outside for whom there'd been no room. *Black pearls . . . black pearls . . . black pearls . . .*

'Do you think they're worth anything?' Polly asked.

'Oh, I should think so. We'll have to get them valued. And re-strung. You ought to wear them. They'd suit you, you're so fair.'

'I wonder why they were hidden,' Polly mused.

'The box is solid gold, I think,' Lennie said. 'So that'll be worth a bit.'

'And we'd never have found it if it hadn't been for that poor boy and his solo flight.'

On their way upstairs to wash off the grime of the treasure hunt, she said, 'Funny to think . . .'

'What?'

'Well, there were probably lots of times when finding the gold box and the pearls would have made a lot of difference to the family. Hard times. Even when my father inherited and all the land had been sold off and the house was in a poor state. But here we are, and you're a millionaire, and Ren left me a fortune, and we really don't need to find hidden treasure at all.'

'You're all the treasure I ever want,' Lennie said, and stopped her on the top stair to kiss her.

Stuffy Elphinstone presented himself at Arlington Street with the utmost casualness, saying he'd happened to be in the neighbourhood; but Molly saw the longing way he looked at Charlotte when he thought she wasn't watching, and promptly invited him to stay for dinner. He was a very different young man now from the days when he had been a red-faced and tongue-tied investor in Dolphin Books. He was tall, well-built, far from unattractive, and now had a gravitas that suited him. It was not that Molly was a match-maker – indeed, she thought interfering in someone else's emotional life was both impertinent and dangerous; and besides, Charlotte had only just parted ways with Launde. But she thought Elphinstone much more eligible in every way, and his attachment to Charlotte had never wavered – he was still unmarried, and his name had never been connected to any other woman's. In the fullness of time, it would not be a bad thing at all if . . . And with war coming, they would all need to grab what happiness they could. Launde, damn his eyes, might have had the decency to run away sooner if he was going to run at all . . . They really ought to stop referring to Elphinstone as 'Stuffy'. What on earth *was* his first name? He had a very decent estate in Hampshire . . .

Charlotte was comfortable with him, chatted with him, no signs of shyness, which might have been a good thing or a bad thing. At the moment she wanted to know about the international situation more than anything.

'There's a lot of negotiation going on,' Elphinstone said. 'Diplomacy and so on. Halifax is still hopeful. It looks as though Hitler was ready to go on the 26th – troops on the Polish border and so on – but at the last minute he heard about our formal treaty with Poland, and called a halt. Oh, and I understand that Mussolini told him he wasn't ready to go to war yet. I don't know how much Hitler was depending on the Italians, but it was another scruple to add to the balance.'

'So we've got a breathing-space,' Molly said.

'There's a suggestion from America that they think Hitler's bluffing, that he can't really want war with Britain and France. And it's a fact that yesterday he presented Henderson – our ambassador to Berlin, you know – with an offer, guaranteeing the safety of our Empire if we let him solve the "Polish problem", as he calls it, without interfering.'

601

'Solve it?' Vivian said, pausing in the dissection of a potato. 'We know what his method of solving problems is. I take it we're refusing?'

'Not right away,' Elphinstone said.

'Of course they didn't refuse, Vivian,' Molly said. 'What kind of diplomacy would that be? You keep on talking – am I right?'

'Yes, ma'am,' said Elphinstone. 'If there's any way we can wriggle through and avoid catastrophe, we'll take it. Henderson's offering to mediate talks between Germany and Poland for a peace, but the last I heard, Hitler handed Henderson a list of demands, including Germany taking back Danzig and the corridor, which Poland would never accept.'

'I should think not,' Vivian said.

'So we're teetering on the edge,' Charlotte said.

Stuffy looked at her, and she saw in his eyes that he didn't hold out much hope. 'He's got troops in place on the Polish border, and some sources say this has been in planning since March. I don't think it's a question of "if" any more. It's "when".'

'And when is "when"?' she asked.

'A few days at the most.' He looked at Molly. 'You were wise to send your children down to the country, ma'am.'

'A part of me keeps hoping I'll have them back by the time school starts.'

'We all keep hoping,' Stuffy said. 'We've got air-raid precautions in place, the National Service Bill ready to enact, our expedition force primed and ready, the French have the Maginot Line, the Poles have mobilised their navy and they have a million men in arms, close to the border. But if it all proved for nothing and there was peace after all, we'd be very happy.'

'Will you be going into uniform?' Molly asked, thinking he looked at his best during that speech – almost noble.

'Oh, yes, straight into the Guards, with a commission. It's all arranged. But I'll be staying at the War Office, at least at first.'

Charlotte smiled faintly. 'You'll look splendid in Guards' uniform,' she said. 'You have the height.'

Stuffy blushed with pleasure, and Molly, on impulse, said, 'What *is* your first name, Stuffy? I can never remember.'

His blush deepened. 'Nobody ever uses it, not even the mater. Everyone calls me Stuffy.'

'But what *is* it?' Molly insisted.

'Eadred,' he admitted. 'Damn silly name. Family tradition, apparently.'

He looked quite put out, and Molly was sorry she'd asked.

There was scaffolding up in the chapel, and the house reverberated to hammering. It was felt that there was a real urgency about getting the roof repaired and as much of the inside work done as possible. It was Thursday, the 31st of August, and that morning the Royal Navy had been mobilised and the reserves of the Army and Air Force had been called up. Who knew how much longer the workmen would be available to do the job?

The day before, Ambassador Henderson had handed Ribbentrop the British government's reply to Hitler's demands over Poland:

His Majesty's Government repeat that they reciprocate the German Government's desire for improved relations, but it will be recognised that they could not sacrifice the interests of other friends in order to obtain that improvement. They fully understand that the German Government cannot sacrifice Germany's vital interests, but the Polish Government are in the same position and His Majesty's Government believe that the vital interests of the two countries are not incompatible.

'Still hoping,' said Lennie. The wireless receiver in the drawing-room was permanently tuned to the Home Service for the news, and he haunted it for bulletins. Just after eleven in the morning, came the news that the government had issued an order to evacuate civilians from cities and towns that were likely targets for enemy bombing.

'That doesn't sound like hoping,' Polly said.

'I can't see the British people going along with it,' Lennie said. 'They might send the children, perhaps. But can you imagine Londoners, for instance, running away with their tails between their legs?'

'You'd never get Londoners to go to the country for any reason,' Polly said, with grim humour. 'Give up their pavements and streetlights and pubs and cinemas for fields full of cows?'

She had been worrying for days about James, from whom she hadn't heard in weeks. France was safe enough at the moment, but if war broke out, would he be able to get back?

Alec, Bibi and Mimi got home from school, gas-masks slung around their necks – the school was insisting that the children all carry one – and Polly intercepted them and sent them straight up to the nursery for tea. Alec wanted to hear if there was anything on the wireless, but she didn't want the little Lohmanns to hear any more unsettling bulletins. She promised to come up after tea and play a game of Ludo with them.

They had hardly gone up the stairs when the station taxi rattled over the drawbridge, pulled up outside, and the dogs rushed out in a flood to engulf it. Polly was passing through the hall, and followed Barlow to the door, and her heart lifted when she saw James climbing out. There were cases tied to the roof, as well, which was even more heartening. 'You've come home!' she cried, running down the steps to hug him. He hugged her tightly but briefly, and put her back just as she noticed someone else getting out of the other side of the taxi, where Barlow had hurried to open the door. A young woman in a beige raincoat over beige trousers, and a shape-less felt hat on her short, dark hair.

James held out a hand to her, and when she reached his side, he said, strangely formal, 'Polly, this is Meredith. Meredith, my sister Polly.'

Meredith's hand was as hard and strong as Polly's, though with fewer calluses.

'How do you do? Welcome to Morland Place.' She looked quizzically at James. 'Is this the Meredith you met on your Canadian trip, all those years ago?'

'The very same,' James said, with a rueful grin. Helmy had found him and he was holding off his ecstatic advances with his free hand.

'I can't believe you haven't mentioned me since then,' Meredith said to him.

He looked embarrassed. 'There wasn't anything to tell, was there? Not until now.'

'What are you talking about?' Polly demanded.

'Meredith and I – well, I've been wanting to marry her for years, but she would never agree, until now.'

Polly looked from one to the other, delight dawning. 'You're engaged to be married?'

'Um, not exactly,' James said. 'We stopped off in London and did the deed. Meredith is Mrs James Morland now.'

'We had everything in place to get married in the American Embassy in Paris,' James said. 'You know, birth certificates and so on. But things were getting more and more sticky over there, and I started to worry that we were going to be marooned. You remember, Pol, Papa telling how all those Americans got caught there last time? The Germans were massing at the Polish border, and we'd moved everything of Hélène's that she wanted moving, plus everything of all of her friends, so there was nothing really to stay for. Then Hélène said, "For God's sake, go!" So we went.'

'I'm terribly glad you did,' Polly said, though with a doubt in her voice.

James heard it. 'What's wrong? Aren't we welcome? I'd offer to take ourselves off to an hotel, but the fact is that we're stony broke, haven't a bean between us. Spent our last *sous* getting married. We can sleep on the nursery floor, and we don't eat much.'

'Don't be silly, of course you're welcome,' Polly said. 'I wouldn't forgive you if you went somewhere else.'

Lennie understood. 'I think what your sister is worrying about is that, now you're back in the country, you'll be eligible to be called up when conscription starts.'

James shrugged. 'Oh, well, can't help that.'

'Unless you went back to the States,' Lennie said. 'You could still get out.'

James and Meredith looked at each other. 'We don't want to do that,' she said. 'We talked about it, and we want to be here, carrying on the fight.'

'It would be very feeble of us to run away,' James said.

Lennie grinned. 'Exactly how I felt when the last war broke out. I was visiting here, and definitely didn't want to go home and miss it all.'

Alec was ecstatic that his uncle had come back. James was flattered, until his nephew said, 'Well, Uncle Lennie is American so he can't fight, and Mummy's a girl and they don't, so I'd have no-one to tell the other boys at school about. But now you're here, and you'll go off and fight, and kill hundreds of Germans, and I can talk about that. It'll be swish!'

'What a bloodthirsty young ruffian you are,' James said dispassionately.

In the early hours of the 1st of September, the German army invaded Poland from three different directions, with one and a half million men, panzer divisions and a relentless bombing from the Luftwaffe.

It was a Friday. The children went to school, everyone tried to get on with their work as usual, and the hammering from the chapel roof continued with even greater urgency. Polly went into York to talk to her staff at Makepeace's. The ARP warden had visited her two weeks before to ask her what arrangements she had made for their safety in an air raid. Makepeace's had a cellar, but the warden had recommended that she got steel and wooden props put in place to support the ceiling as an extra safety measure. Now she addressed the staff to make sure they knew what to do if the air-raid siren went off; that they knew the difference between the warning and the 'all clear'; and that they all had their gas masks with them. The young men from the gentlemen's departments she shook hands with, telling them that when they were called up, everyone would be tremendously proud of them; they shuffled and blushed. She wondered how she would stretch her female staff to cover their jobs, and what gentleman customers would think of being served by girls.

That evening, it was announced on the news that the Prime Minister had addressed the House of Commons at six o'clock. The newscaster read out his speech. "'It now only remains for us to set our teeth and to enter upon this struggle, which we ourselves earnestly endeavoured to avoid, with determination to see it through to the end. We shall enter it with a clear conscience, with the support of the Dominions and the British Empire, and the moral approval of the greater part of the world.'"

And the late bulletin said that Sir Neville Henderson had handed an ultimatum to Ribbentrop at 9 p.m., which declared that unless the British government received satisfactory assurances that Germany was prepared to withdraw from Polish territory 'His Majesty's Government will without hesitation fulfil their obligation to Poland'. The newscaster said that the French ambassador delivered an identical note one hour later.

'So the die is cast,' Lennie said.

'What does that mean?' Ethel asked. She was knitting again, and the more agitated she got, the faster the needles moved.

'It means that if Hitler doesn't withdraw from Poland, we go to war,' James explained. 'And he won't, so we will.'

Further bulletins described various attacks and bombings on Poland. The Polish forces were no match for the German military machine.

That night, Polly lay in Lennie's arms, and said, 'We're for it, aren't we?'

'I think so,' he said.

She pressed closer. 'It sounds stupid, but I'm almost glad the waiting's over. It's been going on for so long. At least now we know what we're facing.'

He held her, and kissed her hair.

'What will happen to us?' she asked, after a while.

He didn't answer at once. It was an impossible question, anyway. She meant them, him and her, but also their household, their family, and she also meant the neighbourhood, York, England. All of them.

'We'll be all right,' he said.

'Do you really think so? I can't help thinking that it's going to be as bad as last time, and look at all the people we lost.' He had nothing to say to that. Then she said, 'But the Lady didn't cry. So we'll survive, won't we?'

'We'll survive,' he said.

Saturday was a waiting day. 'It's like Holy Saturday,' Polly said, and strangely only Ethel really understood her, being an old-fashioned churchgoer. There was nothing to do but wait. She knew the children felt the atmosphere, so she took them over to Twelvetrees, where Jessie did her bit to entertain them, giving the little Lohmanns a riding lesson on a quiet horse, letting Alec take one over the jumps. They stayed for lunch, and then while Jessie went off to do things, Catherine and Ottilie played a protracted game of Monopoly with them. The Lohmanns had never played before, so it kept them thoroughly absorbed. Their English was now quite idiomatic, but they learned a few more words while playing the game.

Polly collected them and took them home for baths and supper. She had a telephone call from Emma, who chatted about her children, and sounded oddly disjointed. 'I just wanted to know you were still there, I suppose,' she confessed at last. 'Everything is so strange. I somehow feel that if Morland Place is still there, if it's all right, we'll come through.'

'Like the ravens at the Tower of London?' Polly said.

'Oh, yes – and goodness, what's going to happen to them? Will they have—?'

'Taken precautions to make sure they survive? I'm sure they will,' Polly said.

Later that evening, there was a most unexpected call from Basil. 'I was just talking to the Aged Ps, and they asked about you. So I said I'd give you a ring. Mum was on the phone to Aunt Molly for an hour today. Everyone's ringing everyone else, it seems.'

'It's that sort of day,' Polly said.

'Yes, a transition day. From the state of peace to the state of war.'

'What have you heard?'

'Nothing from Germany over the ultimatum – unsurprisingly – so the government's going to give them a final deadline of tomorrow morning. The French too, but a bit later. And after that – war will be declared.'

'Oh, Basil!'

'Don't be like that. It's going to be hard – harder than anybody realises, I think – but we'll come through.'

609

'You really think so?'

'Britain's been around for thousands of years. Caesar tried to beat us, and Napoleon, and the Kaiser, and they all failed. You don't think that silly little man with the ridiculous moustache is going to put an end to our magnificent history, do you?'

She laughed shakily. 'Oh, Basil, you do one so much good.'

'Please tell the mater that. She thinks my hair is too long, and that I'm not serious enough about things.'

'Wherever would she get that idea?'

Sunday, the 3rd of September. Not Easter Day, with its triumph and joy and the transcending of death, but a strangely holy day, all the same. Everyone moved quietly about the house, even the children. The world seemed to be holding its breath. The dogs followed Polly, keeping close, sensing the atmosphere. After breakfast, Lennie got out an enormous jigsaw puzzle and set it up on the dining-room table for the children. The picture on the lid was an odd one, of three circus workers playing draughts backstage – a clown, a bareback rider in ballet dress and a scarlet-uniformed ring master with waxed moustaches and a whip. The board was set out on an elephant's stand from the ring, and a black-and-white dog lay nearby, wearing a clown's ruff. Everyone who passed the door went in and looked, and placed a piece or two. It was the strange background to the day that Polly never forgot.

A little after eleven in the morning, there was an announcement on the wireless: 'This is London. You will now hear a statement by the Prime Minister.'

It had been announced the night before that the deadline was eleven on Sunday morning, so everyone was hanging around nearby, waiting to hear. Polly urged everyone into the drawing-room, adults, children and servants.

Mr Chamberlain's voice, with its oddly fluting vowel sounds, came on: clear, but tired, and despondent.

'I am speaking to you from the Cabinet Room at ten Downing Street. This morning the British ambassador in Berlin handed the German government a final note stating that unless we heard from them by eleven o'clock that they were prepared at once to withdraw their troops from Poland, a state of war would exist between us. I have to tell you now that no such undertaking has been received and that consequently this country is at war with Germany.

'You can imagine what a bitter blow it is to me that all my long struggle to win peace has failed. Yet I cannot believe that there is anything more or anything different that I could have done and that would have been more successful. Up to the very last it would have been quite possible to have arranged a peaceful and honourable settlement between Germany and Poland. But Hitler would not have it. He had evidently made up his mind to attack Poland whatever happened, and although he now says he put forward reasonable proposals, which were rejected by the Poles, that is not a true statement.

'The proposals were never shown to the Poles, nor to us, and, though they were announced in a German broadcast on Thursday night, Hitler did not wait to hear comments on them, but ordered his troops to cross the Polish frontier. His action shows convincingly that there is no chance of expecting that this man will ever give up his practice of using force to gain his will. He can only be stopped by force.

'We and France are today, in fulfilment of our obligations, going to the aid of Poland, who is so bravely resisting this wicked and unprovoked attack upon her people. We have a clear conscience. We have done all that any country could do to establish peace, but a situation in which no word given by Germany's ruler could be trusted and no people or country could feel themselves safe had become intolerable. And now that we have resolved to finish it, I know that you will all play your part with calmness and courage.

'At such a moment as this the assurances of support that

we have received from the Empire are a source of profound encouragement to us.

'Now may God bless you all and may He defend the right. For it is evil things that we shall be fighting against, brute force, bad faith, injustice, oppression and persecution. And against them I am certain that the right will prevail.'

Afterwards, everyone went quietly away about their tasks. No-one could bear to speak to anyone else, not yet. Polly and Lennie went out into the gardens, and the dogs followed them, unusually subdued.

They held hands, and walked without speaking, their steps taking them round the moat, the swans following at a discreet distance, in case they should happen to have brought bread with them. The sky was no longer the transparent pale blue of summer, but the opaque, creamy, dense blue of September; the sunshine was more oblique, still warm, but more precious. Autumnal.

At last, after a full circuit, Polly said, 'It was a good speech.'

'Yes,' he said.

'I'm so glad you're here,' she said, the words bursting out of her. 'I'm so glad we're married. I keep thinking, what if I'd had to face this alone? I love you so much – I want you to know that.'

He smiled, and teased her gently. 'Hey, hey, that sounds as if you're going away somewhere.'

'No,' she said. 'I never want to leave this place, or you. I have everything I could ever want here. Let them take it from me if they can!' she added fiercely. 'Whatever happens, Lennie—'

'I know,' he said.

'No, you don't,' she said. She hesitated. 'Not entirely.'

She stood still, and the dogs, who had run ahead, came surging back and pushed up close, staring up into her face to see what she wanted, why she'd stopped. She took Lennie's hands. 'There's something you don't know.'

'What, darling?' he asked, slightly amused by her earnestness, not alarmed by the mystery.

'I wanted to tell you before, but somehow I couldn't while this was hanging over us, while it wasn't certain. Now I can. I'm going to have a baby.'

He had no words. He drew her close and held her, and rested his head on her hair.

'You're glad, aren't you?' she asked, in a shy murmur.

'Oh, my love, more glad than I can possibly say.'

She made a sound of contentment. 'It's right to tell you today,' she said. 'Today of all days, there ought to be hope. Here on the very edge, with so much darkness ahead, there has to be hope.'

'There's always hope,' he said.

An aeroplane went by overhead, a fighter plane, high up and fast, scrawling a white line across the blue. But the sky was reflected in the moat, and the swans were the white on that blue, as they had been for hundreds of years.

POSTSCRIPT

POLLY combined running the estate with war work for the York Refugee Committee. *LENNIE* offered his services to HM Government in the field of radio interception and transmission. They had two daughters, Eleanor and Sophie.

BIBI and *MIMI* Lohmann never returned to Germany. Mimi married a York accountant, and she and her three children were probably as often at Morland Place as at their own home in Knapton. Bibi studied history and mathematics at Oxford where he was recruited by an MI6 scout, and worked as an analyst for the Secret Service. He never married.

CHARLOTTE joined the WRNS and served as an intelligence officer in Whitehall. The war delayed her obtaining a divorce from *MILO*. In 1946 she received information from a solicitor in Geneva that he had been killed in 1943 when a light aircraft in which he was travelling crashed in the Alps. *LORD ELPHINSTONE* remained good friends with Charlotte while he was at the War Office, but felt it wrong to try to engage her affections while she was still married. He transferred to active service in the Guards Armoured Division when it was formed in 1941. He was killed in the advance on Arnhem in 1944. After the war, Charlotte worked for the Prudential Assurance Company at Holborn Bars. She never remarried.

BASIL served with distinction in the Special Services throughout the war, was wounded once and decorated twice, emerging with the rank of major. *GLORIA* ran a social club and canteen in Knightsbridge for serving officers. She was killed in May 1941 when the building suffered a direct hit. After the war Basil returned to journalism, writing opinion pieces for several newspapers and a satirical column under a pen name for *Punch* magazine and later for the *New Yorker*. He married in 1947 an ex-Wren, former colleague of Charlotte, and they had two sons. Basil and his wife remained close friends with Charlotte, who was godmother to both their children.

RICHARD was called up and served in the Pioneer Corps, reaching the rank of captain. He was killed in June 1944 while assisting the landings at Sword Beach and was awarded a posthumous George Cross. *CYNTHIA* undertook war work with a Jewish refugee organisation in Brooklyn. After the war she married a New York Jewish solicitor, a widower with two small children. She never had any children of her own but was much loved by her stepson and stepdaughter.

JAMES was called up in 1940 and joined the Duke of Wellington's Regiment. He fought in the North Africa Campaign, then the Anzio Campaign, where he was wounded, and spent the rest of the war at a desk. *MEREDITH* spent the war at Morland Place, helping Polly and serving in the WVS. After the war James and Meredith emigrated to Australia and managed a sheep station, which they were able to buy in 1952. They had a daughter and a son.

The third child of *EMMA* and *KIT* was another girl. Kit didn't mind a bit.

Have you read them all?

THE
MORLAND
DYNASTY

Discover all thirty-six books in the acclaimed
Morland Dynasty series and immerse yourselves in
the romance, drama and intrigue of every momentous
event in British history.

From the War of the Roses to Henry VIII, the
English Civil War to the War of Independence,
the Victorian era to the sinking of the Titanic, and
King Edward VIII to World War II, if there is a
particular moment in history you love,
you'll find its story, captivatingly told, in the
Morland Dynasty series.

ALL 36 BOOKS AVAILABLE TO READ NOW